PACK LOYALTY SERIES

AMELIA SHAW

CONTENTS

FATE OF THE WOLF

1. Allara — 3
2. Reid — 13
3. Allara — 19
4. Reid — 31
5. Allara — 41
6. Reid — 49
7. Allara — 55
8. Allara — 67
9. Allara — 79
10. Reid — 87
11. Allara — 103
12. Reid — 111
13. Reid — 123
   Epilogue — 131

LOVE OF THE WOLF

1. Tammy — 143
2. Jason — 153
3. Jason — 163
4. Tammy — 173
5. Jason — 181
6. Tammy — 193
7. Jason — 201
8. Tammy — 211
9. Jason — 219
10. Jason — 229
11. Tammy — 237
12. Tammy — 251
13. Tammy — 267

DESTINY OF THE WOLF

1. Kara   283
2. Kara   293
3. Ronan   303
4. Kara   313
5. Ronan   323
6. Kara   333
7. Ronan   341
8. Ronan   351
9. Ronan   361
10. Kara   369
11. Ronan   377
12. Kara   383
13. Ronan   393
14. Ronan   403
15. Ronan   411
Epilogue   423

BABY OF THE WOLF

1. Amy   431
2. Noah   439
3. Amy   447
4. Noah   455
5. Amy   463
6. Noah   471
7. Amy   479
8. Noah   487
9. Amy   495
10. Noah   503
11. Amy   511
12. Noah   519
13. Amy   527
14. Amy   535
15. Noah   543
16. Amy   551
Epilogue   559

CURSE OF THE WOLF

1. Mannix   567
2. Mannix   575
3. Mannix   583
4. Amelie   591
5. Mannix   599
6. Amelie   607
7. Mannix   615
8. Amelie   623
9. Mannix   631
10. Amelie   639
11. Mannix   647
12. Amelie   655
13. Mannix   661
14. Amelie   669
15. Mannix   677
16. Amelie   683
Epilogue   691

PACK
LOYALTY

1

FATE OF THE WOLF

AMELIA SHAW

FATE OF THE WOLF

ALLARA

I grimaced at the clock on the dashboard as I pulled up outside the bar I'd worked at every weekend for the past five years.

Late as always. Mick's really gonna kill me this time.

I jumped out of my car and slammed the door. The old rust bucket was reliable and got me where I needed to go, even if the aesthetics left something to be desired.

I ran through the back entrance, pulled off my woolen coat and dumped my bag in the small cupboard we had for employees, fumbling with my keys.

The bar wasn't one of those dive bars with only two lights bulbs that worked, but it wasn't a fancy two story place with a super-expensive menu, either.

It was warm and friendly, with an affordable menu. The locals considered it the perfect place to hang out after work, or on the weekends.

"Allara. You're late. Again," Mick called out to me, his tone dripping with sarcasm. "You're lucky I love you!"

I *was* lucky.

He really did love me, and as a wolf shifter without a pack... I needed a family. Mick was the only father figure I had in my life these days.

I threw him a grateful smile. "You know I'll make up the time at the end of the night."

He tossed me a chef's apron and I caught it one handed, trying to suppress a groan. He liked us to wear them on nights when more beer got spilled than drunk.

Football finals.

That was tonight! Shit.

"The place is already half-full, so..." He clapped my shoulder with a heavy hand. "Better get out there."

I tied the apron around my waist, covering my new jeans. It seemed a bit of a waste to wear them at work, especially since no-one could really see me from the waist down behind the counter anyway. But... new jeans. I couldn't resist trying them out.

"Thanks, Mick."

I walked through the kitchen, tossed a quick hello to our chef Louise, then strode out to take my place behind the bar. My heart was still pumping from the rush to get here, but my body was beginning to hum pleasantly, my hips swinging to the music playing over the bar's speakers.

I might whine and moan about having to work weekends, but mostly, it was all show. I really didn't have anything else I'd rather be doing. This place, and the people who worked here, had become a home to me. I enjoyed my nights here and there were definitely worse jobs. Even on nights like this, with the rowdy football crowd making extra work and noise.

I grabbed a hair tie from around my wrist and threw my long hair up into a high ponytail. On football nights, the place got stupid hot and people flooded in non-stop until the early hours of the morning. Working the bar on a busy Saturday was basically the equivalent of a free gym workout.

"Hey Tammy!" I called out to the other bartender, who was shaking a tumbler and pouring what looked like a cappuccino cocktail mixture into two glasses.

Ooh, fancy.

"Hey Allara," she called back with a wide grin. "How's it going?"

Tammy was a nice chick, the ideal bar partner for this sort of place. We worked hard—probably *too* hard—but I think she enjoyed the rush as much as I did. The bar was busy enough to warrant hiring a third bartender, but thanks to the fact that Tammy and I could run an eight-hour shift on our feet, Mick didn't need anyone else.

Being a wolf shifter meant I had a fast metabolism and more strength than a non-paranormal human. I could work hard without really feeling it physically. Tammy was driven by pure energy. There was no paranormal in her, but she still worked like a trojan—I assumed, just because she could. She was awesome.

"Hey. Can I get two brewskies?" a guy called out, shaking me out of my train of thought. He threw a twenty on the bar in front of me.

I stopped a sigh from escaping just before I politely plastered on my "work face".

No rest for the wicked, or so the saying went.

"Of course! Can I get you anything else?" I asked, jumping in to work.

I didn't stop for hours. People just kept coming through the door and I kept running, pouring glass after glass. Beers and wines and more beers, and the occasional cocktail for a stray Hen Party reveler foolish enough to come to the bar on a football night.

You could barely hear yourself think above the roar of the men in the bar. As I predicted, it was roasting in here; I snagged my water bottle out from under the counter, and gulped it down before wiping the sweat from my brow.

"Who's winning?" I called out at one point to Tammy, grabbing her elbow as she flew past me.

She rolled her eyes and laughed. "You can't tell?"

I winked at her, grinning, and let her disappear back into the crowd.

She knew I wasn't a football girl by any stretch, but living in Nebraska meant you *had* to follow a team—and know the rules well enough to follow along.

"Hey gorgeous. Aren't you dressed like an angel tonight?" said a man leaning over the bar, his tone sticky enough to trap plenty of honey suckers.

But that wasn't me.

I squashed the desire to roll my eyes at his cheesy pick-up line. That would have been strictly against Mick's "no upsetting the customers" policy. Instead, I flashed the guy a grin. "Thanks. I got this top on sale, actually."

I tugged at the top in question. It showed off my ample cleavage, true. But it was made of a breathable cotton, perfect for running around like a crazy woman for eight hours straight, and serving beers to guys like this one. "What can I get you?"

"What are you doing after work tonight?" he pressed on, ignoring my polite deflection.

The smile I'd stuck on my face threatened to slide off. I forced it to stay put.

This guy wasn't a regular. I'd never seen him before. Which was a pity, really. If he *had* been a regular, he would have known that I don't date.

Barely, at any rate.

And even if I did, I wouldn't choose a forty-something guy who wore a suit to a bar on a Saturday night. Who was he trying to impress?

If it had been a Friday, that would've been forgivable. I understood the whole corporate vibe then; some of the men came straight from work, after all, so they had an excuse to be suited up. But this douchebag had actually made the decision to put on a suit to come drink beer and watch football.

"Um... what am I doing after work?" I struggled to think of something brief and innocuous in response. "Probably going home and face-planting my bed. I don't get off until four a.m."

His eyes lit up and this time, I couldn't disguise my flinch.

Fuck! Rookie mistake. Dammit.

I'd gotten out of practice, apparently.

"Well, I'm sure I can get you off by four-thirty." His tongue darted out and wet his lips. "My place or yours?"

My skin crawled. Jeez, this guy.

I can't say I wasn't used to it. Practically everyone in the place had tried it on at least once. After five years working as a bartender, I'd accepted that this sort of thing came with the territory.

Most accepted when I said no.

If only they knew I could shift into a wolf and bite their faces off if I wanted to...

I didn't know if it was the heat, or the lateness of the hour, but something about this dude made me want to punch him right in his smug expression.

I put up my hands and shrugged. "Look, I'm just here to serve drinks. Do you want something?"

"Uh, yeah. Three beers and your phone number."

I turned away to grab three beers from the fridge, the expensive ones. He hadn't been specific, after all. His mistake.

"Are these all right?"

His eyes widened a little as I set the bottles on the counter between us.

"Oh, sorry. Too rich for your blood?" I asked, trying to sound as confused and innocent as possible.

"Oh, no, not at all. Here, charge it." He handed me a normal blue credit card and I bit my tongue.

What? No black AMEX?

I tapped his card on the machine with a bland smile and slid over to the other end of the bar, trying to calm the tremble of anger rushing through my veins.

You can't hit anything, or anyone, here. Relax.

That guy had actually managed to make my blood boil. I wasn't sure why. I was usually pretty good at brushing past people's shit.

Damn, my blood really was up tonight. Definitely must have been the heat. I needed some peppermint tea and about fourteen hours of sleep to calm down. In that order.

"Hi, what can I get you?" I asked the girl waiting patiently for my attention. She was a tiny redhead, fresh out of college by the looks of her.

"Um, white wine please. Just the house is okay."

I nodded at her with a friendly smile, then turned to open the wine cooler.

College and wine. Luxuries I hadn't been able to afford at her age.

Whatever, I'm doing fine without either.

"Here you go." I slid the drink across the bar.

I was just turning to deal with the guy to her left, when an almighty crash reverberated across the room.

The crowd of rowdy patrons stumbled out of the way to reveal the same douchebag who'd been trying to pick me up earlier.

He'd dropped all three bottles of beer against the hardwood floor. There were shards of glass everywhere, and alcohol pooled at his feet.

Shit.

I glanced around, trying to spot Mick. He was all the way over on the other side of the room, busy with the DJ and his sound system.

"Allara!" Mick called, gesturing to the mess on the floor and miming a dustpan and brush. He gave me a thumbs up before turning away again.

I was officially done with this night. I just wanted to go home to bed.

Fine. I picked up a spare tray, grabbed a broom, and headed out into the fray.

The guy was leaning against a nearby pillar, looking strangely smug.

"Hey, I'm sorry," he said, not sounding sorry at all.

I forced a smile. "No problem."

After all, it was my job to clean up after man-babies like him. I bent down and picked up the big pieces of glass carefully, putting them on the tray, and then swept up as much of the rest as possible, into a pile.

Damn it. The glass had tracked everywhere.

I was going to need the vacuum.

I grabbed the tray and turned to the creep. "Can you keep other customers away from this area? I'll be back with the vacuum in a moment."

"Sure thing," he said, with a shit-eating grin.

I turned to walk away and he slapped me on the ass. Hard.

I bit my tongue as a growl rolled up into my throat.

I swallowed hard. That was unusual. My wolf usually lay mostly dormant inside of me.

I shook myself and kept walking. I located the vacuum at the back of the store room, and allowed myself one single, solitary, *"fuck!"* out loud in the dark, empty space, before I went straight back out there.

That creep didn't scare me. *Hardly.* I'd dealt with much worse.

Eventually, the football game ended. Most of the patrons had called it a night and were wandering home or piling into waiting cabs.

All of them, that is, except the creep.

I'd kept an eye on him after the beer incident, but he mostly kept a low profile for the rest of the night. Foolishly, I let my guard down, deciding he wasn't worth the stress. If he wanted to nurse his beer in an empty bar, fine. Not my concern; I'd get to kick him out soon, anyway.

Finally, there were only two customers left. The creep and some guy slumped over in a booth in the back corner.

Almost done.

As I wiped down the counter, I noticed the creep harassing Tammy over by the DJ booth. She'd gone out to collect the empty glasses. He was pressing her up against a pillar, tugging at the tray in her hands.

Ah, shit.

My heart began to pump faster. Harder.

Tammy was no wilting lily, but she was no wolf-shifter in hiding either.

"Hey, Mick!" I called out, but he was nowhere to be seen. I ducked my head around the kitchen door. "Louise, you seen Mick?"

"Hmm, not for a while." Louise furrowed her brow, stacking plates onto the draining board. "Bathroom, maybe?"

"Do you mind keeping an eye on the bar? Tammy needs help."

Louise narrowed her eyes, understanding my tone. "Sure."

She came out of the kitchen with me as I re-entered the bar area and marched across the floor. The creep had succeeded in tugging the tray out of Tammy's hands and was leering over her, getting right up in her face.

His breath probably smelled horrible.

"Please," Tammy was begging. "Stop!"

She shrank back against the pillar, trying to fend off his groping hands.

My wolf instantly rose, sensing danger to a member of my adopted family. I reassured her enough that she settled, albeit uneasily.

I can deal with this, I told my wolf. *He's just another creep who needs to go home and sleep off his stupidity.*

"Hey!" I poked him hard in the shoulder. "That's enough, now."

"Piss off." He glared at me, his eyes bleary and bloodshot. He reeked of alcohol. "You had your chance. I'm going home with this one."

Over his shoulder, I caught Tammy's eye. The look of horror on her face had my heart pounding and my wolf racing straight back up to the surface.

No fucking way.

"I don't think so." I grabbed his arm and yanked him away, giving

Tammy the chance to scuttle to safety. "I'm calling you a cab. C'mon, let's go."

I did a quick scan of the room. Damn it, where'd Mick go? Patrick, our security guard, was missing too. He was probably outside making sure the drunk patrons got into cabs instead of wandering toward their parked cars.

"You little bitch!"

My attention snapped back to the problem at hand. The hammered, infuriating *asshole* of a problem standing in front of me with an irate expression.

"You let her get away."

"Get *away?*" My jaw dropped. "She's not a fucking rabbit, dude. You're not out hunting."

The veins on his neck bulged as he clenched his teeth. He wanted to hit me. *Well... good. Just try it! Please. Give me an excuse to break your teeth.*

I held my ground. "I suggest you leave, now, before I call the police."

I turned away, but didn't get very far. Wide hands reached out and grabbed me, hauling me backwards. I could feel his soft belly pressing against my back. His beer breath brushed my cheek.

"You jealous, girly? That your problem?"

I tried to lean away from him, but he held on tight. I felt a hot wetness sliding over my cheek, slithering behind my ear.

Ugh. He had his *tongue* on my *face.*

That, right there, was the last straw.

I shoved away from him as hard as I could and twisted around to face him. He stumbled backwards, a look of shock on his stupid face. Shock that turned almost instantly to rage. As his fists clenched and he started toward me, I roundhouse kicked him in the belly.

He flew backwards and collided with the pillar behind him, clutching his stomach.

"What the fuck?" He wheezed. *Good.* "You're crazy, bitch."

When he stumbled to his feet and staggered forward, his dark eyes were filled with hatred.

His fingers tightened into a fist and he aimed what looked like a forceful haymaker at my head.

Shouldn't signal your punches like that.

I ducked under him and came up with a swift upper cut to his jaw, listening to the satisfying crunch it made as my fist met bone.

Unfortunately, I hadn't put enough force behind the punch. He didn't go down as I'd intended. He just staggered sideways, off kilter, and fumbled for a barstool to hang onto.

"Who the fuck do you think you are?" he hissed. "Stupid bitch."

My strength didn't exactly match that of a normal human woman, especially one my size. He was clearly too drunk to register what I really was.

I grinned; that was his biggest mistake.

He got to his feet and tugged on his suit jacket, stumbling away and weaving through scattered barstools. He mumbled to himself as he went, but I didn't bother to listen closely to what he had to say.

Instead, I moved cautiously back behind the bar, watching his progress. To my relief, he made a beeline for the exit and cursed as he yanked the door open with more force than necessary. Before he could walk out into the night, however, someone stepped in front of him, blocking his path.

We'd dimmed the lights in the bar hours ago, and at first I could only make out the man's silhouette against the darkness.

I could tell that this guy was big, though. Bigger than the creep by a long shot, with a broad chest and shoulders.

It was then that I recognized his flannel shirt. The guy from the booth!

Huh. In the rush to help Tammy, I'd forgotten he was still here.

He wasn't slumped in his booth anymore. He wasn't swaying like the creep, either. On the contrary, he moved with the deliberateness of someone who was completely sober.

He leaned forward, saying something to the creep in a low voice. His face caught the light, and I got a good look at him at last.

God dammit.

"You," I whispered. My heart sped up at the sight of someone I had never thought I'd see again.

Before I could process my thoughts or emotions, the creep swung his fist at the newcomer.

Oh, boy. Even bigger mistake.

The flannel-shirted guy moved so leisurely it almost seemed like slow motion. He hit the creep in the face with one brutal blow, and the douchebag went down like a lead fucking balloon.

CHAPTER 2
REID

It took me more than two weeks to track her down. I'd searched every corner of the city and come up empty. I'd had to rake through social media in my shitty motel room and hang around outside dive bars in the hope someone might have seen her.

And yet, there had been nothing.

Until this morning, when I'd overheard some guys outside a cafe talking about a hot girl they'd seen the other night, a shifter with dark hair who worked weekends at Mick's place.

That had caught my attention, and the lucky break had led me all the way here, to a bar in the middle of the city. I'd been watching Allara work all night. She really was a sight for sore eyes, even after all this time.

Her gorgeous thick, dark hair swung in a high ponytail as she took orders. Her blue eyes remained warm, no matter who she was dealing with, and her beautiful face glowed with good health. Her strong, lithe arms moved gracefully, gesturing back and forth as she laughed with her customers.

And those were just her physical attributes.

According to my intel, she worked two jobs now. She'd lived alone out here for five years, supporting herself. The fact that she lived outside of the pack's protection was unusual for a shifter woman, even these days. Obviously, she was doing a pretty damn good job of it. She looked well. Not unhappy.

Damn, it was good to see her again.

I stuck to the shadows all night and slouched alone in a booth near the back. I didn't know why, but I was hesitant to catch her attention. Tracking her down had been one thing, but actually confronting her with everything I had to tell her? That was quite another.

So, I lay low and watched her work. She served drinks, took cash, and got hit on. Rinse and repeat. She dealt with all of it in her stride, and better than most.

I knew her well, though. All those little tells from the past, were still in operation. That tiny crease between her eyebrows when she served the guy in the suit, told me she was royally pissed.

And rightly so. That asshole guy just wouldn't let it go. All night I watched him circling the bar like a fly that just couldn't be swatted away.

I managed to keep my cool, even when the other patrons started to leave and the jerk managed to corner Allara's bartender friend. Though, a moment longer and I would have stepped in.

Funnily enough, I hadn't had to.

The fire in Allara's eyes had flared as she'd stormed over and finally confronted the asshole who had been plaguing her all night. There had been a shadow of her father in her, at that moment. They'd always been cut from the same cloth, with their dark hair and eyes, right down to their hot tempers and their desire to protect others.

When the guy hit the pillar, the thud had reached my booth. I smirked down at the table, hearing her punch meet its mark, right against his stupid face. Atta girl.

Dumb bitch, the guy had muttered to himself as he stumbled away from her. *Probably a whore, anyway.*

I'd heard enough. I wasn't going to let him get away with disrespecting her so easily. I was tired of sitting back and listening to his bullshit. Watching him try to use his strength to abuse and control the women behind the bar.

Time to make my presence known.

Moving swiftly so I could catch him before he disappeared into the night, I blocked his exit, putting my hand against the doorframe so he couldn't slither away.

"What the fuck, man," the guy mumbled. Allara had really done a number on him; with the alcohol and the blows, he could barely stand straight.

I leaned close. "Your pick-up tactics need a little work."

He blinked, his lip curling. "Get fucked…"

He swung at me and that was all the permission I needed.

I punched him. Hard. It was one of the most satisfying punches I've ever landed in my life.

He crumpled to the floor like a sack of potatoes.

I nudged him with my foot, rolling him onto his side. He was out cold. *Huh.* His expensive suit dragged a little, picking up scum from the floor of the bar.

Oops. Hadn't meant to hit him that hard. I kept forgetting humans were more fragile than us.

A wolf would have taken that punch and come back for more.

I swept the hair back off my face and looked up, trying with difficulty to keep my heart rate under control.

Allara, the love of my life, my sweetheart, the one I'd let get away… stood there with her arms crossed, staring at me. I couldn't work out the expression on her face, but I could make a good guess as to what she felt.

Disbelief. Shock. Regret, maybe?

Same as me.

She met my gaze. Her expression cleared, landing firmly on *irritated.*

With her arms folded like that, her boobs looked great. High. Full. Plump. Just like I remembered. I forced my eyes away from that delectable cleavage.

"I had it under control, Reid," she said, forgoing a greeting.

She hasn't changed. Always did cut straight to the chase.

"I know." I grinned at her. "But he deserved it."

We stood there for a moment. Seeing her again, *talking* to her, I was struggling to remember why I'd come here in the first place.

"Uh..." I shifted my weight, glancing around the empty bar. "Can we talk?"

Her arms relaxed and fell to her sides. She rolled her shoulders a little, like she was preparing for battle. "Do I have a choice?"

Always, I wanted to say.

And she did. She could walk away from me right now, disappear again like she had five years ago.

She'd abandoned the pack, her father, all her responsibilities as the Alpha's daughter.

She left me. Even though she'd had good reason to.

I shook the thought away. This was bigger than what had happened in our past; bigger than us. She needed to know what had been going on with the pack since she'd left.

Her pack. *Our* pack.

We needed her now. She was the only thing that stood between us and Jaime.

"You know you have a choice," I said, keeping my voice low and persuasive. "But if you have a minute, I'd appreciate it."

She stared at me, assessing me intently like she used to. And for one unsettling moment, I thought she was going to turn away, tell me to *fuck off* and leave her alone. The thought made me cold.

Then her shoulders relaxed a little, and I realized we'd both been holding our breaths. She nodded once.

"Fine," she said. "I finish in an hour, okay? I can talk to you then. Or tomorrow. It's super late."

I couldn't wait any longer to speak to her. I'd been waiting all night. Longer than that, really. Five whole years.

I wasn't tired. Far from it. Watching her all night, talking with her now, standing up close like this... it was enough to call the wolf in me up to the surface.

I could feel the pheromones shivering through my body, urging me to shift.

But I had to ignore the way my blood was pumping in her presence.

Ignore the enticing scent that filled my nostrils every time she moved.

Mate.

But she wasn't. She had made that choice when she ran.

Which meant, I couldn't act on those urges now, no matter how strong they were.

My desire for her was forbidden.

Sadly, I answered to a higher power than my libido.

With difficulty, I shoved down the distracting feelings and refocused. I had a job to do, after all.

"I can wait." I looked around and pointed to an empty booth. "Can we chat there?"

She wrinkled her nose. "I've been here all night. There's a twenty-four-hour diner just down the block. I'll meet you there, okay?"

"Sure."

Allara turned away, heading back to the bar and picking up a tray.

Conversation closed, then.

It was about what I deserved, anyway.

I stared down at the unconscious guy at my feet, half wondering if I should drag him outside.

A bouncer appeared through the open door behind me and tsked at the sight of him, shaking his head. "Friend of yours?"

I snorted. "Hardly."

With one final, wistful glance toward Allara, I made my way out the door, leaving the creep and his future fate in the hands of the bouncer.

He must have caught something in my expression, because he clapped me on the shoulder as I passed and hooked a thumb toward the bar. Allara had busied herself with the cash register: she'd apparently decided to ignore my presence completely.

"You know Allara, then?" the bouncer asked.

"I..." I opened my mouth and shut it again.

He waited.

"Used to," I mumbled eventually, ducking my head at the sight of the guy's knowing grin and raised brow. He was clearly looking out for her, but must have known her well enough not to try stepping in on her behalf.

As I strode out into the night, it began to dawn on me. This mission was going to be a whole lot more difficult than I'd realized.

Allara had a life here, one that I didn't know anything about. Friends. Maybe even a boyfriend. The latter thought turned my stomach.

After all my efforts, finding her again had turned out to be the easy part.

Convincing her to give up her life here in the city? That was going to be a whole other level of difficult

CHAPTER 3

ALLARA

Reid was the last person in the world I expected to see tonight.
The last person I wanted to see—tonight, or any night, for that matter.

He was the guy—the *only* guy—who had completely broken my heart.

He'd always gotten to me like no-one else, even when we were kids. He understood me in ways I didn't understand myself. And then, one day, he ripped it all away like what we had was nothing.

He was one who got away. Only, it ended up being me that got away. From him, and from everything I had known and grown up with.

As I started packing away glasses, my memories burst through, creating a kaleidoscope of images flashing past me, one after another.

The day I first saw him. We'd been kids then, total strangers. Too young to shift, chasing each other through the trees with sticks and howling like wildcats all summer long, running barefoot over the forest floor.

The picture changed. The two of us in awkward adolescence, struggling to cope with the rush of puberty and our first shift. Reid had withdrawn, avoided me for weeks, disturbed by the new, hormone-fueled feelings that were racing through him.

Then, later, Reid and I in bed together. Our first time together.

My first time... period.

He'd been so gentle, letting me set the pace. I recalled his broad shoulders beneath my fingertips, warm and strong, the silken feel of his hair that always seemed to fall down into his eyes no matter what he did to it. The shape of his mouth, curled up at one corner, right before he kissed me. All the tiny details were still there in my mind as I recalled the memory of that night.

As the years wore on, our connection had only deepened. Couples around us broke up and got back together, found new partners who came and went as the seasons changed.

But not us. Our teenage infatuation morphed into a true, lasting bond. I'd been crazy for him. He was everything I thought a good man should be: strong, warm, funny. He was a part of my pack.

A part of *me*.

I would have done anything for him, and back then I had truly believed he do anything for me in return.

That hope had been snuffed out the night Reid broke up with me.

He had acted so strange that night; distracted. All he would say was that it wasn't right for us to be together. That he knew it was hard, but that one day I'd understand.

I'm doing this for you, he said. *Because I care about you.*

He hadn't given me a reason beyond that. Instead, he'd just stood there, stone faced, while I yelled at him, crying, and begged him to change his mind.

I couldn't remember most of what I'd said after that. I only knew that I could never take any of it back.

I'd packed some things in a small suitcase and left the following morning.

I watched everything I'd ever known shrinking away from the back window of the cab as it drove through the trees.

My pack, my people, my friends, my family.

And now, here he was. The person from my old life I'd fought hardest to forget.

There was only one reason he'd track me down after all this time, and I knew it had nothing to do with him missing an old flame.

Something must be wrong with the pack.

Or my dad.

That was the only reason I hadn't immediately told him to leave.

I finished up my shift by putting away the final glass and glancing around to make sure there was nothing left to do. I walked up to my boss who was counting the money out of the till, and handed my apron back with a grimace.

"You gotta get more security staff. We could have been in a hell of a lot of trouble tonight if I hadn't kicked that guy's ass."

Mick grinned at me as he took the apron. A girl waited for him at other end of the bar, gazing in his direction with big doe eyes.

So *that* was where he'd been all night.

"That's why I have you, kiddo." He ruffled my hair and I ducked away from him.

He chuckled. "You're all the security I need."

"You know I do the work of two bartenders, right?" I stuck out my tongue at him. "You can't count on me for security too. That's just not fair."

"Hey." As he handed me my pay, he pulled an extra fifty from the till and pressed it into my hand with a wink. "Thanks for tonight, hon."

Tammy wandered out from the kitchen, wrapped up in her woolen sweater and hugging herself tightly. The ordeal had clearly shaken her. "Yeah, Allara. I owe you one."

That was my problem, I thought with a sigh. My famous protective streak.

I couldn't walk away from people who needed me, and everyone knew it.

Even people who had crushed my heart under their heel for no good reason, then turned up five years later as if nothing had happened.

Damn it.

I tried to tamp down my pulse rate, which surged at the thought of Reid waiting in the diner down the road.

"I'll see you both tomorrow night, okay?" I managed a smile at Tammy and Mick, and raised my hand in farewell.

Hopefully, Sunday night would be quieter, and far less eventful.

Pulling on my long woolen coat, I shook my hair free from its ponytail and walked out into the crisp night air.

I smelled Reid immediately. The intensity of his wolf shifter pheromones mingled with his cologne and an underlying scent that definitely hadn't changed in the five years since I'd seen him. The evocative smell melted the years away and I had to stifle the moan that rose up from my chest.

I would never get enough of that scent. I would never forget it, either.

"I thought I'd walk with you," he said, the voice coming out of the darkness.

I startled, then looked to the right where he was leaning against a brick wall, his head cocked at a sexy angle like some sort of underwear model about to strip off.

"Okay." I shrugged, like it didn't matter either way, though my heart was thudding through my winter layers. "No problem."

I stuck my hands into the pockets of my coat and began to walk.

I loved how dark the nights became at this time of year. The cold kept the city streets quiet and deserted, but there was still enough light from the stars shining brightly above us to see clearly enough to navigate.

It was a pity we were surrounded by so many streetlights here. Without them, we'd be able to appreciate a lot more of the natural light.

Still, this time of night, after my shifts, was the closest my concrete jungle came to the vast, glittering constellations I'd been used to seeing, growing up.

Reid and I had gazed up at those same constellations once. We had given them made-up names, and I picked out all the brightest stars, pointing them out one by one.

"I'll make them into a necklace, Allie. Just for you."

"Reid!" I'd giggled. "You can't make stars into necklaces."

"I can." He kissed the top of my head. "For you, I can. I promise."

When I glanced in his direction, his head was tilted up toward the heavens.

He glanced over, and our eyes met. Was he remembering those times, too?

It felt like a lifetime ago.

The diner was up ahead, just around the corner. We kept walking in silence.

Was he as weirded out by all of this as I was?

I couldn't think of anything useful to say. I had a million questions rolling around in my head, but my mind turned blank every time I tried to reach for one.

His presence alone was intoxicating. We walked close enough that I could feel the radiant heat from his body, and our hands were inches away from each other as we reached the end of the block.

I tried to tell myself that it didn't matter how sexy he was, or how much heat he put out, inviting my hands to touch and explore. Reid, and everything I had ever loved about him, was in my past. And that's where he needed to stay.

My body wasn't listening.

Heat pooled in my lower belly, and my skin tingled. My heart thumped and blood pounded in my ears.

"It's..." I began, then fumbled when he caught my eye. "Uh. It's right here."

The bell jangled when I opened the door.

He inclined his head, indicating that I should go first. "After you."

A reluctant smile twisted my lips.

What could I say? The guy was a gentleman. He was exactly as I remembered him, and I knew we'd be standing here all night while he pushed to do the right thing.

He always had.

Which was why our breakup had felt like such a betrayal.

The thought pulled at my stomach, and my smile faded as I walked into the diner.

"Hey, Penny," I called out to the waitress standing behind the cash register. "Got room for two more?"

I'd known Penny for five years, ever since I started working for Mick. She was tough, like me, and she'd helped me out of some tight corners when I first arrived in the city.

"Allara, hi!" Penny's gaze darted around the empty diner, and she chuckled. "Yeah, I think we can squeeze you in."

I started toward my favorite booth at the front of the shop.

She raised an eyebrow, as if noticing Reid for the first time and liking what she saw.

Her eyes widened, and her brows waggled at me. "Want some menus? Maybe a candle?"

I gave her a frown, trying to quash where her thoughts were obviously headed. "Menu, yes," I said, sliding into the booth. "Candle, definitely not."

Reid sat down opposite me and drummed his hands against the table. "You come here a lot?"

"Yeah, it's kind of the only decent place open after I finish work," I said. "I'm usually wired and starving, so I need someplace to relax before I head home."

After not being able to speak at all, now I was talking too much, too fast. Trying to fill the empty space between us with words.

His presence in the city felt like a bizarre fever dream, my old life crashing gracelessly into my new one. Part of me worried that if I blinked, he might melt away.

"Night shift munchies." Reid nodded. "Makes sense."

Huh.

For us, it didn't make sense at all.

The wolf shifters of my old pack weren't nocturnal creatures at all. They hunted, fought, and conducted their business in the daylight hours.

Up with the sun, down with the sun, as my daddy always said.

Reid must have been feeling pretty shitty having to stay up so late to talk to me. Maybe that was the reason he was acting so oddly. He hadn't met my gaze once since we'd sat down.

"You want some coffee?" I asked.

"No, thanks," he said. "I'll be bouncing off the walls 'til dawn if I have some now."

Penny came up to our booth with the menus. She looked Reid up and down like she'd never seen a man before. Or at least, not one that good-looking. She turned to me and mouthed, *who is he?*

Later, I mouthed back, hiding my face behind my menu. Reid was paying us no attention, however; he was fixated on his order.

She shrugged, but her eyes glinted with interest, nevertheless. "The usual, Allara?"

I couldn't blame her for being curious. Reid didn't exactly blend in with the city suits. I'd never even seen him wear a tie. His flannel shirt and beat up leather jacket made him stick out around here, and his height and broad physique only accentuated his striking looks.

It wasn't my style to bring random men to my favorite diner at the end of my shift, and Penny knew it. I would have to give her a rundown later.

That'll be an interesting conversation.

I nodded. "Yes, please."

Blackberry tea and a piece of pecan pie. My reward at the end of a long, exhausting night.

Predictably, Reid ordered half the menu. I laughed at him when Penny walked away and propped my chin in my hands, resting my elbows on the table.

"Still hungry as ever, huh?"

"My appetite hasn't changed, if that's what you mean," he said slowly.

I swallowed hard and stared into his dark eyes.

Did that mean that he still liked to have sex every day and twice on Sundays?

Because that was an appetite I could appreciate.

I coughed, crossing my legs under the table and dropping my gaze quickly.

Jeez. I needed to shut down that line of thinking, and quickly.

Whatever sex drive I once possessed had lain dormant for a long time. One whiff of Reid's scent, however, and I couldn't seem to get my mind out of the gutter.

"You wanted to talk." I drew a deep breath, forcing myself to look at him and praying that the heat I could feel in my face wasn't a noticeable blush. "So, start talking."

A shadow fell over Reid's face, and he stared through the window at the darkness outside.

It was bad news, then, just as I had suspected.

My heart sank and I clutched my hands together.

"Your father's sick."

My stomach swooped. "How sick?"

Alpha wolves were the strongest of our kind, and pack leaders were the toughest of all. They rarely got ill, but if they did, it usually signaled the end of an era.

Reid lowered his head, staring at me with an intensity that I remembered well.

"You know what I mean, Allara."

I shook my head. Pain tightened my ribcage until I felt like my chest would burst. "I need you to say it."

"He's dying," Reid said, sounding shaky. "The doctors haven't said how long he has left, but... you and I both know they don't understand our physiology very well."

"But..." I scrambled for words as I tried to process the information. I'd expected bad news, and yet somehow, not this. "Are we talking—what? Weeks, months... years?"

I knew in my heart that Reid wouldn't be here if it was the latter.

"Weeks. At most."

Hot tears sprang up in my eyes and I ducked my head and blinked rapidly, forcing them back. I refused to cry, not here, and not in front of Reid.

"What..." I swiped at my cheek, catching a stray tear. *Damn it.* "What can I do?"

My dad and I hadn't been close, even when I lived with the pack. Not after my mother had died, anyway. It happened suddenly, the year I turned fourteen. Dad withdrew from almost everyone, shutting himself away in his study for months and taking long, solitary walks around the perimeter of the village.

Eventually he'd begun to open up again, but we had never really reconnected like we had in the past. As the years wore on, I had turned to Reid rather than Dad for comfort.

But he was still my dad, and to hear now, that he had mere weeks...

The night I'd left the pack, the look on my father's face was etched onto my memory.

He had stood watching me, like an unmoving stone statue. He didn't say anything. He didn't need to.

"You have to come back, Allara," Reid whispered, breaking me out of my thoughts. "You have to come back with me."

"I..." I frowned, trying to think. "I'll come back, sure. To see Dad. I won't be staying, though."

Reid matched my frown with his own. "You know that's not what I meant, Allara."

"Well, what *did* you mean? Be clear."

Something contrary inside made me want to push at him until he acknowledged the unspoken threat of his presence to my current, comfortable existence.

He glared at me, and I glared back, my sadness temporarily forgotten.

That was the problem with us, the thing everyone had loved to point out in the past. We had been a hot-headed pair. I needed someone calm, like a chilled-out yoga instructor. A guy who could balance me out, and temper the fire in my blood.

"The pack is waiting for you, Allara. It is time to claim your birthright."

I stared at him, dumbfounded.

I hadn't expected *that*.

"I..." I struggled to form a coherent thought. *This cannot be happening.* "You... What are you *talking* about? Dad's been grooming Jaime to take over for...ever!"

Jaime was the son of Terry, my dad's right-hand man. He was a beta like his father, but fierce with ambition. I'd never really gotten on with him, but I'd always chalked it up to my own jealousy; he and my dad had been super close.

Especially after Mom died.

Jaime had become the son my father never had: strong, sharp, and most importantly, *male*. I found it difficult to watch them together, so I'd kept my distance from Jaime out of habit.

I thought back to that time. About a week before Reid broke my heart, Dad had gathered the whole pack together for a huge feast. He'd pulled Jaime up to stand by his side, his arm thrown affectionately around Jaime's shoulders as he made a toast.

He declared then and there that, when the time came for the pack to have a new Alpha, Jaime would be his successor.

I hadn't been surprised. None of us were. That announcement had been years in the making.

I'd never really thought about the timing of it all, though. Jaime was announced as my dad's heir, and Reid ended our relationship a few days later.

In hindsight, that struck me as kind of odd.

Nevertheless, what was done, was done. I'd tried my best to close the book on that chapter of my life for a reason. Re-examining those memories was like poking at an old wound. It wouldn't bring me the closure I wanted.

It would only reignite the pain.

"I know it's not what you want to hear." He looked down at the table top for a moment.

Damn it. It was all I could do not to reach out and comb my fingers through his hair, tilt his face up to mine, and press a kiss onto his lips.

Oh, how I had missed kissing Reid.

I blinked, bringing my focus back to the matter at hand as Reid spoke.

"It's not meant to be this way, Allara. *You* are your father's heir. His *blood.*"

I shrugged off his words, along with my traitorous impulses.

"This is what my dad wanted. Your Alpha. He chose Jaime." I narrowed my eyes. "Then you dumped me, remember? There was nothing left. So, yeah, I got out."

Now it seemed to be my turn to stare down at the wood grain of the table. Anger filled my chest as I raised my gaze back up. "Has anything changed? No, of course it hasn't."

Reid went very still, like he'd been caught in a trap he hadn't realized was there.

"Allara…" He lifted his head and glowered at me.

Like *he* had any right to be angry.

"Jaime isn't the man your father thinks he is. He can't be trusted. And there's no one who can stand up to him worth a damn, not anymore." He leaned forward, capturing my gaze. "No one but you."

His eyes were hypnotic. For one heart-fluttering moment I felt like I would do anything he asked, even dive off a cliff top if he suggested it.

A plate of pie landed heavily in front of me, followed by a steaming mug of tea. I snapped out of my love-struck spell and thanked Penny with a flustered smile. Her answering grin was a little too knowing for my liking.

With my first sip of tea, my faculties returned. Was Reid being *serious* right now?

"I'm sorry to have to tell you this," I said, not sorry in the slightest, "but your trip has been wasted. Eat up, get your strength back, and go home. There's no way I'm going back with you. Not now." *Not unless Dad's really that sick…*

He had the gall to look confused. "Why not?"

I'd been about to take my first bite of pie. Instead, I dropped my fork and it fell against the side of the plate with a clatter.

"Why *not?* I have a life here, in case you haven't noticed. Friends, an apartment. I have work tomorrow, for Christ's sake! And I'm not giving it up, Reid. Any of it. If Dad's that unwell, then I'll make arrangements to come visit. But not to stay. Never that." I picked up my fork again and pointed it at him. "Not for anyone."

"But—"

My words rushed out before I could stop them, buoyed by a tidal wave of past heartbreak and loss. "And *certainly* not for you."

CHAPTER 4
REID

I gazed at Allara. This booth wasn't huge, and she was sitting close enough to touch.

My first love. Hell, my *only* love.

No matter how hard I'd tried to put her out of my mind, I always failed. She'd made a permanent mark on my heart; one I would carry forever.

"Allara." Somehow, I had to make her understand. "This is serious. The whole pack is in jeopardy—every last man, woman and child."

She would come around eventually. I was sure of it.

The Allara I remember was fiercely protective. She cared deeply for her pack and defended them no matter what kind of trouble they got into. She might be tough, but she was also a good person who cared about others. Her heart had always been in the right place. I couldn't see that changing, no matter what she'd been through in the past five years.

The way she'd punched that guy in the face for her friend tonight? That was Allara all over.

Now, she just stared at me with those beautiful dark eyes, and pushed my plate closer toward me. "Eat up, okay? You have a long drive ahead of you."

I stifled a sigh. So, maybe convincing Allara to come back with me wasn't going to be as easy a task as I thought, but I couldn't really blame her.

Her father had distanced himself from her after her mother died—a time when she probably needed her dad more than ever. Then he had passed her over as his successor, and on top of that, I'd gone and ended our relationship. Five years ago, every link she had to the pack must have felt like they had been broken, one by one. She must have felt abandoned by everyone.

I hung my head. There wasn't any point ruminating on the past. I had to focus on the situation in front of me, and consider the future.

I picked up my knife and fork and began to eat. The scrambled eggs were light and fluffy, the bacon crunchy and fatty. Just how I liked it. Focusing on the food gave me time to gather my thoughts and figure out how best to play this.

Allara matched my silence, though I noticed she only picked sporadically at her pie. No matter what she said, I could tell my news had upset her.

She hadn't changed much. Still beautiful, stubborn, and fiery. Everything I remembered. Everything I loved.

If I moved my leg under the table, even slightly, it would brush against her calf. The prospect was enticing, but there was something in her eyes that made me hesitate.

Her eyes *had* changed. They used to glow when she looked at me, lighting up her whole face with a radiance that took my breath away.

I hadn't been naïve enough to expect to find the lovestruck teenager I'd once known. I knew that time was over, and that she had buried her teenage notions when she left all those years ago.

But I hadn't expected the loss of innocent young love to sting this much. She was so close to me, but her face was pale and blank. Her cold demeanor separated us, far more than this table; it made me feel like the miles still stretched out between us.

I didn't know how to get through to her. I didn't know if I *could*.

Suddenly, the Allara I'd known seemed like a figment of imagination I'd dreamt up, a ghost from a happier time. One that was not even real.

Once I'd eaten the breakfast plate and the French toast, my hunger began to abate. I moved on to the basket of fries, eating them slowly and stirring my milkshake.

Time to try a different angle, I guess.

"So..." I leaned my elbow on the table. "Tell me about city life then. Since you love it so much. What's so great about it?"

She smiled tightly, but the show of humor didn't reach her eyes.

"I *do* love it." She drew a shaky breath. "I work at an elementary school during the week, helping children with reading issues. And I work weekends at Mick's bar. I've got a lot of friends out here. Good people. They really, uh, helped me through stuff."

I nodded, ignoring the twinge of guilt in my chest.

Did they help her through what I did to her?

"You live alone?"

Do you have a boyfriend? I desperately wanted to know. I sensed the question wouldn't be a welcome one, though.

"Yeah, I do." She looked down at her empty mug, hair hanging over her face.

With a jolt, I thought for a second she had confessed to having a *boyfriend*. I picked up the thread of our conversation as she continued and shook myself internally.

Stay on track, damn it.

Her presence was getting to me, just like it always had. When Allara was near, my brain still turned to mush.

"To be honest, I really like having a place to myself," she said. "You know what growing up in the pack is like. Everyone's living on top of one another, and everyone knows everybody's business. I have my own space here, independence. The city... you can blend in here. Disappear. No one cares what you're doing. I like that anonymity. It's refreshing."

You can disappear? How could someone like Allara disappear? She had such a presence about her. She lit up every room she entered.

Still, I could see why the city held its charms for her. If she hadn't felt welcome at home, the close-knit pack atmosphere would have only magnified the problem. She must have felt trapped.

Especially after... that night.

"You don't love me anymore?"

Something broke inside me at the forlorn note in her voice, but I kept my gaze stoic and controlled.

"I've made up my mind, Allara."

Shoving down the past with some effort, I managed to catch her eye once more.

"Allara. You gotta come home, okay? Even... even if it's just to spend some time with your dad."

Her lovely face crumpled. I hated having to be the one to hurt her—again, but it had to be said. Her father was dying.

"I have some leave due." She sighed, fiddling with her fork. "I'll apply for some in the next few weeks."

What? No!

"That might be too late," I snapped.

Her face blanked, then her eyes narrowed as she glared at me. "Dad hasn't contacted me in five years, Reid. *Five years.* Not once since I left. He never even checked to see if his own daughter was still alive! Do you know how that feels? Why would I just drop everything I've built here in the city to go running back to a family that so clearly doesn't want me?"

The words were harsh, but I heard the underlying hurt beneath them.

The waitress glanced over at us from behind the counter, looking concerned. I exhaled with frustration and forced myself to lower my voice.

"He does want you, Allara. He's always wanted you." I resisted the urge to reach across the table and grab her hand. "That's not what this is about."

She made a succession of angry noises as she stood, throwing some money down on the table.

I shook my head. I knew she was upset, but *seriously?* She was leaving, just like that?

"Well, thanks for stopping by." She shoved her bag onto her shoulder. "Drive safe. Send my regards to the pack."

As she made to walk past me, my hand shot out and I grabbed her wrist. She tried to shrug me off, but I held tight.

"Reid." She fixed me with an icy gaze. "Let me go."

I could feel her anger rising, and the spark lit the flame to my own temper.

Allara had always done strange things to my insides. As much as we riled each other up, I never felt more alive than when I was with her.

As uncomfortable as this interaction had been, I couldn't deny it: just *being* with her again was exhilarating. I felt more energy sparking through my system than I'd had in years.

"I won't give up that easily, Allara," I assured her. "This is more important than you think."

She twisted sharply and pulled free of my grasp. "Goodnight, Reid."

As she stormed out of the diner, she let the door slam on her way out. I deliberately turned back to my meal rather than see her leave.

I'd already watched her run out of my life once before, and it had been one of the hardest things I'd ever done.

I finished my meal in silence, ignoring the waitress's glower, before heading back to the motel where I'd been staying for the past few nights.

I wasn't leaving this city without Allara. I just had to make her an offer she couldn't refuse.

~

I was so fatigued I practically passed out back in the motel room. I stayed that way all day, trying to catch up on the sleep I'd lost last night. It had been hell trying to adapt my body to the stupid hours these city people keep on weekends. The pack didn't live like this; we went to bed at night rather than dawn. Here, waking up as night fell left me groggy and disoriented.

I couldn't wait to leave this place.

If everything played out as I hoped it would, I would be going home in a few hours.

I just needed to convince Allara that it was a good idea for her to come with me.

I glanced around the parking lot and stared at the small bar. Mick's place, she'd called it, with a note of affection in her voice.

Sunday night seemed to be a quieter affair; only a handful of punters passed through the frosted glass doors, and the noise level was thankfully reduced to a muted hum.

The city could be so loud.

I didn't know how she'd stuck it out for so long.

After a moment of consideration, I decided not to try my luck inside tonight, instead waiting out on the street. I was relieved when she walked out around midnight.

"Hey," I called out, waving at her.

She froze. Her eyes met mine with a mixture of anger and incredulity.

I stayed where I was, leaning against the hood of my truck, letting her assess my presence.

Never catch an unknown shifter off guard, Reid.

But Allara wasn't unknown. I knew the sound of her heartbeat as well as I knew my own.

We'd had sex in this truck I was leaning against... how many times?

God only knows.

I wasn't scrapping the thing, ever. Too many memories I couldn't let go of.

The ghost of a smile flitted across her face as her eyes traced over the scratched headlights and beat-up hubcaps.

"Still got this old junker, then."

"Yep."

I left it at that. There were too many thorns attached to any conversation about our old relationship, and I'd already proven myself adept at stumbling right into them, and scratching both of us in the process.

She cocked her head to the side as she gazed at me. "What are you still doing here, Reid? I told you to go home."

Hopefully my gamble would pay off. After all, the Alpha's daughter had never backed down from a challenge before.

Ever.

"I've got a proposition for you."

Her head came up. I watched her spine straighten into a posture I recognized.

"Oh yeah? What's that?" she asked, lifting her chin.

"A challenge."

Something flickered behind her eyes.

I continued. "A fight, between you and me."

"A fight?" she whispered.

The shifter swirl of silver swam in her eyes.

Wolf shifter eyes. She could try to hide it all she liked from her precious city friends, but she couldn't hide her shifter from me.

"Yeah. If I can pin you, then you gotta come back with me." I lowered my voice and leaned close. "Come see your dad. Come back home, to your pack. Your family. We need you, Allara."

She blinked, seemingly caught off guard, before appearing to recover herself.

"And when *you* lose?" she asked, flicking her ponytail over her shoulder and thrusting out her perky breasts in a cocky move.

I put up my hands, trying to appear as non-threatening as possible.

She'd always been easy to rile up, just like I was. But I sensed that it had been a long time since the wolf in her had been allowed to roam free.

That'll sure make my job easier.

I brushed off my guilt and focused on my task. I had to do whatever it took to get Allara to come back with me, even if that meant using her wolf shifter biology against her.

I gave a loose shrug. "Then I go on my way. I'll return to the pack, admit defeat, and make sure none of us ever bother you again."

I studied her carefully, wondering what she was thinking. If I lost, did she even plan to come home for her father's funeral?

My resolve firmed. It didn't matter what she planned or didn't plan. I was going to win this fight. I had to. I didn't have time to give even a passing thought to the possibility of failure.

She stared at me for a moment longer, and a spark of hope grew in my chest.

Then, she shook her head. "No."

She turned away and walked off without another word.

God dammit.

I took off after her down the street. It looked like she was heading toward that diner where we'd eaten last night.

"Come on, Allara. You know I don't give up that easily."

She stopped in her tracks and pinned me with a stare. "You gave up on *us*."

I felt her words slide like a knife right between my ribs.

"I didn't give up," I forced myself to say. "I made a choice."

She held my gaze for a long time, but I didn't break the eye contact. I couldn't. This was too important.

Eventually, she was the one who blinked and glanced away.

"Then it was the wrong choice." Her voice shook with suppressed emotion.

This time, her words twisted themselves straight into my heart.

I had given her five years to move on, to find someone better, but from everything I'd seen and heard about her time in the city, it didn't seem like she had come close to settling down with anyone else.

I grabbed her arm and pulled her around to face me.

"We need to put our differences aside. It's like I said, okay? There's more at stake here than just the two of us." I understood her position. It was a struggle to think about the bigger picture right now, too. "Accept my challenge, Allara. Let the chips fall where they may."

She bit her lip, and I could tell she was wavering. I gripped her arm a little tighter, pressing my advantage.

"You could be free of me forever. Free of the pack. One fight, that's all it would take. I give you my word. If I lose, I leave."

She lifted her gaze to me, and there was so much unsaid in those big blue eyes of hers. Fear was at the forefront.

Was she afraid of saying no, or saying yes?

Of finally severing her connection to the only true family she had? Our pack.

I hoped not. That was what I had leveraged my challenge on.

Then suddenly her face cleared. She gave a single nod.

"Okay Reid." She cleared her throat, her wide mouth narrowing to a thin line. "I accept your challenge."

Finally.

I knew, somewhere underneath that slick city demeanor, that the Allara I knew was still there.

I shoved my hands into my pockets and projected an aura of casual certainty. Not that I was feeling anything near casual, but I didn't want my eagerness to cause her to switch off again.

"Where do you want to do this?" I asked, resisting the urge to say, *your place or mine?*

This is her territory, after all.

She knew the lay of the land better than I did.

"My condo has a backyard," she said, without hesitation. "The sooner we can get this over with, the better, right?"

I nodded. "Sure."

I couldn't quite get a handle on her emotions. One moment she seemed ready to kick me to the curb and send me packing, and the next, I could swear she seemed almost... *excited* by the prospect of letting out her wolf.

Without another word, she turned and strode away from me.

She's probably just looking forward to body-slamming me a few times.

Feeling strangely like I'd lost control of the situation, I followed her.

CHAPTER 5

ALLARA

The backyard of my condo was dimly lit, and the fences were high enough to deter any prying neighbors.

Perfect.

I shucked off my scarf and shoved it into my bag. "C'mon, I haven't got all night."

I was trying to contain the rush of adrenaline rocketing through my system, but it was proving more difficult than I thought to tamp the runaway emotions back down.

"Yes ma'am." He gave me a mock salute, and I rolled my eyes.

I could hear the thud of his heartbeat in his chest and his breathing picking up. My stomach tingled with anticipation despite everything. It had been... how many years since I'd shifted?

Too many.

I grinned, despite the situation that had led to this moment.

"A few ground rules," he said, tugging off his jacket and tossing it to one side. "No hair pulling, okay?"

"Very funny," I replied.

"I remember your moves well enough." He shook himself out a little and stretched. His biceps pulled tight behind his head and I looked away.

What was I *doing*, getting into this with Reid? I was here in the city for a reason. I had an okay life. I had friends. I was doing fine on my own. *Good*, even.

No thanks to him, or my dad, or anyone from the pack.

They'd cut me loose, and never followed up. Till now.

He smirked; he'd caught me looking. I shook the hair out of my face and straightened, focused on keeping my balance.

If he wanted a fight, he would get one. I wasn't going down easy.

Something in his gaze shifted when he registered the change in my posture. To a human, the change would be imperceptible, but for the first time that night I saw the wolf inside him rear up.

His breathing had deepened and there was a silver glint in his eye. My body was responding, as it had done hundreds of times before. Adrenaline raced along my veins, making my muscles tremble, and a shot of excitement curved my lips upward.

My wolf pushed, hard, desperate to be let out after all this time.

Silently, Reid extended his hand to me.

I stared at it for a moment before accepting the connection. Already, my brain felt totally scrambled.

Right. Challenge accepted.

I took a deep breath, and let him clasp our palms together. The feeling of his warm skin amidst the cold night air shocked me, and I gasped.

This was the first time we had touched each other in five years.

His head lowered and his eyes darkened, unblinking, hungry, and utterly focused on me.

I couldn't suppress a shiver as I backed up a couple of steps. He matched me pace for pace, and we began to circle each other slowly.

Without warning, he snarled, and his eyes flashed silver.

The outside world melted away, and my vision narrowed.

He had been my sole focus since we set foot in my backyard, but as I shifted into my wolf body, that feeling only grew in intensity. My every sense flooded with him: the heat of his fur, the intoxication of his scent, the flash of his eyes. They all melted together with a level of concentration I had long forgotten.

I shrank away from him, disorientated and overwhelmed.

It was surreal to be a wolf again, after all this time. My ears flicked, catching the sounds of distant traffic on the freeway.

I padded toward Reid with a curious huff, absorbing the feel of the damp grass against my paws.

Well, they always said it would be like riding a bike.

Reid's wolf eyed me impassively. His brown fur glinted with silver flecks, just like I remembered. He stood a couple of hands taller than me, and his pelt wasn't quite as sleek as mine.

He made a formidable sight. If he had been a stranger, I might have been afraid.

But I wasn't. Quite the opposite, in fact.

He was trembling a little, muscles coiled. He was holding himself back as he waited for me to adjust to the change.

I thought about the long years I'd spent alone. Without him.

I'd been abandoned at a time when I needed him, more than I ever had before. He knew how much he'd hurt me, and he hadn't seemed to care.

And then, to come swanning back into my life now, like nothing had ever happened.

The dark thoughts swirled in my head, and a growl built in my throat.

He answered it with a low, rumbling snarl.

There wasn't any warning or signal. We didn't need one. Not when we were like this.

We sprang at each other, just as we had done countless times before.

But this was no play fight or teenage sparring session. Not for me.

I channeled every ounce of hurt I had held onto for the last five years and unleashed it on him.

It had always been like a dance, fighting with Reid. I could sense his every breath, perceive his movements almost before he actioned them himself, and he could sense mine. We knew each other's strengths and weaknesses as well as we knew our own.

We sparred for a while, ducking and weaving and play fighting as we had as children, re-learning each other as my body quickly fell back into the groove of the whole wolf thing.

I might not have been as strong as I once was, but I knew I could still put up a fight. He seemed to sense the heat of my anger, too. *Good.*

But he was holding back a little, and that infuriated me further.

He'd challenged *me*, after all. There was too much at stake for half measures.

I snapped at him to show my frustration.

He loped back a few paces, shaking out his pelt.

He couldn't fool me. We were both panting heavily with exertion, but he needed to commit fully, so I could, too.

I let out an impatient whine and charged him. Taking advantage of his shock at my aggressive move, I fastened my teeth into his neck and pulled him over me, trying to lock him into a tussle.

He threw me off with ease, confirming my suspicions that he wasn't using his full strength.

Come on, Reid. What're you so afraid of?

He'd been the one to suggest this, raising the stakes. But now we were here, body-slamming each other into the turf, he didn't seem to want to land a proper hit on me.

Finally, it dawned on me. He was worried about hurting me.

I snorted.

Well, if he wanted to hold back, I wouldn't. I slid under him, rolling him over and forcing him into action. We grappled, and finally, I felt his energy engage.

Good. If I won this, I wanted it to be on my own merits, not because he wouldn't commit.

Neither one of us managed to gain the upper hand. His body pressed itself against mine, eliciting all kinds of long-forgotten sensations.

He wasn't going easy on me anymore; he was finally exerting his full strength. I had to use every trick I had to keep him from getting close enough to pin me down.

We drew apart and he shook himself out with a rumbling growl, glowering at me. His eyes darkened, and his pupils grew larger so that only a sliver of silver iris was visible.

Adrenaline pulsed through me.

Perhaps he'd thought I'd go down easy. I hadn't been in my wolf form for a long time, after all, and clearly, he had only grown in agility and strength.

I still had a key advantage over him. Alpha blood ran through my veins. We were more evenly matched than he'd bargained for.

His sudden attack caught me off guard, knocking me to the ground. I twisted out from under him and we rolled over and over on the grass before thudding into the side of the fence, hard enough that splinters of wood flew everywhere.

Oops. So much for keeping a low profile.

For a split second, I had him exactly where I wanted him. His head pushed into the ground and he relaxed under me, huffing out a breath.

I breathed out too, relief crashing over me.

I had this.

Acting on instinct, I leaned down and nuzzled at the side of his throat.

In a flash, he flipped us over and pinned me to the ground. Enraged, I snarled and snapped up at his neck, struggling against him.

To no avail.

I didn't have him, after all. Far from it. Instead, he had me exactly where he wanted me.

I should have walked away while I had the chance. Everything about him—his voice, his scent, his eyes—had made me weak.

Alpha blood or not, I suddenly realized I never stood a chance.

The fight drained out of me and I felt my body start to shift, melting back into human form. Above me, Reid's wolf form faded too, until I was staring up into wide human eyes.

I wasn't struggling any more. The shock of transformation drained me of any fight I had left.

At any rate, he'd won.

He had me pinned. His bare skin was hot against mine.

In a rush, I remembered why it wasn't a good idea to shift into wolf form wearing clothes. There were probably torn pieces of clothing littering the grass all around us.

Those were my new jeans!

It was a minor annoyance in my current position, but still.

The silver in his eyes faded to their usual dark gray, though they were still burning with heat. The expression of desire on his face was one I remembered well.

Our mouths were mere inches apart.

Involuntarily, I licked my lips, and his gaze dropped immediately to my mouth.

He looked like he'd forgotten why we were tangled together like this.

He wasn't making any move to get up, though. And I wasn't making any effort to push him off me.

I could barely feel the grass underneath us anymore, or see the starlit sky above.

I was consumed with the feel of his body on top of mine. We'd been here a thousand times before.

My body remembered it vividly, even if the rest of me had desperately tried to forget.

He drew his arms up until they rested on either side of my head.

One of his hands found my throat and traced the skin there. He slid his fingers through my hair, tilted my head up, and leaned close so that his hair fell down and tickled my shoulders.

When he brushed his lips against mine, I shivered, my lips parting slightly.

He groaned and exhaled against my mouth, deepening the kiss and pressing down against me.

Heat curled in my stomach and I slid my calves against his. Taking advantage of his distraction, I rolled us over so that I straddled him, before leaning back down and kissing him deeply.

When we broke apart, I stared at him, a million thoughts swirling in my head.

What am I doing? God, I've missed this.

He lay there, chuckling. "Alpha."

Judging by his wide smile, he wasn't mad about me flipping us and taking the dominant position. I brushed the hair off his face and ran my hands down his chest and over his arms. He was breathing heavily, looking up at me with something akin to awe.

A small part of me wondered if he'd known this was going to happen. An even bigger part of me screamed to get off him before I did something we would both regret.

His hands wrapped themselves firmly around my hips and I snapped back to the moment.

He was waiting for me to make the call.

Screw it, I thought.

In for a penny, in for a pound.

My fingers tangled in his hair and I dragged him up to meet me in another messy kiss.

CHAPTER 6

REID

Our fight had gone in my favor. Just as I knew it would.

Allara was still fiercely strong, and faster than any of the other women in the pack, but I had the edge of determination and raw strength on my side.

And a point to prove.

Kissing her hadn't been part of my game plan, though.

It's been too long, the wolf in me snarled. *Take her, right now.*

Her hands threaded into my hair and she pulled me up toward her again.

I went willingly.

No hair pulling. I wound my arms tightly around her as she kissed me.

A surge of desire caught me, and I moved her off me, jumped up and then pulled her to her feet. I lifted her against me and she instantly wrapped her legs around my waist, holding on like a limpet as I carried her to her patio door. After a little fumbling to find the handle, I managed to open the door one handed and carry her inside.

The tiny shred of reason left inside me screamed at me to stop, to back away right now, leave. This wasn't meant to happen.

This was the *one thing* that wasn't meant to happen. Every second I held her in my arms, I was breaking down all the barriers that had kept me apart from her.

Barriers I knew had been put in place for a reason. I had agreed, hadn't I?

She wasn't meant for me. I knew that. She never had been.

But if we kept going like this, tonight, then the strings that had once tied us together would be hopelessly tangled again. *And this time, we might never be able to unravel them.*

Once my shifter impulses had kicked in, red mist had descended. Even though we hadn't been near each other for years, my body reacted to her touch as if no time had passed.

Like we were a mated pair. Soul-bonded.

There was only one direction this was heading in and it was a direction I couldn't continue to travel.

And yet, I was powerless to stop.

It had been so long since I felt whole. Five long and lonely years.

We stumbled through her dark condo and I pressed her up against every surface we passed: her kitchen counter, the back of her couch, a nearby wall. She nipped at the skin between my shoulder and neck and I growled with impatience before finally pushing her up against the door she whispered belonged to her bedroom.

She lowered her legs to the floor. I pinned her there as she shivered and gazed up at me. Her pupils were dark, and even in the low light I could tell that her lips were swollen from my kisses.

"I've missed you." The words tumbled out before I could stop them.

Without giving her a chance to register what I'd said, I leaned in and captured her lips again, delving into her mouth without restraint.

The heat building between our dampening skin would have overwhelmed an ordinary human, but it only intensified our desire for each other.

Her scent was driving me crazy. The smell of her shampoo was different, but underneath it she was still Allara. *My* Allara.

I pressed my nose against her neck and growled, scraping my teeth over her sensitive flesh just to feel her pulse skittering. Her legs trembled, like she would collapse if I weren't holding her against me.

She opened the door and drew me in to her bedroom, urging me forward until the back of her legs hit the mattress. Then she swiveled and pushed at my chest, and I sprawled out backwards on top of her bed. She crawled on top of me, her long, gorgeous hair pooling on either side of me, and she took my lower lip between her teeth and bit down, none-too-gently.

I groaned and rolled on top of her. My hands slipped around her waist, and I pulled her up, inch my inch, not stopping until my cock slipped deeply inside her. I'd wanted to do that from the moment I stepped into that dingy city bar.

I'd waited five years. There was no time for finesse.

She gasped and tightened around me so sweetly I almost finished right then and there. But I clenched my jaw and focused on the beauty of her face. I wasn't coming without her.

The room around us spun as I began to move, riding her thrusts as she countered mine.

In that moment, everything vanished from my head in the blink of an eye: the pack, my mission, Jaime. None of it felt real.

Nothing else mattered. Only her.

She hooked her ankles behind me and urged me deeper, panting in my ear. My desire for her was overwhelming, and I buried my face into her neck and gave myself over to it completely, absorbing everything: the taste of her skin, the feel of her perfect body, the softness of her hair, and the look of wanton bliss in her eyes.

We had been here countless times. I could pick out her scent from a thousand. The feeling of her mouth against mine was one I remembered well.

She had been locked in my head for years, in a hundred memories, a thousand tiny moments that took on a much greater significance after she was gone.

I'd replayed my memories of her when she was like this over and over in my head. This was real. Every memory I had of her paled in comparison to the real woman lying beneath me, and the ecstasy of having her with me again.

And then her breath hitched, and I knew she was close. I wanted to hear that keening cry, feel her spasm around me.

I grabbed her hips and tilted her until she moaned, then I sunk into her as deeply as I could, over and over again. Until she was crying out my name and sucking me into orgasm with her.

I groaned as I spilled myself inside her, feeling the wetness of her tears on my cheek as her pussy spasmed around me and we both fell into perfect bliss.

CHAPTER 7
ALLARA

I rolled over in bed and felt the unfamiliar weight of another person lying next to me.

Well. Not quite unfamiliar.

I'd had more than a few dreams like this, in the hazy moments between sleeping and waking. I smiled sleepily and pressed up close against his back until my body was flush with his, inhaling that gorgeous scent.

Reid.

As I began to wake up properly, it all came flooding back.

Last night. The fight. And then we...

Ah, shit.

Twisting away from him, I yanked the covers back and stumbled out of bed, groping around on the floor for my robe.

I cursed myself for being so stupid, for letting him *get* to me like that. No matter how carefully I stepped, it seemed I couldn't help myself when it came to him.

You helped yourself last night, said a voice in my head that sounded suspiciously like Penny's all-knowing tone.

I grimaced at the memory. On Sunday afternoon, I'd swung by the diner to grab a coffee and fill her in on Reid's sudden reappearance, followed by the disastrous meal we had shared there the night before.

Penny was one of the few people in my new life who knew the truth about who I was and where I'd come from.

This had made explaining the whole *Reid* thing easier in some ways, and much, *much* harder in others.

"So, he's... what? An ex-boyfriend of yours?"

I nodded, stirring my coffee. "I guess you could say that."

Penny's expression grew contemplative. "That explains the weird tension, then. Wait—I thought shifters mated for life?"

I cringed. "He's not my mate. He's just Reid."

"Huh." Penny looked skeptical. "If you say so..."

I'd changed the subject and instead regaled her with my bar encounter with the creep who had harassed Tammy. Penny seemed to take the hint, though I could tell she had a million questions hovering on the tip of her tongue.

Not that I was likely to have the answers for her.

I thought I'd known where I stood. Now, it was like the ground beneath me had crumbled away, and I stood at the edge of a cliff, looking down at the jagged rocks below.

When I walked out of the diner last night, I had wondered if Reid's and my brief reunion inside the bar was the last we would see of each other.

I'd had no plans of returning to the pack until he dropped back into my life, after all. At some point, I would probably have visited the pack briefly, to pay my respects to Dad, but up until yesterday, the thought of seeing Reid again had been too painful to contemplate.

Perhaps, I thought, he would take me at face value and give up.

It seemed hopelessly naïve in the cold light of day. Reid wasn't the type to give up on anything that truly mattered.

Like me seeing my dad before he died, obviously.

I stared down at Reid's sleeping form, lost in thought. His brown hair lay fanned out over my pillows, his face buried between them. A heavy sleeper, just like I remembered.

The smooth planes of his back were toned and lithe, although he had filled out since I'd last seen him. Having now reached his physical prime, he'd lost the rangy appearance of a young wolf shifter, and fully come into his adult power.

He looked strange in my little apartment bedroom, like a puzzle piece that didn't quite fit.

Shaking away my confusing thoughts, I grabbed a towel from the linen cupboard and, after a second's hesitation, fresh clothes. I would change in the bathroom.

I was better off leaving him to his own devices while I attempted to pull myself together.

After my shower, I made coffee and toast, curled up at my kitchen table, and waited for him to make an appearance.

It was a little after eight when my bedroom door finally opened, and he padded into the kitchen. Steam trailed in through the open door; he was wearing one of my towels slung loosely around his hips. Water droplets ran down his neck in an obscenely distracting manner. He flashed a grin and shook out his hair, sending water everywhere. He scrubbed at the back of his head with one careless hand.

"Ugh." I hated when he did that.

I only remembered how much I hated it as he was *doing* it.

I kind of regretted making him a coffee now.

His grin widened. Unrepentant, he stole a piece of toast from the plate in front of me and chewed happily, picking up the coffee mug I pushed across the table at him, and wandered back into my bedroom.

The worst part of all of this?

He *knew* that he had me exactly where he wanted me.

It was imperative I return with him now. It was written into our biology, in the shifter blood running through our veins. A promise that couldn't be broken.

I couldn't decide how I felt about that.

I knew one thing for sure: I should never have accepted his stupid challenge in the first place.

Groaning to myself, I put my head in my hands. Last night had been such a mistake.

Now that he'd given me a taste of what we used to have, walking away at the end of all this was going to be so much harder.

He would just repeat what he did last time, and stroll off without a care in the world. I would be left to pick up the pieces. Again.

There was nothing to do about it now, though. I had to see this thing out to the bitter end.

~

"Haven't you missed it at all?"

Reid's voice startled me out of my reverie. I'd been staring out the truck window, watching the skyscrapers turn into suburbs as we reached the edge of the city, before finally giving way to open farmland.

I turned to him.

"Missed what?" I said, though I already knew.

His hands flexed on the steering wheel. His eyes were fixed on the open road. "Home. The pack."

Of course. Before I came here, it was all I'd ever known.

"Not so much anymore," I said. I pulled the sleeves of my sweater down over my hands and hugged myself. "Feels like a long time ago."

It wasn't a total lie. It *did* feel like a long time ago. I had found new people to protect in the city; in some ways, they had almost become my new pack.

He glanced at me. "You cold?"

I shook my head. "No, this truck has shitty insulation, which you still haven't fixed. Don't think I haven't noticed."

It was a bullshit answer and we both knew it. Wolf shifters ran hot; we didn't need the kind of protection from icy weather that ordinary humans did.

"It does! You never..." His face fell, and his expression shuttered. "You never shut up about it."

A weighty silence followed his words.

Our past together lurked around every corner, and we kept slamming into it like a brick wall.

I rubbed the cashmere weave of my sweater between finger and thumb. It wasn't practical for where we were going, but I hadn't taken much stuff with me when I left all those years ago. Most of my clothes were lightweight now. Sneakers and tank tops were much better for a crowded city.

I thought about Reid's question.

Maybe I'd done a better job than I thought of seeming above it all, like I couldn't care less whether he came or went.

Maybe he truly believed I had moved on from my old life with the pack.

Moved on from him.

I had, right?

"Coming back with you... it doesn't mean I'm staying," I heard myself say. "You do know that, right?"

His face turned grave. "I know."

The fields were disappearing outside the windows. We were nearing the edge of the forest now. I caught sight of the first redwoods up ahead of us, and my heart clenched with a queasy mixture of anticipation and dread.

Out of the corner of my eye, I glanced at Reid, but his focus had turned back to the road.

Although I would never admit it to him in a million years, I was comforted by his presence. The only thing worse than my current predicament would be having to face the pack alone.

The redwoods began to thicken, and the winter sun shone dimly through the trees as we drove. The woods were small and spaced out here; some were barely seven feet tall.

The trees at the heart of the forest were giants. They stood tall enough that you could barely see the tops of them, and their branches seemed to stretch out for miles, forming a leafy canopy overhead thick enough in places to block out the stars.

"Stick close," Reid said suddenly. "When we arrive, stay near me, okay? I'll take you straight to your dad."

There was tension in his voice that startled me. I didn't understand or appreciate his tone, but I nodded nonetheless.

Maybe things back home really had changed?

Did he think I was in danger?

"What's up with Jaime, anyway?" I asked, to change the subject. "You said he couldn't be trusted. Why?"

Reid's face darkened. He was silent for a long moment, like he was choosing his words carefully.

"He wants to... expand our territories." His brow furrowed as he stared at the open road ahead of us. The snow-topped mountains loomed in the distance, blue and hazy. "Roll the border out, right across the creek. He wants to take land all the way out to the plains. Once he becomes Alpha, he's planning to start a turf war in every direction."

"What?" My heart began to pound. "He wants to push the Ferrers pack off their land? And the Thornwoods? That's crazy!"

The neighboring packs had lived in peace with ours for as long as I could remember.

"I know." Reid's jaw clenched. "Even if we had the numbers... it's a suicide mission."

I nodded grimly. Not to mention the fact that we would be betraying the trust of people we knew. Our allies. Packs that we'd fought shoulder to shoulder alongside during countless turf wars in the past.

Strange, I thought, how I've already slipped back into thinking of the pack as ours.

And now Jaime wanted to destroy our pack? Destroy everything my dad had built, in an ill-considered and bloodthirsty quest for dominion?

"How do you know all this?" I asked.

I couldn't imagine Jaime revealing his plans willingly, and to *Reid*, of all people.

They had never seen eye to eye. As the son of the pack's Beta, Jaime was a high-ranking male in the pack's hierarchy. Reid was an unknown element, an outsider who, in the eyes of some, had unsettled the natural order of things when he waltzed in and started dating the Alpha's daughter.

When we were young, Reid had been stronger and faster than the others, and everyone knew it. As a foundling, no-one knew Reid's true heritage, but I always assumed he came from an Alpha line. He was huge in wolf form, and protective as all get out. Not to mention loyal, too.

Jaime had challenged him to more than one fight over the years, usually over something petty and stupid. Reid had always had the good sense to refuse.

The notion that Reid was now somehow privy to Jaime's plans seemed absurd.

Still, what do I know? They might be best pals, now.

Maybe Jaime was planning on making Reid his Beta. I'd been away for a long time, after all.

I almost laughed at the ridiculousness of the image. Things might have changed, but they couldn't have changed *that* much.

"About a month ago, I overheard Jason talking to Paul," Reid said.

"About Jaime, and his plans. They'd both tried to tell him how insane it was, apparently, but he wouldn't listen."

That made more sense. Jason was Jaime's best friend. Paul was a couple of years younger, but he had followed the two of them around like a puppy for as long as I could remember.

It hadn't always been that way. Once upon a time, Jason and Reid had been like brothers.

Reid, Jason, Kara and me.

When we were kids, it was just the four of us... our own little pack.

That was a long time ago.

Things were very different now.

"The Thornwoods would retaliate," I said. "They'd go upstate, get help from one of the bigger packs. Maybe even the State Chapter." I tried to keep the panic out of my voice, but I could hear it, nonetheless. "All the peace treaties would be dust. We'd be wiped out!"

"Allara." Reid took one hand off the steering wheel, grabbed my hand, and squeezed it. "*Listen* to me. I know. That's why I came to bring you back. I realize...I realize this isn't what you want. I would have let you be if I could. But the pack needs you right now."

I need you.

His unspoken words echoed in my head and I sighed with frustration. Why did he make me feel like this—as if I knew what he was thinking and feeling as well as I knew my own mind?

Just like last night, I was misinterpreting things again. Filling in the blanks, equipping him with motivations that might not even be accurate.

"Does Dad know?" I asked.

Reid's mouth twisted. He tapped his fingers against the driving wheel and wouldn't meet my eyes. "No."

Something dawned on me. As I put the pieces together, my feelings of despair grew.

"He's been ill for a while, hasn't he?"

He sighed. "Yes. I'm sorry."

I knew that learning the truth about Jaime would break my dad's heart.

Reid had kept that painful news from him, apparently. For better or worse.

"Thank you for sparing Dad that information."

Reid nodded and I turned to stare out the window.

I had to think fast. It wouldn't be long before we arrived. The trees we passed were taller and denser now, and the air had taken on a familiar dim, misty quality. Shafts of sunlight pierced through the branches and lit up patches of undergrowth as we rumbled along.

"Would the pack stand behind Jaime?" I asked. "Some of them might agree with him."

Reid's brow creased, and he shook his head. "I don't know. Some folks, maybe. But most of them would realize that it's total lunacy."

I exhaled shakily. For the first time since we got in the truck, Reid turned his head and met my eyes properly.

"Allara, you and I both know we won't have a choice. Once Jaime becomes Alpha, he can exert his will over the pack. They'll have to do what he says, even if..."

"It kills them," I finished.

That was how it worked. I'd never appreciated how terrifying the prospect was before, nor how easily the power could be abused.

Maybe because Dad, for all his faults, would never dream of leading his pack into danger. Every single decision he made considered pack safety and happiness first and foremost.

I swallowed. *Except when it comes to me, I guess.*

Reid was silent for the rest of the journey. When the track curved to the left, winding off the main road, he glanced at me.

"You ready?"

"Yeah," I lied.

The first rooftops began to peek through the trees. We passed trucks parked up on both sides of the track, and the tarmac road gave way to dirt.

I tried without much success to quell the flutter of nerves in my stomach.

Reid pulled up outside his house and turned the key to cut the engine.

The truck suddenly felt way too still and silent for my liking.

Although I was eager for a chance to stretch my legs after the long journey, I took my time opening the passenger door and climbing out.

Our arrival had not gone unnoticed. People came out of the meeting house across the street, stopping in their tracks to stare at us.

Who was I kidding?

They stared at *me.*

Their eyes burned into the back of my head as I slammed the door of

Reid's truck louder than I needed to. I mostly kept my head down, but still noticed some familiar faces in amongst the gathering crowd.

On the wide porch of the Briars' house, Jason stood watching us, his sister Kara by his side.

My mouth twitched as I noticed that their faces were perfect mirror images of shock.

I couldn't help but feel the ghost of something at the sight of Kara. A feeling that was akin to regret.

She had been my closest childhood friend. I was an only child, the lonely daughter of the Alpha wolf. Most of the other children had treated me with respect, but they never forgot who I was, or what I was destined to be. They weren't cold to me, but they weren't warm, either.

Except Kara. We had been almost sisters when we were kids, joined at the hip.

Then Reid came along, and the four of us had hung around for a little while. Reid, Jason, Kara and I, making forts in the woods, pranking the other kids, and causing all kinds of trouble.

And then Mom died.

I'd withdrawn from Kara, just like I had from practically everything and everyone else.

I spotted Luke, who had been a kid the last time I saw him. He was now a gangly teenager. He reminded me a little of Reid at the same age, standing in the awkward fashion of someone who wasn't yet certain how to arrange their long limbs.

One by one, everyone in the immediate vicinity fell silent. Every face turned toward me.

Watching. Waiting, no doubt, to see what I would do next.

Run away? Again?

It seemed like the most attractive option, albeit a highly impractical one at this moment.

Instead, I lifted my head high, and straightened my spine, hearing my dad's voice float to the surface of my mind from some long-forgotten memory.

Alpha wolves do not bow to anyone, Allara.

I had to face this situation head on. I had to act like I couldn't care less about the stir my appearance had created.

Easier said than done.

A warm hand landed around my shoulders, a firm, steady pressure that eased the nervous tension a little.

Reid.

He was a solid presence by my side. He turned me slightly, shielding me from prying eyes with his body.

"Show's over, folks!" he called out, waving a hand at the audience we'd gathered. A few more curious glances shot my way, then the crowd began to disperse, murmuring amongst themselves.

After a couple of minutes, we were alone on the dirt road that ran straight through the center of the small village.

Our small village.

I stepped away from Reid, and his hand fell back to his side.

His face fell, too.

"I'll see you later?" I said, before I could stop myself.

He brightened and gave me a crooked smile. "Definitely."

My old house lay at the end of the street, just around the corner. It was set back a little from the other houses, down a small gravel path.

When I reached the house, the long timber beams supporting the overhanging porch, and the swing where I used to sit with Reid... everything seemed exactly the same.

Just like I never left.

There was a light in the small window at the top of the house. The attic, where my dad's study had been. Was it still his study? Or was he too ill to do any work there, anymore?

He had always kept a lamp burning there all through the night. One time, I asked him why. I had been very small and wanted him to keep talking to me so I didn't have to go to sleep.

"Because, Allie," he'd said as he tucked the blanket up under my chin and smoothed the covers beneath his hands. "Sometimes even Daddy has to sleep. And this way, my lamp can keep watch over the whole pack, and keep everyone safe."

"Like a lighthouse?" I asked.

"Just like a lighthouse." He kissed my forehead. "Exactly. It's my job to protect everyone in this pack, honey. And, one day, it will be yours."

I snuggled down under the covers. "Goodnight, Daddy."

"Goodnight, Allara. Sweet dreams."

The memory faded away, and my happiness at the familiar sight mingled with dread at the thought of what I would find up in that attic room.

CHAPTER 8

ALLARA

Before I could talk myself out of what I had to do, I strode up to the porch and fumbled in the pocket of my jeans, drawing out the small key I'd found buried in the bottom drawer of my closet back in the city.

A lump formed in my throat as I slid it into the lock and turned the handle.

Maybe he changed the locks.

The door opened easily. I stepped inside, inhaling the familiar smell of pine leaves, smoke, and... family.

My chest grew tight. I dug my nails into my palm to prevent tears from falling.

Why had I stayed away so long?

Was the hurt back then worth alienating myself from everything I had ever known and loved?

I could barely even swallow. My throat ached at holding back the emotion.

The hallway was dimly lit. As I closed the door behind me, taking care to be quiet, a woman appeared at the top of the stairs.

Rachel. My mom's oldest friend. The woman who'd taken Reid in, raised him practically as her own child. She'd always had my back.

After Mom died, she'd been the only one to defend my relationship with Reid. On one memorable occasion, she had even argued with my dad about it.

He'd thought we were too young to be spending so much time together, and she had reminded him sharply of the way he and Mother were at that age.

After that, he never brought it up again.

"Allara?" She blinked at me, looking as dumbfounded as everyone else in the village.

I raised my hand in greeting and smiled at her weakly.

She seemed to gather herself together, and raced down the stairs, sweeping me into a rib-cracking hug before pulling back to look me over like she couldn't believe her eyes.

"What—how—*when* did you get back?"

"Whoa!" I said, grinning. "Slow down! Just now, I swear. I came straight here."

Her eyes filled with happiness. "Reid found you, then."

I dropped my gaze and untangled myself gently from her embrace. "Yeah."

So, she had known he was coming to look for me.

It occurred to me that I didn't know whether Reid had acted alone. Had he confided in anyone about his plans for bringing me home? Rachel had clearly suspected it, at least.

Was she the only one?

"Your father's upstairs." Her hand pressed against mine, holding tight. "He's... I'm so sorry, Allara. He's very ill."

"Reid told me already." I blinked back a tidal wave of emotions before they threatened to spill over, determined to meet her kind, familiar gaze with calm rather than panic. "Can I see him?"

"Of course, honey." She put her hand on my elbow and led me into the kitchen. "You can take him his glass of water. He needs to take his medication, and he hides the pills otherwise."

I snorted despite myself and grabbed a glass from the cupboard before filling it up.

That sounds like Dad, alright.

Trying to keep my breathing steady, I climbed up the stairs with the glass in my hand. Once I reached the landing, I spared a glance at my old bedroom door.

Had he kept it as it was? Or had he cleared it out?

I couldn't bring myself to peek inside. I didn't particularly like either of those options.

The narrow stairs that led up to the top bedroom were fitted with a stair-rail that hadn't been there when I left. I knocked once on the door, and then pushed it open softly.

"Rachel?" A voice, frailer and quieter than I remembered, floated over from the other side of the room. "That you?"

I hadn't been allowed into the attic much as a child. The adults had been afraid I might overhear something, a pack secret that wasn't meant for a child's ears. My dad and his Beta, Terry, would work in here; maps were often pinned to the walls, plans weighted to the coffee table, almanacs stacked up on the sideboard as they made plans each new year.

Resolving feuds, managing supply runs, chairing council meetings, negotiating trade deals: in the pack, everything was done with the changing seasons, drafted into existence as frost coated the window-panes, golden leaves blustered through the streets, or the first buds of spring curled open on the branches outside.

When Mom died, Dad had taken to sleeping up here.

He'd never come back down. Not really.

I inhaled sharply as pain squeezed my ribs. He was sitting near the window, reclining in his favorite armchair. He was propped up on a stack of pillows. An old TV set buzzed faintly in the background. A stack of newspapers rested on the coffee table beside him. I'd clearly just woken him.

My chest tightened. "Hey, Dad."

He turned, startled. His sudden recognition felt like the clouds parting to reveal the sun.

"Allara?"

The newspaper on his lap slid onto the floor. I approached him slowly, picked it up and placed it on his unmade bed.

I'm being too cautious. Relax. If your body language conveys tension, he'll sense it.

Hell, he *taught you that.*

He looked up at me, blinking.

I gave him a faint smile. "Yeah, it's me."

He angled his head to get a proper look at me. He had aged so much since I'd last seen him. His hair had almost entirely turned white, and his body was completely dwarfed by the chair he sat in.

There was barely an echo of the strong man in the prime of his life that I knew as a little girl. The intervening years, and the losses they brought with them, had obviously taken a great toll on him.

"It's really you, isn't it?" He reached out and touched my hair. His touch was as light as the brush of a cobweb. "After all this time, the prodigal daughter returns."

"Reid brought me home," I heard myself say.

I was still reeling from the sight of my father like this. The proud Alpha wolf he had once been still lurked somewhere behind those clouded eyes.

It must. He can't be gone from me already.

At the mention of Reid's name, my father sighed deeply. "Ah, yes. Of course."

I bristled. Surely, he couldn't be holding onto his old grudges even now?

A thousand defensive comments swirled in my head. Before I could express any of them, however, my father spoke again.

"Allara." He drew a deep, shuddering breath, looking like it took all his energy to do so. "I owe you an apology."

I went still. *What?*

Whatever I'd been expecting, it wasn't *that.*

"Five years ago," he continued. "You left us. I know it was because of me."

He paused and gave a couple of great, hacking coughs. I passed the glass of water over to him, looking around for his medication.

"Dad, it's fine. Just rest, okay?"

"No." He batted my hands away, taking the glass but refusing to drink. "I'm fine."

"You're not fine!" *So stubborn.* Now I remembered where I got it from. "You need to save your strength."

"I've *been* saving it." He met my eyes. "For this. For you, Allara. I had to talk to you. Before..."

He trailed off. His gaze turned inward, like he was looking at something I couldn't see.

I took a seat in the easy chair opposite him, giving him a chance to gather his thoughts.

"I never meant to make you feel like you didn't belong here," he murmured, so quiet that I had to lean forward to hear him. "I think about the night you left all the time. I think about the choices I made back then..."

"Like announcing Jaime as your successor?"

He looked up. His eyes were steel blue, piercing. The clouds vanished. In that moment, for a few seconds at least, he looked like his old, strong self.

"Being a leader is about strategy, Allara," he said, leaning back and folding his hands together. "I had to think about the pack. I didn't know whether they would accept you as my successor. A woman taking the role of Alpha... it isn't unheard of, but in these parts?"

As much as his reasoning made sense, my voice still trembled with anger as I said, "So, you—what? Just decided to keep me out of the loop altogether?"

"I never kept you out of anything!" he barked, refusing to meet my eyes. Instead, he stared beyond me, gazing out of the window at the forest. "I couldn't *reach* you, Allara. As much as I wanted to. I... I didn't know how."

For the first time, I saw our situation through new eyes. Me and Reid grew close after Mom died. Dad had withdrawn from me, sure. But I'd pulled away from him, too.

"Terry and I talked it over. After your mom..." He hung his head. We'd never properly spoken about her death. I could sense that wasn't going to change, even now. "You seemed so lost, Allie. You weren't ready for the responsibility."

"And Jaime?" I asked. "You thought Jaime could take on that responsibility?"

My father's face softened. "It wasn't an either-or situation. I thought he would be a good match for you, when the time came."

Confusion rose in me. "So, you thought that by naming Jaime as your successor, I would eventually become his mate?"

My mouth twisted. On paper, it did sound like a neat solution. The ideal way to appease those in the pack who wanted a male Alpha, *and* those who wanted a leader with actual Alpha blood.

A perfect match.

Too bad I'd refused to play along.

He met my eyes and it was as though his piercing gaze reached into my mind and turned over my thoughts, one by one.

"I wanted you to step up, Allara. You and Jaime had the potential to lead the pack together, side by side. I wanted you to think about your future here."

A new thought nudged at the back of my mind, hazy at first, before it slid abruptly into focus.

"You ordered Reid to end things with me," I whispered. "Didn't you?"

"Like I said..." He leaned forward, placing his trembling hand over mine. "I'm *sorry*."

A jumble of emotions threatened to overwhelm me as I sat there in silence and tried to make sense of it all.

For so many years, I'd avoided thinking about that night; the moment Reid's words had washed over me and broken me apart, piece by piece.

At the time I had been in shock, unable to think straight. The breakup had seemed to come totally out of the blue. It had left me reeling, wondering if there had been signs of his fading affection that I'd missed.

I recalled the things he said that night with excruciating clarity.

Even all these years later, those words had jagged edges; they cut me just as sharply as they had the first time I'd heard them.

We can't be together anymore. I should never have let it get this far.

You had to know... we were never going to last forever.

Allara, I'm doing this for you.

Maybe he really *had* done it for me.

Or... done what he *thought* was the best thing for me.

"The boy wasn't easy to convince, Allara."

My dad's words broke through my reverie.. He sat there, gazing at me. His eyes were overcast once more, full of regret.

"I tried everything I could think of to make him see reason." He stared at the television, but I knew he wasn't really seeing the screen. "I offered him money. That didn't work. Then I threatened him."

My lips parted a little, but no words came out.

A threat?

My dad shook his head. "I'm not proud of it. But still he wouldn't budge. I gave him the chance to pack up, go start a new life somewhere, far away. He wouldn't take any of it."

I swallowed hard, unable to speak.

That sounded like Reid all right.

If my dad had thought any of those options would sway Reid, then he didn't know him at all. Reid didn't care about money, and he was afraid of nothing.

"Finally, I asked him to consider your future," my dad whispered. "As the Alpha's daughter, I told him that you had certain... responsibilities. That, sooner or later, you were going to have to make a choice."

A choice. Between the pack, and Reid.

"You were worried I would choose wrong," I said softly.

He nodded. "I was. And I had every reason, Allara. I couldn't know for certain whether or not you would put the pack's welfare first."

I looked away from him, and watched the bare branches of the tree outside tapping against the glass. "I guess we'll never know what I may or may not have done. But, without him..."

The pack wasn't worth leading. There wasn't anything here worth staying for.

When I'd been cast adrift after my mother had died, he was the one who found me and pulled me back to shore. I couldn't envisage life here without him.

My father seemed to catch the words I left unsaid, because he simply nodded, regret etched across his face.

He'd tried to force my hand, and he'd lost everything. We both had.

"I made a mistake, Allara." He leaned forward and took my hand in both of his. "I didn't understand the depth of your feelings for him. That was *my* failing, not yours."

I sniffed and wiped at my face with my cuff sleeve.

"Your mother and I..." The ghost of a smile flickered across his face. "Well, I knew it from the moment I met her that I would do whatever it took to keep her safe. That I could never be without her. When you find your mate, you *know*."

"I could never be with Jaime," I said, feeling the need to explain myself. "There was no one else. Only Reid."

"Allie," he said, pulling me forward with a surprising amount of strength to gather me up into a hug. "I'm sorry."

"I'm sorry for leaving," I mumbled into his shoulder, realizing that, despite the fact he'd tried to manipulate my life, I'd ended up proving him right. That the pack wasn't the most important part of my life. Reid was.

We broke apart and I wiped at the tears on my cheeks.

"I put you in an impossible position," he said, brushing the hair out of my face and giving me a chagrined smile. "And, for what it's worth, I'm proud of all you have accomplished, out there on your own."

I frowned. "How do you know what I've accomplished? You haven't..."

I stopped. Of course, he had kept an eye on me. I was pack. I was the Alpha's daughter. There's no way they'd have just let me disappear, without keeping some kind of tabs on me.

I wasn't sure whether to be grateful or annoyed that maybe I hadn't been as alone all these years as I had thought.

Tears sprouted, and even then, I couldn't tell what emotion was foremost in my mind. Eventually I rubbed my eyes and shook my head. Given my tears, I must have made an unappealing picture, but my dad didn't comment on it.

"You're proud of the bartending on the weekends? Assistant teaching? Hardly a glittering career, Dad," I managed to say.

"It's all yours, though." His eyes twinkled. "My little lone wolf. You must've learned some mean cocktail recipes, at least."

I laughed. "Totally."

"You know who else would be proud of you?" Dad's voice trembled, but he continued regardless. "Your mom. She loved you very much."

I gave a shaky nod. I worried that if I spoke in that moment, I would start bawling again.

"You're my daughter, Allara." My dad brought my head forward and touched our foreheads together. "My true heir. I neglected you when you needed me, and I'm sorrier for it than I can say. I want to make things right between us while I still can."

The weight of hurt... of betrayal, fell away, leaving me light. I let out a long breath.

"You already have, Dad."

With a peaceful smile, he fell into a doze. I left him and tiptoed back downstairs to find Rachel.

I settled in one of the living room armchairs with a mug of cocoa and tucked my feet up beneath me.

Rachel sat opposite. She took a careful sip from her own mug and fixed me with an unreadable expression.

Although I could barely admit it, even to myself, I wished Reid were here. It might help to diffuse the tension in the room.

"It's good to see you," I said. "It's been too long."

"Five years too long." Her eyebrows drew together as she frowned. "I called you, Allie. Several times. You never picked up."

"I'm sorry." I let out a shaky breath. "I... I changed my phone. I needed a clean break, Rachel. I never got your messages, sorry. I just... had to leave it all behind."

She set her mug down carefully on the coffee table and folded her hands in her lap with a heavy sigh. "You never truly turned your back though, did you Allie?"

I stared down at the mug in my hands, my heart thumping. "What makes you say that?"

"Well, it's obvious." Rachel's voice was surprisingly gentle. I looked up, forcing myself to look her in the eye. "Reid is your mate."

Your mate.

The two words reverberated through me until they were all I could hear.

I stared blindly at the mantel, looking at the photographs set out on display there. Reid and I when we were kids. Rachel and I baking a cake, covered in frosting. My dad, looking about thirty years younger, glowing, with his arms wrapped around my mom.

Rachel had probably put them there. Dad didn't have any photos of Mom in the house when I lived here.

"That's what Dad said. Well, implied," I said, feeling proud of the fact my voice didn't wobble. "But... Reid broke up with me, Rachel. Dad told him to do it. I know that now. But... I thought it wasn't possible to walk away from your mate like that. If you were truly bound together, I mean."

"Oh, Allie." Rachel shook her head at me, just like she used to do when I was ten and she caught me skipping out on homework to go play in the woods. "You think he walked away? He never did."

A sudden surge of irritation caught hold of me at the knowing smile on her face.

"Uh, yes. He *did*. You weren't there. You didn't see his face. It seemed so *easy* for him."

"And yet," Rachel said softly, "after you left, I was here. I saw the effect it had on him. It was like something inside him just... switched off. I'd never seen him like that before. He barely spoke to anyone, didn't want anything to do with the pack. He just went off by himself. Sometimes he didn't return for days on end."

I absorbed her words slowly.

"I didn't see the point in being here if I couldn't be with him," I said. "I'm sorry."

Rachel nodded, sighing. "I understand that. And I'll bet you he felt just the same."

Now, with hindsight, I was sure she was right, but for me, leaving had been the only way to stay sane.

Then again, if I'd stayed, maybe I could have stopped Jaime from making his plans to destroy our pack.

Hopefully it wasn't too late to stop him now.

RACHEL'S WORDS echoed through my head while I wandered the village, saying a few quick hellos to old friends and acquaintances as I passed. I kept my conversations brief and didn't answer any questions about where I'd been, or why I'd gone away.

Rachel thought that Reid and I were... mates.

It wasn't an impossibility. Nobody knew why the "fated mates" attraction happened. It didn't happen to every shifter, but it was common enough for our kind that plenty of tales were told of it.

I had heard many, over the years.

They were spoken of around the campfire on lazy summer evenings. The elders told the stories, and the smoke above our heads framed image after image of love, death, and war. Women who had run away from home after pack-meets to chase after the shifter men that they couldn't get out of their heads. Packs turning to bloodshed and violence over a stolen woman, or a broken marriage pact.

Many people said that my mother and father had been fated.

To be honest, they were probably right, though the phenomenon was shrouded in secrecy.

Bonded mates were something only the council could officially determine.

If they had known anything about me and Reid, they'd kept their cards close to their chests, right up until I left.

The only reason I took Rachel's belief to heart was that Rachel was probably the only person in the world who knew Reid almost as well as I did.

ALLARA

I had been seven years old when Reid came to our town.

My dad had leaned down and scooped me up to sit on his shoulders. My mom walked alongside him, explaining something to him in low, urgent tones.

They'd found Reid on the steps of the meeting house, early in the morning.

He was a scruffy, skinny foundling, roughly eight or nine years of age. His hair was a dark, chestnut brown color, and his eyes were a clear gray.

Even though I'd been young, I remembered his eyes the best of all. They had been wide, and full of fear.

At first, he had glared daggers at everyone who dared to come near him. He seemed half-feral; a little cub dropped into the den by who-knew-who.

He wouldn't talk at all for the first few days, although he'd eaten everything put before him with a ravenous hunger.

No-one seemed to know where he had come from or guess at how he'd arrived in the middle of our village.

He couldn't—or wouldn't—answer any of the questions the pack elders asked him, even after he finally started to speak.

The only concrete piece of information that they managed to get out of him was that his name was Reid.

Finally, it was agreed by the council that he should be taken in and cared for until his identity was confirmed, or until the pack he belonged to came back to claim him.

It was decided that he should live with Rachel, who had no children of her own, a spare bedroom, and a gentle manner. He started going to school with the rest of us kids and, after a few months, it was just as though he'd always been here.

Although my father sent out dozens of lines of enquiry, nobody came forward to take him back to wherever he'd come from. Not a whisper from any of the neighboring packs, nor any indication that someone out there was missing a son.

A single shred of evidence arrived one day, three years after Reid came to us. It was via an unmarked envelope, and it contained a handwritten message which simply read:

He is safe here.

As for Reid himself, the strangeness of his arrival was only the beginning.

He grew into a quiet boy who was far more interested in climbing trees and building forts by himself than playfighting with Jaime and the other boys of his age.

Even as a child, it was clear to the pack that he was a shifter. His strength and speed were incomparable to that of a human child. If his agility hadn't been enough of a giveaway, then the way his eyes swirled with silver a few weeks after his twelfth birthday certainly was.

Not long after that, his first shift happened.

Unlike most of the pack, whose fur colors varied between grayish silver and a light, sandy brown, his coat was rich and dark, a deep brown like his hair color. In both wolf and human form, he stood a fraction taller than the other boys, and his pelt was thicker and shaggier, too.

I experienced my own shift a few months later.

In my wolf form, I was quick and deft, and to my delight I was by far the best at clambering up steep riverbanks and wriggling through tiny crevices. The forest around us was like a giant playground, and we reveled in it. The boys were always stronger than me, but far clumsier, with their overlarge paws. On top of this, they had little regard for danger, and their recklessness came back to bite them more often than not.

I couldn't help but smile at the memories this place held for me.

Reid was well liked by most and grew into a strong and dependable man—an asset for a pack of our size, though the unanswered question of Reid's origin continued to haunt us.

Although he never spoke about his life before he'd come to our pack, even to me, I knew that it bothered him somewhere deep down. The pack's adult members accepted him as one of us under strict orders from my father, but I knew that in many ways he would always be seen as an outsider to them.

Their prejudice was on some level instinctive. Sometimes the wires got crossed in the wolf part of our brains; Reid was no enemy to them, but he was no kin, either. They always treated him with respect, but often kept him at a careful distance.

Nobody had to tell me that my father would have never considered Reid to be a suitable match for me.

The Alpha's daughter would never be partnered with a foundling cub from who-knows-where.

It didn't matter to me, or to Reid. Practically from the minute he'd arrived, we'd been inseparable.

"Allie?"

I started, and realized that I had been so deep in my thoughts that I'd wandered right to the edge of the village. I had come upon the small, babbling brook which cut a path through this part of the forest and provided our village with fresh water, straight from the mountains.

Kara crouched by the side of the stream, rinsing out a beautiful piece of cloth the same color of the redwood leaves behind her. Her arms were green too, right up to her elbows, so that it looked like she was wearing gloves. After a second, I realized she was in the process of dying the material. She'd always been an artist; half the blankets in the village had been woven by her.

She stared at me, waiting for a response.

"Oh." I flushed. "Hi, Kara."

"Long time, no see," she said evenly, drawing the cloth out of the water and wringing it. "Reid said you moved to the city."

That's understating things, somewhat.

I inclined my head. "Yeah, I've been away a while, huh?"

She just nodded. Her expression was unreadable. "About your dad... I'm sorry. How's he doing?"

"Thanks." A ripple of sadness swum through me as I recalled the reason for my return. "He's in good spirits, but... he's worried, I think."

Something flickered in Kara's eyes. I sensed that she caught the fullness of my meaning.

So... that must mean things have *been different around here.*

"Must be difficult for him." Heaving the cloth out of the water, she flung it out onto the boulder next to her and sat back on her hands. "I guess we all do what we think is right, in the moment."

She was talking about the succession. Jaime being named my father's heir, ahead of me. As uncomfortable as the topic made me, I knew that I should get the lay of the land from her. Kara was as good a person as any to talk to. She always gave good advice, and I trusted her judgment better than most.

I leaned against a nearby tree and took my chance.

"Has Jason told you anything? About...?"

I didn't need to finish my sentence. Jaime and Jason had been thick as thieves for years now; wherever Jaime went, Jason was sure to follow.

She snorted suddenly. "Nope. You'd think he'd open up to his twin sister, wouldn't you? But no. He's always with Jaime and Paul nowadays. I hardly see him."

That pretty much lined up with what Reid had told me. Still, I couldn't help but wonder whether there was more to the story.

"They've always been best friends, though," I pressed. "Right?"

She shook her head. "It's not that. I can't explain it, but... something's changed here, Allara. Ever since..."

She trailed off.

Right. Ever since I left the pack.

I really wished people would stop reminding me.

"Come to think of it," Kara said suddenly, "there was this one night.

A couple of months ago, I came down to the kitchen to get a glass of water. I heard something... weird."

My heart rate picked up, but I forced my voice to remain calm. "Jaime was there?"

"No," Kara said. "*Reid*, of all people. He was talking to my brother... and they weren't exactly keeping their voices down. It sounded like an argument if I'm being honest."

"What did you hear?" I said, too intrigued to pose the question subtly.

She shrugged, shooting me a curious look.

"I couldn't make sense of it. Reid said something about Jaime being... dangerous, I think. Then Jason said...ah..." Her cheeks went pink. "Something about you, actually."

"About me?"

"First, he told Reid to stay out of their business." Kara grimaced. "That it was none of his concern. And that he was just jealous of Jaime, because, uh, your dad wanted *him* to be with you, and not Reid."

I didn't reply. I was too busy thinking about what my dad had said earlier.

As the Alpha's daughter, you had certain responsibilities.

"Reid left pretty soon after that," Kara said. "I think Jason might have said some other things, about Reid coming here, maybe. About him being a foundling, and not having any family. Stuff like that. But I didn't catch much of that part."

I frowned to myself, thinking.

I couldn't tell Kara about what Jaime planned to do after he became Alpha. It would only put her in danger, and besides, Jason was her twin brother. I didn't want any of my suspicions to fall on the wrong ears.

Jason had always struck me as a decent person, though. He was kind and thoughtful, just like his sister.

"Does Jason really think that?" I asked. "About Reid?"

After all, they had been friends, hadn't they? Once upon a time.

It seemed difficult to square this version of Jason with my dim memories of the two of them.

Back then, it was simple. The sun had always shone, and we were happy.

But we were older now. Supposedly wiser for it, too, though I didn't know how true that was.

Everything was so much more complicated.

"About him being jealous of Jaime? Probably. But not about Reid's parentage." Kara trailed her hand in the flow of water and looked up at me. "No. That's not like him, Allara. That's Jaime all over. It's like the words were coming out of Jason's mouth, but Jaime was saying them. He's gotten to my brother in some way. Jason's under his influence now... and whatever they're up to, it can't be good. I'm sure of it."

REID

I woke with a jolt.

For a few moments, I struggled to remember where I was. The past couple of weeks had been disorientating, and I hadn't slept in this room in a long time.

Looking around, it was as if hundreds of memories patchworked themselves together with my present reality. Allara's quilt spread across the bed, all her old posters covered the walls... it brought me back to a different time.

On the pinboard above the dresser was a postcard from the day we'd spent together at Gold Beach. Just in front of it was the stuffed bear I'd won for her at the carnival when we were sixteen.

The real woman snuggled closer into my chest, forcing me out of my recollections. Even in sleep, she held me close, like she was worried I would disappear.

I stroked her dark tresses out of her face. After a few minutes, Allara's blue eyes blinked open and she gazed at me with a sleepy kind of surprise.

All the events of the previous day seemed to rush back to her, all at once. She extracted herself from my arms and hopped out of bed, pulling her hair up into a messy bun and securing it with a band from around her wrist.

"Allara." I groaned at the rush of cold air and pulled the covers up over my chest. "C'mon, it's way too early. Come back to bed!"

She tucked a loose strand of hair behind her ear and shot me a cheeky grin.

"No, thanks. I'm gonna go see Dad. I thought I could make him a virgin cocktail today. I don't think it's a good idea to give him alcohol, but I thought it might be fun to show him my skills in some way." Smirking, she picked up my flannel shirt off the floor and slipped it on. "Such as they are."

"So, it went well with you guys yesterday, then?" I said, trying to keep my voice light and casual.

After the visit with her father, she'd been distinctly untalkative last night, eating little and saying even less.

I hadn't seen the man himself for some time, but I shoved down my curiosity. Allara didn't need an interrogation from me on top of every-thing else.

She seemed to be in a better mood today, though. Her eyes bright-ened as she wrapped my shirt around her body. The sight of her in my clothes always did strange things to me. I managed to ignore the surge of arousal and focus on the conversation.

"Surprisingly, it did!" Her voice was warm as she opened her closet and rifled through the coat hangers, pulling out some of her old clothes. "He explained... a lot. In particular, the stuff that happened around the time I left the pack."

She wouldn't meet my eye, but I caught her drift well enough.

"Oh," I said, and left it at that. For now.

I didn't want to ruin her sunny mood, especially not when things were going so well between the two of us.

Plus, I didn't know how much her dad had told her. *Stuff that happened...*

Stuff about Jaime?

About me?

I desperately wanted to tell her everything about that night, but I knew it had to wait.

Once an agreement was reached, an Alpha's word was binding. Allara's father had been very clear. First, I had to break things off between us, and break her heart in the bargain. Second, I couldn't ever tell her why.

Only when the Alpha died would the pact between us be broken. As much as I didn't want anything to happen to Allara's dad, I did want the truth to come to light, one day.

Not that I was certain how she would react when it did. Maybe she would never forgive me. But at least there wouldn't be any more secrets between us.

I'd lived with them—and their consequences—long enough.

"He said he was proud of me." She smiled at me, looking rueful. "For what, I don't know."

I pillowed my head with my arms and appraised her. A pulse of excitement shot through me when I saw her gaze lingering on my biceps. "So modest."

She threw the sweater she was holding at my head, and I ducked out of the way, cackling with laughter.

Our attention was diverted by a couple of knocks at the bedroom door.

Allara quickly buttoned up my shirt on her, then headed over to the door. She was still giving me the evil eye in between her giggles as she opened the door.

Rachel stood on the threshold. Her face was entirely drained of color.

"Allara," she whispered. "I need you to come upstairs with me right now."

FOR MOST OF THE PACK, the death of their Alpha was a once-in-a-lifetime event.

The very oldest members had only been children when Allara's grandfather had died. With one or two exceptions, such as myself, the pack's structure was mostly made up of members from those original families.

By the time Allara had said her last goodbyes and his body had been taken away, we walked outside the Alpha's house and were greeted with quite a spectacle.

Hundreds of candles lined the path leading up to the front door. What looked like the entire pack had assembled outside, huddled into small groups, holding vigil for their fallen leader. They were dressed in black and gray, and tears streaked some of the women's cheeks.

They were waiting for some kind of direction. They wanted to hear what would happen next.

Allara stood beside me, her back straight and her face grim.

She was her father's daughter through and through. It would have been clear, even to an ordinary human, that Alpha blood ran through her veins.

I stood by her side, close enough to see the tension she carried in her shoulders. But then, I knew her better than most. I knew all her little tells, the ways she put on a mask to hide her pain from the world.

She had rifled through the back of her wardrobe and found a simple black dress that had once belonged to her mother. Her face was very pale, but her eyes were dry. She held her head high as she surveyed the waiting crowd.

"My father is gone."

A ripple went through the pack, as though she had thrown a stone into a still pond.

People gasped, and a few cried out. Young children hid their faces against their parents' chests. But most of the pack stood silent and still, ashen-faced.

Every man, woman, and child in the pack—they had all known this was coming for a long time, but that didn't make this moment any easier to bear.

Allara opened her mouth, then closed it again. She lowered her gaze and pressed her lips together hard, obviously fighting grief.

I put my arm around her shoulders and gave her a gentle squeeze, and she looked up at me, her expression beseeching.

"I can take it from here if you want," I murmured, so that only she could hear.

She reached up and slid her hand over mine.

Yes.

"Elder Mason will perform the rites." I raised my voice, so that the entire pack could hear me. My voice echoed through the silent crowd; only the wind in the trees answered. "He has already made the preparations. We gather at noon, at the boneyard."

There was a figure at the edge of the spectators, standing a little apart from the rest of the mourners. Before I finished speaking, he turned and hurried away down the track before vanishing from sight.

Jason, I thought.

Perhaps no one had yet told Jaime the news.

I was sure Jason would be off to do that, now.

I gave a few more parting words to the crowd before guiding Allara back into the house. I shut the door behind us and let out a long breath. I'd always disliked crowds, and it was a relief to be free of the dozens upon dozens of eyes, watching us. More specifically, watching Allara, waiting for answers, most of which she couldn't give.

Allara kept glancing up the stairs. It was like she expected her dad to come walking down them at any moment, hale and hearty.

Part of me wondered whether she was strong enough for what lay ahead.

"Hey, hey." I took her face in my hands and forced her to look at me. "I got you, okay? I got you. I'm right here, I promise."

She nodded and blinked with those blue eyes that always held me so entranced. Her expression wobbled a little, and she flung her arms around my neck, burying her face in my shoulder.

I swept her hair out of the way and kissed the side of her head, just above her ear.

"Don't leave," she mumbled, so quietly I almost missed it.

I drew back and met her eye, tucking a few errant strands of hair back into place.

"I swear upon my ancestors, whoever they might be." I smiled, watching her mouth curl upwards just a little. I cupped her jaw and placed a soft kiss on her parted lips. "I'm not going anywhere."

~

THE BONEYARD LAY about a half mile from the village, down a narrow gravel track. Carved wooden posts covered with tendrils of ivy marked the trail on either side of us.

Burning tapers signified the entrance, and I shivered as we passed under them.

I wasn't frightened of old spirits that might haunt this place. Those ghost tales were for kids. I knew that the dead had no power over the living, even here.

It was the living folk that concerned me.

One in particular.

A raised platform had been erected around a freshly dug patch of earth. At the graveside, Elder Mason stood with the dusty records book and an ancient looking carved staff. His face was solemn, but other than that, he betrayed no emotion.

There were a few scattered sobs from the people behind us, but the scene was eerily silent otherwise.

Across the circle of mourners, I spotted Jaime's sandy blond head of hair. He caught my eye, and a slow, satisfied smile spread across his face.

My eyes narrowed as I studied him. Did he know that I'd figured him out?

We had sparred often enough in the past, but as hot-headed as he could be, he had always known better than to deepen our enmity. I was young and strong, an asset to the pack. If he drove me out, he would weaken his position considerably, and without false modesty, he and I both knew he would likely weaken the pack, as well.

Once or twice, I'd caught him watching Allara in a manner that made the hairs on the back of my neck stand up. Part of it was attraction, and that part I understood. She had always been gorgeous; no-one could deny that.

But there was something else—a deeper, darker undercurrent to his gaze. I sensed that he wanted to possess her, ensnare her like an animal in a trap.

He needed her lineage to legitimize his claim, but I knew he would destroy her if he had to. He would stop at nothing to secure his power.

Before long, he would have everything he wanted.

He would be Alpha.

If push came to shove, I would leave the pack. I would take Allara to the city and leave everyone behind, everything I'd ever known, in order to protect her.

Once Jaime became Alpha, things wouldn't be safe for her here.

I didn't know how long we had. I hoped that we would be given a few days' grace before we had to make the decision.

I wondered if, after the announcement, Jaime would ask Allara to undertake a bonding ceremony with him and make her his mate without wasting any time.

It seemed unlikely that Allara would agree to anything like that.

My stomach dropped at the thought, nonetheless.

If he lays a finger on her...

I forced down the hot surge of anger as images of Jaime in Allara's bed flashed through my head. Him on top of her...

No. I needed to stop that train of thought immediately.

I turned my attention to back to the ceremony.

"He was beloved by us all," Elder Mason was saying. "A strong leader and a worthy Alpha, until the end."

My chest tightened as the casket was lowered into the earth. The man had taken me into his pack and given me a home with Rachel. Cared for me, defended me from the judgment of others...

He was gone.

There was a part of me that still couldn't believe it.

Despite my own sorrow, I needed to stay strong for Allara. She leaned close, pressing into my side as she watched the soil being poured into the grave.

The pack was silent, watchful. The only sound was the wind whistling through the clearing.

The branches above us whispered and stirred, like the trees were passing secrets amongst themselves.

A loud thud startled me. After a moment, I realized it was Elder Mason's staff slamming into the ground. All eyes turned to him.

He gave a creaking cough before he started to speak.

"The time has come for us to announce a new Alpha," he said. His voice reminded me of the rustle of dry, papery leaves. "An Alpha to emerge from the ashes and replace our fallen leader. An Alpha to carry us forward, into a new era for the pack."

I inclined my head so that I could whisper to Allara without being overheard by those next to us.

"I don't think I've ever heard Elder Mason speak publicly before."

"Neither have I," she murmured. "But, shh!"

"My council has consulted upon this matter for several moons now, leading up to this day. The previous Alpha guided us in our decision and offered his blessing. Though some among you may doubt it, I believe that our new leader will prove worthy of the responsibility."

I glanced across at Jaime, who was whispering something to Jason. Jaime's eyes were glittering and his face was pale. His gaze was fixed on Allara, who was too absorbed by the Elder's words to notice.

My hackles rose. My wolf sensed danger.

I slid my arm around Allara's waist, resisting the urge to shield her with my body.

"The role of Alpha shall pass through the true bloodline," Elder Mason announced, and a ripple of surprised noise rolled through the crowd.

Hang on a second...

True bloodline?

But... that means...

"Allara Bane." The Elder turned to her, and held out the thick, dog-eared tome he was carrying in front of him. "Do you accept responsibility for the pack of your father, and his father before him?"

Cold with shock, I could do nothing but stare down at Allara.

Her lips were parted and shock was reflected in her expression. Frozen to the spot, she blinked up at me, and then back to Elder Mason, in turn.

I gave her a gentle nudge.

"I... ah..." She reached out and touched the ancient record book, tracing her fingertips over the tome's binding. "I... do. I accept."

She cleared her throat and raised her chin. "I accept," she repeated, louder and firmer this time.

I spared a glance over to the other side of the circle, where Jaime stood with his fists clenched. His face was almost incandescent with fierce emotion.

"Very well." The Elder inclined his head in somber acknowledge-ment. With slow, reverent movements, he opened the book and drew a small silver knife out of his pocket, laying it down on the page in front of him with the handle pointed toward her.

On the left-hand side, I could see the name of Allara's father recorded in dark red, and his signature and seal, a little faded around the edges.

The right side page was blank, ready and waiting for the next Alpha's mark.

"*No!*"

A piercing cry came from the other side of the circle, traveling over the freshly settled earth of the grave mound. It was Jaime.

Allara paused, her hand outstretched to take the knife.

"Allara." I put my hand on her arm and tried to hold back the rumbling growl that threatened to take over my voice. "Ignore him. Sign the book."

Jaime called out again, his voice echoing through the clearing. Two men jumped forward to restrain him, but even so, his fury was so intense they only just managed to hold him back and prevent him from shifting into wolf form.

His eyes flashed silver, full of disbelief and rage.

"Allara Bane," he shouted. "I challenge you."

Everyone froze to their spot.

He had said the one thing we couldn't ignore.

The one thing that was bound to catch the attention of every single pack member, right down to the smallest child.

"Tomorrow," he spat, shaking himself free of the men restraining him. "We battle. You and me. Whoever wins becomes Alpha."

Jaime stood with his back straight and regarded Allara with a look of visceral hatred.

I let out a growl, unable to hold it in any longer; it was like a switch flipped as I took in his aggressive body language. His stance was enough to trigger my instinctive fight response. If he shifted into his wolf form now, I would be sure to follow, and I couldn't guarantee there would anything left of Jaime for Allara to fight.

I took deep breaths, trying to control myself. I had to let this play out the correct way. The pack had to see Allara step up and take control. It was the only way for her to prove her leadership qualities.

But I didn't have to like it.

"And whoever loses?" she called. Her voice rang out loud and clear, so that everyone could hear.

The way she spoke reminded me of our fight at her condo. The one that brought her here.

It was only a couple of days ago, but it felt like a lifetime.

"Oh, didn't I mention?" Jaime gave her a smirk. He was savoring this moment; I could tell. Making assumptions about his own strength, and her weakness. "We fight to the death."

My stomach dropped out from under me.

No.

"No, no, no!"

It took a moment to realize I'd shouted the words out loud, because Allara tugged on my wrist.

"I got this," she muttered, before raising her voice so that it could be heard all the way across the clearing. "I *am* the Alpha, Jaime. It's in my blood. My lineage. It was always going to be this way!"

"Then *prove it!*" he yelled back. Even from this distance, I could see the way his body still trembled with suppressed rage. To me, he looked to be on the edge of lunacy. The most dangerous kind of shifter to fight.

"What kind of Alpha abandons their own pack?" Jaime jeered. He pointed to her as he turned to address the crowd of funeral onlookers. "Her father's dead, and now she wants to stroll in and take charge. She ran out on us five years ago. She doesn't care about us. She left, and she'd do it again in a heartbeat!"

Allara sucked in a breath. "That's not—"

"You would allow a *woman* to lead you?" Jaime cut across her, before barkingd out a harsh laugh. "The Alpha named me successor years ago. Just because he changed his mind in the end, means nothing. He was right not to trust her. Why should you? She ran off. She betrayed her own kin!"

Murmurs rippled through the crowd. Nobody seemed convinced by Jaime, but nobody was shutting him down, either.

Some of the people around us looked skeptical, but most just looked afraid.

"She's hiding behind that *mongrel.*" Jaime pointed at me, and I bared my teeth at him. "Like he'll save her. Look at her! She's barely even a wolf anymore, she's been away from us for so long. Who would respect a pack whose Alpha has forgotten who she is?"

My pulse raced, and my body trembled. It wouldn't be long before I shifted. Jaime's words were stirring up every protective instinct I had, and every cell in my body wanted to tear his throat out, right where he stood.

Allara's hand gave mine a final, warning squeeze before she stepped forward. Her head was high. Her dark hair flowed down her back like a river, looking almost blue in the places it caught the light from above.

Jaime is wrong.

She is the Alpha.

The light in her eyes was unmistakable. She was proud, unbending, regal.

All the years she'd been away from us fell away like water. They didn't matter; she wasn't changed. She had never belonged to the city, and it hadn't left an indelible mark on her. Her experiences there had shaped her, yes. But she was still Allara.

Still a wolf.

More of a wolf than ever, in fact.

"I accept," she shouted, and my heart dropped. "I will meet your challenge for Alpha, Jaime, and I will win!"

"What are you doing?" I hissed, horror flooding my senses, even though I knew she had to do this.

My actions had ensured that she had no choice.

By bringing her back here, I had put her in this position, where she had to fight him.

After so long, I'd finally gotten her back, only to risk losing her again. This time, for good. I had led her into enormous danger. She would have been safer remaining in the city.

I'd just signed the death warrant of the woman I loved.

"You have to trust me," she whispered. She stared at me, and her blue eyes were filled with resolve.

"I do," I said, brushing my fingers lightly over her cheek. "I *do*."

And I did trust her, more than anyone. I trusted in her loyalty and integrity, and her determination to do the right thing, no matter the cost to herself.

But I knew that the man standing on the other side of the clearing didn't care about trust, or honor.

I knew that, whatever happened tomorrow, he wasn't planning on playing fair.

Jaime met my gaze and smirked, his eyes glittering. He had the taste of victory already on his tongue.

THE PACK WALKED BACK through the forest, past the meeting house. I kept Allara separate from the clusters of pack members who stared at us unashamedly as she passed, walking so that my body sheltered hers from their gaze.

It was the least I could do for her.

Helpless fury burned its way right to my core. She had been placed in an impossible situation. One that I had inadvertently created. If I hadn't meddled with her fate, Jaime would be Alpha right now, and she would be safe and sound in the city, none the wiser.

In the back of my mind, I knew the situation wasn't that simple. The pack would have been screwed, either way. With Allara, at least they had a shot.

And her father had needed to see her, before the end.

But damn it.

Now *she* was in danger, and there was nothing I could do to protect her.

I managed to keep my thoughts to myself, all the way back to the house. Once the front door shut behind us, I couldn't bring myself to hold it in any longer.

The tension had been steadily mounting between us as we walked. Now, I let it spill out into the open air.

"Don't do this."

Through some effort, I managed to keep my voice steady. She had her back to me.

She became still, the line of her shoulders rigid with tension.

"You're putting yourself in danger," I continued. "Jaime... this is what he wants. You're a threat to him, Allara. He'll *destroy* you."

She didn't turn. Instead, she walked away, disappearing through the archway of the kitchen. I followed her, only to find her staring out of the window into the forest, with a pensive expression.

"Allara." I placed my hand on her shoulder, taking care not to startle her or show too much of the panic I felt. "There's still time. You can take it back, you *can*. Just go to him and tell him you won't do it."

She twisted out of my grasp and fixed me with a glare strong enough to knock the wind out of me.

"Take it *back*? Are you serious?"

"Yeah!" Recovering, I threw out my hands defensively. "Screw Jaime!"

She just stared at me, saying nothing.

After a moment, all the pent-up frustration drained out of my body. I was exhausted. I ruffled the hair on the back of my head with one hand, sighing.

Once Allara set her mind to something, there was nothing anyone could say to put her off her course.

To tell the truth, it was one of the things I loved most about her.

Usually.

I huffed out a long breath and sat down at the small table by the window. I had to choose my next words carefully.

"Your dad wouldn't have wanted this, you know that," I said, softly. "He'd want you to be safe."

She made a noise of irritation and slumped into the chair opposite me. She hid her face in her hands, her hair tumbling forward and obscuring her expression.

"I don't have a choice, Reid," she mumbled, so quietly I almost missed it. "You know I don't."

I thought fast.

"We'll leave together, while we still have the chance." I drummed my fingers against the table and pulled up a mental map, plotting our route in my head. "The truck's got enough fuel to get us at least as far as Bridgeport. We can hop around, stay in motels... maybe head for the east coast. See those beaches you love so much."

I smiled wistfully.

Before she could say anything, I continued. "Or up north, far north. Somewhere remote, where no-one will come looking for us. I can pick up work along the way... You wouldn't have to worry about anything, I swear. We'll find a place, Allara. I'll keep you safe."

She looked up at me, her eyes wide. "You... you really mean all that, don't you?"

I bit my lip, dropping my gaze. "Yeah. I really do. We gotta get far away from here, and we gotta go now."

She stared at me as if in disbelief. Then she reached out and took my hand, drawing it closer to her. I wound my fingers through her hair and pulled her forward, kissing her forehead.

She squeezed my hand tight, and then let it go.

"I can't leave," she said, after a long moment.

I growled my frustration. "He'll hurt you, Allara! He'll *kill* you. And he'll enjoy it while he does that."

"You said you trust me."

Her accusation hurt. "I do trust you. But I don't trust him. He won't play fair, Allara. He'll use every dirty trick in his arsenal. He wants you *dead.*"

"I know." She traced a pattern on the tabletop. "But he'll hurt the entire pack if he becomes Alpha. He's crazy, Reid. I saw that, today. So, I can't abandon everyone. Not again..." She stared past me, out of the window at the forest beyond. "He's right, you know. I did leave everyone behind. If I leave now, why did I come back at all? Why did *you* bring me back?"

Her head snapped back to face me; her gaze was sharp and unrelenting.

Maybe it was always going to play out like this. Allara wouldn't walk away from people who needed her. It wasn't in her nature.

And right now, our pack needed her. Whether they knew it or not, she was the only one who could protect them from Jaime.

If she survived tomorrow.

Jesus. Why *had* I brought her back here?

So she could see her dad one last time.

Because she's the only thing standing in the way of Jaime wreaking havoc across the entire state.

Shit, I couldn't lie anymore. Even to myself.

Not now that she was finally back in my arms. No longer a memory, but flesh and blood. Real.

I'd brought her back because *I* needed her. Plain and simple.

My thoughts were interrupted when she gave a heavy sigh.

"If I refuse his challenge, and take over as Alpha anyway..." She paused, lost in thought. "They'll never accept me. You know that, Reid."

I knew. I also didn't need to ask who she meant by 'they'. The council, the pack elders. Hell, everyone in our community. She was right.

Elder Mason had proclaimed her the rightful successor to her father. She could sign her name in that book in her own blood, perform all the rites, and be declared Alpha.

But none of that would mean Jaime's challenge would be forgotten.

She couldn't step into the Alpha role having turned her back on a rightful challenger on her very first day leader. It would be an unforgivable display of weakness, and it went against every code of law followed by our kind.

Then there was Jaime himself.

He had Allara in his sights. Like any vicious predator, he wasn't about to let her get away without a fight.

Even if we left the pack, we would never be truly free of him. He would cast a shadow that would find us, wherever we went.

He wanted to snuff her out.

The realization filled me with dismay, and I couldn't stop myself from pressing my point.

"There's got to be another way," I said. "This isn't a gamble you have to take, Allara."

"Yes, it is."

She stood up. The late afternoon sun shone through the window and she lingered in the light for a moment, bathed by it. The loose strands of her hair glowed, framing her face like a halo.

She had always taken my breath away.

"I've already made up my mind," she said. Her eyes glimmered as she looked at me.

I was transfixed, unable to look away.

"You *know* that. I'm done running away from my fate. It's time to face it, Reid."

In that moment, I could truly see the Alpha she had already become. Her eyes held their own silvery light, like she was on fire from within.

"You should leave." Her hand slid down my arm, her touch cool and reassuring. "If he wins tomorrow..."

She trailed off. She didn't need to finish her sentence.

If Allara lost the battle, the next person Jaime would come after was her vengeful, grieving mate. *Me.*

Her unspoken statement filled me with surprise. Even now, after all this time, she didn't know.

Where you go, I go.

"I'm not going anywhere." In a couple of strides, I rounded the table and was by her side. I cupped her face in my hands and gazed into those sunlit eyes, then softly kissed the corner of her mouth. "I'm with you. Every minute."

She made a small noise and turned her head, drawing me closer for a deep, toe-curling kiss.

And I knew, in that moment, she did understand what she meant to me.

We understood each other perfectly.

CHAPTER 11

ALLARA

I stared up at Reid, hardly daring to believe that we were back in this space, where anything was possible. Where we might get our second chance.

His hands were warm on my face. The look he gave me was blazing, and it heated me right down to my toes.

I turned my head to the side slightly, sliding my own hand up to cover his, and kissed his palm gently.

"Let's get out of here," he breathed. I raised an eyebrow at that, and he said, "Just for a little while. Not for good."

A grin spread across my face as I caught on to his meaning. Our special place.

My wolf surged up, ready to spring free.

With a seductive smile, I slipped out of his arms and padded over to

103

the kitchen's back door. I opened it and stepped with bare feet out into the sunlight.

Hanging on to the doorframe, I cocked my eyebrow challengingly. "Race you?"

For a second, he stood there in the kitchen and stared at me, like he couldn't believe his eyes. After a moment, his brows lowered and his expression darkened, and a new kind of hunger crept into his gaze.

It was enough to make my cheeks heat, and a flush creep up from my neck.

Without warning, he gave a playful growl and sprang after me.

There were times when his wolfish qualities came right to the forefront, even in human form. He had always struck me as particularly wild, even compared to others of our kind.

His untamed qualities made my pulse race and called to the shifter in me.

My heartbeat thrummed in my chest like a trapped bird as I began to run, darting through the trees, his footfalls echoing all around me.

As I ran, I pulled off my drab black dress and let it fall to the forest floor, before shaking my loose hair out over my shoulders. I panted as adrenaline began to flood through me.

This was freedom. And it had been so long since I'd tasted it.

I shifted into wolf form.

Unlike the other day, this time the change was as effortless as breathing. I could run on four legs much faster than two, and I leaped through the air with the sheer exhilaration of the chase.

In spite of everything, it was good to be back.

Home.

It seemed like an eternity since I'd felt the sun on my back like this, or had time to stop and listen to the sounds of nature around me.

For a wolf, city life could be overwhelming.

The first couple of months had been hell. Every car alarm, police siren, and drunken argument outside my bedroom window had startled me, and my finely tuned senses became so rattled I barely slept.

But I'd gotten used to it.

Eventually, I'd managed to put my memories of the woods—memories of this place— in the same deeply-buried box in my mind where I put everything else that hurt too much to think about.

As I ran, I heard a deer chewing the foliage half a mile away. Somewhere nearby, a woodpecker hammered on tree bark. There were distant voices echoing from the village. The wake for my dad was still winding down, most of the tribe having adjourned to the meeting house.

I was aware of Reid's presence somewhere just behind my right shoulder. He was catching up to me, and fast.

I had always been smaller and lither than him. Today I used that to my advantage, ducking under a fallen branch, weaving through tight spaces, and sprinting away before he could catch me. Our destination glimmered through the trees up ahead, and anticipation shot through me. I picked up my pace.

I burst through the tree line at the edge of the lake and dove in without hesitation.

The water was pleasantly cold, and I swam down into the depths, admiring the flickers of silver as fish darted through the dark reeds around me.

Reid crashed through the water after me.

His dive was markedly less graceful than mine. Any remaining fish in the area swam away in panic as shockwaves rippled through the water around us.

When I reached the surface and burst out into the sunshine, I realized I had transformed back into human once again.

The transition had been so seamless, so natural, that I hadn't even noticed.

I yelped with laughter when Reid followed me, emerging from the depths still in wolf form, shaking out his fur and becoming a man again before my eyes.

He was grinning from ear to ear.

"Cheater," he laughed. "I would've won if you hadn't taken that shortcut!"

"If that's what you need to tell yourself." I splashed him playfully, and shrieked when he splashed me back. He grabbed me around the waist, dunking me underwater.

I squirmed away and resurfaced, gasping and spluttering with laughter.

His gaze was bright with unmasked joy. It raked over my torso, taking in the way my wet hair clung to my bare chest, accentuating my curves.

I grinned.

One track mind.

I could admit it, I wasn't much better. The way his water-slicked abs glistened in the sunlight made me want to do things to him.

Wonderful, unspeakable things.

It was amazing to think that, even though we had spent so many years together before being driven apart, my desire for Reid hadn't been quenched desire one bit.

If anything, our five-year separation had only intensified my need—because I remembered exactly what I'd missed.

I wanted to drink him in, have all of him. And this time, I never wanted to let him go.

I traced my eyes over his arms, his shoulders, appreciating the way his hair had slicked back in the water and the sunlight glistened off the hard planes of his body. He was still panting a little, from our race, and from something else.

Desire.

He made me greedy. I could drink and drink him in, take everything he gave me, and it would never, ever be enough.

In that moment, looking at the need etched on his face and then down to the hardening of his body beneath the clear water's surface, I knew that he wanted me just as much as I wanted him.

No more waiting...

He drew me toward him, pulling me through the water. His big hands settled around my hips. The movement was gentle, but firm with intent. I settled against him willingly and brought my arms up around his neck.

"You have no idea what you do to me," he murmured.

"Oh, but I do." I wiggled against him, and he groaned.

One hand came up to cup my breast and I bit my lip at the contact, releasing a moan. "When I'm around you..." His grin was crooked. "It's like I can't think straight."

I slid a hand into his hair and closed it into a fist, tilting his head back so I could bite lightly at his jaw and neck. "Oh, yeah?"

His breathing grew heavier when my lips moved farther down his chest. I could feel his heartbeat thudding against my mouth, and I smiled at the sensation, my tongue darting out to taste his skin.

"Reid." I looked up at him, meeting his lust-filled gaze. "At the diner. You asked me if... if I lived alone. I know what you meant. You wanted to know if... if there was anyone else."

A shadow fell over his face. His arms grew tense around me.

"I did."

My forehead dropped, resting against his chest.

"There's never been anyone else," I whispered. "I thought about it, once or twice, but I just couldn't. It felt wrong. There was only ever you."

His body trembled against mine. His arms gripped me tighter, hoisting me up, holding me close. I put my hands on his shoulders and let him carry me clumsily through the water to the shoreline.

He took me to the lake's edge and deposited me on the grassy bank.

Before, he'd seemed withdrawn, almost hesitant to touch me in the firm and confident way I remembered, after we'd kissed for the first time in five years. That night, he'd seemed content to let me take the lead.

He'd been holding back.

Now, there was no hesitation in the way he crawled between my legs and hooked my knees over his wide shoulders. His movements were quick and instinctive, and they brought me back to a different time.

In that moment, he reminded me of his teenage self, always ready to go in those brief stolen moments when we had the chance to slip away from everyone and be alone.

My head fell to the side and I arched my body up toward him, but his hand snaked over my hips, holding me still. He kissed the insides of my thighs until my toes curled and I grappled blindly for his hand, tangling his fingers with mine.

The sight of his head between my thighs sent an even stronger pulse of heat through me, and I stared up at the leaves above my head, dappled with golden light, wondering how I'd gotten so lucky to have this second chance at happiness.

He licked my flesh and sucked on my clit until I was writhing on the bank and crying out for him to come to me. I couldn't handle any more teasing.

I wanted him close. I wanted him inside me. I wanted to come around him, as he released his hot seed within me.

I grabbed a fistful of his hair and dragged him up my body, kissing him deeply. I moaned at the feeling of his firm chest pressing against mine and wrapped my arms around his torso, clinging to him shamelessly.

His lips brushed against the shell of my ear, and I writhed and bucked as he rocked his hips and thrust his cock into me.

"So gorgeous," he groaned into my neck, and I responded readily, wrapping my legs around his waist and driving his length impossibly deeper. "So beautiful. You're so..."

A wave of bliss bubbled up in my chest at the sound of his low voice, his need for me. I brushed back his hair, staring up into those incredible eyes, insensible with desire.

"Allara. I..." He shuddered. His hair escaped my fingers, falling across his face, and a shadow of silver rolled across his gaze. "I love you."

"I love you too," I managed, moments before he began to drive into me with hard purpose, over and over again.

Every other thought fell from my head so that all I felt was him. Inside of me. Over me. Possessing me. Consuming me.

Reid was my love. My mate.

My one true love.

And as we cried out together, reaching an ultimate climax at the same time, I knew I'd never be able to live without him again.

∾

We lay on the bank at the edge of the lake until the light started to fade. Reid's eyelids were half closed and he seemed about ready to pass out, but I knew he was still alert to our surroundings.

If he'd been in wolf form, his ears would have flickered at the sound of every leaf rustling, every twig snapping. His fur would've been tufted up, standing on end.

I trailed my hand down his bare skin and goosebumps appeared where my fingers had been.

He groaned. One eye blinked open, staring at me. Gray eyes, fringed with dark lashes. No silver, now that he was sated.

They changed like the weather, Reid's eyes. When he was angry, they swirled like a storm, and they grew pale and still when he was sad, or deep in thought. Right now, they were calm. The color of woodsmoke.

I loved his eyes. I loved everything about him.

He grinned, flashing his white teeth at me, before flopping onto his back.

"You don't know what you do to me," he said. He whistled low through his teeth. "It's like, I have a plan. And then you come along, and everything flies off the rails. Been that way ever since we met, Allie."

"Oh, yeah?" Feeling bold, I pressed a kiss onto his shoulder, and then another. Slowly, my mouth trailed down his bicep. "Didn't know I was so distracting."

"Allara," he murmured, cupping the back of my neck and forcing me to meet his eye. His expression grew serious. "Five years ago..."

I tensed.

Way to ruin the moment.

"What?" My tone was carefully neutral.

"I... I made the wrong call. I shouldn't have listened to your father." He pressed his forehead against mine. "I was a stupid kid. The pack should never have come between us. I should have found a way for us to be together, no matter what."

"Yeah?" I breathed, hardly daring to believe that he was admitting such a thing.

His mouth met mine for one dizzying moment, and then he pulled back, his fingers twisting themselves through my hair.

"Forgive me. I didn't stand up for you. For us. I regret it every day."

He did?

I tried to hide the rush of emotion that flooded through me.

"You were obeying your Alpha," I said. "You had no choice."

"There's always a choice," Reid said simply. "And for me, it's always gonna be you."

My heart skipped. "Is that so?"

"Yes, ma'am."

His smile was wide and utterly, blindingly perfect.

I closed my eyes, and let myself believe I could have him like this forever, even though the promise of tomorrow wasn't a certainty.

CHAPTER 12

REID

We slept again at her dad's house that night, though sleep was a relative term, at least for me. I could barely sleep at all, no matter how hard I tried.

I lay with my arms around Allara, watching the dawn creep over the horizon outside and listening to the sounds of the birds rustling in the trees.

A hundred thoughts raced through my head.

I couldn't shake the constant, nagging fear that Allara would get hurt.

I wouldn't allow myself to contemplate the possibility that I might lose her.

For good this time.

I had one shred of hope on my side.

I knew that if Allara was facing death at Jaime's hands, I could step in and offer myself as her champion. I would face execution, and she would be safe.

It may not be her ideal outcome, but it was a hell of a lot better than the alternative.

She would never agree to the idea if I voiced it before the battle. In her mind, she needed to be the one to defeat Jaime's challenge, so the pack would accept her as their leader.

I understood the position she was in, but that did not mean I had to like it. Nor would I accept her death as any sort of outcome.

She mumbled a little in her sleep and my arms tightened around her body. She was so strong, so determined to do the right thing. But the fact remained that she was out of practice in her shifter form. As fast and smart as she was, Jaime had years of training under his belt, a mean streak a mile wide, and a point to prove.

And, if it came down to it, I would gladly go to my death protecting her.

To an outside observer, she would probably seem confident, even laid back.

I knew her better than that. When she was getting ready, her hands had trembled slightly as she wound her long hair into a braid, and she deliberated for too long over what to wear, pulling out every item she had brought back with her as well as everything she'd left behind, and laying it all on the bed.

She'd never been one for fancy dresses. Like me, she usually kept it simple: plain tees and worn-in jeans, with combat boots to top it all off. Perfect for hiking over rough forest terrain.

"What does it matter?" I said. "You're gonna be in wolf form, no-one will care what you wear beforehand."

She glanced at me, her brow furrowed. "It matters, okay? I can't go out there looking like the same old Allie! If I'm destined to be the *Alpha*, Reid, I have to look the part."

I put up my hands in a gesture of surrender. "Okay, okay! Your call."

"I have to go out there like... I already know who I am." She straightened her neck and rolled out her shoulders.

To me, it didn't matter what she wore. Being an Alpha was innate, not dependent on anything external. Allara was an Alpha in my eyes already.

In the end, she settled on a pair of calf length boots over her jeans and her favorite sweater. Her eyes landed on her old leather jacket, that had hung on the back of her bedroom door for as long as I could remember.

Her bedroom was exactly as she'd left it. Her dad hadn't moved a thing. I wasn't sure how Allara felt about that. When she first saw it, she had stopped in the doorway for a long time. A sheen of tears had brightened her eyes, but she hadn't said anything then.

"Reid?" she said now, bringing me out of my reverie. She walked over and took down the jacket, then brought it over to show me.

Up close, I realized that it was an old one of mine.

She had stolen it a lifetime ago.

I had long since grown out of it, but it fit her perfectly. The collar was crooked, and the elbows had been re-patched on countless occasions. It reminded me of happier times, when our only problems revolved around not getting busted for sneaking out into the woods at night.

She slipped on the jacket, adjusted her braid, and looked up at me. The image changed: suddenly, she wasn't the carefree teenager I'd once known.

She was a woman.

A strong Alpha.

She's mine, I thought, and quelled my inner wolf before it could emerge. It wasn't the time, or the place to claim her.

Up until then, I hadn't realized how detached from the pack she'd been when she traveled back to us in her city garb. How uncomfortable she had seemed in her stiff funeral attire.

Now, it truly felt like she was a part of the pack again. The battered leather jacket, with its clinking hardware, was all the battle armor she needed.

"What do you think?" She fixed me with a challenging stare, her mouth lifting at the corners.

"Perfect," I said. "Ready?"

She nodded. "Let's do this."

∼

As Jaime had been Allara's challenger, he was the one to choose the arena for the fight.

He had selected a clearing about a mile away from the village, surrounded by overhanging trees on one side and a rocky outcrop that tumbled into the ravine below on the other.

I did my best to hide my irritation.

Leave it to Jaime to go all dramatic.

He was a showman of the worst kind, and he clearly wanted to give the pack something to remember.

He wanted to defeat the last symbol of the old bloodline. He wanted to be the victor of a story that would be told around endless campfires for years to come.

The whole pack gathered at the edge of the tree line, ready to watch the action.

I couldn't see Allara anymore; she had greeted everyone with a quiet confidence when we first arrived, and then wandered off, presumably to prepare herself mentally for what was about to happen.

There were some ancient, uprooted trees that served as benches, and a few hollows in the rockface that the elders settled in, whispering amongst themselves. On closer inspection I realized that these carved-out spaces were manmade.

Somebody had taken the time to make seats, like this place had been used for gatherings before.

Battles, I guessed. Or... rituals. I traced my fingers over the grooves in the rockface, and the back of my neck prickled with anxiety.

There was a light touch on my shoulder, accompanied by a soft, familiar voice.

"This place is famous," Rachel said. "Must have been used to settle hundreds of scores. It's been around since before Allara's grandfather's time."

I forced myself to appear relaxed. I turned and gave her an uneasy smile.

"Too showy for me," I said.

She chuckled and grabbed me into a hug. I hugged her back tightly and she whispered into my ear, her voice low and urgent.

"Allie needs you. Go to her." She pulled back and looked me over, reaching up to brush the shoulders of my jacket. "Whatever happens out there... you keep your cool, all right? Promise me, Reid."

I gazed down at her. Even though she barely came up to my chest, she always had a way of making me feel like the little kid who had shown up on the pack's doorstep with nothing but the clothes he stood in.

It was a lifetime ago now. But in so many ways, she was the only mother I had ever known.

Unable to meet her gaze, I glanced away. "You know I can't promise that. If she's in trouble..."

Out of the corner of my eye, I watched her expression fill up with sorrow. When she spoke, it was with understanding.

"I know." She rested her hand against my face, sighing. "You'd do anything for her. But I had to ask. I'm proud of you, Reid. Whatever happens, remember that."

I nodded. "Thank you, for everything, Rachel."

I walked away from her with a heavy weight in my chest, and made my way through the trees in the direction Rachel had pointed, until I came upon Allara.

She was sitting on a boulder, staring into space. She didn't seem to hear me approach, because when she looked up, her expression was startled.

I knelt in front of her and took her face in my hands, staring deeply into her eyes. "You got this," I said, more to reassure myself than her.

"Jaime has the edge." She hung her head. Her braid swung toward me, and I tugged on it lightly. "He's strong. He's ready for this."

"He's arrogant. He thinks he has this in the bag." I extended a hand, pulling her up. "You can use that arrogance; turn it against him. Plus, you're faster than him. You're *smarter*. Remember all of those things, Allie."

She nodded, but doubt still flickered in her eyes. My chest went cold.

She can't doubt herself. Not now.

I could fight on her behalf, but she could hold her own against Jaime, at least for a little while.

She had to.

"Reid." She smiled softly. "I—"

Before she could finish, a howl pierced through the forest. A flock of birds took off from a nearby tree, their wings beating at the undergrowth.

"I know." I kissed her forehead for a final time. "I know. Me too."

This was not the time to declare our love once again, or to wish that things might be different. She had to concentrate.

She nodded, lifted her chin, and stepped away from me.

Maintaining eye contact, she slipped off her leather jacket and laid it on a nearby log. Her sweater followed, then her boots and jeans.

Finally, she stood naked before me. Framed by greenery like this, she looked ethereal, like a goddess of the forest.

"I believe in you, Alpha," I said, and in that moment, hope filled me.

She could do this. She could save our pack.

Her eyes glimmered with silver, and my whole body tingled. I had to back away before I shifted into wolf form alongside her.

Not yet.

Not knowing entirely why, I picked up her jacket and hugged it against my chest.

She gave me one final, unreadable glance before she turned away, padding off into the trees. I followed her through the forest, back to the clearing where Jaime and the others waited.

I rubbed the old leather between my fingers. It was stupid, but I wanted something of hers to hold onto while I was forced to watch...

No. Don't even think it.

Allara would survive.

I trusted her, and I trusted myself to back her.

I would do whatever it took to ensure that she survived this.

The alternative was unthinkable.

Rachel stood at the edge of the gathering. As I approached, she beckoned me to her side.

My gaze wandered over to the group of elders. Jaime's father Terry sat among them, looking as stoic as ever. He met my eyes and gave me a brief nod of acknowledgment.

Although he shared his son's fair hair, that was where the resemblance ended.

As far as I knew, Terry had always been faithful and supportive, the ideal second-in-command for Allara's father. He had never treated me with the disdain that some of the pack members showed, and he could usually rein in Jaime's more fiery impulses.

Usually.

I wondered if he knew what his son had in store for the pack, if he won today.

Did he know the extent of his own flesh and blood's craziness?

Before I could contemplate any further, a vicious growl erupted from the other end of the clearing.

Jaime.

I bristled with tension. If I had been in wolf form, my fur would have been standing on end at the sight of him.

Allara, in wolf form, loped into the clearing with her head held high, circling wide so that she could acknowledge the crowd of spectators up close. She looked regal; her carriage remained unbowed, as was befitting a wolf of her status.

Jaime dragged up the earth, raking it with his claws. His growl built until it seemed to shake the ground beneath our feet.

He was trying to rile her up, bait her into attacking first.

She appeared to pay no attention to him. One of her ears flicked back and forth, like she was trying to swat away an annoying fly.

Finally, she turned to her opponent.

Silence fell as they faced each other down. From where I was sitting on a fallen log next to Rachel, I could see Jaime's flank rising and falling rapidly. The muscles in his back legs were coiled with tension.

Although he was bigger than her, he was slighter than most of the male wolves in the pack. He had a wiry, deadly strength, and a reputation for using it with an unbridled savagery; a chunk was missing from his left ear, and even from a distance I could see his muzzle was heavily scarred.

He was glowering at Allara, practically frothing with bloodlust.

My fingers dug into the bark of the log, anchoring me in place.

I have to let her do this.

Without warning, he leapt for her.

His jaws were already wide, preparing to close around her throat.

He'll snap her neck in an instant. It'll be over before it has begun.

Moving impossibly fast, she met him halfway. They clashed in mid-air, their two bodies crashing down to earth in a blur of claws, fur, and teeth.

Snarls and growls filled the previous silent arena.

In a flash, I was transported back to our fight in Allara's backyard, before we left the city.

It had been a close call, too close for my liking. Both of us had pushed to the edge of our strength and dexterity. But that battle had been completely different to this one.

Death had never been the chosen outcome for either of us.

Our battle's undercurrent had held a different kind of intensity. Our passion for each other had been obvious, even then; we wanted to draw each other as close as possible, taste the other's delicious scent while we had the chance.

This was... different.

The fight between Jaime and Allara was vicious, frantic, and merciless. They were both going for the kill, snapping at each other's jaws with an impossible speed and ferocity. If either one reached the other's neck, it would likely be over in an instant.

Jaime had the size advantage, and he used it. He kept pressing forward, forcing Allara back onto the defensive. I watched with bated breath as he manage to close his teeth around her back leg, but she shook free and slid out from under him before he could fully bite down.

Although she was giving it everything she had, I could tell Allara was flagging. She kept feinting to the left, and I realized she was trying to draw Jaime away from the crowd of watching pack members.

I growled in frustration.

Allara. She was too busy thinking about danger to others, when she should be focusing fully on her own peril.

Typical.

Jaime lunged again. His bite didn't manage to gain purchase, but he did tear at Allara's ear. She whined, blood dripping down from her wound and soaking the earth between them.

Jaime loped back a few paces. His movements were unconcerned and almost lazy. He was enjoying this, taking his time.

Arrogance. There it was. *Use it against him*, I willed her.

Rachel placed her hand on my arm. I realized that my fists were clenched, and my knuckles were white. I forced myself to relax my muscles and concentrated on slowing my ragged breathing.

In, out.

Allara backed up, drawing Jaime farther away from the tree line.

In, out.

He lunged at her again, crowding over her until she bore down into the earth. He was forcing her to lie flat to protect her stomach. Her ears were peeled back, and her eyes were wide and fearful.

She was showing her fear? That wasn't good.

In, out.

Jaime's jaws closed around the scruff of her coat. Too close. Far too close to her neck.

He dragged her to her feet and shook her violently between his teeth.

I couldn't stand it any longer. I had to help her.

Shaking Rachel's hand off my arm, I felt the air around me grow hazy and distorted. Adrenaline raced through me, and my heart beat a mile a minute.

Jaime dropped Allara into the dirt and nudged at her with his paw like he was playing with his prey. Though they were some distance away by now, I could see her chest rising and falling rapidly.

"Allara!" I bellowed, dropping with a thud onto my knees.

I was dimly aware of Rachel and a couple of others pulling at my chest, holding me back. They were trying to stop me from shifting. I gritted my teeth, heeding their warning, but ready to throw them off if I had to.

Jaime held Allara down, right at the very edge of the outcrop. One wrong move and he would send her tumbling over the edge onto the jagged rocks below.

Allara give a soft whimper. Though my blood still raced, and I felt like I was about to explode, the noise caused a memory to flicker in the back of my mind.

Allara doesn't sound like that.

Although panic was flooding my body, I held my breath for a few seconds and thought about that noise.

I'd sparred with her hundreds of times. When we were mad at each other, when we wanted to solve an argument, when we were happy, sad, bored, or for any reason at all.

I had never heard her make that whimpering sound before.

Except... once.

It had been years ago, when we were teenagers who would skip out on long and boring pack meetings to go spar in the forest for hours.

I scrambled to my feet after shifting back to human form, and kicked moodily at the dust, glaring at nothing in particular while Allara picked up a blanket and wrapped herself in it, laughing and laughing.

"You look so mad!" she said, delight in her tone.

"Yeah," I said, feeling belligerent. "You tricked me!"

"I did not!"

"Did too!" I snagged my jeans and tugged them up quickly. The conversation would be much more embarrassing if we both remained naked. "You pretended you were scared. Made me hesitate. I would've pinned you otherwise."

"Well..." She chuckled at the look on my face. "It worked, didn't it?"

I grumbled and took her hand, pulling her close to me. "I won't be such an idiot next time."

"Maybe you won't underestimate me next time." She flicked my ear with the tip of her finger, and I couldn't help but grin at her. I threw my arm around her shoulders as we headed back through the woods to the village.

My vision cleared.

Jaime wasn't toying with Allara.

Allara was toying with *Jaime.*

She was doing exactly as she should, taking advantage of his arrogance; his cocksure bravado. She knew he wanted to put on a big show for the pack and take out his competition in a public show of dominance.

She knew he would assume his victory was set in stone the moment she appeared to back down.

Even though I was focused on what was happening here and now, part of me reconsidered our fight, back in the city.

Had that gone her way as well?

I thought about what had happened after I pinned her. Maybe, after all that... she had wanted my win just as much as I did.

Maybe she'd *wanted* to come home, but had been too stubborn to admit it out loud.

Lightness filled my heart. She wanted to come back. With me.

Then I narrowed my eyes, studying them. Nothing was guaranteed. She was still in a great deal of danger.

After all, it wasn't over yet.

I calmed down enough that I wasn't about to shift into wolf form, but the sight of Allara so close to the edge of that precipice still had me on the verge of panic.

She told me to trust her.

And I did, down to my bones.

Jaime still had Allara pinned to the ground. One paw rested on her chest, almost like he couldn't be bothered to fully restrain her. His ears pricked up and he looked out over the pack, surveying the scene.

Letting everyone drink in his superiority.

The Alpha's daughter... defeated. About to be silenced forever, along with any memory of her father's legacy.

In a move so quick that everyone watching let out a collective gasp, Allara twisted out from beneath his restraining paw, and sprang up. The move swept Jaime's front legs out from under him, and he yelped, obviously shocked.

He staggered for a moment, caught off balance, before falling sideways and scrabbling. He couldn't seem to get purchase, and slid backwards towards the rocky edge of the ravine.

Before he had a chance to fall, Allara pinned his forelocks to the ground, holding him firmly in place.

Making sure he didn't fall to his death, I realized. As, indeed, did everyone watching.

Silence fell over the pack.

Then, into the silence, Allara threw back her head and howled.

The sound reverberated through the forest, sending shockwaves down my spine. The faces of the people around me were tight with tension.

The only figure of calm was Elder Mason, who stood near the center of the gathered crowd, surveying the scene with his cloudy, half-blind gaze.

"It is as decreed," he declared in his strange voice. He glided to the front of the crowd, his walking stick hitting the ground with a resounding *thud* at every step. "The Alpha's daughter shall take her place as the rightful heir."

A shiver went through the pack as they processed the outcome of the fight. Then, moving as one, every member of the council lowered their gaze to the earth and raised their right hand, placing it over their heart.

"Allara Bane!" they cried, and their hands flew upwards as if they were offering her name to the sky.

Thud. Thud. The wooden staff struck the ground.

It was done.

Allara was the new Alpha.

Her name echoed through the trees once more as the pack declared her their rightful leader.

I rushed forward, wanting to reach her, but Rachel put out a hand, stopping me in my tracks.

"Wait."

I turned toward her with a small growl. I had waited long enough.

What now?

CHAPTER 13

REID

But Rachel simply placed a woven blanket in my arms and gave me a gentle push.

"Go to her."

I gave her an apologetic smile and mumbled my thanks. I was grateful for her foresight, even if every cell in my body screamed at me to go to Allara *right this second.*

I held up the blanket. "You brought this for her. You knew she'd win?"

"I had a hunch." She patted me on the arm, smiling fondly. "Now go."

On impulse, I grabbed up Allara's leather jacket off the ground from where I'd dropped it, before I strode into the clearing, unable to stop myself from jogging the last few feet until I reached her crouching form. She had morphed back to human again, and was naked.

She had her back to me, and even from my angle of approach I could tell that she was panting harshly.

"Allara." She didn't seem to hear me. "Allara," I repeated, keeping my voice as soothing as possible. "I'm here."

Her head turned then, but just barely. If she were in wolf form, her ears would likely be twitching back and forth.

Moving slowly, I draped the blanket over her shoulders, covering her bare skin. After a moment her fingers came up, and she drew the blanket around her, wrapping herself in it.

She stood then, revealing her fallen adversary. Jaime lay sprawled out at her feet, staring up at her with an expression of hatred. The elder had decreed Allara the winner. There was no way for Jaime to win the fight now, even if he cheated and took her out after the fact, while in human form.

He would be shunned by the whole pack, and I would kill him.

Allara arranged the blanket so that it sat evenly over her shoulders. Her graceful movements made it seem like she wore a coronation gown rather than an old woolen blanket.

"The pack have declared it," I said in a low voice. "Once and for all. You are their Alpha, Allara."

Finally, she looked up at me. Her blue eyes were shining. She had never looked more beautiful.

"Don't I always tell you to trust me?" she said, granting me a soft smile.

I chuckled. "Maybe I should start listening."

She moved closer to me and pushed her forehead against mine, sighing. The sun glowed through the trees, and the wind flooded my senses with her gorgeous scent. It was a perfect moment.

Well, it would have been, except...

I pulled away and ran a thumb over her temple, snarling when I found blood there. "He hurt you."

Her face turned grave, and she glanced down at the silent figure lying at our feet.

"It looks worse than it is," she said, reaching up to touch the side of her head gingerly. "Reid... this isn't your fight."

"Your fight *is* my fight," I said simply.

Jaime sneered at me and his eyes glimmered with a hint of silver. I had to look away before I did something stupid.

Allara tugged at the jacket I held in my hands, distracting me.

"You brought my jacket," she said, giggling.

It *was* kind of silly, given the situation. But it felt right for her to have it while she faced the pack for the first time as their leader.

Careful not to jostle her, I lay the jacket loosely over the top of the blanket and brushed stray strands of hair away from her face with my fingers.

Now that my heart had stopped racing, I noted every scratch and bruise on her skin. They were scattered all over her face and jawline, and trailed over her collarbones and the exposed portion of her chest. My gaze drifted down to the monster at her feet.

"Reid," she said firmly. My eyes snapped back up to meet hers. "It's my call."

I inclined my head. "Yes, *Alpha.*"

The heat of my gaze contrasted with my deferent tone, but I couldn't bring myself to change it.

If I were in her position, I would kill Jaime without remorse.

He had done enough damage—to us *and* to the pack, and if he had his way, he would do even more, destroying anyone who dared to stand in his way.

It wouldn't take much. He'd shifted back to human now and was already at the edge of the cliff, the perfect picture of submission. One push, and he would be out of our lives forever.

Allara seemed to be mulling over the same thought. She stared up at the sky and closed her eyes, standing perfectly still for what felt like an eternity.

Then, she opened them.

"No." She turned to me, and I knew her mind was made up. "Jaime lives."

I shook my head, readying myself to challenge her with everything I had. "It was a fight to the death. You have to do this."

"I won't." She stumbled a little and pressed her hand against her side, groaning.

I darted forward to catch her, but she refused to let me take her weight. *So stubborn.*

"I can't let bloodshed be my first act as the Alpha of our pack, Reid."

"Allara—"

"I knew it," Jaime spat. "She hasn't got the *stomach* for it. Just like her dear old Dad."

He sat back on his elbows and glared up at us. My blood was boiling, but I knew what the outcome of the fight meant for him. Some considered it a fate worse than death to be defeated. Humiliated in front of everyone.

Voices murmured behind us, and I looked up to find that the rest of the pack had come closer. They stood in a crowd a few paces away, watching and waiting.

"James Fletcher." Allara raised her voice so that everyone could hear. "As victor, I decide your punishment." She looked down at him, her demeanor cold and regal. "I will not kill you. Instead, I banish you from this pack. From this day until your last, you may never return here. When you die, your bones will not be laid to rest with those of your ancestors."

I spared a glance at the pack, wondering what they made of all this. Were they relieved by the outcome of the battle, or enraged?

I couldn't really tell. Only Terry's face stood out to me; the man looked white as a sheet.

A long silence followed Allara's words.

Slowly, Jaime got to his feet, grunting with pain. I felt a shadow of satisfaction that Allara had managed to give as good as she got. For someone so out of practice in her wolf form, she'd really done a number on him.

He straightened up, looking her right in the face. No deference to her status showed at all. His eyes were like ice.

"You'll regret your weakness," he said in a low voice that trembled with rage. "Someday soon. I promise you. You and your mongrel mate."

A growl built in my throat. Allara linked her arm through mine, pulling me away from Jaime until he stood alone at the edge of the cliff.

"Leave it," she murmured. "He knows it's over."

Without breaking eye contact, Jaime circled around us and backed away, his hands in the air in a mocking show of innocence.

Once he reached the edge of the clearing, he stopped and turned back, shouting,

"When the time comes and you're all sick of this little girl and her mutt, don't worry. I'll be there to take her place. She turned her back on you, but I never will!"

Without waiting for a response, he loped away, vanishing into the undergrowth.

I stared at the spot in the trees where he had disappeared, fighting the urge to follow and finish him. I knew that his threats weren't empty; this wasn't the last we would see of Jaime.

Allara's fingers threaded through mine, and I smiled as a new thought struck me.

We might have to watch our backs, but so would he. Allara was a force to be reckoned with. And she would have me by her side, from this time forward.

Casting my gaze over the crowd, I noticed that Jason was watching Allara with an unreadable expression. He glanced away when I caught his eye.

Kara murmured something in his ear, and he nodded.

Paul stood beside him, looking devastated. I told myself that it didn't mean anything. He'd just lost his best friend, after all.

Terry was a far bigger concern.

He stood a little apart from the others, staring out into the valley with a blank look on his face.

As the Beta of the pack's old leader, he would always have a place on the council, and the ear of the pack.

Not for the first time, I wondered whether he'd known about Jaime's plans. He'd always been a thoughtful man, the complete opposite of his hothead son.

Terry had counseled Allara's father for decades. I fervently hoped that he would understand the position she had been put in.

Then I understood the logic of sparing Jaime's life, as well as the compassion. The pack's new Alpha would have made a powerful enemy if she had killed Terry's son.

Rachel smiled at me, relief and hope in her eyes, and I smiled back. I owed her so much. I'd had nothing when she took me in...

Nothing worth holding onto, anyway.

"Looks like you got your wish, after all." Allara tugged on my hand, and I looked down at her.

"What's that?"

In spite of her tiredness and injuries, her face glowed. "You're stuck with me. I can hardly go back to the city now, can I?"

Acting on impulse, I picked her up and raised her off her feet. She squealed with surprise before laughing brightly.

"I'm sure we can find something for you to do here," I replied, burying my face in her hair and kissing her head before setting her down gently. "Alpha Bane."

She gave me a wicked grin. "At your service."

EPILOGUE

ALLARA

I sat in front of my dressing table mirror and peered at my reflection. I might just change that little strand...

Kara slapped at my hands as I tried to rearrange the wedding hairstyle that my friend had thoughtfully done for me. "Stop fiddling with it!"

I dropped my hands into my lap, trying to tamp down the guilt. *Oops. Busted.*

Time to put my trust in Kara.

She threw a smirk at my reflection via the mirror before continuing to weave her seemingly magic fingers through my hair. It was looped into a simple half-up, half-down style that looked simple and yet elegant.

As much as I loved what she'd done, my fingers itched to pull my hair free of its style, slip out of my fancy dress, and run far, far away.

I was about to get married, to the man I loved more than life itself, and I couldn't control my nerves.

Rachel appeared in the room, and I met her gaze in the mirror, smiling gratefully as she passed me a cup of herbal tea.

"Something to settle the nerves," she said.

"Do all brides feel like this?" It seemed ridiculous, to be stressed over something I actually wanted!

"Most do." Rachel patted my shoulder. "You'll have to get used to being stared at, Allara. You're the Alpha now."

I huffed a sigh. I knew that, of course. *But...*

"Everyone knows that Reid wasn't my father's first choice." Kara glanced at Rachel before resuming her fussing with my hair. "What if they all think I'm making a mistake?"

"But he's *your* choice." Rachel's hand on my shoulder squeezed gently. "It was always meant to be this way. In time, they'll come to understand that."

I prayed that Rachel was right about the others. I wanted them to accept Reid fully as one of us.

I hadn't lied to Reid when I told him there hadn't been anyone else. There had never been anyone else. I realized that now.

And I wanted to bond forever with my mate.

For me, and for Reid.

We'd been apart for so long. It seemed unthinkable now, that either of us had let the situation drag on. He had been following his Alpha's orders, at least, but I had been driven by hurt.

After we had picked up where we left off, the intervening years had melted away like a bad dream. I had a lot to be thankful for, and I couldn't wait to make my love for Reid official with the bonding ceremony.

But part of me knew that the mystery surrounding his origins would always leave people wondering, who was the man at the right hand of the Alpha?

Would he be my Beta wolf? My co-counsel? Would we lead the pack together?

They were only some of the questions that I didn't have the answers to, yet.

Finally, Kara finished fussing at my hair. I stood and straightened my skirt, turning to face her and Rachel. "Do I look okay?"

They nodded.

"More than okay. You look perfect." Rachel put a hand against my cheek. "You look so much like your mother."

"One finishing touch," Kara said. She picked up a simple circlet fitted with small amber stones, and reached up to drape it carefully over my head, so as not to disturb my hairdo. "There. *Now* you're good to go. You look awesome."

I don't feel like I'm good to go! I wanted to scream. *I feel like I'm about to melt into a puddle of tension.*

Nevertheless, I gathered my nerves together and made my way downstairs. Rachel helped me down the front steps of my house, and together we walked through the village, coming to a stop outside the meeting house.

"Just relax, take it one step at a time," Rachel said. "Remember, it's your day."

I felt some of the stiffness in my spine drain away as I climbed up to the entrance of the building.

Briefly, a wave of sadness hit, that my parents would not be here to see me wed Reid. But somehow, I felt their energy, their presence, and I knew that they would both be happy for me in this moment. I nodded, took a deep breath and released it, letting the sadness go. Then I entered the hall. As I did so, soft music began to play.

Elder Mason stood at the front on a raised dais that had been constructed for the occasion, holding a length of red velvet in his hands. The pack surrounded us on either side of the aisle. They stood patiently, about to witness the bonding of their Alpha to her mate.

Beside Elder Mason stood Reid.

As soon as I saw him, my tension melted away.

He was always the focus of my attention in whatever room he stood, but today I truly couldn't take my eyes off him.

He'd ditched his trusty leather jacket for the occasion, trading it in for a simple button down in a soft gray that fit his broad frame perfectly and made his eyes look even more striking. He had even tamed his hair somewhat, pushing it back so that I could see the strong line of his jaw as I approached.

He was everything I had ever wanted.

I came to a stop opposite him, meeting his gaze. The look on his face was hard to read, but there was a storm of emotion in his eyes.

You look beautiful, he mouthed.

My lips curved into a smile.

You too, I thought, and hoped he could read the appreciation in my gaze.

I'd never seen him so polished, though I'd always loved him best in flannel and his old boots.

Or naked... of course.

The music began to crescendo, swelling with intensity, and the drumbeat thundered around us, keeping time to the beat of my heart.

As one, we held out our right arms. Our wrists met in the empty space between us.

"The time has come," Elder Mason said, "for these souls to join together as one."

He held the velvet fabric up for those watching to see, and then wrapped it around our joined wrists, tying it once.

"Allara Bane," he continued. "You are bonded to Reid, body and soul, as the fates have foretold."

I inclined my head. The elder wrapped the cloth around us a second time, tying it again.

"Reid." His attention turned to Reid. "You are bonded to Allara Bane, body and soul, as the fates have foretold."

Reid bowed. Against the wrist that was now bound to his, one of his fingers brushed my arm gently.

"She is yours," Elder Mason said, magnifying his voice so that it filled the whole room. "And you are hers. As the fates have foretold!"

As one, the pack got to their feet, stamping on the floor and echoing his words in unison as a drumbeat started to play once more.

"As the fates have foretold!"

With his free hand, Reid pulled me forward by the waist and I melded into his body. He kissed me with a fierce intensity, our bound hands trapped between us.

When we broke apart, I flushed at the way we had displayed our passion for the whole pack to see.

I was faintly aware of applause, some scattered cheering, and a few wolf-whistles, but I pressed my forehead into Reid's and ignored it all, focusing only on him.

"Finally," he breathed, and then captured my lips for a brief, dizzying moment before pulling away and laughing softly to himself, like he couldn't believe it. "You're back. And you're *mine*."

"As you are mine. Now, and always," I said simply.

We stood there, soaking in the moment. Then, Reid tugged at the ties that bonded us together.

"Do we have to keep these on forever?" he whispered, quirking an eyebrow. "Because I could work with that."

I chuckled, shaking my head.

"I think you're meant to untie us at some point. If you can figure out the knots," I added, winking.

Toward the back of the hall, I spotted my old boss Mick, Tammy, and Penny chatting to Kara and Jacob, and my heart skipped a beat or two.

I gave them a wave and a grin, and then tilted my head at Reid. "I didn't know they were coming!"

"I invited them. What?" he said. "City life can't have been all bad, right?"

With difficulty, given our current entanglement, I wrapped my arms around his neck and kissed his cheek. "I love you."

"I love you, too," he murmured, kissing my hair. His eyes were warm, and calmer than I'd seen them in a long time. "Always have. Always will."

THE FESTIVITIES WOUND on well into the evening. A long table was set up in the clearing, and lanterns were hung in the trees. Children ran back and forth, trying to catch the fireflies that glowed in the fading twilight.

Dancing began after the feast, and people spun around each other, skirts swirling, shouting with laughter. Reid was at the center of it all, playing ring-a-rosie with the smallest children and letting them clamber all over him as he chuckled.

I stood to one side and watched the people—*my* people—without really seeing them.

Too much stirred in my head to get completely lost in the joy of the moment.

I'm the Alpha now.

The thought shocked me still.

But my dream had come true.

Reid *had* stayed, just as he said he would. My duties weren't mine to carry alone.

Wherever you go, I go.

We had to protect everyone here from whatever lay out there, in the darkness beyond the trees. But we would do it, together.

"Most women look happier at their bonding ceremony," said a voice beside me.

I turned. Terry was holding a can of beer and studying me with interest.

"Don't fancy a dance with your new mate?"

I swallowed and shook my head, fiddling with the trailing edge of my sleeve. "Just tired, I guess."

The truth was, I did feel kind of weird. I had for a few days, now, but I'd chalked it up to bonding ceremony jitters.

"Hmm." He nodded. "The road ahead is long and winding, Allie. Better keep your strength up for what lies in front of you."

Before I could figure out what he meant, or formulate a reply, he drifted off, mingling with the revelers until I lost sight of him altogether.

What lies ahead?

Was he in contact with his son? What did he know?

My niggling worries could be paranoia on my part. Nevertheless, something made the hairs on the back of my neck stand up.

He was your dad's closest friend, I told myself.

So, we'd better keep an eye on him, replied another inner voice, which sounded remarkably like Reid.

I wonder what he'll do next...

Penny came bounding up to me, flushed with exertion from being spun around by the inhuman strength of dozens of wolf shifter men. "Hey, cheer up, sour face! It's your wedding! Or, close enough, right?"

"Right." I laughed, forcing a smile onto my face. "Having fun?"

"Tons." She grinned back at me. "Your hubby—or is it soulmate? Whatever. Reid's waiting for you! Go dance!"

At that, I shook off the niggle and grinned back at her. Penny was right; I could put away my Alpha responsibilities for just one night.

I wandered out onto the dance floor, where Reid waited for me. His eyes reflected the light of the flickering tapers around us, and his lips were stretch up into the most gorgeous smile I'd ever seen.

It might have taken a few bumps along the road to get here, but I knew now that we could take on whatever the future brought to our doorstep.

Because, finally, we were together.

The End

LOVE OF THE WOLF

USA TODAY BEST-SELLING AUTHOR

AMELIA SHAW

LOVE OF THE WOLF

TAMMY

The forest outside my window flashed past in a blur as we drove. The landscape was breathtaking this far outside the city, but I wasn't in the mood to take in the natural beauty that surrounded us.

Up front, Mick and Penny were chatting—no, *gossiping*. Their topic of conversation was fixed on one thing—the mysterious stranger Allara had eloped with a couple of weeks ago.

"I'm just saying, it's crazy she just ran off with him like that." Penny swivelled in her seat to catch my eye, and I gave her a half-hearted nod. That seemed to satisfy her, because she turned back and continued her discussion with Mick. "If any of my ex-boyfriends showed up, I wouldn't be taking them out on any dates, that's for sure."

Her long earrings swung from side to side as she talked. Penny was pretty, petite, and vivacious. A real firecracker. She'd had to fend off a guy or two from time to time.

"Nah," Mick said. I could see his profile, his lips drawn into a frown, in the side view mirror. "I saw the way he looked at her. It was deeper than some past fling, I'll bet."

"Allara said he dumped *her*," Penny mused. "What?" She laughed, catching Mick's raised eyebrow look. "So, I eavesdropped a little! It was past midnight and there were no other customers in the diner. You can't tell me you wouldn't have done the same."

Mick just harrumphed and caught my eye in the mirror. "Check the map, will ya? This place must really be out in the sticks." We were in a remote area that provided no signal for a GPS.

Sighing, I opened the map and spread it over my knees, running my finger over the route we had marked out.

Of all the road trips I'd taken, this one had to be the weirdest.

First, the highway we were on was narrow and winding, with steep banks cut into the rock on either side of us. It was completely unmarked on the map itself, so we were basically following a series of crosses Reid had drawn for us and praying we were on the right track. We were in remote territory now, and if we got lost, nobody had any bars of reception on their cell phones to call for help. I couldn't ask Allara for advice, even if we had reception. Reid had invited us as a surprise for her, so she didn't know we were coming.

Secondly, Allara had disappeared from our lives, practically overnight. The only reason we knew she was all right was a short note she'd left for Mick, saying that she was fine and that she had to take care of some things at home. She said she'd only be gone a few days.

And finally, rather than appearing once again after a few days, we'd received an invitation from her hunky guy Reid to their wedding in Allara's hometown. Out here somewhere, in the middle of nowhere.

Only he didn't call it a wedding. He'd called it a *bonding ceremony*.

I had to admit, the wording intrigued me a little. I didn't have Allara pegged as the type to be into all that New Age, crystal healing stuff.

"Looks like we're on the right track," I said, glancing up at the road ahead. "We passed that cave thing on the left a couple miles back, right?"

"I think so," Penny said, sounding uncertain.

She and Mick resumed their debating and I tuned out, letting the sound of their voices wash over me as I went back to staring into space.

Truth be told, I hadn't known Allara very long. She was a good co-worker, and I loved working with her, but I'd always known the bar job was just a stopgap for her. A way to make ends meet, just like for me.

I was fresh out of college, having finally completed my last semester and had gained enough credits to earn my degree in child development. Allara and Mick had both surprised me by showing up at my graduation ceremony, which had been lovely.

All my friends and family wanted to know when I would start grad school to become a social worker. It had been my goal from the minute I'd started college, and they all knew it.

I blew them all off and kept my answers vague and non-committal. There would be time for all that later on. I was burned out and, if I were honest, I was fine where I was. Mixing drinks wasn't exactly the ideal way to spend my weekends, but it paid the bills.

Besides, it wasn't like I had anyone to spend my weekends *with*.

Not anymore.

I shook off the dark thoughts and focused on Allara. This was going to be *her* day, after all.

I knew the other two were curious to witness the mysterious bonding ceremony as well. Reid hadn't really described what would happen, but I got the sense that it wasn't like anything I'd seen before. I should be excited too.

But I couldn't shake off my misery so easily. It had sunk its claws into me a month ago, and it wasn't going away any time soon.

Time heals all things.

I wished I could believe it, but the advice I had heard from everyone around me was empty and meaningless. I was alone, and there was no disputing that fact. No way of inserting sunshine and rainbows into my life. The years stretched out ahead of me, barren as a desert.

No matter how I looked at the situation, the pain was still as deep as it had been that night.

The night that had changed everything and turned my whole world upside down.

Nothing made sense anymore. I didn't know when things would turn right side up again, when the pieces of my life would fit back together as they did before.

In my heart of hearts, I suspected they never would.

～

It was midday by the time we rolled up the narrow road and into Allara's hometown.

There were trucks parked on the side of the road, mud coating their wheel guards. We hadn't seen any signs of life since we turned off the freeway, so it was a relief to see evidence of civilization this deep into the woods.

The trees were just like Allara had described the few times she talked about home. Their trunks were thick; some stood wider than our car's width, and they were so tall I had to crane my neck up to see the treetops. Their branches were so high, it was like they held up the skies above us.

Mick parked on a small patch of grass littered with dirt bikes and other cars, and turned off the engine. Our arrival had not gone unnoticed. Several people were staring from outside a nearby house, and more than a few had stopped in their tracks.

Some of the kids were peering curiously, trying to get a better look at us. I waved at a small girl with long, braided hair, and she smiled at me before hiding her face in her mother's skirt.

"Well," Penny said, confident as ever. "I guess we should find out where to go. Wouldn't want to miss the fun."

With that, she opened her door and slid out the passenger side, landing daintily on her tiptoes so that her heels didn't sink into the grass.

I'd opted for simple flats for the occasion, as the invitation had suggested. The ground was firm beneath my feet, and as I inhaled, the first lungful of cool, forest air cleared my head, leaving me with a calmness that I hadn't felt in weeks.

"We're here for the... uh... bonding ceremony?" I heard Mick say to someone nearby.

"We have our invitation," Penny added, offering the stranger a card identical to the one I'd received. "Which way is the town hall, please?"

"Social hall," a man corrected her, sounding gruff. His eyes were narrowed, and he stood hunched over with his hands in his pockets. Another man wandered over and put a hand on the gruff man's arm. The first guy backed off immediately.

Huh. That was weird.

"Sorry about that," the second man addressed us with a warm smile, and we gravitated toward the friendly face. He shook each of our hands in turn as he spoke. "I'm Terry. The hall is right this way. I'll take you, as I was just heading there myself."

"Thanks." Penny smiled as we fell into step beside him. "We're not exactly from around here."

Terry threw back his head as he laughed uproariously. "No kidding! Everyone knows everyone else round here; that's just the way it is. Some don't take kindly to new faces, but they'll get over it soon enough."

"We're friends of Allara's," Mick explained. "From the city?"

Something flickered behind Terry's eyes, but other than that, his expression didn't change. "Sure, of course. Our Allara's always been one for adventure. Loves new experiences, all kinds of people. Here we are." He pointed to a building, slightly larger than the others surrounding it, with a low, pitched roof. "This is the social hall. The center of our little community."

We climbed the steps and found ourselves in a room with a vaulted ceiling made from roughly cut logs, some as large as tree trunks. The ceiling held a light fixture made from antlers, and the wooden benches were beautifully carved with leaping salmon, prowling mountain lions, and soaring bald eagles.

It was rustic, but beautiful. *Feels like home.*

Which was admittedly an odd feeling for me to have. I'd never been anywhere quite like this before. It certainly didn't look anything like what I'd always thought of as *home.*

The room was already packed. Practically every person in the village must have been in attendance.

With a shared look and an unspoken agreement, we chose a bench at the very back of the room and took our seats.

"Hey," Penny murmured, leaning in close to me. "Check out the eye candy."

I glanced over, following her sightline.

On the other side of the aisle were a group of youngish guys, sprawled out over the back benches and conversing lazily amongst themselves. Despite their casual demeanor, there was an alertness in the way they kept glancing over to the doors of the entrance that suggested they were keeping a close eye on the proceedings.

Almost like they're guarding the place.

But... from what?

This was a wedding, after all. Were they expecting someone to make a scene?

I didn't have time to wonder about what was going on, before Penny's elbow caught me sharply in the side. "Dibs on the cutie!" she whispered, giggling.

Which one is the cutie?

The truth was, they were all as good-looking as each other. I couldn't work out which one in particular she meant.

Even though they were all seated, I could tell they were unusually tall. They were broad, too, the width of their frames causing their suit jackets to sit almost awkwardly across their shoulders.

All of them cut an impressive figure, with firm jawlines, and white teeth that complemented easy, perfect smiles. Country living certainly seemed to agree with these men.

For a brief, heart-stopping second, a pair of hazel eyes met mine.

My cheeks flushed with heat and I looked away quickly, my heart hammering in my chest. I furtively wiped my palms against my skirt and looked intently at the invitation that lay in my lap.

God, it's hot in here.

I told myself I must have been mistaken. It wasn't like any of them would be looking at me for any reason. They were probably staring at Penny, who was naturally attractive and vivacious, and I just happened to be in the way while they were scoping her out.

I was too nervous to check and see if I was right. So, I decided to keep my eyes to myself from now on. There were plenty of other things to hold my attention, after all. Up at the front, a group of musicians were performing a piece that involved a pair of huge drums. Although I couldn't see much from my position, I was intrigued by the braided hair of the women playing the music and the long, sweeping robes of the elderly man who stood at the front of the hall.

"There's a buffet after, right?" Mick mumbled to Penny, who *shushed* him as the music cut off abruptly and an eerie silence filled the room.

The double doors creaked open and a man entered through them, alone.

Reid... Allara's ex-boyfriend turned fiancé. The man who'd invited us here today in support of her.

I had a vague recollection of him from just a few brief moments when he'd stood in the doorway of our dim, smoky bar after Allara had punched that jerk who tried to hit on me and wouldn't take no for an answer. I'd only caught a few glimpses of Reid that night, but the two things that stuck out to me most were his height, as well as the rough, battered leather jacket he'd worn.

Just like those other guys across the aisle.

Just like the owner of the hazel eyes.

I forced my attention to remain on the groom—if that was what he was called, at a bonding ceremony. He was a lot more well-dressed than I remembered. His hair was combed, for one thing, and he was wearing slacks and a button up shirt that brought out the color of his eyes, which were just as piercing as those of the hazel-eyed guy.

Reid strode up the center aisle and came to a stop at the platform, just in front of the elderly man. The older guy looked like some sort of religious officiant, but I didn't recognize the denomination of his church. His robes didn't look like any that I'd seen before.

The drums picked up again, and soon the entire room was filled with the sound. There was buzzing through my feet and my body unconsciously began to move with the music. I didn't notice for several seconds, and when I did, I continued. Those around us were also swaying, as well as stamping their feet in time to the rhythm.

The doors opened once more, and Allara entered, accompanied by a few women who were also dressed to impress, but none of them could hold a candle to Allara.

My friend looked supremely radiant. Her long, dark hair was looped up into a complex pattern, fastened at the nape of her neck. She must have had someone else arrange her hair, because the Allara I knew would never have the patience to create that.

Her long dress was beautiful in its simplicity. The only decorative element was the embroidery that shimmered around the sleeves and hem of the garment.

As she passed us, I realized that the design emulated the foliage that surrounded this place. The forest was echoed in her headpiece, too; the delicate silver band was fitted with amber pieces. Their golden hue stood out against her dark hair, making her look regal.

Once she reached Reid, she turned to face him. The expression on his face at the sight of her was enough to send a shiver of envy all the way down my spine.

I sighed, wondering what it would feel like to have someone look at *me* that way.

It wasn't that I didn't feel happy for Allara. I did. Extremely happy. I knew she'd had a tough time, and it seemed as if she'd finally found her place in the world again. She was back where she belonged, with her people; her family.

And she had this gorgeous guy by her side, who clearly adored her. Anyone could tell that he would do absolutely anything for her.

I watched as they murmured their unusual vows to each other. They sounded arcane, almost mystical. Like nothing I'd heard before. He leaned in close to her to whisper something, and I watched her lips curve into a smile as she stared up at him with adoration.

I couldn't begrudge Allara her happiness.

And yet, there was a tiny part of me that ached with longing.

They were both equally gorgeous, and they looked utterly content together. Two halves of a perfect whole.

The beautiful ceremony unfolding in front of my eyes only exacerbated my feelings of loneliness.

I was sure to the depths of my being that no one would ever look at *me* that way. Never cradle my face like I was something precious and irreplaceable to him. Never kiss me like he couldn't get enough of my lips against his own. Hold me like there was nobody else in the room.

Allara's slender body curved to meet Reid's strong form. She was so lithe and feminine, her dress skimming over her body like water. I couldn't help but wonder what it would be like to look like her.

Next to women like Allara and Penny, I always felt so frumpy and ungainly. I knew I would never be petite like them. My weight had always bothered me, but in moments like this, it really came to the forefront.

Above all, I envied Allara because I could tell that she was totally secure. I envied her the security of Reid's love, even as I celebrated for her.

She knew the man she loved would never leave her or look at another woman. She knew that the love she felt was returned by her partner completely, and she had her whole community around her to celebrate this day.

It was a life I would never know, and I was humble enough to admit that it crushed me a little inside to acknowledge that fact.

Still, I held up my chin, smiling widely, and applauded with everyone else when Reid and Allara stood, their arms bound together, flushed and glowing with happiness.

It was a perfect day, and I wasn't going to let my private sorrow ruin it for anyone.

No way.

JASON

A trio of folks I didn't know entered the social hall, led by Terry. Were they shifters, from another pack? After some deliberation, they sat across from us on the other side of the aisle. They were obviously invited guests and didn't seem threatening, so I barely looked at them, being more focused on the hall and my own pack, until Paul elbowed me in the side.

"Must be Allara's friends from the city," he hissed. "Don't cha think?"

Huh. Must be human, then.

We didn't get many ordinary humans up in our neck of the woods. Our settlement was deliberately hidden away, far from the main highways that cut across the state. Some of the children had barely seen outsiders before.

Humans weren't that interesting to me. They couldn't hike, run or climb like we could, and their senses were notoriously feeble. I hated the avalanche of noises and smells that greeted me any time I visited the city, and the way they gawked at us when they saw our eyes change always made me want to head straight back home, where I didn't feel so out of place.

But, just for a moment, I gave those city folk a brief look.

Not like there's anything better to look at right now, anyway.

The one on the end was a woman with a loud voice, bright lipstick and dangly earrings. Human as they came. She seemed to have spotted something she liked, though, over in this direction. She kept glancing over to us and giggling. To my annoyance, Eli and Paul didn't seem to mind this at *all,* judging by their identical smirks.

It was all I could do not to roll my eyes at their juvenile posturing.

Paul noticed my glowering face. "What?"

"Nothing," I muttered.

"She's hot, right?" he continued, indicating toward Dangly Earrings. Like I was going to miss the way his tongue was practically hanging out as he studied her. "D'you think I should go for it later?"

I shook my head, this time not hiding the eye roll. To avoid having to respond any further, I looked back to the humans and pretended to consider them.

Next to the loudmouthed chick was an older guy who didn't look quite as thrilled to be there as his friend did. I vaguely remembered hearing Reid talk about Allara's job as a bartender, and that she'd gotten to know the owner pretty well. From his description, this guy looked like he could fit the bill.

My attention turned to the woman sitting at the far end of the row.

She was dressed more soberly than the other woman, and her curves were nicely plump. Her features were softer than those of her companions, a kind and gentle friendliness on her face as she glanced around the room. When her more garish friend nudged her, she looked across and caught my eye, and a jolt shot through my system.

Whoa. What the hell was that?

I almost glanced away from her, but something inside stopped me doing so.

Sweet. The word struck me out of nowhere as I continued to stare into her eyes, which had widened a little.

Did she feel this strange connection, too?

Around her face, her hair fell in loose, natural waves over her shoulders. The style, as well as the rich auburn color, was striking against her creamy pale skin.

Not my usual type at all. And yet, something about her arrested my attention and held it. I couldn't look away.

She folded her hands in her lap and stared down at them, breaking the moment.

I blinked hard a few times before slouching down in my seat. I tried to ignore the way my pulse picked up as a tingle of awareness sparked in every part of me.

It felt like my body had betrayed me with its reaction, and I didn't understand where it had stemmed from. I'd slept with more than a few women over the years. The corners of my mouth curled upwards as I thought of the women I'd bedded.

Confident shifter women, from packs out of state who'd been passing through our area to trade with us or to look for a mate. Hot women. Skinny, fit women.

In truth, not one of them were anything at all like the sweet human female sitting opposite me.

I had thought about bonding with a few of those ladies over the years. I genuinely liked a lot of them, and they liked me. But something had always held me back before I took that final step.

I could never put my finger on the reason. The humans would probably call me a *lone wolf*. I had just figured I wasn't a commitment kind of guy.

I glanced at the woman again, surreptitiously this time, and told myself to pull it together. This was clearly a good girl; someone who would never look my way, let alone spend a night in my bed with no strings attached. I could already see that as plain as day.

As much as I was a commitment-phobe, she was a woman who would want it all from her partner. All, or nothing. This was a lady you wed; you didn't just bed her and move on.

The doors opened behind us and Reid strode through them, looking as uncomfortable in his fancy get-up as I felt in mine.

Every time I thought about bonding with someone—spending the rest of my life tied to another person and sharing *everything* with them —the whole idea seemed so crazy. It almost made me break out in hives.

Had things gone differently, it might have been Jaime up there right now about to bond with Allara, the Alpha of the pack.

And me as the proud Beta, standing by his side and supporting him every step of the way.

In the back of my mind, I knew it was a ridiculous thought. Allara would have never gone along with the bonding. Not with Reid already there in her heart.

And Jaime...

Well, the less I thought about *him* today, the better.

Allara herself came in soon after, and I watched the ceremony with a mixture of envy and sadness.

The envy confused me. Surely, I didn't want to be bonded to one woman, like Reid was about to do with Allara? Even if they both did look the happiest I'd ever seen them.

The sadness, on the other hand, was understandable.

Jaime had had a dream of being Alpha, and I'd been caught up in that dream right along with him. The dream had been snatched away in the blink of an eye, and I was still getting used to the new status quo.

But... maybe this is what's best for the pack.

Allara and Reid together, are strong, and that can only be good for us all, moving forward.

The sound of the drums carried me to my feet, and I hollered and stamped like everyone around me, but inside there was an empty, hollow feeling in my chest.

I wasn't quite sure what was causing it.

Without meaning to, I darted another glance over to our human visitors and caught an expression on the auburn-haired woman's face that seemed to mirror exactly what I was feeling.

On the surface, she looked supportive and happy. But there was something in her features that hinted the opposite. I sensed that she carried something sad deep inside her, just like I did. Something dark, like regret. Whatever it was, I could tell her emotions in that moment weren't so different from my own, despite the wide smile on her lips.

Hell, I need something to amuse me. Just so I can make it to the end of this confusing day.

I decided to make it my mission to find out just what that *something* bothering the mystery woman might be, and see if a little wolf company could put a more authentic smile on her face.

Maybe I was wrong, and she *would* consider a no-strings attached night of fun. The thought lifted my lips in my first genuine smile since Jaime had been defeated by Allara in the fight for Alpha supremacy of the pack.

⁓

TAMMY

THE RECEPTION WAS HELD on the lawn just behind the hall. It was a beautiful day. The decorations were perfectly set off by the sun glistening through the trees, and my heart warmed to see so many children making a dash for the open space after being cooped up inside for so long.

To the delight of Mick, the buffet table was laden with food and drink, and he immediately made a beeline for the victuals. Penny made a similar move for the wide lawn, predictably throwing herself into the thick of the social action without a second's hesitation.

I didn't know which one of them to follow. Getting a drink seemed like the smartest idea right now.

A strong one, preferably.

The people flooded out onto the grass, chattering, and laughing. The musicians came with them and struck up a square dance. Smaller children linked hands and persuaded some of the more enthusiastic adults to take turns swinging them around in a circle while they squealed with joy.

I smiled too, as I watched them all dance. The joy was infectious.

Allara and Reid came out of the building arm in arm, chuckling as they untangled the red velvet cloth that tied their arms and bound them together. Reid spun her around in his arms and tied the cloth around her waist, fastening it with a bow at the back and kissing her neck while she batted his hands away in mock protest, her eyes shining with pleasure.

I was so glad for my friend, who had obviously found her perfect man.

I found myself alone, sitting on the back porch of the social hall. I clutched my glass of white wine like it was a lifeboat and occupied myself with people-watching.

It was one of my favorite activities, especially at large social events like this one.

Reid was the life and soul among the kids, letting them clamber all over him. Now that his gruff exterior had dropped and he was back in his natural environment, I could see his playful spirit shining through.

He'd make a great partner for Allara. And maybe someday, a great father to their children.

I searched among the group for that captivating pair of hazel eyes from inside the hall, but they were nowhere to be found.

I didn't know whether to be relieved or disappointed.

The frisson of awareness that had shivered down my spine when I met his eyes, had been more than a little disconcerting.

A low, smooth voice traveled down to me, coming from somewhere above my left shoulder. "Don't fancy joining the party?"

I looked up slowly, my heart jumping in my chest when I realized to whom the voice belonged.

Hazel eyes. Black hair. Just the right amount of stubble.

Holy shit. He's actually speaking to me.

The man had undone his tie along with the top few buttons of his shirt, leaving a tantalizing glimpse of his chest on display. I wasn't sure whether he had purposefully sought to emphasize his impressive physique, but it was certainly working for me.

"Oh, I don't know this dance," I said carefully, pointing to the mass of partygoers, who were now weaving in and out of each other in pairs and spinning their dance partners around with enthusiasm. "Or any of the dances, to be honest. I'm happy to sit here and watch the fun."

To my shock, he took a seat next to me on the steps. He was a perfectly respectable distance away, but a shiver passed through me, nonetheless.

"Are you really happy to sit here and watch? That doesn't seem to be the case for your friend," the guy said, resting his elbows on his knees in a careless way and pointing in Penny's direction.

Sure enough, she was reveling in the music. Occasionally, she missed a step or trod on someone's foot, but she just laughed it off and carried on regardless.

"That's Penny," I said, feeling the need to explain. "She's extremely confident. She's just making it up as she goes along, by the looks of it."

"And you can't do that?" I turned to meet those devastating eyes. He was studying me with an intent expression that I couldn't quite read. "Make it up as you go along?"

"Definitely not," I mumbled, feeling inadequate as always. "Spontaneity isn't exactly my default setting."

"Maybe you just need to meet the right man to lead you in the steps." He flashed me a cocky grin. God, his smile was so alluring. "Don't let life pass you by, Red. You never know what could be waiting for you right around the corner."

Red? My face heated as I registered the reference to my hair color. *How original.*

"I've tried the whole *man* thing, and it didn't exactly work out for me," I snapped. He looked askance at me, and I sighed. "Sorry. My faith in guys isn't exactly top tier right now."

He clicked his tongue and ran a hand through his hair. "So *that's* your damage," he drawled. "I was wondering. Back in there," he hooked a thumb over to the doors that led into the social hall. "You looked..."

He trailed off without finishing the statement. I decided to push further, feeling irritation rising in spite of myself. "Looked what?"

"I don't know... conflicted?" He stared at me, narrowing his eyes. "Now, maybe you just hate bonding ceremonies. But there's more to it than that, right? I could tell, just by looking at you."

I hope no one else could tell. Especially Allara and Reid.

I got to my feet and smoothed down my skirt, trying to rein in the hot rush of embarrassment and annoyance that flooded through me.

Why do all the hot ones have to be such assholes?

And why was he even talking to me, anyway? A guy like him could have any woman he wanted, most likely just by crooking his little finger or shooting them an inviting look. Women with gorgeous bodies, women who would laugh at his jokes, women who weren't too shy to get up and dance in front of strangers...

Women like Penny. Never women like me.

"I'm not a puzzle that you can just *pick apart* to satisfy your own amusement," I managed, after an awkward pause. "Allara's a good friend of mine and I'm thrilled that she and Reid are married... or at least, bonded."

He regarded me with a wry smile. "Same thing, in our world. And, I never said you weren't happy for your friend."

He hadn't moved from his position, comfortably sprawled out

across the step. For some reason, the casual, arrogant display only served to inflame me further.

"I *am* happy for her," I said. I was telling the truth, after all. "I wanted to be here for her on her wedding day. End of story."

He didn't need to know anything more than that. I'd already given him too much ammo as it was.

And he definitely *doesn't need to know that he hit the nail right on the head without even trying. Bullseye. Fifty points to the arrogant jerk with the hypnotic eyes.*

"If you're referring to what just happened in there," he said slowly, "maybe you don't know her as well as you thought."

What does that even mean?

I stood and began to walk away, unwilling to entertain any more of his cryptic nonsense.

I had a half-formed plan to rescue Mick, who seemed to have gotten himself backed into the buffet table by a couple of angry husbands. I grimaced. Knowing Mick, he could have been hitting on any number of ladies.

Penny was still out there somewhere, flinging herself around the dance floor.

I tried to focus on my friends, managing to push the arrogant man out of my mind and assuming the caregiving role, which came naturally to me.

Dang, guess I'm the designated driver. Lucky for them I'm responsible.

Responsible enough to walk away from guys with loose ties and easy smiles, that's for sure.

"I didn't catch your name," I heard from somewhere behind me.

I looked over my shoulder. Him again.

I debated ignoring him, but innate courtesy won out. "It's Tammy."

His hazel eyes glittered, and in spite of my conflicted feelings, it was like the first time we locked eyes, all over again. My breath caught in my throat and my heart thundered.

"Jason," he countered. He didn't raise his voice at all, but it traveled over to me nonetheless, clear as a bell.

"Nice to meet you, Jason."

God, I'm losing my mind. Did I really say that, with a "come hither" huskiness in my voice?

The sooner I get out of here and back home to the city, the better.

CHAPTER 3

JASON

Her words washed over me with the effect of lit gasoline. My blood ignited and the heat rolled right through me, from head to toe.

I watched Tammy walk away with a strange feeling in the pit of my stomach. I had a strong desire to catch her before she disappeared into the crowd, which was unusual. Women chased me, not the other way around.

I was so lost in my thoughts that I didn't notice Reid approach until he spoke.

"Hey." Reid shoved his hands in his pockets and looked at me, tilting his head. "It's almost time for the race up by the creek. You still coming, or what?"

I gave him a tight smile. "Wouldn't miss it, man."

He grinned back, a relieved look on his face, before strolling off, whistling to himself.

Reid and I had exchanged a few brief yet civil conversations over the last few days. Our awkwardness had a lot to do with Jaime's absence. As the pack's new Beta, Reid wanted to bring everyone into the fold, and make sure those previously closest to Jaime were happy.

And to keep an eye on us, of course.

Shifter packs were old-school when it came to allegiance. In our minds, one was either with us, or against us. There was no middle ground. No Switzerland.

Which put me in a bitch of a situation.

Many years ago, Reid and I had been like brothers. Back when everything had been simple. When we were kids, it didn't matter that Reid wasn't of our blood, that he might challenge one of us for control of the pack one day.

It was obvious—to those of us who would admit it to themselves, at least—that Reid was of strong blood. His size alone dictated he was at least born of a Beta wolf. More likely an Alpha.

But what kind of Alpha would give up his son? None of us knew.

Jaime was unstable; always had been. If he'd been allowed to lead, he would have walked the pack off the edge of a cliff if he thought it would further him in his quest for domination.

The way he ranted and raved about Reid was sickening. Allara, meanwhile, was nothing but an obstacle to him, to be used or destroyed as he saw fit. As Jaime's preferred second-in-command, I had found myself in a situation that was growing increasingly untenable, and yet I hadn't quite known how to extricate myself. The more Jaime seemed to lose it, the more I felt like I couldn't leave him, without somehow making the situation worse.

Allara had shown unexpected mercy toward Jaime, the day she let him go free. It was a mercy that he would not have shown her, had their roles been reversed.

We hadn't seen the last of him.

I also knew that, as Jaime's proposed Beta, I could easily have been left out in the cold along with him on the day he lost the challenge to become Alpha. I had been loyal to him for too long, and a wolf's loyalty was not easily broken. It would have been simpler in the eyes of everyone if I had been banished. Safer, too.

But Allara and Reid weren't like that. They would never banish one of their own, not without a good reason for doing so.

The only problem was, it was clear to everyone in the pack—and especially to me—that the two of them didn't trust me.

And what's a wolf without the trust of his Alpha?

I stared into the distance. The isolation sank into my bones as I watched the joy of the revelers shouting with laughter, celebrating the bonding of their Alpha with her mate. Without meaning to, Allara and Reid had doomed me to a purgatory I couldn't escape.

Even though it was a purgatory of my own making, through my own actions, it still hurt.

I was with my family, with the people I loved most in the world. And yet, I didn't belong. Not anymore.

I wanted to be part of the pack again. To be part of the future that the new Alpha was building, to gain back the trust of my former friend.

But this was my new fate. To exist on the fringe. Always on the outside, looking in.

I'd always been considered a bad boy as far as women were concerned. So, if I was gonna be cast as the pack lone wolf bad guy now, then so be it.

～

TAMMY

IT WAS early evening by the time I finally convinced Mick and Penny that it was time to head home.

"If we get lost in the dark, in those woods..." I trailed off, looking between the two of them imploringly. "There's no cell reception out here, no gas stations, nothing. We'll be stranded."

"So what? We'll stay here for the night!" Penny flung out her hands, staggering sideways, as Mick almost fell into the back seat of the vehicle.

They had obviously both imbibed rather generously. Very lucky for them that I hadn't indulged.

Penny had taken off her heels, and they dangled precariously from one manicured finger. "There's more than a few warm beds to hop into," she giggled, hiccupping. "If you catch my drift."

I struggled to shut out the hazel eyes that popped into my head at her words.

No! Forget about him, damn it.

Penny cackled when she caught sight of the look on my face. "You're blushing! Was it that guy you were talking to earlier? He was *delicious.* You got his number, right?"

"No point getting his number," I muttered. "No cell reception, remember?"

But she wasn't listening, already staring around at the crowd as if looking for one of the other sexy young men.

I turned away, willing my flaming cheeks to settle, and pretending to check on Mick. He was stretched out in the backseat of the sport utility vehicle. Every now and then he gave a light snore.

Well, at least that's one of them taken care of.

Penny's arm landed around my shoulders like a lead weight as she hung off me, listing a little to one side until I flung out my arm to steady us both.

"Hey, hey! *Tammy,* I said—"

"Nope," I cut Penny off, gently maneuvering her until she was safely situated in the front passenger seat. "I didn't get anyone's number."

Women like me don't ask for phone numbers from guys like him.

I realized with a jolt that there was no sign of my purse. I checked the vehicle footwells and the hatch, frantically retracing my steps in my head.

Damn it, I must have left it somewhere at the reception!

With a frustrated sigh, I turned and made my way back toward the social hall, picking up my pace when I heard the distant laughter of some of the villagers nearby. They sounded like they were on the move. If I could catch them, someone might have seen my purse lying around somewhere.

To my surprise, once I reached the lawn, the area was almost completely deserted. Only the whispering wind greeted me, stirring the leaves of the trees overhead.

Trying to ignore the sudden anxiety making my heart pound, I scouted around for my missing purse. My search came up empty.

Shit. Maybe I should just leave. It's going to get real dark soon.

Allara would mail it on to me, anyway. It contained nothing that I couldn't live without for a few days.

I was mulling over my options, staring into the tree line where the grass met the edge of the forest, when a strange light caught my attention.

One light became two, which then became four. I narrowed my eyes. There were about a half-dozen of them, all bobbing and weaving through the trees like fireflies.

What the hell?

Then I put two and two together. They were the lanterns from earlier. They had been unhooked from their poles and carried into the trees.

The party hadn't disappeared, after all. It was on the move, winding its way into the forest.

I glanced back the way I'd come. I should turn back. We had a long journey ahead of us. I shouldn't follow those lights. I shouldn't...

Penny and Mick are waiting for me. I have to drive them home. Come on, Tammy. It's time to leave. Walk away. Just turn around...

The hairs on the back of my neck stood up, and the flesh on my forearms rose with goosebumps.

Something was calling me, in that forest, and I had no idea what it was.

My feet carried me forward without my permission. I padded across the lawn, following the progress of the lights as they flickered like a beacon in amongst the dark foliage.

"I'm going to regret this." I spoke aloud, even though I was on my own. I couldn't seem to stop following.

What are they doing? Where are they going?

I kept a distance from the stragglers at the back of the group, using the sound of distant chatter and shouting from the party up ahead to guide me through the darkness.

I reasoned to myself that I was Allara's guest. This was her wedding celebration, wasn't it? It was her day, and we had been invited here, after all. I wanted to be there for her. She would not begrudge me my curiosity.

The trees were starting to thin, becoming smaller and more spaced out. I was nearing a small clearing. I kept a careful distance, wincing when a twig snapped under my heel and made a loud, cracking noise. Luckily, those nearest to me seemed to be too caught up in the excitement of whatever was happening to notice any noise I might have made.

A male voice floated over to me, carried in snatches by the wind,

"The rules... simple... three laps from... to the ravine... no shortcuts, okay?"

I crept closer, daring to peek through the leaves to get a proper look at what was going on.

Most of the adults from the party were gathered around the perimeter of the clearing, clustered together in small groups. There was a gap at one end, and someone was dragging a tree branch through the dirt, drawing a rough line.

There were about ten people gathered at the center of the circle. I spotted Reid and Allara among them, along with Jason and a few of the other guys from earlier in the day. They formed a sort of huddle before breaking apart, whooping, and playfully shoving each other as they made their way over to the marked line.

Looks like they're about to run some kind of race. But why are they doing it all the way out here?

From where I was standing, the foliage seemed too thick to run through. The branches would snag their clothing and shred it.

I spotted Jason drop his suit jacket on the ground, pull his tie off his neck, and roll up his shirt sleeves.

Okay, so maybe him *losing his clothes wouldn't be such a bad thing.*

They all crouched down, like they were taking their marks or something.

Then, the strangest thing happened. In the fading light, it looked as if everyone's eyes flashed, swirling with an odd, silvery light.

And then those in the center of the circle... changed. Morphed into something non-human, right in front of my eyes.

I inhaled deeply, frozen to the spot with the shock of what I was witnessing.

Some humans remained around the outskirts of the huddle, but everyone in the center of the circle was gone. *Allara* was gone, and Reid. In their place stood a pack of enormous wolves.

The smallest of them could have comfortably looked me right in the face, even on all four paws. It was easily my height. The largest among them dwarfed the nearby spectators, with paws larger than dinner plates.

Oh, my God. They're wolf shifters.

And, suddenly, everything began to make sense.

Allara's sudden disappearance. This small community, so isolated, all the way out here in the middle of the forest. The strange ritual that

I'd witnessed this afternoon, and the weird looks we got when we arrived here.

Jason's words rang through my head once again.

Maybe you don't know her as well as you thought.

Shit.

My fingers dug into the bark of a nearby tree, gripping it for dear life. I needed to grasp onto something real, and concrete, as everything I had ever believed about my work colleague and friend was turned on its head.

I let go of trying to make sense of my thoughts and focused on breathing, aiming to slow my pounding heart. The effort was futile.

Frantically, I tried to remember everything I'd learned about wolf shifters from movies and books.

They were much stronger than the average person. Faster, too. All their senses were heightened. They had sharp instincts, and knew how to use them.

They're also fiercely territorial, and they don't like outsiders coming onto their turf.

Right. That would explain the cold shoulder we'd received on arrival. Lucky we weren't shifters ourselves, or else it could've gotten ugly, and fast.

A howl pierced through the air and I jerked, startled out of my reverie.

Several more joined in, until the air was filled with the sound. It should have been terrifying, and it was. But it was also hauntingly beautiful, almost like music, and I shivered in excitement as well as fear, as I listened.

How many humans had ever heard such a thing?

I heard a couple of human-sounding yells, and I realized the race had begun. The wolves leapt into a run with impossible speed, racing into the tree line and melting into the forest like shadows.

My thrill of excitement mixed with a new unease.

I shouldn't be here. This wasn't for human eyes.

I was about to turn away and try to fumble my way back through the trees, toward the relative safety of the village, when I froze. A new realization dawned on me.

A pack of superhuman wolves was roaming somewhere in these woods, and I was, quite possibly, their ideal prey.

Allara wouldn't eat me. I was certain of that. But I didn't know the others well enough to be sure. Would they all be as good and kind as my friend? Would... *Jason* retain his humanity, when he was roaming the forest in his wolf form?

I was about to blunder off blindly, in the dark. Straight into their path.

On one side of me, the clearing was filled with pack members in human form, talking and laughing amongst themselves. If I moved that way, they would soon discover me.

On the other side was the forest, were the wolves. If I started back the way I came, my shitty human senses would be no match for a stray wolf shifter.

They're at a wedding, Tammy! They're just having fun.

Still... what kind of fun did wolf shifters get up to, other than racing each other? Maybe the party earlier had just been the appetizer.

I swallowed.

Maybe I'm about to become dessert.

CHAPTER 4

TAMMY

A leaf rustled nearby and I closed my eyes, my heart hammering a mile a minute.

Allara wouldn't let them harm me. She'd always looked out for me. Every time a creep harassed us at the bar, she'd kicked them to the curb.

Allara can't protect you forever, said a voice inside my head. *You're all alone. You'll always be alone.*

Stop being such a baby, and learn to stand up for yourself.

I gritted my teeth, forcing myself to focus.

There was only one course of action. I had to walk into the clearing and show myself to the pack members who had remained behind in human form. Hopefully, they would take pity on me and take me back to the village.

I thought longingly of the SUV, where I had left Penny and Mick waiting, and cursed myself for my recklessness.

Serves you right, wandering into the forest so impulsively.

Okay, so, I had a plan. But unfortunately, my feet weren't getting the memo that it was time to move. They remained stubbornly rooted to the spot. Frustration and fear welled up in me once more, and I trembled. Just do it. Take a step forward and let them know you're here.

Thud.

The noise came from somewhere behind me. It was a heavy sound, like a weight being dropped onto the ground. Or...

Or the sound a gigantic paw might make when it landed on the floor of the forest. The sound of a predator advancing on its prey, slowly and deliberately, so that the prey didn't startle or run away.

My heart clenched and I almost whimpered out loud. Very, very slowly, I turned my head.

Out of the corner of my eye, I saw the wolf.

It was one of the bigger ones. Its shaggy fur was black, with a few patches of gray here and there. Its eyes were slivers of silver, and its gums were peeled back, teeth fully exposed in a silent snarl.

It must have caught my scent while racing the others.

But clearly, I was a more entertaining prospect.

My heart hammered in my chest, thudding with the speed of a high-performance engine, zinging adrenaline along my veins.

There was no point in running or shouting for help. I could tell from the look in its eye that this would all be over before anyone could reach me. Knowing my luck, I would only end up attracting more unwanted attention, anyway.

The massive wolf hunched down and backed up a few paces as it prepared to spring.

I closed my eyes and waited for the end.

Please God, let it be over fast.

But the death blow never came. Instead, I heard a growl, then a high whine and a loud thud, like the sound of a body hitting the side of a tree trunk.

Still paralyzed with fear, I inched one eye open to get a look at my surroundings.

My attacker was lying on his side, unmoving, next to a nearby tree.

What on earth...

Panting heavily, a second wolf stood where the downed creature had been a moment before. This one was also large, with dark fur.

I had escaped unscathed. For now.

Maybe this second wolf just didn't like to share his food.

Out of the frying pan and into the fire.

But my rescuer was... different from the other one.

His posture was upright, not crouched low. He didn't seem to be stalking me like the other one had, even though he was growling at me. A low, rumbling growl that I felt all the way through my chest, right down to my toes.

There was a sharp contrast between this growl and the one from the other wolf.

The first wolf had been ready to kill. I had read death in its eyes, and it had let out a snarl that was all vicious, blood-curdling aggression.

This one almost sounded like... a warning.

Like the wolf was pissed off at me, but didn't want to hurt me. In my head, I heard a human voice, more panicked than anything.

What the hell are you doing all the way out here by yourself? You're not safe!

I grimaced. Yep, I was *definitely* losing my mind. Hearing voices in my head, that weren't actually my own.

The newcomer loped his way closer to me. I inhaled sharply. Fear prickled every one of my senses and I couldn't move a muscle. It was probably my imagination, but as I stared into his eyes, unable to look away... I swear I recognized him.

Jason?

And even stranger, I saw a flicker of recognition in return.

I moved backwards, flattening myself against the tree trunk as the wolf loomed over me. He had me pinned. He was so close I could feel the heat coming off his fur. It was a stark contrast to the chilly night air, and I shivered, fighting a sudden urge to lean in and rest my body against his warmth.

My reaction was as frightening to me as anything else in this moment.

And then, everything stopped.

The cold of the wind and roughness of the tree bark pressing into my back disappeared. The trees no longer rustled and the dull whining of the other wolf lying somewhere nearby faded into nothing.

The only thing I registered was the press of a very human body against mine. His eyes still glowed silver, before they faded a few seconds later into a familiar hazel color.

Jason was human once again, and his gaze was wide with astonishment.

I fell into those entrancing eyes headfirst and felt like I could never climb back out. He stared at me, conveying the same amazement that I felt as my body flooded with something I'd never felt before.

"Huh," Jason breathed. "Hey."

His face was so close to mine, our mouths were a few scant inches apart, and his bare torso pushed me insistently against the tree like he wasn't even aware of his own movements. His arms bracketed my head on either side, solid and strong. My gaze flickered to them, watching the tendons shift beneath his skin.

I swallowed hard. "Were you going to kill me?" I whispered.

"What?" He sounded dazed.

I felt like I had just been hit over the head with a sledgehammer. He sounded like he did, too.

What was happening between us?

"Your buddy almost tore out my throat," I managed. "Weren't you tempted?"

It was difficult to concentrate when we were so close, his body still pressed up against the full length of mine. To an outside observer, I wasn't sure if it looked like he was shielding me, or making love to me. His proximity was making my pulse race, nonetheless.

"No." Shock flashed across his features. "*No*, of course not. I—"

"Jason!"

Allara's voice from nearby was sharp, startling us both. He finally dropped his arms, allowing me to slide free of my confined position. Funny, there was a part of me that didn't want to step away from the warmth of his embrace. That thought sent heat racing to my cheeks, and I ducked my head, trying to regain some kind of equilibrium.

As he stepped backwards, I realized that he was completely naked. *Well, then.*

My face heated even further and I averted my eyes from his body. I doubted it was humanly possible for my blush to intensify at this point.

"There you are." Allara burst through the undergrowth, breathing heavily and loosely buttoning up her shirt. Reid appeared just behind her, looking worried. "Oh my God, *Tammy*!" My name came out almost as a screech. She was obviously shocked to see me. "What are you doing here? I thought you'd left ages ago!"

"I..." Everyone turned to look at me, and the words dried up in my throat. I swallowed and tried again. "I lost my purse, and I saw... everyone heading out this way. I just automatically followed. I didn't know... I'm so sorry."

I wrapped my arms around my middle, trying to contain my nerves.

Allara's lovely features softened as she took me in. She put a hand on my arm and sighed deeply.

God, I must look like a complete mess right now.

"This is all my fault," she said, to my surprise. "I should've told you the truth about us. I thought it would be easier for everyone if I didn't. And now, I've put you in harm's way. *I'm* the one who should be sorry, Tammy."

"Are you hurt?" Reid murmured, stepping forward to stand by Allara's side.

"No," Jason said, before I could answer. "Paul just got a little carried away, that's all."

We all looked at Jason. He was sitting at the base of the tree he'd held me up against only moments before. The dazed look was still clouding his expression, and he couldn't quite meet anyone's eye.

"What happened?" Allara demanded, her voice authoritative. Reid slid an arm around her waist and she relaxed visibly, but her tone was clear, and the steel in her eyes didn't fade one bit.

So, she's in charge?

Hmm. Interesting.

"We'd just taken the corner next to... to the waterfall," Jason said, haltingly. "We were up ahead from some of the others, out on our own. I was on Paul's heels, hassling him a little, y'know? Trying to figure out a way to get ahead."

Allara nodded and Jason sighed, rubbing a hand over his face before continuing.

"Then I saw Paul turn, just a little. He lifted his head, scented the breeze, and immediately changed course." Jason swallowed. "Then I smelled... *her*."

He inclined his head at me, still refusing to meet my eyes. I forced myself not to shudder.

I wonder what I smell like to them. To him.

Attractive? In a sexual way? Or... like dinner?

"Paul took off, full tilt, through the forest," Jason said. "Like the devil was on his tail. You know how it gets sometimes. The mist descends... he was just acting on his instincts. But I knew she... I knew she wouldn't be safe, if he got to her. So, I took off after him."

A few feet away, someone moaned faintly.

Paul.

"Sure enough, he was about to spring," Jason said. For a split second, there was nothing but pure fury in his eyes. I was glad it didn't seem to be directed at me. "So, I jumped in the way before he had the chance to pin her. The end."

Allara was silent for a few moments, processing the information. She exchanged an unreadable glance with Reid, before turning to me.

"Tammy?" Her voice was gentle. "Did anything else happen?"

Yes. But I couldn't tell you what it was, that passed between me and Jason. Not for love nor money.

"No," I muttered. "That's... that's everything."

"I can give you guys a ride home," Reid said. "You've had quite a shock and you probably shouldn't be driving."

"Oh no, you don't need to do that—"

"They should stay," Jason cut in. I turned to him, surprised to find that he was staring straight at me. "Just for one night."

I'd fallen into his eyes again. Damn it. Nobody who spent enough time amongst these people could mistake them for normal humans. Jason's eyes smoldered even in the darkness. They gave off their own, almost hypnotically powerful, light.

"Of course," I heard myself say. "I couldn't possibly trouble you, Reid. It's your—"

I was about to say *wedding night,* but that wasn't quite right.

God, I didn't know what *was* right. I didn't have the first clue

"—the night of your bonding ceremony." I finished lamely. "It's a once in a lifetime thing, right? We'll be fine here until the morning. The others are probably asleep by now, anyway."

With any luck, Penny and Mick would remain passed out in the SUV until tomorrow.

"You're welcome to stay," Allara smiled. "It's the least we can do."

She linked her arm through mine as we set off back through the trees. The distant lights of the village soon began to twinkle through the undergrowth, and the knot in my chest eased at the prospect of a warm bed.

It had been one of the longest, most confusing days of my life, and I wanted nothing more than to put my head on a pillow and forget about it for a few, blissful hours.

"Thank you," I said to Allara, glancing behind me. I expected to see Reid or Jason following in our footsteps, but there was nothing but dark foliage.

"Don't be silly." Allara gave me a strange smile. "I'm happy to have you around a little longer." Her words were friendly, but she gazed off into the distance, as if she was lost in thought. "Besides... I'm not the only one."

My stomach flip-flopped as I considered the implication of her words. I knew who she meant, and I didn't know how to reply.

I wanted to tell her the truth about what had happened out in the woods. I knew I could trust her.

But what *was* the truth? I honestly didn't know. However, one thing was certain.

Tomorrow morning, I had to find Jason. We needed to talk.

CHAPTER 5

JASON

Allara walked off with Tammy, leaving Reid and me to pick up the half-conscious Paul and drag him back through the forest.

I was grateful to have something physical to do, to occupy my mind for at least a few minutes.

I was still gobsmacked over what had happened with Tammy—a *human* woman—and my brain needed time to process it.

In an unusually thoughtful gesture, Reid had tossed me some jeans and I was grateful for the cover as we made our way through the undergrowth on the way to the village. Wolf shifters didn't feel the cold like regular humans, sure, but it was nice to have *some* semblance of modesty when I was feeling so... unsteady.

I made sure not to manhandle Paul any more than necessary. The guy was still groaning from the hit he'd taken. And while I knew that he'd be fine by morning, I still felt bad. A bit. After all, I'd taken him down for a good reason. To protect...

Her.

He'd been about to attack Tammy, kill her most likely. If I hadn't been there, he would've finished her off in seconds.

I hadn't meant to slam him against the tree quite that hard, though. The poor guy actually bounced, before hitting the ground and staying there.

Reid was silent for the first few paces, which suited me fine. He was clearly deep in his own thoughts. After all, the night had taken an unexpected turn for everyone.

The adrenaline of my wolf form hadn't fully left me, and every leaf rustling and twig snapping underfoot increased my tension and agitation.

It was crazy. Tammy had left with Allara only moments earlier, but every inch of me wanted to abandon Paul and Reid and tear through the woods after her. I craved her with a ferocity that would be unsettling if I could think about it logically.

But that was impossible. I was on fire, and I couldn't do anything but burn.

"You know she'll probably head back to the city tomorrow."

It took me a minute to register that Reid had broken the silence. His voice was low and cautious, like he was talking to a wild animal or something.

In a way, he is.

"What?" I hefted Paul's arm, so that it was wrapped more securely around my shoulders. He was staggering like a drunkard, forcing me to steady him. It gave me a handy excuse to focus my attention on him instead of Reid.

"The human girl," Reid said.

"Her name's Tammy."

"Yes. I know that, Jason. I'm the one who invited them here." I could hear the almost-eye-roll in his tone. "I'm guessing they'll head back at first light. No reason for them to hang around here all day, after all."

I grunted. "What makes you say that?"

Reid shrugged his free shoulder. "Nothing."

We were silent for a few minutes. The trees were beginning to thin out, and I knew we were reaching the edge of the woods.

"Reid," the name tore out of me as I stood at the edge of the village and looked up at the dark shapes of the houses silhouetted against the starlit sky. "Just... just a minute."

Reid gave a nod and we stopped moving. Paul was pretty much a dead weight at this point, a dark shape hanging between us. Reid looked at me, unblinking, his expression imperceptible.

"When I threw Paul off the girl, I... I went to check on her." I swallowed, hearing my voice shake and I clenched my fists tight. "When we touched..."

"She's the one, isn't she?" Reid murmured. He wasn't looking at me anymore. His gaze was blank, staring in the direction of the treetops. I mirrored him. A large, pale moon hung in the sky, washing the grassy field with pale light. "Tammy. She's your Fated Mate."

My mouth dropped open at how perceptive he was. "How is it even possible?" My voice was hard as flint. I evaded answering his question directly, but I couldn't deny the truth of his words.

She's who I've been waiting for. All this time...

"She's a human," I said, more to myself than to Reid. "How can we be *destined* for each other?"

"It's not unheard of." Reid glanced at me, deep in thought. "All humans have shifter blood in them, you know that. For most of them, it stays dormant all their lives. Unless..."

Unless they are destined to mate with a shifter.

I couldn't argue with the genetic side of things. Tammy wasn't a shifter, and she never would be. But our children...

Our children will be like me.

Jesus, children. I'd only just met the woman, and suddenly I was picturing her having my pups? It was all happening so fast.

How was I so far removed from the person I was when I woke up this morning?

Reid seemed to catch onto my state of mind, because his expression grew consolatory. "I'll talk to Allara. I'm sure she'll convince Tammy to stay for a few days. This whole world—who and what we are, and how the Fated Mates thing works—is all new to her. She'll need some time to come around to the idea."

So will I.

Whenever I pictured bonding with someone, in the idle moments I'd entertained the prospect of settling down, the woman in my mind's eye had been... like me.

A wolf shifter. Strong, fast, confident. A little too sexy, maybe.

Someone who would fit in with the pack, who knew the way things worked with our kind. Someone I could share everything with. No secrets.

Someone who understood my world completely, because it was her world, too.

I turned to Reid, frowning. "How did you know?" I asked. "What you said, about Tammy." I paused for a moment, even her name on my lips sending a shiver down my spine. "It's like you knew what had happened in the forest before I said anything."

Reid's mouth twisted into a wry smile. "It was pretty obvious."

"Really?"

"Really," Reid echoed. "It was written all over you both. I've never seen you look like that before, man."

Ouch. If Reid knew, that meant *Allara* knew.

Which meant that I had lied to my Alpha's face.

As if reading my thoughts, Reid gave a loud bark of laughter. "Don't worry about it. You've just found your mate, Jason. Give yourself a break! Why do you think Allara wanted them to stay the night?"

I'll admit, I had entirely missed the subtext on that one. I'd been so wrapped up in my own shock over what happened, I hadn't realized how damn *obvious* I was.

Then something Reid had said penetrated, and my muscles relaxed a notch. *It was written all over you both.*

"So, you think she felt it, too? As strongly as me?"

Reid raised a brow. "That's how it works, with Fated Mates. I'm sure she did."

I parted ways with Reid with a murmur of thanks and headed home, taking a half-awake Paul the last few meters on my own. After depositing him on the sofa, I headed upstairs.

On the landing, I lingered for a moment outside the closed door of Kara's bedroom.

Call it a twin thing. Whatever it was, I was struck by a sudden urge to tell my sister everything that had happened tonight, and get her take on it all.

She hadn't come out to the forest to race. She'd been too tired, so she'd missed seeing the whole thing with Tammy.

She would probably give me a shove and tell me to get over myself. She'd say that some people waited their whole lives to meet their Fated Mate, and that many never got the chance.

You should count yourself lucky, idiot.

I couldn't decide whether that was the advice I wanted to hear right now.

So, in the end, I headed off to my own room, falling face-first onto my bed with a groan.

When sleep eventually found me, my dreams were riddled with the sound of running feet hitting the forest floor and feral snarls.

~

DESPITE THE LATE NIGHT, I woke before dawn, and lay staring up at the ceiling for a long while.

I knew that I had to see Tammy today and speak with her properly.

It was inevitable. And necessary.

Half of me – the wolf half – ached to be with her again. My human side told me that things were never straightforward, even in more favorable circumstances.

Regardless, whatever the day held for me, I would learn where my fate lay. Somewhere out there, just beyond my front door. Close enough to touch. Close enough to taste all its heady promise.

And, sooner or later, I would have to go and meet it.

~

TAMMY

When I woke, I lay for a moment in the comfort of the warm bed I found myself in. I ran a hand over the soft quilt and basked in the morning sun that streamed in through the window.

The room Allara had found for me last night was in a house belonging to a woman called Rachel. It was simple but cozy, and much of the furniture looked handmade. A bunch of herbs were arranged in a jar on the bureau, and their scent filled the space with a soothing aroma.

I was so relaxed that it took a moment for my brain to catch up, and for yesterday and last night's events to come flooding back.

Jason found me in the forest. He rescued me. Why?

Maybe he didn't want his friend to have blood on his hands?

But one thing was certain. Something had happened between us when he held me against that tree.

The connection wasn't like anything I'd felt before, and the more I thought about it, the stranger the whole thing became.

The way he'd stared at me... Like, I was the only thing in the world he wanted to see.

I'd never been looked at that way before. It was the same way Reid had stared at Allara during their bonding ceremony.

Even now, as I sat in Rachel's small kitchen nursing a cup of coffee between my palms, I could run through every detail of the previous night in my mind with perfect clarity. The feel of Jason's skin pressed against mine, his hot breath on my face. The way his eyes had burned into mine so powerfully, even in the dim light of the forest. The warmth of his body, enticing me impossibly closer.

I felt an ache in my lower belly and between my legs, that I hadn't felt in a long while. But the connection was more than that; more than lust. I just didn't know *what* it was.

It was still too early to head back to the vehicle, but I couldn't sit still any longer. I wanted to be out in the fresh air again and enjoy the beauty of my surroundings while I had the chance.

I didn't know why, but something about this strange forest community cleared the cobwebs from all the dark corners of my brain and left me feeling lighter than I had felt in months.

I slipped out of the front door and shut it behind me as quietly as possible, so I didn't disturb my kind hostess. Outside, the grass underfoot was damp with dew, and drops of moisture clung to my shoes as I made my way outside.

There was a chill in the air this morning, and I wrapped my jacket tightly around my shoulders, taking in a few invigorating breaths of air.

It was so quiet here, so different from the bustle and noise of the city.

There wasn't another soul to be seen, which suited me just fine. I had always been content with my own company, and I wanted more time to process everything before I was faced with the entire...

Pack.

The word was so alien to me.

Allara had a pack. More than that, she seemed to call the shots. Last night, it had been clear that Reid and Jason deferred to her judgment. She had the final say over whether or not the three of us from the city stayed the night.

I glanced around at my surroundings, surprised to find that my feet had taken me back to the social hall. All closed up in the light of morning, it looked sleepier than it had yesterday.

My gaze snapped to the steps that led up to the wide entranceway.

"What's your name?" The voice belonged to a little girl of around seven, sitting neatly cross-legged on the top step, gazing at me with undisguised fascination. I thought I recognized her from the day before. She had been among the crowd of kids who'd waved at us so excitedly when we first arrived.

I wondered about shifter children. Did they shift into wolves, like the adults, or was that something that only happened at adolescence, or in adulthood? There was so much about Allara's life—about *Jason's* life —that I didn't know.

"I'm Tammy," I answered the girl, taking a seat on the bottom step and folding my hands in my lap. "What's your name?"

The girl blinked at me and twisted a long braid in her hair around her finger. "Lyra."

"That's pretty."

"Where are you from?" Lyra asked. "I haven't seen you before."

"I'm Allara's friend," I explained. "I used to work with her, when she lived in the city."

"The city," whispered Lyra, as if to herself. I smiled at the look of wonder in her eyes. "I've never been to the city before. Did Allara have her own pack there? Were you in it?"

I laughed as I caught onto her assumption. "Oh, no! We weren't in a pack." I paused before continuing. "I'm not like you, Lyra. I'm not a wolf shifter."

Lyra's eyes rounded. "Wow," she whispered. "That's what Sage said, but I didn't believe her!"

"Sage?" I tilted my head to the side, curious.

"My sister." Lyra bit her lip, frowning. "I've never met a regular human before. What's it like?"

I chuckled again, unable to stop myself. It had been a while since I'd been around kids of Lyra's age, and I'd forgotten how much I liked their forthrightness and honesty.

It's refreshing. Everyone else around here seems to speak in riddles.

"Being a human? Probably not as interesting as it is to be a shifter," I confessed, and watched her eyes light up with interest. "What's *that* like?"

"It's the best!" Lyra grinned widely, revealing two missing front teeth. "Well, I *guess.*" She pouted a little bit. "I can't run fast yet or climb the tallest tree. Mom says it's because I'm too little."

"Well, I'm sure you could still beat me," I said, and watched her brighten at the idea.

I fervently hoped that she wouldn't take me up on it.

Getting into a foot race with a kid that would probably run rings around me? Not exactly number one on my agenda this morning.

Luckily, Lyra seemed to be more interested in quizzing me about life in the city than challenging me to a race.

Over the next half hour, I told her about my life. About the fancy drinks with the little umbrellas I made for bar patrons, the deep dish pizza from my favorite pizza place around the corner from my apartment, my upstairs neighbor's three noisy dogs that barked in the middle of the night for no reason.

I talked about the noise, and the traffic, and the hustle and bustle and general busy-ness of life in the city.

She listened to it all with astonishment, drinking in my words like she was committing them to memory.

"I much prefer the peace and quiet out here, though," I admitted, and she laughed.

"I don't," Lyra said. "I bet I would love noise and bustle best!"

I grinned at her, wondering if she would change her mind as she grew older.

For me, life here in the forest felt like an idyllic escape from all the chaos and misery I had left behind. But I could see that, for a kid like Lyra, the world beyond the forest probably seemed like an exotic fairytale.

I left out all the distinctly un-fairytale parts. She didn't need to know about them.

Let the kid believe that the world is good and kind, while she still can. I won't be the one to take that fantasy away from her.

I was halfway through explaining the concept of a karaoke bar when a shadow fell across the step I was sitting on, blocking the light from the early morning sun.

"Making friends?"

That voice had grown so distinct, so familiar to me in such a short span of time. It startled me, and I couldn't help but look up with trepidation. Had I imagined that moment last night? Was it all in my head?

"Lyra was just giving me a rundown of how things work around here," I said, shielding my face so that I could better make out Jason's form, backlit by the sun. My heart flipped. "She's been very—"

I turned back, but the little girl was nowhere to be seen. The spot where she'd been sitting only moments before was empty.

"Helpful," I finished, feeling confused.

"It isn't you." Jason extended his hand and I took it by instinct, letting him help me to my feet. The chaste touch shouldn't have affected me the way it did, but I couldn't help focusing on the warmth of his hand and the way it made my insides curl with pleasure.

This was the second time we had touched.

The real question here is... why am I keeping count?

I blinked and realized I was still holding onto him. I dropped his hand quickly and took a step back, my cheeks burning.

He's waiting for you to reply. What did he say, again? My sluggish brain finally clicked into gear.

"What isn't me?" I asked, blinking stupidly, and he chuckled.

Great, now he'll think I'm an idiot.

"She didn't leave because of you." Jason shoved his hands deep into his pockets and rocked back and forth on his heels. Despite his nonchalant posture, I could tell that he was holding something back. Something that made him uncomfortable, and faintly sad.

I couldn't say how I knew that, but it was as if I were tuned in to his emotions, almost as clearly as my own.

Then he added, "It's me, not you. If that's what you were wondering. I'm not exactly Mr. Popular around here these days."

"Why is that?" I asked softly.

He fixed me with an inscrutable look and ducked his head. We had to be around the same age, but there was a boyishness about him that was equal parts frustrating and deeply attractive.

He didn't answer my question, instead changing the topic swiftly. It didn't fool me, but I let it ride, for now.

"Were you satisfied?" Jason asked.

I released a shaky breath, my mind flashing to the night before.

His body had been so close against mine, the heat of him bleeding through my clothes. His arms encircling me, holding me steady. If the others hadn't arrived, I don't know what would've happened. The possibilities had seemed endless, and I had been unusually open to exploring them.

Satisfied? Nowhere near.

He gave me a crooked smile, his eyes glittering like he could read my thoughts.

Oh God, I hope mind-reading is not one of their super powers!

He cleared his throat. "I only meant... did Lyra answer all your questions about life here in the village?"

"Oh." Was I ever going to stop blushing around this guy? "Well... no. I still have tons of questions," I confessed. "But we got kind of side-tracked talking about human stuff instead."

"Oh?"

"I guess those tiny cocktail umbrellas sound *really* exciting when you're seven years old." I scrunched up my face, and he laughed. "I do genuinely have more questions we didn't get around to, though. I mean, last night was a bit of a shock, all round, actually."

There. I'd said it. Kind of. At least I'd put the ball in his court in relation to whatever it was that had happened between us.

I stared challengingly at him, and he stared back. After a moment, he leaned in and offered me his elbow. The gesture was so unexpected and slightly old-fashioned I wanted to laugh, but instead, I bit my cheeks to hold in my amusement, and took his arm. The supple leather of his jacket was warm against my fingertips. Now he was wearing what I assumed were his usual clothes, he looked much more comfortable than he had in the more formal wear from yesterday.

"Come with me," he murmured.

"Where are we going?" I asked, picking up on his light, mischievous tone. It felt like we were playing hooky from school or something.

He smiled. "It's a surprise."

"I've had a few of those already in the last twenty-four hours," I muttered.

Unexpectedly, he laughed. "This is a good surprise. I promise. Trust me?"

Surprisingly, I did. My heart was a little lighter as he led me out of the village.

CHAPTER 6
TAMMY

"Okay, you can open your eyes now." Jason's voice was soft and lingering, so close that his lips barely missed brushing the shell of my ear.

I shivered at the sudden proximity and did as he said.

"Oh," I said, my mouth dropping open.

We were standing beside a small stream, on a bank carpeted with moss and long, trailing ferns. Toward the water's edge there were a few rocks scattered in amongst the foliage, creating the kind of natural spot I had only ever seen in movies before now. The sunlight dappled the water and the breeze ruffled my hair off my shoulders.

"It's so very beautiful," I said, sighing at the tranquil vision before me.

When I turned, Jason was watching me rather than the picturesque setting.

I looked away from his intense gaze, feeling suddenly self-conscious. "What?"

"Nothing," he said, but out of the corner of my eye I saw a wide smile break free.

We sat beside the water in silence, and I listened instead to the trickle of water, warbling birdsong, and the rustle of leaves above us. So different to the noises of the city, and so much more in tune with what my soul craved, deep down inside.

I just hadn't known that, until now.

I'd never been in a place as calming as this.

It was surprisingly comfortable being here with Jason, too, in spite of how little I knew him. It felt as if we'd known each other for many years, and we'd just returned to a favorite place only the two of us knew about.

I hadn't felt that close to anyone before.

Not even with...

No. We're not thinking about him. *Not today. Not ever.*

"No one else from the pack knows about this place," said Jason. His voice was low, confessional, like he was letting me in on a secret. Which, I suppose, he was.

"No one?"

He shook his head. "I haven't shown it to anyone else. It's a good thinking spot." He fixed me with one of his intent looks, his gaze piercing.

I felt honored that, for some reason, he'd decided to share his secret place with me. I wasn't quite sure why. It wasn't like gorgeous men were forever taking me to their secret hideouts, after all.

I suppressed a self-deprecating laugh. *So many gorgeous guys. I can hardly keep track of them all.*

"I won't tell. Promise." I smiled. "Thank you for sharing it with me."

He looked at me wonderingly for a long moment, until I was forced to drop my gaze. I fiddled a little with the sleeve of my jacket, at a loss for what to say.

"You do that a lot, huh?" he said.

"Do what?" I asked.

He replied slowly, carefully. I could hear a hint of curiosity in his tone. "Look away from me. Do I make you nervous?"

Very!

My heartbeat was strong but steady. I took a long, shuddering breath. I felt safe here, with Jason. "A little."

He chuckled. The timbre was loose and easy, strikingly melodic to my ears. "Don't be nervous. I won't bite."

Ha! Said the wolf to Little Red Riding Hood.

"Questions," I blurted out, my cheeks burning. I had to get the conversation back on track before this got out of hand. "I... I still have questions."

"Fire away." Resting a hand against the ground, he leaned back, tilting his head up to stare at the sky.

"Allara," I said. "I've noticed she seems to have the final say over things here. She called the shots last night. What's up with that?"

He shrugged. "Allara's our Alpha."

The way he said it was blunt. An open and shut case. *She's the Alpha.* Like there was nothing more to it.

I thought about that. "That means she's like... the leader around here, right?"

"It's more complicated than that," Jason said. "She looks out for us. She's responsible for the big pack decisions, though she takes counsel from others."

I heard the implication in his voice. "But?"

"*But.*" He threw me a crooked grin. "It runs more deeply than that. When a wolf shifter becomes the Alpha of a pack, the members of that pack are... beholden to the Alpha. You humans have your leaders, sure, but those bonds can be broken pretty easily, right?"

"Are you saying you *have* to do what Allara says?" I couldn't even imagine having that sort of power over someone else.

"In a way. My biology *wants* me to." Jason's mouth twisted. He looked like he was choosing his words carefully. "I could go against her wishes, but it would be overriding all my instincts to do so."

"Wow." I whistled. "That's crazy."

"Not if you're like us," he said, amused at my tone. "It's totally normal for wolf shifters. She has final say, but she's not a dictator. Reid's her Beta. He helps with decision-making, and tries to keep the rest of us in line. That sort of thing."

"That's kind of a crazy set-up for a marriage," I pointed out. "Running a pack together... I could see that getting in the way of a relationship."

He threw me an odd look. "Reid and Allara are Fated Mates, Tammy. They're meant to be together. It's literally in their blood. They're a... a perfect match, I guess you could call it. Brought together by Fate."

There was an odd undercurrent in his words, a tension that I couldn't read. I filed away that detail for now, deciding to examine it later. I had more pressing questions.

I was silent for a moment. "How do they know they're fated to be together?"

Now it was his turn to look abashed. He rubbed a hand over his mouth and turned his gaze toward the water, though I suspected he wasn't really looking at the stream.

"You just... know." His voice was low, so quiet I had to lean forward in order to hear him properly. "It's like... hearing your own name for the first time, coming out of the mouth of a stranger, and it just sounds so right on their tongue. Or solving a puzzle you didn't realize was a puzzle. One that you've been trying to solve your whole life, and then, suddenly everything falls into place and the answers are right in front of you."

"That sounds pretty good," I said faintly.

"It happens differently for each person," Jason continued. "For Reid and Allara, they've known each other forever. Since we were all kids. They just *fit*, you know? They were apart for a few years, sure, but they weren't *whole* until they found their way back to each other in the end."

I thought about the look on Allara's face the night Reid had turned up in the bar. She must have been so lonely, without her mate, for all those years.

"Yes," I said. "I can see that."

"Sometimes it's like a first-sight thing." Jason picked up a pebble and turned it over and over between finger and thumb. His hands were like the rest of him, tan and angular, with smooth, rounded fingernails. "*That* one's a shock to the system, or so I've heard." He caught my eye. "Sometimes, you know your partner by their scent. And sometimes—" He ran a hand through his hair, pushing it back off his forehead. "Sometimes you know you've found your Fated Mate the first time you touch."

My skin tingled at the memory of his hands on my body.

Don't be ridiculous, Tammy. You're not a wolf shifter! And you're not special enough to be anyone's Fated Mate.

What I felt yesterday was nothing more than late night excitement fueled by a near-death experience. It had to have been simply that, and nothing more.

"Feels like... like electricity, I guess." Jason gave a shaky laugh. "Tammy, come on. I don't need to explain to you. I think we both know what it feels like."

Ahh... what?

A flood of emotions crashed through me as he stared at me. He was acting as if I should know what he was talking about. But he couldn't be serious. I was no one's Fated Mate. It didn't make sense. What on earth was he thinking?

I don't know what Jason had been expecting from his freaking *soul mate*, but I couldn't be it.

"You can't mean..."

Jason grinned at me, as if happy I'd finally caught on. "That we're Fated Mates? Yep. Didn't you feel it?"

I blinked at him. "Well, I felt something. But... how is that even possible?" I rubbed at the spot between my eyes, where I could feel a stress headache developing. "I'm not like you, Jason. I'm not a shifter, I'm just..."

Me. Fat... average... human... me.

"It happens." Jason's brow creased as he looked me over. Strangely, his eyes were reflecting the same uncertainty. "It's rare, but it happens. I'm sorry, Tammy. This—" He gestured around us, to the forest, the trees. "—I know this isn't your world. You didn't ask for any of it. And I've gone and trapped you here with me."

I could have laughed in his face, but I bit my lip instead. It was crazy that a guy like him could feel bad on *my* behalf.

He's acting like he's Hades, leading me astray down into the Underworld.

Except he'd gotten it backwards. The story was all wrong.

"You could be wrong, you know," I said. "Maybe this is just some sort of... glitch?"

Because if what he was inferring was true, everyone would believe I was the one to trap him. This gorgeous, sexy, funny guy belonged to a world of danger and adventure.

Of sexy women and perfect bodies. I was nowhere near good

enough for him, and I'd spend the rest of my life knowing he'd settled for me when he could have had so much more.

Someone better. Someone more exciting, more sexy... more everything.

And if he didn't already know that, well... I knew it was only a matter of time before he would come to the same realization.

But I couldn't seem to get up and leave. For better or worse, I wanted to stay close to Jason, for as long as I would be allowed.

CHAPTER 7
JASON

I sat on the rocks and watched her out of the corner of my eye. Her hair was truly gorgeous. As the sun rose, it blazed with color, curling over her chest and framing her ample cleavage.

My pulse raced at the sheer sight of her abundant curves and beautiful face. I wanted her badly, but I had to hold off for now. She was clearly disoriented from recent revelations and was probably struggling to adjust to all the new information I'd given her.

It wasn't typical for a human to end up in this situation. The last thing I wanted was to hurt her or make her feel uncomfortable.

It had been so long since I'd spoken with someone who wasn't a shifter.

One thing that kept confusing me was the way she shied away after every compliment I paid her, every glance between us that lingered a little too long.

At first, I thought it was her nerves showing, or some sense of modesty at the acknowledgment of our mutual attraction.

But I was beginning to think that she was simply *unused* to any attention.

I struggled to believe how anyone could fail to notice how gorgeous she was. She was not rail-thin and athletic, but that made her more unique. And far more attractive, in my eyes.

I had been struck like an arrow through the heart the very first time we locked eyes. I could tell that her reserved nature pushed her into the background, but she was the kind of soul who you glanced at once and then couldn't look away from.

She was lovely and, above all, I could tell that she was kind.

There were so many questions she wanted to ask. Every time I looked at her, I could see them shimmering behind her eyes.

Questions about Allara and Reid. Questions about why Lyra was so reluctant to remain in my presence.

Questions about the bond between us. How it worked, what it meant, and why it had happened.

She had every right to know the answers to all of those questions, and more. But she wasn't forcing them out of me, by any means. Instead, I was happy to talk.

I was used to sharing my innermost thoughts with those closest to me. I'd grown up with Kara's incessant poking and prodding, and Jaime would have never allowed us to hold information back from him.

It just wasn't the way a wolf pack operated. Having everyone up in your business sure got irritating at times, I could admit that much, but it was our way of life.

Tammy was different, though. She wasn't pushing me.

My heart raced when I thought of her simple acceptance of this fragile new thing between us, even if she seemed unsure about what it might actually mean for the two of us. I got the impression that maybe she saw herself as inferior in some way. Was that because she was human, and I was a shifter? In my mind, one wasn't better than the other. We were just different.

A desire grew in me, to protect her from hurt. Not only physical, but emotional hurt. I sensed that maybe she had been hurt badly in the past, and while I didn't know for sure, I wanted to help her let go of anything in her past that had made her feel bad about herself.

This was all new territory, though. I had no idea what to do, to protect her.

My new purpose—my innermost desire—was to keep her safe, and make her happy. I smiled to myself.

In her own way, by worrying about whether or not she was good enough, it seemed she wanted to protect me in return. I had been so focused on protecting *her*, it hadn't occurred to me that it could go both ways.

And to tell the truth, I wasn't sure what to do with that information.

I SAT WITH TAMMY, talking and laughing, until the sun rose fully in the sky and my stomach growled with hunger.

Half the morning had gone by without either of us noticing. *Huh.*

Time seemed to move differently when I was around her.

I held off on taking her back to the village, unwilling to face the rest of the pack. This place was a haven away from all the judging eyes and silent suspicion. We were in our own little bubble of bliss, and I was loathe to give it up before I had to.

Eventually, I was forced to concede that it was time to head back. I loved Tammy's crestfallen look when I mentioned it. Perhaps she felt the same way I did, and wanted to stay in our private little piece of heaven for as long as possible.

Reid waylaid me as soon as we reached the clearing outside the social hall.

Allara was at his shoulder and she drew Tammy over to her with a firm but gentle hand, fixing me with an unreadable look as she turned away.

Reid skipped the preamble. "So, I take it you told her she's your Fated Mate?" I nodded shortly. "I did. What's going on?"

"It's been decided that it's best if Tammy stays here with us." Reid crossed his arms over his chest. "For a few days, at least. I can't imagine that you'll have a problem with that."

I didn't, but I couldn't help but resent the intrusion on her behalf.

"Decided by who?"

"Allara. The pack."

Tammy wasn't a chess piece on a board, to be moved around as we saw fit. I wanted to get to know her properly, sure, but...

"It's up to *her*, Reid," I growled. "I'll go back to the city with her if I have to."

Reid snorted, probably at the mental image of me in the heart of the concrete jungle. Ugh.

Whatever. If Allara could stick it out for five whole years without her mate, then I could deal with it for as long as it took. Provided I could be with Tammy.

Something flickered behind Reid's eyes. Silver.

Uh oh.

I had to watch my step.

I wasn't scared of him. Strength-wise, I knew we were pretty evenly matched.

Why was I even thinking like that, anyway? We were on the same side now. And, even if it irritated me, at the end of the day, I recognized that he was only looking out for me.

Getting into a fight in the middle of the lawn with Reid was the last thing I wanted to do.

Like it or not, I knew I had more than myself to think about now.

∽

I GAVE up on the idea of finding Tammy until later that day. The expression Allara had sent my way as they walked away said *back off* in about a dozen languages, including wolf shifter Alpha speak. So, I swung by my house with the vague intention of fixing a sandwich and quieting the rumbles of hunger in my belly.

As soon as I entered, however, I froze in my tracks.

"Jason?" Kara called from somewhere inside the house. "That you?"

Shit. Shit shit shit.

My first instinct was to run out the door, but it was pointless. There was no hiding from the visitor sitting in my kitchen. The scent—*her* scent—made me want to leave Idaho and never return.

Quit being dramatic, you pussy. Just get it over with.

With a deep sigh that was almost a growl, I padded toward the kitchen and stuck my head through the open door. Kara was hovering around the stove, making pancakes. And sitting at the dining table, a grin stretched across her face, was—

"Hello, Jason," Naomi purred. "Long time, no see."

My gut tightened but I forced myself to casually lean against the door frame. "Hey, Naomi. What's up?"

Naomi tapped her fingernails against the table and smiled, flicking her gaze up and down my body. "Not much. Just back for a visit, same as always."

"Sure." *Except nothing is the same, anymore.* I swallowed, heading over to the breakfast bar and pretending intense interest in the bowl of batter sitting on the counter.

Before I could stick my finger in it, Kara yanked it away. "Uh uh. Not for you."

Naomi smirked. "Oh, Jason's not very good at keeping his fingers away from things that don't belong to him, Kara."

Kara screwed up her face. "*Ew.* Gross."

Jesus, the woman is all class. This was going to get very awkward, very fast.

"Where have you been?" I asked, just to steer the conversation away from dangerous territory.

"Around," said Naomi, her eyes glittering as she fixed her gaze on me.

I frowned and looked away.

She was bad news. Bad, *bad* news.

Naomi and I went way back. She was part of the pack that lived over on the other side of the creek. And every spring, at the big pack meet-up that happened every year...

There had been a time I thought about sealing the deal with her. But I was just a kid then, too young and stupid to realize that she had a mean streak a mile wide and a habit of skipping town when her various misdeeds finally caught up with her.

She was hot, sure, but she was a mistake, and always had been. Like a forest fire, she was beautiful and bright, and consumed everything and everyone in her path.

"How long you sticking around?" I asked, trying to keep the tone of my voice level.

"Depends." Naomi looked up at me through her thick eyelashes.

Shit!

Once upon a time, I might have said *on what?* I'd have matched her smirk with one of my own and probably fallen into bed with her to forget how lonely I was.

We'd danced this dance before, after all. Many times.

I folded my arms across my chest and stared at her with nothing more than annoyance bubbling inside me.

Did she come here to stir up trouble? Did she know about Tammy already?

I had a mate now, and a sensitive one at that. She wouldn't like one of my old bedmates hanging around. Hell, *I* didn't want my old bedmate hanging around.

We may not have had a bonding ceremony yet, but my wolf was settled, for the first time in my life. My wolf and I were in perfect synch—completely happy with the choice Fate had made for me. Tammy was perfect, and even now, when we had only just parted, I ached to be near her once again.

Naomi, on the other hand, was just plain, old trouble.

I had to get out of there as soon as I could.

~

TAMMY

I MAY NOT HAVE FULLY WRAPPED my head around the way things were done around here, but I knew an ambush when I saw one.

Still, I allowed Allara to drag me away without putting up a fight. We had a lot to talk about, and if she was the Alpha around here, I imagined she'd be pretty busy most of the time.

"Good morning, was it?" Allara winked at me as we walked, and I shook my head with wry amusement at her cheery tone.

"I don't know what you're implying," I said, my voice light. "Jason and I talked, that's all."

"It's good to see you smile like that," Allara said, her eyes crinkling as she looked me over. "I haven't seen a smile on your face for a long time."

I shrugged, keeping my attention fixed on the trees overhead as we walked. "Something about this place makes me feel like smiling. As soon as I got here yesterday..."

It was true. I had felt like I was home, as soon as we pulled up in the car.

"I'll bet," Allara replied gently.

The path she led me down wound through the central group of houses, toward a slightly larger house with a wide porch that was set back from the others. She caught my look of surprise and smiled as she led me up the front steps.

"C'mon, you look like you could use something to eat."

Up until that moment, new emotions and nervousness had kept me preoccupied. But as soon as Allara mentioned food, I realized I was ravenous. Jason and I had skipped breakfast so he could show me his "surprise".

I followed her into the house and smiled at the coziness of the interior décor. "It's so homey here," I said, trailing after her into a rustic, sunlit kitchen. "So different from the city. In a good way, I mean."

"Well, we are out in the sticks." She laughed, rifling around in the cupboards for ingredients. "But I'm glad you approve! It can be peaceful, I guess, but my return was a bit of a culture shock."

"I'll bet."

"Tammy..." Allara had her back to me as she pulled out some pasta and various spices from the cupboards and the fridge. "I *am* glad you like it here. It's a relief that you do, honestly." She used her hip to shut a cupboard door and turned around to face me. "I'm not sure how to say this, but we're going to need you to stay with us. For a few days, at least."

Her tone was somber. Confusion struck me.

"Okay... But why?"

"Do you know what happened last night?" Allara tilted her head to one side, regarding me intently.

"Jason and I talked about it," I said. "He said something about Fate, bringing us together?" I chuckled a little and ran my hands through my hair. "Listen to me! It all sounds crazy, saying it out loud like that."

A soft smile crept over her face. "You really like him, huh?"

My cheeks heated. "I don't really know him, yet, but... I guess I do. He seems like a decent guy, and... well." I raised an eyebrow, trying for nonchalance. "They don't make 'em like that back in the city."

God, keep a lid on it! You only met the guy yesterday!

Allara grinned more widely. "So, you'll stay?"

"What about Mick and Penny?" I asked suddenly. "I was supposed to drive them home! I completely forgot all about them!"

How had I so completely forgotten my friends? *Because of the whole Fated Mates shock with Jason, that's why.*

"Oh, they left hours ago, while you were off in the woods with Jason." Allara set the pasta on the stove to boil. "I told them you would stay a while, and we'd drop you back to the city if and when you're ready."

If and when?

Fragrant smelling steam began to rise from the pot as Allara stirred. "I promise we'll take good care of you, Tammy," she added.

I thought about the big pile of nothing that waited for me back in the city and compared it to the excitement of everything that had happened here. There was no contest, really.

Screw it.

"Why not?" I said, my heart beating rapidly. "I'll stay." I couldn't even imagine leaving now. Not until everything with Jason was sorted out, one way or another.

A part of me still assumed he'd made a terrible mistake, and he would wake up to that, very soon.

CHAPTER 8

TAMMY

Allara squealed with joy and leaned down to give me a tight hug. "Thank *God*, that's a relief." She returned to her cooking, looking like a weight had been lifted off her shoulders.

I folded my hands in front of me and fiddled with the bracelet that encircled my wrist. "So, what's the deal with Jason?"

"What do you mean?" Allara asked. Her voice was suddenly noncommittal, deliberately casual.

"What's he like?"

Allara shrugged. "I know his sister, Kara, better than I know him."

"You guys must have all grown up together," I pressed. Something about the way she was dancing around the subject struck me as... *odd*. "C'mon, Allara. It's me, Tammy!"

"We did grow up together." Allara folded a dish towel, smoothing it flat. She began twisting it round and round in her hands, lost in thought. "We were inseparable as children, actually. The four of us— Reid, Jason, Kara and me."

I heard the wistful sadness in her voice. "So, what happened?"

Allara opened her mouth, then closed it again. She seemed unsure of what to say.

"Don't say nothing happened." I held up a hand to forestall her. "I sense a sadness in Jason; a regret that he tries to hide. And I'm sensing the same thing now, with you. And if he's my Fated Mate, then I deserve to know. Don't I?"

Allara sighed heavily. "When I came back here," she said. Her voice was hushed, a stark contrast to her usual confident tone. "Reid *brought* me back. At first, I didn't want to return."

In halting tones, she told me about the night Reid found her in the bar and let her know her dad had been sick. Dying.

Poor Allara. I couldn't imagine how alone she must have felt.

Just as I suspected, there was more to the story. I listened to the tale that unfolded and it made me shiver. This was a world of rage and retribution, of bloody battles and territorial conquests. Allara's fate could have been so different if things had gone the other way.

"So. This Jaime," I said, once Allara had finished her story. "Where is he now?"

"I don't know," Allara said simply. "Reid's pretty sure we haven't seen the last of him, though. And I agree. A wolf doesn't just give up like that. And a crazy wolf like Jaime will only stop once he's dead."

"What's any of this got to do with Jason?" I asked.

"Jason?" Allara blinked, surprised. "Didn't I mention that part? Jason was Jaime's best friend. He would have been his Beta, if Jaime had defeated me and become Alpha."

My stomach dropped. "What?"

As soon as I think I have a handle on this place, something comes along and knocks me off my feet once again.

So *that* was why Lyra disappeared as soon as Jason had shown up. That was why Jason always seemed to be on the fringe of things, like he was on the outside looking in, even though this place and its people were all he'd ever known.

"Ever since the day I banished Jaime, Jason's kinda... kept to himself," Allara explained. "There were those who believe I should have cast out the both of them." Her face hardened. "But that's not the kind of Alpha I want to be, Tammy. Where do I draw the line? Do I banish everyone who might have sided with Jaime if he had become Alpha?"

I shook my head, helpless. "I don't know."

I'm just glad I don't have to make those kinds of decisions.

"I refuse to punish someone who hasn't committed a crime against this pack," Allara said. "And, whatever happened in the past, Jason is loyal to his family. I trust Kara, so I trust Jason."

I wavered, thinking about every encounter I'd had with him. Behind the cocky bravado, there was an underlay of something warm. Gentle, even. Maybe behind those glittering hazel eyes, there was a kind heart.

He must have felt so alone, for a long time.

"Jason was Jaime's right-hand man for years." Allara slid a steaming bowl of pasta in front of me, and I inhaled the delicious aromas gratefully. "If Jaime were Alpha right now, Jason would be the pack's Beta. It just didn't shake out that way."

Wow, that was rough. To have an expectation of your life going a certain way, only to be left out in the cold through circumstances beyond your control.

I can relate.

Pushing my dark thoughts aside, I took a bite of pasta and chewed, thinking hard. "Was Jason on board with Jaime's plans for the pack? Would he have gone along with everything Jaime had planned?"

Bloodshed, brutality and domination. Whatever cultural differences lay between us, there were certain lines I wasn't willing to cross.

Allara gave a deep sigh, taking a seat opposite me with her own bowl. "Who can say? It's complicated. Our kind... I'm afraid that it's in our nature to be loyal to those closest to us. Even if they bring us nothing but pain."

I stared out into the forest, feeling a sharp ache in my chest.

Maybe humans and wolf shifters weren't so different, after all. And that wasn't necessarily a good thing.

I spent the afternoon wandering aimlessly around the village. The conversation with Allara had cleared up a lot for me, but I was left with the realization that once again, I was standing on the outside of this world looking in.

My thoughts were interrupted by a crowd of small children led by Lyra, who waylaid me on the gravel path in the center of the village.

"Hello, Tammy!" Lyra bounced up to me, taking my hand like we were old friends. My heart warmed as I let her drag me forward. "Come and meet everyone!"

In due course, introductions were made. I met Lyra's older sister, Sage, a girl of about ten who seemed to have adopted a teenage eye-rolling habit a couple of years early. JJ and Ethan were identical twins with identical tooth gaps. Eva, a shy little thing with long plaits who spoke in a soft, whispering voice, and Teddy, who had even more questions for me than Lyra.

Before I knew it, I was sitting with them all in a circle in the long grass and quizzing them on everything I could think of.

If there was one thing I'd learned from college, it was that kids were like tiny sponges. They soaked up everything at this age, and it was clear that these children in particular were hungry for knowledge of the outside world.

"Don't you have class?" I asked, puzzled.

In truth, I didn't see how they could go to an ordinary school out in the middle of nowhere, like this.

"We used to have Miss Jackson," Teddy informed me solemnly. "But she left a couple of months ago. She lives with another pack now, but she promised to visit. Sometimes one of the other adults teaches us stuff, but..." He shrugged, and it was obvious from their responses that these children had been allowed a rather ad hoc approach to education.

"We do have a schoolhouse, though," Lyra piped up. "Wanna see?"

"Absolutely!"

~

TRUE TO THE children's word, it was clear that the schoolhouse hadn't seen regular use in some time.

With effort, I managed to get the doors open. A cursory peek around at all the facilities told me that this place could do with a serious update. The windowsills were full of cobwebs and one of the lightbulbs was busted.

A few rows of desks were set up in a small semi-circle, with a large teacher's desk in front of a blackboard at the other end of the room.

There were a few plant pots in a row on the windowsill and the walls were covered with craft displays and other projects.

All in all, it was old-school, but serviceable. Underneath all the dust, I saw a bright, happy place in my mind's eye.

While I was here, I reasoned, I might as well make myself useful.

With that thought in mind, I set about putting the room to rights. I explored a little, and found a spare bulb in a box under the teacher's desk. I showed the kids how to sweep away the cobwebs from the windowsills and desks with a feather duster.

I got so absorbed with my self-appointed task, I didn't even register the knocking until JJ tugged on my sleeve and pointed in the direction of the open door.

"Rachel!" Lyra rushed over, jumping into the arms of a woman I remembered from yesterday's ceremony. *Rachel.* This must be the woman whose house I stayed in last night. She hadn't been home when Allara dropped me there and showed me up to my room. "I made a new friend!"

Rachel laughed, hugging the girl tightly before setting her down and looking up at me. Her eyes were kind and I returned her smile easily.

"You must be Tammy," she said, extending a hand and grasping mine warmly. "You stayed in my guest room last night."

"Yes." I scanned my memory frantically, hoping I'd left the room in a decent state. "Thank you so much! It was lovely."

"Don't look so worried," Rachel chuckled. "It was a pleasure! I've had far messier house guests, believe me."

I must have looked puzzled because she patted my arm a couple of times as if to reassure me. "I raised Reid, from when he was about this high." Gently, she pulled Teddy toward her and ruffled his hair. Teddy giggled and tried to duck. "And believe me, when Reid hit teenager-hood... well, there's nothing like a teenage boy to wreak havoc." She kissed the top of Teddy's head and the boy wrinkled up his face.

"*Rachel!* I'm not little anymore!" Teddy looked up at me, eyes wide. "I'm almost *nine.*"

"Wow," I said, nodding to show how impressed I was. "Almost into double digits!"

Apparently satisfied with my response, Teddy ran off to join in the game the others were playing. They had abandoned the feather dusters in favor of chasing each other around the desks and shouting with laughter.

I smiled, watching them for a moment.

"Yes, Reid was borderline feral at that age," Rachel murmured, smiling to herself. "He, Allara, Jason... all of them."

"Jason?" I struggled to keep the interest out of my voice. Judging by the twinkle in her eye, something told me that I hadn't succeeded.

"Oh, yes," Rachel said. "They were the best of friends, once upon a time."

Huh.

Things seemed to have cooled off considerably since then. Still, I guess kids weren't kids forever. Life got complicated sometimes. I should know.

"Do you have kids?" Rachel asked suddenly.

I shook my head. "No. I've always wanted them, but I never found the right guy."

I paused as I realized how insensitive that sounded. This woman had just told me she'd raised Reid. Did that mean she'd done it all by herself?

"I'm so sorry," I bit my lip. "That came out wrong. I didn't mean..."

"Darling," Rachel put a hand on my shoulder, gently silencing me. "It's perfectly all right. It's wonderful if you can find a partner to do these things with. But it's clear to me that you're more than capable of going it alone, if you choose."

"Really?"

"Sure!" Rachel smiled. "You kept this bunch occupied for most of the afternoon, didn't you? These are shifter children, Tammy, with a whole bunch of pent-up energy that never seems to wane. That's no mean feat, to hold their focus so long. How do you think I found you? I was wondering why it had gotten so quiet around town all of a sudden."

I burst into laughter, and she joined in.

Strange. I actually feel happy.

All the pain I'd felt over the past few months... maybe it hid something deeper.

I didn't know how, but it was like I belonged here. Almost like...

I blinked a couple of times as the thoughts hit, hardly daring to believe it. It seemed impossible, ridiculous. And yet...

It's like I've finally arrived home.

CHAPTER 9
JASON

After making my excuses to Kara and Naomi, I ducked out of the house and spent the afternoon deep in the forest, after first shifting into my wolf form.

I'm not running away. I'm just clearing my head.

Who was I kidding? I was totally running away.

Being in wolf form felt as exhilarating as ever. The other night had been a maelstrom of confusion and panic, and it felt great to leave all that stuff behind for a few hours. The thud of my paws through the undergrowth, and nothing to focus on but the sounds of nature around me...

Naomi, Tammy, Allara, Reid, Jaime...

I needed the space to stop thinking about any of them and just enjoy the rush that always came with shifting.

I pounded across the forest floor, the trees flashing past on either side of me in a blur of greenery.

Eventually, I knew I'd have to return and face the music.

I was finding it increasingly difficult to ignore the magnetic pull somewhere deep inside my chest. The pull toward Tammy. My mate.

I trusted that Allara would look after her friend, but to be a lone human in the midst of a wolf pack would be unsettling. I had to get back, and check that she was okay.

By the time I returned, dusk had settled over the village. The pack had built up a large bonfire in the middle of the lawn, and several rough wooden benches were scattered around it.

I spotted Tammy sitting at the edge of the circle and made a beeline for her. "Hey."

She looked up, and her eyes softened visibly at the sight of me. "Hello."

She shuffled up a little to make room for me on the bench and I sat beside her. We watched the flames flickering in silence for a minute or two.

"I'm staying," she said.

It sounded like a challenge. I caught her gaze and watched the fire dance in her eyes. "I'm glad."

More silence. I was very aware of our close proximity. This was the nearest we'd been to each other since...

Since it happened.

"How was your first full day here?" I asked, and her face lit up with a wide smile.

God, she's beautiful.

"Really good," she said, her voice full of happiness. "Tons of new people," she giggled. "Mostly the kids, but I'll get around to everyone else soon enough, I'm sure."

She spotted Rachel, who sat across from us, and waved. Rachel waved back, smiling broadly at Tammy. To my surprise, the older woman's smile even extended to me.

My gaze snapped to the fire to hide my shock. I had become so used to my outcast status, I'd forgotten what acceptance felt like.

"You like kids?" I asked, swallowing the lump that had lodged itself in my throat.

She nodded. "My degree was in childcare, so..."

I waited for her to elaborate, but she didn't. Instead she just shrugged, and trailed off to nothing. I sensed there was more to the story, but something told me to leave it alone for now.

"Maybe you could help with the schooling situation round here," I said. "The kids are all kinda running wild at the moment."

I winced. *And that's an understatement.*

She let out a knowing chuckle. "Yeah, I gathered that. They're sweet kids, though."

"They'd rather play in the woods than learn their times tables," I grumbled, and ducked my head at the sound of her answering laughter.

"And I'm sure you were *so* well behaved at their age." Her white teeth nibbled at her plump lower lip, and an ember of something hot flickered between us.

"Sure, I was," I drawled, picking up a stick off the ground and poking at the edge of the bonfire with it. "Nah, you're right. Jeez, I remember when Reid and I—" I broke off, running a hand through my hair. "It was a long time ago now."

Curiosity was written all over her face, but she didn't question me further.

I decided to change the subject. "What's it like for a human? The whole..." I waved a hand between the two of us. *Soul bond.*

I didn't know why I couldn't say the words out loud to her, all of a sudden. It felt too... intimate. Especially out here, surrounded by everyone else watching us.

Jesus. Harden up!

Tammy's expression grew reflective. "I don't know. Like nothing I've ever felt before. What's it like for a wolf shifter?"

"I told you." I grinned at her, appreciating the way the color rose in her cheeks. "It's pure electricity."

"Why me?" she asked. I watched her eyebrows draw together as she gazed at me. "You could take your pick, Jason. So many young, strong and attractive shifter women for you to bond with."

So, I was right. She *was* worrying about the fact she wasn't a shifter.

"The bond doesn't work like that, Tammy. You don't pick and choose for yourself. Fate chooses for us."

"What if Fate chose wrong this time?"

I opened my mouth to reply, but snapped it shut again. I couldn't deny it, the thought had been weighing on my mind, too. Not that Fate had chosen the wrong mate for me, but that I wouldn't be able to protect her properly, living here among a pack of wolf shifters. I couldn't bear the thought of something happening to Tammy, and all because I happened to live in an environment that might not be safe for a human.

How could a human live among us? *Would* it be safe for her here, in the long run?

But she was already surprising me. Various pack members were greeting her like she was an old friend, and she'd clearly won Rachel over with ease.

Most of all, when it came to the kids, she'd clearly hit her stride. The pack was in desperate need of a tutor for the younger children and Tammy would be perfect, especially if she'd studied childcare at college.

Maybe this can work out after all.

I was getting way ahead of myself. Just because she fit in with the pack didn't mean all our problems would be solved.

She's not like you. You can't ask a woman you barely know—a human, at that— to give up her whole life for you.

"For my kind..." I swallowed, thinking about how to explain. "This bond is a pull like no other. Undeniable. Irresistible. And it only happens once. And for me, it was you, Tammy." I edged my hand close to hers, brushing our fingers together. "Only you."

For our pack, a bonfire signified one thing. Being together. A family.

Food, booze, music, stories, and conversation. Everything flowed freely between everyone on bonfire nights. The air was thick with smoke and laughter, and even the kids were allowed to stay up late to listen to the elders tell stories about the old times.

It was the best kind of night.

Usually.

Tonight, I couldn't appreciate any of it. I was so distracted, I barely even noticed when the festivities finally wound to an end and I was staring vacantly into the dying embers of the fire.

Beside me, Tammy was chatting easily to Terry.

I was half paying attention to their conversation, but the bulk of my attention was focused on the lock of hair that fell loosely across Tammy's shoulder. It shone like copper in the firelight. I wanted to run it between my finger and thumb to see if it was as soft as it looked.

"Jason?"

I looked up to discover Terry had already left, and Tammy was staring at me with a concerned expression.

"Are you okay?" she murmured.

In a movement that seemed almost unconscious, her hand slid over mine, bringing me back to the present. Grounding me.

In answer, I slid my other hand into her hair, tilted her head up, and kissed her.

She gasped with surprise and I took the opportunity to flick my tongue against hers, groaning at the sensation and the taste. She tasted like strawberries and her skin was fire-warmed and as soft as silk to the touch.

We broke apart after a moment and I rested my forehead against hers, panting. "Does that answer your question?"

She melted into me, and our mouths met again, over and over. It wasn't long until I was completely lost in her.

~

TAMMY

I FELT weightless in Jason's arms, like floating on a cloud.

His skin was hot to the touch, his muscles firm under my hands. Pleasure pulsed through me when he buried his face in my neck and his hand slid down the front of my dress.

His thumb grazed one of my nipples and I let out a wanton moan, forgetting we were still out in the open, where anyone could see us.

The fire pit was long deserted.

His arms are so strong and steady. I could stay here forever, just like this.

Soon, though, my desire for him started coiling sharp and hot in my stomach. I needed more.

I shifted into his lap and gazed up at him imploringly, hoping he'd decipher what I couldn't bring myself to say out loud.

He did, letting out a feral growl before hoisting me up like my weight was nothing to him, manhandling me until he had me in a bridal carry.

I wrapped my arms around his neck. He dropped kisses on my parted lips as he carried me into the darkness. I wondered vaguely where he was taking me, but I couldn't bring myself to care, as long as it was somewhere away from prying eyes.

It was dark in the forest, which suited me just fine. The low light made everything so much more potent. His scent was everywhere, and I could feel every one of his ragged breaths against my lips. The pulse of his heart thundered in my head, drowning out my own.

It was like I couldn't tell where one of us ended and the other one began.

He lay me down in the soft moss and guided my hands up under his shirt, my eyes fluttering shut at the brush of his bare skin against my palms.

"Tammy," he rumbled. "I need you."

I whimpered at his words and pulled at his shirt, needing to get closer.

He reared back for a moment, stripping himself of his clothes, pulling his shirt from his shoulders and pushing his jeans to the ground.

My breath caught in my throat at the beauty unveiled to me.

I had seen him naked the night we connected, but now I had the time and the focus to see him properly, with no one else around to judge if my gaze lingered too long on his beautiful strong body.

I reached out to him, and as he lay back down between my waiting thighs, I arched up, capturing his mouth in another searing kiss.

I hadn't been with a man since... well.

It was crazy to be out here like this, about to have sex under the stars, but everything about it felt perfect.

We'd been dancing around each other from the moment we locked eyes at the bonding ceremony. It was always going to end like this, I could see that now.

I still couldn't believe that someone as amazing as Jason would want someone like me.

But it was clear how much he *did* want me from the way he licked his way down my neck and held me firmly against him, allowing me to feel the thickness of his cock against my belly. I groaned, grinding against him.

What was also clear was that Jason knew exactly what he was doing. His moves, his touches, were practiced and skillful.

How many other women had he done this with? Was I the fifth girl this month he'd taken out into the forest to ravish? Or the tenth? I had no way of knowing, and though I needed to know, something in me shut that line of thought down.

Consider it tomorrow. Tonight, just focus on the here and now. On his talented fingers slipping under my skirt, sliding his fingers against my clit while his mouth found a sweet spot just behind my ear that made my eyes roll back in my head when he explored there.

Eventually, I couldn't stand the torment anymore. I needed him inside me. I panted the words into his ear, my toes curling at his answering groan.

He drove into me without warning, then froze, and we both gasped.

"Oh, God," he said in a deep, husky voice. "I'm trying to not hurt you..."

As he began to move slowly, rocking inside me, it was obvious he was holding himself back.

"Fuck me," I whispered. "Like I know you want to. I can take it. Fuck me hard, Jason."

His head dropped onto my shoulder, his teeth scraping my throat.

Then he did exactly as I asked, driving into me over and over again. The pleasure was incredible, making me cry out and grab for him until my core tightened around him.

I was close and didn't have the time to warn him. I bit into his shoulder and moaned, shaking as the climax crashed over me. Wave after wave of bliss rippled through my body, leaving me boneless and exhausted and clinging to the gorgeous man above me.

He followed soon after, his eyes rippling with a glint of silver as he came. Aftershock pulsed through me as I reveled in the moment.

Then the thoughts started crowding back in. He'd clearly been with a lot of women.

But... how many *human* women? Was I the first? I hoped so.

I pressed my face into his shoulder and felt my satisfied smile curve against his skin.

Guess I'll have to wait to find out.

~

J*ASON*

· · ·

It didn't take much persuading to get Tammy to come and stay with me that night. Kara was off somewhere, so we had the house to ourselves.

Once we got inside and I realized we were alone and could take our time, I almost regretted my impulsive actions earlier.

Almost.

Taking Tammy like that, in the middle of the forest... it hadn't exactly been part of my game plan. I was usually the smooth type, wining and dining a woman before undressing her piece by piece. I liked to savor my conquests.

But this was different. There had been no calculation on my part, only a wild need that seemed to be mirrored in Tammy, and it drove the both of us crazy.

She brushed past me into the house, looking around the dark hallway with interest. I could smell myself all over her and the wolf inside me growled with satisfaction.

She's finally mine. And tomorrow, everyone's gonna know it.

The rational side of me knew I should think about the logistics of what that actually meant, but right now I couldn't feel anything but relief. I had finally satisfied my instincts, cleared my head enough that I could start to think about other things.

She pressed up against my shoulder, standing on her tiptoes to kiss my cheek. The gesture was unusually chaste, given what we'd just done in the woods.

Okay. *Tomorrow* I would start to think about other things.

She looped her arms around my neck, and I walked her upstairs, listening to her giggle with happiness in my heart. It felt good to hear her laugh. The sound was a world away from the withdrawn, reserved woman I'd met just a couple of days ago.

I ran my hands over her generous curves, appreciating her softness. She was still flushed, warm to the touch, and it made me almost ready to go again.

However, by the way her eyelids were drooping, it wasn't going to happen again tonight.

Sure enough, once she was in my bed, she was out like a light, molding herself into my side like she belonged there.

And the crazy part was... she did.

That's another first to add to my list. I don't think I've ever had a female stay overnight in this house before.

For some reason, I couldn't keep the grin off my face.

I wrapped my arms around Tammy, and fell into a deep sleep almost the minute I closed my eyes.

CHAPTER 10

JASON

When I woke, I felt totally replenished in a way I hadn't felt in possibly forever. I opened my eyes, stretching my arms above my head. The window was open, and the white curtains billowed out, filling the room with fresh air.

Outside, I could hear faint voices. The community was stirring, ready to start the day.

I wasn't, however. Not yet. I just wanted to stay in this little cocoon for a while longer.

I rolled over, flinging out my arm, finding only a vacant pillow. The space next to me was empty, only rumpled sheets beside me now. I sat up.

"Tammy?" I called.

She edged into the room. A dressing gown was wrapped tightly around her form, and she looked strangely shy. I frowned.

That's weird. I thought she enjoyed last night. Did I read something wrong?

"Come back to bed?" I pulled the covers back invitingly.

Her cheeks flushed and she bit her lip, adjusting the tie on her robe. She sat on the edge of the mattress, taking care to avoid sitting on my feet.

"You could try getting under the comforter," I joked, and she smiled back hesitantly.

I couldn't figure out her sudden reluctance, but I decided to just charge ahead anyway.

I flung back the covers, my feet hitting the floor. "Breakfast, then?"

If you can't beat 'em, join em, right?

A warm smile crept across her face. One hand stroked the material of her robe, back and forth, like she had a nervous tic. "Sure."

I bit my lip, looking her up and down once I realized that the robe was mine. Something about seeing her wearing my clothes excited me in a new and unfamiliar way.

Her gaze met mine. She'd caught me looking. I grinned at her, unrepentant.

"I don't have any clothes with me," she explained, looking sheepish. "I wasn't counting on staying so long."

Huh. I hadn't thought about that.

After some digging through my closet, I managed to find an old flannel shirt and some sweats that fit her well enough. She made me leave the room while she changed, which only heightened my feelings of puzzlement.

What's happening? Is this a brush off?

Feeling disheartened, I wandered downstairs and set about making us some French toast. It was the only fancy breakfast thing I could make, and *dammit,* I wanted to impress her, at least a bit.

Maybe this had only been a bit of fun for her. To be with a wolf shifter, the novelty of it... Maybe, now that she'd had me, she'd be on her way?

Fuck 'em and leave them. That was my style, right? There would be a certain irony in having my own moves thrown back at me.

Especially if it was done by the only woman I'd ever really wanted to stay.

I heard her coming down the stairs and shook off my morose musings, forcing a smile onto my face. She took her plate gratefully and we curled up on the sofa together.

"What's your morning usually look like around here?" Tammy asked.

I shrugged one shoulder. "Depends. When it's lumber season, I'm out in the woods for days on end. Sometimes I go hunting."

We lived a rural life around here. I couldn't sugarcoat it for her, it was a life totally different from the world she was used to.

"How often do you..." She broke off, giving me one of her adorably shy smiles. "I mean, how often do you, uh, *transform?*"

I laughed. "It's good to shift at least a couple of times a month, otherwise my wolf gets a bit antsy, but most of the time it just happens, y'know? Running on two legs can get boring."

She chuckled. "Fair enough."

"It's different for everyone, I guess. Apparently Allara wasn't in wolf form for *years*, and she *still* got close to beating Reid's ass," I snickered. "According to my sister, anyway."

"Can I meet her?" Tammy said. "Her name's Kara, right?"

My stomach flipped. I must have looked unsure or something, because Tammy's expression dropped in an instant.

"Oh, God, I'm so sorry. That was forward of me."

"No!" I cut in quickly. "No, you'll meet her later, I promise. I don't know where she is right now, is all. She's gone off somewhere, probably with..."

Naomi.

Jesus, this was gonna get complicated if I didn't play my cards right.

Naomi arriving here a split second after Tammy showed up and I bonded with her, was like some kind of cosmic bad joke.

"Never mind," I finished lamely. "We can hang out today, though."

I had to stop myself from saying *if you want,* like some kind of awkward teenager. I couldn't help it. Tammy made me feel clumsy, like I was putting the moves on someone for the very first time, and doing it very poorly.

"I'd like that," Tammy said softly. My hand found hers where it rested against the couch cushions, and I laced our fingers together, squeezing tightly. "Very much," she said, and the warmth in her tone chased my awkwardness away.

~

Tammy

Jason's plaid shirt was a little long in the arms, but other than that it fit me okay. The material was soft, and I couldn't stop running my hands over it as we talked.

It was distracting, wearing his clothes. The scent of him all around me was heaven.

It made my heart race when I saw his eyes lingering over my frame, drinking in the sight of me. It made me feel special. Wanted.

In spite of that, I hadn't been able to bring myself to get changed in front of him this morning.

You're being ridiculous. You've slept together, what do you have to hide?

But it had been very dark in the forest the night before. And I wasn't sure I was ready for him to see *all* of me in the cold light of day.

As much he seemed to want me, I couldn't fully trust in this Fated Mates bond thing, quite yet. I sighed to myself. My insecurities over my body had always gotten in the way of me feeling comfortable in my previous relationship. Sex with my ex *always* happened with the lights off, no exception, and he had always made it clear he wanted me to lose more than a few pounds.

Jason's gorgeous body didn't exactly help matters. He would never understand the insecurity that came with not being overly attractive, and I wouldn't expect him to.

Things were so warm and safe between us this morning. He was so beautiful, his expression open and happy as we talked.

I didn't want to screw things up, but the worst part of it was, I *knew* that I would.

I always did. It was inevitable. Now and always.

Only this time, when things ended with Jason, I had the feeling it would hurt a whole lot more than anything I'd ever experienced. There was good *and* bad about being someone's Fated Mate.

"You're doing that thing again." He reached out and pushed a lock of hair behind my ear. My skin tingled at his touch, the sensation lingering long after he withdrew his hand. "What are you thinking?"

"What thing?" I deflected, tucking my feet up under me.

"Like at the bonding ceremony," he explained. "You looked... I don't know. Sad. Regretful."

Inwardly I flinched at his perception, but I made sure my facial expression didn't show my discomfort. "I told you, I was happy for my friend."

He was silent, waiting for me to say more.

"Doesn't everyone have some sort of damage, Jason?" I said eventually, and let out a deep sigh. "It's... complicated."

He frowned. I could see his concern for me was growing. His brow furrowed as if he was trying to figure me out and not quite succeeding. "Try me."

I bit my lip, hesitant. "It's a long story."

He slid his arm along the back of the couch and brushed his fingers against the nape of my neck. The evocative touch made me melt into him even further, and he shot me a crooked grin, clearly pleased at the reaction he'd elicited.

"I've got time," he said simply.

"Okay." I paused, giving myself a moment to gather my thoughts. "Well, I guess I should start at the beginning. I was sixteen when I started dating Johnny." I stared into the distance as the memories flooded my head. "We were high school sweethearts."

I caught Jason's eye, and he nodded. He was listening with that unique, wolf-shifter intensity of his, giving me his undivided attention.

"No one thought it would last, but we dated all through high school, then college." I sniffed. "I believed that I'd found the man I would marry. We talked about it plenty... where we'd have the wedding, what kind of cake we'd have, all that stuff." I let out a laugh, cringing a little at the broken sound. "It seems so stupid now, saying it out loud. Then, on the night before my college graduation, I came home to find him in bed with another woman."

My eyes flicked up to ascertain Jason's reaction to my words. His face was impassive, but there was an angry steel in his eyes that made me shiver. I glanced away again.

"Cliché, right?" I shrugged, trying to hide my hurt. "Turns out he'd been seeing Christine—a woman from his office—behind my back for over six months," I said grimly. "The worst part of it was the way he yelled at me after I walked in on them. Like it was somehow *my* fault I'd caught him screwing around with someone else. In our bed."

"What an asshole," Jason growled, and I huffed out a fake chuckle.

"He said he was going to tell me after I graduated. Apparently, he didn't want to *distract* me from my studies." I couldn't keep the bitterness out of my voice. "After that, he told me we were over. That he was leaving me."

"Good riddance." Jason's eyes were hard, burning with their usual intensity. "At least the trash took itself out."

My chest warmed at his protectiveness, which cut through some of the resentful residue left by Johnny's betrayal. I shook my head, fiddling with the hem of my shirt. "I guess. It didn't feel like that at the time, though." *Still doesn't.*

"So... Reid and Allara's perfect relationship, and their bonding ceremony..." He trailed off, waiting for me to fill in the blanks.

"Yeah, it kinda stung a little, even though I was so happy for them both." I looked him in the eye, proud of the way my voice held steady. "All my dreams for the future, the life I'd built with the man I thought I was going spend the rest of my life with, disappeared, just like that."

Jason nodded, seeming to understand. His index finger traced random patterns across the back of my hand. I focused on the comfort of his touch, letting it soothe me before I went on.

"Meanwhile, Allara's childhood sweetheart comes out of nowhere to sweep her off her feet. They have a beautiful ceremony, they're perfect for each other in every way..."

"I can see how that would be hard to watch," Jason murmured. "It's *normal* to feel the way you felt, after what happened to you."

"And yet, I still felt like an asshole," I said flippantly, giving him a rueful smile. "Allara found the one person she was destined to be with, right in front of her. Imagine being that lucky."

"Ah, hello? Fated Mate over here." He waggled his hands and raised his brows, and all of a sudden my heart lightened.

I giggled, then sobered. "It's not quite the same thing, you and I, is it?" Allara and Reid were from the same world, an Alpha and a Beta, destined to be together in every way.

Jason and I were worlds apart—literally. And I knew, deep down, that this thing between us could only ever be temporary.

"Well... sometimes things don't shake out in exactly the way you think they will," Jason pointed out. There was a twinkle in his eye when he spoke. "Doesn't mean you should close yourself off from the world forever."

"Are we still talking about *me* right now?" I tilted my head, watching his expression change to puzzlement, then defensiveness.

"What do you mean?"

"Maybe you're right," I said. "I got burned by a guy, and it's been haunting me ever since. But you're haunted too, Jason." I leaned forward. "I can see it. There's a sadness in you, too. What happened with Jaime?"

He ducked his head, his hair falling over his face. I brushed it away, tilting his chin up so I could look into his eyes.

"You can't change the past," I said. "Neither of us can. We have to carry on."

He surged forward and captured my lips. I wrapped my arms around his neck, holding him close. There was a desperation inside me as I kissed him and I could feel equal desperation in Jason. I wondered if I would ever get tired of this. The thrill of having a guy so attractive want me as much as I wanted him.

I was giddy with it. I would take whatever he gave, for as long as he gave it.

There's more to it than that, isn't there? A small voice said, coming from somewhere in the back of my mind.

You just don't want to admit it to yourself, but it's true. You're falling for him. Hard. Even though you've only really just met.

CHAPTER 11

TAMMY

The next week with the pack flashed by in a blur. Allara had sent someone to the city to collect some of my things, so I now had some more of my own clothes and personal belongings, which was easier than borrowing stuff from others.

I managed a couple of static-filled phone conversations with Mick and Penny from Rachel's ancient landline, just to let them know I was doing okay. From her tone of voice, I quickly realized that Penny *knew* that Allara was a wolf shifter, and that she was the Alpha of the pack.

I rolled my eyes when she said, "Oh my God, I am sooo jealous right now! I can't believe you're sleeping with one of them! How hot is that?"

She should try being in my shoes for a minute.

I couldn't deny that being with Jason was going great—way easier than I expected, actually—but I couldn't stop the niggling doubts. When would the penny drop for him, that I didn't belong here?

I lay awake late at night, soaking in the warmth of Jason's arms around me. It was a struggle to believe that it could always be like this. The two of us, here, a human and a wolf shifter. Side by side. Forever.

It was hard enough to make a relationship work when you were both the same. But other than the couple of phone calls, I was completely cut off from the outside world. And the weird thing was, I didn't mind one bit.

Nobody objected to me taking over the schoolhouse and giving lessons to the kids. A few days in, I realized that wolf shifter kids *really* didn't like being confined to a classroom all day.

After that, I tried to keep their curriculum as outdoorsy as possible, collecting jars of tadpoles and sketching different types of leaves while we sat out in the fresh air, letting them run around and burn off some of that endless energy in between lessons.

Some of the adults continued to give me suspicious glances every so often, but those grew fewer and fewer as the days wore on, especially when the children seemed to enjoy their lessons and kept coming back each day for more. To be honest, the pack adults seemed relieved to have the kids occupied rather than getting underfoot or running amok like wild things. The fact that I was a human, was apparently something they were willing to overlook.

There was one woman, however, who never seemed to want me around.

She was Kara's best friend, back for a visit. Naomi.

She was tall, slender, and toned, like all the shifter women, with long, wavy hair the color of honey. She never spoke to me, but I saw the way her eyes flashed whenever I walked into a room. The perfect shape of her mouth twisted, like she'd caught the scent of something she didn't like.

I tried not to let it bother me, but it was difficult. She was way too obvious about her dislike of me. And ignoring beautiful women was not easy for me. It took a level of confidence I didn't have.

There was something else about the woman that bothered me. I didn't like the way she talked to Jason, one hand resting loose against his elbow, leaning into him.

She was familiar with him, clearly. *Intimately* familiar. And she was at pains to make sure I knew it.

Every time they were together, it was like she was marking her territory. Telling me without words that there was something between them. I was powerless, watching her hands move over his arms with casual confidence.

The worst part was, I *couldn't* match her actions.

I didn't know how to touch him like that. I wasn't sure I had the right.

On a logical level, I knew my insecurities were skewing things between us. Jason held me so tight, night after night, worshiping my body unlike any man I'd ever known before, whispering adoration into my ears as I moaned my pleasure and we wrapped ourselves around one another.

But when Naomi was around, it brought back so many bad memories. I'd tried to forget them, but they kept bubbling up out of nowhere, disturbing my peace.

Memories of Johnny. And his other woman, Christine.

He'd loved me once, too. Or so he'd said. Until I caught him in bed, in the arms of the woman he'd sworn up and down was just a friend.

It wasn't fair to Jason, I knew that. He and Johnny were polar opposites in so many ways. Johnny had been professional and clean-cut, always in a shirt and tie. He was hard to read. Pleasant to everyone, but distant.

By contrast, Jason was as rough and ready as they came. After the soul-bonding ceremony between Allara and Reid, I hadn't seen him in anything close to formalwear. He favored plaid flannel, jeans, and solid boots, like everyone else here. He often had a five o'clock shadow, and the feel of his stubble against my skin drove me crazy with need.

He wasn't one for cologne, but he always smelled so good to me. The soap he showered with mixed in with the scent of forest foliage and a tang of something Allara told me were his shifter pheromones that were apparently perfectly aligned to my system.

You're not a wolf shifter, she explained. *But he smells so good to you because you've bonded with each other. It'll be the same for him whenever you're near.*

I'd blushed at that but decided to take the whole thing in stride. It certainly made better sense to me now why I wanted to launch myself at Naomi every time she so much as *looked* at Jason.

I wanted her greedy hands off my man.

I guess the possessive wolf thing goes both ways.

The whole thing drove me crazy, and that damn woman knew it. She was dangling him in front of me like a prize to be won, and I couldn't do a damn thing about it except watch, and seethe inside.

~

"What's *with her*?" I asked Allara, hours later.

She looked up from where she'd been swirling her tea around in her mug, lost in thought. We were sitting on her porch, the place where I spent many evenings when Jason was out of town for work. Dusk was beginning to settle, and twilight turned the skies a pale violet above us. I could hear grasshoppers chirping in the undergrowth.

"Who?" Allara asked after a moment. She sometimes lost the thread of our conversations, too caught up thinking about pack business.

"Naomi," I whispered. "She seems to *hate* me."

"Oh," Allara snorted. "*Naomi.*"

The name in her mouth seemed to carry a lot of significance. I raised an eyebrow at her, and she sighed heavily.

"Naomi grew up across the creek. Officially, she's still part of the Thornwood pack, but she's been kind of a nomad for the past few years." When she noticed my expression, she shrugged. "Not all wolf shifters want to settle down, Tammy. Naomi... she's different."

Having lived with the pack for only a short while, I found myself struggling to imagine any other kind of life. What could be better than having a family around you, supporting you? Protecting you?

"What *aren't* you telling me?" I challenged Allara.

Her mouth twisted, but she looked amused. I think she enjoyed having me around—a human, not blood-bound by loyalty, and someone who wasn't afraid of her.

"Jason met Naomi when we were kids," Allara said. Her voice halted a little and she fiddled with the handle of her mug. "They had an on-again, off-again thing for a while. Jason might have considered bonding with her, I don't know. But Naomi..."

I waited for a minute before nudging my foot gently against hers. She shrugged.

"The point is, I don't think either of them were ever *serious* about it. Jason's never been serious before, not about anyone." She gave me a warm smile. "Before you came along, I mean."

My chest grew tight. Over the last few days, I'd felt the walls I had so carefully constructed around my heart splinter a little. Cracks were beginning to show in the protective walls, and the light was creeping in for the first time in what felt like forever.

I'd started to allow myself to believe that Jason actually *cared* about me.

It was dangerous and dizzying, but I couldn't help it. He *got* to me in a way that no one ever had before. To be honest, I was addicted.

"How can I know how he *really* feels, Allara?" I heard myself ask. "We've only known each other for a couple of weeks. What if he gets tired and moves on?"

I hated showing this much vulnerability, but Allara was a good friend. I knew she'd understand.

"I guess you never *can* know for sure," Allara said. "But, for our kind, the soul-bond is a once in a lifetime event. It's impossible to ignore, Tammy. It means that you two are fated."

I had to admit, all the talk of *fate* and *souls* around here scrambled my head. I sighed, giving her a reluctant nod. Maybe I understood it as much as I was ever going to.

"Besides..." Allara leaned forward, shooting me a conspiratorial look. "Forget about *him* for a moment. What do *you* want, Tammy?"

"What do you mean?"

"Do you like living here with us?" Allara asked. "Does it make you happy?"

"Of course!" I wondered how anyone could *not* be happy here. "It's... it almost feels like... home."

I whispered the word, hearing the longing in my voice. Being here, I felt an overwhelming sense of peace, safety, and contentment. Some mornings I woke up and wondered how I could have gone without it for so long.

It was like I'd been walking around with a piece of me missing. And being out here, with Jason, with the pack... I felt whole.

"And your life in the city?" Allara asked. My head jerked up. "What about your grad school for social work? Have you applied yet? You told me you were working on it a while back."

"Uh..." I stalled. "I guess I haven't... quite finished it yet."

That was an obvious lie. I knew perfectly well that those forms were sitting on top of my dresser in my apartment, untouched, as they had been for months.

She raised an eyebrow at me, and I flung out my hands. "Come on, you *know* I like bar-tending! The tips are *good—*"

"They're really *not* —" Allara cut in.

"And *besides*, it's... fun." I fixed her with a determined look. Her sceptical expression didn't budge, however, and before long, my shoulders sagged with defeat. "Okay, fine. Sometimes it sucks. But..."

"You wanna know what I think?" Allara prodded me.

No... but I suspect that you're gonna tell me anyway.

"When I took that bar job," Allara said, "I was running away from something. And I think you're running too, Tammy. Maybe not from a crazy wolf pack, like I was." Allara smirked. "But you've got your own demons, I know you do. In the city, I was lost. And maybe you were, too."

I opened my mouth, ready to protest, but no words came out. I ducked my head.

"You might not be a wolf shifter, Tammy, but you fit in here. Everyone can see it." Allara rested a hand on my shoulder, ever the Alpha. I sniffed, my emotions threatening to spill over. "Maybe it's time to stop running. Things don't always work out exactly the way you think they will." She gave a snort. "*Trust* me."

"I can stay?" I whispered.

"Of course, you can!" Allara pulled me into a tight hug. After a moment, I returned it. "As long as you want."

We pulled away from each other and smiled.

Something struck Allara and she giggled.

"What?" I asked.

"You'd really be doing *us* a favor." She leveled a grin at me. "Those kids were running rings around us. We need you, Tammy. We need you as our kid wrangler."

I spluttered with laughter and shook my head, but I couldn't deny it. The idea was exciting. It meant I had a purpose here, a place. Maybe it didn't matter that I wasn't exactly like them. As Allara said, sometimes even individual wolf shifters didn't fit in with a pack. Was it really so unlikely that the reverse could be true, too?

Maybe I have, at long last, found my dream. A place to call home, for real.

~

ONE WEEK TURNED INTO TWO, and then three.

Before I knew it, a whole month had passed. A month of waking up in Jason's bedroom. Of slow, lazy mornings, of exploring the woods and swinging around giggling children by the hands. Baking in Rachel's cozy kitchen and chatting with Allara over cups of peppermint tea.

The only dark spot in my happiness was the occasional nausea I felt creeping in here and there, disrupting my day. Herbal tea usually helped, but there were days I was about ready to throw up. Jason made me chicken one evening and it made me so queasy I had to lie down on the sofa.

A crazy thought struck me. *Could I be pregnant?*

It seemed impossible. After that first, wild time, out in the woods, we'd been so careful.

It was too much, too fast, too soon. Almost as soon as I had the thought, I pushed it to the back of my mind, unwilling to examine it any further.

I was feeling particularly rough one afternoon and I'd gone to lie on the sofa, trying to shake off the sickness that swept over me. I heard faint sounds of movement in the kitchen.

Thinking it was Kara, I called out, "Hey, Kara, would you mind bringing me a glass of water, please? I'm not feeling very well."

A voice traveled in through the open doorway. "Well, looks like you've made yourself right at home already."

The tone was pointed and full of barely concealed hostility.

I craned my neck, sitting up just enough to look over the back of the sofa. Naomi was leaning against the doorway, arms crossed, looking at me with narrowed eyes.

"Oh," I said, brushing the hair off my face. I hoped that I didn't look as much of a mess as I felt. "Sorry. I thought you were... never mind."

I heard her scoff, and I felt a twinge of irritation in my stomach.

What's her problem?

"Can I help you with something?" I sat up as straight as possible, trying to project an aura of confidence that I didn't feel.

"Not at all," she said, giving me a sweet smile that didn't reach her eyes. "You'll be gone soon enough, won't you?"

"What's that supposed to mean?" I whispered.

I felt like I had just missed a step on the stairs. I was grasping at the empty air around me, but I knew I was going to fall, no matter what.

She didn't move from the doorway, but she leaned forward, looking me right in the face. I saw the wolf in her eyes, the predator that lurked just beneath the surface.

She could tear me to shreds if she wanted to, physically and mentally.

"Jason doesn't *settle down*," she said, her voice coated with venom. "Don't make the mistake of thinking he's actually serious about you, *human*."

"You don't know anything about us," I said. I heard my voice tremble, and a slow smile spread across her face. Oh, yes. She'd heard that tremble, too.

"You're a play-thing to him," she continued, letting out a humorless laugh. "You're nothing more than a game. Think about it. Why would he settle for someone like you?"

I was silent. My mind raced and my palms began to sweat.

I shouldn't listen, but I couldn't help it. Everything she said confirmed all my worst fears. I wasn't good enough for Jason. I wasn't a wolf shifter. I wasn't slender and sexy. I didn't have stamina or agility or a killer instinct. I had none of the qualities that were prized among shifters and humans alike.

"The truth is..." She shrugged, giving me a brief, calculating glance up-and-down, before looking away, as if she couldn't bear the sight of me. "You're just a fat, unremarkable human. You don't fit in here, and you never will."

Before I could respond, she turned on her heel and sauntered out, leaving me reeling in her wake.

❧

Jason

THE MOMENT I stepped into the house, I could sense something was wrong.

Nothing was out of place, as far as I could tell from a cursory glance. All the furniture was exactly as I'd left it this morning. My old flannel shirt was draped neatly over the back of the sofa, and my books were stacked equally neatly on the coffee table.

Nevertheless, my eyes narrowed.

I stalked through the house and peered into every room. The kitchen, my bedroom, Kara's room... no one was home.

That was weird. Tammy was usually back by this time in the afternoon.

Maybe she got held up at the schoolhouse or something.

Still, something felt wrong in a way I couldn't put my finger on. I thought back to this morning, trying to remember if anything had felt out of the ordinary.

Nope. The past couple of days had been great.

So good, in fact, that I'd been working up the courage to ask her to move in with me permanently. I thought we could make a weekend trip to the city and pack up the rest of her things. Maybe check in on some of her friends along the way.

I wandered back into my bedroom and noticed that her handful of items, which had previously been littered over my bedside table, were gone.

My puzzlement began to give way to panic. I strode over to the window and looked out onto the assortment of trucks and dirt bikes that littered the turf outside.

My truck was still there, but...

I raced down the stairs and out the front door, snatching up the scrap of paper that was fluttering on my windshield.

Jason,

I'm sorry. I needed to get out of here. I've gone back to the city. Just give me some time to clear my head.

Please don't follow me.

Tammy

I released a growl of frustration and crumpled the note in my fist. My blood was pumping, and worry flooded through me as I pictured her out there in the woods alone.

What is she planning? To hitch a ride with some stranger?

If she'd gone on foot—and my instincts told me she had—she must be heading for the main road, which lay a couple of miles out of town. I didn't know how much of a head start she had on me, but I figured I could catch up.

My body screamed at me to shift into my wolf form. It would be faster that way. I could track her down using all my senses.

I managed with some effort to restrain myself.

She's clearly upset over something. It won't do her any good if a giant wolf comes bounding out of the forest and transforms into a naked man in front of her.

I leapt into my truck and turned on the ignition. Several people gave me curious glances as I trundled up the dirt road toward the highway, but no one stopped me. I caught a glimpse of myself in the rearview mirror and understood the curiosity. I looked like a madman, with my hair sticking out and my eyes glinting with silver.

Calm down!

It was impossible to calm down. Tammy was out there somewhere, alone. Before long, it would be dark. Her human senses would make it impossible for her to navigate the rough terrain.

I hurtled down the road, pressing the gas pedal hard, until the truck was flying along. The darkened trees flashed by me on either side, and I pounded the dashboard with one hand, willing the vehicle to go even faster.

I began to wonder whether I'd made a mistake. Maybe she hadn't gone on foot toward the main road. Maybe she'd persuaded Allara or Reid to give her a ride back to the city, or she'd wandered off into the woods...

But something deep in my gut told me that I was on the right path. She was somewhere along this road, I knew it.

I rounded the next corner and saw a lone figure walking by the side of the road. My brakes screeched, and the figure whipped around.

Tammy.

Her face was pale and her eyes were shadowed and red-ringed, like she'd been crying. They widened when she saw me, and her lips pressed into a thin line, like she was trying to stop herself from bursting into tears.

A strange feeling pierced through me at seeing her distress, like a blade lodging itself in between my ribs.

I exited the truck and hurried toward her, taking her face in my hands. "Tammy! *What—*"

"You followed me!" she exclaimed. To my rapidly growing bewilderment, she *glared.* "I told you not to, Jason!"

Why was she angry? What had she expected—that I'd just let her run off and not follow? Not do whatever it took to convince my mate to come back where she belonged?

I rubbed my hands up and down her arms. She was cold to the touch, only wearing the dress she'd arrived in all those weeks ago, and a thin cardigan overtop. A small bag sat at her feet where she'd dropped it when she turned.

"I was..." How could I explain the feeling of dread that caught hold of me when I read her note? Instead, I focused on the practicalities at hand. "*Why* are you out here on foot? You're freezing!"

She shrugged my hands off her. "I'm fine!"

So stubborn. "If you're not happy—" I forced my voice to sound as neutral as possible. "You should've just said something. Your note scared the daylights out of me!"

"You don't get it, Jason." To my horror, her eyes filled with tears. "I don't belong there, and I never did! And it's *stupid* to keep pretending..."

"Pretending *what?*" I felt like she was speaking a completely different language.

Where was this coming from?

"That it's going to work out between us." Her voice was trembling with suppressed emotion. "We're just kidding ourselves, Jason." Her shoulders slumped, and her voice was weak. "At the end of day, you're *you* and I'm *me.*"

"What's that supposed to mean?" I asked, feeling a twinge in my stomach I felt ill, as if I were about to lose anything I'd eaten in the last day.

I thought she'd gotten over the fact that we were from two very different worlds. Clearly, she hadn't.

"It means that I'm doing us both a favor! With me gone, you'll see that..." She bit her lip as splotches of red appeared in her otherwise pale cheeks. "That there are other options. *Better* options."

I shook my head. "No. There's just you, Tammy." I took a deep breath. "It's only ever been you. The moment we met, I realized that I'd simply been waiting for you to arrive in my life."

"You think that now," she said weakly.

I wished we were having this conversation in the relative warmth of my truck. She looked exhausted and cold.

"Jason, I can't stay here."

I tried to imagine life with the pack without her in it, and I found that I couldn't. "Tammy, *please.*"

"Come with *me.*" Her usually soft gaze was pointed. Her brows drew together imploringly. "Let's just *go*, Jason. Back to the city, to my place. I'll never belong here, and we both know it."

I'd run out of words. All the fight fizzled out of me as I stood before this lovely, impossibly stubborn woman. I could go with her, to the city, but whatever it was holding her back from being with me, wasn't mooted in location. I had the feeling we would simply take the issue with us, even though I wasn't quite sure what the issue was.

I found myself tracing over the planes and angles of her face in my mind, committing it to memory.

"I..." She gazed up at me, and I faltered. "I don't think that's a good idea, Tammy."

Her gaze dropped. "Well, then."

"We can work this out," I said. "We *can*... just come back to the truck. At least let me get you warm."

After a moment she nodded and, in silence, we walked back to my truck. She climbed into the passenger seat with obvious reluctance. The line of her back was stiff, and her face, usually so kind and open, was shut off like the light inside her had been snuffed out.

I started the engine, letting the truck heat up inside. With Tammy, I had to constantly remind myself that she couldn't weather the harsher elements like I could. As a shifter, my body temperature ran a little hotter than a non-shifter human. Her relative fragility was kind of terrifying whenever I thought about it too much, though I was always more than happy to lend a little body heat.

"I can't leave my pack," I murmured again. "I'm sorry. It's not that I don't..." I ran a hand through my tangled hair, at a total loss. "It's my *family*."

It wasn't just Kara. If I left now with Tammy, I would be abandoning Reid and Allara at a time when they needed strong people around them. I had to prove my loyalty to them, all over again, and leaving now would send the opposite message.

"Please Tammy. I can't bear the thought of life without you in it."

She just stared at me with big, sad eyes, and I could almost hear the words in my head. *But you won't leave your pack for me.*

It was a crazy realization. I was loyal to them now. I would protect the pack until my last breath, if I had to. But in that realization, my heart was torn in two.

Tammy didn't realize what she was asking of me. She wasn't forcing me to choose between the two things that tethered me to earth, of course.

But if she left, it would likely destroy me. And if I left with her, it would likely destroy us both.

"I understand," Tammy said. Her voice was so quiet I would have missed it if I hadn't been hanging on her every word.

A small spark of hope caught in my chest. "You do?"

Does that mean she'll come back with me? Will she stay?

"Yes." She turned to me. "Could you drop me off at the nearest bus station, please?"

The spark died. Something broke inside me, a silent howl rising up in my chest, but I kept my gaze steady. I didn't want to cause her any more pain than I clearly already had.

I turned my gaze to the road and nodded, forcing out the words past the lump in my throat. "As you wish."

CHAPTER 12
TAMMY

Walking back into my city apartment after all the weeks I'd been away, I expected to feel a sense of... I don't know. Relief, maybe. Or comfort.

I was back where I belonged, after all. Back in the human world, where I knew the rules, kept my head down and never stood out as different from everyone else around me.

Closing the front door, I leaned against it and let out a heavy sigh. I dropped my bag at my feet.

After a minute, I began to open curtains and windows to allow some air through, and shook out my bedsheets. I rifled through my kitchen cupboards in search of something to eat, but aftr all this time there wasn't much left that was edible, so I gave up and ordered takeout, resolving to spend the evening watching trashy TV.

I refused, categorically, to allow the sorrow in my heart to take hold. I had done the right thing.

He deserves someone amazing. Someone strong and athletic. Someone he doesn't have to worry about every second of the day.

Someone as beautiful as him.

I ignored the gnawing ache deep inside, and picked up the university forms that still lay on top of my dresser. I took them into the living room and, with the help of the white wine that came with my takeout, I set about filling them in.

Allara is wrong.

This is my dream. It was waiting for me, right here. I got distracted for a long minute, but now I'm back where I actually belong.

I'm home.

I repeated the mantra to myself, over and over while I worked on the forms. I said it so much that, by the time I crawled into bed in the small hours of the morning, I had almost convinced myself it was true.

~

Jason

I SPENT most of the following morning in a total daze.

When Kara asked me where I'd been, and where Tammy was, I dodged the question. I grabbed a piece of toast off her plate, trying to keep to normal behavior so she wouldn't ask anything more, ignored her protests and headed outside without a backward glance.

I walked around and spoke to people, like I always did. I even cracked a few jokes, I think. But I wasn't really there. I felt hollow inside, like my soul had been cut out of me and there was only an empty shell left.

All I could think about was my mate.

I'd dropped her at the bus station as she requested, and waited at a distance until the coach had pulled up and she was safely aboard before heading back to the village.

A hand landed heavily on my shoulder and I started, whirling around and automatically lowering my posture into a defensive position.

Reid put up his hands to indicate that he wasn't a threat. "Hey, c'mon man! I called your name, like, three times."

I blinked and straightened. "Sorry. I was…"

I threw out a vague hand, unable to finish. Reid seemed to catch my meaning well enough.

"Yeah, no shit," he looked me over, frowning. "You look like crap."

"Thanks," I said dryly.

The last thing I wanted to do was get into it with Reid right now. It all felt too raw, too sudden. I'd lain awake half the night and it still felt like a bad dream. Surely, I'd wake up from this soon enough?.

"Where's Tammy?" Reid asked.

My expression must have raised some alarm, because he dragged me over to the edge of the trees and looked me up and down, concern growing in his eyes.

Then he waited, eyebrows raised, and didn't say anything. Obviously, he wasn't going to let it go like Kara. I couldn't easily run from the Alpha's mate.

I drew myself up, finally ready to speak the horrible truth. "She went back to the city," I said shortly. "What can I say? I guess Fate doesn't always get it right."

The touch of bitterness in my voice masked the loneliness and loss that ate away at my insides. I wasn't used to feeling so wronged by a woman.

"Just give it some time, man," Reid said. I knew he was thinking of Allara. "She'll come around."

Reid had waited five years to get Allara back. I didn't think I'd last that long, without my mate by my side.

I wish I had the same confidence. It wasn't just the miles that separated us. A rift had opened up, and only time would tell if it could be healed.

TAMMY

I SAT DOWN HEAVILY on the edge of the bathtub and held the small plastic wand in my hand.

I prayed under my breath to every god or goddess that I could think of, begging, *imploring* the thing to show me that my worries were unfounded.

After a minute or so, I stared blankly at the result. Two narrow lines. It was funny how such a tiny thing could make me feel like a hole had been punched through my chest.

It wasn't possible. It *wasn't...*

We'd been careful. Hadn't we?

Aside from that first time, the voice in the back of my head piped up. *You lost control, remember? He took you right there, in the middle of the woods.*

I groaned and slid to the floor, the cold bathroom tiles pressing against my butt. Getting pregnant the first fucking time we had sex? What were the chances?

Maybe that meant we really were destined by fate? As if the constant empty sadness in my heart hadn't already convinced me of that.

I rested my head against the side of the tub and ran my fingers over those dreaded lines.

In my heart, I had already known the truth; hadn't needed to see the test result to know I was expecting. I'd known for a while, if I was being honest with myself.

I curled up right there on the bathroom floor and took stock of my situation.

I was pregnant. The father of my child was miles away, and was probably already hooked up with another woman right now. No doubt the time we spent together was just a memory to him. One chapter in a long line of his conquests. That thought made me close my eyes and press a hand over my mouth to stop the tears spilling down my cheeks.

How could I have a child here, now? How would I earn money, provide for us? My hand found my stomach and curved around it protectively as I thought about the tiny spark of life in there. It would just be the two of us.

And yet, I had never felt more alone in my life. I had no one, nothing. Every man I had dared to love had disappeared out of my life, scattered like dust in the wind.

If this was fate... then she sure had a sick sense of humor.

～

Jason

. . .

THERE WAS a knock on my bedroom door and I rolled over and shoved my pillow over my head. I wanted to tell whoever it was to go away. I didn't want to speak to anyone.

After a moment, when I didn't say anything, the door creaked open.

I groaned into the pillow before removing it and rubbing my eyes, a wave of tiredness cresting through me. "Kara, I told you. Just leave me alone, will ya?"

"It's me."

My eyes snapped open and I turned my head to stare at the intruder. I knew that voice too well.

Naomi.

I half-sat up and rested on my elbows, watching her warily as she moved through the room and sat at the edge of my bed, crossing one long leg over the other.

Her proprietary attitude annoyed me. I decided not to beat around the bush. "What do you want?"

"Wow, someone's in a bad mood." A smirk slid across her face. "You used to be so much fun, Jason. What happened?"

I didn't answer. Lying back down, I slung an arm over my face, hoping that my obvious disinterest would be enough to send her packing.

No such luck. Her voice dropped to a low, seductive purr, and my skin prickled with discomfort as she sidled closer.

"You know..." Naomi's fingers found the edge of my leg, brushing lightly against my calf atop the bedcover. "We were almost mated, once upon a time. It's not too late, Jason. I'm right here." She leaned close until I could feel her breath. "I could give you everything. I'm like you, you know that. We understand each other."

I removed my arm from over my eyes and studied her.

Naomi was perfect to look at. She had the sharp features of our kind, high cheekbones, pointed chin. Her hair was glossy and her body was lithe and toned.

I knew all this, objectively.

None of it affected me physically in the slightest.

She was pretty wrapping concealing a fucked-up present.

As gently as I could, I sat up and pushed her hand off me. I maneuvered so that we were no longer touching and leaned against my headboard.

"I'm sorry." I shook my head, rubbing a hand over my face. I just wanted her to leave so I could return to my pity party. "I just don't feel that way about you, Naomi. It might have seemed like a good idea, once upon a time. But now... no. It will never happen."

Her eyes narrowed. "Don't tell me it's because of that woman. *God, Jason...* I thought you had standards. A *human?*"

I narrowed my eyes. She didn't have the right to swan into my bedroom and talk disrespectfully about Tammy. My silence seemed to enrage Naomi.

"It was never gonna work out with her, babe." She flicked her long hair over one shoulder, fixing me with her calculating gaze. "You know that. She's not from our world. You'll be happier in the long run, believe me."

I shook my head and pointed to the door. After a long pause, she gave a huff and stood up, marching out of the room and leaving me alone in the silence.

∼

I HOPED I could fly under the radar of the Alpha for a couple of months and do all my brooding in peace. I'd been a pariah around here for long enough, I didn't think anyone would miss me.

Unfortunately, I had no such luck.

For some reason, Lyra had gotten over her nerves around me. More than that, she'd developed an annoying habit of trailing me everywhere on the rare occasions I ventured outside my house. She kept up an endless stream of questions. Where was Tammy? When was she coming back? Did she leave because she was angry? Did I make her go away? Did she miss being around other humans? Did I know if she missed Lyra, now that she was back in the city?

I didn't have any answers for Lyra but she kept going, nonetheless.

Lyra I could deal with, and even Kara's pointed looks and attempts to get me out of the house were manageable, but Allara and Reid kept giving me searching looks, and *they* made me nervous.

Had they changed their minds about letting me stay with the pack?

Were they questioning my loyalty? Hadn't I already proven it when I watched the one woman I had ever truly *wanted,* whom I'd genuinely seen a future with, slip away?

It all came to a head one day when Allara gathered us on the steps outside the social hall to make an informal announcement.

"I'm traveling for a few days. There are some obligations I have to fulfil with a pack in Denver." Ignoring the hushed murmurs that followed her statement, she put a hand on Reid's shoulder. "In the meantime, Reid is in charge. If there are any problems, bring them to him. Got it?"

There were a few mutterings of acknowledgment and Allara nodded, satisfied. The crowd began to disperse and I turned away with them.

"Jason?" Allara called, and I swung back. Outside Kara and young Lyra, nobody had spoken to me in about a week. Everyone was giving me a wide berth, like I was an unexploded bomb that could go off at any moment. "I'll need back-up on the road. You're coming with me."

It wasn't a question. I met her solid gaze and lifted my chin, giving her a short nod.

Looks like I'm hitting the road with the best friend of the woman who broke my heart. Awesome.

I sighed. At least it would provide a distraction against the constant thoughts of Tammy. Whatever else, this trip was certainly going to be interesting.

Tammy

I SPENT A FEW LISTLESS, restless days drifting around my empty apartment in a daze.

And then, I did what I always did when life threw a curve ball my way.

I picked myself back up, dusted myself off, and made a new plan.

First off, I was keeping the baby. I knew that it wouldn't be easy, but I couldn't fathom the alternative. I'd lost Jason, I wasn't losing the only piece of him I had left.

I didn't know how it would work, of course. A wolf shifter's baby would surely be a wolf shifter. At the very least, he or she would likely have non-human traits.

I filed away all those fears, resolving to worry about them later. Jason had said shifting abilities only came about near puberty, so I had at least a decade, hopefully, before I had to figure anything out.

With a baby on the way, I wouldn't be able to continue paying the rent on this apartment.

I handed in my notice and moved in with Leah, an old friend of Mom's who lived out in the suburbs. Her kids were long since grown and her husband had died a few years back. Alone in her big house, she lived with three dogs and had a whole load of chickens in the backyard. We'd struck up an odd kind of friendship after Mom died. She had always looked out for me, especially during the low points of my life.

I was pregnant, alone, and soon to be homeless. As far as I figured, that was about as low as it got.

When she heard I was looking for a place to stay, she offered me her spare room for free. I think the arrangement suited both of us. She ended up with company and someone to cook for her, and I got a roof over my head without having to worry about how to make rent each month.

I gave up on bar work completely, instead, taking a job part-time at Penny's diner. I dipped into my savings for the rest, spending my weekends gardening in Leah's yard and sitting in my favorite armchair, staring out the window, thinking about everything and nothing.

The day I was accepted into grad school, Leah, Penny and I shared a bottle of non-alcoholic bubbly in celebration, much to Penny's disgust. We sat around the kitchen table, and I listened to the two of them talking baby names.

Try as I might, I couldn't shake the feeling that I was still... drifting.

It had been a whole month since I'd left the pack. I walked around the city streets, went to work, cooked, did laundry, and all the while felt like I was under some kind of spell.

This was the world where I belonged. A world that made sense to me. Yeah, it would be difficult, raising a child on my own. But I'd made the best of a bad situation before, and I could do it again.

My time in the forest felt like a sunlit dream. And the thing about dreams... they weren't meant to last forever. Sooner or later, I was always going to wake up.

Allara had been wrong. I wasn't Jason's soulmate and he wasn't mine. We were just two people who got tangled up with each other, taking a detour from the path we were meant to travel. But we were always destined to return to our own separate paths, in the end.

I knew all of this, for certain.

So why did it feel like an essential part of me was missing?

~

JASON

WE'D BEEN on the road for about an hour and my head was buzzing.

Allara sat in the passenger seat, silent. There were so many things I wanted to ask her, but I kept my mouth shut, unwilling to stoke the tension that I was afraid would overwhelm the trip if I wasn't careful.

"I know what you want to ask me," Allara said, in a calm voice.

"You do?" I shifted in my seat, uncomfortable. She was the Alpha. She probably knew everything about everyone in the pack, including me.

"You want to know if I've heard anything. From her."

I was silent. I didn't need to ask which *her* she was referring to. As usual, Allara had hit the nail on the head. I didn't want to give her the satisfaction of knowing it, though, so I let out a noncommittal grunt.

"I'm sorry, Jason," she said. Her tone was surprisingly soft. "I wish I had good news."

"I'm just trying to put it in the past," I murmured. My voice barely cut above the roar of the engine, but Allara's head jerked in acknowledgment. "Anyway, she was right. She's a human, and I'm a shifter. It was never going to work. It doesn't even make sense."

Allara didn't reply. A strange expression settled across her features. She glanced out the window, and I watched as the corner of her mouth tilted up a little.

That's kind of a weird reaction to have when someone tells you their soulbond was doomed.

Then again, Allara *was* kind of strange.

We fell back into silence, but it was no longer an uncomfortable one. I focused on the open road for a few minutes.

"You know, I asked Reid something the other night." There was a gleam in Allara's eye that I'd only seen on rare occasions. "And his answer surprised me."

"Oh?" I couldn't keep the curiosity out of my voice.

"I asked him a simple question. If he were the Alpha, who would he pick as his Beta."

I shrugged, tapping my fingers against the steering wheel. "You, surely?"

"I wasn't in the running." Allara smiled at me, not unkindly. "It's totally hypothetical, obviously, but he told me that, if he had to pick, he would've picked *you*."

I frowned. That didn't make any sense at all.

"*Why?*"

Allara let out a bark of laughter, no doubt at my shocked expression. "Why *not*, Jason? You're strong, smart, and you've proven your loyalty to this pack a hundred times over." She gave me a serious look and I saw the spirit of the old Alpha—her father—reflected in her eyes. "You're a good man."

I had to blink a couple of times and I coughed once or twice. Something must've blown off the windshield into my eye. It was the only explanation as to why I felt so choked up all of a sudden.

"I didn't know you guys, uh," I flexed my hands against the wheel, unsure. "*Trusted* me so much."

I'd been on the edge of things for so long, the bad guy with a chip on his shoulder. I didn't know how to *be* anything else. Sincerity, softness... it wasn't a script I was much familiar with.

"I've seen the way you act around Tammy," Allara said. "That's all the reason I need to trust you, right there."

I noted her use of the present tense, but I didn't dare correct my Alpha. It was oddly comforting. For a moment I could kid myself that Tammy was still a part of my life.

That, when I got home, she would be waiting for me.

"I don't know what to say," I mumbled.

"I know a thing or two about divided loyalties," Allara said gently. "For what it's worth, I'm glad you stayed with us—with our pack— when all that shit went down with Jaime. And I'm glad you found Tammy."

Emotions whirling, I managed to give her a nod of acknowledgment. That seemed to satisfy her. We spent the rest of the journey in silence, but I sensed that something integral had shifted between us. Allara and Reid... and me.

In spite of how bleak everything else looked, there was a tiny glimmer of hope on the horizon at long last.

I was back in the fold. Welcomed, with open arms. I *belonged*.

I allowed a small smile to ghost across my face. *It looks like I finally have my family back.*

~

By the time we arrived in Denver, dusk had fallen.

It was chilly this time of year. I caught Allara rubbing her hands together, a rare acknowledgment of the temperature, as our kind didn't easily feel the cold. I turned up the collar of my jacket before following her toward the gated entrance of the large compound we'd pulled up outside.

The Denver pack resided, unusually enough for our kind, on the outskirts of the city's urban center. Like us, they had built their settlement out of materials found in the landscape around them. Scrap metal, corrugated iron and old tires formed the walls that surrounded the small community, and each house looked to be built similarly.

We followed the sound of whooping laughter to where a massive bonfire had been constructed. It towered over the pack members that gathered around it, at least six feet tall. In the fading light, it flickered and burned, stacked with crates, boxes and old furniture.

A hulking figure approached us, flanked by several others. I immediately identified the huge man in the middle as the Alpha of this pack. He and Allara exchanged a polite, if formal greeting, inclining their heads to each other and clasping their forearms in a universal show of respect.

After a few minutes, Allara moved off to talk with the Alpha alone. She signaled for me to stay put, and I did so, even if part of me was frustrated.

I should be going with her. Why did she bring me here, if not for protection?

I slouched down at the edge of the group of revelers and stared into the flames. I could feel my misery rising once more. These people were strangers to me and offered me no distraction from my state of mind.

After a moment or two I became aware of a small presence hovering near my elbow.

I looked down. A petite woman smiled up at me. She was near middle-age, with gentle, smiling eyes and a motherly expression. She was holding out a plate of cupcakes to me. I caught their aroma under the fire smoke and inhaled deeply. They smelled delicious.

"Want one?" she asked with a grin.

I nodded gratefully, suddenly aware of how starving I was. "They look good. Thanks."

I was halfway through the cake when something strange occurred to me. I stopped mid-chew, glancing down at her again.

She was watching me with a contented expression. That wasn't what stopped me in my tracks, though.

It was her eyes.

They were clear and bright, a perfectly pleasant green color. They reflected the firelight...

And that was it.

There was no unearthly tinge of silver around her pupils, no predator's glow. Nothing about her marked her as a wolf. She didn't have the sharp jawline, the arrogant tilt of the head. All the little tells that were easy to read, if you knew what to look for.

She's not a shifter.

The realization was like a shot through the chest. I felt my heart clench and then thud extra-loud, and something dangerously close to hope flooded my system.

She's human. As human as Tammy. And she seems to live here, with the pack.

"Can I help you?" she asked cheerily. She looked amused by my fairly obvious reaction, but not offended.

"Sorry, ma'am," I murmured, polishing off the rest of the cupcake and brushing the crumbs off my hands. "I'm Jason."

I extended a hand, and she took it. I wanted to apologize again for my rudeness. I was totally flabbergasted by the presence of a human right in the middle of a wolf shifter pack. In spite of recent events, I couldn't get it to make sense in my mind. It was like a hen co-habiting with a den of foxes.

"Cecily," she offered. She was assessing me with a sharp, perceptive gaze. "And what are you doing all the way out here, Jason?"

"I'm escorting my Alpha," I said. I turned to try and catch sight of Allara in the crowd, but she was nowhere to be seen. "I can't say I'm doing a great job of it, though. I seem to have lost her."

I turned back to her with a rueful grin, and she laughed, tipping her head back. "Yes, I can see why they like you."

I'd lost the thread of the conversation somehow. This human was running rings around me, while I blundered in the dark.

They keep doing that, don't they?

I shook off that critical inner voice and refocused my attention. "Who?"

"Reid and Allara, of course." Her eyes twinkled up at me. "You have a good heart. I can tell these things."

I couldn't help but feel charmed by the lady. Other than the human thing, in many ways she really reminded me of my mom.

For many years now, it had just been Kara and me. I'd forgotten what it was like to have someone reassure me, even in such a basic way.

"Can I ask you something?" I queried. The fire in front of us flared, golden sparks flying up into the darkened skies above.

"Ask away, dear."

"You're... human." My voice trailed off, into the night air between us.

"That isn't a question." She leveled a glance at me, her expression warm. "But, yes, I am." She folded her hands and stared into the flames. "The Alpha of this pack, Embry, is my mate."

My eyebrows flew into my hairline. I didn't bother trying to hide my astonishment. An *Alpha* mated with a human? I had never heard of such a thing.

Does that mean what I think it means?

"We met by accident," Cecily explained, in her soft, lilting voice. "Bumped into each other outside a train station. At first, I thought he was crazy. He kept telling me I *had* to come with him, that it was important. I almost turned tail then and there. But..." She spread out her hands, shrugging. "There was something about him. I just couldn't get him out of my head, no matter how hard I tried."

"You're bonded to him?"

She nodded. "Our children are shifters, like him. I like to think they got some of their better traits from me, though." She twinkled at me again. "When they've got themselves filthy from playing outside, they're *his* kids."

A booming voice sounded from somewhere behind us. "She's right. Their better traits are definitely from their mom."

I jumped to my feet, turning as I did. Embry, the Alpha, pressed a kiss to the top of his mate's head and gave me a short nod. I touched my hand to my chest in a sign of deference.

"Embry, meet Jason." Cecily stood up, sliding her small arm around his waist. Even standing, she didn't quite reach his shoulder. "I was telling him about the day you and I met."

The Alpha's face turned soft and fond, a surprising expression on such a big, stoic man. "I guess it was a little unusual."

"It's clearly worked out for you, though," I pointed out. They both chuckled.

"It has had its ups and downs." Cecily tilted her head, resting it against Embry's upper arm. "But so does every relationship. He's a shifter, I'm a human... but we're right for each other. And at the end of the day, *that's* what matters. All the other stuff? It's just window dressing."

I couldn't argue with that, especially when I saw the expression in Embry's eyes as he stared down at Cecily. I had rarely seen two people more clearly in love with each other than these two.

Allara wandered over, a drink in her hand. When I made eye contact with her, the corners of her mouth lifted in what looked like a satisfied smirk.

Something hit me out of nowhere. It was totally obvious in hindsight. I couldn't believe that it had taken me so long to see it.

This is a set-up!

Allara had brought me here for one reason, to meet Embry and Cecily. She didn't need my protection. She'd wanted me to see that the situation I was in, that seemed so impossible to reconcile, could work out just fine, if only I would let it.

It was possible for a human to live in the middle of a wolf pack.

Not just live, but *thrive*. Have children, raise them in safety, and become a valued and loved member of the community in her own right.

I couldn't believe Allara had tricked me like this. She'd used my loyalty to her advantage, and I'd walked right into it.

Still, I couldn't bring myself to be mad at her. She had obviously done it with Tammy's and my best interests at heart. And I knew as well as she did, that if she'd been upfront with me, I would never have come. I'd been shut up in my house for weeks now, wallowing in my own self-pity.

Hope began to stir somewhere inside. Seeing Cecily and Embry's successful relationship firsthand changed things. If they could do it...

Why not Tammy and me?

Even *thinking* her name struck a chord of loss somewhere deep inside me. I knew I had to see her again, touch her. Make her mine in every way possible. Prove to her that she was the one I wanted, now and forever, and that I could make her happy, if she'd let me.

I didn't care that she was a human. It had never bothered me, except insofar as it had made her feel like she didn't belong.

All those worries at the start about her not fitting in, not finding her place with us, had turned out to be totally *wrong*. She did belong with us and, looking back, I knew she had been happy living in the village.

Why did I let her go so easily? Why had I not tried to convince her to stay?

It was me who had been too much of a coward to let her in fully, to let her know, truly, how I felt about her.

There had to be a chance that she still felt something for me.

I wasn't done fighting. For her. For *us*.

For the life we could have together.

And if she wanted to stay in the city, then I would stay there, too. *She* was my destiny; my future. I didn't care where we ended up; I just knew I needed her by my side again.

I felt a fire kindling inside me. It wasn't over. Not yet.

I knew exactly what I had to do.

TAMMY

The day had started like every other.

Just another morning, adding to the countless mornings I had woken up since I'd left Jason. Ordinary hours passing by in my ordinary life.

As usual, I got up, ate breakfast, and got dressed in my new tailored jacket and trousers. I waved goodbye to Leah and headed out the door before eight. I liked to arrive a little early to give myself a chance to prepare for the rigors of the day ahead.

I'd been accepted into my post-graduate course and was working part time around my studies, at the local social worker's office. Just answering the phones and making appointments, but I loved the people. And it was great experience for when I graduated.

I was right where I wanted to be.

So why do I feel like a zombie?

Images of the future crept into my brain without warning. I could see the next five to ten years mapped out in front of me with startling clarity.

My baby would arrive in the late summer. I pictured the makeshift nursery, the sleepless nights. Finding a kindergarten, reading school reports, swimming lessons, pushing a tiny bike down a long drive. Watching him or her blow out a cake with two candles on it, then three, then four.

As I drove to work, I pictured breaking the news to Jason.

I couldn't even imagine it. That small town in the woods felt so far away, almost like it didn't exist at all.

The pain of those memories flared up, sharp and hot, but I suppressed them as best I could.

My child wouldn't grow up with a father who had one foot permanently out the door. That much, at least, I could guarantee. My baby would be surrounded by adults who provided unconditional love and support. People whose loyalties weren't divided between their pack and their loved ones.

I wasn't going to compromise any more. I wanted someone who would fight for me. Love *me* as fiercely as I loved the child growing inside me. And I wouldn't settle for anything less.

I would choose my own path from now on, and count my friends among those who were there for me when I needed them most.

I pulled up in the parking lot of the office building where my reception job was based. I could see the first clients through the window already. A family of two, mother and daughter.

I got out of the car and walked inside.

"Hey, Julie!" I smiled at the tiny girl with pigtails and she lit up when she saw me, bouncing up and down in her plastic seat. "How are you today?"

Julie's mom, Rosa, put an arm around her daughter and squeezed her shoulders. "She's a bundle of energy, I'm sorry." She threw me a chagrined smile.

"Oh, please don't apologize," I shook my head fervently. "I love it! I wish I were that much of a morning person."

I wasn't lying. I *did* love my work, and seeing children like Julie.

But it wasn't the life-defining passion I had once thought it would be. It was... perfectly fine.

And that's good, right? That's more than most people get. You should be grateful.

I turned away from them, toward the check-in desk. I fished my lanyard out of my bag and slid it around my neck, then almost slammed right into the guy waiting up ahead of me.

I put my hands out, prepared to launch into a volley of apologies. "I'm *so* sorry, I didn't see..."

My words died in my throat when the man turned and I got a good look at him.

It was Jason.

His hair and beard had grown out a little in the weeks we had been apart, and he looked weather-beaten, like he'd been spending even more time outside than usual. But other than that, he was just as I remembered. Well-worn jeans, sturdy boots, and a plaid shirt. A world away from the office environment we stood in. I ran a hand over the edge of my neatly pressed blouse, suddenly self-conscious.

The other receptionist, Stacy, poked her head out from behind him and caught my eye. "Tammy, do you know this guy? He came in a couple minutes ago, saying you guys know each other." She glanced at him and then mouthed, "Do you want me to call security?"

"It's fine, Stacy." I took a deep breath. My eyes returned to Jason's piercing gaze. Those eyes—both hazel and silver versions—had haunted my dreams. Right now, they were like a dagger through the heart. "He's..."

I paused, unsure of how to finish. *A friend? Ex-boyfriend? My soulmate?*

"I know him," I said eventually. "It's okay."

Hearing the weight in my words, Stacy tilted her head to the side then she shrugged. "You're in early, anyway. Take your time."

Maybe I could use the staff room to chat with him for a minute.

My brain scrambled through possible explanations for what he was doing here; what he could want.

Answers? Gas money? A map? He was here in the middle of the city. Maybe he was lost.

He probably wants his shirt back. You know, the one you keep under your pillow at night.

I fought down the blush that threatened to rise in my cheeks and tried to get a handle on the situation. The sheer fact of his presence here was enough to send me reeling.

This was my world. The human world.

He looked as out of place here as I was deep in the forest among the wolf pack.

You didn't feel out of place there, a traitorous voice reminded me. *You felt like you'd come home.*

Despite his obvious discomfort, he looked me straight in the eye. There was nothing cocky or overconfident in his demeanor. The snarky guy I had first met back at the bonding ceremony had vanished. He looked calm, steady. In spite of the circumstances, there was an openness in his expression I hadn't seen before.

"Stacy, is it okay if I use the staff room to chat with Jason for a minute?"

The other receptionist nodded, indicating to the files in front of her. "Yeah, of course. I've got this."

"This way," I said, pointing down the corridor that led to the staff room. I didn't bother asking him anything. Out here, it felt too public. There were too many curious eyes and ears.

Silently, he followed me. He kept a respectful distance between us, but I still fancied I could feel his warmth radiating against my back the whole way down the hall.

I opened the door and told him to take a seat on the sofa next to the fridge. I internally debated taking a seat behind at the table. It felt too formal, too defensive. In the end, I perched awkwardly on the edge of the dining table, pushing aside some files as I did so.

"You've cut your hair," Jason said.

His voice was decidedly neutral. I couldn't get a read on his intentions at all.

Does he like it? Is he happy to see me? Sad? Bored?

I decided to ask the obvious question. "What are you doing here?"

He looked down at his hands, turning them over, like he was trying to find the answers in his palms. I ached, wanting nothing more than to slide off the desk and take those big hands in mine and hold them close, feel his fingers cradle my face like they had done so easily, so instinctively, not so long ago.

Finally, he looked up. "I needed to see you."

I fought back the emotions that welled up inside me. Even his mere presence was enough to quiet the panicked voice buried deep inside my chest, that emptiness that had me lying awake at night, wondering if he was okay.

"Tammy," he spoke again, and my attention returned to the present moment. "I wanted to give you space. I tried to stay away from you. I thought if we went back to our separate lives, maybe this feeling would fade over time." He drew a deep breath. "I'm not strong enough to stay away from you anymore."

I froze.

Whatever I had been expecting to come out of his mouth, it wasn't *that.*

"What are you saying?" I whispered.

He leaned forward on the couch, forcing me to meet his gaze. Even though I was the one in the dominant position, I felt cornered. I crossed one leg over the other, trying to exude a control over the situation that I didn't feel.

"I'm saying that being apart from you isn't an option for me." His voice rumbled out of his chest and I shivered. "I can't do it. So, either you're gonna have to force me out of here right now, or we work this thing out."

I gaped at him. All my careful plans for the coming years were crumbling before my eyes. I hadn't factored Jason into the equation.

Then again, Jason had never failed to surprise me in the past.

It's one of the things I love about him.

I turned the thought over in my head and realized that it was true. Terrifying, *impossible,* but true. I loved him, completely and utterly.

In some ways, I still barely knew him, but it didn't matter. I *loved* him.

Unbidden, my hand slid over my belly. Jason's eyes tracked the movement without comprehension.

"What did you have in mind?" I asked in a small voice. "My work... my *life*... it's here, Jason. I'm *happy.*"

His eyebrows drew together and his head fell forward, his curls tumbling. It was such a familiar sight. One that I'd missed so much.

"Okay," he said. "Then I'll come to you, Tammy. I'll pack up and move to the city for you. I don't care where I live, I just want us to be together."

I thought about the wolf shifters. Each pack was different, but I remembered Allara telling me that forest dwellers particularly struggled in urban centers. The noise, all the bright lights... it drove their elevated senses haywire.

"You would do that?" I asked. "For me?"

I was struggling to raise my voice any louder than a whisper. I worried that if I spoke at full volume, I would break the spell and this fragile thing between us would snap like a matchstick.

"Anything, Tammy." Jason reached out and put his hands over mine. When I didn't resist, he tugged one of them toward him, tangling our fingers together. Warmth flooded through me, and the emptiness I'd carried for so long dissipated. "I'd do anything, go anywhere. I don't care, as long as I'm with you."

I thought of all the careful plans I'd made, the life I'd laid out for myself in his absence.

I pictured the forest, which stretched out in my mind's eye. Mysterious, endless, full of promise and adventure.

Home.

"What about the pack?" I asked. Part of me still wanted to test him. We had been away from each other so long. Whatever he felt for me, I knew his loyalties would always lie with them.

His expression shadowed. "It will be... difficult," he conceded. "I want you to come back with me, Tammy. But I know that's not what you want."

I swallowed, watching him rise from the couch completely and erase the space between us. His hands slid either side of me, resting on the table. I looked up at him, his proximity making me dizzy.

"I..." I trailed off. "I don't know what to say."

"I know you didn't ask for this." He flung out a hand, indicating between us. "Me coming into your life, our bond. Any of it. But I can't keep pretending any more. I'm done. I can't hide the way I feel."

I leaned into his heat, unbidden. It had been only about six weeks, but it felt like forever. He was intoxicating. Suddenly, I couldn't fight against it any longer. I was tired of pretending I didn't care. "Then don't," I whispered. "I'm right here, Jason."

His hands came up to brush the hair out of my face. One of his thumbs traced down the soft part of my jawline, ghosting around the outer corners of my mouth.

"Tammy." His gaze was serious, his eyes scorching. "I love you."

His mouth met mine, searching at first. It wasn't enough. My fingers grasped the collar of his shirt and dragged him closer, and the kiss rapidly deepened into something heated and desperate.

I broke away with a gasp, leaning my forehead against his. "I love you too." I giggled, light-headed and giddy. I was floating. "I'll... I'll come back, Jason. You don't have to choose."

Jason *loved* me.

He loved me so much he was willing to give up everything he'd ever known in order for us to be together. To leap into the unknown, to build a new life for himself. For *us*.

Suddenly, every reason I had for leaving the pack seemed tiny and insignificant. All of Naomi's words, so spiteful and vicious in my memory, faded away. They couldn't hurt me anymore. They didn't matter.

Because, to Jason, I wasn't some low-grade amusement. I wasn't a fling that he had bedded and abandoned when he grew bored of me.

As it turned out, he couldn't live life without me. And I felt exactly the same way.

"You'll come back?" he asked. His voice was full of wonder. His arms drew around me, pulling me up off the desk and into a tight hug. He lifted me up off my feet a little, and I squealed. "You'll come home?"

"Yes!" I kissed him again, reveling in the luxury of it. I *could* kiss him again, touch him. I could do anything.

We could do anything.

"What about all this?" His eyes flickered around my office, taking it all in. "I thought this was your dream."

"I thought so too," I shrugged. "But the truth is, I think I've been pretending. I've been pretending that all my plans would work out exactly the way I expected them to. Pretending that I would be better off without you in my life." I drew him closer. We stood there, holding each other, for a long moment.

"I'm not okay without you," I admitted huskily.

Jason paused, and then let out a chuckle. "I guess I didn't see you coming. You took me by surprise."

"You threw a monkey wrench into my plans, too." I smiled. "Guess you can't argue with destiny."

He drew back just enough to look me in the eye. His gaze had turned serious again, roaming over every inch of my face. "It's not because of fate, or prophecy. I'm *choosing* you, Tammy. I'm choosing you for *you*."

In all my life I'd never heard anyone say those words to me. I could feel myself let go, surrender to the reality of loving him, and for once it didn't terrify me.

It was time to trust him now, with everything.

～

It was surprisingly short work to pack up the life I'd built for myself over the past six weeks in the city.

Jason and I ended up staying for the week with Leah. I had to tie up loose ends with work; and organize to defer my studies for a year.

The other stuff—the people I would be leaving behind—that was much harder.

I said my goodbyes to Leah and Penny, who both hugged me tightly and made me promise to keep in touch. From the way they behaved, you would think I was disappearing into the forest, never to be seen again. I assured them I wouldn't be a stranger, struggling to make my point while balancing the stack of boxes I carried in my arms.

Penny placed my favorite cherry pie on top of the pile, which made the whole thing severely unstable. Luckily, Jason swooped in before I dropped the load and took everything out of my hands. He paid particular interest to the pie on his way to the truck, and out of the corner of my eye I caught Penny batting his hands away from it before he could dig into the thing himself.

The sight made me chuckle. I had a healthy appetite myself, but the wolf shifters were on a *whole* other level.

Leah drew me aside in the midst of the chaos. Her kind eyes betrayed a quiet concern. I knew she was happy for me, but I couldn't help but feel bereft, leaving her like this.

She had taken me in when I had nothing, no one. I pulled her into a hug and murmured my thanks against her shoulder. She stroked my hair, just the way I remembered Mom used to.

"Are you going to tell him?" she whispered, quietly enough so that only the two of us could hear.

I nodded. *Yes.*

I had to, and sooner rather than later. It wouldn't be long now before the physical evidence would be impossible to hide.

Leah caught my eye, and I could sense that she wanted to say more. Advice, maybe. Or a word of warning for the dangerous new world I was about to enter?

Before she could, however, Penny launched herself at me. I giggled, catching her before she could bowl us both over.

"I'm coming to visit you guys." She grinned toothily. "As soon as—" Cutting herself off, she glanced around. Jason was busy strapping my luggage down on the roof of the truck, none the wiser. *"You know what,"* she finished in a stage whisper, pointing at my stomach.

"Sooner, I hope." My smile for Penny was broad and genuine. She had become a good friend to me, and I would miss her.

"Don't keep *all of them* to yourself." Penny reached out and squeezed the bicep of an alarmed-looking Jason before bursting into laughter. "You and Allara better not forget about me, that's all I'm saying."

I shook my head, unable to stop myself giggling. Her laughter was infectious. "We could never forget about you, Penny."

After that, there was nothing more to do. No more goodbyes to be said, no more suitcases to be packed. We were waved off from the sidewalk, and in the rearview mirror I watched my friends grow smaller and smaller before they vanished from view completely.

"You okay?" Jason glanced over at me. One of his hands left the steering wheel, coming to rest in the space between us, palm upwards.

I slid my hand into his and squeezed it in response. "Yeah. I'm more than okay."

I was finally, truly, happy.

～

Jason

After spending a week in the city, my offer to move there permanently began to seem more and more crazy.

A week was more than enough. The noise of the traffic, the bright neon signs, the humans and all their chaos...

I didn't know how Allara had coped for so long.

I couldn't help but be relieved that Tammy was returning to the pack with me after all. The fact that she actually seemed *excited* about it made me happier than I had any right to be.

We said goodbye to her human friends and hit the road, settling into a companionable silence that I had missed. It was the simple things that made me feel so good. My hand in hers, the open road ahead of us, and her presence by my side.

Sure, we may have problems along the way, but Cecily's voice rang in my ears. *It's all just window dressing.*

As we left the city behind us, Tammy turned to me. The expression on her face was radiant, but there was a touch of nervousness in her eyes. She looked like she was hanging onto the edge of something and she was suddenly unsure of how to let go.

"What's the matter?" I murmured, bringing her hand up and pressing a kiss against her skin.

The sunset glowed ahead of us, lighting up the landscape with golden rays. The forest looked beautiful, like it had caught fire.

"Nothing," she said. "Um, can you pull over for a minute? I have something to tell you."

My heart stuttered. She hadn't changed her mind, had she? My heart couldn't bear it. Quickly, I pulled in to the verge and turned to her. "Tell me."

She smiled at me with those gorgeous, shining eyes. "It's all good. At least, I think it is." Her smile turned shy. "I'm pregnant, Jason. We're going to have a baby."

A wave of shock hit me, followed by a pure wave of elation that made me grip the steering wheel tightly. Thank God she got me to pull over. I might have crashed the truck, otherwise. "That's... that's..."

I couldn't speak, but I shot her a huge grin, hoping it conveyed my joy.

"I know, Jason." Her hand came up, gently curving against my cheek. I focused on the gentleness of her touch, letting it soothe the pounding of my heart. "I love you."

"I love you more," I murmured. I wanted to kiss her properly. Tangle my fingers in her beautiful auburn hair and make her swoon, but this spot on the side of the highway wasn't the best place to express how I felt. I settled for turning my head and kissing her palm. "That is the best news I have ever heard, Tammy."

"You're happy?" she asked, her eyebrows flickering up as though she was still a little unsure.

I laughed. "I wish I could show you just how happy... but I think that will have to wait until I get you home and into our bed."

Tammy laughed happily and settled back into her seat, one hand spread over her still flat stomach.

I covered her hand with mine and left it there for several seconds, imagining what our child might look like when it arrived. Boy, or girl? I didn't care. I just knew I would love it as much as I loved Tammy.

I finally tore my gaze away from my beautiful mate and started the car once again. We had a long journey ahead of us, after all.

Tammy. Me. The baby. But we would make it. Together.

We were going home.

THE END

PACK LOYALTY
3
DESTINY OF THE WOLF
USA TODAY BEST-SELLING AUTHOR
AMELIA SHAW

DESTINY OF THE WOLF

KARA

I was on edge today. Not for any reason I could put my finger on. The atmosphere around me, inside me, just felt tense, like the air before a storm.

Across from me, on the other side of the lawn, the pack Alpha, Allara, sat with her feet up, watching over the children running about. Although her body language was lazy, I could tell that she was on alert in the way that Alphas always were, scanning for threats over at the tree line and ensuring the safety of pack members, even while appearing relaxed.

Not that she could spring into action right now, though, even if something did turn up to threaten us. Not in her condition. The sundress she wore couldn't hide her large, round belly. She chewed her bottom lip, deep in thought over something.

Reid, her mate, crossed the lawn to join her, carrying two large glasses of lemonade. Allara accepted one, smiling up at him with a softness she reserved only for him. He bent his head to press a kiss to her lips. His fingers were gentle as they slid through her hair. The way he treated her—as if she were made of glass and the most precious thing on earth—was surprising for such a big man.

Bitterness spiked through my chest and it only took me a second to realize what the feeling was.

Envy.

As Reid and Allara got to talking, I bent my head back over my needlework and tried to shake away the feeling.

Those two had always known they were fated to be together. Ever since we were kids. Back then it had made us all laugh, the way they were with each other.

Not now. Now, it made us all yearn for something similar to what they had.

Unlike Allara and Reid, though, I'd never had even an inkling of that feeling toward anyone in the pack. I'd never experienced the pull they all talked about. That unshakable certainty that *this* shifter was the one for me.

So, I kept to myself. The other members of the pack didn't bother with me, which suited me just fine. It ran both ways; most of the time, I was happy enough in my own company.

Since my brother Jason had found his mate Tammy, I'd withdrawn even more. It wasn't anyone's fault I didn't feel right in company anymore. Besides, it meant I had more time to work on my art. I should be happy about that.

I smoothed a hand over the pattern I was working on: dozens of trees embroidered in shades of green. The forest scene would eventually become part of a quilt for Allara's baby. The room they had planned for him, or her, was spectacular.

Yeah. I have all I need, right here.

Allara and Reid were still deep in conversation. Even from this distance, I could see they were arguing about something. Allara's brow creased. It was an expression I knew well.

She doesn't want to hear whatever he's saying, but she knows he's right.

Sure enough, a few moments later, Allara threw up her hands.

Fine, fine.

Reid sat back, satisfied, and I smothered a laugh. Allara wasn't one to lose a fight and she wouldn't take it well. Reid brushed his hand against hers, and she relented, tangling their fingers together. Like all their disagreements, it was over before it had really started.

I shook my head and returned to my embroidery.

Kids on the lawn played under the watchful eye of half a dozen shifters. Beyond the grass, a group of pack members emerged from the trees carrying a deer between them. No one would go hungry tonight.

At the other end of the village, the vegetable garden was blooming; come Fall, we would be laden with fresh fruit and vegetables.

Everything was exactly as it should be. And yet, there was something I couldn't put my finger on... Why did I feel so unsettled?

Is it my imagination, or can I smell a storm on the horizon?

It was late evening by the time Allara and I were alone and we could catch up properly. We sat on her porch together drinking iced tea and listening to the cicadas flitting in and out of the grass around the house.

Allara had one hand on her belly, and the other absently stirred her drink.

"It's any day now, Kara." She patted her stomach and grinned. "Ugh, I'm so *done* being pregnant."

I chuckled as I remembered how Tammy had gotten in the weeks leading up to her due date. Jason had been almost as bad as his partner, fussing over Tammy and the imminent event as if everything else in the world had come to a stop. Which I guess, for my brother and his mate, it had.

Setting foot in that house was like waiting for a bomb to go off toward the end. By the time baby Mae finally arrived, we were all at our wits' end, only to be greeted with the most placid, easy-going kid ever.

Not for the first time, I wondered what Reid and Allara's baby would be like. I took a sip of tea, hiding a little grin. Whether male or female, the coming bub was bound to be a leader of some kind. "How's Reid holding up?"

Allara shrugged. A smile played about the corners of her mouth. "Put it this way, I'm gonna miss having him wait on me hand and foot. Though it has started to get a little ridiculous—he carried me into the *bath* yesterday. Like, actually ran me a bath and *put* me in it."

We both laughed aloud this time. How well Reid treated his mate came as no surprise to me. Few men looked at a woman the way Reid looked at Allara.

Her smile slowly faded, and her eyebrows pinched together. "Honestly, I'm frustrated. Until this baby is born, I'm stranded here. It makes my business as Alpha kind of limiting."

"Yeah." I put a comforting hand on her arm. "I can imagine."

It wasn't a situation an Alpha typically found themselves in, especially since most wolf shifter Alphas were male. As much as Allara had flourished in her role as pack leader, she now had a new priority: motherhood.

"I'm gonna confess something..." Allara turned to me, setting her drink down on a table next to her.

Her expression was serious, so I mirrored her posture.

"This isn't purely a social visit. I need to ask you a favour."

"Oh?"

Allara and I had been best friends since we were kids. We'd reconnected almost immediately after she'd returned to the pack, picking up right where we left off. The fact she was now my Alpha hadn't changed that relationship between us. There was little I would refuse her.

"I've been in contact with Elder Frey, from the Thornwood Clan. He's been keeping things running round those parts, ever since..." Allara's face twisted with discomfort. "Well, you know."

Right. Their Alpha's passing.

I'd never met the Thornwood Alpha face to face, but over the years he'd nurtured an alliance with Allara's father. News of his sudden, recent death had spread like wildfire to every shifter pack in the state.

Shifter packs fiercely guarded their secrets, especially upon the death of an Alpha. The risk for any pack was greatest just after an Alpha passed, and before the new leader was chosen. But the Thornwoods had been in open disarray for months now.

"They haven't chosen a new leader yet?" I couldn't keep the shock out of my voice. I'd never heard of such a thing—a pack running wild for so long with no sworn Alpha. How had they survived a takeover bid?

Allara's face darkened. "Oh, they had chosen one. The Thornwood Alpha's son was all set to inherit, but for some reason, on the day he was set to be sworn in, he took off."

"He... what?"

"He ran off somewhere." Allara looked *pissed*, and I sensed it wasn't a good idea to point out right this minute that *she* hadn't embraced the role of Alpha with open arms at first, either. Instead, I tried to keep my face totally blank of emotion.

"The truth is," Allara continued, hefting herself back in her chair with a heavy sigh, "I'm worried. Jaime's still out there, and the Thornwood pack—the one closest to our borders—currently has no Alpha. Honestly, I don't know what Jaime's capable of. If he stepped in and took over..."

I caught a flicker of real fear in her expression.

I shared her fear. Jaime was unstable and if he stirred up trouble with our nearest neighbor, that trouble could spill over to us. I stared out at the clearing in front of us. Earlier that day, it had been full of kids playing chase, giggling and play-fighting with each other.

The thick line of trees at the edge of the grass seemed darker than usual, full of shadows. I knew it was simply my mind playing tricks, but it felt like danger could be lurking around every tree trunk or branch.

I shook the thought away.

"So, what does this have to do with me?" I asked.

"Reid is going to meet with the Thornwood Clan," Allara said. "Normally, I'd go with him, but I don't feel strong enough at the moment. I want you to go in my place."

I stared at her, shocked. *"What?* Why me?"

"Because I trust you," Allara said simply. "And I don't say that about many people. I need people I can trust right now. Your brother and Tammy are busy with Mae, and besides, you were my first choice."

She smiled and squeezed my hand.

"But..." I fumbled. "I don't know anything about politics!"

It might have sounded like a feeble excuse, but it was true.

I wasn't like Allara—bold, confident and strong. She'd left our village without a backward glance and lived for years in a strange city before returning to take up the role of pack leader. She was born for it. I'd always been content to spend my days here with my weaving and craftwork, making beautiful things for my community.

I couldn't just step into her role next to Reid and do the job well. I didn't believe in myself that much, and I was positive no one else would, either. There was no way I could do it.

"Kara." Allara caught my eye and held it in that instinctive, unyielding way that only an Alpha could. Damn. When she pinned me with *that* look, I knew I wouldn't be able to refuse. "Look at me," she insisted. "I *know* you can do this. I wouldn't have asked you otherwise."

I opened my mouth and closed it a few times, discarding excuses that I knew she'd throw aside as soon as I uttered them out loud.

What if I messed up? One wrong move could wreck whatever alliance Allara wanted to build and make things worse for *both* clans.

But the look on her face told me that I couldn't argue. Allara had already made up her mind. More than that, I could hardly disobey a direct order from my Alpha.

"Fine. When do we leave?" I mumbled.

Allara brightened immediately. She sat back in her chair, looking like a weight had been taken off her shoulders.

At least she's confident. That makes one of us.

"Tomorrow."

So soon? I almost squeaked. Allara caught my expression anyway and draped an arm around my shoulders, squeezing tight.

"You'll be perfect, Kara." A soft smile played around the corners of her mouth. "You'll see."

～

IT WAS STILL dark outside when my alarm started blaring, far louder than I expected it to be.

With a groan, I gave it a couple of smacks to turn it off. I rolled over, every muscle in my body tensed, and listened with bated breath for the sound of a baby crying. Had my alarm woken Mae?

There was nothing but silence from the rest of the house. I let out a long sigh of relief and allowed myself to relax into my pillows.

Tammy would never forgive me if I woke Mae up with my stupid alarm.

On the chair beneath the window, the bag I'd packed yesterday lay in wait. I glowered at it, but it didn't burst into flames. It remained exactly where it was, mocking me. Ready to leave.

With a heavy sigh, I knew I couldn't delay any longer. I clambered out of bed and threw on my clothes. I was meeting Reid outside in half an hour. I had just enough time to eat some toast and brush my teeth before he'd be here.

There was no point waking Jason and Tammy. I'd said my goodbyes to them yesterday, and with Mae well and truly making her beautiful presence felt, like all babies do, the sleep-deprived parents needed as much rest as they could get.

Tammy had hugged me tearfully and asked when we were coming

back. She didn't need a shifter's advanced senses to pick up on the tense atmosphere. Jason had not said anything, but his body language when he moved in for a hug and the way he'd squeezed me so hard my feet lifted off the floor, told me how worried he was about me going on this mission for Allara. Jason was more than a big brother to me. Since Mom and Dad had died, we were all the family we had left.

Once I had my bag on my shoulder, I glanced out the window and into the dark street. I could see Reid heading toward our house in the dim light cast by the street lamps. Tension was written across the broad line of his shoulders.

I didn't blame him. My own shoulders were tight with apprehension. I knew this mission wasn't his first choice, either. He'd much rather be with Allara and his unborn child right now. Like any expectant dad, he wanted to be around just in case Allara went in labor earlier than expected.

Sometimes pack duty has to come first.

I tip-toed down the stairs and shut the front door behind me as quietly as I could. Reid nodded as I came down the front steps of the house and gestured for me to follow him.

"Morning Kara. C'mon." He hitched up his own bag on his shoulder as I fell into step beside him. "Truck's all packed and ready to go."

I stowed my bag in the bed of his truck and climbed into the passenger seat, trying not to feel awkward. It wasn't often that Reid and I were in each other's presence without Allara. I was hoping we'd find things to talk about along the way, and not spend the whole trip in quiet discomfort.

If he sensed any of my awkward feelings, he didn't show it. He looked a million miles away as he turned the key in the ignition and we headed down the road that led out of the village. There were dark circles under his eyes, like he hadn't slept in a month.

He glanced at me properly once we were on the main road. "All good?"

I nodded. "Sure." I must have sounded unconvincing, because he grinned briefly.

"We'll be back before you know it, Kara. All will be well."

Judging from his expression, I could tell he wanted to believe that just as much as I did. This trip was the last thing either of us wanted to be doing right now. But orders were orders, whether you were the Alpha's friend, or their mate.

The trees rushed past as we drove. The sun began to rise, and golden light dappled the hood of the car. I tilted my head up, looking through the sunroof at the crows circling high overhead.

"What are they like?" I eventually asked, breaking the comfortable silence.

"Who? The crows?" He followed my gaze upward, then concentrated back on the road again.

I rolled my eyes and looked directly at him. "No. The Thornwood Clan, of course."

Reid drummed his fingers against the steering wheel. "Oh, ya know."

"No, I *don't*." I frowned out at the road ahead. "It's a genuine question, Reid. I've never even been to the other side of the creek."

Reid's brows shot up. "I didn't realize."

I could see he was turning my question over in his mind, trying to find the right words. "They're... secretive," he said eventually. "They keep to themselves, you know? The same as any shifter pack."

Huh. That wasn't much to go on.

We fell into silence for a few more miles until eventually, Reid spoke up again.

"You know Naomi, right? She's one of the Thornwood Clan. Or she used to be, anyway." He shrugged. "Who knows where she's at, these days."

I wrinkled my nose. Of course, I knew Naomi, and I have to admit, I really did not like her. My brother's on-again, off-again ex. In the old days, she'd stick around just long enough to mark her territory and get Jason hooked on her before prancing off again. She reminded me of a poisonous flower: lovely to look at, but you didn't want to get too close.

When Tammy had entered the picture, I wasn't the only one in our clan to breathe a sigh of relief. Naomi had scampered away once she realized Jason wasn't coming back to her. I didn't know where she was, now, and frankly, I didn't care, as long as she stayed away from my little family.

Reid caught my scowl and broke into laughter. "Aw, c'mon! You can't judge a whole clan by one wolf, Kara."

I made a noncommittal noise and crossed my arms. "Fine. What about the others? The old Alpha had a son, right? A son who has mysteriously run off somewhere?"

"Uh, yeah." Reid shifted in his seat. "He had two of 'em, actually. I've only met the younger one, though. Kit Thornwood."

"What's he like?" I pressed.

"He's cool."

Ugh. I would get so much more out of Allara.

The clan was secretive, and the younger son of the old Alpha was cool. I couldn't tell if Reid was holding back on me for some reason, or if he genuinely didn't have any other information to share.

I might not have traveled far in my life, but I was still a shifter, and my shifter senses were on high alert. The farther we drove from the village, the edgier I became. The wolf in me was wary as all hell. Every bump in the road made me flinch in my seat.

If I'm heading into an unknown, I'd rather go in with my eyes open.

But I didn't bother trying to pry any further. For whatever reason, Reid clearly had no more information to provide. I would just have to wait and find out for myself when I arrived.

KARA

It was mid-morning by the time the truck rolled to a stop at the edge of the Thornwood settlement. The perimeter was surrounded by a high wall and, as we approached the gates, a couple of figures stationed in a watchtower turned around to look at us, then disappeared from view.

A guarded perimeter, with watchtowers? *That's not creepy at all.*

The gates slowly started to open. Reid tapped the steering wheel a couple of times, then drove forward, toward the small group of shifters clustered around the entrance. He brought the truck to a standstill and glanced at me as he put his hand on the door.

"Wait here, yeah?"

"Sure." I nodded and watched as he climbed out of the car, my heart pounding in my chest. I was perfectly happy for him to take the lead at this point. I had never done anything like this before—visiting as the representative of our Alpha. I hardly even knew how I was supposed to behave.

I sat bolt upright in the passenger seat as a group of shifters approached Reid. They looked like a welcoming party, of sorts, though the expression on their faces was not what I'd call friendly.

Reid reached the group and clasped hands with a couple of the men, exchanging a few words with them. I tried to read their lips, but they were too far away.

Reid's posture was loose and easy. I allowed myself to relax a fraction, taking a deep, calming breath. I would take my cue from him.

They're our allies. They're not gonna hurt us—not without good reason, anyway.

Most of the men in the group peeled away after they'd spoken to Reid, and wandered out of sight. One of them remained. He continued to speak with Reid, his hands waving in the air in an expressive way that looked more human than shifter.

Reid nodded at whatever he was saying, so I took the opportunity to study the other man. His hair was lighter than most of the shifters I knew. Burnished strands caught the light, flashing auburn when he moved into a patch of sunlight shining through the trees. He had a soft, easy smile, and even from this distance, that smile made me want to smile, too.

He clapped Reid on the back before turning away and loping off in the same direction as the others.

Reid jogged back to the truck and slid behind the wheel. He seemed happy enough. "Let's park, and then I'll introduce you to everyone."

Another twinge of nerves shot through my chest as my heart continued to pound like I was running a marathon. I had to let some of my nervous tension go, before I ruined this for Allara.

"Sounds good." I forced a smile as he swung the truck around, and we trundled over to a small patch of grass where several other vehicles were parked.

This time, I was first out of the truck. I pushed the door open as soon as Reid turned off the engine, anxious to stretch and move. The second my feet touched the grass, my wolf wanted to bolt off into the forest.

Don't be stupid. There's nothing to be afraid of. Don't screw this up!

I swallowed the thickness in my throat. Reid came around to my side of the vehicle. He grinned down at me, and I wondered whether he was oblivious to the anxiety thrumming in my chest, or simply ignoring it in the hope I would get myself under control. Knowing Reid, and his heightened senses, it was probably the latter.

"You ready?" he asked.

My stomach churned. Still, I nodded.

"C'mon. Their meeting house is this way."

I followed Reid across a clearing toward a collection of small homes. Other than that first group of men who had assembled to greet Reid, I hadn't seen more than one or two others. Where was everyone? A couple of people passed us as we made our way down what I took to be the main street, but I caught movement at some of the windows. One of the chimneys was belching smoke.

My shifter senses told me that we were being watched and it made the hairs on the back of my neck stand on end. I hadn't expected anything else of course, but it was creepy being here, knowing that there were eyes on us, but not being able to see exactly where they were.

Like us, these people probably weren't used to outsiders, and given the fence and the watchtowers, they seemed even more guarded in this community than our own.

I recognized the meeting house. It was the biggest building in sight, for one thing. Unlike ours, it had a second floor, and the wide porch area underneath the jutting balcony was crowded with what looked like most of the Thornwood pack.

Okay, so that's where everyone is hiding. No wonder the village seems so empty. Looks like all the action is here.

Several heads turned as we approached, eyeing us as we climbed the stairs to the main doors. A couple of women had auburn hair similar to the guy Reid had spoken to. Theirs was brighter, like copper, and braided back into an intricate fishtail pattern.

As we headed inside, everyone moved back, leaving a wide berth around us, before following us inside, albeit at a distance.

I couldn't shake the worry that we were surrounded by people who could turn on us in a heartbeat.

Inside, the meeting house was already half-full of pack members. They were clustered in small groups on several rows of low benches that faced an empty stage, like they were waiting for something to begin.

We were halfway down the central aisle when a man sidled in front of us, blocking us from going any further. I tensed up. Reid put a warning hand on my arm, and I forced myself to relax somewhat, at least on the outside. Nothing I could about the inner nerves, except keep them hidden.

The man held up his hands, catching my expression. "Whoa! Didn't mean to startle you there, missy."

I took a closer look at him. He had a broad, open face, and his hair had that same deep auburn color as many of the others, but his was streaked with gray at the temples, as was his beard.

"Elder Frey." Reid identified the speaker before moving forward, his voice warm as he clasped the other man's hand and forearm. "It's good to see you again."

"And you, my boy." The Elder looked Reid up and down. "Not much of a boy these days, I see! You've grown into a fine man."

Reid chuckled. "Left boyhood behind a while back. It's been a long time, huh?"

"Too long." Elder Frey clapped a hand on one of Reid's shoulders. "I hear congratulations are in order. Allara's expecting, I take it?"

Reid's expression warmed, and his eyes lit up. "Yes. It won't be long now."

"Wonderful news." After another thud of approval on Reid's shoulder, Elder Frey stepped back. "Well, hopefully we can get this business over and done with so you can return to your family."

"That's the plan."

The Elder's gaze traveled over Reid's shoulder and landed on me. "And you must be Kara."

"Yes." I found my voice, glad it didn't come out on a squeak, and raised my chin before extending a hand for him to shake. "I'm—I'm here on our Alpha's behalf."

Elder Frey nodded. "Yes, Allara sent word. Very well. Follow me, you two. Let's go somewhere quiet where we can talk properly."

Reid and I followed the Elder to the back of the room, then through a small door that led up a narrow flight of stairs and into an upper room. Thick, wooden beams supported the high ceiling, and the desk in front of the window was overflowing with papers.

The guy Reid had spoken to earlier—the one with the contagious grin—stood in the middle of the room. He raised a hand in greeting, throwing us a lopsided smile.

Up close, I realized that he was young—in his late teens, by the look of it. His limbs had a coltish, awkward look to them, like he hadn't grown into his frame yet. But I'd been right about his manner. He gave the impression of friendliness rather than hostility, and I relaxed more in his presence.

"Hey." He came bounding up to us. "Kara, right?" He reminded me of Jason, back when we were still growing up and didn't have a care in the world. He shook my hand enthusiastically and I forgot, for just a second, to be afraid at all.

"Yes." I grinned back at him, charmed already.

"Kara," Reid interjected. "This is Kit Thornwood."

The Alpha's youngest son? "Nice to meet you," I said.

So this is the 'cool' younger brother. Where's his older brother, then? The supposed next Alpha?

The rest of the room was empty. There was nowhere for anyone else to hide. And besides, hadn't the other brother run off? He was probably out there lurking in the woods somewhere.

I glanced at Reid, but he wasn't looking in my direction. Instead, he was studying Kit and the Elder.

"Take a seat," Elder Frey said as he sank into a well-worn armchair.

Reid and I sat on the couch opposite it. Kit dragged over the desk chair and sat in it, crossing his ankles and swiveling back and forth in an annoying manner.

"Kit..." The Elder put a foot on the edge of the chair and brought it to a halt. "Stop that."

Kit bit his lip. His eyes darted toward the door, like he expected it to open, but no-one else entered the room.

"Fine." He spread out his hands and turned to Reid. "Where do you wanna begin? Do you want to go first, or shall I?"

Elder Frey coughed, but Reid didn't seem bothered by the informality. If anything, he looked more relaxed by the way this meeting was being handled.

As did I. If this was a pack business meeting, with an Alpha's son swinging on a chair, then surely, I could handle this, too?

I reminded myself that stuffy bureaucracy was never Reid's thing, either. *The guy didn't want to wear a suit to his own wedding, for crying out loud.*

"How about I start?" Reid said.

Kit shrugged. "Works for me."

"Great." Reid's deep voice filled the room. He'd settled into the leadership role with ease, even here, on another pack's land. He was the kind of person who naturally drew a crowd. A born leader, alongside his mate. "As you know, we had some trouble a few months back with one of our pack members, Jaime."

Kit nodded, exchanging glances with Elder Frey before waiting for Reid to continue.

"Jaime was like a son to Allara's dad. After she left, everyone assumed he'd take over as Alpha." Reid paused, his jaw tightening. "When the old Alpha died, he named his daughter as his successor."

I thought back to the day Allara had returned to the village. The five years she'd been gone had melted away almost immediately. She came back almost the same brash, outspoken girl I'd grown up with. Only there were subtle differences, too. Her experiences in the city had matured her into a formidable woman. An Alpha, through and through. We were lucky to have her as our Alpha.

"Allara claimed the position of Alpha by defeating Jaime in combat." A shadow fell over Reid's face. "But she chose not to kill him. Jaime's still out there. That's the reason we're here. Allara wants to strengthen the alliance between the Thornwoods and the Banes before Jaime has the chance to spread his poison any further."

Silence fell over the room. Reid leaned forward, addressing Elder Frey directly. "Tell me, has Jaime made contact with you in any way?"

The Elder shook his head. "No. We keep our borders secure, as you saw on your way in. There's no way he could breach our defenses. Not without us knowing about it."

Don't be so sure about that. You don't know him like we do.

I'd known Jaime my whole life. Like all shifters, he didn't give up easy, and he had a cunning streak a mile wide. Sometimes I used to think he was more snake than wolf.

Reid seemed satisfied, however, as he leaned back against the sofa and turned his attention to Kit. "Why don't you give me an update on your news. What's been going on here that's got everyone so riled up?"

We both knew, of course, about the Thornwood Alpha's death. It was the event that had caused the power vacuum, but it was obvious there was more to the story.

I spoke up then, knowing it would be something Allara wanted said upfront. "Our pack sends its condolences on your father's passing, Kit."

Reid shot me a look laced with approval.

"Thank you." Kit's bright features dimmed a little as he recounted his father's death. I caught a glimpse of the sadness underlying his cheerful personality.

"So, my brother was considering accepting the position of Alpha, and things were all set for him to take over." Kit started jiggling his knee up and down again, but catching a look from Elder Frey, he stopped. "Then on the day of the ceremony, he just... took off. Shifted and disappeared into the forest before anyone could do anything to stop him, or ask what was going on. Nobody's seen him since."

Reid and I exchanged a glance.

"Did he say anything before he left?" I asked.

Kit shook his head. "Nothing. I don't know what happened... and neither does anyone else. But now we don't have an Alpha, and everything's screwed up."

So, it was as bad as Allara had suspected. Not only did the Thornwoods not have an Alpha, but the one who should rightfully inherit the role was AWOL, and the next in line was just a kid.

Kit seemed like a delightful person, but he didn't strike me as someone strong enough to lead a pack. From the look on Reid's face, he shared my thoughts on that, but when he spoke, his tone remained even and calm. He was doing a good job of masking any concern he might be feeling. "Do you know where he might be? Can we assist in searching for him?"

Kit hung his head. "Nah. The truth is, I don't think he wants to be found. And when my brother wants to disappear, it's pointless trying to look for him. He's likely long gone by now."

My heart thumped in my chest. The small office suddenly felt too cluttered, too hot and stuffy.

I stood up and crossed over to the window, cracking it open and inhaling a lungful of fresh air. It was clear and crisp outside, and the deserted village scene served to calm my senses. It would be a while before I adjusted to all the new smells and sounds that this place had to offer, but I wasn't getting any impression of threat. On the contrary, with Elder Frey and Kit temporarily in charge, I felt like we were with allies.

Then my body tensed as something strange prickled at my senses. My attention was drawn to a flicker of movement. It was coming from the edge of the square. The same direction Reid and I had come in from.

My skin crawled with alarm when a huge wolf loped into the clearing. Its long, reddish-brown fur was matted and its paws dirt-crusted. Even from this distance, I could see leaves and mud in its fur. But its movement was confident and sure.

The wolf didn't seem hurt. On the contrary, it was walking like it owned the place. Its head was high, and its strides were long, as if it were familiar with this place and knew exactly where it was headed.

Once the wolf reached the middle of the square, it stopped and gave a full-bodied shake, dislodging most of the leaves and muck. By the look of what fell off it, the beast had dragged half the forest into town on its back.

The wolf lowered its huge head, and the air grew hazy with the tell-tale sign that a shifter was transforming. Once the haze cleared, a man stood in place of the wolf.

He was one of the tallest and most impressively muscled men I'd ever seen. Like Kit, he had burnished auburn hair, although his was longer and darker, partly obscuring his face. His body was strong and well-built. A heated flush rose in my cheeks at his brazenness. The way he stood naked outside the meeting house, totally at ease with his body, did something to my insides.

He shook the hair out of his eyes and looked up. His gaze locked straight onto mine.

The breath left my body when our eyes met. I bit my lip, embarrassed to have been caught spying, but for some reason I couldn't look away. He held my attention like he had every right to it.

Suddenly, I was the one who felt naked.

I'd been so caught up in the arrival of this stranger, I hadn't noticed that the others in the room had moved to the window and were all standing next to me, gazing down at the guy in the town square.

"Who..." My voice sounded husky. I cleared my throat and didn't finish.

It was Kit who eventually answered my unspoken question. "That's Ronan." He said it slowly, like he couldn't believe his eyes. "That's my missing brother."

RONAN

I knew I had to return to town as soon as I saw the truck approach the gates. Elder Frey was too old, and Kit was far too young, to face down any potential threat on their own. I needed to be there to protect them, and not just by keeping watch within the tree line.

From my vantage position in the forest, I was perfectly positioned to watch everyone who came and went, and I had been keeping a close eye on all movement in and out of my pack's village. I knew every vehicle by sight; every dirt bike, every rust-bucket on wheels that my packmates drove.

This truck, carrying strangers, made my internal alarm go berserk.

As they had approached the perimeter wall I padded through the trees, my belly low to the earth. It was easy to track the rumble of their engine along the straight road, and I ducked back into the undergrowth every time I felt too exposed.

I got the sense that they didn't know I was there, following their truck right up to the gate.

I wasn't close enough to see who the visitors were, but something in my stomach twisted with unease. Was this the threat that sought to tear my pack apart?

My hackles rose as the gate opened and the visitors were allowed to pass through without incident. My lips peeled back in a silent growl when a tall man jumped down from the driver's side, striding forward like he owned the place.

That one was an Alpha, for sure.

At the sight of my little brother jogging forward to greet him, I couldn't help the snarl that rumbled through me. My muscles coiled, preparing to spring...

The man got back in his truck and the high gates closed behind them, cutting off my view of what was happening inside the village.

Strange, being on the outside of my own pack like this.

My exile might have been self-imposed, but it wasn't without good reason. No matter who I'd hurt by my decision—my brother, my friends, Jake and Noah, and even Elder Frey—I knew eventually they would understand.

I hadn't left them unprotected, as they all likely thought. I hadn't run off, due to cowardice. Was it time to come forward, out of hiding at last?

I brushed the leaves aside and trotted out into the open, ducking my head to examine the track marks in the dirt.

I sniffed at the air and a barrage of different sensations hit me.

With a deep huff, I forced myself to separate them out, so I could identify them, one by one.

The truck contained only two individuals, by my reckoning. Both shifters, one male and one female.

Mates?

No, they weren't a bonded pair. They were definitely from the same clan, though—and I knew the scent. I'd picked it up from somewhere before.

But which clan? Silverback? Ferrers?

I inhaled again, more deeply this time. *Bane.*

Though unsettling to scent a neighboring pack member or two on our land, it wasn't the smell of the Bane pack that had me on such high alert.

It was the female. I had never smelled anything like her before; she had a sweet, light scent that made my mouth water and my system switch into hyper-alert mode. It was like finding a clear, bubbling stream after crawling through the desert for years.

I wanted to throw back my head and howl into the sky.

With effort, I restrained myself.

I loped back into the trees, horrified at the urges I could barely control. After weeks of carefully evading the attention of the pack, I'd almost blown my cover over some random chick.

Don't think about that. Come on, focus. Why do you know that scent? You've never visited the Bane Clan.

Maybe not, but some of their members had come around these parts in the past. I must have picked the scent up from Kit. He'd run into them once, several years back.

He was always the more sociable one of us.

Fate had some sense of humor, making me the firstborn.

I circled the edge of the village a few times, sticking close to the walls of the perimeter. There was no sign of life from either the forest or the watchtowers that were stationed around the outside of town. Everyone must have gathered in the meeting house.

Trying to decide what to do in my absence, undoubtedly.

A stab of guilt shot through me. It was no use. I couldn't stay away from my destiny. I was the Alpha's firstborn, for better or worse, and I had to go back. I'd always known I would. Otherwise, I would have been halfway to Canada by now.

Instead, I'd stayed close, watchful and aware, in case my pack needed me. And now they did.

I had to set things right, or at least be held accountable for my actions.

With a deep sigh, I turned around, heading back toward the front gates.

~

KARA

I tried to speak, but it was no use. My muscles were all locked up, and the air had deserted my lungs. *What the heck is wrong with me?*

Luckily, Reid broke the silence for all of us.

"Wait, *that's* Ronan Thornwood? The next Alpha of the Thornwood Clan?"

It was clear, judging by the tone of his voice, that he was in just as much shock as I was. However, he didn't seem to have experienced the same intense, dizzying bolt of electricity as me at the very sight of the auburn-haired shifter.

On the contrary, Reid was frowning through the window at the figure making his way up the steps of the meeting house, and he looked confused rather than impressed.

"Where the hell's he been all this time?" Reid's tone was laced with bewilderment.

Kit shrugged, pure joy written across his features. He clearly didn't care whether his brother had been. He was focused only on the face that Ronan had returned. Kit bounded over to the door.

"Come on!" he called, before vanishing through the doorway.

Reid and I glanced back at Elder Frey, who merely threw up his hands in an *I-have-no-idea* kind of way and slumped down on the sofa with a weary expression.

Reid and I headed down the narrow wooden staircase, more slowly than Kit. When we reached the bottom, Kit didn't head into the main room, where the majority of the pack were still waiting for the meeting to start, but slipped out the front door and onto the porch.

Reid looked at me, shrugged, and followed after him.

After a split-second hesitation, with my heart thumping a mile a minute in my chest, I headed through the door, too.

Ronan, the next Alpha of the Thornwood pack, waited for us on the porch.

The air around him had a sharp, earthy smell, like it was going to rain.

I was suddenly aware of every little detail of my surroundings. The uneven floorboards beneath my feet, the weathered siding on the wall, and even the uneven rasping of my own breath in my ears as I came face to face with Ronan.

He was barefoot. Mercifully, he'd pulled on a pair of beat-up looking jeans from God-knows-where. I'm not sure what I would have done if he was still fully naked. Judging by my skittishness, quite possibly turned tail and scurried straight back up to sit on the sofa with Elder Frey. His chest was still bare, though, and he was breathing heavily from the aftermath of shifting. A fine sheen of sweat coated his skin, high-lighting the defined muscle and sinew of his arms.

Damn, he's gorgeous.

His eyes slid from Kit to Reid and then me, and his expression darkened, like clouds drifting to cover the sun. "Who are you?"

His voice was dark and rough, and rippled over me in a strange yet compelling manner. When he spoke, all the hairs on the back of my neck stood on end.

Reid seemed to be affected, too, which made me feel slightly less embarrassed at my reaction. I was used to Alpha's—I was the friend of Allara, for heaven's sake—but this one seemed to leave everyone around him breathless.

Reid visibly took one breath, and then another. It was a familiar trick that shifters often used when they needed to ground themselves in an unfamiliar environment, or deal with someone their inner shifter perceived as a rival.

Ronan had no such compunctions. I caught a flicker in his eyes. His shifter was still close to the surface, waiting and watching.

"Reid, of the Bane clan." Reid held out his hand with a thin smile that held little humor. His eyes never left Ronan's. "And this is Kara. She's standing in for our Alpha—my mate Allara—who couldn't make it here today."

A muscle in Ronan's jaw twitched. He grabbed Reid's forearm, and they shook in the traditional shifter way.

Then Ronan jerked Reid closer, teeth bared. "And *what* are you doing on my pack grounds?"

Reid's lips pulled back into an open snarl. My hands were on his shoulders before I could think, tugging helplessly. He shook me off easily. He wasn't rough—Reid was still in there, after all—but it was clear his shifter was rearing up and angling to be in the driver's seat.

Opposite me, Kit murmured in Ronan's ear, obviously taking the same conciliatory role as me. Ronan's eyes flashed as he continued to square up with Reid, but slowly, he began to back down from his aggressive stance.

Reid stepped back as well. He glanced at me, giving a small nod as if to confirm he had himself under control.

"We were hoping to rekindle our alliance with the Thornwood pack," he said, stone-faced. "We had a situation a couple of months back. One of our young males went rogue. He almost killed my mate."

Reid stared at the ground, taking a further moment to calm himself. His eyes were dark when he looked up again. "Allara and I hoped we might be able to come to an understanding that would benefit both packs."

Ronan tilted up his chin. The glint in his eyes told me he was listening closely. Despite only being clad in the old jeans, he looked every inch a leader.

"I see." He glanced toward the door. Through the glass panel to the side, several pack members watched the drama unfolding out on the porch.

They whispered back and forth to each other, and I couldn't tell if their interest lay with me and Reid, or if it was Ronan's sudden reappearance that had captured their attention.

"Why don't we continue this conversation inside?" I realized that Elder Frey stood in the doorway of the meeting house. He stepped out and put a hand on Kit's shoulder, steering him toward the front entrance. "Good to see you, Ronan. I'm sure the rest of the pack deserve to hear whatever this is about. In the interest of transparency, of course."

There was a note in his voice that spoke of annoyance. Was he annoyed with Reid and me, or Ronan? I couldn't tell, but Reid and I followed the Elder and Kit inside. Ronan moved fast, stepping past me to hold the door open for me and as I passed him, I was once again forced to inhale that intoxicating scent.

To my surprise, we didn't head to the long benches, where the rest of the pack were gathered. Instead, the Elder led us all the way down the aisle, toward the raised platform at the end of the room. At first I almost veered off, to sit to one side, but then I remembered.

Right. I'm meant to be standing in for Allara.

It was strange, playacting the role of Alpha. I felt like I was wearing someone else's clothes, and everyone could see how ill-fitting they really were. Like a child playacting at being an adult.

When we reached the foot of the platform, Ronan murmured to me, "Watch your step."

His gruff voice sent a shiver down my spine.

I wanted to roll my eyes, but I wasn't sure if it was at his words, or my physical reaction to his closeness.

I know how to walk up a few steps, thanks, was on the tip of my tongue, but in the end I bit my tongue. The stairs were a little uneven, and as I started to climb up to the stage, I faltered.

Ronan grabbed my hand to steady me. As soon as his fingers closed around mine, every nerve in my body lit up.

The sensation was instant and intense, like an electric current passing under my skin, flowing through his hand into mine. Our eyes locked, and my own shock was reflected back at me in his astonished gaze.

What the...?

For what felt like years, we stood there, connected by a single point. My hand in his. Nothing else mattered: the rest of the pack, even Reid. Everything faded into the background, except for the touch of Ronan's fingers that convulsed on my skin.

Abruptly, he dropped my hand and the moment dissipated. We climbed up onto the stage, but I couldn't forget. What just happened?

I glanced at Reid, who stared at me with a mild frown. *You okay?* he mouthed.

I nodded. It was only half a lie. I was okay and yet, somehow I wasn't. Something had changed deep inside me.

The eyes of the crowd passed over me and then Reid with mild curiosity. They seemed to be more focused on Ronan, who I didn't dare look at after that moment. I still felt his touch tingling all the way up my arm and down my left side. I was itching to touch him again, but managed to refrain, clenching them into fists by my side.

Whatever the hell just happened, it must have taken mere seconds.

Remember, you're here for Allara. You have to make a good impression. Don't blow this for her—or your pack.

I let myself be ushered by Elder Frey into one of the high-backed wooden chairs, the kind that council members usually sat in when our own meeting house was in session. I shifted in the seat, hot and uncomfortable, feeling the need to shift and head out for a run. I swallowed a couple of times, dry-mouthed.

Ronan's voice crept over me. I didn't know how he was just standing there, talking to his people like nothing had happened. Maybe he hadn't felt... whatever it was. Maybe it was just me whose world had suddenly shifted on its axis?

"Our visitors from the Bane Clan have come to strengthen the bonds between our two packs."

The crowd murmured, and a few pairs of eyes flicked over to Reid and me with a little more interest this time.

"I want everyone to show them a warm welcome. I know I have some explaining to do regarding my recent absence." Ronan paused. The silence was deafening. "The explanation will come in due course, but for now, I'm afraid you will have to wait. In the meantime, I can assure you, I'm back now. For good."

"Does this mean the Alpha ceremony is back on?" someone from the back called out.

Several people clapped in agreement, until Ronan held up his hands and a hush fell once more.

Damn. He may not be the official pack Alpha yet, but his presence is compelling. These people certainly respect him.

"The truth is, both our packs are in danger—the Thornwoods, and the Banes. There are those out there who want to tear us apart, and not just from the outside. I want to stop that before it can take root. So, Reid and Kara will be staying with us indefinitely as ambassadors on behalf of their people," Ronan continued, ignoring the way Reid's head jerked sharply in surprise. "I hope their visit will bring our clans closer."

The murmuring grew louder. Eventually, scattered applause broke out.

Oh... crap. Were we prisoners of the Thornwood pack now?

Once it became clear that the show was over, the pack members began to get up from their seats and file out. The whole time I just sat there, frozen.

Once we were alone, Reid stood. All pretense at civility was forgotten as he rounded on Ronan with renewed aggravation.

"That's a kind invitation," he growled. "You could've told us you wanted us to stay before you announced it to your *entire* clan. And didn't give us a chance to refuse without looking boorish."

Ronan shrugged. At first glance, his posture was loose and easy, but the slight tension in his shoulders told another story.

"Look, if I'm going to agree to this alliance, I want to know who I'm getting into bed with. We only met a few minutes ago. I need more time." His eyes skimmed over mine. I couldn't stop the heated flush running up my neck. "Besides, it's a win-win. This way, we both get what we want—right?"

"My wife is giving birth in a matter of *days,*" Reid hissed. "There is no way I'm staying here. I will *not* miss the birth of my child."

"Fine." Ronan's voice was like steel. "Then you can leave. We'll take the girl."

"*What?*" Reid spluttered. *"No!"*

"The way I see it, your Alpha should've killed the one that betrayed your clan while she had the chance. You've brought this danger on all of us." Ignoring Reid's thunderous expression, Ronan's eyes wandered over to his brother and Elder Frey. "I'll keep my word, but I need to know that you'll keep yours. My pack is everything to me."

"Kara isn't a bargaining chip," Reid said firmly. "She's coming home with me, and that's that."

The two men stared at each other. Reid was clearly frustrated, but Ronan seemed impassive, like he couldn't care less one way or the other.

I don't buy that attitude for a second.

Time to do what Allara sent me here to do. I took a deep breath, and released it slowly. Finally, I spoke up. "I'll do it."

KARA

The loudness of my voice startled me.

Everyone turned in my direction. Kit and Elder Frey seemed mildly surprised, and Reid's eyebrows drew down.

But it was Ronan whose expression intrigued me the most.

His eyes pierced mine as he gazed down at me. Most of the shifters I knew had eyes that ranged from warm, chocolate brown to light hazel, the color of sunlight shining through spring leaves.

Ronan's, however, were a sharp, unyielding amber. Every detail of his features overwhelmed me. The line of his jaw, his rumpled hair.

Not to mention the fact he's still half-naked. Can we postpone this thing and find the guy a shirt already?

"Kara." Reid's voice drifted in from the sidelines. "You don't have to—"

My head jerked to catch his eye. "I know. But I *want* to."

I tried to communicate everything I couldn't say out loud in a look. I knew that we didn't have much time left, and I wanted him to tell Allara I would be okay.

This is the right thing to do. If I can get these people to trust me, we have a real shot at standing our ground against Jaime, if and when he does decide he wants to make a move.

Reid blinked. Something in my face must have communicated what I was thinking, because he gave a short nod and stepped back.

With the other three men, Elder Frey, Kit and Reid, standing behind us in a loose half circle, Ronan and I were face to face.

My skin prickled uncomfortably. Something about the setting—the fact we were still in the meeting house—made this feel like more than a political agreement.

It feels like a bonding ceremony.

I shoved the thought out of my mind just as Ronan held out his arm.

Taking a deep breath, like I was about to plunge into an icy pool, I gripped his forearm, just beneath the elbow. He did the same to mine.

Sensation flooded through me. It was exactly like our encounter on the steps, except...

Stronger. Much stronger.

I couldn't let go of him. I didn't *want* to let go. I was trapped like a fly in those amber eyes, and I would happily drown if it meant he would continue touching my skin. Frenzied thoughts raced through my mind, my imagination spiraling beyond control.

If a simple handshake feels this good...

I went weak at the knees. For a split second, I was terrified I'd literally melt into the floor, but I managed to stand my ground.

And yet...

There's something else. Something that wasn't there before.

I couldn't chase the thought to its conclusion. In the heat of the moment, I couldn't bring myself to care. I just needed more—needed him to pull me close so that I could feel the heat of his skin through my clothes.

It was only when I wrenched my hand away in a panic, gasping, that I realized *what*, exactly, was different.

This time, we weren't alone.

This time, everyone else had noticed it, too.

RONAN

"The two of you are fated mates," Reid declared in a shocked tone, the words booming around me like a cannon.

The hall was empty now. The rest of the pack had returned to their usual duties after I dismissed them from the meeting. Only the five of us remained. The Elder, my brother and I, along with our visitors.

The Alpha male of the Bane Clan, Reid, rambled on, but I was only half paying attention to the explanation.

I heard the words *bonded* and *ideal partner* in a strange, muted way. Like I was deep underwater, and the words were floating down to me from the surface. With each passing moment, my heart beat faster and faster, like it was searching for a way out of my chest and would explode if I didn't let it out.

Eventually I'd had enough. I looked up, my jaw so tight I could barely force the words out.

"All right. I understand." When Elder Frey frowned I realized my tone was too rough. I growled out a belated, "thank you," in the direction of Reid.

I couldn't even look at the girl.

Kara. My brain seemed determined to acknowledge her, even though my heart did not want it. *Her name is Kara.*

She wasn't the type of woman I usually gravitated to. Not that I'd dated anyone seriously, but my brief flings of the past had all tended toward the blonde, bubbly variety. Human women, for the most part. I liked that they knew nothing about me, nothing of who I was. They had no expectations, beyond wanting a bit of fun. Which suited me just fine.

This girl was a dark brunette. Her blue eyes were so pale they verged on gray. With her pointed chin and dainty, slender frame, it was difficult to see the shifter in her at all. She certainly didn't look like she knew how to party. She looked like she'd never even heard the word, fun.

I'd never given much thought to finding a mate.

And even if I had...

This petite, quiet creature? Really? Where's the fierce she-wolf they say all Alpha women must be?

In all the stories my mother had read to me growing up, fated mates were like two halves of one soul. They hunted together, fought off rivals, raised their young, and basically did everything that made up a shifter's life, together. Most Alpha wolves in the old tales were fierce warriors, and their women were more than a match for their strength in battle.

I'd always assumed that if I ever found a mate, she would match my passion in bed, also.

This one—Kara—looked like she'd snap in two if I tried anything close to passionate with her.

"It's literally *fate* that you came here!" Kit piped up, throwing a sunny smile in Kara's direction. Despite my misgivings, my heart warmed at my brother's optimism. He was always the one of us to see the best in people.

Kara smiled back at him. "It seems so."

I had to admit, standing here with her beside me was becoming increasingly uncomfortable. When she thought I wasn't looking, her eyes kept dancing over my torso in a way that made me think she'd prefer it if I wasn't wearing any pants.

The wolf in me wanted to gather her into my arms and head off into the woods, far from prying eyes. The *man* in me, luckily, knew that that was an insane idea.

You don't even know this girl, and now you want to kidnap her? You're losing it, Ronan.

"When will you head home, Reid?" Elder Frey got to his feet, addressing the male guest.

"I'm not sure. Tomorrow at the latest, given Allara's condition..." Reid stopped, his gaze sliding to Kara. He clearly felt guilty about even thinking of leaving her here alone. In fact, he looked downright pissed at the idea.

She gave him a quick smile. "I'll be fine."

Elder Frey cleared his throat. "Maybe you and Kit would like to show our guests around the village, Ronan." He turned to Kit and me with a smile. "I would join you, but I'm afraid I have some matters to attend to."

"Yes. All right," I said. Anything to break the strange tension encapsulating us.

The four of us headed out into the town square. Reid was frowning again, not at anything in particular. He still seemed displeased by the revelation that Kara and I were connected in some way.

When Kara caught hold of his arm, a jolt of jealousy mixed with a twinge of anxiety shivered through me.

Has she changed her mind already, so soon?

The thought of her leaving was suddenly impossible to contemplate. I blinked, trying to rein in my errant and irrational feelings.

"You should go now." Kara looked up at Reid. Her face was full of warm understanding. "I'll be all right, Reid. It's time for you to return to your wife."

Reid looked down at her. His eyes darted from me, to Kit, back down to Kara, then off to the side, downcast. "I... I can't just..."

"Yes," Kara said, more firmly this time. She squeezed his arm to draw his attention back to her. "You can. You said it yourself, Allara's due any day now. There's no way you're missing the birth of your first child because of me. Allara would never forgive me!"

"C'mon, Kara—"

"I don't need babysitting." Kara tilted her head, affection and exasperation coloring her voice. "I'm a grownup, Reid. I can take care of myself, all right?"

"I know that," Reid grumbled. "Are you sure?"

"Absolutely." Kara gave him a smile that didn't quite reach her eyes, but Reid didn't seem to notice the underlying tension in his pack mate.

I noticed. I wanted to fold her into my arms and tell her she really would be okay. I scowled at the direction of my thoughts.

Reid frowned down at her, then pulled her into a bear hug, his biceps tight around her slender shoulders.

There it was again, unmistakable this time. *Jealousy.* Like acid eating at my gut from the inside.

I wanted to drag him off her, and settle this in a fight. Our shifters would resolve it soon enough. It was a crazy thought, but it was there, nonetheless.

When they pulled back from each other, he ruffled her hair like she was his kid sister, and she shoved his hands away from her. They both laughed.

All the amusement drained from Reid's face as he stepped in close to me. A muscle twitched in his jaw, and his hands flexed by his sides, like he was itching to throw a punch.

He clearly cared for her, which was the only reason I kept my shifter reined in tightly against his aggressive stance.

"If you hurt her," he said in a low, deadly voice, "I'll end you. Got it?"

I met his eyes. The shifter in me wanted to fight back, to challenge him right there and then, but my survival instincts told me to hold back.

"Got it," I said in a carefully neutral tone.

Besides, I kind of respected the guy. I liked the fact that Kara had someone who'd protected her up until now. And I wasn't going to hurt her. Not unless she liked it rough in bed, and then I could get as creative as she wanted.

Apparently satisfied, Reid stepped back. Kara was wide-eyed. Her gaze darted between the two of us, like she was expecting a full-on fight to break out at any moment.

Kit broke the silence, sidling up to Reid.

"Come on." He shoved his hands in his pockets and nodded in the direction of the road leading out of town. "I'll walk you back to your truck."

With one final stony look at me, and a parting, anxious stare for Kara, Reid allowed himself to be led away.

Which left the two of us—me and Kara—alone.

For the very first time, my brain pointed out helpfully. *Let's try not to screw this up, Thornwood.*

I could barely look her in the eye. Which was ridiculous; especially if we were destined for each other. And every instinct was telling me we were.

Yet we were still total strangers.

Where were the rose petals and violins, the tearful vows of eternal devotion? All that crap was nowhere to be found. This was worse than an awkward first date.

"Come on," I muttered, before the silence stretched out even longer. "I'll give you the grand tour."

~

Kara

I was doing my best to concentrate as Ronan led me down the main street, but my head buzzed wildly.

What the hell are you doing? You're smack in the middle of a rival pack, totally alone. No protection except my wits and whatever strength my shifter wolf gave me.

What made you think this was a good idea?

Of course, the answer lay ahead of me in the form of Ronan, the muscles of his back flexing as he strode onwards ahead of me. He occasionally glanced back to make sure I was keeping up with him, but he made no real concession for my shorter legs in his stride.

Every time our eyes met, the rush of electricity was almost overwhelming—and definitely like nothing I'd ever felt before today.

The truth was, I'd never even been with a man—*any* man, much less one who ignited such a strong spark of desire in my belly. There hadn't been much opportunity back at our village; my options were kind of limited. There was Reid, who had always been Allara's and who I saw as a brother more than anything else, and Jaime and his gang. They were my brother's friends, which was kind of a turn-off.

Who was I kidding? It wasn't like no-one had offered. I knew several men in our clan who would have happily taken me for a mate if I'd shown them any interest whatsoever.

I'd just never felt that *spark*. Damn spark.

It was stupid, but on some level, I'd always craved what Reid and Allara had, but had come to the conclusion a while back that it likely wasn't going to happen for me.

I'd grown up with Allara and Reid, after all. I'd had a lifetime of knowing what a true bond was supposed to look like. A perfect relationship with someone who was my ideal match.

I knew it was naïve. Even with Reid and Allara, it hadn't been smooth sailing, but I couldn't help the way I felt.

Now, it looks like I've got my wish. And I'm not sure how I feel about it.

Ronan Thornwood was nothing like my idea of an Alpha. All the Alphas I'd known—Allara and her father, even Reid—were all warm, gentle, and extroverted. Tough when they needed to be, but always quick to pull anyone who looked like they needed it into a hug.

It was difficult to imagine this man acting that way.

I was so caught up in my thoughts that I didn't realize Ronan had come to a halt outside a wooden dwelling until I almost crashed into his muscled back.

The dwelling was a simple A-frame structure, bigger than the ones farther down the street. A claw-print was carved into the crossbeam above the front door.

"This is the Alpha's house." Ronan swept a careless hand up at the façade of the building. "My brother and I live here."

I made some noise of acknowledgement that seemed to satisfy him, because we moved past the house and continued down the street.

The scant information he'd given me was intriguing. The way he'd said *the Alpha's house*, was strange. Like the house itself didn't belong to him and Kit. It sounded like they were just occupying it, for now.

A million questions crowded in the back of my mind, but I didn't have the nerve to voice them.

What was it like growing up here, with your parents? Does the house feel too big, too empty now that they're gone? Where did you run off to, and why? And why did you come back, today of all days?

We walked around the perimeter of the town, sticking close to the high fences that surrounded it. My stomach twisted. It all felt unnatural, existing so close to the forest, yet being cut off from it by a manmade structure.

Completely unlike our pack village, which was more in tune with its natural surrounds.

"This is the East watchtower." Ronan pointed up at a tall structure at the edge of the town.

A man inside spotted us and waved.

"You can see the forest for miles around up there."

"Impressive," I said. "But why?"

Ronan looked puzzled. "What do you mean?"

"No offence. It's just that this place is like a fortress."

Ronan smiled ruefully.

My heart sank. "I'm sorry. I haven't seen much outside my own village, you see, and ours doesn't look like... this."

"Don't apologize. I get how it must look to an outsider." Ronan stared up at the high wall, but his expression was distant, contemplative. "My father was a vigilant man, I guess you could say."

At my questioning look, he shrugged. "Some might call it paranoia. It got worse as he got older. He started to question old alliances and treaties. He had it in his head that the other clans were out to get us. He used to tell my brother and I that they wanted to steal our land and take our women, all that crap. So, he built these walls. In his mind, he was keeping us safe."

I couldn't stop the shiver that ran through me.

"Anyway." Ronan threw me a forced smile, as if slightly awkward about sharing anything personal. "Mom reined him in, when she was alive. They were... y'know..."

Fated mates, I finished in my head. *Got it.*

As we turned back toward the main road, I couldn't hold back the curiosity that itched inside my chest.

"Back there." I glanced up at him. It was getting easier to meet his eyes. "Why did you agree to let Reid go? I'm... I'm nobody, Ronan. I'm not an Alpha. I'm not Allara. We all know that. So, why me?"

"I didn't want Allara," Ronan said simply. "Or Reid."

I blinked. "Oh."

He turned away, leaving me to stare at his retreating back and ponder what the hell, exactly, he meant by *that*.

CHAPTER 5

RONAN

It was nearing lunchtime by the time Kara and I made our way back to the village square. Several people were milling around; a couple of them looked like they might talk to me, so I skirted near to the edge of the clearing until I found my brother leaning against one of the posts outside the meeting house.

He brightened up when he saw me, offering a familiar, sunny smile. Something in my chest tightened. I'd missed him more than I realized.

"Hey!" Kit waved at us as we got within talking range. "I was about to head home and grab something to eat. You guys wanna come with me?"

I glanced down at Kara, who nodded. "Sure, I could eat."

"Awesome." Kit fell into step beside me as we walked toward the main track. "I was thinking mac 'n cheese!"

It was obvious how relieved Kit was to see me, but he kept the flow of conversation light and casual as we walked. I knew he wouldn't ask about what happened until I opened up and told him. Nobody knew me better than Kit, and he knew not to push until I was ready.

As I walked side-by-side with Kara, our arms occasionally brushed. Every time, it sent a spark of electricity through me. I clenched my teeth, forcing myself to focus on the discussion.

"So, is this place any different from what you're used to?" Kit asked Kara.

Kara shrugged, scuffing the edge of her shoe against the gravel path. Her eyes wandered over to the high fence.

"Some things. But the people seem nice." She gave Kit a friendly smile, clearly unwilling to criticize anything here in front of Kit. I appreciated her kindness. "You've all been very welcoming so far."

I thought back to the moment at the meeting house, to my insane decision to have her stay here in a flash of pure, unadulterated instinct. I was regretting it more and more with each passing moment.

Now I've trapped her here. This meek, shy girl who has hardly set foot outside her own village. Of all the people I could hold here as a bargaining chip, Kara is the least suitable for that role.

When we reached the Alpha's house, we climbed up the steps to our front door. Kara's eyes wandered over the bear claw carving. As Kit opened the door, I came to stand beside her.

"My grandfather's handiwork," I said. She looked up at me with those sweet blue eyes and it was an effort to turn my face away. "He carved it the day he and my grandmother were bonded together."

She stared up at the carving, a soft smile crossing over her features as she studied it. What was she thinking? Then she dropped her gaze, her eyes shuttered, as she entered through the doorway. I reached up and ran a hand over the carving before I followed her. I had never properly noticed it before today. It was just a part of life, as familiar as the sky, but the way she had looked at it—*really* looked—made me take more notice, too.

Kit and Kara had already gravitated into the kitchen. Kara stood to the side, her arms wrapped protectively around her middle. I pulled out a barstool and she hopped onto it, swinging her legs back and forth like a kid.

"I hope you don't take this the wrong way..." She bit her lip and stopped speaking.

I had to look away from the sight of those perfect white teeth sinking into reddened flesh. Internally, I groaned, my mind going to exactly where I wanted her to bite me.

"Your house is *way* tidier than I expected for two young guys living alone."

Kit smirked. He was pulling pots and pans out of the kitchen cupboards and laying them on the sideboard with swift, confident motions.

I wish I could be anywhere near that level of calm right now.

"Kit's the neat freak," I admitted as I pulled out the stool beside hers. Her cheeks reddened as she tucked a loose strand of hair behind her ear and laughed. "I can't take responsibility for any of this."

"Yeah, it's been way easier than usual keeping this place clean over the past couple of weeks." Kit averted his gaze from mine as he opened the fridge. It was the first time he'd brought up my disappearance, and there was a note in his voice that stung. I'd clearly hurt him, with my disappearance, but he was too kind to say that straight out.

By the time he turned, his arms full of ingredients, he was smiling again and it was as if he hadn't said anything untoward. "Hey, why don't you show Kara around while I cook? No offense, dude, but it'll be awkward having you two sitting here staring at me the whole time."

I raised an eyebrow. If my extroverted, cheerful brother was feeling awkward, then that was really saying something.

Not to mention, there's not much to see. It's just a house...

Kara was already on her feet. "Oh my God, can I do anything to help? I'm kind of a useless cook, but I can peel vegetables, or..."

"No!" Kit flapped a tea towel at her before she could get too close to the stove. "Seriously, I'm fine. Go with Ronan."

He shot a look at me that was followed by something dangerously close to a smirk.

Oh, God. Was my brother... *matchmaking*?

"Go have fun, okay?" Kit said, and Kara's face flushed even darker. As she scurried out of the kitchen, I glared daggers at my brother, who was struggling not to laugh.

You're welcome, he mouthed to me, with a wide grin.

In the hallway, Kara was waiting for me. She smiled as I approached, and I found myself smiling back. Something inside me wanted to open up to her, to show her how I truly felt. It was an unnerving sensation and one I was definitely not used to.

"No pictures."

I frowned, thrown off-track by her statement. "What?"

Kara pointed to the faded square patches on the walls, the cluster of bare hooks. "You don't have any pictures. No family photos?"

"I guess not."

She didn't press further, but she glanced behind us as I led her into the living room. There was a spare hoodie lying over the back of the couch, and I shrugged it on, pulling up the zipper.

"That's better," Kara mumbled, seemingly to herself.

"Sorry, I didn't catch that."

"Oh, nothing. Doesn't matter."

We wandered toward the staircase. As we reached the landing, I realized belatedly I was leading her in the direction of my bedroom.

She paused outside Kit's bedroom, poking her head in and smiling at the collection of colorful posters and the guitars arranged in the corner.

"Kit's, I take it?" At my nod, she said, "Your brother's really sweet." She leaned her head against the doorjamb as she spoke, and my heart ached. She looked so soft, so pretty. I wanted to reach out, but my hands remained firmly by my sides. "You guys seem close."

I nodded. "It's just the two of us, you know?"

"I do." She let out a soft sigh.

Before I could question the reason behind her sigh, she skirted around me and headed for the door at the end of the corridor. "What's through here?"

I came up behind her and leaned over the top of her head to nudge the door open so that she could peer inside. "My bedroom."

She blinked, looking apprehensive. "May I?"

"Go right ahead."

She slipped into the room. I glanced behind me at the empty hallway, to make sure that we were alone. After picking up the distant clatter of pots and pans, and the sound of Kit whistling to himself, I followed her.

～

KARA

My breath caught in my throat as I stepped over the threshold into

Ronan's room. I could feel his presence at my back. He wasn't leaning into me or anything, but my body sensed him anyway. It was like my synapses had rewired themselves: I could feel him whenever he was standing nearby.

His scent was strongest in this part of the house. As I neared the rumpled bedspread, his distinctive smell grew even stronger.

It was delicious, and heady, and it made me want to rip off my clothes and turn to press my naked body against his.

Damn. I couldn't believe where my thoughts kept heading.

The curtains were partly closed. I reached out and pulled one of them open, letting a beam of light fall across the hardwood floor. Ronan watched me, his face shrouded in darkness.

"Not much to see, I'm afraid." His gaze flicked between the dresser to the bed and back again. "I left in kind of a hurry."

"I can see that." I swallowed. My eye was drawn to the walls—or rather, their emptiness. Just a vast expanse of bare white space...

"What are you thinking?" he murmured.

I fought not to react. He was right behind me. I could feel his hot breath against the side of my neck.

"I can see a question burning in your eyes," he said. "Tell me."

I reached out until my fingertips touched the nearest wall. "Don't you get tired of waking up to a load of empty space?"

He huffed a laugh, as if I'd surprised him with my query. "I guess I'm kind of used to it."

You don't have to be. I didn't say anything, just trailed my hand over the bare whiteness. "That's... sad."

"How so?"

I shrugged. I hadn't meant to say it out loud. "First the pictures, now this..." Ronan curled his hand around mine. His fingers brushed over the space I'd just vacated, like we were doing a weird kind of dance. "Are you into art?"

"I guess." I allowed his hand to guide mine, higher and higher, until I was standing on tiptoe. "I make homewares for people in my pack. Cushions, rugs, pottery, that kind of thing. Sometimes I paint. It depends, really."

"On what?"

I giggled. With his longer arms, he could reach way higher than me. I teetered on the balls of my feet before giving up and slumping back against his chest. He slid his arm around my waist, catching me.

He didn't let go.

Suddenly, it became much harder to breathe normally. "Inspiration."

I felt him take a couple of breaths, processing what I'd just said. "Sounds like you're an artist to me."

"Oh yeah?" I turned in his grasp.

His other arm came up to join the first, holding me in place. His body language was loose, casual, but his eyes burned with a heat that made me shiver.

"Uh huh." His gaze tracked over my face.

I tilted up my head, hungry in a way I'd never been before today.

He touched the side of my face, cradling it loosely. I let my part, acting purely on instinct, and his eyes widened a fraction.

His index finger traced below my mouth and his thumb skimmed over my bottom lip, pressing down slightly. At the feel of his roughened skin against my flesh, I almost moaned out loud.

I wanted him to kiss me... I imagined how it would feel, when he did...

"Dinner!"

We sprang apart like we'd both received an electric shock. I was certain I was flushed all over. Ronan, for his part, just shook his head and a rumble filled his chest.

"My brother has great timing." He strode over to the door and held it open for me.

"I can hear that."

My body still felt like it was alive with electricity. How would I be able to concentrate on dinner now?

We made our way down to the kitchen without incident, although I felt Ronan's eyes on my face, particularly my mouth, the entire time we were getting settled at the table. Kit brought out a delicious-smelling stir-fry, and my mouth watered. I hadn't realized how hungry I was, until this moment.

"Thank you." I smiled up at him as he handed me a bowl. I didn't know whether it was the stress of the morning, or the close encounter in Ronan's bedroom, but I was ravenous.

"You're welcome." Kit's voice had a hint of smugness in it. When I looked up, he was eyeing Ronan with open amusement. "Did you get the full tour, Kara?"

"Kit." Ronan's sharp tone made his brother laugh out loud. "C'mon."

"It's okay." I winked at Ronan before turning my attention to Kit. "Ronan showed me *everything,* including your secret stash hidden in your bedroom. So, who is she? One of the girls in your pack?"

Kit's mischievous expression switched to shock. "Wh-what?"

He hurried across the room, mumbling something about fetching the salt and pepper, before disappearing altogether. A few seconds later, we heard the tell-tale thud of footsteps rushing up the stairs.

Ronan raised an eyebrow at me. "What the hell was all that about? We didn't even go into his room."

"I know we didn't." I laughed. "But I know teenage boys, okay? If it's not a stash of love letters he's hiding up there, it's porn. Either way, I figure he'll leave us alone now."

Ronan's mouth fell open, and he spluttered with laughter. "Oh, *wow.* You're a genius."

"Nah." I ducked my head at the compliment, my face heating up all over again. "Just used to handling obnoxious younger brothers, is all."

Ronan said nothing, but his face was open and curious as he took another bite of food. The plates were stacked high. Like the men in my pack, Ronan and Kit could clearly put food away. I played with my fork before trying the food. It was as delicious as it smelled.

After several mouthfuls, I spoke. "I have a brother too." I picked up my glass and took a sip, keeping my eyes firmly fixed on Ronan. "His name's Jason."

"How much older are you?"

"Hmm... twelve minutes?" I laughed at the surprise in Ronan's face. "We're twins. I never let him forget that I'm the oldest, though."

Ronan shot me a grin, all sharp, white incisors. He must have been living in his shifter form for a long while, because I could see the wolf in him still. It had been hours since he'd shifted, but there it was, right near the surface.

Watching me.

I swallowed hard, and his eyes trailed down my throat, noting and tracking the motion.

Kit slid back into the room and took his seat at the table. At our questioning looks, he threw me a rueful smile. "Well played, new girl. Well played."

I inclined my head in a small bow.

"I like her." Kit sat back in his chair, folding his arms behind his head. He sat opposite Ronan, and I was struck by the family resemblance.

"Me too," Ronan murmured.

When I looked up at him, his pale amber eyes were fixed on me, with an expression so hungry that all coherent thoughts fled out of my head.

CHAPTER 6
KARA

By the time we finished dinner and returned to the town square, a huge bonfire was standing, half-built, in the middle of the clearing. A group of guys emerged, each carrying a vast log over his shoulders. They were all shouting with laughter and trying to shoulder-barge their friends so that they'd drop their cargo. At the site of the bonfire, they dumped the logs, with others bringing handfuls of kindling to add to the pyre.

Early evening had fallen. The sky above us was faded blue, and fireflies darted through the loose clusters of pack members who surrounded the pyre. The people's chatter and laughter filled the open air, growing louder as we approached.

A sharp pang pierced through me.

The atmosphere was familiar, and yet not. If I closed my eyes, I could imagine, just for a second, that I was back in my own pack, with the people I'd known my whole life, getting ready for an evening of celebration. I could almost reach out and touch them—the people who loved me just as fiercely as I loved them. My family.

Back where I belong.

And then the bubble of familiarity was gone and I was surrounded instead by strangers, on a rival pack's land, and the only people I knew here were Ronan, Kit and Elder Frey.

"Hey." Ronan moved his head closer to mine. Even over the noise of the gathering, his deep voice made my skin tingle. "We can head home if you want, get an early night. No-one would mind, I swear."

Home. He meant the Alpha's house. The place with the empty walls.

"I'm fine," I whispered. Then I said it again, a little louder, and found myself believing it.

I *would* be fine. I would make sure of it.

Ronan squeezed my fingers, so brief I barely had time to react. "Come on. I'll introduce you to some folks."

I let him lead me over to the log bearers, who all looked up as we approached. They were almost done with the bonfire. It was taller than I was by a good foot and a half. They were all panting with exertion, but they had bright smiles for both of us.

"What did you do to build this?" Ronan walked toward them, nodding at the structure. "Chop down half the forest?"

"I guess you'll never know, since you weren't here to help us," the nearest one shot back, before rushing over and pulling Ronan into a hug. "Where've you been, man?"

Ronan extracted himself and hooked his thumbs into his pockets, giving a loose shrug. The guy who had hugged Ronan didn't seem bothered by his lack of response. Instead, his gaze slid over and landed on me. Unlike Kit and Ronan, this guy's hair was sandy and short. A deep scar ran through his left brow.

"Aren't you gonna introduce us?" he said to Ronan, grinning at me.

Ronan sidled in close to me, as if he didn't like the other man's gaze on me. "Kara, this is Noah." He pointed to the shorter guy just behind. "That's Jake. And the guy with the burning torch is Zac."

Noah whirled around. "Zac!" He strode away from us with his hands flung wide. "C'mon, man, not cool! We were gonna light it up together, you know that!"

He and Zac started to bicker over the torch, which burnt out, unnoticed, between them. Ronan and I were breathless with laugher as we wandered away, weaving through the crowd.

"Are they always like that?"

"Pretty much, yeah." Ronan's eyes were soft, still glowing with amusement. "They're good guys. We grew up together. They never treated me any different for being the Alpha's son or anything, and I appreciate that. I know I can trust those three."

I thought of Allara. My best friend, the person who, aside from my brother, I knew the best out of anyone.

That was how I knew her—not as my Alpha, but first and foremost, as my friend. It was how I still thought of her. My *best* friend. Growing up, it had never occurred to me that she had a huge weight on her shoulders, an expectation that one day, she would follow in her father's footsteps.

When she ran off to the city, it had hurt. But I understood why she had done it. Now that she was back, it was as if she'd never left. I hoped that she felt about me as Ronan clearly did about his friends.

Trust in friendship was important, and rare, and when you found it, you had to hold onto it.

"Sure," I said eventually. I took Ronan's hand in mine like I'd done it a thousand times before. He looked down at our entwined fingers, surprise in his eyes, but he didn't let go.

Hand-in-hand, we made our way over to a long trestle table, where food and drinks were being laid out.

I became aware that we were being watched. A tall, willowy woman stood nearby, leaning against a wall with her arms folded. Her eyes were fixed on us. When I glanced at her, she raised an eyebrow as if in challenge.

I froze. It couldn't be. But it was.

Naomi.

"Hey, what's wrong?" Ronan asked me.

I nodded over to where Naomi was standing. She hadn't taken her eyes off us. Her gaze remained challenging, like she was daring me to start something.

"What is *she* doing here?" I hissed.

Over the past few hours, I'd been growing more and more relaxed in this new environment. But one sight of Naomi was all it took to get my hackles back up.

"Wait, Naomi?" Ronan glanced in her direction, looking confused. "Do you know her?"

"Yes. We've met before."

Something in my tone must have registered my dislike, because his eyebrows crept toward his hairline. "Oh, this should be good."

"She used to visit our pack," I said. "She managed to get her claws into my brother Jason. He even considered making her his mate. When his *true* mate came along, she wasn't happy and she didn't care who knew it. I haven't seen her for months. It's just a shock, that's all."

Ronan let out a low whistle. "Damn. That sounds like Naomi all right."

I gave him a questioning look, and he shrugged.

"She's still a part of the Thornwood Clan, but only in name. She comes around here when she wants something. The rest of the time, she's out causing trouble somewhere else. Shifters, humans, who knows?" He shook his head. "Who cares? As long as she's not making trouble here…"

"I guess every pack has its own poison," I said, thinking of Jaime. "Though, if she's still considered Thornwood, then anything she does would reflect on your pack's reputation, wouldn't it?"

"Like Jaime and the Banes?"

Touché. Ronan was probably as responsible for Naomi's bad behavior, as Allara was for Jaime's. Which was to say, not at all. Naomi and Jaime, and others like them who behaved badly, were responsible for themselves. No one else could be blamed for any adult's poor life choices or decisions.

Naomi's lip curled in a sneer, as if she could hear the negative train of my thoughts. I turned away from her, determined to put the toxic woman out of my head.

Ronan and I lingered by the refreshment table. He poured me a drink of something sweet and fruity, and I sipped it as we turned back toward the center of the clearing. The bonfire was alight now, yellow tongues of flame creeping along the dry kindling, sending smoke into the sky.

We only look a couple of steps in the direction of the bonfire, before Naomi intercepted us.

"Kara." Her smooth voice set my teeth on edge. "Fancy running into you here. Long time no see."

I forced my features into a smile. "Indeed. Hello Naomi."

Without meaning to, I shrank into Ronan's side, as if my body already knew I would receive support from him, even if my head hadn't quite caught up. His hand tightened around mine.

Naomi's gaze flicked down to our joined hands, and her eyes widened slightly, as if she'd only just noticed.

Oh, come on. You clocked us from twenty feet away, bitch. Enough with the theatrics already.

"Oh, wow." Naomi let out a warm chuckle, but her eyes remained calculating. *Snake eyes.* "I see *you* didn't waste any time."

Don't rise to her bait. That's exactly what she wants.

"I'm here on business," I said, my voice tight. "Now, if you'll excuse us..."

"It sure doesn't look like it." Naomi folded her arms. The movement pushed her breasts forward, emphasizing her ample cleavage. She flicked a glance at Ronan as if checking to see if he'd noticed. My eyes narrowed. "How long has it been, a few hours? I have to say, Kara. I really didn't think you had it in you."

"Naomi." Ronan's voice was firm. An Alpha's command.

Naomi flinched a little, but then rallied. "I'm serious! You always seemed so... meek, so shy. Just like a sad little mouse, trailing around after me and your brother."

A deep rumble began in Ronan's chest, and I tugged quickly on his hand. *I've got this.* "Funny you should mention Jason." I tilted up my chin, meeting her narrowed gaze. "He and Tammy have a beautiful new baby. They're doing amazingly, all three of them. I've never seen my brother so happy. How are *you* doing, Naomi?"

Naomi opened her mouth, then closed it. Her face turned red and she swiveled and rushed away.

Good. She could choke on her own poisonous tongue for all I cared.

Ronan released a huff of laughter. "Remind me not to get on your bad side," he murmured, and I shrugged. All the grief that woman had given Jason, and the empty promises she'd made, was all in the past. She would never be able to hurt him again.

Together, Ronan and I made our way toward the bonfire.

"You okay?" Ronan bent his head close to mine. His eyes were full of concern.

I nodded. "I'm fine. I can handle her."

He glanced behind us with a furrowed brow. "I'm sure you can. You just proved that. Only, be careful with her, okay? She doesn't take kindly to insults. I've seen her strike back, and strike hard. I don't want that to happen to you."

I looked up at him, warmed all the way through by his concern. "I will be careful. I promise."

I have no intention of going anywhere near that bitch.

His face smoothed out at my expression, and he softened, putting an arm around me. His arm felt good over my shoulders, warm and protective.

"I guess we should make the rounds," he said. "That's the sort of thing one does at a party, right?"

"You don't sound stoked at the prospect. Aren't Alpha's supposed to be extroverted and genial?"

His answering glower made me laugh; I leaned into his body and slid an arm around his waist.

"I'm just teasing," I whispered. "You'll be a great Alpha; you've got the command needed for the job. You got this."

CHAPTER 7

RONAN

Attending a party thrown in honor of my return and ascendancy to Alpha wasn't high up on the list of ways I wanted to spend my time.

Having Kara by my side made things even harder. Everywhere I turned, I caught curious glances. I could see people's minds turning over, wondering what could possibly have happened at the meeting house, and why she was now pressed into my side as if we were joined at the hip.

As if we were mates.

Kara seemed to shy away from the attention almost as much as I did.

To my relief, however, people mostly left us alone. The other members of the pack had been told by Kit that I wouldn't be answering any questions tonight about where I'd been. I felt Naomi's eyes burning into my back more than a couple of times, but I was careful to evade her.

I did not want my first job as Alpha to be stopping a fight between that annoying woman, and Kara.

I was given the prime spot in front of the bonfire, with Kara beside me, on the low wooden bench that my mother and father used to sit at, watching over the rest of the clan. For once, I didn't refuse the honor. I could see that Kara was more rattled by Naomi's sudden appearance than she was letting on, so we sat on the prime bench and people-watched for a while.

My thigh felt warm where it pressed against hers.

"That's my Aunt Clarissa, and my young cousin Molly." I pointed out the two redheads as they passed, giving little Molly a wave. She giggled and ducked behind her mom, but her tiny hand stuck out from behind Clarissa's legs, waving back.

I talked Kara through the dynamics of our clan: who was considering who for a potential mate, which ones were competing, who had broken up, and the couples who were fated for each other. As I discovered, it was a perfect mirror of her own clan. All the rivalries and friendships that made up the rich tapestry of a shifter pack, were laid out for all to see, and though the people may have been different, the dynamics within my pack, and hers, were pretty much the same.

"Let me get this straight." Kara laughed. "Noah was with Lacey, but then he broke up with her for Ruby, but when Lacey started dating Jake, Noah wanted *Lacey* again? How does that work? So, who does Lacey want?"

I groaned and dropped my head into my hands. "Ugh. When you put it like that, it sounds even crazier."

"And I thought our pack was dramatic." Kara smiled, her gaze drifting toward the glow of the bonfire. "This is lovely," she said, and a warm feeling grew in my chest.

There were so many stories, so much I didn't yet know about her. I wanted to know everything.

We have time.

Kara wasn't going anywhere, after all. As I remembered the deal we'd struck, the warmth inside me mingled with a twinge of uncertainty.

She's only here because she has to be, remember? The moment you allow her to leave, she'll be home to the Bane clan in a shot.

"So, what about you?" Kara's hand on my arm jolted me back to the present. "Where are you in all this drama?"

"Nowhere," I answered truthfully. "I steered clear of all that. I had the occasional fling with human women, but nothing serious."

"Human." She looked surprised. "Why specifically human and not another shifter?"

I chuckled. "Yeah, I guess it sounds a bit strange. But with shifters, everything gets so... messy. All the pheromones and hormones flying everywhere. I've seen first-hand what kind of chaos it can create. I didn't want to risk my position like that, not over some casual hook-up."

Kara was silent, staring into the flames. From the moment I saw her, I thought she was beautiful, but in the dusk and the firelight, she looked extra stunning. Her dark hair pooled around her shoulders, and her eyes glimmered. I resisted the urge to reach out and tuck a soft strand behind her ear, to stroke a finger over the delicate blush on her cheeks.

"What about you?" I said instead, scrambling for a distraction. "You must have had offers from many of the men in your pack. Or other shifters passing through the area, perhaps?"

I struggled to keep the jealousy out of my voice at the thought of other shifters around her, competing for her attention, for the chance to mate.

"Yes, there were a couple, I guess." Kara bit her lip, sounding evasive. She shrugged. "Your parents must have wanted you to find a match. You were the future Alpha, after all."

Now it was my turn to dodge the question.

"They did," I said shortly. "But, like I said, it never interested me."

But that was before.

Now Kara was here, and I couldn't deny that her presence had changed everything.

"Kit was always the extrovert," I said. "Even with the age gap, he was always the one following in Dad's footsteps. He's more cut out for the Alpha role, than I'll ever be."

I'd always preferred to be off exploring the forest with my friends than learning about pack politics. Now that I was older, I'd learned to mask how uncomfortable I felt when people looked to me as their leader, but that was all it was—a mask.

Deep down, underneath the mask, I knew it should have been Kit who was the first born. The Alpha.

"He just needed a few more years to mature, and he'd have been a perfect leader for the pack, but unfortunately we weren't given that opportunity with the passing of our father."

Kara seemed to read my thoughts exactly. The firelight flickered in her gorgeous eyes, and I drew a sharp breath when she took my hand and our fingers tangled together.

"Look, I know my opinion doesn't mean much to you." She drew a shaky breath, continuing before I could argue. "We don't really know each other that well—hell, I'm not even supposed to be here at all—but from where I'm standing, I think what you just said is a load of crap."

My mouth dropped open. Whatever I'd been expecting, it wasn't *that*.

"What?"

She tilted up her chin, her expression full of defiance. In this light, she was a far cry from the quiet, withdrawn girl I'd met that morning. "I've seen how people look at you around here. They respect you; look up to you. They listen when you talk. And the way you talk about them! You care about them, Ronan. Their wellbeing, their wants, their fears. That's what's important. Being an Alpha is about so much more than being the life and soul of the party. I was joking before, when I said an Alpha is usually extroverted. That's a plus, but its not a requirement for the job. Commanding respect, and having the ability to lead in a clear and rational manner, is what people need, in their leader."

She let out a huff, and her shoulders slumped. Her bottom lip trembled, like she was on the verge of pouting at me.

She was adorable.

I couldn't resist any longer. I reached out and tucked that loose piece of hair behind her ear. She turned her face toward my palm, closing her eyes as if in bliss at my touch, before flushing deep red and jerking away.

"I'm so sorry," she mumbled, covering her face with her hands. "I don't know what that was."

"Hey." I tried unsuccessfully to pry her hands away from her face. "C'mon, it's okay!"

She lowered her hands to her lap. Her gaze darted down to the cup of punch I'd poured for her earlier, resting on the bench beside her.

"Did you spike my drink?" Her mouth curled up at one side to let me know she was joking.

"I can assure you, I didn't." I spread my hands wide. "That was all you."

"Uh huh." She tilted her head to one side. "I'm onto you, Thornwood."

"Is that right?" I leaned closer. From this distance, I could smell her intoxicating scent underneath the smoke from the fire.

I tilted my head to mirror hers. We were inches away from each other. I couldn't tell if the rapid drumbeat I heard was my heart or hers.

A loud *whoop* sounded from nearby, and a light rain of punch fell all around us. Some of it got on Kara, but most of it fell on me. We jolted apart, and I stood up, enraged.

"Oops," Noah called from nearby. "Sorry, Ronan! My bad."

Kara stood up too, her hand falling onto my arm. She must have seen my expression, because she laughed. "It's no big deal."

She stood up on her tiptoes and whispered, "It was getting just a tad hot there, for a bit."

I looked down at her. She had a small, secretive smile on her face, and her thumb rubbed back and forth over my arm, light and teasing.

"We could just head back to your place." She raised her eyebrows. "And get a change of clothes."

Oh.

"Good idea." I returned her smile.

The walk back to the house was thick with a different sort of tension than earlier. Every time her hand brushed against mine, I wanted to grab her right then and there, pin her up against the side of the nearest building, and claim her as mine.

I clenched my hands into fists and forced myself to keep moving. We sped up our pace as the house came into view around the next corner. The street was dark and deserted; it appeared that everyone was still at the bonfire.

By the time we reached the stairs of the porch, I couldn't handle the need anymore. I *needed* to kiss her, to hold her, to drown in her essence. Kara had one foot on the top step when I grabbed her and spun her round so fast that she gasped.

We stood there, drunk on each other. I could tell from her somnolent features that she felt the same way as me. The full moon above us lit her face perfectly. I drank in every detail: her wide eyes, her parted, full mouth. Her lips, crying out for mine.

She surged up and dragged my mouth to hers.

I groaned and hitched her up. We stumbled across the porch, and I pressed her back against the front door.

The kiss grew in urgency, deeper and hotter than before. I groaned as our tongues slid against each other, my hands on either side of her head. She submitted eagerly, tilting her head up and arching her body against mine.

Why had I ever thought she would be too timid? Afraid of my passion?

She was ready and willing, and I couldn't wait to explore more of her body.

The wolf in me wanted to take her, right here, right now, under the night sky and the stars sparkling above us.

The man knew better. She deserved more than a quick fuck. Kara deserved everything I had to give, and more.

I reached around her and pushed open the door, guiding her over the threshold and into the darkened house.

~

Kara

We stumbled through the door and somehow made it into the lounge, pressing kisses onto every inch of skin we could reach.

It was dark, but we managed to reach the dark shape of the sofa, more by instinct than anything else. I collapsed back onto the cushions and Ronan fell on me like a starving man. He suckled on my lower lip, taking it between his teeth, and I gasped.

The gasp turned to a whimper as his hands slid up over my shirt, skating over my ribs, cupping my breasts. His touch felt so good. I needed to get closer.

Ronan moved back and grabbed my jeans, tugging them down my legs so there was nothing between us but my damp panties and his jeans that barely held in his erection.

Then he was back, kissing me, stealing my reason. But I had to tell him the truth...

"I lied," I gasped. "There's never—I've never—"

"What are you trying to say?"

I shuddered at the sound of his voice—half wolf, half man. The shifter was there, right at the surface, and it wanted to claim its mate.

I knew, because mine was right there, ready to leap out and claim my mate, too.

I shook my head, moaning, overwhelmed by his touch, and most of all by the sensation of his tongue dragging over my skin.

It was almost impossible to concentrate. His tongue trailed over my bare stomach, lighting up my nerve endings like a switchboard. Still, I had to get this out. I persisted, somehow, between gasps and moans. "I've never—never done this before."

Ronan went still.

He looked up. His face was unreadable in the dark, but his eyes glinted with arousal. I shivered, wanting his body on mine but not knowing how to ask for it. I settled for squirming and arching my back, trying to encourage his mouth to return to feasting on me, but he shifted away so that we were no longer touching.

I bit back a whine at the loss.

"What do you mean?" He was breathing heavily, short, punched-out breaths. Or was that me? I couldn't tell any more. We were both breathing so hard I could barely hear anything else.

"I've just... I've never." I turned my face into the couch cushion to avoid his piercing gaze. "*You* know."

He sat back completely, slumping down against the back of the sofa. "You've never been with a man before."

I squeezed my eyes shut, nodding.

He was silent. I lay there in the dark, breathing in and out and trying not to panic. Why was he suddenly so quiet?

"Time for bed." The softness of Ronan's voice startled me into awareness once more.

I jerked my head up. My hair, I could feel, was all over the place, but I couldn't bring myself to care. I was too shocked. "What?"

"It's time for bed," Ronan said slowly, like I hadn't heard him the first time.

"With... you?"

"No."

But... I'm not tired." I sat up and slid across the couch until I was pressed up against his side. He didn't reach for me, but he didn't shift away, either. I dropped my head and kissed his shoulder, the side of his neck, sliding my thighs until I was straddling one of his knees. I kissed the side of his neck again, groaning and clenching my thighs around his leg.

A tiny groan slipped past his lips, but that was the only sign he was as affected by our closeness as me.

Gently but firmly, he took my shoulders in his hands and pushed me back.

"*I* am."

From the sound of his voice, he was anything but tired, but his jaw was set and firm. I tried to rock forward into his lap again. His arms tensed around me, and all of a sudden, I was up off the couch, cradled in his thick arms.

"Ronan!" My feet flailed in the air, but it was no use. He carried me across the room, heading toward the stairs. "Ronan, put me *down*."

He ignored me, climbing the stairs and heading in the direction of his bedroom. *Maybe he'd changed his mind?*

My heart started hammering, jackrabbit fast, when we reached the threshold, but when he deposited me on his bed he didn't climb in after me. He just stood there, one hand rubbing at the back of his neck as he stared down at me.

"You can sleep here tonight." His gruff voice, such a stark contrast from his warm, easy tones earlier, shocked me. "I'll take the spare room down the hall."

He crossed over to the door.

"Ronan!"

At the sound of my high-pitched, desperate cry, he turned his head. I sat up in the middle of the bed, panting.

I felt shameless, but it was no use. My breath hitched as something like a sob escaped me.

"Please..."

Holding his gaze, I let my legs fall open. I stared at him imploringly. *Don't leave me here like this.*

In a flash, he was at the foot of the bed. His hands circled my ankles and dragged me to the edge of the mattress. I moaned at the sight of his mussed hair between my thighs. My jeans were long gone, abandoned somewhere. His hands climbed up my shins, over my knees, my thighs, mapping every inch of skin. His hot, panting breath huffed against my bare skin, and my core throbbed with need.

"You want this?" he rumbled, and I whined out loud, feeling the vibration of his voice more than I heard his words.

"Yes," I moaned. "I can't—"

"Shh." Ronan buried his face in the soft part of my thigh, teeth scraping the sensitive, overheated flesh. "I've got you."

He slid his mouth up higher, over my panties, and I almost screamed out loud when I felt the first sweep of his tongue over the center of my pussy. Even through the sheer fabric barrier between his mouth and my skin, it was almost too much.

My hips tried to ride forward but he pinned me in place, his broad hands firm on either side of my hips holding me spread-eagled. I sobbed and squirmed, but he was relentless in his teasing, circling my clit with his tongue until I bucked and thrashed.

He pulled away for a brief moment, giving me just enough time to catch my breath, before he dove forward once more and took me in his mouth.

By the time he pulled back yet again, my face was on fire and I was on the verge of tears. I took one heaving breath after another, trying to gather myself.

I knew that, with one word from me, it would all be over.

But I didn't want that. I wanted this agony to go on forever, if it meant that Ronan kept his hands on me.

He slid my panties aside and spread me apart with his fingers. My hands clenched and unclenched in the bedsheets. Now that he'd relinquished his hold on me, I was free to move, to push my hips forward to where they wanted to be.

I did just that, back and forth over his tongue. After all the teasing, it was heaven, pleasure like I'd never known, and nothing stopped me from taking all of it for myself.

When my climax finally hit, it was almost a shock; I'd been on the precipice for so long that when I finally tumbled over the edge I could do nothing but hang on for the ride as Ronan wrung wave after wave of ecstasy out of me.

At last I collapsed back onto the bedsheets, utterly exhausted.

In a weakened daze, I reached out for the fuzzy shape that was Ronan. He pulled away from me; this time, it was gentle, almost reluctant.

I was just present enough to see him leave the room, softly closing the door behind him, before my exhaustion took over and I slipped into unconsciousness.

CHAPTER 8

RONAN

I woke with a sore neck, a sore and aching groin, and a whole heap of guilt.

Groaning, I shuffled around on my bed, trying to find a less lumpy part of the old mattress. Eventually I gave up and sat upright, shaking my hair out of my eyes.

My head gave a throb, and I winced, pressing a hand against my temple.

Damn. I didn't even drink that much last night.

I chalked it up to the stress of being in human form, after spending so long as a wolf. My body was still calibrating itself, reorienting to the environment.

And, of course, to the base need that had roared through my system half the night, every time I relived Kara's gasping cries as she climaxed beneath my mouth. Those remembered cries prevented me from getting to sleep until the early hours of the morning.

I rolled up and out of bed, pulled on a pair of old jeans and a t-shirt, and stumbled my way toward the kitchen. When I passed something on the floor in the lounge, I scooped it up and my fingers closed around the crumpled pile of fabric. I lifted it, holding it up to the light.

Kara's sweater. She must have dropped it last night, while we were...

I closed my eyes, letting the sweater fall back to the floor. Her scent clung in the air around me; my cock stirred yet again at the memory of her in this exact spot the night before, and then after that, in my bedroom...

Now I knew exactly what she looked like when she came. I glanced up at the ceiling. My room lay directly above the lounge, and I listened carefully for any signs of life.

The house was totally silent. It looked like I was the first one up.

In more ways than one.

I groaned out loud before clambering to my feet and slinking off in the direction of a cold shower.

~

I took advantage of the early start, busying myself with preparing breakfast. By the time I heard signs of life coming from upstairs, I had a stack of pancakes ready on the table, and I was slicing up strawberries while I waited for the last pancake to be done.

Kit wandered in first, yawning widely. The sight of him was a shock. I'd almost forgotten he lived here. I'd been so focused on Kara and what we had almost done last night.

"Hey man."

"Hey." I jabbed the spatula toward him in warning as he reached for a pancake. "Use a plate. And leave some for our guest."

Left to his own devices, Kit would just shove the whole thing into his mouth and then dive in for more. But we had company this morning, and I wanted to make a good impression.

That is, if I haven't squandered the opportunity already.

As if she'd heard my thoughts, Kara appeared in the doorway. She looked between us shyly, and I gave her an encouraging smile.

"You hungry?"

She nodded, sitting down opposite Kit and helping herself to a pancake. I nodded to Kit as we watched her fill the pancake with strawberries and roll it up neatly.

"See?" I turned back to the stove and slid the final pancake onto an empty plate, then wandered over to the table and sat beside her. "Manners."

"Whatever." Kit stuck his tongue out at me. "What did you guys get up to last night, anyway? I totally lost track of you, and by the time I got back here, it was dead quiet."

I looked at Kara, and she looked at me. We both started to speak at the same time.

"We were just—"

"We decided to take a walk and—"

"Stargazing." Kara's voice was firm and steady. "We were stargazing."

"Oh." Kit grabbed another pancake and slathered it with an unholy amount of maple syrup. "Cool."

"Cool," I echoed, meeting Kara's eyes and giving her a soft, secretive smile.

～

JUST AS WE were wrapping up breakfast, we were interrupted by a volley of knocks on the front door. I excused myself from the table and went to answer it, only to find Noah, Jake, and Zac waiting for me with identical expressions of excitement.

I looked between the three of them. "What's up, guys?"

"Hunting season is what's up, man!" Noah reached out and cuffed me on the shoulder. "C'mon, we're heading into the forest on guard duty. We were gonna grab something to eat on the way back. You coming, or what? Been a while since you joined us."

I glanced behind me toward the kitchen, where Kit and Kara were still sitting, finishing up.

Patrolling, followed by a hunt? How long will that take?

It stood to reason that my friends—brothers in spirit, if not in blood —would expect me to keep to my regular duties like nothing had changed. But the truth was, everything had changed. Like Noah said, I'd been gone for some time, and...

The memory of Kara's sweet face, the way she'd gazed up at me last night, was enough to harden my resolve.

"I'm kind of in the middle of something right now." I started to draw the door closed, shaking my head. "Sorry. I'll take the flack from the Elders, okay? Don't worry about it. I'll join you next time."

Jake nudged his foot into the gap before I could shut the door completely. "Ronan, c'mon. You've been AWOL for weeks, and now you don't even wanna *hunt*? What's wrong with you, man?"

In unison, I was met with three pairs of wide, dejected eyes. Guilt prickled inside me. Here I was, abandoning guard duty with my pack mates, after everything I'd put them through...

A voice sounded in the back of my head. The last voice I wanted to think of right now: my father.

Remember your duty, Ronan.

What the hell *was* my duty? Things had gotten so muddled... I pressed my fist against the side of the door, one foot on the threshold, torn.

Soft footsteps sounded behind me, and Kara appeared at my elbow.

She smiled at the three visitors, then directed her gaze at me. "Can I talk to you for a sec, Ronan?"

"Sure." I moved away from the door, leaving it open. Out of the corner of my eye, I watched Zac slump down onto the decking. The other two leaned against the doorframe, their downcast mood obvious.

"I think you should go with them," Kara whispered, once we were in the other room.

My mouth fell open. "What? You heard all that?"

Kara's mouth tilted up at the corner. "Your friends weren't exactly whispering. Also..."

She raised an eyebrow.

Right. Shifter hearing.

I was so used to dating only human women. I kept forgetting that Kara had the wolf in her. Gentle and breakable as she seemed, I knew there was a tough core underneath the soft, sweet exterior. Every so often she let it show. Perhaps that seeming gentleness made her stronger than many others, rather than weak. She clearly had control of her shifter side.

"Are you sure?" Something twanged in my chest at the thought of leaving her here without me. What if something happened to her? "I can send them away."

"You have your duty," Kara said, like it was as simple as that. "And I have mine. Go. I'll still be here when you get back."

"You better," I grumbled.

"Absence makes the heart grow fonder, you know."

"Hmm. So they say."

She huffed a laugh and reached up to drag my head down toward hers.

The kiss was short and chaste, nothing like the fiery passion from last night. Nevertheless, pure need pulsed through me, hot and greedy, just from the brief contact.

When we pulled apart, her eyes were full of challenge.

"I'll see you later." Her words dripped with intent.

I wanted to devour her. Again.

With a deep sigh, I stepped back from her and headed for the door.

KARA

Once Ronan was gone, I found myself at a loose end.

Kit disappeared shortly afterwards. It was a weekday, and he said he had a study group with some of the other teenagers in the pack. After a brief internal debate, I decided to slip outside and head out to the town square once again.

After all, I had a job to do. A purpose, a reason I was here.

I tucked away the memory of Ronan's intense, hungry gaze. For now, at least, I had to be vigilant. I was here as an ambassador, after all. It made sense to get to know as many people as I could, and try and establish some rapport within the pack.

The thought made my heart sink. I was a loner by nature, far more comfortable with my paintbrushes than with making small talk.

Luckily for me, I ran into a familiar face almost immediately. And it wasn't Naomi, thank goodness.

Halfway down the road that led to the meeting house, a small vegetable patch lay between two cottages. Elder Frey waved me over, one hand resting on his spade and the other wiping his brow.

"Good morning, Kara!" His face broadened into a smile as I grew closer, and he beckoned me forward. "Come in, come in, don't be shy."

Hesitantly, I slipped open the wooden gate and picked my way over the narrow gravel path that ran between the raised beds. Broad beans trailed off on pitched wooden frames, and a grapevine crept on a trellis over the back wall. Elder Frey was in the middle of the patch, pulling out weeds from a bed of frothy green stems. Once I got close enough, he tossed me a pair of spare gloves.

"Anything that looks like it doesn't belong," he said, pulling up a dandelion and holding it up to demonstrate, before tossing it into a nearby wheelbarrow, "just root it out."

I pulled on the gloves and got to work beside him. We worked in companionable silence for a few minutes until he sat back on his heels, turning to face me.

"So, are you settling in around here? I know it's only been a short time, but are you comfortable?"

I nodded. "I am, actually. Surprisingly." I glanced around at the peaceful garden. Somewhere in the distance, I could hear faint laughter, and a gentle breeze rustled through the plants around us. There were many things that reminded me of my own pack village—enough that I didn't feel completely out of place. "When I first arrived, everything seemed so…different. But I think I might have been letting my nerves rule, at that point."

"The Bane Clan certainly have their way of doing things, and we have ours." Elder Frey nodded. "There are differences, of course, which is natural, but there are also many things that remain similar in most shifter communities. I hope that the Thornwood brothers are making you feel welcome in the Alpha's house."

"Yeah, they're great." I couldn't help but smile as I thought back to the morning. "Kit and Ronan… they remind me of my brother and I. The gentle ribbing, but underneath, they really care for each other."

"And you have everything you need?"

You could say that. I didn't answer, but the flush that I could feel cresting my cheeks told the story without me wanting to share it.

"Kara…" The Elder's face furrowed as his expression turned pensive; solemn. "I consider it my duty to tell you this, and I hope you will accept my advice. I assure you I speak only as a friend. I knew your Alpha's father very well, and I know he would want me to look out for one of his own."

I pulled my hands back from the vegetable patch and frowned, confused. "Tell me what?"

"What happened yesterday, between you and Ronan."

For a wild second, I thought he was referring to the night I'd spent in Ronan's bed. Then I realized he meant before, in the meeting house. *Oh.*

"I didn't want to say anything then. I didn't think it was my place."

"You mean... the fact that we seem to be fated?" I was totally puzzled as to what the Elder might be about to say.

Is being fated to a mate a bad thing? Where's he going with this?

Elder Frey looked regretful. He heaved a deep sigh, and for some reason the sound sent a chill creeping down my spine. Whatever he was about to say next, I wasn't sure I wanted to hear it.

"How many men have you known, Kara?" He spoke kindly, but his words didn't reassure me. "Not many, I'm willing to bet. A handful in your own pack, perhaps. And Ronan is the only one who has ever elicited these... feelings?"

"Nobody has even come *close.*" I felt like it wasn't his business, but equally, I felt the need to be honest.

Whatever brief, passing interest I'd had for anyone else, none of them could hold a candle to the way I felt around Ronan.

"But," the Elder pressed, "given your—forgive me—lack of experience, who's to say that there isn't someone else out there? After all, how are you to know? Perhaps these feelings are an infatuation. One that, over time, will fade."

"Why are you saying this?" I bit out. I didn't understand his motive. My hands trembled, and anxiety sent my senses reeling. "I don't want anyone else. I don't—"

"Kara." Elder Frey's hand on my shoulder steadied me enough to take several deep breaths, and I felt my heart settle inside my chest. "I'm so sorry, my dear. I didn't mean to upset you."

"Well," I snapped, "you did."

"I can see that." There was a note of genuine regret in his voice. "Look, the bond between fated mates is a mysterious phenomenon. Nobody truly understands how it works. We only have the word of the individuals who experience it. All that those on the outside see more often than not, are two people who rush into a lifelong commitment without thinking through the long-term consequences."

"He hasn't promised me anything." I sniffed. "If that's what you're worried about."

"All I'm worried about is *you.*"

Why is he only worried about me? What about his Alpha? Shouldn't he be worried about Ronan? Is there something about Ronan that he's not telling me? Something that might change my opinion about this whole situation, if I found out?

"I've told you, I'm fine." My voice wobbled. *Don't cry, dammit. Don't you dare cry.* "Look. I know that this is a curveball. I get it. This is your future Alpha, and I'm some stranger who showed up out of nowhere. But I promise you, the last thing I want to do is stand between him and his destiny."

I stood up shakily and brushed the soil off my jeans. Elder Frey looked up at me. In the glare of the midday sun, I couldn't read his expression.

"Just think about what I said, Kara." His soft voice wasn't soothing any more. I didn't want to listen or think. I just wanted to get away as fast as possible. "There are things you don't know. Some shifters... they just aren't meant to have a mate."

I'd heard enough. I mumbled something unintelligible in response and ran back through the garden, letting the gate clang shut behind me.

He didn't try to stop me.

I ran all the way back to the Thornwood house, tears blurring my eyes the whole way.

I waited until I was inside, safe and secure with the door locked behind me, before I finally let my tears fall.

CHAPTER 9

RONAN

Despite my initial reluctance to join my friends, we ended up staying out in the forest for most of the day.

It felt good to be back in shifter form, but not to be alone this time. To feel the wind through my fur, the dirt under my paws. After so long spent as an outcast—albeit self-imposed—having my packmates surrounding me again was nothing short of exhilarating. The joy of running with friends sang through my bone marrow, and when I put my head up and howled, snatches of their own song echoed back to me through the trees.

By the time I arrived back in town, I was spent. I shoved on the spare clothes we'd stashed in the gatehouse earlier, dressing in a daze. Noah nudged my shoulder as he wandered past.

He grabbed a bottle of water off the side of the gatehouse, chugging half of it in one go and wiping his mouth. "Tell us about the chick."

Jake bobbed up beside him and snagged the bottle for himself, ignoring Noah's protests. "Yeah, man! She's *hot*."

My eyes narrowed and my teeth bared, lips peeled back to reveal my sharp incisors. My shifter growled; it was a struggle to wrestle it back down beneath the surface.

"Whoa." Zac appeared with spiky hair and a towel draped around his neck. He'd fallen into the creek as we were heading back and was none too pleased about it. "Dude, relax."

I shrugged off the guys as they attempted to calm me. "She's not just a *chick*. She's…" I hesitated, not sure how to explain Kara, and they seemed to get the message. Crowding me only made it harder to control the wolf within. It was easier when all of them backed off a touch.

"Wow," Noah whispered. He looked awed. "You're *actually* fated mates. Everyone was gossiping about it last night, but I didn't think it was true."

I didn't reply. The look on my face must have said enough, because the other two dropped down to a nearby bench, dumbfounded.

"We thought it was just a crush or something," Noah said. I stared at him with a raised brow, and he shrugged. "What? It seemed kinda far-fetched, is all."

"Is that why you're all tensed up?" Jake asked. "Man, you need to get it out of your system. All the crazy shifter stuff—it won't go away until you… you know."

"No," I rumbled. "I *don't* know."

Jake and Zac looked a little nervous. Noah came over and laid a hand on my arm. I didn't try to throw him off, but I did glare, hoping that the sheer force of my rage would get him to back off.

Ha. As if I'm ever that lucky. Noah has a set of balls the size of coconuts.

"What we're trying to say is…" Noah quirked an eyebrow, fixing me with his serious, steady gaze. "Don't try to fight this one, Ronan. I know how stubborn you get, but you just gotta let fate do its thing. The rest will fall into place. You'll see."

I grit my teeth, but managed to nod.

I want to see her. Right now.

It was the oddest thing, like a magnet dragging a compass needle due north—the urge to get back to her, now that I was close by, was almost overwhelming.

I left them soon afterwards, but only after I'd endured as many encouraging backslaps as I could handle.

I approached my house in good spirits.

The day had been more fun than I expected, but the conversation after had set my mind on one thing.

Kara.

From the look in her eyes as I left that morning, I was certain that she wanted to take things to the next level.

I wanted to go slow, to take my time with her. She was a virgin, and that state needed to be protected. Valued. Enjoyed. My shifter wanted to rush in, to claim, to devour.

Time would tell which instinct would win out.

I unlocked the door of the house and slipped inside, heading for the living room. At the sight of Kara's dark head resting at the edge of the sofa, my heart leapt.

She looked up as I moved closer, and I almost froze in place. Her eyes were red-rimmed, and she was pale. She sat up and curled her hands over her knees as I sat down beside her. Instead of meeting my gaze, she hung her head.

"What's wrong?"

My mind flashed through a thousand possibilities. I wanted to demand answers, to ask who did this. Who made her miserable?

"Hey." I reached over, putting my hand on her cheek. She let me tilt her face upwards readily enough, but her gaze skittered away from mine. "Talk to me. Did someone do something to upset you? Hurt you?"

She shook her head and wiped a hand over her face. "No, I'm fine. It's nothing like that."

"Doesn't look like it." I took her hand between mine, turning her palm over and pressing a kiss against it. She let out a soft sigh, so I did it again. "C'mon. Tell me."

"I'm just..." Her voice trembled. I thought she was about to burst into tears, but she didn't. She steeled herself before continuing. "I'm scared of this. Of *us*. What if it's not... right?"

Not right? My heart beat in alarm. "What do you mean?"

"I mean..." Kara shook her head. Her dark hair fell in a curtain of loose waves, hiding her face. "We barely know each other. I don't want to... pressure you, or..."

I sat back. Realization was dawning on me, slow and sure. She didn't understand if this really was a fated mates situation. I wracked my brain for something to say. Some way to make her see how certain I was about this. About her.

Even at the best of times, words were never my strong suit.

I stood up from the sofa, and she looked up sharply.

"Wait here," I said. "I want to show you something."

~

KARA

I curled my feet into the sofa cushions and pressed my head back against the couch, closing my eyes.

I thought of the soft, thick, woven blanket that I had at home. I'd made it with wool I'd dyed myself, in bright orange, red and purple. My favorites. The colors of a sunset.

A tear slid down my cheek.

I wiped it away impatiently. There was no sense being homesick. I was fine.

The things that Elder Frey had said haunted me. His words had been going round and round in my mind since this morning; by the time Ronan had come home, I'd been half-convinced I'd be sent packing immediately.

But Ronan hadn't done that. He'd kissed me, and spoken in a soft, soothing voice.

Then he'd disappeared again. The minute I thought I'd gotten a handle on him, he did something like that; just took off without a word.

I wonder if I'll ever work him out.

I wonder if he'll ever give me the chance.

I squeezed my eyes shut and focused on breathing. Several thuds came from upstairs, like he was rummaging around for something.

A few minutes later, I heard him back in the doorway. I opened my eyes and saw him standing there, with a slender black file tucked under his arm. In spite of my low mood, my curiosity was piqued. I sat up straighter as he dropped down beside me.

His face was unreadable as he pulled out the file and held it to me. At first I just blinked at it, uncertain.

"Here." He brandished the file until I eventually took it. He tapped the cover, eyes flicking between me and it. "Open it."

"What's this?"

"Just open it. Please."

I opened the folder. As soon as I laid eyes on its contents, I let out a small, involuntary breath.

A loose pile of photographs was tucked inside. I picked up the top one and held it to the light, my pulse racing.

"Is that..." I trailed off, looking at him questioningly. "You?"

He nodded.

I stared at the tiny child in the photograph. His head was thrown back in uproarious laughter. The woman carrying him was smiling too, a broad, wide smile that crinkled the corners of her eyes.

I pointed at her. "This is your mom?"

"Yes."

I looked down at the photo, then up at Ronan. "You have the same eyes."

Ronan smiled sadly. He took the photo from me and tucked it into the back of the pile.

We shuffled through the rest of the photos together. There were more shots of him, a little older, barefoot and wild, holding baby Kit's chubby hand in the forest. On the shoulders of a tall, bearded man; cuddled up on the sofa with his brother; running with his packmates in the woods. And laughing—always laughing.

Ronan held up another picture. "Here. This was the one I wanted to show you."

Ronan's mom and dad stared up at us from the photograph. They were seated on the front porch of a house. I recognized it as the one we were in. The wooden beams were neatly painted, and their smiles were shy, but their eyes were bright and glowing with happiness. His mom wore a lace veil and had a bouquet of wildflowers in her hands. His dad's hair was smoothed down, and aside from the beard, he looked very much like Ronan.

"This was taken after their bonding ceremony." Ronan's voice was low and hushed. I leaned in closer. "My grandma took it. Mom and her were just visiting the pack. They lived a couple of states over, in another pack at the edge of the city. But Dad took one look at my mom and she looked at him, and that was it. She was the one for him. His one true mate."

My eyes met his. Even in the low light, they were such a piercing shade of amber. For a split second, I lost my breath.

"Were they happy?" I asked, mostly to distract myself from the beauty of his eyes.

"Yeah." Ronan took the photo back and closed the file, setting it down on the coffee table. "Very happy. Everyone thought they were crazy, bonding with each other so soon after they met. But they didn't care what anyone else thought. They knew it was right."

I didn't know what to say. For some reason, I found that I was on the verge of tears. Without looking up, I reached out blindly and took his hand, tangling our fingers together.

"Thank you for sharing that with me." I finally got the courage to look at him, blinking away my blurred vision. "I would've liked to meet them."

"No problem." Ronan squeezed my hand. "I just wanted to show you... my parents couldn't help the way they felt. And neither can I, Kara. I know that what we have is real. No-one else can weigh in on that. I don't know if someone said something, or if the doubts you were having stem from you and no one else. But I wanted to make it clear, that this thing between us... it is no one else's business but yours and mine. And it is up to us what we want to do about it."

My heart was light as he drew my hand up and pressed a kiss onto it.

How could I have doubted him? How could I have doubted this?

"Mom would've loved you, by the way." Ronan ran his thumb over the backs of my fingers, his eyes soft.

I allowed myself to smile up at him. The heaviness weighing down my insides was gone. "Seems like you were born into the perfect family."

Ronan's smile seemed to freeze on his face.

Then the moment passed, and I was left wondering if I had imagined it altogether.

I mentally shrugged, and snuggled further into his solid chest.

It's been a long day. Stop being paranoid.

Everything is perfect... All you have to do is not screw it up.

CHAPTER 10

KARA

Ronan and I sat on the couch for a while longer, talking quietly about nothing in particular. My head rested on his chest, and I pressed into the warmth of his shirt, listening to the slow, steady beat of his heart.

The knot of anxiety in my chest began to ease.

I was used to keeping my own company. I didn't mind it most of the time; sometimes I even appreciated the solitude and drew strength from it. I'd convinced myself that my creative passions were enough, and that I was content to while away my days in the pack, watching other people be happy.

Meeting Ronan had changed all that.

For the first time, I allowed myself to imagine what it would be like:

to stay here, in the Thornwood pack. A day ago, the idea would have filled me with horror.

But now...

Once the thought materialized in my head, I couldn't stop thinking about staying here, with Ronan. I kept mulling the idea over as we moved from the living room to the kitchen, where Ronan threw together a simple but delicious stir-fry after refusing to let me help with anything.

"You're still our guest, Kara!" he said, then dug out place settings for two.

With Kit still gone, it felt a little bit like, well, a date.

"I should've dressed fancier," I joked, as Ronan sat down opposite me.

He'd found a candlestick in the back of one of the cupboards and set it in a holder in the center of the table. It was a little bent out of shape—it clearly hadn't been used in years—and in the glow of the candlelight I caught him making a face.

"You don't need to dress up. You're gorgeous all the time." He picked up his fork and played with it absently, gazing at me with obvious interest. I managed to meet his eyes. I was getting better and better at accepting the attention instead of shying away from it.

"Thank you," I managed, though part of me didn't believe him. No one had ever shown me this level of interest, or if they had, I had never picked up on it. With Ronan, everything was different in that sense. New and undeniably exciting.

"All that other stuff is just... surface level. It's *you* that I want," he said.

"My inner soul?" I tilted my head at him, only half-joking.

He shot me a crooked grin. He didn't seem offended though, just... curious.

"Maybe." A spark entered his eyes. "The wolf in me wants the wolf in you."

"Is that all?"

Ronan stared at me for a long moment. I ached under his heated gaze. I pressed my thighs together under the table, wanting things I couldn't even put a name to.

"No, that's not all." *I want all of you.*

He didn't say that last bit out loud, but I could almost hear the words hovering there between us. I knew, because those words were on the tip of my tongue, too.

I grasped about for a new conversational topic, something that wouldn't result in me crawling over the table and into his lap right then and there.

"When I got here, I thought this place was so different from home." I clenched my fork. My mouth suddenly felt dry. I lifted my glass and took a sip of the wine before continuing, letting its sweetness flood over my tongue. "The people, the watchtowers... everything. But now I'm not so sure."

"What do you mean?"

I gestured around us, and Ronan looked around the kitchen, frowning. "I'm not sure I follow."

I let out a soft sigh. "I *know* this house, Ronan. These walls. I've lived inside them too, at least metaphorically. Ever since I lost my parents."

My voice was gentle, but there was an undercurrent of sadness in it that I couldn't hide. No matter how long it had been, I knew the sadness would never go away. Not completely.

"For the longest time, my brother Jason and I were on our own. We had the pack, sure, but..." I bit my lip. "There were times when it felt like all we had was each other. The house we grew up in, our parents' house, became a memorial to them. It wasn't a place to live any more... just a reminder of everything we'd lost."

I gazed around at the kitchen. Like the rest of the house, the walls in here were bare of decoration.

"I'm sorry," Ronan murmured.

I reached out and grabbed his hand over the table. "I'm just saying... I get it."

"What changed?"

A smile blossomed across my face. "Jason found his mate. Tammy. A human girl, of all things."

Ronan's eyebrows shot up. "Wow."

"I know." My smile faded as I thought of them in that house, happy with the new life they'd just brought into the world. Making new memories to fill the space with love once again. "I'm happy for him."

"But...?"

I tilted my head, confused. "There's no *but*. All I want is for the people I love to be happy."

A wrinkle appeared between Ronan's eyebrows. "Of course. But you deserve happiness too, Kara. You deserve to make your own memories."

"I'm happy enough," I countered.

"I beg to differ."

I wanted to put an end to this conversation that had suddenly taken a ridiculous turn. We were debating my happiness, for some reason, when I was the happiest I'd ever been, sitting across from Ronan with nothing but a beat-up old candlestick between us.

I opened my mouth to say something to that effect, but before I could get any more words out, Ronan stood up and circled the table, hoisting me up out of my chair.

I gasped and flung my arms around his neck to steady myself. I wanted to protest. I could walk on my own two feet, thank you very much. Before I could say anything, he pressed his mouth against mine, hot and demanding.

It was exactly what I'd imagined doing to him, only a few minutes earlier, and now that he'd taken the initiative, I melted into the embrace.

I moaned as his arms tightened around my body, reveling in our closeness. When he pulled away, his gaze was determined behind the heat in his expression.

"You deserve everything," he growled. *"Everything."*

Well, when he put it that way... "I *want* everything," I whispered, and I had never spoken a truer word. I pulled his face down to mine, and we kissed with an intensity that left me trembling and weak on the inside.

In a move that left me dizzy, he lifted me up, encouraging my legs to wrap around his waist, and then he carried me upstairs. This time, he wasn't as controlled about it. Judging by the way he kept pausing to press hot-mouthed kisses over every inch of my skin he could reach, he was struggling to contain his desire. I shivered as I realized he was holding himself back from just taking me right there, in the hallway or on the stairs.

I wouldn't have cared at all. I was shameless, wanton. I needed to *feel* him, against me, around me and *inside* me, more than I had ever needed anything in my life.

I slid my hands up his back, clenching my thighs tighter around his waist and feeling his muscles shifting underneath his shirt. Once we reached the landing, he placed me down. I stumbled onto my tiptoes, arching up into his form, pressing the length of my body against his. My hands fisted into his shirt as I dragged him backwards toward the door of his bedroom.

I wanted him to be in no doubt at all, that this is what I wanted. Him, right here and right now.

My heart beat like a trapped bird inside my chest. I was dizzy with arousal, helpless to control the ache deep within me.

The night was only going to end one way.

I need to feel him inside me.

We made our way through the threshold of the room, and he backed me toward the bed without breaking his stride. There was none of last night's cautious restraint; he wasn't holding back anymore as he pressed down on top of me. The mattress sagged down under our combined weight, and I shifted and writhed up against him, giving as good as I got.

He pulled away from my mouth to look down at me. There was a wildness in his face; his hips thrust into mine, like he was unaware of the action. His tangled hair fell over his face, and in the half-darkness, there was no mistaking the wolf in him.

Good. I want it—I want it all.

He growled as my legs fell open around his hips, and my mouth parted in a wordless invitation. He leaned down over me and seared a kiss against my neck, tasting my fluttering pulse.

"No-one has touched you," he murmured, "before me?"

"No-one," I gasped.

He slid his fingers down and teased over the waistband of my jeans, and I bit back a needy moan.

"Only you."

His clever fingers worked open the zipper and brushed down, skirting the edge of my pussy until he had me panting with frustration. Before long, we both grew impatient, tired of the teasing. I worked off my jeans and fiddled with the buttons of my shirt, but Ronan had had enough. The fabric came apart between his fists, and shreds of fabric littered the bed around us. My bra soon followed, and before long I was naked beneath his hot, heaving chest and wild eyes.

Last night, Ronan had been the picture of control. He hadn't seemed worried for his own pleasure; he'd been content to drive me to orgasm and retreat downstairs for the rest of the night.

This was different.

This time, we were in it together: that crazed hunger that overcame all shifters when they found their true mate.

I squirmed a hand free and pawed at his t-shirt. He tugged it off, getting the message. My hands roamed over his chest as he stared down at me. When my hands made for his jeans, his fingers encircled my wrists and pushed me back down.

I wanted to cry out. To beg and plead, if I had to.

In the state I was in, I would do or say just about anything to get him to touch me.

"You've never been taken like this before." Ronan's voice rumbled through my own chest. "Have you?"

"Never." The word was almost wrenched out of me. "Please, I need you. I can't—"

My hips bucked up into his. I was so wet, and I would have been shame-faced if not for the feel of Ronan's hard cock pushing against the inside of his jeans. In spite of my impatient movements, he seemed unsure. His eyes flicked over my face, searching for something.

"What is it? I want you, Ronan. I need you. Don't stop."

Evidently, my permission must have been what he was looking for. My words galvanized him into action. His hands sprang from my wrists and he jumped up to drag off his clothing and free his erection before rejoining me on the bed. We both groaned as he shifted forward, and the head of his cock brushed over my clit.

"Ronan." I squirmed as he bore down against me, his mouth pressing into my neck, teeth and tongue working over my heated skin. "Please."

When he finally slid inside me, I was so wet and ready that there was only minimal resistance. He paused, then thrust a little harder, and the virginal barrier was gone. He filled me, the heat and intensity of being possessed like this almost too much to bear. I spread my legs as wide as I could, shameless in my need, and arched up into him.

He put his hands around my waist and pulled me into him. Then one of his hands found its way to the side of my head, fingers tangling in my hair. I buried my face in his heated neck, and he began to thrust into me.

He drew back and forced me to look at him. I wanted to blush, to duck away, but I couldn't escape his eyes.

Those damned eyes. After tonight, I'd never be able to look into them the same way again.

"Mine," he said. "You're mine, Kara. Mine to claim."

"Yours," I managed to gasp out.

In that moment, I knew it was true. Body and soul, he had me.

His thrusts were slow at first, testing, making allowance for this being my first time, but when my moans and gasps proved I was enjoying this as much as him, he picked up the pace and started driving into me in a steady, unrelenting rhythm. I was spread-eagled against the mattress, pinned in place with the force of his possession, helpless in the face of my mounting orgasm.

It crashed over me, wave after wave of pleasure coursing through my body as Ronan fucked me through it. I sobbed, loving the feeling of him surrounding me on all sides. One of his hands came down to rub my clit and I wanted to pull away—it was too much, too intense—but there was nowhere to go. I could only buck into his touch as he changed his angle slightly, and with another deep thrust, a second orgasm rolled through me.

After what felt like an endless sea of pleasure, Ronan buried himself deep and spilled into me with a groan. He tugged my head back, and he laid an open-mouthed kiss against my lips. I swallowed the sound of his orgasmic cries, drinking him in as eagerly as my body rippled around his cock.

A shiver ran down my spine at a sudden realization.

We didn't use protection.

There was a possibility that he'd claimed me in more ways than one.

I ached as he slowly pulled out of me. He hadn't been overly rough as far as I could tell, but the unfamiliarity of the act left me exhausted, physically and emotionally. He slumped down next to me and gathered me into his arms, rolling me into his side and pressing a kiss against the back of my shoulder. I pressed back into him. We were lying in a tangle of hot, damp sheets and the remains of my shirt, but I didn't care.

The long day, with all its emotional highs and lows, had finally caught up with me.

Beside me, Ronan's breathing settled. He mumbled something into my hair as he drifted off to sleep, but I didn't catch it.

I lay still for a few minutes, trying to process what had just happened, unable to fight the huge smile that lifted my lips. Pretty soon, I followed him into sleep.

CHAPTER 11

RONAN

Now that Kara and I had laid all our cards on the table in relation to how we felt, a strange sort of peace settled over the house.

Over the days that followed, we fell into a routine. Each morning, I headed out to attend to my pack duties. On good days, this meant patrolling with Noah or Jake, and on bad days it meant sitting through a seemingly endless council meeting and listening to the Elders strategize about this or that.

Usually, I returned in time for lunch with Kara. Sometimes Kit joined us, or it would just be the two of us. After, we'd sit out on the porch people-watching, and Kara would tell me about her morning.

She had taken it upon herself to renovate the house. It started with, in her words, sprucing up the kitchen and living room, before unfolding into a full-on transformation. After the morning I came home to find her cursing at the wall and holding her wrist, I enlisted the help of some of the guys for the manual labor, and by the end of the week, the wall that divided the kitchen and dining room was mostly gone, replaced by a couple of rustic beams that opened up the space and somehow made it cozier at the same time.

I began to notice small things appearing. Colored cushions on the sofa one day, followed by a throw in a soft, loose knit the next. Things that I hadn't seen for years—an old wind chime, a rusty planter, a watering can—all rescued and restored, or else repurposed into something new.

At first, she would ask me if I liked each new thing.

I always said, truthfully, that I loved it.

After a while, she stopped asking.

People around town—some teasing, some sincere—began to point out the change in me. How there was a new purpose to the way I walked, a true Alpha's glint in my eye. Even Kit, who had always been a happy kid but full of excess energy, seemed calmer, no longer skittering around the house like he was full of nervous tension.

It was all down to the positive influence of Kara.

I couldn't believe how lucky I had been to meet her. One day, I would have to visit Allara at the Bane pack and let her know how grateful I was that she had sent Kara in her place.

The peace and happiness for all of us was new, and it was welcome. But in my experience, good things didn't last.

I woke up in the night to the sound of movement coming from outside my bedroom window. I stirred, half-awake. Kara lay beside me, still deeply asleep, her hair spread out on the pillow and one of her hands curled up against her cheek. She looked adorable, and my dick stirred immediately.

Until I realized what had woken me. At the sound of a distant shout, I sat bolt upright in bed, amorous thoughts on hold.

Silently, I climbed out of bed and moved over to the window. My shifter senses were on high alert. I could hear more shouting in the distance, and the thud of running feet on the street outside.

A sleepy voice came from the bed behind me.

"What's the matter, Ronan?"

I turned around. Kara was gazing at me and rubbing her eyes.

"What's going on?" she asked.

"I don't know." Trepidation filled me. It sounded like some kind of attack. I glanced back outside, but it was too dark to see anything clearly, even with my shifter-enhanced vision. "Stay here, and lock the door behind me."

I quickly threw on some clothes and strode out of the room, taking the stairs two at a time. I slipped out of the house as silently as possible, praying that Kit was still asleep upstairs. He was too young to become involved in a battle, if this truly was an attack of some kind on our pack.

It was pitch dark outside. The rest of the houses were still and quiet. Whatever was happening, most of the pack still seemed to be oblivious.

I followed the sound of voices, my heart thudding under my shirt. I couldn't shake the feeling that something wasn't right, but I couldn't put my finger on what.

Then it hit me. Everything was dark, but it shouldn't be.

The lights from the watchtowers, those familiar beacons that shone over the town every night, were gone.

Thud.

I tensed up as I smacked into something warm and solid, and my hackles rose, instincts telling me to fight. A low growl slipped out of me.

"Ronan?"

At the sound of Jake's voice, I relaxed a touch.

"What's happening?" I asked. "An attack?"

My pack is in danger. The thought thrummed through my whole body. *I have to protect them. I have to protect Kara.*

"I don't know." The seriousness in Jake's usually carefree voice sent a chill down my spine. "I woke up and heard noises. Figured I'd come and find you."

I blinked, touched by his loyalty.

"Come on. This way." I tapped his shoulder, indicating that I wanted him to follow me.

Together, we crept through town, sticking to the sides of buildings to orient ourselves. Even with our shifter eyesight, it was nearly impossible to see much in the darkness.

Jake and I had been packmates all our lives, friends for years, and had done many guard duty hours together. We didn't need words as we soundlessly worked our way through town.

As we neared the edge of the square, we ran into Noah and Zac, who were crouched behind a high fence. A fire burned nearby and a spark of relief flooded me when their faces came into view, despite their grave expressions.

"The gates are open," Noah said. "Ronan, I think it's a coup. There's a group of people—shifters I'd say—and they said they're looking for you. And when they find you..."

My blood froze. I sprang to my feet. "I left Kit and Kara back at the house. I have to go back for them—"

Zac yanked me down again, ignoring the growl I sent his way. "No way. If you go back to that house now, you're a dead man."

"I don't care."

I wasn't thinking logically. I wasn't thinking at all.

"You may not care, but we do," Noah interjected. "We need a living Alpha, Ronan. Not a dead one."

"I'm no-one's Alpha," I hissed, forgetting that I'd started to slide automatically into the role over the past couple of weeks. Right now, I didn't want to lead a pack. All I cared about was the safety of my younger brother, and the woman I—

"Guys, we can debate this later." Jake peered over the fence. I realized that the area beyond our hiding place was brighter, like more fires had been lit nearby. "We have to leave now, before they see us."

As we skirted around the edge of the square, I caught sight of a few of the figures gathered in the center, holding torches.

A woman's long hair shone in the firelight. As she turned her head, I got a good look at her.

Naomi.

A man I didn't recognize slid up alongside her and wrapped an arm around her waist. Her lips thinned, but she didn't push him away. He whispered something in her ear and a smile stretched across her face.

Something about that smile chilled me to the bone.

Enough of this. I wasn't born to crouch in the shadows, or slink away like some coward.

I turned to Jake and Zac. "Circle back to the front gates. Then close them. Cut these other shifters off from escape, make sure no-one else gets in."

I used my commanding tone, knowing they couldn't refuse. They turned away without a word and vanished into the night. I trusted them completely to get the job done.

I turned back to the clearing, my eyes narrowed as I considered and discarded options. In the end, there was only one option that made sense.

"Wait." Noah hovered at my shoulder. "I know that look. Ronan, this is a bad idea."

"I know," I muttered. "But it's the only idea I have."

It's me they want. Nobody else has to get hurt.

With a deep breath, I straightened upright and swaggered into the clearing.

CHAPTER 12
KARA

The minute Ronan ordered me to stay put, my hackles rose with fear mixed with a healthy dose of anger.

There's no way I'm staying here!

I wanted to yell after him as he swept out of the room, but the words stuck in my throat. Furious, I flung back the covers and stumbled into the clothes that had been abandoned by the side of the bed earlier that night.

I remembered the way Ronan had torn them off me, frenzied with passion.

I squeezed my eyes tight shut, and drew a deep breath.

Now is the time to be brave.

Without thinking twice, I pulled on my clothes and headed for the door.

The landing was dark. As I crossed over it toward the stairs, the door cracked open behind me and a chink of light appeared, along with Kit's sleep-tousled hair.

"Kara?" His voice was rough and gritty with sleep. "I heard something."

I glanced back at him. "I know. I'm going outside. Stay here, okay?"

"Where's Ronan?"

I paused, one foot hovering over the top step.

I couldn't lie to him. Ronan was his brother—he deserved the truth. It was what I would've wanted in his position. "He left already."

We exchanged a long look. With each minute that ticked past, I was more awake, more alert. The silence prickled against my eardrums.

Something was wrong.

Kit slid out of his room, flannel PJs and all, and shut the door behind him. Even in half-shadow, I could see the determination on his face. "I'm coming with you."

"No, Kit—"

"If you try to tell me it's too dangerous..." His eyes flashed at me, and I caught a hint of his shifter beneath the surface. Young, feral. Ready for action. "Save it, okay? He's my *brother*. I know you understand."

I nodded. I understood all too well. I had just been angry with Ronan, because he had assumed I was too weak to help, and demanded I stay put. It would be hypocritical of me if I did exactly the same thing to Kit now.

"Be careful, okay. Ronan loves you so much, Kit..."

"I know. That's why I need to help."

After a moment I nodded. There wasn't time to argue. We headed downstairs together, slipping on the first pairs of shoes we could find in the darkened hallway, and snuck out into the night.

The streets were mostly empty, but there were a handful of other people from the pack who had heard the noise and come out like us to see what was going on. We found ourselves in the middle of a group of people who were heading toward the town square. It seemed to be where the action was, with the flicker of flames in that direction drawing us all like the proverbial moths.

By the time we made it to the edge of the clearing, the crowd was thick enough that we had to nudge our way through to the front.

My heart plummeted down to earth and I had to clench my hands into fists to stop them trembling.

Ronan stood alone at the center of the clearing. He was surrounded on all sides by shifters. They didn't seem to be from this pack. Even though I didn't know everyone here on a personal level yet, I'd seen a lot of Ronan's pack around the village since I'd been here and at least knew them to look at. These shifters were strangers, stony-faced and threatening.. Some of them were in wolf form, and they padded around the edge of the square like moving shadows. Circling Ronan, as if he were prey.

One of the strangers stepped forward into the light, and my heart all but stopped.

He wasn't a stranger, not to me.

Jaime.

He looked unchanged from the last time I'd seen him, when he'd turned up to fight Allara, assuming he was going to kill her and win the Alpha spot. Same smug, smirking face, same sandy hair. Only a deep scar, bisecting his left eyebrow and carving an ugly crevice down his cheek, spoke of his fight for dominance against Allara all those months ago.

A smaller figure slunk up beside him. *Naomi?* Was she with Jaime, now? A sick feeling settled in my gut. Individually, Jaime and Naomi were poison. Together, they would likely be deadly.

The two of them moved forward like some twisted parody of an Alpha pair, coming to a standstill about five feet away from Ronan.

He wasn't moving. The only indication of the emotion I knew must be bubbling inside him were his clenched fists. Even from here, I could see his white-knuckled grip.

"I guess we have an audience now," Jaime said, his voice ringing out through the clearing. "It looks like this takeover won't be as peaceful as I hoped."

Ronan's face twisted. "You mean you can't kill me in my sleep, now that the pack is here to bear witness?" He swept out a hand toward Jaime and whirled around. "Behold, your would-be Alpha, everyone. A coward who attacks under the cover of darkness, because he knows he'd never win in a fair fight. The Bane pack's Alpha proved that, already."

The smile on Jaime's face instantly disappeared. His eyes glittered coldly. "At least I know what I am. What I *can* be. You had all the power at your fingertips, there for the taking, and you ran away. What sort of Alpha runs away and leaves his pack unprotected? Why do you think

I'm here? There's a power vacuum, Ronan." He shrugged. "You didn't step up."

"You will never be Alpha of this pack," Ronan said. His voice rang out clearly, strong and sure. The flames burning around the clearing flickered, and several people gasped. "Get out of here, before I tear you apart."

Jaime's smile reappeared. "The truth is," he said, obviously playing to his captive audience and making sure we all caught every word, "deep down, you know you aren't the man for the job. Everyone knows it."

His eyes narrowed, and his voice dropped into a hiss. "Your *father* knew it."

Ronan let out a growl so powerful, I felt it rumble through the ground beneath my feet. Everyone around me held their breaths. Even Naomi took a small, involuntary step back. Jaime looked surprised, but he held his ground.

A mist was churning up in the center of the clearing. Dust rose from the ground, and static flashed in the air.

Ronan was shifting.

Jaime's eyes flashed with something. I couldn't tell if it was panic or anger. But he damn sure hadn't expected to have to fight Ronan. The coward had planned to kill Ronan in his sleep.

He didn't have any choice, now. Jaime crouched low in the dirt, a cloud of mist rising up around him to mirror Ronan's own.

The wolves patrolling around the edge of the square threw back their heads and howled.

My chest grew tight, and my gut churned. I felt it: that familiar urge, the instinct to let the wild creature inside me run free. It was the strongest call I'd had in years. Stronger than my first, uncontrolled shifts, stronger even than the first time I'd laid eyes on Ronan and realized he was my fated mate.

I bit my lip so hard I tasted blood. Now wasn't the time to lose control.

Beside me, Kit shifted his weight from one foot to the other, as if he were fighting against the same urge as me.

Unable to drag my eyes away from Ronan, I reached out blindly and grabbed at Kit's wrist, shaking my head.

Don't do it, Kit. Control yourself.

Young shifters couldn't always help it when they shifted sometimes

—especially when they were scared, or angry. The skill only became more controlled with time and experience.

Inside the clearing, Ronan drew himself up to his full height. He was a massive wolf. His russet fur gleamed in the firelight, and his thick pelt rippled across his broad, bulky frame. Despite Jaime's taunts, his features were unmistakably those of an Alpha's bloodline and it was strikingly apparent to everyone there that they were looking at an Alpha wolf.

He shook himself off in a familiar motion, and his head dropped low, eyes narrowed and deadly as he readied himself to fight.

Poised to strike, he stood taller than Jaime in wolf form, and every muscle in his body tensed. One-on-one, he was in a good position to defeat the rogue intruder. But he was outnumbered. Already the other wolves were crowding in, ready to defend Jaime at a second's notice.

The back of my neck prickled, and my mouth went dry.

Unconsciously, one of my hands came up to rest over my abdomen.

Jaime's ears flicked, and he glanced at the wolf to his left side. The wolf slunk backwards, and the others followed.

Okay. So this isn't a pile-on. Not yet, anyway.

This is a fight for control of the Thornwood pack.

Something in the air shifted. Ronan's muzzle came up and his eyes slid past Jaime—and landed on me.

I poured everything I felt for Ronan into my expression, praying it would give him strength.

Then Jaime lunged at Ronan.

I jumped, my heart pounding as I watched the man who should be my mate, handle an attack from a man I knew to be vicious and unhinged.

There wasn't going to be any mercy here tonight. This would be a fight to the death.

Both were going in for the kill.

Ronan twisted away from Jaime, then lunged in, his jaws latching onto the back of Jaime's neck; he lifted him into the air and shook him before slamming him back down to earth. Jaime snarled and shook himself free, slinking backwards, his belly against the earth.

I was fixated on the fight. I didn't even blink.

I sent out a soundless, desperate prayer into the darkness.

Please, Ronan, you have to finish this.

For me. For us.

I was barely conscious of who I meant. Us—the pack? Me and Kit? Or something else? Something that I was too elated and afraid to even name. Perhaps it was for the tiny something that could be growing inside me right now as I watched the man I loved fight for his life.

Sharp, vicious snarls and growls pierced the air, and I snapped back into the present.

Naomi had joined the fray and advanced while Ronan's back was turned. She was sleeker than Jaime, with fur that shone white in the shadows.

Ronan's ear flicked outwards as she grew closer. He knew she was there, but he was too busy fending off Jaime's snapping jaws to do anything about her.

Then I realized that my hand, the one that had been locked on Kit's wrist, was empty.

Shit.

Russet fur flashed at the edge of the clearing. My heart thundered in my chest and adrenalin zinged along my veins. Kit was in wolf form and advancing around the circle, keeping to the shadows but obviously trying to position himself to launch into defense of his brother.

Several of Jaime's wolves turned to Kit.

My mouth formed a single, soundless word. *No!*

As if we were psychically connected and he'd heard me, Ronan's head snapped up. He immediately saw what was about to happen, and charged Jaime, tossing him to one side. He bounded past Naomi like she wasn't even there. His eyes were wide with fear, and fixed on his brother.

He was too far away. Jaime's wolves sprang on Kit and dragged him down in a blur of teeth and fur and snarls. Kit whined and tried to lash out, but the wolves were too big to fight, too strong to throw off, and too many to defeat.

Ronan skidded to a halt in front of Kit's fallen form and let out a snarl so powerful it was almost a roar. He grabbed the nearest wolf in his jaws and tore him away, sending him tumbling to the ground in a mess of blood and fur. Another of Kit's attackers snapped at him, but he twisted aside and then lunged for him, knocking the wolf aside and slashing out with his huge paws.

Kit lay on the ground, curled onto one side. From this angle, I couldn't see if he was still breathing.

My vision blurred. My heart thundered in my chest.

I couldn't control my shifter any longer. My family needed saving.

I dropped to my knees and the world around me dissolved. When I blinked and straightened up, I wasn't fully Kara anymore. My shifter was in the driver's seat.

For once, I didn't try to suppress my wolf instincts. I simply got out of its way and let it take control.

I crept forward.

Being a wolf again was surreal. It had been months, maybe even a year, since I'd been in this form. Every blade of grass under my feet, every brush of wind on my face, every subtle movement of the crowd surrounding the square flooded my senses.

I couldn't get distracted.

Ronan was caught up with Jaime again. Naomi was watching them, waiting for a chance to jump in and help Jaime. She hadn't noticed me. I had the element of surprise.

I bounded forward and lunged at her, sinking my jaws into her neck without hesitation.

I'd never attacked anyone like this in my life.

It felt surprisingly good, given the recipient was Naomi.

My human mind, buried deep under thick layers of shifter instinct and rage, replayed every encounter with her over the years. The sly comments, the casual cruelty. The way she'd tossed Jason aside when it was convenient, then came running back the second he found someone better. Her shameless greed, her ambition for power.

And now, her desire to destroy Ronan. I could not forgive, nor let that slide.

Not anymore.

She managed to roll me over, dislodging me off her neck, but I had drawn blood, and I wanted more. She snarled in my face, long teeth glistening. I arched up and growled straight back at her, baring my lips to reveal my own shifter teeth.

It was obvious she was the more experienced fighter of the two of us. But I had something she didn't have: unstoppable anger, and the drive to protect my family.

With a sharp twist, I pounced and pinned her to the ground, my front paws on her neck and chest. Her white fur, so flawless before, was marred and tangled. I probably looked similar, but I didn't care.

A crack rang out like a gunshot over the square.

I jerked up my head, looking for Ronan, and felt the jolt of shock through Naomi's body beneath my paws as she arched her head in the same direction as me.

Jaime lay at Ronan's feet, still and lifeless.

Cold shock rushed over me. A couple of whining noises from the edge of the clearing caught my attention. The wolves from Jaime's pack were crowded together, pinned down by three newcomers that I suspected were Noah, Zac, and Jake.

A small, pained sound came from a few feet away.

Kit.

Like a spell had been broken, I climbed off Naomi and left her on the ground, walking away from her toward Kit. She didn't try to get up.

Ronan was already standing over Kit when I got there, nudging at him with his muzzle. He looked up as I approached but allowed me to press up against his side. Another shifter approached, but Ronan snarled at him until he backed away.

Kit's chest was rising and falling in short, shallow breaths. Ronan nudged him again and whined, a low, awful sound that set my fur on edge.

I couldn't imagine this village without Kit's smiling, happy face in it, and I'd only known him a short time. Ronan must have been so scared at the thought of losing his only sibling.

Out of the corner of my eye, I caught movement.

The crowd parted to let someone through. Elder Frey strode into the middle of the clearing and spread his arms out wide.

"The challenger has been killed," he said. Even from this distance, I could see his expression, grave and stone-like. "Go home, all of you."

Something flickered in my chest. Doubt, maybe. Or confusion.

Why wasn't he declaring Ronan the victor?

I shook my head and refocused on Kit, who was just beginning to stir. I'd held a grudge against the Elder ever since he'd taken me aside and told me Ronan wasn't cut out to be a mate.

Ronan is the perfect mate. For me.

I stared again at Elder Frey, whose lips were tight as he glared around at the crowd.

It's probably nothing.

We had far bigger problems right now.

RONAN

The next few days passed in a blur.

I couldn't keep track as days faded into nights. I sat beside Kit's bed, the changing light outside the window my only source of company.

Kara brought me food occasionally, slipping in and out of the room and closing the door softly behind her. I must have eaten, but I barely registered what passed my lips. Sometimes she sat with me, and together we shared the silence that lay like a thick fog over everything.

I couldn't even begin to face the thought of life without my brother by my side.

On the third day, Kit woke up.

I was dozing face down on the bedspread when I felt a soft poke against the top of my head. I jolted, mumbling and blinking the sleep out of my eyes.

"Kara?" I muttered.

"No." The voice was scratchy with disuse, but it made my heart sing. "Your brother."

My eyes opened properly and I sat up so fast I felt dizzy. Kit was resting against his pillow. He was still pale, but he was awake. And smiling at me.

"Hey." I poured him a glass of water from the bedside table and handed it over. He drained it in one swallow, then wiped a hand over his face. "How do you feel?"

"Like I got run over by a truck." Kit ran a hand through his mussed hair and cocked his head to the side. "What happened?"

"What do you remember?"

"Not much." Kit struggled to sit up, shuffling around and ignoring my hand on his shoulder, trying to get him to lie still. "I remember the fight. Those other wolves getting ready to attack you. I thought I might be able to distract them... help you... But after that, it's all a blur."

"The coup failed. Jaime's dead. It's over."

Kit raised an eyebrow.

"You killed him."

He said it as a statement rather than a question, like he had every confidence in me.

I nodded slowly. "I did. But it was close."

"Are you okay, Ronan? And Kara?"

"We are. The storm has passed, I swear, Kit. We're safe."

Kit grinned. "You beat the challenger. Congrats."

I didn't smile back.

When I thought of the life I had taken, mixed emotions rose in my chest. Bitterness, sorrow... and the sure-fire certainty that I would do it all again if I had to.

I'd do anything to keep the ones I loved safe.

But I wasn't ready for Kit to learn about the guilt that came with killing a man, yet. To see the look in his eyes when he learned the truth. Killing didn't bring triumph. Killing was a last resort and always something that weighed heavily on a person's soul, even if the death was deserved, or in self-defense.

"Does this mean you've accepted, then?"

I blinked, snapping back to the present. "What?"

"That you're our Alpha," Kit said carefully, like I was slow on the uptake. "The ceremony doesn't have to be a huge deal, Ronan. It's just a formality, right?"

I said nothing, plucking at a loose thread in the duvet cover.

Luckily, Kit's attention had already wandered to other things. Now that he was awake, that restless teenage energy was back with a vengeance. He moved under the covers, as if about to get up, and I shook my head, pushing him back down.

"No way, man. You're still healing."

"Ronan." Kit's voice had gone full little-brother-whine. His eyes widened as I climbed to my feet and headed toward the door. "C'mon, I'm *fine.*"

"Even shifters need time to recover." I remained firm, even when Kit rolled his eyes and slumped back down again. "Give your body a chance to heal, okay? At least until tomorrow."

As I left the room, I hoped the palpable relief in my voice wasn't as obvious to my brother as it was to me.

Three days ago, we weren't sure he was going to wake up at all.

I stood outside his door, and gave an involuntary sigh of relief. Soaking in the reality of the fact that my brother was alive and going to be okay.

I didn't have a chance to bask in the relief for long. Already, the respite was draining away. I had other problems, and now there was nothing to distract from them.

Like an echo, his words filtered through from the back of my mind.

You're our Alpha.

My ribcage felt several sizes too tight. I tried to draw in a deep breath, but my lungs were being squeezed inwards.

Fresh air. That's what I need.

My heart hammered as I jogged down the staircase. I hadn't so much as set foot outside in days. A good run through the forest would clear my airways and soothe the tension thrumming along the length of my spine.

Kara came out of the kitchen. Seeing the look on my face, she buried herself in my arms. "He's awake?"

"He is." I pressed my face against the top of her head, comforted. "Thank you," I mumbled, pulling away to kiss her properly. "For everything."

Her eyes shone up at me, and I cupped a hand against her cheek, tucking a few loose strands of hair behind her ear.

"I've got a surprise for you." Her smile was soft. "Look... just here."

She led me away from the foot of the stairs, across the hall to the wall on the other side.

I came to a standstill.

The wall, which had been bare for almost a year now, had been transformed.

The photos from the file I kept buried in my closet—the same ones I'd shown Kara, all those weeks ago—had been arranged in a pretty collage on the wall. I didn't recognize the eclectic bundle of frames that housed the pictures: they were mismatched, but they all somehow fit together.

Some pictures were of Kit and me, down by the creek, arms slung around each other's shoulders with matching smiles. Noah, Jake and Zac were holding beers in one of the photos, while my teenage self frowned from the corner of the frame. There was even a recent one of me and Kara, in the garden behind the house, standing amongst the sunflowers. I think Kit took that one, a couple of weeks ago.

Dad was everywhere. Standing center stage in the meeting house, swinging Kit in his arms, laughing and clapping a man on the shoulder. I leaned closer, realizing the other man was Elder Frey, just a less grizzled version than the one I knew.

In the central frame, my mom and dad stared out at me. I was perched on Dad's shoulders with a wide, cheery grin; in Mom's arms, baby Kit was sleeping peacefully.

I tried to speak, but when I opened my mouth, nothing came out.

All the tiredness, rage, confusion and frustration that had been building up over the days I'd spent at Kit's bedside rushed over me. I swayed backwards on my feet, unable to take my eyes off the picture in the middle.

From my father's unyielding, frozen gaze.

You're our Alpha.

Kara put her hand on my arm. "What do you think? Do you like it?"

~

KARA

With each passing moment, each second of silence that dragged out, my anxiety grew.

I thought he'd love the collection of photos. I'd spent ages picking through them all to find ones that resonated with who I believed Ronan to be. I wanted to give him this reminder of all the relationships he valued; everyone who had cared for and supported him over the years.

Ronan stared at the collage with an unreadable expression. He was so still, he could've been a statue. Only the slow rise and fall of his chest told me otherwise.

I glanced again at the wall, my stomach sinking.

I'd wanted to channel all the nervous energy I'd built up over the past week into something productive. Something that would brighten up the barren hallway. Something that could remind Ronan what he had right in front of him.

The life he had, the people he'd loved. Even those he'd lost.

I thought it would help him come to terms with what had happened.

Now, doubt flooded through me. Had I overstepped the mark?

Ronan seemed to appreciate all the other little changes I'd made around the place. Maybe I'd gotten carried away, this time.

Finally, Ronan's shoulders hunched forward, and he turned away. His eyes dragged past mine without meeting them on his way over to the door. He opened it, then paused with his hand on the door handle.

"The kid's restless already," he said. "You should go see him."

I glanced back toward the photos on the wall. With the light of the sunset flooding in from the porch, the glass of the frames glimmered.

Ronan's eyes were fixed on the floor. He couldn't seem to look at either the photos, or me any longer.

"I will." I was proud of myself for holding my voice steady. "But only once you've told me what's wrong."

"I'm fine," he shot back, his eyes hard.

It wasn't an expression I was used to getting from him. All that affection and warmth seemed to have vanished. This was not the Ronan I knew.

He moved to close the door, but I swept forward before I knew what I was doing and pushed my way through, following him outside.

"No," I said. "You're not. Ronan, I'm sorry. I wanted it to be a surprise. I thought it would cheer you up."

"It's fine." He dragged a hand over his face. "Kara, I just need some air. I need to take a walk."

Stupid and irrational as it was, a surge of crushing panic swept over me.

The part of me that was human—the rational, level-headed part—knew the panic was ridiculous. But I couldn't help it. The other part was terrified of losing its mate. It wouldn't listen to reason. The fear was primal, lodged deep in my chest.

The worst part was, I couldn't fight it.

He got halfway down the steps before I put a hand on his shoulder. "Ronan. Please. Just *talk* to me."

Stay. The word hovered in the air between us, unspoken.

Under my hand, his body stiffened. He turned his head to the side so that I could see his darkened profile. "I'm done with talking right now."

"Well, I'm not! You've been watching over your brother for days, barely talking to anyone. And now you can't even *look* at me!"

The mention of his brother seemed to crack through the surface of whatever wall Ronan had put up. He wheeled around at me. "Because I've been trying to take care of the only family I have left!"

I bit down hard on my lip to quell the tears that threatened to spring up. My shifter was growing frustrated, and with frustration came anger.

My throat burned, and my breath came out fast and uneven. "And what are the rest of us meant to do? You're acting like you're alone, but you're *not*. My clan—"

Ronan's mouth curled bitterly. "Your clan? Your clan let Jaime go free. Your *reckless* Alpha almost got my brother killed."

"Don't you *dare* talk about Allara like that."

We were almost nose to nose, staring each other down without blinking. I hated how Ronan's sheer proximity always made my heart race in my chest. It was totally inappropriate, but heat coiled in my gut, and not entirely for the right reasons.

Ronan's gaze darted to my mouth. He huffed out a long breath. "I don't endanger me and mine, Kara."

"Neither does she." I looked up at him, and my breath caught at his burning gaze. "There's a difference between protecting people and holding them prisoner."

"What are you saying?"

"This place, these walls. You're not keeping people safe—you're locking them in. I have a brother too." The words were coming out fast, harsher than I intended, but I didn't care. "One I haven't seen in *weeks*. And a sister-in-law—and a niece."

I let out a short laugh that bordered on hysteria. "What am I even still *doing* here? If you would turn like this, so cold and unfeeling..."

Something flashed across Ronan's face. For a brief second, he looked anguished. "Kara."

"Maybe it's time for me to go back to my own family. My *clan*." My breath hitched as I held back a sob. "Now that Jaime's gone."

"Kara, *wait*."

I shook my head, darting out of his grasp as I descended the steps of the porch.

"That's why I'm here, right?" I whirled around toward his stricken face. "You needed collateral. Something to keep your truce with the Bane Clan. I was so stupid. I thought... well, it doesn't matter what I thought. I was wrong."

Ronan growled. He started after me, but I skittered out of reach.

"Don't be ridiculous," he shouted.

"Ridiculous? I'm being ridiculous?" The fire inside my heart was burning, and nothing could put it out. "Jaime's dead now. The clans are safe. There's no-one left to challenge you. You don't need me here anymore."

"Kara!" Ronan's voice resonated through my chest. From the way he was holding himself, I knew he was on the verge of shifting.

I didn't want that to happen, because I knew that, if he did, I would shift too.

I backed away slowly, shaking my head.

"Just..." Tears tracked down my cheeks, flowing freely. "Don't."

I couldn't look at him anymore. I turned and fled, ignoring his booming voice, and the sound of my name fading into the distance. Only one thought consumed me.

I have to get out of here. Away from him.

I MADE it to the edge of the village in one piece.

Nobody tried to stop me. Here and there, people gave me vague smiles, or raised a hand in greeting, but I hurried on. If my tear-stained face raised any eyebrows, I didn't stick around to find out.

Only one face stood out among the townsfolk I passed. Elder Frey stared at me as I hurried past the meeting house. He was in the upper window, standing in the same place I'd been when I first laid eyes on Ronan. His face was unreadable, not smiling or frowning, just... watchful.

A tremor ran down my spine, but I kept going.

As I reached the gates, I'd worked myself into a rage so powerful I was fully prepared to start kicking them down if they didn't open.

But they did. I didn't see who was manning the watchtowers, but I passed between the high fences for the first time since I'd arrived.

I didn't stop running until I was deep in the forest.

Only then did I allow myself to break down. I sobbed for what felt like hours, until I had no more tears left to cry. Until I trembled on my feet, light-headed and empty. I wanted to curl up on the forest floor and sleep. I wanted to sink down into the earth and just forget everything that had happened in the past few days.

Behind me, the foliage rustled. I inhaled sharply, pressing my back against a nearby tree, and held my breath.

A deer trotted out into the open. Relief flooded through me, so powerful that I almost laughed out loud.

I can't stay here. I'm too close to the Thornwood boundary. I have to get over to the other side of the creek.

I dug deep, feeling around for my shifter. It was curled up, burrowed away from the light. Slumbering. Heartbroken.

Tough shit. I needed my shifter now, in order to get home safely.

I couldn't travel like this. My frail human body couldn't trek through the forest, especially with my emotions torn to shreds. I needed my shifter's speed and agility.

After a few deep breaths, I finally felt my shifter stir. The change spread through me, starting at my feet, building in my chest. The wolf was here.

Time to go home.

CHAPTER 14

RONAN

For the longest time, I stood on the porch, gob-smacked that she had ignored my commanding tone.

I dismissed the thought of running after her. It was no use. I'd seen the look on her face before she turned away. Her mind was made up. We were both alike in that way. We made decisions and followed through on them.

Stubborn, a voice in the back of my mind whispered.

I snorted. Eventually, I slouched down onto the top step, staring out at nothing. I was in shock, the argument that had come out of nowhere still drumming through my head on a loop. I didn't know how it had escalated so quickly from one minute to the next.

I squeezed my eyes shut. Maybe when I opened them again, Kara would be back, and all the terrible things we'd said would be undone.

I opened my eyes.

I was alone.

A hopeless certainty filled me. Kara wasn't coming back. Even if I went to the Bane Clan, crawling on my hands and knees, that Reid guy, Allara's mate, would run me out of their territory on principle.

Fuck.

A floorboard creaked behind me, and I looked up to see Kit hobbling toward me.

"Thought I told you to stay in bed," I grumbled, although there wasn't much heat behind the words. "What happened to resting up?"

"I heard the angry voices." Kit dropped down beside me, like it wasn't weird to him that I was sitting out here on my own. "What's up? Where's Kara?"

"Gone."

Something in my tone of voice made Kit stare hard at me. I could feel his gaze, but I didn't turn and look at him, just frowned into the middle distance.

"What did you do?" His tone dripped with suspicion.

I was offended enough to look up. "What makes you think it was *me*?"

Kit just gave me a look. I slouched forward, resting my elbows on my knees.

"Told her the truth," I said. "I've got one job, as far as I can see. Since Dad died, I'm your only family, Kit. I have to look out for you."

"That's what you told her?"

I nodded. My chest felt hollow.

"You're an idiot."

My head snapped up. "What?"

If he wasn't still recovering, I would've put him in a headlock. *First my mate turns against me, now my brother?*

I was so indignant that it took me a second to realize I'd just thought of Kara as my *mate.*

"Do you really feel that way?" Kit gaped at me, outraged. "That it's just the two of us? That she's not *family*?"

"I—" He was right. I knew it deep down in my soul. Kara *was* family, and I had just watched her walk out of here on her own. I had let her down, just like I'd always done, with family. With obligation.

Kit dropped his head to his chest when he saw the look on my face.

He scrubbed a hand through his hair, tousling it in every direction, then looked up again.

"Wait, is this about those pictures in the hallway? I saw them on my way out here." He wasn't indignant anymore. His voice had gone quiet. He sounded older than usual. His boyish expression was gone, replaced by something sober and deep with understanding.

For the first time, I realized that he was growing up.

I set my jaw and said nothing. I didn't need to. My silence said it all.

"I like them," Kit whispered eventually. "Especially the ones of Mom."

I still didn't trust myself to speak. I just nodded and dragged a hand over my mouth, wincing at the coarse stubble around my chin. I needed to shave.

"When you were little," I said eventually, my voice rough, "you broke your arm climbing in the forest."

"I know," Kit replied slowly. "I was there. Hurt like a bitch."

"I was meant to be watching over you." I turned to face him. "But Noah had found something. A cave near the mouth of the river. I lost track of you up in the canopy. You were like a spider-monkey."

I smiled at the memory.

Then, the smile faded. "I heard this *crack*. And you were bawling your head off. I carried you on my back, all the way home."

Kit snickered, shaking his head. "I don't remember any of *that*."

"Dad was so mad," I continued. "He got right up in my face. I still remember his exact words. *You'll never make an Alpha like this, boy. Alphas watch out for their own. It's in your blood. Never forget that.*"

Kit, for once, was quiet.

"I failed you, Kit. I didn't keep you safe. And you almost died again a few days ago." I punched my hand hard into the side of the porch. "Because of me."

With slow, hesitant movements, Kit grabbed onto the stair rail and got to his feet.

"Bullshit. I wanted to fight. I'm grown, Ro. I can make my own choices." He jabbed a finger into my arm. "Stop using me as a distraction, and start thinking about how you're gonna win back the only woman you've ever truly cared about."

He began to limp toward the door, and I called out after him. I knew better than to offer a helping hand. I'd only land myself another poke, or worse.

"When did you get so perceptive?"

"Always have been." He shot me a sunny smile as he opened the door. Then his smile dropped, and he shot a glance inside, expression turning serious. "Want me to take those down?"

He jerked his head at the wall where the photos were hanging.

I shook my head. Kara had worked hard on that, for me. It was time I showed her my appreciation. And so much more. It was time to go get my mate back. If she'd have me.

I got to my feet, stretching out ligaments that were stiff with disuse. "You're right, Kit," I admitted. "I *am* stupid. And I gotta go fix things, before it's too late."

∼

KARA

By the time I reached the road that led toward home, the sky had opened, and it was pouring with rain.

Droplets hammered down onto my back as I raced through the forest, sliding through my fur and turning the forest floor into a muddy quagmire. I dashed through wet leaves and slithered under low-hanging branches, relying on my shaky mental map of the area until I hit a familiar track.

My paws thundered on the ground, and I let the rhythm soothe my senses and lull me into a state nearing calmness.

I was going home.

Back to my life, the place I knew best. The only place, up until recently, I had ever been. Back to my family and friends, familiar rhythms and routines. Old, well-worn patterns.

My haven, where I could hide away from the world.

I came to a halt near the edge of my village, my heart crying out with relief. I'd made it. I was home.

A familiar figure trudged through the downpour carrying a bunch of sodden firewood on his back. If I'd been in human form I would have burst into tears at the sight of him, but instead I let out a low whine.

Reid.

He heard me and whirled, and the logs tumbled to the ground, forgotten.

I let out a soft bark in greeting and managed to stumble forward a couple of paces before exhaustion washed over me, and I fell to the ground at his feet. I was distantly aware of the thud of more footsteps rushing toward me, but I didn't have the energy to raise my head and see who it was.

The sound of my brother's voice, shouting something in alarm, was the last thing I registered before everything went black.

~

WHEN I WOKE UP, I was me again. Human, tucked up in my own bed, under a pile of soft woolen blankets.

Pale light drifted in from the window, and the long shadows across the floor told me it was late afternoon.

Groaning, I pulled the covers over my head and sank back into unconsciousness without another thought.

~

I WOKE up properly early the following morning.

I ached all over from yesterday's mad dash through the forest. Inside, my shifter was quiet again, still licking its wounds.

I curled onto my side and pressed my face against the pillow, willing myself to go back to sleep. I didn't want to be awake, and have to start thinking about what had happened with Ronan.

All I'd wanted was to come home. Now I was here: back in my own room, surrounded by familiar things. Paint pots littered the desk under the window, and a half-finished blanket lay over the back of the armchair in the corner.

My bedroom was like a time-capsule. A snapshot of my life on the day I'd left the pack with Reid. I hadn't expected everything to change that day. I hadn't realized that, when I did finally return, I would be vastly different to the innocent girl who had left.

More than anything, I wanted to go back to that day. To tell myself not to get in the truck, and not to leave pack territory.

But it was no use. There was no going back.

I dragged the pillow over my head and tried desperately to push down the tight feeling that squeezed my chest.

I can't believe I've been so stupid.

I'd actually begun to let myself believe that I could have... more. More than this room, this life.

I had thought that Ronan and I belonged together. That he saw me as *family*—someone worth protecting, someone to make new memories with after laying old ghosts to rest.

Now I saw how naïve I'd been. How childish.

Elder Frey had been right all along. Ronan didn't want or need a mate. He wasn't going to step up and become Alpha of his clan. Nothing would change that, especially not a woman he'd only known for a few weeks.

The pillow grew damp under my face as tears leaked onto it.

I'll just stay in bed today. I'll deal with the fallout from all of this tomorrow.

I wasn't ready to show my face around the village just yet. I couldn't face the questions. The looks of confusion. Or worse, pity.

Would they all know—would they be able to tell—that I had met the person I thought would be my mate, and he had essentially rejected me?

I'd just begun to drift back into a light slumber when a sharp knock jolted me awake again.

"Go away," I called out. My voice was weak and scratchy. I slumped down, defeated, when the door opened anyway. "Jason, just go…"

I trailed off in surprise, blinking. Tammy shut the door behind her, then turned to face me with her hands on her hips.

"Oh," I said stupidly. "I thought you were my brother."

She leveled me with a look, then grabbed the chair from my desk and dragged it over to my bed before plopping herself down on it.

"I don't wanna talk," I said weakly.

"Yeah?" Tammy raised an eyebrow. "Well, I don't want to be awake at the ass-crack of dawn. But here we are."

I fell into a miserable silence, slumping back on my pillow. Her expression softened slightly as her eyes raked over my face.

Oh God, my hair is probably a bird's nest. Running through the forest, even though in wolf form, was not conducive to a good hair day the next morning.

"Allara put you to bed last night," Tammy said. "You were pretty out of it. She thinks this is all her fault. She's the reason you left in the first place."

"It's not her fault." I raked a hand over my face. Every movement was exhausting. "I just…I didn't belong there."

My throat was sore from holding back the misery.

"With the Thornwoods?"

I stared up at the ceiling. "I guess I don't really belong anywhere," I whispered. "Tammy, I can't go out there. I can't face it."

"Reid told me…" Tammy paused, like she wasn't sure she should continue. "You found your mate. The Thornwood heir. That's why you stayed."

I let out an empty laugh. So everyone *did* know. "Ronan and I… no-one will understand. Destiny, fated mates, what does it matter? We're from totally separate worlds."

She *snorted.*

At my shocked, affronted look, she just shook her head at me, folding her arms over her chest. We were roughly the same age, but suddenly, I felt like I was about to get told off.

"Nobody will understand?" Tammy scoffed. "Kara, I'm a *human* living in the middle of a wolf pack!"

"Tammy—" I managed to sit up properly, chagrined at the look on her face, but she wasn't finished.

"You think you're the only one who fell for someone they didn't expect?" Tammy's eyes flashed. She might not have been a shifter, but her strong will was more than a match for my own. "The only one who comes from a different world?"

I twisted my fingers in the bed sheets. "That's totally beside the point!"

"Is it?" Tammy demanded. "Because I'm not gonna let you wallow around in bed feeling sorry for yourself over this."

"I'm not feeling sorry for myself!"

Yes, you are.

Tammy grabbed my hand, forcing me to look up at her. "Kara, running away from this isn't going to fix anything. You can't hide away forever. When I first got here, I was terrified, but you made me feel welcome." Her eyes softened. "You made me feel like this was my home, too. You've been nothing but kind to me. So please, for the love of God, let me take care of *you* for a change."

CHAPTER 15
RONAN

I had my mind made up.

Even though I was walking through town alone, my heart was racing a mile a minute in my chest. I didn't know what lay ahead of me on the other side of the creek; from the look on Kara's face the last time I'd seen her, I was guessing there'd be a whole load of pain and rejection.

But I had to try. I had to know for sure, if she'd forgive me, or if it was too late.

If she never wanted to see me again, she'd have to tell me that to my face.

Buoyed up by the thought that, either way, I would at least see her again, I felt a new spring in my step as I made my way into the center of town. Kit's pep talk had done the job. I took a deep breath, inhaling the forest air gratefully.

A sharp voice from the steps of the meeting house made me stop in my tracks.

"Ronan." Elder Frey stood with his arms crossed, staring me down. "Where are you going?"

A sharp prickle ran along the back of my neck. My hackles began to rise, and I tamped them down before I did anything stupid like snap back at him.

"I have business to attend to," I said shortly, striding onwards. "I don't know when I'll return."

"I was hoping to speak to you, Ronan." He unfolded his arms and started down the steps. "Inside."

"It'll have to wait."

"No, I don't think it can."

I stopped. *What did he mean?* In a flash, Elder Frey had crossed over to me and laid a hand on my arm. I shrugged it off.

We met each other's eyes for a long moment, my steel gaze clashing against his steady, severe countenance.

Eventually, I pushed past him and strode toward the meeting house. "Whatever it is," I said with a snarl, "make it quick."

He followed me inside without another word.

By the time we were ensconced inside the tiny office on the upper floor, my skin was itching with impatience. I'd made a decision. I needed to find my mate, to fight for her. Everything else was an unnecessary distraction, and my shifter was growing more restless with every second that passed.

The Elder sat at the desk, and I dropped down into the chair opposite. All of a sudden, I felt thirteen years old again, about to be told off by my father.

"Well?" I bristled. "What is it?"

The Elder heaved a deep sigh. There was a strange, calculating look in his pale blue eyes that I didn't like one bit.

"I'm sorry that it's come to this, Ronan." He folded his hands together. With another sigh, he pulled some papers out of the lower drawer in the desk and slid them over to me. "But you've given me no choice."

My eyes darted over the writing. The more I read, the more my stomach sank, leaving a hollow pit in its place.

"What is this?" I asked, my eyes darting up. My head was lowered in challenge, and I forced myself to straighten up, to feign indifference.

I could tell that he wasn't buying my forced pose one bit.

He tilted his head. The look on his face made me feel like I was a troublesome insect he couldn't squash. "I always knew that you would never make an Alpha."

I opened my mouth, but he continued on like he barely noticed me sitting there.

"We use the bloodline as our guide, of course. And nine times out of ten, it's right. The mantle of Alpha passes from one generation to the next, uninterrupted. Strength begets strength, strong leaders make strong heirs, and so on and so forth." His mouth twisted in contemplation. "But sometimes... it fails. Sometimes, there's a weak link."

I was frozen in place. Every word he spoke fueled the hot ball of rage inside my chest, but I couldn't find the words to counter him.

"Your father didn't believe it, at first. The memory of your mother, it softened him." Absently, Elder Frey turned his attention to the rafters above us, to the claw marks from Alphas gone by. Generations of my ancestors had carved themselves into history, right above our heads. "I spent years persuading him of the truth. That your brother was the better—the stronger—choice. Friendly, amiable, eager to please. Given time, I knew I could mold him into something truly great."

"You wanted a puppet, you mean," I spat out. The mention of Kit had shaken me back into speech. "Someone who would listen to your every word."

Elder Frey leaned forward across the desk. A thin smile lingered on his face. "We'll never know, will we? He hero-worshipped you from the start. His perfect older brother... no matter how arrogant you were, you could do no wrong in his eyes. I knew that there was no way he would ever betray you."

A spark of warmth glowed in my chest despite the curl of bitterness in the Elder's voice.

You got that right.

"We look out for each other." I glowered at the man opposite me. "It's called *loyalty*. It seems you're unfamiliar with the concept."

The Elder laughed, but there was no joy in the sound. It was harsh and cold, and I had to fight not to flinch back from it. "Loyalty? I didn't see much loyalty on the day of your Alpha ceremony. You shamed your father's memory, Ronan, by running off. That day, I knew I was right. You could never step into his shoes."

His face darkened further. "And then you returned, just in time to meet our *dear* visitors from the Bane Clan." His expression twisted; he looked unrecognizable. It was like a stranger occupied the chair, instead of the man I'd known my whole life. "Their Alpha's mate, that Bane idiot, and his whore companion."

I was out of my chair so fast I barely registered moving at all. I loomed over the Elder, hands clenched into fists. I wanted to punch the smug look off his face for daring to use that term about Kara. The urge was almost overwhelming, and I fought to get my breathing under control and quell the red mist that rose up.

"You do not—*ever*—use that language in relation to Kara."

"Or what? You'll hurt me?" Elder Frey rolled his eyes.

A growl erupted out of my chest. "She is my *mate*. You will not disrespect her."

"When I realized that you were fated for each other, I must admit, I was worried." Elder Frey chuckled. "But she was so meek, so afraid! No strength, no passion in her. Hardly a fitting mate for an Alpha. Even my attempts to drive her away, to make her see the truth, were wasted. She was as blinded to your faults as the rest of them."

The words were the final straw. With an angry roar, I lunged over the desk and hauled him up by the collar. His eyes glittered with triumph as they stared into mine.

"You don't know a damn thing about that woman," I said. "You're the one who's blind, you old fool."

Elder Frey laughed. Through the haze of anger, something in his words stuck out to me.

Even my attempts to drive her away...

"What the hell did you do to her?" I shook him, senseless with rage. "If you hurt her, I'll kill you."

"Why would I hurt her?" He wrenched himself free, straightening up. "I didn't need to. You managed to hurt her all by yourself. You might have killed Jaime in combat, but your mate is long gone."

At the mention of Jaime, something twinged in the back of my head. Slowly, I looked up to meet those cold eyes.

"You let him in. *You* brought him inside the gates," I whispered. "Didn't you?"

When he didn't respond, my voice rose up into a roar. *"Didn't you?"*

"I'll admit it." Elder Frey's lip curled. "You surprised me, Ronan. Jaime was easy enough to persuade. He was hungry for power, and the honor of leadership. I expected you to go down without a fight. Maybe you have some of your father in you, after all."

He shoved the papers in my direction. "I think we're done here."

I glanced down at the document before me. The opening sentences chilled me to the core.

I, Ronan Thornwood, do hereby relinquish my right to the position of Alpha of the Thornwood Clan.

"What is this?" I hissed.

"Sign it," he snapped. "You've poisoned this pack enough. Step aside, Ronan. Go and live like the outcast you were born to be."

I picked up the document. "If I sign this, my claim dies with me."

Elder Frey's voice turned soft, persuasive. "It won't trouble you again. Or your children, or your children's children. It's a fresh start, Ronan. You should take it. Think about Kit. What would he want?"

I looked up at him, making sure I had his full attention.

Then I ripped the paper in half, clean down the middle. The pieces fluttered down onto the desk.

"You forgot the most important part of being an Alpha. Nobody tells you how to live your life." I loomed over him. This time, I was gratified to note that he actually began to look afraid. "And *nobody* threatens your family and gets away with it."

I spared him one final, dismissive look, before heading for the door.

"Running away again?" he called after me. "Or are you worried you'll lose to an old man?"

I paused in the doorframe.

"When I get back," I said, my voice low and dangerous, "you'll be long gone. I will not allow you to set foot in Thornwood territory for the rest of your days. I'm not sparing your life out of *mercy*. Your exile will be punishment enough, after I make sure the other clans know of your treachery. No one will take you in. You don't deserve the dignity of an Alpha's challenge. You are nothing."

If he said anything in reply, I didn't hear it.

I was already out of the door.

∼

KARA

I clutched my jacket around me and shivered. The wind blowing through the trees had grown cool, and the dark clouds overhead told me that thunder was on its way. I'd spent a long time with the Thornwoods. The peak of summer was long gone, and fall was fast approaching.

"I don't like this," Reid said.

He had been the hardest one to convince, having not warmed to Ronan on their first and only encounter, but he'd accepted my choice to return in the end.

"I know." I gave him a quick hug. "I'm sorry. I'll see you soon, okay? All of you."

Allara's face broke into a smile. Careful not to jostle the sleeping baby in her arms, she wrapped one arm around my shoulders and squeezed.

"You got this," she whispered in my ear. "Good luck."

When she pulled away, we regarded each other for a moment. It didn't matter how many years passed, or what was going on in our lives: Allara always brought out that shy teenager in me, slightly in awe of her feisty best friend.

We were standing at the edge of the forest. I'd said my goodbyes to Jason and Tammy already. I was ready to go. After all, I had little more than the clothes I stood up in.

Most of what I need is in Thornwood territory.

My heart, for one thing. I couldn't ignore it for a moment longer. I had to find Ronan and tell him how I truly felt.

I was done being angry, or afraid.

With one final smile for my friends, I turned away and walked into the trees. I had a full day's hike ahead of me, but I wanted to do it this way. I didn't want to turn up with Reid or Allara. As much as I loved them, this was my journey to make alone.

The thick canopy of trees overhead protected me from the rain as it started to patter, soft and light, through the leaves. I tilted my head up as I strode onwards, oddly comforted by the gentle sound.

Soon, the downpour was coming thick and fast. The foliage still protected me from the worst of it, but by the time I neared the edge of Bane territory, where it abutted Thornwood land, my hair was damp and curling at the ends and I was pretty much soaked through.

Once, Ronan had told me that it didn't matter to him what I looked like, that it didn't change his feelings for me one bit.

I guess it's time to test that theory.

As I neared the creek that formed the border between territories, trepidation set in. What if I was wrong, and he really didn't want me back? What if, in my quick rush to anger that day we fought, I had destroyed what we had, once and for all?

There was no turning back now.

I didn't know what waited for me on the other side of the river.

My future, bright and glittering with possibility? Or a heartbreak so devasting I would never recover from it?

Only time would tell.

I took a deep breath as the trees around me started to thin out. It wasn't as dark here; bright patches of sunlight pierced the forest floor around my feet. The rain was still falling, but the clouds overhead were starting to clear.

I stepped out of the trees. I'd reached the creek.

On the other side, Thornwood territory stretched for miles. I shivered. Once again, I was a stranger in these lands.

He won't hurt me. No matter what.

Not physically, anyway. My heart would be in pieces if this didn't work.

The creek was at its widest point here. The shallow waters swirled at ankle height, and large stones littered the crossing, forming a natural bridge.

I hopped onto the first one easily enough. I looked up at the opposite side, toward my destination. Through the rain, everything in sight glittered with refracted sunlight.

My heart caught in my chest when a hazy figure came into view.

I took another step, keeping my eyes fixed on the man in the distance.

The clouds cleared, and a beam of sunlight fell onto his face. I just about stopped breathing.

Ronan.

His gaze was intense, piercing. Even from this distance, the light in his amber eyes took my breath away.

He strode easily from rock to rock, like he'd done it a thousand times before. I was less graceful. Nerves and impatience churned in my gut, and more than a couple of times I slipped on a damp stone surface.

By the time we reached the middle of the creek, I was trembling with anticipation. I put a foot wrong, and almost fell headlong into the river. He caught me around the waist.

"Kara," he said, his eyes drinking me in. "What are you doing out here?"

I bit my lip. Now that the moment had come, the words stuck in my throat. I closed my eyes briefly, and swallowed down my nerves. "I wanted—"

I reached up and tangled my fingers in his hair. The touch sent a shock of electricity down my arm. It had barely been two days since I'd seen him, but it felt like a lifetime. It felt unbelievably good, being able to put my hands on him again.

"Why are *you* here?" I asked.

He was still holding me close, and I curled my hands around his forearms. I pulled back, looking him in the eye.

"I was coming to get *you*." His eyes blazed. It might have been the light, but for a brief flicker, I thought I saw his shifter rise up from their depths. "I've come to take you home, Kara. Come home with me."

The way he spoke was simple, and appeared as easy as breathing to him. I leaned into the seductive promise of him, closing my eyes. Warmth flooded through my chest, and I forgot about everything else. Nothing mattered, only the sunlight on my back, the rain on my face, and the feel of Ronan's arms around me, our chests pressed close. His heart beat against mine.

"Are you sure?" I whispered.

I didn't want to ask the question. That was why I was standing here, after all: to come back. To come *home*.

Allara's pack would always accept me, but I didn't belong there anymore. My spirit longed to return with Ronan. But there was a shard of doubt still lodged in my chest, a terror that this was all too good to be true.

"It was never about a treaty," Ronan said, his voice deep with emotion. "You weren't here because of some political pact, or because I saw you as collateral. From the moment I first saw you, I wanted you with me—always."

He slid his hand up my neck, tilting my head back until my eyes met his. "*You* are my family, Kara. As much as Kit is. More, in some ways. You are my future."

I hardly dared to believe what he was saying. It was more than I hoped for. It was everything.

"What are you trying to say?"

"I'm saying I want you to be my mate. Properly." He dug around inside the pocket of his shirt before pulling something out.

I squinted in the sunlight, and my heart started to hammer even harder than it already was.

"I should have done this sooner," he said. "I'm sorry."

I couldn't find the words to reply.

He held the ring between his thumb and forefinger, fumbling for my hand. The metal was warm to the touch from having lain against his chest. "Kara, this has been in my family for... I don't know how long. It's a human tradition I know... but I want you to have it." I could only nod, overwhelmed, as he slid the ring onto my ring finger. "It's a promise."

The ring was gold, two hands linked by a heart. I ran my thumb over the design, and tears blurred my eyes.

"It's beautiful," I murmured. "It's *perfect.*"

A smile lingered around the corners of his mouth as he took my face in his broad hands and pressed a soft kiss to my lips. The second our mouths met, I felt the same rush as I did the first time. Every moment with Ronan was fresh and new and exhilarating. It only lasted a second before he pulled away, and I bit down a sigh of frustration.

"The life of an Alpha's mate won't be easy," he said, absently tucking a strand of hair behind my ear.

I leaned into the touch before his words fully registered.

"Hang on...did you say, *Alpha?*"

"I'm done hiding from this, Kara." His expression shifted, turning serious. "It's who I am. It's time to stop worrying about living up to someone else's expectations and start making my own."

I tilted my head. "Why did you run away from the pack, Ronan? I need to know."

He pinched the bridge of his nose, and sighed. "Um... I don't have a good reason."

"Tell me anyway," I said. "And I'll never bring it up again. I promise. I just want to understand why."

He nodded. "I... my father had made it clear since I was pretty young that I wouldn't be a good Alpha. That I just didn't have it in me to lead. He said it constantly, in fact. That's why they had Kit, I think. So that there would be a second heir to inherit the title. But Dad died earlier than expected, and Kit just isn't old enough... so they told me I had to take on the mantle. I felt like a fraud, stepping in to take something away from my brother, when everyone knew I couldn't do the job well. I couldn't handle the judgment from the pack. From Elder Frey..." Ronan shook his head and *tsked* loudly. "But I couldn't leave. That would have left the pack vulnerable. I ran out of the compound, got about a hundred yards down the road, then turned back. I couldn't leave my pack unguarded. What if something had happened to one of them? I would never have been able to forgive myself."

"Damn," I said faintly. "You really are an Alpha, aren't you, protecting the pack even then."

He laughed suddenly, smiling down at me. "I... I suppose I am. I never thought of it that way, before. I just figured it was one more thing I couldn't do right, only half-running off, and not letting Kit get on with it."

Then he grew serious once more. "Are you okay with that? With me being an Alpha?" Ronan's brow furrowed as a sudden spark of concern entered his eyes. "You didn't sign up for any of this."

"Neither did you. Ronan..." I couldn't hold back my smile any longer. "I'm proud of you."

Ronan shot a crooked smile back at me. "You came out here, all this way, by yourself..."

"For you," I finished for him, in a rush. I took his hands in mine and stood on my tiptoes to kiss him properly. When I pulled away, we were both breathing heavily. "I know the life of an Alpha and his mate, all the responsibility... it's not what either of us pictured, but that doesn't have to be a bad thing. Maybe we can figure it out together."

I shrieked as he hitched me into the air, and my legs scrabbled for purchase around his waist. He didn't seem fazed, just pressed burning kisses against my cheeks, my neck, my nose, and forehead.

I submitted to the attention, laughing, before drawing him into a proper kiss.

By the time we walked back together to the village, hand in hand, we were both soaked from head to toe.

I couldn't have cared less.

EPILOGUE

KARA

Ronan straightened and brushed off his hands. He was grinning from ear to ear, and I couldn't help but grin back at him.

"That's the last one." He stared down at the pile of wood at his feet. Here and there, pieces of barbed wire glinted, poking through the long grass. "Time to start building another bonfire, I reckon."

I wanted to take him to task about the barbed wire—someone was going to slice themselves up if they weren't careful—but Ronan looked so happy I couldn't bear to dampen my mood.

The project had been a couple of weeks in the making. The plan had been to pull everything to the ground at first, but then it was agreed that one of the watchtowers should stay.

But the fences were gone, at long last.

The open forest stood around us. Pack members wandered past us in a daze, staring like they couldn't believe their eyes. After years of being penned in, they were free to roam their whole pack territory to their heart's content.

It was like Ronan had said, getting up to the platform to speak after our bonding ceremony.

You can't protect the ones you love from danger by hiding away from the world. Danger is out there, but it's our bonds with each other that will keep us safe. The forest is our home, our territory. We won't be cut off from it any longer.

The applause was the loudest I'd ever heard. The pack had rallied around Ronan in his decision, just like I'd hoped they would.

Allara came to stand beside me. She was holding a beer, and a soft smile played at the corners of her mouth. Reid's foster mother was looking after the baby in honor of the occasion. It was nice to see my best friend get the chance to let her hair down a little.

"Thank you," she said, tilting the neck of her bottle in my direction.

I blinked. "Uh... you're welcome?" I narrowed my eyes at her. "What did I do, exactly?"

"Exactly what I asked you to do." Her voice was soft. "You've helped to unite the Bane and Thornwood Clans. Because of you, we don't have to fear them. Your children will be our kin."

I opened my mouth, then closed it. I ducked my head, heat flooding my cheeks. "I hadn't thought about it like that. I just..."

"Fell in love," Allara finished for me, smirking.

"Shut up." I nudged her with my elbow. "Wait, did you plan this?"

Allara scoffed. "Don't be stupid. I couldn't have known! I couldn't go with Reid, and I needed someone to go in my place. Simple." It might have been a trick of the light, but I could've sworn that she winked at me. "Maybe I was *hoping* you'd find a match along the way."

Allara the matchmaker. I shook my head, dumbfounded.

"Anyway, it all worked out in the end," she said happily. "Now all we have to do is get those two to behave themselves."

She pointed toward Ronan and Reid, where they were dragging one of the fence posts in from the edge of the woods. It was a huge log, the size of a tree trunk. Both men were having an intense debate about the best way to carry it, but they kept waving off anyone who tried to come over and help shoulder some of the weight.

I sighed. "I think I preferred it when they were locking horns."

Allara snorted into her drink. "Agreed. They're a liability like this, I swear. They're going to lead each other into mischief."

"Well, we'll just have to lead them straight back out of it, won't we?"

She laughed, and shot me a look filled with respect.

We watched idly for a while. Ronan brushed his burnished hair out of his eyes in a gesture that had become achingly familiar. The sun was low in the sky, and his eyes, always striking, were particularly vibrant in the evening light. His eyes met mine, and his features softened. The change was only slight—nobody noticed but me—but it was enough to send a spark of warmth through my chest.

The tang of fall was in the air. Dead leaves crunched underfoot, and debris from the old fences littered the ground around us. A cool, fresh wind rippled through the trees, and blue smoke began to rise behind the rooftops ahead of us.

Allara linked her arm through mine and raised her beer. "Here's to..." She tilted her head at me. "What?"

I smiled as the sound of laughter reached me. The sound of family, of home. My hand slid down to my still-flat belly, where my child grew. The next Alpha of the Thornwood Clan.

I clinked my bottle of water against her beer. "Here's to beginnings."

THE END

PACK LOYALTY
5
BABY
OF THE
WOLF
USA TODAY BEST-SELLING AUTHOR
AMELIA SHAW

BABY OF THE WOLF

AMY

The morning that stick turned blue two years ago, I didn't celebrate like other expectant mothers may have done in the same situation. I turned around and vomited into the toilet bowl, for the third time that morning.

I'd been sick for weeks but hadn't thought much of it, putting the sickness down to stress from work, or maybe a stomach bug. But when I'd added up the dates and realized I was three weeks late on my period, I'd known it was time for a test.

Pregnant. Becoming a mom was the last thing I'd expected at twenty-three and still single. I couldn't blame anyone but myself, though. And luckily, or unluckily for me depending on how you looked at it, I knew exactly who the father was. I'd fallen, or rather, jumped, into bed with a guy I'd met at a bar. So cliché, and yet that's exactly how it happened. Not my usual style, but I hadn't been able to resist him.

Noah.

I couldn't forget him even though I'd tried hard ever since to do so. More than two years on and I still dreamt about him almost every night. When I look at his child, the daughter he'd made with me that night, a replica of Noah's piercing blue gaze stares right back at me.

I shook myself out of my reverie as I walked up the two flights of stairs to my tiny apartment. It was small, but it was rent controlled, and a short walk to my parents' house which was essential, since my mom did most of the babysitting while I worked.

I put my key in the door and pushed it open. "Hello!"

"Hey Amy!" Mom called out as she walked toward me, holding my daughter in her arms. "How was your day?"

"Mama. Mama," Trixie said, leaning forward, reaching for me with her chubby hands.

I dropped my bags, the exhaustion of the day disappearing into thin air as I pulled my beautiful girl into my arms.

"Hello baby. Have you been a good girl for Grandma today?" I squeezed my daughter tight to me and kissed the golden curls on her head. "Thanks for looking after her, Mom."

"No problem," Mom said, reaching for her bag which sat on the small table by the front door. "I put some soup on the stove and did some washing. You should try to get an early night tonight. You've got circles under your eyes."

Gee, thanks.

I sighed. "Yeah. Trixie hasn't been sleeping well. She's teething again, I think."

Her cheeks would bloom bright red, and she'd cry with her hands stuck in her mouth for hours.

"I think you might be right. I saw her canines trying to pop through her gums on both sides," Mom said, opening the front door to leave. "They're notorious for being the worst of all the teeth for pain."

Damn. I knew it. Maybe we're in for another sleepless one tonight.

"Thanks, Mom. See you tomorrow." I kissed her on the cheek and closed the door behind her.

I sighed, resting against the door and thinking about all the things I still had to get done this evening, before I could enjoy the luxury of going to bed. A bone-deep tiredness washed over me. A single mom's life wasn't easy, and anyone who said so was utterly insane.

Trixie launched herself toward the ground, and I carefully set her on her feet. "Are you hungry, sweetheart? Let's see what sort of soup Grandma cooked for us."

Trixie took off in the direction of the kitchen, running at a rate reserved for kids much older than herself. She was fifteen months old, but had been walking for almost six months already.

"Oh.... pumpkin soup." I inhaled as I lifted the lid off the pot. "From scratch! Grandma is the best."

Trixie smiled up at me in seeming agreement.

I settled us into our nightly routine: dinner, clean up, bath, and then bed.

"Such a big, strong girl, aren't you?" I said while dressing Trixie for sleep, and not for the first time, noticing how muscled she was. Her arms were thick and her biceps defined.

"Mama," Trixie said, reaching for the diaper beside her and handing it to me.

"Thank you, baby."

I dressed her into her pajamas and zipped her into her toddler sleeping bag. "Bedtime, sweetheart."

I popped her down into her crib and handed her the only toy she liked to sleep with, a gray wolf that my dad had gotten her for Christmas last year. At the time I'd thought it was such a strange toy to give to a little girl, but Dad said that Trixie had picked it out of all the toys he'd offered her at the store.

In fact, she'd been so adamant, my dad hadn't been able to convince her to accept anything other than the wolf.

He'd been right to give it to her, though. She loved it. She wouldn't go anywhere without the grubby thing.

I stared down at her and watched as she nestled into the wolf, clenching it with her chubby little fist, then she closed her eyes.

I snuck out of her room and sighed as I closed the door behind me. She was an angel when it came to her routine. I was really blessed compared to other moms, from what I'd heard. But the likelihood of her sleeping through the night was low, especially if those teeth were trying to come through, so I figured I'd better get into bed myself soon.

I walked into the kitchen and put away the rest of the soup, then flicked on the TV to relax for an hour. I deserved a little bit of adult normalcy, surely?

I had only stopped working for the first three months of Trixie's life, and I had no intentions of doing so now. Trixie and I were going to survive and thrive, with a little help from my parents but not much else.

My daughter deserved the best of everything, and just because I was a young, single mom, didn't mean I couldn't provide for her. Quite the opposite. The love I had for my daughter drove me like nothing else ever had.

I was dozing off around episode two of some supernatural drama on TV when a strange, high pitched growling noise came from Trixie's bedroom.

I jumped to my feet. "What the hell?"

I bolted toward her room. Had some wild animal managed to get inside? No way! The window was closed. Or at least, I *thought* I'd closed it...

My heart pounded in my chest as I pushed her bedroom door open. I looked around, narrowing my eyes in the dim light.

A growl sounded again, and I glanced in the direction it had come from. Toward the crib. I crept over, icy fear trickling down my veins. *No, not my baby.*

I looked into the crib, half afraid I was about to find a wild raccoon in there with her, but there was nothing abnormal going on around my daughter. Nothing at all. Trixie was fast asleep, her wolfy clutched tightly at her side.

The growl came again, followed by a sharp bark. I stared in horror at my daughter as her little mouth opened to make the noises that had woken me. Again and again, she barked and growled, her face contorting in her sleep as though she were fighting some fierce beast.

Oh, God. What the hell is happening to her?

I slammed both hands over my mouth so that I didn't scream and wake her. Instead, I just stared in disbelief as she snarled and chomped her little teeth together like she was biting down hard on something. Then she relaxed, her face clearing of any animal-like signs, and once again she was my angel, fast sleep.

I stood at the side of her crib, waiting for another showing of this strange animal-like side of my daughter, but it didn't surface again.

Exhausted beyond belief, I staggered back to my own bed and crawled under the covers, tears of worry streaking down my cheeks.

I had no idea what had just happened, but it was another thing to add to the growing list of things I didn't know about my baby. And unfortunately, I knew why I didn't know.

It was because so many of her traits presumably came from her father, a man I barely knew and had no contact with. Mom had told me that I hadn't walked until I was thirteen months and was super-talkative at Trixie's age. Mom described my physique as being 'Michelin man'. Dough boy soft.

My daughter was super advanced physically, and yet she barely talked. She was strong and fit in a way that toddlers just shouldn't be, and now made animal barking noises in her sleep.

There was also the fact that I was certain her eyes changed color at times. Mostly, they were blue, an electric, bright blue that reminded me of Noah, but I'd seen them swirl to yellow, or even silver sometimes, in a way that didn't seem... natural. My mom and the doctor had told me I was crazy when I finally got up the courage to mention it, and I'd never been able to get a good photo of the shift. But it was there. Something... odd.

Was that little piece of weirdness connected to her father, too?

Who was Noah, really? And what did he have to do with all of these strange things in Trixie's development that I couldn't quite explain?

I closed my eyes and pictured him in my mind's eye. He was six foot three, with a body most underwear models would die for. He had a six pack so defined that I had been able to literally run my tongue around every muscle, through every groove. And I remember how much he'd liked it when I did that.

The base, animal attraction between us had been so intense, it was embarrassing to admit how quickly I'd said yes and gone home with him.

Our eyes had met across the dance floor, and heat had flooded my body so fast my legs had trembled from one single glance. His blue eyes had darkened so much that they'd appeared black by the time he stood in front of me.

A few words were spoken—to be honest, I can't even remember what we said to each other in those first seconds—and then a minute later he was kissing me, pressing me into the wall behind us and making it clear for the whole room that he wanted me. That I was *his* for the night.

I hadn't been much better, gripping his shirt and hauling him into my suddenly-aching body. I'd needed him that night, in a way I've never needed anyone before, or since.

He asked me to go back to his place with him, an hour's drive into the forest.

I'd been terrified, but excited at the same time. Despite normally having pretty good common sense, with that intense, throbbing need clawing at my belly, I'd had no choice. That feeling had overridden whatever smart voice in my head had been saying 'don't go'.

I went home with him, much to my shame afterward. But at the time? What a night it had been!

We'd arrived in a small town I'd never heard of and once getting past the massive wall and gates that seemed to be designed to keep everyone out, Noah had parked in front of a log cabin that he said was his. We made it up the front steps, but no further.

He took me against the wall outside the front door because neither of us had been able to go another step without giving in to the craving. We hadn't even made it inside before my first orgasm had crashed into me. But it had been the first of many. Noah had made love to me all night, showing a stamina and level of care that I'd never experienced ever in my life before then.

As the memories of that night crashed over me, I shivered in my cold lonely bed, and the tears began to fall in earnest this time. Noah had scared me, on a deep level. My need for him, and my inability to resist him, was one of the main reasons I'd stayed away ever since.

Not to mention the shame. First, because I'd had unprotected sex with a complete stranger, and then because I'd stayed away so long since then. And the longer I waited to tell him the truth about Trixie, the harder it became to reach out. Even if I could find him, after that night, how in God's name could I tell him he now had a two year old daughter?

I'd never looked for him after that morning. When I woke up around dawn I'd walked to the nearest road, called an Uber, and gotten back into the city without a backward glance. I'd never gone back to the club where he'd picked me up. Never tried to find that town where he lived.

Now, I didn't think I could put off the inevitable any longer. Something was wrong with my baby girl, and I knew, in a bone-deep way, that her biological father would have the answers.

I fell asleep and dreamt of Noah, making love to me all night long. When I awoke, I began making plans for our trip to find him, and hoped to God I'd be able to locate that town that wasn't on any map.

CHAPTER 2
NOAH

The sun was hot on the back of my neck, and the pick in my hands was getting heavier as the hours wore on. The shadows of the forest nearby beckoned but it would be a while before I could go for a run beneath the cooling foliage and take relief from this incessant heat.

We had work still to do, for our village.

I stood up straight and stretched out my back, then wiped the sweat out of my eyes.

I called out to the men around me, all still working but, like me, moving slower than they had a few hours ago. "It's looking great, guys. Let's keep going."

I dropped the pick and reached for another fence pillar and my shovel. We'd taken down the walls around our pack months ago, but it was slow going to rebuild normal-height fences and more housing to accommodate the pack. Now that land was available, everyone wanted more space. We'd been hemmed in for too long, and now, finally, the Thornwood pack was reveling in its freedom.

"Hey, you okay, Noah?" Ronan asked, walking up to me and tossing me a bottle of water.

I caught it and twisted open the cap, then chugged down the coldness in a few grateful swallows. I wiped my mouth and grinned at my Alpha. "Yeah. Though that was much needed. Thank you."

"I don't mean now. I mean..." Ronan made a strange noise, almost a groan, and crossed his arms over his chest. He looked annoyed and uncomfortable, not normal traits for the guy I'd known my whole life and the leader of our pack.

I dropped my shovel and narrowed my gaze at him. "What's up, Ronan? You need something? Or..."

"No. It's not me. It's Kara. She was wondering if you wanted to come to the pack dinner tomorrow night?"

The pack dinner? Between us and Kara's old pack? Why would I want to do that?

I frowned. "Ah, what?"

Ronan stared heavenward as though this was the last conversation in the world he wanted to happen. "She thinks you might want to meet some of the women from Allara's pack. She's got this idea of playing match maker, and although I think she's crazy, I promised her I'd ask you."

I laughed; I couldn't help it. "Thanks, mate, but I'm fine."

I found it kind of hilarious that a guy like Ronan was so easily influenced nowadays, by his mate. Obviously a fated mate changed you, because back in the day, Ronan wouldn't have done anything he didn't want to. Quite the opposite, actually. Our pack leader had quite the stubborn streak. Except, it seemed, when it came to Kara.

Ronan tilted his head to the side. "So, you're already seeing someone we don't know about? Because that's the only answer I can give my mate where she'll be satisfied. That, or you're gay. And I think she'd still want to set you up with someone if it's the latter."

I stared at the ground, to avoid looking into Ronan's eyes while I lied. "Tell Kara I'm seeing a human in town. I don't need fixing up. But thanks."

The untruth ate at my gut, and unfortunately, Ronan didn't leave.

I dragged my gaze up from the dirt to see my Alpha frowning at me. "What?"

He raised a brow. "What do you mean, *what*? I'll lie for you, no problem. Kara's need to make everyone in the pack happy is driving me half insane, but I was kind of glad when she wanted to help you. You're a good man, Noah, and a great pack member. She and I both want you to be happy."

I swallowed the lump in my throat. "Thanks, man, but I'm all good. How is Kara feeling with everything?"

"You mean with the baby due any second? She's sick, and grumpy, but you know..." Ronan shrugged. "I wouldn't have anyone but her. She's good for the pack. And for me."

I smiled. "She is. We're all really glad you found her."

There was suddenly too much emotion in the air.

Ronan and I both coughed and cleared our throats.

"Right. Well. I've gotta get back to this fence," I said.

"Yeah. Great."

Ronan left and the awkwardness in the air finally dissipated as I got back to work. Surprisingly, the Alpha's visit had buoyed my spirits. He and his mate cared about my happiness. There was little else a Beta wolf like me cared about. And yet, the lie I'd told to get them off my back sat like a lead weight in the gut.

I'm good. I'm seeing a human in town.

I felt bad, not because I'd lied, but because I wished what I'd said was the truth.

There was only one woman I wanted, and that was the human I'd had a one night stand with around two years ago.

It was pathetic to still be pining, and I would never admit it out loud, but she was the only woman I'd ever been with who had left me sated and happy on a level that was almost a miracle. The sex had been mind-blowingly amazing. And sleeping next to her afterward in my bed had been bliss. Against my nature, usually, to bring people back to my own home, but I'd curled my body around hers and my soul had been at peace in a way I'd never felt before, or since.

When I'd woken up to find her gone, I'd searched for her, first through the pack grounds, then in town. I'd gone back to the bar I'd picked her up at, every weekend, for six months. There had been no sight of her. Nothing.

Unfortunately, I'd had nothing to go on but a first name and a description. No phone number, no last name. It was like she just disappeared into the ether.

I hated that I'd lost her, and worse, I hated knowing that she'd deliberately run away from me, when I'd thought our experience the best night of my life. I'd tried to forget her, but there wasn't a woman in my bed, nor a bottle of scotch in my hand, that had made me forget the way her body had felt wrapped around mine.

Perfection.

I shook my head and got back to work. There was only one way to sleep at night nowadays, and that was to work myself into the ground during the day. I needed to be physically exhausted, and then I could rest, otherwise my mind raced and my wolf howled, all for a woman I'd spent scant hours with and would likely never see again.

My obsession with her made no sense, except for one unfortunate belief. My shifter believed he'd found his mate in the little human Amy, then I'd gone and lost her.

Whether it was true or not that we were fated mates, didn't seem to worry my wolf. He was convinced, and because of that, deep down, so was I.

∾

THE NEXT DAY, I woke up with the same gnawing pain in my gut that I always did. *Loneliness.* The sensation was cold and heavy, and made me want to pull the covers over my head and pass out once again. But nature called, and the morning sun shone into my room. It was another hot day, with work to be done, and I needed to harden up. Amy was gone, and I had to figure out a way to keep living.

It was pretty obvious to me, and likely others too, that I was existing, and not much else.

I crawled out of bed, went to the toilet, then walked back to the bedroom to get dressed. Draven, my housemate, was already in the kitchen cooking up breakfast, judging by the smell of charred bacon on the grill.

"Bacon's burning!" I yelled out to him.

"Shit!"

I shook my head at the clatter of pots and pans in the kitchen. He was young and a bit naïve, but a good kid overall. Compared to some of the other guys I could be sharing a place with, I was lucky to have Draven.

I pulled on jeans and a t-shirt, and headed down the long hallway to the kitchen.

"You want a coffee?" I asked him, going straight to the coffee maker to turn it on.

"Nah, I'm fine, thanks," he said as he pulled out plates and began serving us breakfast: toast, scrambled eggs, and crispy bacon. My favorite.

"Thanks," I said, taking the plate he offered me.

I ate without real enjoyment, appreciating the food more as a way to stuff my body with fuel, then washed the dishes.

Draven grabbed his tool belt from the couch and walked over to the front window, pulling aside the curtains to look outside.

I grabbed my own bag and stuffed a few bottles of water inside, and bananas. It was going to be another scorcher. Better to be prepared.

"Hey, Noah," Draven called out from his vantage point at the window.

"Yeah?"

"Are you expecting company?"

I frowned at the kid, who stood peering out like a peeping tom. "No. What are you talking about?"

"There's a car out the front of our place, and I don't recognize the girl in the driver's seat. Thought maybe you were expecting someone."

My heart thumped in my chest and my mouth went dry. Settle down, I told myself. After all this time, it won't be her. But I couldn't help swallowing hard before asking in a pseudo-casual tone, "What does she look like?"

"She's still sitting in her car, so it's hard to tell, but I think she's got blonde hair. Hang on... she's getting out."

If the woman was blonde, there was a chance it was Amy.

I raced to the door and flung it open, unable to stand the suspense.

There she was. The woman of my dreams, in the flesh. She stepped out of the car, her lips turned down in a frown as she shut the door, then twisted around to stare up at the house. At me.

She looked older, more tired, but just as beautiful as I remembered, with long blonde hair and a pretty, heart-shaped face that I'd never forgotten.

I had to fight the urge to run down the stairs and grab her up into my arms.

My wolf, so often dormant nowadays, lifted its head and howled inside me. Adrenaline pumped in my veins, and I shuddered at the intensity of all the emotions that rushed through my system.

She smiled in recognition and raised a hand to wave at me, though I noticed the smile didn't reach her eyes. "Hi Noah."

I jogged down the steps and stood on the same level, staring at her. She wore blue jeans, a black tank, and a red checked shirt over the top.

"Hang on a second... is that *my* shirt?" It was way over-sized for her, and she'd rolled up the sleeves.

This time, her smile was more genuine and her brown eyes sparkled a little. "Yeah... I took it the morning I left because I was cold, and kinda kept it. Sorry."

I shook my head. "Don't be sorry. I... ah... Are you here to see me?"

I should be calm. I should be cool, but all I could do was stammer over the fact that she was here. She was *here*!

What if she wasn't here for me? What if...

She nodded, cutting off my racing thoughts. "Yeah. I came to chat. Hope that's okay?"

Okay? "Sure! About what?" The fences could wait.

"I don't know how to say this." She pressed her lips together, then dropped her head and stared at the ground.

"Whatever it is, you can tell me."

Draven walked down the steps behind me and said, "I've gotta get to work. See you later?"

"Yeah, sure." I waved him off.

As he walked away, Amy gave him half a smile before turning back to me. "Who's that?"

"My housemate. As one of the single guys in town, I get lugged with the younger kids on occasion. He's nice enough."

Her eyes went wide and round. "You're still single then?"

There was a hope in her tone that made me long to reassure her. I'd waited for her. Had she waited for me too?

My heart squeezed tight in my chest and my wolf paced, impatient to have the woman he felt was our mate back in my arms. "Yes. Very single. You?"

She nodded. "Same."

Thank the heavens for that!

"Do you want to come inside?" I asked, gesturing to the house.

She bit her lip and took a few steps backward, reaching for the car door handle. "Yes, please. But I've just gotta grab something, hang on."

"Sure."

She was back. And single, and quite possibly, here for me!

My stomach was tight and my muscles trembled with excitement.

Amy stuck half her body in the car, looking for whatever she wanted to bring inside. A bag maybe? What had she brought? Something to show me?

She whispered something I didn't quite catch, then she emerged once more, and I fell back a pace.

What the hell...

"Sweetheart, time to wake up," Amy whispered to the toddler in her arms, a little girl with curly blonde hair, clinging to a gray wolf toy.

"Mama..." the little girl said, moaning in annoyance, then she opened her eyes and looked up at me.

There were my very own eyes, strikingly blue, staring right back at me.

That was when the biggest piece of my life's puzzle fell into place. Amy had left, and she'd taken my child with her.

My daughter.

Holy shit.

CHAPTER 3
AMY

I trembled as I stood before Noah, clinging to my child. *Our child*. A daughter he hadn't known existed at all, but now he did. I could read the recognition in his shocked gaze as he stared down at Trixie without blinking.

What was he thinking? What was he going to do?

Trixie made an annoyed noise and I hoisted her to a more comfortable position on my hip.

"Can we please go inside?" I asked Noah.

He was still gaping, frozen in place, his eyes wide and staring.

He may have been in shock, but I needed to sit down and feed Trixie, or she'd have a melt down and that was the last sort of first impression I wanted to make.

"Ah, yeah. Yeah. Of course." He blinked a few times and seemed to come to his senses. Sort of. "Can I help you? Do you... Does she... have a bag or anything?"

I pointed to the passenger side. "Actually, yeah. Could you grab the bag out of the front seat? That would be great."

He rushed around the car, pulled out my massive black baby bag, and slung it over his shoulder. "That it?"

I could have cried, right there and then. Why had I waited so long to contact him if he was going to be this good about the news? This thoughtful and helpful? God knew, I could have used the parenting help over the past year or two.

"Yeah." I nodded at him, clinging tighter to Trixie. "Um. Thanks."

Noah hurried up the steps in front of us and opened the door wide. He didn't say anything else, just stood there waiting for us to move past him and into the house.

My heart thumped so hard I doubted I would have been able to hear him properly even if he had spoken.

"Mama," Trixie spluttered.

Right. Move!

I raced up the stairs, past the wall he'd first taken me against, and tried to ignore the way my body shivered in response to the delicious and decadent memory.

"Okay, sweetheart, hold on just a moment," I said to Trixie as we reached the lounge room and she lurched to get down and walk around.

I set her on her feet and put my hand out for my baby bag. "Thanks for carrying that. She needs something to eat."

Noah handed me the bag and I sat down on the couch, rifling through the inside until I found the fridge bag with the yogurt snacks I'd brought with me.

"Here you go, sweetheart." I held out the opened pouch and she raced over to me, taking the yogurt and sucking it straight into her mouth.

Noah walked over to the other couch and sat down on the cushions. His movements were loose, as if his limbs were a bit shaky. He stared at me with what looked like a hundred burning questions in his gaze.

I swallowed hard. How did I even start this conversation?

Noah's gaze dropped to Trixie, then flicked back to me. "She's mine."

There wasn't any question in the words, but I felt the need to respond anyway. "Yeah, she is."

He jumped to his feet and walked toward the small kitchen. "Do you want a drink?"

"Coffee if you have it. I've been up and driving since six. She's an early riser."

He didn't respond but busied himself around the kitchen.

I got down on my knees and started pulling out some of Trixie's favorite toys so that she didn't break anything in the house, not that there was a lot to break. No photo frames, or vases, or even pillows on the couches. No decorative items at all. Nothing spoke of a feminine touch, or even... a home.

"There you go, sweetie," I said, handing Trixie a box with blocks that she loved.

She sat down on the floor to play with them.

Noah walked over to me with a mug. "Here."

I stood up and took the coffee. "Thanks."

The whole situation was so stilted, and my nervous tension rose. I stared at him with what was likely a hungry gaze, but I couldn't help it. God, he looked good. Older, more tired, like me, I guess. But my belly was tight and heat flushed up my cheeks from being this close to him.

He was still gorgeous, with his bright blue eyes and dark blond hair. But it was more than just simple good looks that had me shaking. My attraction to him hadn't diminished at all but luckily for me, it had settled to a simmer, rather than the flash burn it had been in the beginning.

"Why didn't you tell me?" he asked all of a sudden, and my stomach lurched.

That was it. That was the question I'd been dreading from him for almost two full years. Why didn't I hunt him down and tell him the moment I'd found out I was expecting his child?

"Well, ah..." I walked back to the couch, afraid my legs might give out on me. "I..."

Anything I said from now on wasn't going to be good enough, so where did I even begin?

Noah plonked himself back on the couch, and I noticed he had a beer in hand.

I raised an eyebrow. "Is that normal for you? To drink at breakfast time?"

Hopefully not, because then we would have another issue to talk about.

Was I throwing myself at the mercy of someone with a drinking problem?

He glanced down at the bottle, then back at me. "Hardly. But this conversation needs a drink."

I kind of agreed. So, without further ado, I took a deep breath, held tight to my mug, and plunged on. "I... should have told you. But I wasn't sure how to at the beginning. And to be honest, I wasn't sure what I was going to do to start with, either. So I just put it off, then it got too hard, and I wasn't sure I'd be able to find you, or if you'd moved on... or...."

"I brought you here, to my home. How would you not be able to find me?"

Heat flushed my cheeks. The heat of shame. "I'm so sorry. I... the truth is, I simply didn't know how to tell you. And then somehow, I convinced myself you wouldn't want to know."

"I wouldn't..." His voice trailed off as his lips tightened to a thin line.

"I'm sorry," I repeated, in a small voice.

The words seemed so inadequate, but it was all I had.

He nodded slowly. "So, what changed?"

"What do you mean?"

"Why are you suddenly here?" He narrowed his eyes at me. "Is she okay? Do you two need help? Money?"

I shook my head. "Oh no, no, we're fine. I work and earn enough for us both to live comfortably. I've managed pretty well, I think."

And I had. I was proud of how I'd gotten by on my own. With a little babysitting help from my mom, of course.

"Then why are you here?" he asked. "Not that I don't want you here —I do. I wish you'd come back straight away. But why now?"

I inhaled sharply. "I have some questions about, well, you. If that's okay?"

Noah's eyebrows lifted up. "Yeah, sure. Go for it."

How did you ask someone about their family line in a respectful way?

When I couldn't come up with the proper questions, I changed the subject. "Your town has changed quite a bit. Wasn't there a huge wall around the place last time I was here?"

Noah nodded, a smile tugging at his lips. "Yeah, until about six months ago. The new Alpha... I mean, ah, our new leader, decided it was time to open the town up a bit."

"Alpha?"

"That's what we call our leader, or whatever. He's in charge around here."

I pressed my lips together. Did he just say Alpha? Was this some sort of military base? Should I even be here?

I stood up. "I shouldn't have come here without notice. I'm so sorry. Would you like to come into town and meet somewhere else? I can give you my cell number, and our address."

"No!" He bolted to his feet. "Don't go. I don't want you to leave when you've only just got here."

"But this probably isn't the time to ask you personal questions about Trixie."

"Trixie?"

"Yeah." I gestured to the perfectly well-behaved little toddler sitting on the floor. Thank goodness this was a good day. Being a toddler, it was pot luck whether or not she would behave, or be a little more demanding. "Her full name is Beatrix, but I call her Trixie for short."

I reached down and grabbed my daughter up in my arms, feeling the need to hold on tight. I'd had Trixie completely to myself for her whole life so far, and while I knew Noah wasn't a threat, it was difficult to adjust my instinct to protect her.

Noah stared at her. "She has my eyes."

"Yes, she does."

Trixie reached out to him, her little hands opening and closing as she tried to grab at his t-shirt.

I gaped, amazed at the way she was acting. "She doesn't usually go to anyone she doesn't know."

Trixie grunted and tried to dive for him when I didn't act fast enough for her.

"Whoa, honey. Wait."

"I'll take her," Noah said, rushing to grab her up in his arms.

A strange zing ran through my body when Noah settled her on his chest, holding her against him as easily as if he'd done it from the beginning. They stared at each other with such a look of wonder, and growing love, that my heart all but broke for the time they'd lost.

My fault. I kept them separated from one another, and for what? Because I was scared? Because I was afraid of rejection? Not just for me, but for her.

"She likes you," I whispered.

Trixie reached for Noah's face, patting his cheek.

"What's wrong with her, Amy?" he whispered back, as if not

wanting to startle our child. "She looks so healthy—she looks perfect, actually."

Tears came to my eyes at the wonder in his tone.

Then he added, "But you've come here for a reason. And I know it's because there must be something wrong."

I swallowed hard and forced myself to forge forward with the questions swirling in my brain. I'd gone through a lot harder tasks than this, in my life. Namely, her birth. That had almost killed me. Quite literally.

"Well, Trixie is a little unusual for my family. She doesn't talk much, but physically, she is advanced. Really strong, and muscled, and fast."

Noah grinned. "Sounds like my side. We don't talk much until we're about three, but our reflexes and strength come in early."

He hoisted her up on his chest and wrapped both arms around her, holding her tight. He looked slightly awkward, but Trixie nestled closer, as if she craved his embrace.

"There's something else," I said quietly, fear creeping into my heart. What would I do if he didn't know what I was talking about?

He turned his head to look at me. "Tell me."

"Last night, she was fast asleep and dreaming, and started making really strange sounds."

"What sort of sounds?"

"Well..." I ran my hands through my hair, tugging at the long tangles. I wasn't quite sure how to explain it. "Barking. Growling. Biting. Sounds a dog would make, if I'm honest. Scared the hell out of me."

Noah's eyes widened, but beyond that, he didn't respond. The silence stretched between us.

I continued when he didn't say anything. "I mean, she doesn't see any dogs. I don't have one, and my parents don't either. I don't know how she would have even seen one, except in books and the occasional movie. Certainly not enough to mimic one in her sleep."

Trixie sighed and put her head down on his chest. Then she closed her eyes.

I put my hand over my mouth. They made the most beautiful picture together: Noah with all his height and strength and masculine power, and Trixie with her sweet face and golden curls, trusting the man who held her enough to fall asleep on him. "What should I do?" he asked.

I shrugged, feeling confused, but my smile was genuine. "You're done for now. So, I suggest you get comfy. On the couch maybe?"

He did as I suggested and crept over to the couch, sat down slowly, then lay back.

Trixie crawled up his chest and settled her head into the crook of his neck.

Noah was frozen, his eyes wide with shock. My expression probably mirrored his.

But as the minutes ticked on, Noah's beefy arms came up and cuddled Trixie to his chest.

A sense of calm and happiness settled over me as I watched them. In all the different first meetings I'd imagined, this moment surpassed even the best scenario I'd created.

"I know why she's barking, and whatnot," Noah whispered, stroking Trixie's little back.

"You do?" I asked, perching on the edge of the couch. "Thank God! Tell me."

Surely there was a reasonable explanation for all the strange things about Trixie that worried me.

He looked up to meet my gaze. His eyes were an electric blue, but a silver mist swirled within them that wasn't usually there. Damn it! I knew I hadn't been imagining when that happened in Trixie's eyes, too!

"I do," Noah said, "but you're gonna have to keep your mind open, because I've heard that humans don't take this news too well."

Hang on a minute. Did he just say, humans?

CHAPTER 4
NOAH

Amy's mouth dropping open and her eyes widening in nervous anticipation of my explanation was not exactly encouraging, but I knew what needed to be said. How she would respond to it? Well, I couldn't exactly control that.

"Um, did you just say... human?" Amy asked. "Does that mean you're, ah, saying you're not one?"

I nodded, stroking the back of the little girl I held in my arms. She was so light and soft, and yet I could feel the strength Amy was talking about. She definitely had my genes.

Pride swelled inside me.

"I may as well just get down to the truth of it all. Are you okay with that?" I asked.

I knew next to nothing about the woman in front of me.

Nothing except for the fact that our attraction burned brighter than a forest fire, and that my wolf believed she was our mate.

How true that was, was yet to be seen. But the proof of our child, half human, half shifter, lay curled in my arms.

Did she like straight talking? Or should I soften it some? I wasn't sure. I hadn't known her long enough to make that judgment call.

"Hit me with it. I'm ready." Amy curled her fingers into fists and lay them on her thighs. She was thinner than last time I saw her. Probably from the stress of having to work to support them both.

Something I decided to change as of this very minute.

"I'm a wolf shifter," I said. "Everyone in this town is. That's why we live out here in the forest, away from town. We need the space, and we're pretty private."

"You...." Amy shook her head and frowned at me. "Say that again?"

My throat was thick, and I stroked my baby's back to soothe both her and myself, given the sudden tension running through my body.

"My whole family are wolf shifters. It's not like the movies. We're not "werewolves", or creatures that have no control over ourselves. We choose when to shift into a wolf, and when not to. And when we are in wolf form, we can hear and see, and feel, just like we do when we're human. So you never have to be afraid of me, or anyone for that matter, if you see us in our wolf form."

Amy clenched her hands together tightly in her lap and began to rock a little bit. What was she thinking? Was she about to freak out completely?

"Holy shit," she whispered. "I don't want to believe you, but I knew there was something strange about this town. About you. Something... otherworldly."

I nodded, feeling the heat pour through my veins from just looking at her. Damn, she was beautiful. Her skin, and those dark eyes, called to me like no other woman ever had.

But I pushed my desire down. We had a lot of shit to sort out before we got back to that.

Amy swallowed hard, her throat working. "So does that mean that Trixie, is a... you know... wolf. Person."

I grinned at her. "The term is shifter. And honestly, I don't know. It sounds like she's already displaying characteristics of our pack, but we don't often breed outside our own people, so I'd have to ask someone who knows. An elder maybe."

"Breed," Amy repeated, shaking her head. "That sounds so strange."

"Not to us." I kissed the top of Trixie's head, and she gave a little sigh. I squeezed her tighter, amazed at the amount of love I already felt for this little one. "I can't believe I have a daughter."

Amy stood up, wrapping her arms around herself. "I'm sorry I stayed away so long."

"Why did you?" I asked. "Really."

She squeezed herself tighter. "So many reasons. Firstly, because I was ashamed that we'd had a one-night stand and I was pregnant to a guy I didn't even know. That isn't something I usually do, you know."

His gaze softened. "I know. I would have seen you again, Amy. I would have asked you to move in here if I'd known. I would have looked after you, and her."

"How was I to know that?" Amy hissed back at me, throwing her arms in the air. "I didn't even know your last name. I still don't. All I knew was that we had this insane chemistry, and a hot night... and then nothing. I didn't have your cell number or anything. Hell, it's taken me three days to find this place! Even though I was here before. When I left, I certainly didn't memorize anything about the place!"

She was panting, her eyes flashing with anger.

Trixie whimpered on my chest.

"Shh..." I rubbed her back, and then stared at Amy. "Don't wake her up."

"Don't give me orders about my own daughter!"

After a moment, her gaze relaxed and she let out a sigh. She ran both hands through her hair, pushing it back off her face.

"Look," she began, putting both hands on her hips, "I made the wrong choice. It's clear now. But I promise you that I have taken very good care of her on my own. I've worked hard, saved money, kept a roof over both of our heads..."

It was obvious she'd done a good job, and all on her own, but she hadn't needed to suffer the way she had.

I sat up straighter, wishing I could hug Amy, but not wanting to let go of Trixie. "Amy, I'm not trying to give you a hard time. But I have... regretted that morning for the past two years."

Amy's eyes went wide. "Oh. What do you mean?"

She sounded hurt.

I rushed to correct whatever wrong idea she had. "I mean that I wish you'd never left. I wish I'd woken up and stopped you from creeping away. There was nothing to be ashamed of, or apologize for. Our connection is undeniable, and I hope you'll give me, and our town, a second chance to prove that to you."

I kissed Trixie's head again so that I had an excuse to look down and away from Amy's intense stare.

I'd missed her more than I wanted to admit and there was no way I was saying any more now. Not when the only reason she was back was because she needed answers about Trixie's genetics. If our daughter hadn't shown any signs of the wolf, would Amy be here? Probably not.

I had to be careful not to scare her away. Because if that happened again, I might never get either of them back in my life.

Amy sat down in the chair with a sigh. "I had no idea you felt that way."

I wanted to laugh but swallowed down the impulse. "Of course, you didn't. We barely know each other, just like you said. But I want you and Trixie to be here, and I'll do whatever you need to prove to you I'm worthy of being her father."

"You want me here?" Amy whispered.

Damn it, she didn't let things slip by her.

I nodded, then tried to back track. "Yeah. Of course, I do. It's the right thing to do, for Trixie. Don't you think?"

"Well, I hadn't thought about you and I together." Amy glanced away, her cheeks red with a heated blush.

I smirked, knowing she'd just lied to me, then pulled my mouth back into a neutral line. She was lying, but there was no reason to point that out to her. She didn't understand fated mates, but I did. I burned for her, and she would burn for me. I would make sure of it, this time round.

But if she needed time and closeness to be reacquainted with those feelings, then I was more than happy to oblige.

"Great. So, you and Trixie can move in here, and I'll get you set up with the Alpha's wife so you two can talk and get more knowledge about what's happening with Trixie."

"What? No! I can't move in here," Amy said, shaking her head. "I have a job, and an apartment. My parents are expecting me for dinner tonight."

The very idea of letting my daughter go again was like a knife to the heart. I couldn't do it.

What did I have to say to get Amy to stay?

I sighed heavily, my mind swirling with options. What would keep her here, even a little while longer? Long enough for me to convince her we were right together. "But what about her wolf characteristics? They may become more frequent, and more obvious. Do you really want her around humans when she's developing her strength?"

Amy's eyes went wide, and a touch of regret for my exaggeration flashed through me. I still felt justified in saying it though, if the words kept Amy with me.

"Do you really think…"

"I think, now that Trixie is manifesting some signs, it's a lot safer for both of you to be here, at least for a couple of weeks. We'll talk to the elders, and the neighboring pack, see if any of them knows anything that can help."

Amy nodded, but tears filled her eyes. Was it because she was overwhelmed, or did she feel helpless? I didn't want her to feel either.

I wanted to help, and I wanted to make her life just that little bit easier and less lonely.

"Go open the left drawer on the desk over there." I nodded toward my dad's old desk pressed up against the wall near the kitchen.

She didn't ask why, but she got up and walked over to it.

"Open the drawer and grab the white envelope."

She did as I asked and brought the envelope back to the couch.

"Take it, and go pay your rent, buy some stuff you need for Trixie, whatever you want. A crib maybe?" I had no idea what my daughter needed.

Amy opened the envelope and gasped. "I can't take this!"

"Of course you can! Think of it as two years of child support. I don't want you worried about your job, or bills, or anything like that. So, go back to town if you need to, but take the money. Pay your bills for the next month or so, and then come back and spend time with me, here. I promise you won't regret it. Please, Amy. I want to do this for you, and for Trixie."

It was a gamble, letting her leave at all. What if I never found her again?

Amy nodded. "I suppose I could tell work I need family leave. And she'd need a crib and diapers, and some things for your house."

I didn't correct her when she said my house. Soon, hopefully it would be *our* place, and she wouldn't need her apartment.

But I was patient; I'd wait for that day.

Amy inhaled loudly. "I think I can do that, but I'll need to make some calls. Does cell reception work out here? Because last time I tried, I had to walk halfway back to town to message an uber."

I laughed. "Of course we do. Check your cell."

She stood up. "Are you okay to hold her if I go call work, and my parents?"

Would I hold my own child so that my mate could tell the world she was spending time with me? A rumble of laughter started up in my chest. I swallowed it back down with difficulty. Did she really need to ask?

I cuddled my daughter closer, breathing in her scent. "Absolutely."

Amy stared at us, then popped out the front and shut the door behind her.

I couldn't help the huge grin that stretched across my lips. How was it possible that in one single morning, my whole world had turned around in such a momentous way?

I'd woken up this morning with a hole in my heart and a gut ache that never seemed to go away. But now Amy was back, and she'd brought with her the best surprise I'd ever had.

Now, I just had to work out a way to keep them both.

CHAPTER 5
AMY

My parents were much happier to hear that I was cancelling dinner with them than I'd expected. Once I told them the reason, of course.

In fact, they wholeheartedly agreed that I should stay with Trixie's father until we'd sorted everything out. I'd been a little shocked they agreed so rapidly, but then again, they'd always wanted me to contact Noah and tell him about Trixie.

Next was work, and they were actually pretty good considering I was giving them next to no notice, but I hadn't taken any time off in the past twelve months.

When I went back to the apartment, I just had to pay rent in advance and get Trixie a crib so that she could comfortably sleep here at Noah's with me. Although, I had a pack-and-play back at the apartment that I barely used, and I considered using that one instead of wasting money on a whole new one. It might do the trick for a short time. Then we'd be right to stay for the next fortnight. Or longer if we wanted to.

As long as I could deal with the fact that Noah thought he was some sort of wolf... werewolf... what had he called himself?

I shivered as I walked back inside the house where I'd known the most incredible passion imaginable. How was I going to keep my hands to myself with Noah always within arm's reach?

He hadn't moved from the couch, but he had twisted around to lift his legs up and was lying back a little more comfortably.

My baby girl was fast asleep on top of him and looked so trusting and peaceful, the image of them both, in turn, relaxed me.

"How'd you go?" he asked.

"Everything's all set," I said, though my heart was so full I could barely speak. "Work is sorted, and my parents are happy. All is... good."

I was on an unofficial, and definitely unplanned, vacation. With my baby's daddy.

"So, you'll stay?" he asked, his gaze finding mine. "Here? With me."

I nodded. "I need to go back to the apartment for some clothes and things. The porta cot, blankets, bottles. But yeah... we'll stay. At least until we've worked everything out and I can understand more about what's happening with Trixie."

Noah nodded but his eyes shuttered a little, and he didn't say anything else.

I wanted to know what he was thinking, but I was too afraid to ask. He was so honest, more so than I'd expected from a man I didn't know well and who had every reason not to trust me.

There was a knock on the front door, and a man called out, "Hey Noah, you home?"

"Can you answer that?" Noah whispered. "He won't stop calling out until we answer."

"Oh, sure." I ran for the front door, pulling it open to stop whatever pounding knock was coming next.

The man on the other side of the door was huge and vicious-looking.

I inhaled sharply, clinging to the wood to try and avoid automatically stepping back. Was he one of the wolf people, too? What was going to happen once he worked out I wasn't one of them?

Instead of growling at me, the big guy raised his eyebrows as if in shock, and then he hunched a little, making himself smaller. The deliberate act turned him instantly from someone scary, to someone who obviously had kindness in his heart. "I'm sorry... Is Noah in?"

"Ah, yes, but our daughter's asleep, so we're just trying to be quiet," I said. The term *our daughter* rolled off my tongue without thinking.

"Your... *what?*" The guy at the door spluttered, and I laughed a little at his shocked expression.

"Yeah, he was a little surprised too." I stepped back and gestured to the couch where Noah lay holding Trixie.

Noah lifted his hand and waved at the guy at the door.

"Oh, my God," the big guy said. "My mate's gonna love this."

Then he grinned and all the remaining fierceness in his face disappeared. "Hey. I'm Ronan. Alpha around these parts."

He stuck out his huge hand and I looked at it, before extending my own. "Nice to meet the... Alpha. I'm Amy."

He shook my hand briefly then dropped his arm away. "And you're human... I'm not sure what to say now. Did Noah tell you..."

I shoved my hands into my jeans pockets and rocked back on my heels. "You mean about the wolf man, person, thing? Noah just told me, but I haven't seen it in action yet."

And part of me still didn't believe him. Men turning into wolves? Seriously.

Ronan's gaze shot to Noah. "You know the rules."

His tone was accusatory.

"What rules?" I asked, feeling defensive of Noah. I'd gotten him in trouble already. *Shit.*

The Alpha turned to look at me. "We don't usually tell humans what we are."

I laughed, then put my hand over my mouth. "Sorry. That was inappropriate. But maybe you should. If I'd known, I might not have gotten pregnant, and then found my daughter growling and howling in the night."

I wasn't sure anything could have stopped me the night we conceived Trixie, but a little heads up might have done the trick.

"Sorry." The Alpha blinked a few times. "What?"

I gave the Alpha a quick run-down on the past two years, and by the time I was done, he'd invited himself in and sat down on the couch next to me.

"Wow. What a story," Ronan said, grinning. "I will see to Draven being reassigned straight away."

He got to his feet and headed toward the front door.

Shit. These people did not mess about.

I called out to him, quietly as not to disturb Trixie. "Oh, we don't want to inconvenience anyone."

"It's no trouble."

Trixie woke up then, loudly yawning and mewling like a little puppy.

I froze, watching her as she opened her eyes and took in her father for only the second time ever.

She didn't flinch even though I half expected her to. Instead, she simply smiled at him, then pushed herself back so she could sit up.

"Hey baby, did you have a good sleep?" I asked, rushing forward to pick her up.

She came straight into my arms, and then I took her back to meet Ronan. "Um, Alpha. This is Trixie."

I wasn't sure how my baby was going to respond to meeting another huge man, but she reached for his face.

The Alpha came forward and offered his cheek to her. She patted it gently, then moved back.

Ronan made a soft growling noise that sounded more like a happy purr than anything else.

"She's beautiful, Amy." He turned to Noah. "And there's no doubt she's yours. Look at those eyes."

"Of course, there's no doubt," I said, slightly miffed he'd even brought it up. "Don't worry about that."

Several people over the years had accused me of not knowing who the father was, and suggested that was why I hadn't chased him down for child support.

But Noah had been the only man I'd slept with that year. When I'd met him, it had been months since I'd been to bed with anyone, and then I didn't go near a guy afterwards. Maybe that was another reason my poor starved body ached every time I looked at Noah now.

Ronan glanced down, looking embarrassed. "I didn't mean... I just meant... those eyes."

"Yeah, I know."

The Alpha cleared his throat and shuffled to the door.

Noah finally stood up and rolled his shoulders as though stretching his back. "Did you need something, Ronan?"

"You didn't turn up for work, so I was a bit worried about you. I've seen you dig a trench with a broken arm, so I thought you might be bleeding to death in your shower or something."

I shuddered at the thought, but Noah laughed it off. "All good, but are you all right if I take the day off? I'm going to drive the girls back to town to pick up some clothes and baby stuff. Then they're coming to stay here."

Ronan grinned. "Sounds like a plan. Just let her know some of the pack rules, yeah?"

Noah nodded, and the Alpha left.

"You're driving us back?" I asked Noah, turning to look at him as he walked over to us.

Trixie put her arms out to him, and he picked her up out of my arms as though he'd done it a thousand times before.

Again, my heart broke a little for them both, thinking about all the times he should have held her when she was a baby.

Oh, the things I would do differently if I'd known he'd be this good a father.

"I'm definitely coming with you guys," he said, shaking me out of my guilt-ridden thoughts. "I'm not letting you two out of my sight."

I grinned at him. "I won't disappear again, I promise. In fact, we should exchange numbers and details, like now."

He chuckled and walked over to the desk to grab a set of keys. "Am I driving, or...?"

I shook my head. So, we weren't discussing the fact that he'd decided he was coming with us. We were just doing what he obviously needed to do, which in all fairness, I understood.

I'd run out on him once before. He probably wanted to make sure it didn't happen again. But things were different now. Everything was different. I would not run out on him again. He had a right to know his daughter, and she had the right to get to know her father and his kin.

"Well, Trixie has to sit in a baby seat, so we probably need to take my car."

He rolled his eyes. "Damn it. I have a lot to learn."

I walked over to the baby bag and grabbed out my keys. "You learn fast when you need to, trust me."

Noah shrugged. "Okay. Let's go. And grab the money."

I reached for the envelope of cash still sitting on the coffee table with shaking hands. I didn't want his money—I never had—but not working for a month was going to eat into my savings something fierce and we needed those in case of emergencies.

Even so...

"I really don't need it—"

"I want to help," he said firmly, cutting across my words. "So use it for whatever she needs. Rent. Food, clothes. Whatever."

I finally conceded that he was probably right and slipped the envelope into the baby bag that doubled as a handbag. "Thank you. I appreciate the gesture more than you can imagine."

Maybe I could start an account for Trixie and leave it to grow into a college fund. Then at least the money would go to her and not me.

Noah opened the front door, and with our daughter held safely in his arms, called out to me, "Let's go."

We drove back to my apartment, and I packed a huge suitcase of stuff for me and Trixie: toys, blankets, and the porta-cot.

Excitement built inside me at the chance to do something new and different. It really did feel, strangely, like we were going on vacation. Even if it was just to a log cabin in the woods an hour away.

Noah was the perfect gentleman. He played with Trixie while I packed up all our things, then carried everything down the two flights of stairs without a single complaint.

Next, we had to deal with the cash I had floating around in my bag, so he drove me to the bank and made me put the money in my account. I refused twenty times, but the wolf man had a will of steel and in the end, I did what he asked for the sake of time, and my daughter.

Who knew what would happen in the future and maybe one day we'd need the cash?

For today, we were going back to the 'pack', and on to an adventure I wasn't sure I was ready for.

CHAPTER 6

NOAH

By the time we got back from town, Draven had already packed up his room and moved on. Where he'd gone to, I wasn't sure, but I was going to miss his cooked breakfasts. Even if they were burnt most of the time.

"Do you want to set up in the second bedroom?" I asked, opening the door and showing Amy the room that had been Draven's.

It was now empty, save the bed and a chest of drawers.

"Oh, yes, please. It's lovely," Amy said, walking into the room and putting her bag down on the bed.

I glanced around. "I suppose it is."

The room was large, the bed was hand carved, and the nice ruby red drapes on the windows gave the room a little splash of color. "Room for the porta-cot too," she said.

I hated the fact she wasn't moving straight into my bedroom but decided against offering her that option. I didn't want to be turned down, not today. My nerves were already stretched thin as it was.

A silence fell between us and I wanted to grab her, hold her, and kiss her. All the things I wasn't allowed to do. All the things I craved.

I clenched my teeth tight and forced the desires away. I needed something constructive to do. Something physical, that would distract me from thoughts of touching Amy.

"I'll go grab the bags out of the car," I told her.

I didn't wait for a response, just turned and went outside to grab the suitcases and bags she'd wanted to bring with her. I hadn't realized a baby would need so much... stuff. But what did I know about kids?

I brought everything in and dropped it in her bedroom, as my little girl toddled around the room checking everything out. She tugged on the curtains and examined the walls like they held a mystery only she could see.

My body was burning with energy and normally this would be the perfect time to shift and go for a run. But I didn't want to do that, not today. Not when everything with Amy was so fragile, the trust so thin. I needed to stay close by.

And I needed her to understand a little more about shifters and our pack, before I gave in to my wolf side and maybe scared her half to death in the process.

"I'll walk up to the shops and get us some dinner, if you want?" I didn't think Amy would necessarily want to buy a meal at our only eatery. People would stare and I doubted she'd be comfortable there at this early stage.

"Oh, that would be great. I'll feed Trixie and get her ready for bed. Do you have a bath?"

"Just a shower. Which you're welcome to use." I pointed to the room opposite her bedroom, across the hall. "There's a full bathroom in there."

She smiled happily. "Showering her is a two-person job, so I think I'll just wash her down with baby wipes and be done with it. Thanks."

I opened my mouth to offer to help her with showering Trixie, then realized how stupid that would sound to her. We weren't a couple yet, and we weren't a family that could be free and easy and comfortable with each other like that. Not yet.

I turned away and marched toward the front door. "Back in about an hour."

I headed out into the cool night air.

"Fuck." I ran my hands through my hair and squeezed my skull.

What I wouldn't give to have Amy naked before me once more, but I wasn't seeing any signs that she wanted me the way she had the night we'd met in the bar. She didn't look at me the same way, and I wondered what having the baby had done to her. Did it change her hormone levels to a point where it might be permanent, and she might not want me anymore? Ever?

I hoped not but what did I know about any of that?

I walked up the main road and through town, making my way to the only eatery we had here. It was run by Bailey and his wife, and they made hot meals similar to a pub meal in town. They also did take out, which would suit me just fine tonight.

I walked into the shop.

"Hey Noah." Bailey's wife, Maeve, greeted me with a curious look while wiping down the counter top. "I heard you've got a woman staying with you. And a baby. Is that right?"

I shook my head as I wandered up to the counter. "Why am I not surprised that you already know my most private business, Maeve? You got her shoe size and everything as well?"

Maeve picked up her pad and pen that had been lying on the counter and grinned at me. "Not yet, but I will soon enough. What can I get you?"

"Two house specials, extra chips, and.... should I get something for Trixie? She's... fifteen months old."

If my math was correct, that was about right.

"Do you know what she likes?" Maeve asked.

"Nope. Sorry."

"I'll put in some extra chicken and vegetables. Something plain. Little ones don't like seasonings or sauces much. Will be about twenty minutes, love." She ripped off the paper and set it alongside the other orders.

"Thanks, Maeve."

She went back into the kitchen, and I wandered outside to take a deep breath of fresh, country air. Going into town today for only an hour was enough to make me grateful for the fact that I didn't live there.

Kit bounced up to me, grinning. "Heard you've got yourself a human girl! What's she like?"

I couldn't help but smile at the Alpha's younger brother Kit. He was all happiness and sunshine in a world where most of the men were rough as a bag of nails. But Kit wasn't, and that was fine by me. He was a good guy, a loyal shifter. A man who'd die for his family and almost *had* done so when Jaime attacked our pack a few months ago.

I'd always liked Kit, even though he was an unusual kid. But that day had proven to me, and a lot of others too, that he really had more heart than sense.

"She's good," I told him. "Her name's Amy."

"Amy? That's cool. So, is she hanging around?"

I nodded. "Yeah, at least for a while. I asked her to stay."

Kit came to stand beside me, then whispered, "Is it true she had your baby and you didn't know? Now she's back and you gotta deal with like a... two-year-old?"

I laughed and shook my head as I swung around to stare at him. This town. Word spread faster than a wolf after a hare. "My daughter's name is Beatrix. She's not quite one and a half."

"Wow," Kit said, shaking his head. "That's crazy."

"That I didn't know I had a kid? Absolutely." I'd never even considered it a possibility before.

"I wonder what Lacey's gonna say," Kit said in a pseudo-whisper.

I grimaced at the mention of my ex. "Well, not really her business anymore, is it?"

Lacey and I had been on and off again for years. She'd been a good distraction while I was looking for, and waiting for, my fated mate. I'd always harbored some hope that I had one out there somewhere, and I'd refused to settle for less than that.

Meeting Amy that night had proven to me that those feelings of perfection were possible, so anything I'd shared with Lacey over the past two years had been me searching for a little comfort in the darkness.

But Amy was back, and I wasn't letting her go. I just had to hope that Lacey didn't get too jealous, or act out, because she could be a nasty bitch when she wanted to be. She was a pretty powerful shifter, too.

I shook myself out of the negative train of thought. "She'll be fine."

Kit chuckled. "Good luck, mate."

He slapped me on the shoulder and headed off.

I groaned. He was right. I had better give Amy a bit of a heads up about Lacey, before she heard it from someone else.

"Dinner's ready, Noah," Maeve called and I went in to get our take out.

"Thanks, heaps."

"Enjoy."

I took the aluminum rectangular dishes and headed back to my place, my heart aching with anticipation, and my excitement thrumming.

I pushed open the door and called out, "I'm back."

The extra bedroom door opened, and my gorgeous little girl came barreling out wearing nothing but a diaper. She was all chubbiness and bulky strength.

She giggled, her little legs pumping as she ran.

"I'm gonna get you!" Amy called, running out of the room after Trixie wearing a thin summer dress and her hair still wet from the shower.

"Oh, hi," she said, scooping the baby up into her arms. "I decided to have a shower myself while she just played at my feet. I hope that's okay."

I nodded, my throat thick and my body instantly tight with tension and longing. Damn, she was gorgeous. Such clear, beautiful, soft skin. And her scent. It rose around me, mingling with the smell of my soap to become something altogether exotic and delicious. I swallowed hard.

"Yeah. Of course. You guys hungry?"

"She's always hungry," Amy joked, "But let me just dress her. I won't be long."

Amy disappeared back into the bedroom with Trixie and closed the door.

I went to the kitchen table and set down the food. We just needed some cutlery and we'd be right. I grabbed glasses and water, then set the table for three. How Trixie would eat, I had no idea, but she may as well have a place at the table too.

The baby came running to me and grabbed me around the legs.

"Oh, hello," I said, glancing down at her.

She stared straight up at me, those bright blue eyes unnerving to a degree. It was like looking in a strange mirror, but that didn't make sense either. The child was only one year old, and a girl too, and yet I could see so much of myself in her face.

She made a noise, as if she wanted something from me, but I couldn't figure out what.

"She wants you to pick her up," Amy said, walking up to the table and smiling at me.

"Oh, okay." I scooped her up in to my arms and held her tightly to me. "Maeve put some chicken and vegetables in here for you, little one. Would you like some?"

I unwrapped the packaging and Amy made agreeable noises. "Oh yeah, she'll love that. Perfect."

We sat down to eat and I got to enjoy my first ever family dinner, with the woman my wolf knew was our mate, and the child we'd created together. I'd missed so much, since that night I met Amy. Her pregnancy, Trixie's birth. The first year of my daughter's life. I wasn't going to miss out on any more firsts.

We finished dinner, then we walked together to the spare room so that Amy could put Trixie to bed.

She went down easily in the pack-and-play in Amy's room, simply cuddling her little toy wolf and going to sleep.

We crept out of the room together and grinned as though we'd shared in a great and successful adventure. Then we walked back into the living room and sat down on the couches, just like any other two parents who had just jointly put their child to bed.

But the sudden tension in the room belied how easy and natural everything else had been about the day.

Amy jumped into the silence. "So, what do you do at night?"

"Watch TV. Go to bed early. The pub maybe. A friend's house. Whatever, really."

Probably the same sort of things she'd done before she had Trixie.

Amy stifled a yawn, though the action didn't look very natural. "I'm pretty tired. Trixie gets up early, so maybe I should turn in, too."

She gave me a forced smile then stood up.

I got to my feet too, my heart pounding in my chest. I didn't want her sleeping alone, in my house, while I tried to get some sleep in my own bed.

"I haven't shown you the rest of the house," I managed.

She swallowed hard, her pupils dilating to huge black pools. Was that desire I could read in her gaze? Or was it something else, and I was just projecting what I wanted to see? "What else is there?"

"My bedroom," I said, feeling daring, and then held out my hand. "Wanna see it?"

She glanced down at my hand, then nodded, reaching forward to take mine. "I'd like that."

I tugged her out of the living room and down the hall.

It was time to find out if the fire of passion that had raged between us two years ago was still present, or if it had turned to ash.

CHAPTER 7
AMY

I couldn't believe I'd agreed to go into his bedroom with him, but here I was. My legs quivered as I walked down the hallway, past the bedroom where my daughter slept and on toward the back of the house.

The silence around us was deafening, and out of sheer nerves I asked, "Do you have your own bathroom? Or is the one we used the only one in the house?"

I didn't care either way, of course. One bathroom, two. Made no difference to me. But I felt like I had to make conversation, or I would burst into flames from nerves and excitement.

"Yep. Got my own," Noah said as he pushed open a large door and indicated into a dark room. "Come see."

He flicked on the light, and I stared around the room.

"It's lovely." The room was made up well but was once again devoid of any real personal touches in terms of decor. I stepped in to the room; it was almost as big as the whole living area. "It's huge."

"Yeah…" Noah said from behind me, his words rolling over me like a vibrating massage. "I spend a lot of time in here."

I could see that. There was a small couch on one side and a TV. Then there was his huge bed. A bed I'd been in before.

"You know, now that I think about it, I've actually been in this room before," I teased, walking forward. "Just not in the daylight."

The morning I'd run from him, the sun had barely been up, and I hadn't taken the time to look around and study my surroundings before I left.

"Hey, I want to ask you something. Why did you leave that morning?" His question caught me off guard.

I turned around and stared at him. "I told you. I was ashamed of my behavior. Embarrassed beyond belief, actually."

And I had been. I couldn't believe I'd gone home with a guy I didn't know, had sex with a stranger, and then gotten myself stuck in the middle of the forest.

I'd gotten up and taken my independence back quick smart.

He shook his head as he sauntered toward me. "I'm not sure I believe you on that. It was something else, wasn't it?"

My heart pounded in my chest like a bongo drum, a tingle of fear zinging along my spine even as my core melted in anticipation of being touched by him again.

"No." I swallowed hard, my throat constricting tight. "What else could it be, than what I've already told you?"

He chuckled. "Oh, I don't know. Me, perhaps? Did you wake up, look down at my face, and realize you'd made a horrible mistake?"

He ducked his head so I couldn't read his expression, but he reached for me at the same time, sliding his hands around my waist.

"Was that it?" he whispered as he tugged me closer.

Our hips met and I gasped at the intimate contact, his warm breath on my face.

"Was it me?" he asked again.

I couldn't do anything to stop the way I responded to his closeness. I placed my hands on his broad chest and groaned at the heat that radiated off him. "I thought there was a fault in my memory when I remembered your heat. But I was right... You're super-hot. Literally as well as..."

I broke off and my cheeks heated as he laughed and finished for me. "Figuratively?"

He chuckled again, and readjusted his height to stand tall and span his hands out to cup my hips. "You're pretty hot too. And I don't mean in temperature."

The embarrassed heat spread from my cheeks down my neck and I found myself reaching for deflection. "Is that a wolf thing? The heat? Because Trixie has always been the hottest, sweatiest baby."

He smiled gently, as if he could see through my thinly veiled deflect technique, and I shook my head.

"Sorry. Not sexy to talk about the baby, I know."

Bad move, Amy. Bad.

"Anything you say is sexy, Amy. But I want to take you to bed. Will you let me?"

I inhaled sharply, fear of rejection clutching at my heart. "My body isn't the same since I had the baby..."

I was saggy in places that had never sagged, and thinner in places that were once strong.

He bent his head and kissed me gently on the forehead. He looked deep into my eyes as he said, "You're beautiful. So much more beautiful than I remember. I want you, Amy. So much."

I closed my eyes to block out the look in his eyes. The look that told me he was speaking truth. It scared me, that truth. But I wanted more. So much more.

I opened my eyes again, enjoying the feeling of his lips on my skin, and the closeness of his body to mine. Still the uncertainty dragged at me. I pulled away and stared up at him, worry making me second guess myself. "I haven't been with anyone since I got pregnant, and I'm not sure..."

My next words were lost as Noah cupped my face and kissed me, hard and firm.

Well, that's one way to silence the anxiety, I thought, and then I forgot to think at all as desire took over.

I couldn't remember what I was going to say next, but it didn't seem relevant anymore. My mind melted into pleasure. I didn't want to think. It had been so long since I'd felt anything but pain, discomfort, and stress. I deserved to feel good for a moment, surely? I wanted to just luxuriate in his lips, in his presence. In the love I had always held for this man in my heart. The love for the man who'd given me my beautiful, cherished baby.

A groan escaped my throat as he moved closer, grabbing my ass and hauling me against his body. I ached so badly for him, and although the fear of how much I wanted this man had tormented me over the past two years, now that I was here, I wanted nothing more than to dive into bed with him again, to assuage the ache deep inside me that had never gone away. Not since that night we were together.

I tugged at his shirt, wanting to feel his skin against mine. *Needing* the skin-to-skin connection, like it was some kind of wonder drug.

He pulled back and stared down at me. His eyes swirled with color, and I bit my lip to stop from moaning aloud. Far from being scared, the exotic nature of his wild side enticed me in as much as the man himself. Even with everything I had learnt, the animal side of him didn't scare me. Not in this moment. Not as much as I knew it probably should.

"Do you want me?" he asked, his voice deep and sexy.

I nodded. I'd never been asked such a thing and found it as confronting as hell. But I understood that he wanted to be sure.

"Say it. Please." He groaned. "Tell me you want me between your legs, making you come over and over again."

This time I couldn't stop the moan that escaped my lips. "Yes. Please, yes. I want that, Noah. I want you."

That was all it took for him to lift me up and kiss me again. I wrapped my arms around his neck and my legs around his waist, and kissed him back with all the longing in my soul.

He walked me over to the bed then fell with me so that I landed on the mattress on my back, still wrapped around him. He pulled away just long enough for us to tear at each other's clothes.

I wiggled to help as he stripped my dress off my body in a few easy pulls, and my underwear fell away just as fast. Standing up, he yanked his t-shirt off over his head and dropped his jeans before kicking them away.

I got one look at his gorgeous body before he was on top of me again, hot and urgent. I lifted my legs, encouraging him to enter me straight away. I ached for him. It hurt inside, like an actual physical pain. I'd been empty for so long, and no one could fill that void, except Noah.

Instead of thrusting inside of me, he pulled back and began working his way down my body, kissing my throat, kneading my breasts, and generally tormenting me with this build-up of pleasure.

"No. Please." I tugged at him. He was going the wrong way.

He glanced up and frowned at me. "What's wrong?"

"I want you inside me." It was almost shocking to say the words, but if that was what I needed to say to get him to fuck me, then I'd gladly oblige.

He didn't come up to me like I wanted. He grinned like the wolf in the Little Red Riding Hood fable, and continued to devour me, inch by shocking inch.

"No... no...." I cried out as he kissed my belly then held open my thighs. "You shouldn't..."

"Oh, I most definitely should..." He growled, then flicked his tongue over my throbbing clit.

I exploded, jerking beneath his mouth and crying out as my first orgasm hit in a wave of pleasure.

He groaned and set his mouth over me, sucking at my clit while I grabbed for his head, anything to anchor me in the storm of passion.

He didn't stop his pleasuring. He licked me and suckled my tender flesh until I was peaking once more.

"Noah... please."

He thrust his fingers up inside me and my pussy clamped down on him, greedy and wanting more.

He worked me from the inside and the outside, and I was helpless to do anything but writhe on the bed and cry out to the gods above to slow the torment as wave after wave of pleasure washed over my starved system.

This is what I remembered from that night. The unending pleasure crashing over me in waves. I had missed this with Noah, so damn much...

I gasped and arched my back, my belly tightening to a crescendo once more under his talented fingers and tongue.

Finally, he withdrew and climbed back between my legs. "This time we come together."

He set his thick cock at my entrance and nudged at my flesh. I tilted my hips up to him, opening for him eagerly.

As if we were made for each other.

Yes. Please.

He slid inside me slowly, and I gasped at the slight pain as I stretched wide. "You're too big."

He shook his head and moved over me so we were touching from our noses, all the way down our bodies. "No. You're just tight. I'll be gentle, don't worry."

I didn't want gentle, but as he forged slowly inside me, I held my breath, waiting for more pain.

He was as gentle as he promised he would be. He rocked his hips slowly, thrusting into me deeper and deeper until he was finally buried to the hilt and the need clawing at me was at its peak. I was so tight, and hot, and sweaty, it felt like I would explode if he didn't move. Now.

I sunk my teeth into his shoulder, loving the salty taste of sweat on his skin. "More. Please."

He growled above me, the sound as dangerous as it was sexy.

I should have been afraid of the animal he'd told me was lurking inside of him. Instead, I lifted my thighs, wrapping them tight around his waist, and held on for the ride.

He pulled back then thrust into me, hard.

I gasped and clung to him tighter.

He did it again, and again, until he was fucking me into the mattress, into the headboard. I was crying out, he was growling, and all of it was a mess of pleasure and yearning and pure, unadulterated need.

I came on him once, then twice, rippling around his ever-hard cock, but he kept pounding into me.

The sweat rolled down his back, and the pleasure inside me kept building, until I reached up for his face and dragged him down to kiss me. Our lips met, and he thrust into me one more time before he came.

His tongue plundered my mouth as heat flooded my belly.

I threw my head back and screamed as orgasm after orgasm hit me, over and over again. The waves of sensation didn't stop until finally, he collapsed on top of me, and my mind let the world go, falling into the deepest sleep I'd had in years.

CHAPTER 8
NOAH

Waking up an hour later to find Amy still beneath me was a shock. I'd never passed out during sex before, but it had felt like she practically ripped my soul from my body in that last exchange.

She was breathing softly, fast asleep, and my sated cock lay on the sheets between us. I pushed up with my arms and moved off her slowly, not wanting to disturb her. Then I gently nudged at her shoulder until she rolled over and I could spoon her from behind.

She moaned a little, then nestled in and went back to sleep.

I glanced at the door, still wide open. We would hear the baby in the night if she needed us.

I smiled as I closed my eyes and put my head on the pillow beside hers. The baby... *our* baby. Despite how new the idea was, that was a concept I could get used to.

~

WHEN I WOKE up the next time, the sun was shining and the warm body in my bed was gone.

My heart plummeted and I jerked upright, for a moment reliving the last night of passion we'd shared. And its aftermath.

Shit. I called out, "Amy?"

She couldn't have gone far. Surely?

Please don't tell me you've run off on me again.

She didn't answer so I rolled out of bed and quickly pulled on my jeans before heading off to find her, my heart beating unnaturally fast. She wouldn't have left me again, would she? Not after all her promises?

The fear tugged at me, so I hurried down to the baby's room to make sure she was still there.

"Ah, there you are," I said, releasing a sigh at the sight of Amy in the spare bedroom, now known informally in my head as *Trixie's room*. She was lying on the bed next to our baby, who was drinking a bottle.

"Oh hey. I didn't mean to wake you," Amy said, sitting up on the mattress.

"You didn't." I walked over to where she was resting in an oversized t-shirt. "Will she go back to sleep, or should we take her back to bed with us?"

"Oh, she won't sleep anymore," Amy said, swaying in place, her eyes half closed. "But I sure as hell could. After last night..."

She sent a slightly shy smile my way, and then shook herself and made to stand up.

I put out a hand to her, staying her movement.

"Why don't you go back to sleep?" I said. "I'll take Trixie out to see the town, assuming that's okay with you?"

Amy frowned. "Oh, I don't know. She's never been here before."

And Amy had never trusted me with her before. That part I understood.

"How about I just take her for a walk to the store, get some milk, and come back? Give you an extra hour? Is she fed and warm enough?"

Trixie handed her mother the bottle, rolled over, and crawled straight to me.

Amy rubbed her eyes. "She's okay in her pajamas. And her diaper's changed and her belly's full. She's okay for an hour or so. But... just don't put her down. She'll run off and she's really fast."

I almost laughed. Of course, Trixie was fast. She was a shifter's daughter. But then, with me being the shifter in question, I knew she'd be safe with me.

"I'm sure I can catch her, hon, but I have no problem carrying her. She's light," I said, picking up the little one and stepping toward the door. I flicked the switch to turn off the light. "You sleep there. We'll be back in an hour."

"Come straight back if she's any trouble," Amy said, though she was already pulling a blanket over her body. "A little more sleep would be amazing. Thank you."

I shut the door quietly and crept back to my room with Trixie to finish getting dressed and pull on some boots.

"What do you think, little one?" I asked my daughter as I popped her on the floor and went in search of a pair of a fresh t-shirt and a hoodie. "Wanna go meet your grandmother?"

My mom would freak when she found out I had a daughter I never knew about. It was probably better that I tell her first, if she didn't already know. This town was like most small towns. Gossip, especially the juicy kind, spread quickly.

While I pulled on some clothes and shoes, Trixie played happily with her little wolf toy

"Gray too," I said with a laugh. "Just like me."

Once dressed, shoes and all, I picked her up and crept out of the house. As soon as I'd shut the front door, I grinned at my little girl. "Your mommy is tired. What have you been doing to her for the past year and a bit?"

Trixie patted me on the face, then pointed to the road ahead.

"You want to go walking? Exploring? Yeah, I bet you do. Let's go."

I'd never had to talk to myself like this before, but it felt strangely normal to chatter away while Trixie listened.

It was early, even for wolves. Barely six a.m. I walked through the town, pointing at things as I went. The birds in the trees. The houses and the people. Even the shops that were still closed, except the small bakery. The staff there would have been baking bread since before four in the morning.

"Should we go in, sweetheart?" I asked her, and she reached for the door handle.

"I'll take that as a yes, and we'll get your mommy, and mine, some fresh bread."

I walked through the door and froze when I saw the woman behind the counter. *Hell.* "Lacey. I didn't realize you were working here."

Lacey was stocking the shelves when her dark gaze landed on me, then slid across to my daughter. Her eyebrows lifted in a way that would have been comical, if I weren't suddenly full of concern for Trixie and Amy. "Who's that?" she said.

"This is Trixie," I said, though my mouth was dry. "Can we get a couple loaves of white bread? Just put it on my tab."

We didn't carry a lot of cash around town, but I settled my tabs at the end of every month.

Lacey turned away with a flick of her dark ponytail and grabbed the bread I wanted from the shelf behind her.

When I stepped closer to pick up the bags, Lacey hissed in surprise.

"She has your eyes." Her gaze clashed with mine as she asked, "Why the fuck does she have your eyes?"

Trixie squirmed a little in my arms and then began to cry, clawing at me to snuggle closer. I hoisted her higher on my chest, her little hands grabbing at my neck and her face dropping into the crook of my neck, most likely to get away from Lacey's vitriolic gaze and tone. "Thanks for that," I muttered to Lacey.

I turned and walked out of the bakery, half afraid Lacey would follow me. Not that I was worried about her for my sake, but Trixie was still sobbing, and I didn't want her more upset.

"Come here, little one. It's okay." I pulled her around to the front of my chest and held her tighter against me. "She's just a mean girl that you don't have to see again. Don't worry."

Trixie settled down as we walked further away from the bakery. She could read a room, that was for sure, even at her age. A good skill to have.

"Let's go see if Grandma is awake."

My mom was going to be—I wasn't quite sure. Furious? Surprised? Elated? She didn't have any other grandchildren, since I didn't have any siblings, so perhaps this would be a good thing. I had no idea, and there was only one way to find out.

The strong scent of coffee brewing hit me as soon as I stepped up to the front door. "Hmmm." Then I knocked softly.

"Who is it?" my mom called out.

"It's me, Mom."

The door opened and my mom stood in the doorway wearing an old floral dressing gown. "Noah, what are you doing here so early?"

Trixie made a cute little gurgling sound and my mother's gaze darted straight to the little girl in my arms.

Mom's eyes went wide and her mouth dropped open a little. We both stood there awkwardly for a minute, until Mom blinked a couple of times and shook her head as if to clear her brain. She pushed open the screen door. "Who is this?" There was note of something in her tone I couldn't read. Was it... hope?

"Can we come in? I brought bread." I held up the loaves.

"Of course. Come in.Not just for the bread!" Mom ushered us inside. "Is she hungry?"

"She might be. She had a bottle a little while ago, but hasn't had breakfast yet." I followed Mom into the kitchen where she started immediately getting out plates and food.

She seemed to be bustling even more than she usually was. I wondered if maybe it was nerves about what she likely knew I was about to announce. Anyone looking at Trixie would know we were related.

She pulled out a piece of bread, cut off the crust, and handed the slice to Trixie.

"Here you go, baby girl," Mom cooed.

Trixie took the bread happily, gave my mom an enormous smile, and stuck the food straight in her mouth.

"What's her name?" Mom asked, still staring at Trixie like she was afraid she'd disappear.

"Her full name is Beatrix, but her mom calls her Trixie."

"Trixie..." Mom repeated. "She's glorious, Noah. But... where'd she come from?"

"Well." I shuffled my feet a little from side to side. "She's mine."

Mom laughed.

"Yeah, that's pretty obvious, Noah," she said, when she'd calmed down. "So why haven't I met this gorgeous baby girl until today?" She made herself a cup of coffee. "You want one?"

"No, I'm fine. And I only met her yesterday. I didn't know about her, before then."

Mom sat down with her coffee. "Start from the beginning. And explain everything."

I told Mom about the night I met Amy, and what had happened after she ran off.

"So, you think Amy is your fated mate? This... human?" Mom seemed surprised, and I didn't blame her. Fated mates weren't that common, and to have a human mate, in our pack anyway, was unheard of.

I nodded. "I do. I don't know how it's possible though. A human and a shifter. Fated mates. Do you know anything about it, Mom?"

She pressed her lips together. "I don't, but I heard from Kara that her sister-in-law is human."

"Really?" Kara and Ronan had met a few months ago and it had been obvious to everyone from the moment they'd set eyes on each other that they were meant to be.

"Yes, and she had a baby with Kara's brother, so obviously it's possible."

I bounced my baby on my knee, loving the way she giggled and laughed. "Obviously."

"So, what are you going to do?" Mom asked, buttering a piece of bread and cutting it into tiny squares for Trixie to eat.

"What do you mean?"

"I mean about Amy, and Trixie. Are you going to convince Trixie's mom to stay? Or are you going to let her go and visit every other weekend."

A growl rolled through my chest. "They'll stay."

I couldn't stand the idea of just seeing her for a couple of days every month. That would drive my wolf insane.

Trixie looked up at me, frowning. Then she patted my face as if to say, 'calm down'.

I forced myself to breathe slowly and evenly. They couldn't leave; I wouldn't handle it well. I wouldn't handle it, at all. "If Amy wants me to move to be with her, I'll do it."

"But you hate town," Mom reminded me, like I'd forgotten.

"I do, but I'll move if it means keeping my family together." There wouldn't be any other choice. I couldn't handle being so far away from Amy, or Trixie. Not again. The past two years had been hard enough missing Amy. But to miss my daughter as well... I couldn't live through that.

My mom gave me an assessing look, then nodded once. "You look well, Noah. Happier than I've seen you in a long time."

I looked down at Trixie, and unfamiliar emotions swelled within my chest. "I was missing something vital."

A knowing look passed across Mom's face, and her expression relaxed.

"Mama," Trixie said, patting my face again. "Mama."

"Okay, baby," I told her, getting to my feet. "I better take her back. Amy's probably missing her."

And I was pretty sure Trixie would be able to feel it when it was time to go back. She was an intuitive little thing.

Mom stood up and started packing food into containers. "I'll send you with some sandwiches. Give me two minutes."

I set Trixie down to run around, and when our picnic was ready, we headed home.

This was what I'd craved for more years than I cared to admit. I'd enjoyed playing around with women when I was young, but it had gotten old, fast. I wanted a family, a woman, and a real home.

What I hadn't known for the past two years, was that I already had a family. A woman, a child. They'd just forgotten to pass along the message.

Well now she was back, and I wouldn't let Amy go, not without a fight. I'd lost her once, and I wouldn't lose her again.

CHAPTER 9
AMY

I woke up to the sound of a door closing, then Noah's voice calling out, "Amy? Are you up?"

"I'm awake!" I said, though my body was still heavy with sleep.

I glanced at the time on my phone. Eight a.m.? Shit!

I sat bolt upright in bed and swayed, "Whoa, too fast."

I swung my legs off the bed then waited for a minute. God, I was more tired than I thought, and my body definitely wanted more rest.

"Everything okay?" I called out. "Trixie behave herself?"

"Yeah. All good."

I got dressed slowly, my body aching with tiredness still.

"Come on," I told myself, shaking my head from side to side. A coffee, that was what I needed. Then I'd be all right.

I walked out of the room. Noah was unpacking food onto the table, and the smell of coffee permeated the air.

"Hmm, smells good. Whatcha got there, baby girl?"

Trixie held up her hands, both stuffed with what looked like white bread.

I glanced up at Noah, heat flooding my cheeks when he stared back at me with the same hunger on his face that he'd shown last night. He obviously hadn't gotten enough of me yet, which was reassuring and terrifying in equal measure. I was a little afraid to get too invested again, in my feelings for Noah. Next time I wouldn't have a little Trixie to assuage the heartache and the sense of loss when it was time to head back to the city.

With heat unfurling in my belly, I knew I hadn't gotten enough of Noah. Would I ever have enough of this sexy, enigmatic man? "Did you go to the bakery?"

"Yeah, it was the only shop open at this time of the morning."

He went over to the cabinets to pull out mugs for coffee.

I picked up my girl and sat down with her in my lap, hugging her sweet little body to mine. "Thank you so much for the sleep in. It was really great to have someone to help with her this morning."

That was something I'd missed out on, raising her on my own. Mom and Dad had helped when they could, but they'd left me alone to raise her mostly and that meant I did all nights, weekends, and mornings. It was a lot.

He smiled at me like it was nothing, but to me the couple of hours extra sleep, knowing Trixie was in safe hands, had been everything.

"No problem," he said. "We had fun, didn't we, little one? Oh, by the way, I took her around to meet my mom."

I picked up the mug of coffee and froze when it was halfway to my lips as his words registered. "You... what?"

"Took her around to meet her grandma. My dad died a few years ago, but at least my mom got to meet her."

Noah sat down across from me and I just stared at him. He'd... what? I couldn't quite process the idea.

"What's wrong?" he asked. "You look upset."

"Oh, no. I'm not upset." *Shocked. Worried, maybe.* "I just, uh, suppose I hadn't really thought about her having grandparents on your side of the family."

Noah snorted. "Yeah, I don't think you really thought about anyone in that regard, me included."

Horror slapped me right in the face. He hadn't sounded bitter, but what he'd said was correct. In keeping Trixie from him—and from his family—I had been very much in the wrong. "I know. And I'm sorry. Truly, I..."

I was going to have to apologize for my choice to withhold Trixie from him for a long time. Every time he mentioned it, I felt the need to run and hide from the shame of my actions and decisions.

"Don't worry," he said. "I'm just teasing you. We've just gotta make up for lost time."

He grabbed plates and served the food, which turned out to be cheese, ham, and fresh buttery bread.

"What did your mom say?" I asked, desperate to know if some older she-wolf was about to hunt me down for hurting her son.

He shrugged. "She was a little shocked, but she takes most things in her stride. She and Trixie seemed to take to one another, which was great to see."

"So, will she be coming over here to yell at me later?" I asked, only half-joking. "Should I be running for the hills again?"

Noah shook his head. "Don't worry about my mom. She's pretty cool, actually. And no, you won't be taking Trixie away from me again."

Despite his words earlier, about not to worry, there was an edge to his voice now. I swallowed hard at the thinly veiled threat.

I pushed back the need to fight him, because I was in the wrong and we both knew it.

"I won't," I said. "No matter what we decide about where we're living, or any of that stuff in the future, I promise you can always have access to her."

He made a strange growly noise and drank his coffee.

My heart ached. "Did I say something wrong?"

Again? He seemed different this morning. I felt a little bit as though I were walking on eggshells around him.

He shook his head and kept his gaze low, obviously not wanting to talk at the moment about whatever was bothering him.

I drank my coffee and ate some of the food, trying my best to enjoy our first breakfast together, but worrying too much over what he was thinking to really get into it.

Trixie grew grouchy and tired, so I put her to bed and cleaned up the kitchen.

Noah hung around, not really saying much.

"If you need to go to work," I said, "it's fine. I'll just potter around here. Clean up, make dinner if you show me where everything is."

Noah shook his head. "I'll stay with you today."

"Worried I'll run away again?" I joked.

His face went deadly serious, and his eyes grew dark.

"You are, aren't you?" I forced myself to ask, though my throat was thick with sudden emotion.

I put down the dish cloth and walked across the room toward him. "Noah, I don't know what else to say or do to show you how sorry I am that I left two years ago. That I didn't tell you about Trixie."

He crossed his arms over his chest and still didn't speak.

I pressed my hands together in front of my body. "I am so sorry, Noah. I really am. I wish I could go back and change it all, but I can't. I'm here now, wanting to find a way to make this work."

"Make what work, Amy?" he asked. "You only came back because Trixie is going to turn into a wolf shifter and you need some help understanding that and managing her. If it hadn't been for that, you would never have sought me out, and I would never have met my child. Never known I *had* a child at all."

He was huffing a little now, and I wrapped my arms around my chest to try and comfort that part of me that was breaking. I'd thought he was okay with it, in some small way. That coming back now had made up just a little, for what I'd done. But I could see now that it wasn't nearly enough. I wasn't sure if it would ever be enough.

"Noah..."

"No," he said, his voice harsh. "It's true, and you can't change that fact. I just have to get used to the idea that you didn't come back for *me*."

"What are you talking about?"

"Nothing." He shook his head, then stormed for the front door. "You're right. I probably should get some work done."

"I won't leave," I said, even though part of me was aching to run from all the paranormal craziness surrounding me. "I promise."

"I know you won't, because you know I'll find you two again."

I shivered from the rage in his voice, but shook my head. "That's not why. I won't leave this time, or any time in future, because you're already a great father, and I want that for Trixie. She should have had you from the start and I did her as well as you a disservice by what I did. I'm sorry she didn't have you from the beginning, Noah."

Noah growled a little then shook his head like he was deciding against talking further. He walked out the front door, slamming it behind him.

I stared after him, tears filling my eyes. What the hell had that been about? I sat down on the couch and let go of the sobs that had been building in my chest since this little fight had begun.

It had come out of nowhere, but it was clear that Noah was very distressed. Now, I was, too.

I grabbed the tissues nearby and balled some up, sobbing into them through the pain. I knew I'd done the wrong thing when I made the choice not to involve Noah in my pregnancy or the birth, and that mistake had haunted me ever since.

Now I was realizing that I would never again be able to make decisions for her and me, without Noah's involvement.

Was that something I wanted, that I'd miss? I didn't know. But it was a scary thought to have after being independent for so long. To be held accountable and liable by another human being... Well, was he even classified as a human? I had so much to learn about this life of wolf shifters.

There was a knock at the door, and I tried to swallow the tears. Shit, I needed to get myself together. I grabbed more tissues and wiped at my eyes.

The knocking sounded again then a female voice called out, "Hello? Is anyone home?"

I stood up and took a few quick breaths before walking to the door to open it.

"Um, hello," I said, biting my lip as the tears rose again.

I was such a mess. How embarrassing.

The woman on the other side of the door looked about the same age as me and had a kind face. "Hi, you must be Amy. I'm Kara, Ronan's wife."

The Alpha's wife.

I nodded but couldn't really speak. I should be able to pull myself together, but I was struggling today.

"Can I come in?" she asked.

I nodded and stepped back. *Get yourself together.* I wiped at the tears on my face and hoped to hell Kara was as nice as Ronan.

"I heard you brought a baby with you. Is she awake?" Kara asked, shutting the door then walking into the living room.

"No. She went down for her nap about an hour ago, but she'll be up soon."

I noticed the swelling of Kara's belly and the way her loose t-shirt clung to her. I swallowed the pregnancy question, because that was not a question any sane person asked another woman. I looked six months pregnant for at least a month after I had Trixie.

"Do you have any kids?" I asked her, settling onto the well-worn couch.

"Oh, I'm expecting my first in about three months," she said with a grin, cupping her hands around her belly.

I was happy for her. "You look beautiful."

"How was your pregnancy?" she asked, then groaned. "I've been feeling so sick."

"Oh, the pregnancy was okay. The birth, not so much for me. But that might have been because I'm human and Noah's, well... not."

Kara sat down on the couch opposite me. "So, you know what we are?"

I nodded. "Technically, yes. I've heard the words, but I'm not sure I totally... get it yet."

Or fully believe him.

Kara grinned at me. "Noah will show you his wolf when you're ready. I'd show you now if I could, but the pregnancy makes it almost impossible for me to shift, and then shift back. It's a horrible feeling, like denying half of myself an existence."

I shook my head. "It's such an incredible concept. I don't think I've grasped all of this yet."

Kara sighed. "Yeah, I can only imagine. I was born and bred out here, in a pack about an hour away. My brother mated with a human from town, so she's probably a good person you could talk to you about everything. I could ask her, if you like?"

"Really?" I asked. "There's more of us here?"

"Absolutely. And honestly, I think you'll love Tammy. She's so strong and fiery."

"I'd love to meet her," I said, because any type of alliance in this strange new world would be a good thing.

"Great. I'll set it up," Kara said. "But while I'm here, is there anything I can do for you?"

I shook my head. "Not at the moment, though I appreciate the thought."

"You wanna tell me why you're crying then?"

I sighed. "It's just... everything. I'm a bit overwhelmed, and Noah is angry about me keeping Trixie a secret for so long."

Kara sighed. "Yeah, wolf shifters have huge hearts and are the most loyal men there are, but they're also stubborn and have egos the size of a house."

I laughed at how aptly she'd put it. "Thanks for the tip."

Kara stood up and held out her hand. "Welcome to the pack. If you need me, I'm about three minutes away."

"Thank you, Kara."

She left, but my heart felt stronger. If I had some help easing into this life, maybe I could stay here long term?

I sighed and sat back down on the couch. That was, if Noah could forgive me for what I'd done, because from where I was standing, it didn't seem likely.

CHAPTER 10

NOAH

I was so angry, my fingers had shifted into claws, and I'd had to run out of the house so that Amy didn't see my loss of control. I didn't want the first glimpse of my wolf to scare her.

Another part of me was confused and annoyed because I didn't really know why I was so pissed. Sure, the existence of my child had been kept from me, and that needed to be dealt with, but surely berating Amy when she was right in the middle of owning up to her mistakes wasn't the way to go?

Especially after what had occurred last night.

I felt like a heel, talking in such a way to her this morning. If I wanted her to stay, I would have to figure out what the hell these feelings were that kept rising up inside me.

One moment I was as joyful as if I'd found my fated mate and our happy-ever-after, and the next I was rearing up in anger and fighting to keep my wolf from bursting out and howling at the proverbial moon.

I groaned as I ran a hand through my hair, pushing myself to continue to work, digging holes, building houses. Physical work that was meant to drive the voices from my head.

But it wasn't working. All I could see in my mind's eye was the way Amy writhed on the bed beneath me. How right it had felt to be near her, inside of her. Nothing had felt so perfect for me as last night. But every time she talked about staying, or going, the conversation only revolved around Trixie.

She never said anything about how she felt about *me*. Whether we should be together. That was what was pissing me off more than anything.

My wolf had yearned for her, for years. Literally. Had she thought about me once in that time? As more than Trixie's sperm donor?

I worked until my shoulders ached and sweat ran down my back. I wasn't interested in talking to anyone. Not Ronan, or Kit, or any of the other guys. I kept to myself until the bell rang to end the day.

There was relief in the sound. Time to go home. To my house. To my woman and child.

And yet she wasn't my woman. Not yet. But God, I wanted her to be.

I raised my hand in farewell to some of the guys I'd worked alongside today and started the walk home. I lifted my t-shirt to wipe the sweat off my face.

A high-pitched wolf whistle came from ahead of me. I glanced around only to see Lacey walking down the street swinging her hips.

Uh-oh.

"Hey lover," she called as she stepped closer.

"Excuse me?" I said, glancing around. "Who are you putting on a show for?"

She ignored my question and went up on her toes to kiss me.

I grimaced and pulled back, frowning at her. "What the hell are you trying to pull, Lacey?"

She shrugged. "Just offering you something I'm sure that little human isn't giving you. There's no way she could keep up with a wolf for strength or stamina. No way."

She grinned at me like she had already won the argument and I suppressed the urge to shudder.

"We haven't been lovers for a long time, Lacey, so I suggest you move on to the next guy on the list. I'm taken."

"Taken?" She crossed her arms over her breasts, pushing them up so her cleavage popped up above the neckline of her tank top. "You're not taken until you're mated, Noah, and I sure as hell can't see any new ring on you."

I clenched my jaw against the need to snap at her. "I've got a child, Lacey. That's more than enough commitment for me. So, just stay away, okay? I'm not interested."

I stormed off without looking back because I knew she would be throwing daggers with her expression. Lacey had never been the woman I wanted. I'd fought with her and gotten jealous when she'd been with others only because I wanted someone of my own.

Even if that person didn't fit me properly.

I knew who fit, with me and my wolf, and she'd left me. Now, she'd come back. So how hard was I going to fight to keep the right one around?

Very hard is the answer.

I jogged up the steps to my house and opened the front door.

And there was my little family, on the floor playing dolls. Amy was sitting cross legged on the rug, with Trixie's pink toys everywhere.

"Oh, hey!" she said, jumping to her feet. "I didn't know what time you were expected, so I only put dinner on a little while ago. Sorry."

I shook my head. "I'm not used to being waited on, Amy. You don't need to worry about that sort of stuff."

It was nice to come home to a kitchen smelling of beef and spices, though.

Trixie got to her feet and ran for me, her chubby little arms open.

"Hi!" I bent down to scoop her up.

She hummed at me, and I realized she had no name for me.

"Hey, Amy. What's Trixie going to call me?"

She walked over from the fridge, a beer and a bottle of water in hand. "What do you want her to call you?"

She handed me both, and I grabbed the water.

"Just this, thanks."

What had I called my dad? Just... Dad? "I haven't thought about it."

"Well, most of her friends from my mothers' group call their dads, Daddy, or some variation of it. But if you have another word, or something your family uses, go for it."

"Daddy." I liked the sound of that. My heart swelled and a grin split my face.

"Done," Amy said, like it was the simplest thing in the world. "That's what I'll call you when I'm talking to Trixie about you, and she'll pick it up soon enough, I'm sure. Now, dinner. How long do you want to wait to eat? Trixie kind of needs dinner soon, then I can get her to bed."

"Soon is great," I said, "though I need a shower. Can you take her and I'll just be ten minutes?"

I handed my little girl off to her mother and jogged through the house to the bathroom. I wanted to get back to my little family as soon as possible.

I washed, changed, then walked back down into the living room to be confronted by Lacey. In my house.

She was standing in the middle of the room looking angry, her eyebrows lowered and her cheeks flushed. The front door was shut and Amy stood beside her like they'd been talking. About what, I didn't want to imagine.

"What are you doing here?" I demanded.

Amy glanced away and down, avoiding looking at me as she walked away to the kitchen. Trixie came straight over to me, tears in her eyes.

"It's okay, sweetheart. Come here." I picked her up and she nestled into my chest. I glared at Lacey. "You're not welcome here."

Lacey laughed like I'd made a joke. "That's not what you usually say when I come over, Noah. What's wrong? Worried your little human will get jealous if we climb into bed together?"

My ribs squeezed tight around my heart, but I forged forward to the truth. "Amy, can you come here, please?"

Amy turned around and came back to me, though her arms were crossed and she stood too far away to touch. I needed to get this out in the open, and over and done with as soon as possible.

"Amy, this is Lacey. We dated on and off for years, while she was also doing whoever else she wanted in the pack. We aren't together now and haven't been for months. So don't let her get under your skin."

"Oh, don't be like that, Noah." Lacey grinned. "Just because this chick had your baby, doesn't mean you two need to be together. She'll never fit in around here. She needs to go home. And you need to stay here with your people."

I opened my mouth to retort, but Amy jumped in.

"Don't you have any self-respect?" she said, glaring at Lacey. "He's made it pretty damn clear he doesn't want you. So go home to whatever slop bucket you live in and leave my family alone."

Lacey whirled on Amy, her eyes shifting to her wolf.

"You're not a family." She spat. "You bore his bastard. Any woman could have done that."

"But *any* woman didn't," Amy all but growled back. "*I* did! So, fuck off and leave us alone."

I saw the shift in Lacey sooner than most would.

I jumped in front of my mate and shoved a whimpering Trixie at her. "Take her. Quick."

Lacey's humanity disappeared and a large black wolf stood in her place.

"My bedroom. Go," I managed to get out as my own wolf ripped through me.

Amy screamed, but I blocked out the pain that came from the sound. I needed to protect her first. I'd explain afterwards. I bared my teeth and growled at Lacey.

She launched at me.

I lifted my front paw and swiped at her face, hitting her square in the side of the head. She staggered sideways. I bore down on her, my teeth at her throat. She gnashed at me, fighting and scrabbling for purchase. Her claws scratched the floorboards, making a terrible screeching sound in the room.

She was a small wolf compared to me, so I didn't let up. Nothing had been more worth fighting for than the woman whom Lacey had just tried to attack. I tightened my jaw and pressed into her neck harder, tasting blood as my teeth cut into Lacey's throat.

Lacey dropped to the ground and lay still, her chest heaving with her frantic breath.

I made a final loud warning growl in my throat, then opened my jaws and backed away to allow her room to rise. If she tried to attack again, I'd rip a hole in her.

Lacey shifted back to human, now naked and practically sobbing on the floor. "It's not fair, Noah. You and I were always meant to be together. This wasn't the plan. *She* wasn't the plan."

I shifted back and grabbed for my ripped jeans, then threw them down again when I realized they were beyond salvageable. "You were never in my plans. Amy's my mate. She always has been."

"Your mate?" Lacey repeated, her eyes going wide and fearful. "No, she can't be."

I laughed and the sound was harsh even to my ears. "She is, and as soon as she agrees to be mine officially, you'll see the announcement go up around town. Now get out of here, before I do something we'll both regret."

Lacey grabbed her clothes and ran for the front door.

I turned around and marched down the corridor to where my bedroom door was closed.

Shit! What if the fight had scared Amy into leaving? That wasn't how I'd wanted my mate to meet my wolf.

I stepped closer and pressed my ear to the wood. I couldn't hear anything on the inside of the room, but hopefully she was still in there.

I didn't want to frighten her, so I called out just in case she needed the advance warning. "It's okay. It's all over."

The door flew open, and Amy's tear-stained face greeted me.

"Noah!" She threw herself into my arms and sobbed her heart out.

I wrapped my arms around her and held her tightly against my body. "It's okay, sweetheart. It's okay. I'll never let anyone hurt you. You're safe."

I consoled Amy while our daughter happily played on the floor, growling and barking with her little wolfy toy in her arms.

CHAPTER 11

AMY

I'd never been so terrified in all my life. Not going into labor. Not the day I found out I was pregnant. Never.

When Lacey shifted before my eyes from human woman to a snarling black wolf, and Noah had told me to grab Trixie and run, I'd done what he asked. Who wouldn't have turned tail and fled when a massive wolf wanted my blood? But as soon as I was safe, or as safe as one could be behind a single wooden door, I became terrified for Noah. What if Lacey hurt him? What if he died? What would I do if something happened to him now that I'd finally found him again?

Then he'd knocked on the door and the knowledge that Noah was alive and well flooded my highly stressed heart. I didn't know what to do with all the emotions pulsing through me. So, I burst into tears and cried all over him.

I cried like my heart was broken. Like someone had actually died. I cried for all the pain and misery, and shame and sadness that I'd dealt with over the past two years, walking this road alone when I should have been standing beside Noah the whole time.

Such a waste. So stupid.

"Come on," he said, "let's get you more comfortable."

He picked me up and took me further into the bedroom where our daughter was still playing on the floor with her wolf toy.

"The door," I managed to say, clinging to his shoulders. "Trixie."

I didn't want her wandering around the house, or out the front door. Not with those monsters hanging around.

He kicked shut the door behind us, then walked me over to the bed and sat down holding me.

"Are you okay?" he asked, stroking my hair.

I nodded, sniffing loudly. "Yes. I'm fine."

The silence stretched as he held me, and I realized suddenly that he was completely naked.

"Um." I sat up and wiped at my face. "Where are your clothes?"

He shrugged. "Shredded in the lounge. Unfortunately, shifting without warning has its disadvantages."

"What about Lacey?" I asked, images filling my head of the two of them rolling around on the lounge room floor naked. "Did she end up naked, too?"

Jealousy exploded inside of me. Not that they'd had time to fuck. It had felt like I'd been in that bedroom for hours, but I was pretty sure it had only been a few minutes.

He chuckled. "Does it worry you that much?"

You, rolling on the floor naked with another woman? In anger, perhaps, but anger was closely aligned with passion. I almost laughed, but instead I pressed my lips together, trying not to say something stupid, or mean. "I suppose not. It's just so strange to me."

He grinned. "You were more worried about the naked thing than the wolf thing?"

I shook my head. "No, that part was freaking terrifying, I admit. Part of me didn't believe you when you told me about it. Though..." This time I couldn't suppress the almost-hysterical laughter. "I guess I have to believe you, now."

I'd kind of hoped his explanation was a metaphor, or maybe like... a spirit animal. Anything but the truth, that he truly turned into an actual huge, hulking, wolf.

"Why would I lie?"

I huffed out a laugh while I traced patterns on his skin. "I didn't think you were actually lying, but... it didn't seem possible. In my world, where I come from, things like that are just myth and legend."

He sighed and pressed my head back to his chest. "What a mess this is."

I nodded, tears sliding down my cheeks at the relief of surviving such a stupid act of jealousy on Lacey's behalf. "And it's all my fault. I never should have left you in the first place."

If I hadn't left two years ago, then Lacey would never have been with Noah. The whole spiteful jealous show she'd just put on wouldn't have happened.

"No, you shouldn't have." Noah sighed, squeezing me tight. "But that can't be changed now. So we just need to work out a way to move forward, don't we?"

I nodded, feeling miserable. Those weren't the words of a man who really wanted to be with me. He was putting up with what I'd done, and who I was, for the sake of Trixie.

I had to ask. "You're never going to forgive me, are you?"

"It's not that I don't forgive you..." he said, then groaned. "It's just that..."

"Just, what?" I asked, sliding off his lap and sitting on the bed next to him. I handed him a pillow, which he looked at confused for a moment, before understanding dawned. He placed the pillow across his lap, hiding the enticing view.

Trixie was still happily sitting on the ground, playing with her wolf. She was growling and hissing like Lacey had.

I huffed a small laugh and nodded to Trixie. "She knows what sort of sounds wolves make now."

Noah didn't even crack a smile. "Yeah. Hopefully she wasn't scared."

"She's okay," I said, then assessed her again quickly. "She isn't clinging to me, or crying. I'd say she really is fine."

In fact, she hadn't seemed that perturbed at all. It was me that was a shaking mess.

Noah stood up. The pillow dropped away, and I tried not to look. Well, I looked a little. It was impossible not to, when his magnificent physique was right there in front of me. "Maybe I made the wrong call here."

"Which call was that?" I asked, hoping he didn't mean anything huge.

"Asking you two to move in here."

Oh, fuck. That was big.

Pain squeezed my heart. "What do you mean?"

Was he rejecting us now that I'd seen the truth and hadn't acted like I should have? Sure, he turned into a seriously scary-looking big gray wolf, but I could handle it. Couldn't I? He had come to our aid in an instant, and part of me knew he would never let any harm come to Trixie or me, if he could help it. I was just surprised, was all. Next time, I'd be better.

"I know that I don't exactly fit in here, but Trixie is going to need you guys. And Kara said I could talk to her human sister-in-law, Tammy. Maybe that will give us the answers we need about how Trixie's going to develop and... stuff."

Noah ran his hand over his jaw and through his hair.

"What wrong, Noah? Talk to me."

He was really worrying me now.

"I just think.... maybe Lacey was right, and we need to take you two back to town. I can't protect you twenty-four seven, and Trixie is still so young. Maybe's its better if you come back when she's older."

We'd been in danger for a few seconds and now he was pushing us away? That wasn't fair. It wasn't my fault I hadn't been raised to deal with wolves. Or the she-devil woman who had turned into one.

"Hang on a minute," I said, getting to my feet. "What about us?"

"What about... *us*?" Noah repeated. "You never even mention, *us*."

I did. I was sure I did.

"When I came back here," I began, worried that I'd put two and two together and come up with seven, "you said you wanted me. And Trixie."

He stared straight at me. "I did. And you haven't said once what you want."

"Oh." Maybe I was still trying to work out what I wanted. Or maybe I knew what I wanted, but didn't think it would ever be possible. "I haven't considered my own feelings in a long time. Trixie has been my whole world for so long."

Noah crossed his big arms over his beefy chest and stared at me.

"Well, she has me now too. And I'm asking you, Amy, what do *you* want to happen, between us?"

He was putting me on the spot, and I didn't like it.

"I don't know," I hedged, because I didn't. I knew that we were fantastic in bed together, but could we build a life on that? "We haven't spent any real time together, so how can we judge?"

Noah spun away, growling.

I went straight to him, wrapping my arms around his naked waist from behind. "Please don't turn away from me. I'm trying. I promise. I just..."

He pushed away from me and went to his closet to pull out another set of clothes. He didn't speak as he tugged on black jeans and a gray shirt. "You just don't know. Yeah right. So, as always, I'm stuck in no man's land. The last one considered on your list of priorities."

Ouch. Arrow straight to the heart. "That's not true."

He did the last of his buttons on his shirt and glared at me. "Okay, then tell me right now. How do you feel about me? What do you want from me? A father for Trixie? A relationship between us? What?"

I covered my eyes with my hands, wanting to cry and run from the room. Everything had been too much to deal with. "Don't put me on the spot like that. It's not fair."

"No. What's not fair is that if you were a wolf, you'd know what this is. What we are to each other. And you wouldn't be afraid of it."

I dropped my hands from my eyes and glared back at him. "Are you serious right now? You're saying that it would be better if I was a wolf? Well, I'm so sorry that I'm not some snarling, nasty beast like Lacey. I'm only a poor, weak, stupid human woman who doesn't know anything about anything."

Noah's eyes widened until he narrowed his gaze back at me. "Nasty? Snarling beast? Is that how you see me?"

"Well, ah..." Of course, I didn't see him that way. I'd been talking about Lacey, not Noah. Lacey, who'd just tried to attack me and my child.

"I suppose that's how you're going to see our daughter too when she shifts for the first time." Noah sounded more like he was talking to himself than me, and there was a note of sadness in his tone that did not bode well.

"No... that's not what I meant. Don't be ridiculous."

"Ridiculous?" Noah marched over to the bedroom door and threw it open. "I was right. You need to go back to town and be with your own people."

I hurried over to our daughter and scooped her up into my arms. "But I came here for help with her. I still don't have any answers."

Noah twisted his head away, an angry muscle in his jaw tight and ticking away.

Then he swiveled back. "Okay. We'll get you the answers you came for. Who did Kara say to ask for advice?"

"Um." I bit my lip, searching my memory for the name. I was so flustered by Noah and this whole situation, that I couldn't remember. Then it came back to me. "Her sister-in-law. Tammy, she said."

He nodded. "I'll go talk to Kara. There's food in the fridge. You do dinner and all your nightly routine stuff with Trixie and I'll be back when I can. Don't wait up."

He marched off toward the front door and I hurried after him, Trixie grunting and trying to get down from my arms so that she could get to her father.

"That's it?" I called out, shocked he was leaving so abruptly after such a heavy discussion.

He opened the door and turned back to look at me. "What do you mean?"

"You're just leaving us? Right now?"

He heaved a heavy sigh. "I'm not leaving you. I'm going to find someone who can help you."

"But we haven't finished talking." The wounds were all broken open and weeping, and he just wanted to walk away? This was when we needed to push through the uncomfortable parts and get to the other side.

He finally muttered, "I think you've said enough."

"And you haven't said anything," I shot back. "You haven't told me how *you* feel, or what *you* want."

His face went blank and cold. "I've told you everything, Amy. And if you can't hear what I'm saying, or feel what I feel, then we're not fated mates like I thought."

Fated mates? What did he mean? But before I could ask, he walked away, shutting the door behind him.

Trixie cried out as I set her on the ground. She sobbed as she ran for the door, "Dada. Dada!"

"Oh baby," I cried, tears sliding down my cheeks. "Daddy will be back soon. Don't worry."

He'd missed her first words for him, and that broke me. He'd missed so much, and if we couldn't sort out this shit, he would miss a hell of a lot more.

I cuddled Trixie into my chest as she sobbed and I cried. So much hurt, and rejection and pain. On every side.

"It's okay, baby. It's okay. Mommy will find a way out of this."

But hells if I knew the way right now. I got my tears under control and focused on my daughter. Her needs were all that mattered. I made her dinner, gave her a quick wash down with baby wipes, and put her to bed.

Then I sat on the couch with a cup of tea and waited for my baby-daddy to come home.

CHAPTER 12
NOAH

Walking away from my home, and my mate, and my daughter, was one of the hardest things I'd done to date. But I had to, or I'd lose control of myself, and perhaps my wolf. I was so angry I could barely speak.

I could feel my teeth shifting in my mouth, and the heat of my body ratchet up to the point I had to breathe deep and force my shifter back down inside.

I had a job to do. So instead of running into the forest like I really needed to, I found my Alpha and his mate at home. They invited me in and quickly agreed to help me by getting Tammy to speak to Amy.

"I can call her tonight if you want?" Kara offered. "Ask when you can drop by."

"Yes please, as soon as possible," I said. "I'll drive Amy and Trixie over tomorrow morning if that suits them and Tammy."

Kara grabbed her phone. "Back in a bit."

She stepped into the hall.

Ronan offered me a beer and we sat down on the couch. I was jittery as all hell.

"So," Ronan said casually, taking a sip of his beer, "things not going quite to plan?"

I snorted, pushing my hair off my face. "It's a fucking farce, is what it is. I can't believe I thought a human was my mate."

I had to be wrong about that. Things were not meant to be this hard.

"What makes you think she isn't?" Ronan asked quietly.

I groaned and took a sip of beer. "It's meant to be easy, isn't it? Natural. Fated mates just fit together, without any effort at all. And yet, with Amy, everything is a fight. A slog. I feel like I'm walking on eggshells every time I speak... my moods are all over the place. It shouldn't... I don't know. This is not how I thought it would be with her. If she really is my fated mate, why is it this hard? Not only for me, but for her, too? I can see she's not happy with how it is with us, either. Maybe I was wrong. Maybe she isn't my mate."

Instead of nodding and agreeing with me, as I expected, Ronan chuckled, setting his beer down on the coffee table. He leaned back and folded his hands behind his head, studying me. "You think everything with Kara has been easy from the start? She left me, ran off home. Remember?"

"Yeah, but—"

"But nothing. Relationships, even when they're fated, are messy. There's always fights and mistakes made along the way."

I groaned. "Yeah, but you two sorted it out pretty fast. I don't know how Amy and I are going to get past everything, Ronan. There's too much history. I thought I could just forget what she did and move on. Forgive her for lying to me for so long and keeping Trixie away."

"And you can't forgive that?"

"I don't know."

It wasn't that easy, to just decide I could or couldn't forgive something. And it didn't help that I still didn't know if Amy even wanted me at all. She hadn't admitted to having any feelings for me in a current context, and until she did, we were at a stale mate, with me wanting her for life, and her too afraid to come forward and be honest—one way or the other.

Or maybe that was the problem. She *didn't* actually want me at all, and hadn't said anything because she was afraid of hurting my feelings and making me feel rejected, or some bullshit like that? That would make sense. Maybe she'd only fallen into bed with me last night because the poor thing had been so starved for sex. I mean, she'd practically said that. Lust and forever love were too entirely separate things.

Maybe... I dropped my head into my hands and rubbed my face. My thoughts felt tied up in knots. I didn't know what I was thinking, anymore, let alone being capable of figuring what Amy wanted. Or didn't want.

"Fuck." I sighed, the weight of defeat crushing the hope in my chest. "I think I need to let her go. For all our sakes."

Kara walked back into the room at that moment, phone in hand. "Tammy said you can bring Amy and Trixie over in the morning. The baby's down for the night, otherwise she'd come straight over now."

I stood up and smiled at my Alpha's mate, feeling a sense of relief.

"Thanks, Kara, I appreciate that." I stretched my back, pulling my arms up and over my head. "I think I need a run. I feel... restless."

It was more than that; my wolf was practically on the verge of shifting. He was always there, vibrating at the edges of my control. I'd shifted only a few hours ago to fight Lacey, but the adrenaline was still zinging through my system and I had to work it off.

I needed a run. A proper one.

"I'd offer to come with you, but my mate has requested we go to bed early," Ronan said, with a boastful grin.

To make it even more obvious what he was talking about, Kara blushed prettily and whacked Ronan on the arm.

I laughed and opened the front door, jealous of their easy, happy relationship. "Thanks again for your help."

"I'll come with you in the morning, if that's okay?" Kara said, rubbing her belly. "I'd like to catch up with my brother, and it'll be easier to navigate if I show you the best road there."

"That would be much appreciated," I said.

I walked down the front steps of their house and started to unbutton my shirt. "Do you mind if I leave my clothes here, and I'll come back after my run?"

"Not at all. Go for it," Ronan said.

"Isn't Amy expecting you back?" Kara called out.

I shrugged. "She's got Trixie. She doesn't seem to need anyone else."

I took off my shirt and pulled off my jeans. My wolf rose up inside me and took over, making my human side disappear. The feelings that came with the shift were fantastic. My mind slipped away from everything, the worries, the stress, and the pain.

In its place was power, strength, and a hunger for life that wasn't present in human form.

I dug my paws into the dirt and took off, running through town, across the back streets and into the forest. The sun was just dropping from the sky. Rabbits bolted out of my way, and I could sense a deer nearby as well. Senses were always heightened during the shift. Hearing and smell in particular, as well as physical speed, were at their peak.

But I didn't want to hunt. I just wanted to run. To feel free and happy. Something I hadn't felt in too long to think about.

I reached halfway to the main town when I slowed down.

Something tugged at my heart to stop, and I did. I wanted to go forward, but it was like the ground had rooted me to the spot.

I had to go home to my mate and child.

The run home was slower, as I carried a heavier heart. My wolf was certain that Amy was my mate, and yet the same woman had left me after our first night together. She would never have sought me out even now, if it wasn't for Trixie's wolf-like characteristics.

It tore at my heart, and my pride, that she didn't feel the same way I did. But could I expect her to, when she was human? Maybe it wasn't the same for humans as it was for shifters. Maybe she didn't have this aching certainty in her heart—in her *soul*—the way I did, that we were destined for one another if we wanted it.

I reached Ronan's house when it was full dark, changed into my clothes, and walked back to my house. I was pretty sure I'd missed more than dinner. I would have missed Trixie's bath time, sleep time, and perhaps even Amy going to bed.

There were no lights on when I arrived home. I snuck in quietly, locking the door behind me.

Dinner was sitting on the kitchen table, a cold stew in a large bowl. I had no appetite, but heated the meal in the microwave and ate it anyway. Amy had gone to the trouble to cook, and the stew was tasty once reheated, salted well with lots of big chunks of potatoes and pumpkin along with tender meat.

It should have made me happy to see signs that she was trying to settle in, and that she possibly wanted to stay with me. But all I saw were the advantages of living with a woman who was used to caring for herself and her child.

Once I'd cleaned up, I snuck by the spare bedroom. The door was shut. I paused there for so long I forgot what I was waiting for. Did I want to talk to Amy about what had happened tonight between us? Probably not.

Did I want her to come out and say goodnight? No. That might not end well for either of us.

Was she even in there? Or would I find her asleep in my bed? *Our bed.*

With a heart that was a little too happy at the prospect that I would once again be sleeping alongside her warm body, I crept up the hallway to my room.

When I pushed open the door and found the bedroom empty, the disappointment was crushing and far outweighed the expectations I should have had. I'd walked out on her after a fight. After her life had been threatened, by a woman who turned into a wolf in front of Amy. Then she'd seen me change. Confirmation that the father of her child was not human, after all.

Why would she sleep with me?

I slunk into my room and shut the door, had a quick shower, and crawled into bed.

Was Amy asleep in the spare bedroom? Or was she wide awake and aching with loneliness and confusion, like me?

I slid between the sheets. My wolf wasn't happy, and neither was I.

What the hell was I going to do about this situation now?

Should I fight to spend time with them? Should I keep them here while we worked out the best way forward?

Or should I let Amy go? Back to her own life in the city? Try and co-parent together, like so many other parents did—parents who were not together, but still shared a child or children. I could do weekends with my daughter. Was that really a life for a wolf like me? Especially with the way I felt about Amy.

I closed my eyes and tried to get some sleep, even though my chest was tight and I was the closest to shedding a tear I'd been in my adult life.

Everything about this just felt wrong, but at least we had some kind of a plan. We would talk to Kara and Tammy tomorrow morning, and hopefully another human woman would give some clarification to the situation. For Amy, and possibly for me.

Ronan's words stuck with me though, casting a little light in the darkness. He'd said that the road of a relationship, even with a fated mate, wasn't always smooth.

I clung to that thought through the long, lonely night.

CHAPTER 13

AMY

I had a truly shit night's sleep. Not because Trixie woke me up, or cried through the night. She was a little angel.

It was me. My mind whirled. I couldn't think anything nice or positive to concentrate on, and a strange type of depression chased me, even in my dreams when I did finally drift off.

After waiting hours for Noah, I'd gone to bed angry. So, I'd been awake when Noah had finally gotten home. I'd heard him enter the house, eat the dinner I'd cooked, then stand outside my bedroom door. I'd been so mad at him for staying away, I was half ready to jump up out of bed and yell in his face if he opened the door to check on me. But he never did.

After what felt like an eternity of holding my breath and lying super still on the mattress, I'd heard him sigh heavily and walk down to his own bedroom, all without even checking if I was awake or not. Thanks to that frustrating moment, I'd tossed and turned for most of the night.

When I woke up the next morning, I was exhausted and wanted to sleep the day away.

"Mama, Mama," Trixie called from her pack-and-play.

I didn't move a muscle, hoping she would lie down and go back to sleep if she thought I was still out for the count.

Instead, the creaking of the thin mattress as she jumped up and down sounded. She was obviously excited to see me in a bed in her room.

I lifted my head and glanced down at her. "Agh, sweetheart. Please tell me you're going to have at least two naps today. I'm gonna need them!"

I hauled myself up out of bed and reached into the crib for her. She looked just as gorgeous and sparkly as ever, with her beautiful blue eyes and clear, pale skin.

"Are you really going to turn into one of those wolves one day?" I asked her, even now doubting the truth of those words. "Because if you do, I'm going to be the odd one out around here."

I crept to the door, opened it, and went out to the kitchen to make her a bottle.

I'd been shocked by the transformations I'd seen yesterday between Noah and Lacey. And yet, despite how vicious and nasty they'd seemed when facing each other down, I'd known that Noah was only protecting us. That fact was strangely comforting. Noah had shown that he would defend us against any enemy, including his own kind. Not to mention he would clearly be able to kick any human's ass, that was for sure.

I made Trixie a bottle, put on the coffee maker, and took her back to bed with me to cuddle with her. I lay with my head on the pillow and stared at the beautiful daughter I'd created. With Noah. I stroked her cheek and cupped her little ear, enjoying the few minutes of quiet that we had together in the morning, before the day really started and the whirlwind of life took over.

Trixie finished her bottle, handed the empty thing to me, then rolled over to sit up. She was so independent now, so big. My little baby was mostly gone.

There was a knock at the door, and I twisted around to look. "Hello?"

The door opened and Noah peek into the room, his blue eyes dark and sad. "Morning."

"Good morning."

Trixie slid off the bed and ran for him.

"Dada," she chanted, and Noah laughed as he scooped her up.

"She's saying *Dada* already."

I swallowed hard against the lump of emotions in my throat. "Yeah, she is. She's very clever."

He nodded, wrapping his arms around her. "I'll make us some breakfast, then we've gotta get going."

"Oh yeah? Where are we going?" I asked, getting to my feet and reaching for my bags with all our clean clothes.

"When I went to see Ronan and Kara last night, we organized to head over to Tammy's today. Kara thought you might be able to ask her sister-in-law more questions about cross-mixed babies, since she has one, too."

Relief filled me at the news. That sounded like a great idea. I took out diapers for Trixie and got our things ready for the day. "That sounds perfect, thank you."

Noah handed our daughter back to me, then pointed his thumb at the kitchen. "I'll get on the food, then we can go."

"Great."

Noah left without another word, and a huge hole ripped inside my heart. What little friendship we'd built over the last few days had been stripped away, leaving nothing but the burning awkwardness usually felt between exes. That feeling made everything seem insurmountable. The wolf thing. The single mom thing. The fact that I'd lied to him for so long. Everything.

Suddenly, my life was too hard and I couldn't see a way to fix it.

Trixie tugged at my leg and held out her clean diaper for me. My clever girl. I sighed and took a slow, measured breath. This little one depended on me, so there was no falling in a hole today. Not tomorrow either.

Maybe later. When she was all grown up and capable of taking care of herself.

"Okay, baby. Let's get you clean and dressed."

Once we were both ready to face the day, I wandered out into the living room and was met with a simple yet yummy-looking breakfast.

"That looks great. Thank you."

Noah glanced at the table. "I can't cook much, but I can chop."

He'd cut up strawberries, apples, bananas, and pears. There was yoghurt and toast and bread rolls.

"It's perfect. Thank you."

My heart lifted at seeing him trying so hard with us once more.

He handed me a coffee, his face as quiet and still as the surface of a mill pond. Equally as unreadable. "Let's eat."

We sat down and ate our food, Trixie passing between us to eat snatches of each of our breakfasts. A bite of toast from me, a piece of banana from Noah. It was lovely and gave my foolish heart hope that this is how things could be between us, if we could only figure out a way forward.

When we were done, having not talked about anything other than how cute Trixie was, we cleaned up and packed the car in virtual silence.

"I'll sit in the back with Trixie if you don't mind driving," I said to Noah, throwing him the keys.

He caught them, surprise in his face. "You sure?"

"Yeah, of course. Kara should sit in the front with you since she'll need the leg room. Plus, she can help navigate. I don't even know where we're going."

And I didn't care. I'd drive clear across the country and back again if it got me answers about Trixie's health.

We hopped in the car with me in the backseat with the baby, then Noah drove us over to a huge house at the top of the hill.

"Whoa. So that's the Alpha's house?" I asked.

"Yep. It's big, isn't it?"

I nodded. "Huge."

Kara waddled out, a grin on her face. "How are you guys this morning?"

"Fine, thanks," we both said, as she climbed in. Then, off we drove.

"How far is this place?" I asked no one in particular.

Kara twisted around to grin at me. "Oh, it's about an hour's drive on the main roads, but I know a few tricks to get there faster."

We drove through the forest, up hills and around corners, Noah heading wherever Kara pointed. If I'd been worried about my safety with these two people, then the fact that we were driving into the wilderness with no signs of life would definitely have sent up red flags.

But I didn't have anything to worry about with these two, so I dismissed the silly thought. A pregnant woman, and a man who loved my daughter, weren't going to cause any issues in that regard.

I just sat back and listened to them chatter about the pack while I entertained Trixie with food, toys, and my phone when she got too restless for anything else.

When we arrived at another small town, with gorgeous little houses and developed roads, I sighed. "Wow. This place is nice."

"Yeah," Kara said softly. "I grew up here, and although we've gone through a few rough times, it's a great town. If we have time to stop and see Allara, I think you'd really like her."

"Who's Allara?" I asked.

"My best friend."

"The Alpha," Noah elaborated.

"You mean the Alpha's mate?" I asked, assuming that Allara was the wife of the Alpha, the same way Kara was Ronan's mate.

"No, she's the Alpha," Kara said. "She was the only child of our old Alpha, and even though Jaime challenged her, she won in a death match."

"Wow." That definitely sounded like a woman I wanted to know. Only, *death* match? That sounded pretty scary.

Kara chuckled. "Yeah, she's pretty kick ass."

No kidding.

We drove up to a small house, and a smiling woman walked out the front door holding a baby girl in her arms.

"Tammy!" Kara cried, stepping out of the car and waddling over to meet the woman.

I unclipped Trixie from her car seat. My daughter was dying to get out, thrashing about and crying as I released her.

"I'll get her," Noah said, coming around to Trixie's side of the car and opening the door.

"Oh. Okay. Thanks." What else could I say? That *I* wanted to get her, like I always did? That would sound petty.

Instead, I grabbed my bag and Trixie's things and walked up toward the woman who looked as human as me. And Kara. I would never have been able to pick Tammy out as being a human when Kara wasn't. On the surface, they both seemed just like every other human woman I'd ever known.

"Hi," I said, smiling at Tammy and the little girl in her arms. "I'm Amy."

"Hey! I'm Tammy and this is Claire."

Tammy had a strong, sure voice, and a sweet face. She was also slightly more curvy than the wolf shifters I'd seen in Noah's town.

"Hi Claire." I waved at the little one, and she gave me a shy smile. "Oh God, she's beautiful."

Tammy groaned. "Well, she might look cute, but she kept me up half the night for God knows what reason, so come on in and let's have some coffee. I apologize in advance if I'm grouchy."

I laughed as I followed her. "Been there. Done that."

Kara hung by the door, but didn't come in. "Hey Tammy, do you mind if I go say hi to Allara?"

"Of course not. Go for it. I think she might be at the council building this morning."

Kara snuck off and left me alone with Tammy, Noah and the two little ones.

Tammy went to the kitchen and turned on the coffee maker. "So, guys. What's going on?"

I glanced over at Noah, who was still holding Trixie and seemed to have gone mute. "Well... I've got a few questions, if you don't mind."

"Yeah? About what?"

"About, you know, babies of wolf shifters and humans, and what it's like to live out here when you're not... one of them."

Tammy popped her daughter in a highchair and grinned at me. "Have you seen Noah shift yet? How fucking scary is it, right?"

"Seeing as how he shifted in the lounge room to protect me and Trixie from another wolf—a woman—who wanted to attack us, I'd say it was pretty fucking scary."

I glanced toward Noah, who was avoiding my gaze and didn't see that I'd softened my words with a grin. I turned back to Tammy, whose mouth had dropped open, and was unable to stop the laugh that bubbled up and out of my throat. "It was kind of surreal, actually, to witness that shift. I'm still not sure I've assimilated it all."

"No kidding," Tammy said, with a quick head shake.

Noah shot me a sharp look when I laughed, and though he still didn't say anything, something about the line of his jaw seemed to relax a notch.

He sat on the floor with Trixie and let her rummage through Claire's toy box.

"Well, have a seat," Tammy said to me, gesturing to one of the dining chairs that surrounded the nice wooden table. "Sounds like we've got lots to talk about."

AMY

I thought about what to ask, and a hundred questions popped into my head. Then I realized that my first questions had to be about Trixie. After all, that was the main reason I'd sought Noah out, wasn't it?

"Well, I suppose I should ask, how was your labor with Claire?"

Tammy blinked at me, and I blinked back. Yeah, that wasn't what I'd thought would come out of my mouth either, first up, but here we were.

Tammy ran her hands over the table in front of her as though she were nervous. "Okay, weird place to start, but I guess it was good. I had her here, at home. It wasn't fun. I screamed the place down. But no drugs, no stitches, no intervention. Was a dream labor compared to some of my friends in the city. Why?"

Wow. That sounded like heaven in comparison to me, and not what I'd been expecting her to say.

"I thought maybe the wolf-human mix might cause a harder birth. That's all."

"Not for me," she said, then grinned. "But I've had these lovely childbearing hips my whole life."

She wiggled on her seat and her breasts wobbled as she moved.

I smiled at her openness. She had a lovely curvy figure.

"You're perfect," I said shyly.

"You had a hard time with Trixie's birth?" she asked.

I could feel Noah's eyes on me, but I didn't want to look his way. We hadn't really talked about that. To be honest, we hadn't really talked about a lot of stuff, yet.

"I did. Once I found out about Noah, I was kind of hoping it might have been the wolf-human genetic mix." I shrugged. "But it might have just been me."

Which was what I'd always assumed until I found out Noah wasn't human.

"Or the medical intervention," Tammy said with a frown. "How bad was it?"

I shrugged. "Almost died, but you know. I didn't."

Noah jumped up to stand beside me. "You almost died?"

I glanced up at him, my chest tight with strain. "Yeah. They needed forceps to get her out because she got stuck, and they tore something that caused me to almost bleed out. But they stopped the bleeding, got me into surgery, and I got a few pints of someone else's blood in a transfusion."

I tried to make light of the situation; after all I'd survived it. Other women hadn't.

Noah's jaw tightened, and his gaze hardened as though he was angry.

He shouldn't be. It wasn't like it was his fault.

"Oh my God," Tammy said, drawing my attention back to her. "You must be terrified to have another."

"Oh, I have no plans for any more," I said, and then it hit me.

Oh, my God. I had unprotected sex with Noah. Again.

My gaze shot up to Noah and he stared right back as if the same thought had just crossed his mind.

Oh, crap. Not again.

"Well, maybe a C-section next time?" Tammy said, breezing on with the conversation. "Not that I've heard that's any better, but at least it's more controlled."

I nodded. "That's what the doctors said at the time." *What day am I on in my cycle? Ten? Eleven? Shit! I don't know.*

Was it really possible to get two for two?

"Anything else you want to know?" Tammy asked, glancing between us.

Yes, I thought. *A million things. But I don't know where to start.*

Noah walked off to play with Trixie, as if wanting to give us space, and I shook myself. I could deal with that issue later.

Focus.

I swallowed hard and forged on. "Trixie is already showing wolf-like signs. She howls in her sleep, and her eyes shift color too. Do you know what the likelihood of her being a full shifter, is?"

The words came out robotically, as my head spun with the possibilities. What would I do if I was pregnant again? Could I do another baby on my own? How would Noah feel about this one?

If it happened again, I would have to be up front and honest with Noah from the beginning. I owed it to him, and to the child. If there was another one.

"To be honest, I don't know. No one's really talked to me about it. I'd say, just assume she will and educate her accordingly. And if she doesn't, well, you can deal with that then." Tammy took a sip of her coffee, then went to the cupboard and pulled out a container of biscuits. "Are you planning on staying with the Northwood Pack? Will Trixie grow up knowing about the wolves?"

"We haven't really decided on that yet," I said, glancing at Noah, who wasn't looking at me. He was squatting down next to Trixie, looking at the her while she played her little games.

I wasn't lying though; we hadn't even discussed that topic, let alone come to any decisions.

"Well, that will really determine how much she knows and is comfortable with," Tammy said. She stared at me long and hard.

I tilted my head at her. "What's up?"

She turned in her chair. "Hey, Noah. Can I chat with Amy for a bit by herself? Is that okay?"

Noah picked up Trixie and walked over to us. "Yeah, sure. I'll just take Trixie for a walk."

Tammy jumped to her feet.

"I'll walk you out." She looked at me. "Can you watch Claire for a second? I'll be right back."

"Yeah. Of course." I slid closer to the little girl and handed her one of the toys that had been out of reach.

My ears strained to listen to what Noah and Tammy were saying, but I could barely even hear whispering. Either they'd walked too far away for me to hear, or they had ultra-sonic whispering skills.

"What do you think they're saying?" I said to Claire, then sighed because I was hopeless.

I forced myself to concentrate on Claire, enjoying her tiny hands and smile. Then Tammy walked back in.

"I think I've got the lay of the land now. So, tell me what's going on with you." Tammy sat down again opposite me and grabbed a cookie with the air of a woman on a mission.

"I'm not sure what you mean."

Wasn't I the one who was meant to ask *her* questions?

Tammy took a sip of coffee from her large mug, then gestured at me with her hand. "How are you dealing with the whole... wolf thing?"

"Which bit?" I asked with a nervous laugh. "The fact that Noah is one, or the fact that my daughter might become one?"

Tammy grinned. "Well, both."

I worried my bottom lip with my teeth for a moment before answering. "I don't really know. It's scary and still seems totally surreal, but I suppose I'm okay with it. I mean, it could be worse, right?"

Even as I said the words, I was thinking, not sure how, but there had to be worse scenarios.

Tammy nodded. "Think about all the kids that inherit syndromes that cause disabilities. As a wolf shifter, Trixie will have a lot of advantages that we humans don't have."

"Like what?"

"Like speed and strength, not to mention an awesome metabolism. And their ability to heal is off the charts."

"Really? I didn't know about any of those things." Some of those sounded very cool.

Tammy cackled. "Yeah, that's because Noah's finding it hard enough just to think clearly around you, without sitting down and explaining all the wolf concepts."

Before I could jump in with a question about what she meant, she continued on. "Plus, they don't really think about all the cool things they've got that we don't. It's only us that notice the differences because we're not wolves. They pretty much take all those things for granted."

I inhaled slowly through my nose, conflicted in which way to take the conversation. "You, um, seem totally fine with it all."

"I am," Tammy said, and her tone was truly happy. "A wolf shifter mate is the best husband, or boyfriend, or whatever you want to call it. They're insanely loyal, and if you're lucky enough to be fated mates with one, then they'll never leave you. Never look at another woman again, no matter how old or chubby you get. And turns out it's the same for me, even though I'm human. Once someone commits to their fated mate, whether it is two shifters, or a human and a shifter, they will never want or need another partner."

Tammy picked up another biscuit and chomped on it, the ordinary action belying her momentous words.

Was she serious?

"What actually is a fated mate? Is it like... a soul mate?" That sounded awesome.

Tammy nodded. "That's a good description. Some of the wolves say they feel a special attraction to their fated mate. It's a person who is absolutely perfect for them, and because of that, they can't be with anyone else. That's what it was like for me and Jason, and Allara and Reid."

"And Kara and Ronan?" I added, thinking of those two and suddenly knowing exactly what she was talking about.

She nodded with a grin. "You've seen them together?"

"Yeah, there's this... happiness to them. A glow. I can't quite put it into words."

Tammy placed her elbow on the table and leaned on her hand. "That's the bond. With Jason and I it was a bit harder to deal with. Obviously, not being a wolf shifter, I didn't understand how intensely Jason felt about me. Or how hard he struggled with the fact that I was human."

"What do you mean?" I asked as she stood up to pick up Claire, who had begun to fuss.

Tammy hoisted her baby up into her arms and popped a pacifier in her mouth. "I mean, the wolves don't really like dating outside the pack. In the past it has brought with it too many issues, which was part of the reason Jason didn't really want to date me." She shrugged. "But what can I say? When it's meant to be, it's meant to be."

"I wish it was like that for me and Noah," I said with a sigh, then realized I'd said that out loud. I slammed my hands over my mouth. "I'm sorry. I didn't actually mean to say that."

Tammy laughed. "You and Noah need to talk this thing out. You've already lost two years when you could have been together and deliriously happy. Do you really wanna lose more time?"

I frowned at her. "You think Noah still wants to be with me?"

"Not sure what's changed from me talking to him ten minutes ago," she said matter-of-factly.

I stared at her in wonder. Had Noah really told her that he wanted me? No, he couldn't have. I frowned. That didn't match up with what he'd told me.

"He said it was better I leave. That I was safer in town, away from the wolves."

And any psycho exes that had the ability to bite my head off. Quite literally.

She shrugged. "Maybe you are. I don't know. But what I do know is that these guys are insanely protective and would rather cut off their own right arm, than see you fall in harm's way. So even if it kills him, Noah will send you away if he thinks you're better off without him."

Even if it kills him? Is it really like that, for Noah? Tears gathered in my eyes and began to block up my nose. I opened my mouth to speak, then closed it and shook my head instead. Nope. Couldn't talk.

Tammy sighed, juggling the baby from one hip to the other. "Amy, look, being out here can be rough, and leaving your whole world behind... yeah, that takes a bit to get used to as well. But these men... if they love you, they will move heaven and earth for you. That sort of love is worth any sacrifice, in my view."

I swallowed hard and brushed the tears off my check. "How will I know if he loves me like that or not?"

I didn't know if he could ever really love me in the way she had spoken about. Love like that involved trust, and that would mean he would need to forgive me for what I'd done.

Tammy grabbed a box of tissues and handed them to me. "You really need to just sit down and talk to him, Amy. He'll be honest with you, as long as you're honest with him."

"But I am honest with him!" I told her. "I try to tell him everything now."

She frowned. "Well, he thinks you're holding something back. About why you left. And I can't tell you much more, because we only chatted for a few minutes, but if you want to save this relationship, you've gotta tell him everything. No holds barred. I mean, you have a child together. And if you do love Noah, then full honesty is the only thing that might save this situation."

If I do love Noah? My heart jiggled in a strange erratic beat. Tammy was right. It *was* time for full honesty. With Noah, and with myself.

I nodded and wiped up my tears, just as a knock sounded on the door.

It was Kara and Allara, ready to chat and do a meet and greet. I put on my happy face and tried to focus on the women in front of me, but in the back of my head my thoughts were spinning.

From what Tammy was saying, *I* was the one standing in the way of my happily ever after with Noah.

But what did he need to hear for us to move forward?

CHAPTER 15

NOAH

I played with Trixie in the woods, enjoying the sunshine and her bubbly company. She was such a content child. She giggled and chatted away in her own little language, radiating happiness.

I'd had no idea, until Amy turned up with Trixie, that being a dad could feel so damn wonderful.

What would I do when they returned to town without me? My heart sank at the thought of not being with them. Either of them. Trixie had wriggled her way into my heart the moment I saw her. Just like her mom.

My woman. My child. My family.

Could I simply continue my life as a bachelor? A single wolf whose mate lived an hour away?

No, not my mate. I shook the thoughts from my head. Just because my wolf thought of her that way, didn't mean it was true.

I was just walking back to town with Trixie snuggled in my arms when Allara found us.

"Hey Noah," she called out. "I think the girls are ready to leave."

"Yeah. Cool. Coming."

Had Amy found any of the answers she'd been searching for? And did that mean she now felt safe to take Trixie back to town and away from me until she was older?

Most wolf shifters didn't start their transitions until they hit puberty. I hadn't told Amy because I wanted to keep her around. Now, I should probably reassure her that Trixie wouldn't have any issues for ten years or so. Hopefully. I didn't know anything about what happened with a half human, but I had to assume the shifter traits were likely to be diluted rather than amplified.

When I got back to the car, Kara and Amy were already packed and ready to go.

"Trixie really needs a nap, and she'll fall asleep in the car on the way home," Amy said, reaching out for our daughter.

There was a look in her eye that I couldn't read as she studied me. It made my stomach wobble. I nodded, pretending calm, and loving the way Amy said 'home' when she described my place. It was probably just a slip of the tongue, but even so, it warmed me for a long moment.

I said my goodbyes to Allara and Tammy, and then hopped in the car.

"Did you get the information you needed?" I asked Amy as we began the drive back to our pack.

"Mostly," she said quietly, fussing over Trixie in the back seat and not meeting my eye in the rear view mirror.

We didn't talk much for the drive home, all three of us deep within our own thoughts. We dropped Kara back at her house, and she staggered up her front stairs, holding her back and her belly at the same time.

"Is she okay?" I asked Amy, frowning as Kara finally disappeared inside. "Is she meant to look like that?"

She didn't respond at first, then said, "Probably just some sciatica. Happens when you sit for too long. She'll be okay, but I can check on her tomorrow."

"Tomorrow?" I repeated, twisting around in my seat to look at her. "You're staying?"

She stared at me with an unreadable expression. "I'd like to. Can we talk about it at home?"

This time the use of the word home seemed to be deliberate, and I couldn't stop the wave of hope that swept through my chest.

"Yeah, of course. Let's go."

I drove back to my place as fast as it was safe to do so, and Amy carefully picked up the sleeping Trixie and carried her inside. I held the bedroom door open and watched her place our daughter in her crib. Trixie kept her eyes closed, and she cuddled into her blanket and wolf toy with a little sigh of what sounded like contentment.

Amy snuck out and shut the door, grinning with relief. "She doesn't always transfer well, so you must have done a good job of wearing her out."

"I didn't do much. Truth be told, she kept me going, with all her energy. It was probably all the fresh air as well." Of which we had lots, being out in the forest.

Nothing like town.

"Can we chat now?" Amy asked, her dark eyes big and open.

My stomach twisted into knots. I couldn't tell where this was headed. What was she going to tell me? "Sure."

We walked back into the lounge room and sat down opposite each other on the two couches surrounding the coffee table. I stared at her, waiting for her to begin. She wanted this discussion, so I was going to let her lead.

Besides, my throat was closed over with nervous tension, so I needed a moment before I could get any coherent words out.

She shifted on her spot on the couch, and cleared her throat with a cough. "I really enjoyed meeting Tammy today. It was really good of you to organize that and take me over there. Thank you."

I nodded, then had to do a little throat clearing of my own. Finally, I felt I could trust my voice not to betray my nerves. "Sure. Anything in particular you learnt that you want to talk about?"

She bit her lip, then jerked her head in a nod. "Yes. Tammy told me that wolves have fated mates."

I froze. *Shit.* I hadn't wanted Tammy to tell Amy that. "Yeah, some of us do."

"Do you have one?" she asked, staring at me intently.

Fuck. Talk about being backed into a corner.

I straightened up on my cushion. "Well... that's still to be decided."

She frowned at me. "What do you mean? I thought you just... knew."

We did, which was why lying about this was almost impossible. "Well, if I'm honest, I thought *you* were my mate."

She moved to the edge of the couch. "When? When did you think that?"

I waited a heartbeat, then dove right in with the truth bomb. "The moment I saw you standing across the bar that first night."

Her jaw dropped open. "Really?"

I nodded, partially annoyed that she hadn't realized when I had. Especially after the incredible night we'd shared.

"Yes, which was why I was totally blown away when I woke up the next day and found you were gone. During the night I thought you must have felt it too—the fated mate bond. But it's obvious you didn't then, and I guess it's equally as obvious, judging by the dumbfounded look on your face that you don't feel it now, either. So, I must have been wrong. If we were fated mates, both of us would have felt it."

Tears glimmered in Amy's eyes and I glanced away. I didn't want to see her shame at not feeling for me the way I felt for her. Worse, I couldn't bear to see her pity.

I stood up and walked away, pacing around the room and needing to move. "It's okay if you need to move back to town, Amy. I won't stop you from leaving if you don't want to be here."

Could she hear the pain in my tone? Finally, I turned to look at her. She was simply sitting there staring at me.

"We can organize some sort of custody thing, if you want. I can't walk away from Trixie now that I know she's alive. I already love her." I stopped, my chest tight and burning with pain.

Amy jumped to her feet. "I'd never take her from you. Never. I can see how much she means to you already. And... well, I can see how much *you* mean to *her*. She loves you too, Noah."

She does? It was something wonderful, at least, from this terrible situation.

If only Amy loved me, too.

I nodded and crossed my arms over my chest. "Thank you." Emotion clouded my voice, and I swallowed hard.

What else could I say? Amy had kept her from me for almost two years and I still believed she never would have brought her back to me if it wasn't for the wolf-like characteristics Trixie had begun to display.

"So that's it?" I asked, the tightness in my chest beginning to double up and burn. "You'll stay while we work out custody, then leave?"

She shook her head. "I need to tell you how I feel."

"You do?" I asked, my heart beating harder and faster in my chest. Did that mean there was more? That I could be... wrong?

She nodded. "Tammy pointed out to me that you didn't know how I felt about you, and this... relationship."

She gestured around us.

"No. I don't know how you feel," I said. "Everything you've said and done so far has revolved around the fact you were too ashamed to even wake up next to me, let alone tell me you were pregnant, or come to me for help with the baby."

She stared at me, more tears building in her eyes, turning them luminescent.

I pushed forward. "And I assume the only reason you're here is because Trixie has wolf genes, otherwise you'd still be in town, raising her on your own, and I would never have known I had a child at all."

Amy's tears overflowed then, slipping down her face, but she brushed them away. "You're right. I was a coward. I ran away from you, and I kept running."

"But why?" I demanded. "I would have cared for you, and loved you both! Was I really that scary that you had to leave and not come back for *two years*?"

Surely, I wasn't that ugly, or fearsome?

She shook her head. "It wasn't that. I wasn't afraid of you. I was afraid of myself. I'd convinced myself that I was weak, and naughty, and slutty for going home with you. I didn't want to be tempted again. So I stayed away."

"But what we have is fucking amazing! The attraction! The electricity in bed! That's what I've dreamt of my whole life. And I found it with you, Amy."

She shook her head. "Please don't say that."

"Say what? The truth?"

She put her hands over her ears like a child trying to block out a loud noise. "If that's the truth, then all that I've suffered and gone through— and all that I've kept from you in not allowing you to see our daughter till now—is for nothing and I'm not sure I can bear it. If I was wrong, then I've hurt us all, so badly..."

I stormed over to her and grabbed her hands, tugging them down so that she had no choice but to listen to me. "What are you talking about?"

"I convinced myself that you were... too sexy."

I huffed out a disbelieving laugh. "Thanks for the compliment, but not sure I'm understanding the problem yet."

"It *is* a problem! I don't feel like I have any control over myself with you! I feel weak... and stupid... and..."

I didn't let her finish the sentence. I grabbed her up in my arms and kissed her hard. I pressed my mouth into hers as though we were one person and not two. I separated her lips with mine so I could plunder her with my tongue.

When she moaned and grabbed for me, I picked her up and she wrapped her legs around my waist.

When she eventually broke our kiss, she panted out, "See, this isn't fair. It shouldn't hurt so much to be apart from you."

A groan ripped up through my chest as I carried her up the hallway and into our bedroom. I threw her onto the bed and tore at my clothes. She needed to feel how much I wanted her; know how much I needed her.

"This is how it's meant to be with a fated mate, Amy. You'll always need me. I'll always need you. And when we're apart, we'll yearn for one another like we're missing that other half of ourselves."

I threw my t-shirt on the ground and ripped off my jeans.

"That's what being a fated mate means."

Amy was lying on the bed, still clothed, tears in her eyes again. "Is that how it was for you too? Did you miss me over the two years I was gone?"

I stared at her, connecting our gazes. "Every damn day."

"Oh, God. So did I, Noah. I missed you so damn much."

I crawled onto the bed to make sure my mate knew just how much I had truly missed her.

CHAPTER 16

AMY

I grabbed for Noah's shoulders, desperate to feel his heavy body on mine. When I connected with his hot skin, I wrapped my fingers around his deltoids and pulled him down to kiss me again. We hadn't worked much out yet, but admitting finally that the feelings I had for him scared the shit out of me seemed to have unleashed something wholly amazing in him.

Was this just a bad case of lust? Or was this what being a fated mate felt like?

I knew in my heart this was not simply lust. I had never felt anything as strong as this pull toward Noah before, and I couldn't imagine ever feeling such a thing with anyone else.

I kissed him hard and moaned when he pulled back. "No. Don't go."

"Don't worry. I'm not going far," he said, putting only enough space between us to tug at my clothes.

I hurried out of my leggings and t-shirt with his help, then my underwear. I was hot and uncomfortable, and so ready to have his hands on me again. I wanted him. So much. And I didn't want to be afraid to want him anymore. If this was how it was meant to feel between us, why had I been so worried about it?

I pushed those thoughts to the back of my mind as he moved down my body.

I stopped him with a firm hand. "This time, it's my turn," I told him, pushing him back so that I could crawl on top of his huge, delicious body.

He lay back against the pillows with a lazy smile on his face. "Really? We get to take turns? Sounds pretty good to me."

I grinned back, excitement curling inside me. "Thank you."

"I'm all yours," he said, and even though there was a jesting tone in his voice, seriousness colored his blue eyes.

He was mine. All mine.

And he was letting me know it right here, and right now.

I kissed him gently on the mouth, then slid further down, exploring his body as he had mine. I kissed the indentation of his throat, and then his chest. Such beautiful thick muscles. It was hard not to gasp and moan at how hot he was.

I went lower, running my tongue around his abs and down one side of his hip into the sexy V that all women love on a really muscled guy. I couldn't believe such a man wanted to be in my bed.

When I reached his cock, already thick and hard, I took the flesh into my mouth and loved on him, sucking and licking his salty shaft until his gasps grew desperate and he tugged at my hair.

"Come up here," he said, his voice hoarse, like he'd been yelling.

After one more long lick, I crawled back up to him.

"Sit on my face," he demanded.

A blush swept up my cheeks. "I can't do that."

I was so wet and ready for him, and if I did that, there was no hiding from my desire. *How embarrassing.*

"Oh, yes, you can," he said, grabbing me around the waist and hauling me up his body.

I squealed at being manhandled, then grabbed onto the thick

wooden headboard. My knees were on either side of his head and I was sitting on his chest staring down at his face. He shuffled down the mattress to get under me.

On that first lick of his tongue against my pussy, I screamed. I was so naked and exposed in this position. I wanted to hide, and yet I couldn't ask him to stop. It felt amazing to be pleasured like this, and my embarrassment floated away, to be replaced by nothing but need.

He grabbed my ass with both hands and ate my pussy like a starving man, flicking his tongue against my clit and tasting me as I cried out against the pleasure. Over and over again he licked me, nibbling at my throbbing flesh until I was so tight and ready, I was sobbing for release.

"Please. Don't stop. Please. I need more."

He pulled me down his body and held me over his cock.

"Ride me," he demanded, and I couldn't think of anything I'd rather do.

I settled on my knees, raised myself up, and slid back to find him. The head of his cock slipped between my folds—so wet already from my own desire, and from his mouth—and as I twisted my hips, his cock nudged inside of me.

I gasped at the feeling of pressure, wanting more. Needing him to assuage the ache inside of me. I dropped my head to kiss him, his hands on my waist tightening as I found his cock and pushed back to envelop him. I broke our kiss to gasp out my pleasure as he filled me. He gripped my hips and thrust up, meeting me halfway and making it impossible not to sob with how good the connection felt.

I began to move, riding his cock, up and down, getting faster and faster until my belly tightened to screaming point.

He took over then, grabbing my waist and pounding into me. I came, the sensation plowing through me in an unending wave of orgasmic, pulsating pleasure.

I dropped my head to his chest, and he groaned as he thrust deep inside me. Another orgasm hit just as he came inside me, my body greedily milking him as I shuddered on top of him. When I collapsed, I could barely breathe and had tears in my eyes.

I was finally whole. And happy.

"Oh God, I love you. I love you so much." I sobbed into his chest, finally feeling like I could tell him the truth about how I felt.

He wrapped his arms around me and squeezed me tight. Though he didn't say anything back, I knew he'd heard me. I didn't need any words back from him, in this moment. I felt his emotions in the beautiful, all-encompassing hug of his arms around me.

I sighed and closed my eyes, loving the sound of his heavy breathing in the room, and the feel of his thumping heart beneath our sweaty skin.

I rested with my head against Noah's shoulder. I was in the safest, best place in the world.

"I can't believe Trixie is still asleep," I said, grateful to my daughter for staying asleep long enough for this time to fix things between Noah and me.

"She's a good girl," he said, his voice more serious now than it had been earlier.

Eventually though, the atmosphere cooled, changed, and I knew it was time to slide off him and talk.

I rolled off him and sat up, wrapping myself partially in the sheet, since I knew this conversation was going to make me feel vulnerable enough. I didn't need to be naked for it, too.

He shuffled up the bed, grabbing the second pillow to put behind his head so he could rest comfortably against the headboard.

He nodded at me, all serious now. "You said you loved me."

I inhaled sharply. "Yes. Yes, I did."

I bit my lip and waited for him to continue.

He cocked an eyebrow at me. "Did you mean it?"

Surprise rippled through me. He still doubted? "Of course I meant it. I wouldn't say it if I didn't."

He glanced away. "I thought it might be just a, you know, heat of the moment thing."

I shook my head. "I think... I think I fell in love with you the moment I saw you too." Or at least I fell in lust. "But I didn't know anything about you then. Now... well, I've seen how respected you are in your community."

The Alpha had come to check on him in the first moments I'd arrived.

"And how you are with Trixie." My heart swelled at the thought of the two of them together. It took a special sort of man to bond so effortlessly with a little girl the way Noah had bonded with his daughter.

"So you did feel it," Noah said. "Even though you're not a wolf."

I nodded. "I felt something, very strong. Intense. Overwhelming. For you, that was probably a signal of the fated mate bond. But to me, it was terrifying. I'd never felt anything like it before, and it scared me half to death."

"Do you still feel that way?" he asked. "Terrified, I mean."

I shook my head. "I don't. Not now that I understand what it is. And that you might feel this crazy pull, too. If you feel the same way, then we're just two people in love. Nothing wrong with that. And nothing to be scared about, at all."

"Nothing at all," he said, reaching for my hand to link our fingers together. "So, you'll stay? Here? With me?"

Joy flooded through me. "I will if you'll have us."

Speaking of which.... I opened my mouth to tell him that our unprotected sex might have consequences, but Trixie called out to us.

I turned my head. "Trixie's awake."

"Let's go get her then," Noah said, swinging his legs over the side of the bed and getting to his feet, gloriously naked. In the past, I'd have averted my eyes, trying to avoid being so affected by his sexiness. Now, I drank my fill. I couldn't believe that this magnificent man loved me. And our daughter. It was like a dream coming true, and I so hoped I could make him as happy as I knew he would make me.

"Come on," he said when I hesitated, cocking his head to look back at me over his shoulder.

I laughed as I chased him down the hall, naked too. Who was here to see us and pass judgment? No one.

Noah pushed open the door and walked into the room, and I gloried in how happy he was to see his daughter. No one was going to love her the way he did. No one but me, of course. And that was exactly as it should be. Both of us here for her. And for each other.

"Mama," Trixie called, reaching out her arms for me.

I grinned at Noah as I walked around him to grab her.

"You do know that it's very possible I'm pregnant again," I said to Noah, hoisting our baby up out of her crib and holding her in my arms.

Noah blinked at me, stunned, before a wide grin split his face. "I hadn't even thought about it."

I laughed at him. "Seriously? Well, I suppose that's how we got into trouble the first time."

Noah grinned as Trixie reached for him. "Trouble? What are you talking about? This little one was meant to be."

He settled our daughter in his arms and dragged me into his side to join the hug. "We're a family, and I love you both. I'm not going anywhere, so if you are pregnant, then I'll be there, right by your side the whole time."

I sighed and closed my eyes, nestling into my big wolf shifter mate. "I can't think of anything I'd like more. Sounds like a dream come true, to me."

EPILOGUE

NOAH

Nine months later

I stared down at the pink, squealing little infant in my arms and my heart expanded in my chest. Love, as strong as what I felt for Amy and Trixie, flooded through me for my new son, and the woman who'd birthed him.

"He's absolutely perfect, Amy," I told her, as the midwife tied off the cord and helped to wrap him in a light blue, thin blanket.

"That's great." Amy panted, turning over to lie back on the bed after giving birth on all fours.

She looked happy but exhausted. To my eyes, she was still perfect, but anxiety flared suddenly. "Is she okay?" I asked the doctor who was between Amy's legs and examining her still. Amy had been so concerned after her trauma around Trixie's birth, that we'd hired a specialist from the city to attend our home for the birth.

"She's very okay," the doctor said, and my anxiety died down to nothing. Thank God. Amy was my everything. Amy and our daughter. And now our perfect son.

"She did beautifully," the doctor added with a smile. "I'm just going to check for any tears, but there's no excessive bleeding, which is wonderful."

"Can I hold him?" Amy asked, putting her arms out for our son.

"Of course!" I walked him to her waiting and open arms.

She sighed as she took him, putting him straight to her breast. I kissed her forehead, which was hot and sweaty from exertion. "Do you want me to go and get Trixie? Or do you need some peace for a bit?"

Trixie was over two years old now and had started talking at a rate of knots. We couldn't get her to be quiet, even if we'd wanted to.

"Oh, I'd love to see her. Please," Amy said, stroking our newborn son's head. "I think she should meet her brother as soon as possible."

I nodded, thanked the doctor, and headed off to Kara's place to pick up Trixie. We were often at Ronan's house nowadays, their new little family enjoying the company of ours, and Trixie was besotted with the new Alpha heir.

As I walked up the street, I waved at my pack members and shot them thumbs up all round, and congratulations were shouted from every direction. I grinned, my chin high, and kept walking.

The past nine months hadn't been without their trials, but Amy and I had worked through them together, one obstacle at a time.

I'd learnt to trust her, letting go of the past and forgiving her the choices she had made surrounding Trixie's birth. I'd learnt that without that trust in one another, we couldn't build the relationship we both craved. So, I'd made the choice to accept what had been, and then to let it go and focus on the present and the future. And with that release had come the ability to truly love Amy, and be loved by her in return.

Neither of us were afraid of the fated mate pull any longer. Instead, we had come to cherish it as the gift it truly was.

Trixie seemed to be flourishing living here in the forest with the other children like her—one or two half-wolf, half-human children, and the rest full shifters. And Amy said she loved being part of such a tight-knit small community.

I was thrilled that everyone in the pack had accepted her and Trixie in without question. They were part of our pack now, and that would never change.

When I knocked on the door, Kara answered with her baby, Tennessee, on her hip. "Hey Noah! Is the baby here yet?"

"Yes! We have a beautiful and very healthy son. And Amy is doing very well, according to the doctor."

"That's wonderful! Congratulations," Kara said with a huge smile.

"Daddy!" Trixie cried, running toward me and hurling herself into my arms.

"Hey beautiful girl. Have you had a good day with Auntie Kara?"

"Oh, yes," she said with a smile, "but I wanna see Mama."

"Funny about that, because she wants to see you, too!" I hoisted Trixie higher in my arms and glanced back at Kara. "Thank you so much for keeping an eye on her for us."

"Of course! Anytime. Is Amy really doing okay?"

"She's doing beautifully," I said, pride blossoming in my chest. "Especially after everything she went through with Trixie's birth. You know how nervous I was when she wanted to try another natural birth, but it worked out perfectly, with the support in place. I'm so proud of her, though."

It had taken many chats with multiple doctors, and a lot of research, for Amy to want to try a natural birth this time around. I'd been happy to support whatever choice she wanted for her body either way, but I couldn't describe the level of pride I felt for her succeeding in her goal.

"She's an amazing woman, Noah. She is a perfect match for you."

"I know." I grinned happily at Kara, and gave Trixie, still in my arms, a little squeeze.

"Send my love, and I'll pop down later with dinner," Kara said. "It's just in the oven."

I grinned again at the Alpha's mate. "You're the best, Kara. Thanks."

Kara closed the door, and I took Trixie back home to see her mother.

"Guess what?" I said to her, as we went along the path.

"What Daddy?"

"Mama had the baby!"

Trixie screwed up her little face. "You mean the baby's here? Like... out of her tummy?"

"Yep. Out of her tummy. You have a little brother. Shall we go meet him?"

Trixie nodded, though I could see how concerned she was. We entered the house, still warm and heated for the birth.

"Mama, guess who's here?" I called out as I strolled up the hallway and into our bedroom.

Most of the mess had been cleaned away and new sheets already put on the bed. Amy still held the baby in her arms, against her naked body.

Trixie ran for the bed and jumped up beside her mother.

Amy put her arm around Trixie and whispered to her how much she loved her, and then told her all about her little brother. "He's too little now, but when he starts to grow, he's going to love his big sister Trixie so much."

"He will?"

"Of course, he will," Amy said. "He'll love you just as much as me and Daddy do."

Trixie peered at her brother, and then a smile graced her face. "He's little," she said, and then reached over to touch his cheek with a gentle finger. "Nice."

Amy pressed a kiss to Trixie's forehead. "He is nice, and so are you, beautiful girl. I love you very much. So does Daddy."

I stood back and watched, reveling in the amazing woman my mate was. We'd overcome so much together.

Being by her side through the whole pregnancy had been a dream, and being at the birth was a miracle. I finally had the chance to experience everything I'd missed out on with Trixie, and now the circle of love was complete.

"Does Daddy wanna hold the baby so I can cuddle Trixie some more?" Amy asked me with a small wink.

I reached for our son. "Gladly."

My family.

Life was truly perfect.

THE END

PACK LOYALTY

4

CURSE
OF THE
WOLF

USA TODAY BEST-SELLING AUTHOR
AMELIA SHAW

CURSE OF THE WOLF

MANNIX

My father was a crazy, A-list asshole. I didn't like admitting it to anyone or saying the words out loud, but there was no changing the facts.

What sort of man, let alone an Alpha shifter, would drive his eldest child one hundred miles from home, leave him in the wilderness, and tell him to find his own way back?

Because that's exactly what my father did to my older brother, Reid, when he was eight years old.

For years, the pack believed Reid had died. What eight-year-old could survive the harsh winters of our state? After all, my father had chosen one of the most bitterly cold days of the year to drop Reid off. At least that was what I'd been told by others as I'd gotten older.

Within our pack, people would often gossip and speculate on how my brother had likely died. He'd been too young to shift. Too young to hunt. So how had my father ever expected him to survive? The simple truth was he probably hadn't. Which made my father... what? A murderer? Insane? Or both?

The pack said my father was cursed. And when he died in a fire a later that same year, no one had been surprised. He'd killed himself and my mother. I'd only been five years old at the time, so I don't remember much about that time.

I was saved by my father's best friend and the man who raised me, Alfred. A kind man. A loving beta who took on the role of Alpha after my father's passing, only because there was no one else in the pack to do it.

But the biggest shock of all had come the night before Alfred died. He confided in me that he'd heard whispers that my brother Reid was still alive.

I hadn't wasted any time. In the same week that I buried the man who'd raised me, I set off in the same direction my father had apparently driven off in with my brother all those years ago. I'd traveled from pack to pack, asking everyone I met about a man named Reid.

Eventually, I found someone who knew of a man with an Alpha's size, height and strength. He was apparently quiet but a good leader. That description sounded just like the man I'd always envisioned my brother would have been. But was it him? And what would the passage of time have done to him?

I turned off the engine of my truck and stared out the front window at the buildings set around this village square. I'd been driving for a month, and I finally arrived at the Northwood pack grounds.

My heart pounded a little too hard in my chest and after all this time, I hesitated to get out of the vehicle.

Suddenly a fist pounded on my window, and I jumped, glaring at the guy staring at me.

"Can I help you?" he called out.

I sighed and pulled the keys out of the ignition before pushing open the door, my hesitation at an end.

"Hey, man." I shut the door and slid the keys into my jeans pocket.

"Hey," he repeated. "Are you looking for someone?"

My heart thudded again, sending stress bucketing through my system. "Yeah. I'm looking for Reid."

The guy's eyebrows fluttered high on his forehead and his eagle-like gaze scraped over me. "Oh, yeah? I was heading over there myself to have a chat with the Alpha. Wanna tag along?"

I inhaled sharply, a pain like being kicked in the gut hitting me square in the solar plexus. "Sure. I'm Mannix, by the way."

I held out my hand and the other guy took it, shaking my whole arm with the strength of his grip. "I'm Jason. Come on. They should be home now."

"They?" I asked, walking side by side with the guy who had to be one of the pack's betas. He was large and looked fit but was still an inch or two shorter than me.

"Yeah, the Alpha and her family."

"*Her* family?" I repeated. "Your Alpha is a... her?" How did that work? Didn't Jason say we were going to see Reid?

Jason frowned at me. "I thought you said you knew Reid."

"I do... kind of," I muttered as we stepped up in front of a large log house. It was double story and surrounded by gardens.

I glanced around. It was the only two-story house in the area. "This is the Alpha's house," I said, knowing I was correct without needing Jason to confirm it.

Jason frowned at me, suspicious now of a stranger, which made him a good beta. "I think you're going to have to explain to me what you're doing here before I let you in to see Allara and Reid."

"Allara?" I repeated. "Is that my brother's mate?"

"Brother?" Jason gasped, his shock visible in the way his frown disappeared, and his mouth dropped open.

I wanted to smack myself in the head. "Look. I..." I'd royally fucked this up. I hadn't wanted it to come out like that. "My brother went missing twenty years ago. His name was Reid. We all thought he'd died, but I was told only a week ago that he was still alive."

"So, you're here to find out if our Reid is your brother?" Jason asked. A grin stretched across his mouth.

"Yeah. Sort of." I glanced at the house, then back to Jason. "What's this Reid like?"

Jason assessed me, crossing his arms over his chest and staring me down. I must have passed some kind of test because he relaxed a notch. "You kinda look like him, you know."

"I do?"

Jason nodded. "Yeah. Same eyes, and that cleft in your chin. Anyway, Reid's a great guy. He's mated to our Alpha, Allara."

"Was he born in the pack?" I asked, hoping he wasn't and assuming that Jason wouldn't waste my time if he was.

Jason shook his head. "No. He was a foundling. One of our women discovered him in the forest, half dead, starving and dehydrated, when he was about ten."

Ten? Jesus. He'd survived two *years* out there, on his own?

"Or that's what we all thought because he was tall. They never found out where he came from, and he wouldn't talk about it. Was mute for months after they found him, but he came good."

Every word was like a punch to my heart. "They... you..." I swallowed hard, tears clogging my throat. "You found him?"

"Not me." Jason said, shaking his head. "Emma. She raised him."

I stared at the large house, too many emotions to mention running through my mind. "What's he like now?"

"Why don't you come meet him yourself?" Jason said, knocking me in the shoulder as he walked past me and headed up toward the entrance. "Come on."

I was rooted to the spot. How did I approach the man who should be my Alpha? The man my father had thrown away as if he were trash.

"I..."

Jason groaned, turned away and knocked on the door.

Oh, fuck.

The door opened and a woman answered, a baby in her arms.

My stomach clenched tight in my abdomen, adrenaline coursing along my veins. I wanted to run. Away, preferably. And yet I couldn't move at all. Indecision froze me.

Jason spoke to the woman. I had to assume she was the aforementioned Allara, then they both started to walk toward me.

My feet shifted on the spot where I stood, and I was glad to learn that I could still move.

"Hi, there," the woman said as she moved closer. The babe in her arms only looked a few weeks old but was content and sleeping. "I'm Allara, the Alpha of the Northwood Pack. Jason says you're looking for Reid."

I nodded, swallowing hard. "I'm Mannix."

She smiled softly. "And you're looking for Reid?" she repeated.

"Did Jason tell you?"

Allara glanced at her beta. "He did. He said you might be part of

Reid's family. He never talked about the time before my pack found him, so I don't really know what to say or do."

"My father was our pack's Alpha," I said swiftly, wanting to get the information out as quickly as possible. "Your husband is my older brother, if your Reid is the same Reid I'm looking for."

I sounded like a bumbling idiot, but I didn't really care. Well, I did, but my pride was a small price to pay if I got my brother back.

Allara smiled broadly this time. "I think it's safe to say that he is. How many other men are the size of an Alpha, but were found wandering the woods alone when they were a child?"

Jason frowned at me suddenly. "Was your father sick?"

"Sick?" I tilted my head, pretending to think about it. Mentally sick? Probably. But how could I explain that in this moment? I ignored the question for now. "My parents died in a fire."

"Oh my God." Allara's hand covered her mouth. "I'm so sorry."

"It's okay." I shrugged off her concern. "It was a long time ago."

An entire lifetime ago, for me. I barely remembered my parents, and from what I'd been told about my father, I was glad I didn't recall much.

"Okay, well, Reid should be back any minute. He went out for dinner a little while ago. He won't be long."

Allara's gaze slid past me, and her face lit up like it was Christmas morning. "There he is. Reid!"

She waved her free arm in the air like she was hailing a cab.

I turned slowly and stared as a huge man walked toward us. They'd said he was Alpha-sized, but this man was even bigger than I'd expected.

His eyes were dark as was his hair, and in his chin, I saw the family cleft that neither of us had escaped.

This man was my brother. I was certain of it.

He walked up and went straight to his mate's side, possessively sliding a hand around her waist while simultaneously dropping a kiss on top of her head.

Only then did he turn his attention to me. "Hey, I'm Reid." He introduced himself with an easy smile, not a glimmer of recognition on his face.

"Hey." I nodded at the large man, no doubt staring like a wide-eyed fool.

Allara frowned at me, then glanced up at Reid. "Sweetheart, this is Mannix."

I wasn't sure if it was my name or if he suddenly recognized something in my features, but Reid's face transformed. His eyebrows drew together, and his mouth dropped open.

"Man... Did you say, Mannix?"

He was staring at me now with suspicion etched into every line in his face.

I nodded. "Yeah. That's me."

"Jason, take Allara and the baby into the house for me," Reid said, and his tone brooked no argument.

He was all Alpha, from the commanding voice to the straightening of his spine, to the flaring of his nostrils.

He didn't even look at his mate or Jason, he simply directed Allara into Jason's arms and stepped in front of them.

Allara threw me a worried look before she did as Reid had asked and walked back into the house.

The aggression in his stance was sparking the Alpha also in my bloodline. I pushed down my wolf as he rose inside my chest. He wanted to protect me from the threat Reid posed. I'd been raised by Alfred to be the Alpha of my pack, and every part of me wanted to respond to the anger Reid was throwing my way.

But I would not fight him, no matter what happened. I forced my wolf to calm through sheer willpower.

Reid crossed his arms over his chest and stared me down as if sensing the struggle inside me. "What the fuck are you doing here, Mannix? What do you want?"

CHAPTER 2

MANNIX

My mouth dropped open, then my wolf flared back to life inside of me too quickly to stop him. And with that flare-up came the anger.

I stepped forward and only just stopped myself poking him in the chest. My teeth were bared as I growled at him. "What do you mean, *what the fuck am I doing here*? I've been searching for my brother. The one I thought I'd lost decades ago."

Reid crossed his arms over his chest. "Well, that kid died in the woods the way his father wanted him to."

I glared at him. "Really? Because I feel like I'm looking straight at him, so what does that make you? A ghost?"

Reid's mouth tweaked up a little as though he wanted to smile, but he tugged it down quickly.

"Mannix, I don't know what you're looking for, but you're not going to find it here."

"I told you," I said through clenched teeth. "I'm looking for my brother."

"Why now?" he pushed. "What do you want from me?"

I groaned and threw my hands in the air. Of all the different scenarios I'd run through in my head, this was not how any of them had gone.

"Because I only found out you were alive last week! And it's taken me that long to find you."

Reid narrowed his gaze at me. "Oh, really? What changed last week?"

"Alfred died," I said, the pain that sentence brought with it still fresh, still sharp.

"Alfred?" Reid repeated, finally dropping his arms down from the defensively crossed posture he had going on over his chest. "Dad's beta?"

I nodded. "Yeah. He raised me."

Reid's eyes widened. He was shocked. Good. It was about time he felt something of what was going on with me.

"Raised you? Why? What happened to—"

"Mom and Dad died almost twenty years ago," I interrupted. "The same year you disappeared." The year I'd lost my whole family.

Reid's shoulders slumped. "They're *both* dead?"

I nodded. "Yep. Dad set fire to the house and killed them both. Alfred saved me." I'd been unconscious for two days, but I didn't mention that.

Reid sighed and shook his head. "So, he really was insane."

"Pretty much." Just about summed it all up. So much loss and pain. And we were now left standing together, but with a chasm of what seemed to be impossible to fix space between us.

There was a long stretch of silence, and neither of us seemed to be able to break it. I opened my mouth to speak once, then closed it again.

What could I say after that?

As we stood there staring awkwardly at each other in continued silence, a woman came walking up to us, her sunny disposition obvious on her happy face. "Hey, Reid. Is Jason around? I can't find him."

She stepped close enough for me to smell her and I inhaled sharply. "You're human."

Since when did wolf packs invite humans to live with them?

The woman laughed, then stuck her hand out to me. "I'm Tammy, Jason's mate. And you are?"

I liked the woman's spunky attitude and couldn't stop myself from reaching out and shaking her hand. "I'm Mannix."

"Mannix? That's a cool name."

She glanced from Reid to me, then back again. "Are you Reid's family? Visiting town?"

I tilted my head at the human woman. "You can see the resemblance?"

She laughed out loud at that. "You're kidding, right?"

I glanced over at Reid, whose face had transformed into a storm cloud of frustration. Did I look like that? I certainly felt frustrated enough right now. "Yeah, you're right. There are a lot of similarities, I suppose."

"What's the link?" Tammy asked, ignoring Reid's scowl.

I waited for him to answer but when he didn't, I told the truth. "Reid's my older brother and rightful Alpha to my pack."

Tammy's mouth dropped open, and Reid let out a strange growl. "I'm not your Alpha, and that's not my pack. They've got you. I'm sure that's enough."

I glared at him, my hands tightening into fists. "I didn't say I'm not enough! I said that you're the fucking true Alpha of our pack, and if I'd known you were alive, I would have come and fetched you back years ago."

Reid and I glared at each other until Tammy coughed and cleared her throat. "Uh, I didn't mean to say anything to upset everyone. Sorry guys."

Reid tore his gaze away from mine and looked at Tammy instead. "Not your fault. Jason's inside if you want to go see him."

Tammy nodded and raced off.

I slumped. "This was a mistake. You're right."

"You can't seriously think I would just leave my pack—the pack that saved my life twenty years ago. My mate and child. I have a *life*, Mannix. You don't get to walk in and just up-end everything." His voice rose as he spoke, until he was all but yelling at me.

"That wasn't my intention!" I hollered right back at him, unable to believe he'd egged me on into a shouting match.

Why was my brother being such a selfish dickhead? In my mind, he'd always been the perfect one. Obviously, I'd been wrong.

Allara came running down the path, her infant child now missing from her arms. "Hey, enough yelling. I think you two need to come inside for a bit."

"No, I was just leaving," I told her, grabbing my truck keys out of my pocket.

Allara stepped forward and put a warm hand on my arm. "Please. Come inside."

Her words were soft but like with all Alphas, there was steel behind the softness.

I opened my mouth to refuse but she squeezed tighter on my arm. "Come and meet your nephew, Mannix."

My nephew? How could I possibly say no to that request? My heart squeezed so tightly in my chest that I couldn't speak. I just nodded and ignoring my brother, followed her up the path and into the large, double-story house.

Inside, Tammy was holding the baby and her smile lit up her whole face when she saw me step inside. "Oh, good. You came in."

I glanced toward the female Alpha. "Well, I didn't think it would be a smart move to say no to Allara."

Tammy laughed and Jason walked up next to her. "You got that right."

Tammy glanced up at her mate. "How about we give these guys some family time and we go pick up our little girl from your mom?"

Jason grinned down at his mate. "Sounds like a plan."

Allara took her now-sleeping son back from Tammy, and the couple said their goodbyes.

As soon as the front door shut behind them, Allara turned her gaze on me. "Would you like to hold him?"

I put up my hands, palms facing her. *Hell, no!* "Oh, uh… I've never held a baby before."

Never. Ever.

Allara just kept coming at me. "That's normal for men, but it's easy. Here, just hold his head and cradle his back. There you go."

I don't know how it happened, but between Allara pressing the warm bundle into my chest and her soothing words, I soon had my arms wrapped around my nephew. Reid's son.

I stared down at him in wonder. "I can't believe he's still asleep."

"Of course, he is," Allara said. "He's safe with you. He knows that."

I nodded because a lump lodged itself firmly in my throat. Allara didn't know me and yet somehow, I felt her acceptance. Too bad my brother didn't feel the same way.

"So, tell us," Allara began. "How did you come to be here in our town?"

The Alpha moved over to the couch opposite me and sat down. She indicated to the large chair behind me. "Sit."

I didn't know how I was supposed to do that while holding a baby, but I managed to hold him tight, then squat until finally I was seated. "Phew."

Allara grinned and crossed her legs, sitting up straighter. "Talk."

I glanced around and realized Reid had also come inside. He was in the kitchen, busying himself with something. What, I wasn't sure. But his mate was in charge now, that was clear.

"I... like I told Reid... my parents died the year my brother disappeared."

"What do you mean disappeared? What happened to cause him to end up in our forest? And how far away is your pack?"

She was all business now, and I didn't mind. It soothed my frazzled nerves to answer questions rather than think of things to say. I had nothing to hide.

"Our pack lands are around two hundred miles north of here."

"Two hundred? What the hell was a kid Reid's age doing down here, alone, barely dressed for a winter's day?"

I glanced up from the angelic little face I'd been looking at and stared at Allara. "My father dropped him off in the forest and told him to find his own way back."

Allara shot to her feet, her eyes blazing as her wolf rose. "He. Fucking. *What?*"

"Allara, leave it," Reid called from the kitchen. He'd obviously been listening to our conversation, and he moved to the doorway to stare at us.

"You never told me that!" she hissed at her mate.

I looked over at Reid, who shrugged. "It's pretty hazy to me. I was half dead by the time Emma found me and you guys took me in."

Allara bristled and growled some more, then huffed and sat back down again. "So, your dad was an asshole. Got it. Go on."

"A crazy asshole," I corrected her. "The pack all assumed Reid had died, then that same year, my dad started a fire in our house, killed my mom and himself, and I was saved by my dad's beta, Alfred, who raised me."

She gulped, silent for a long moment. Then she said, "I'm so sorry. That must have been terrible."

"To lose my whole family in a single year? Yeah, it was. But at least I had Alfred."

I still remember the crash of the glass as Alfred broke through the window to drag me out of the smoke and flames into the cold night air. He'd saved me and the pack, that night.

"Okay. So, what brings you to this point?" she asked, getting back on track. "Coming here, to find Reid."

"Well, like everyone, I'd always been under the impression Reid had died. No one expected him to survive what my dad did to him, and I was only five at the time. When I was told Reid had died, I believed it."

Reid made a hmph noise from where he'd retreated to the kitchen, and I continued, "But last week, the night Alfred died, he told me he believed Reid was still alive. That he'd heard stories at town meetings and from other pack Alphas, that there was a female Alpha far down south who'd married a foundling. A man everyone said was an Alpha's size." I stopped to swallow the lump that had risen once more. "That he was kind and gentle. Quiet. But as loyal as the day is long."

The tears actually blinded me now, so I dropped my head and stared at my nephew. "The description sounded like how I remembered Reid."

"That is Reid," Allara said quietly.

I nodded, not looking up. "So, I made sure my betas had everything they needed to survive without me for a while, bought a cell phone even though I detest the things, and I headed south."

"To find him? To find Reid?"

I nodded again. "Yeah." The only family I had left.

CHAPTER 3

MANNIX

The silence around me was heavy and hot. Like a day with too much sun, a little rain, and clouds that blocked it all in.

Allara cleared her throat. "Well, you've found him, Mannix. You've found your older brother. So... what's the plan now?"

I sighed. I didn't really have a plan. "I don't know. The odds of finding Reid were so slim, I... didn't really think past that point." And if I had, I probably would have wanted my brother to come home with me.

Now that I looked at it properly, it was becoming clear that half-formed plan wasn't even a consideration.

"Well, there's a lot to discuss," Allara said, sitting straighter and taller, if that were possible.

"Like what?" I asked, then shifted position on the chair.

I must have done it wrong because the baby began to squirm, his little face scrunching up in an angry way.

Panic hit me and I extended my arms out to the female Alpha. "I think he wants you."

Allara got up from her chair and scooped up the baby with a practiced move. "Thanks. He'll be getting hungry."

She walked over to Reid in the kitchen and whispered to him so quietly that even my wolf hearing couldn't pick up her words.

"Back soon," she called out to me. "I'm going to go feed him in the bedroom." Then she disappeared from sight, and I was left alone with my brother.

I slumped against the back of the recliner, finally feeling the exhaustion from the week of travel. The high expectations, and the subsequent low outcome. What had I anticipated, really? For Reid to just welcome me into his new family with open arms?

I got to my feet, bone-weary. "Is there anywhere I can stay tonight? I'd head back to my pack now if I could, but I haven't gotten much sleep this week." And I honestly wasn't sure it was safe for me to drive at the moment.

The last thing my pack needed was another dead Alpha.

"There should be. There's a couple of people in town that have accommodations they rent out to pack visitors."

"I've got money, so I can pay," I confirmed, lifting my chin. "I don't need charity. Or, if you'd prefer, I can find a motel somewhere nearby."

"No." Reid shook his head as though fighting with himself. "Allara... uh, she wants you to stick around today so we can sort some shit out."

"What sort of shit?" Why did they keep thinking I'd come here with an ulterior motive?

Reid frowned at me. "I assume I have to sign something to say that I relinquish succession to the title. I don't want to be Alpha. It's all yours."

Oh, that. Yeah. Whatever.

I nodded. "There probably is, but I didn't bring it with me."

Hadn't even thought about it. Not really. I'd just gotten in my truck and left. Alfred had always said I was too impulsive, but I'd never agreed. Until now.

Reid crossed his arms over his massive chest. "You came all this way to find me and didn't bring anything with you that would let me sign over the role to you?"

I squeezed the bridge of my nose and inhaled sharply. I'd had a dull headache for a couple of days, but it was building into one hell of a migraine. "Look, brother, I don't really care what you believe or don't. I'll head home tomorrow, with or without your stupid signature. Just point me in the direction of a bed and somewhere I can rest for a few hours. I'd appreciate it."

It took everything in me to say the words with a little patience and not bite Reid's head off. He may not care one way or the other if he had a brother, but I did. Even a bull-headed one like Reid. His rejection was strange and painful, to say the least.

"Okay. Yeah. Let me walk you over to Amelie's place. She could use the extra cash if you're willing to chip in for food and stuff."

"Sure," I said, sighing heavily. "Let's go."

I turned toward the door as my brother walked past me. Then I followed Reid outside into the sunshine, blinking rapidly as pain exploded in my head. I must have groaned or something because Reid turned around. "What's wrong?"

I glanced down, unable to open my eyes fully now. "Migraine. I can't... see properly."

Shit. The flashing lights, the tunnel vision. I was in trouble now.

Reid's hand grabbed my elbow. "Amelie's place is only about a hundred feet up the road. Just walk, and I'll get you there."

I nodded and let him lead the way, though the panic in my gut was intense. I hated this. The vulnerability. I had no idea where I was going or who could see me stumbling along the road like an idiot.

It was the worst feeling for a wolf shifter, let alone an Alpha. Someone could attack me right now and I'd have no way of defending myself.

"Almost there," Reid said gruffly.

"Stop it. I'm fine," I growled back. He was feeling sorry for me, I could hear it in his tone. But I didn't want his damn pity.

"This happen often?" he asked.

I shrugged, tripping over something on the pavement, but Reid held me firmly and I didn't hit the deck. "Ah. Not really. Once or twice a year." Sometimes more if I was stressed.

"We're here. Two steps up to the porch, okay?"

I forced my eyes open to slits and lifted my legs to walk up the stairs. Fuck, the pounding had begun like a tiny pixie stood inside my brain, hitting it like my neurons were an anvil.

Reid knocked loudly and I leaned into him a bit. This sucked. Big time.

A woman spoke, and she had the sweetest voice I'd ever heard. "Reid. Who's this?"

I would have laughed at how suspicious she sounded, if it wasn't for the pain in my head.

"This is Mannix," Reid said, then paused.

I waited. Was he going to introduce me properly or brush over it like our connection was nothing? Probably the latter.

"He's my brother," he said, surprising me, though the anger behind the words hinted at the fact he wasn't happy about the connection.

Amelie's gasp was audible. "Oh my God. How... Why..."

"I'll explain later, but he needs your help. Can he stay here tonight?"

"Sure. I've got the guest room set up. But what's wrong with him?"

"He can speak for himself," I grunted. Then I groaned, destroying any illusion of being all right. "Migraine," I managed, and Amelie gasped again, loudly. I frowned in her direction though I didn't have a hope of seeing her. "Are you okay? I'm sorry, my head's so bad I can't open my eyes at the moment."

Which meant I couldn't gauge her reaction to a stranger turning up at her house.

"Bring him inside, Reid." Her no-nonsense attitude was one I was very familiar with. She sounded faintly like Allara. "I'll draw the blinds and bring you water. This way, Mannix."

I stumbled forward and Reid grabbed me again. Together, they managed to get me inside, with Amelie calling out instructions and Reid stopping me from falling on my face. Being inside and out of the sunshine helped with the pain a tiny bit, at least.

Then I was led to a dark room, where I sat down on a soft bed.

I sighed and relaxed my eyes so I wasn't keeping them squeezed shut any longer. The pain wasn't better, but it wasn't getting any worse, which was a good sign.

Amelie sat next to me and handed me a glass of water. "Drink this and take a couple of Advil." She placed the pills into my palm, and I squeezed them to avoid dropping them.

"They don't really help," I told her, inhaling her scent.

"Take them anyway. They'll help you sleep."

She smelled amazing. Even in my pain-drenched state, I couldn't help but notice her scent of honey and cinnamon.

"Have you been baking?" I asked to make conversation, then put my hand to my mouth and swallowed down the painkillers.

"No. Why do you ask? Are you hungry?"

I was, but I couldn't eat when I was like this. It wouldn't stay in my stomach long. "No. I didn't mean it like that. I can just smell honey and cinnamon. It's really strong."

There was silence around me. Why, I had no idea. Had I offended her in some way?

"It's a nice scent," I reassured her, then swayed where I sat. "I'm sorry, but I think I'm going to have to lie down." Before I did something stupid like fall down or vomit in front of her.

"I'll just wait in the kitchen." Reid said, and seemed to disappear, the room seeming bigger all of a sudden.

Amelie jumped up, then she softly pressed on my shoulder. "You can lie down now."

I did and groaned. The whole bed smelled like fresh honey cakes. Must be her detergent or something. "Thank you."

I lifted my legs and Amelie pulled off my shoes.

"I'm sorry they're not clean," I apologized. "And thank you for this. I... didn't time this too well, did I?"

I felt like a complete fool and must look weak to both of them. What sort of Alpha let himself get turned inside out by a simple headache?

"My dad used to get migraines. Bad ones," Amelie said, her sweet voice floating around me. "So I know how bad they can be. The water's on the nightstand next to you."

Footsteps sounded and I turned onto my side, nestling into the pillow, the scent now fading as Amelie walked away.

"Thank you again," I managed, the throbbing intensity in my head lessening as sleep called.

"If you need anything, call out and I'll come immediately," she said. "Get some sleep."

"Thanks."

The door shut and I sighed heavily. What a fucking horrible day. It had its perks, of course. My brother was alive, which meant my father hadn't killed him all those years ago. That was a great thing.

But Reid wanted me to leave. That definitely wasn't a highlight of the day.

I let sleep claim me. The faster I could get better, the faster I could return home and get back to my old life.

Such as it was.

AMELIE

My heart was thundering a million miles an hour. The smell of Mannix, the sound of his voice, were too much for my starved system to take and now every single part of me was on high alert.

"Reid... he... ah..." I was shaking like a leaf as I stood in my kitchen, trying to get myself together. This was never meant to happen.

I put my hand up to my mouth, feeling the quiver right to my lips. "I..."

Too shocked to speak further, I didn't know what to say.

Reid, my Alpha's mate, stood in the kitchen nearby, staring at me like he had no idea what I was so worked up about. Even I didn't know what was going on. Not really. I'd heard of this happening, of course. But I'd never experienced it, not personally.

"Amelie," Reid said quietly, taking control of the conversation after words failed me. "Did you just... well... I don't even know how to phrase this question."

I wrapped my arms around my body and nodded my head. "He smells better than anything I've ever come into contact with. And the sound of his voice..."

A shiver coursed through my body at the memory of Mannix's voice. The moment I laid eyes on him I'd known something strange was going on, but after he spoke... Wow. Everything inside of me—my heart, my belly, lower down even—it all lit up like fully charged lights on a Christmas tree.

"Makes you happier than you ever thought possible?" Reid finished.

I nodded before I even thought about it. But how was this even possible? Mannix was a complete stranger. He had no right to make me feel anything at all, much less happy.

I lifted my gaze and stared at Reid. His eyes told me that he knew exactly what I was talking about.

"Is this how it feels?" I asked, a cold wave rushing over me followed by a hot ripple. It was like my system had kicked into overdrive and didn't know how to behave.

"When you find your mate?" Reid asked. "Yeah. Though I was only eight when I met Allara, so it didn't feel quite as intense for me back then."

I shook myself and stared hard at him. "Did you just say mate? I *had* a mate, Reid. You know that. And you also know he's dead."

Reid tilted his head and pressed his hands onto the countertop. "Yes, I know. You were mated to someone you loved, Amelie. But that's not the same thing as being fated. We both know that."

I trembled, adrenaline coursing through me. I needed to run. Shift.

"I have questions, Reid, but I need to go."

"Yes, go," he said. "I'll stay, in case Mannix wakes and needs anything."

The shift was coming, and without any control left whatsoever, I could barely speak. "If Lacey comes back. Tell her... I..."

I shook my head. Words were gone. He could see that, and he moved to the front door and opened it for me.

"I will. Go."

I allowed my black wolf to come forward, bursting up inside of me and taking over my humanity. I dropped to the ground, my skin sprouting with fur and my hands turning into paws with long nails that clicked on the floor.

My wolf took over and I didn't fight it, I just ran. Out the front door, down the road and into the woods.

I had to get away.

It couldn't be true. It couldn't.

I knew what Reid had been trying to tell me. That Mannix was my fated mate, the same way Allara was Reid's.

Fated mates had been considered a myth when I was young. Something only the rarest and most special couples had. But it was becoming more common, and often talked about in our pack and neighboring ones.

That was fine for them, of course. For people like Allara and Reid. But I'd never thought the same thing would come for me. I'd had my mate. My husband. My childhood sweetheart, Evan.

We'd been married for five years before he was killed in a pack war. My heart had been broken beyond repair, but our daughter Lacey had been only four years old at the time, and she'd needed me. My love for her was the only thing that wouldn't allow me to follow my husband into an early grave.

My daughter had needed me. She still did. She was nine now, and the love of my life. She was all I needed. I had told myself that for years, and I was certain it was still true despite the scent of Reid's brother that enticed me the way nothing had ever before.

I ran and ran, until my breathing was labored and my heart pounded even faster than it had when I first met Mannix and realized how special he was to me.

When I was finally exhausted, I turned and headed home again. I didn't know what I was going to do, but having another mate wasn't of any interest to me. And my daughter didn't need a stepfather.

By the time I got back to my house—the house my husband had built for me—I was calm. Well, calmish. Mannix didn't need to know we were fated mates, and he could go back to wherever he came from, none the wiser.

I trotted up the front steps, still in wolf form, to find Reid standing in the foyer waiting for me. "Hey, you okay?"

I didn't want to shift back and have to answer him, so I brushed past his leg on the way to my room. I did appreciate him waiting to see if I was all right.

As soon as I reached my room, I shifted back and shut the door. My skin was covered in sweat, so I jumped in the shower and washed. I could be hospitable enough, surely? I mean, Mannix was still likely out of it if his migraines were anything like the ones my father used to get.

I dressed quickly, in old jeans and a long-sleeved sweater. For some reason, I assumed that if I was more covered up, Mannix wouldn't be able to sense the truth. As I left the room, I checked my hair, and pulled it up into a high ponytail.

When I was finally satisfied that I looked presentable but in no way sexy, I walked out of my bedroom and into the family room once more. The Alpha's mate was still standing in my kitchen.

"Thank you so much for staying, Reid. Has Lacey come home yet?"

He shook his head. "No. It's just been me, here alone. Other than Mannix, of course, but I checked a little while ago. He's still sleeping."

I grinned at him. "Alone? You make that sound like a horrendous thing."

Personally, I kind of liked being alone.

He crossed his arms over his chest. "I've never liked being alone. Not since I was a kid."

I nodded and sighed. "Yeah, I get that."

Reid had been abandoned by his family and found by our pack. He'd been alone for a long time, wandering around trying to survive the elements and hunger. Probably trying to make his way back to his pack, the poor kid.

"Are you sure it's okay for Mannix to stay here?" Reid asked. "If you're not comfortable..."

"No. I'll be okay. It won't be for long." Surely, he'd want to go home soon?

Reid nodded his head. "Once he's better, I'll sign whatever I need to, and he can go back to his own pack and be the rightful Alpha."

I swallowed hard, my throat thickening with emotion. "He's the Alpha of his pack?"

Reid grunted. "Yeah, he is."

There was definitely a story there, but not one Reid wanted to talk about, obviously. "Okay, well, I'll let him sleep and look after him until he's better. You go home to your mate and new baby."

Reid walked to my front door. "All right. But come get me if you need me."

"I will." I showed him out the door.

Once Reid left, taking his bristling energy with him, I could breathe a little easier. Not long after, there was a little knock on the door. "Mommy."

"Oh!" I twisted around and opened the door for my little girl. "Hey, baby."

She rolled her eyes at me. "Not a baby."

I laughed. "I know. But you're *my* baby, and you'll always be my baby. Now tell me, how was school?"

Lacey chattered away while I made her an after-school snack, and I was grateful for the way she filled the silence. It went at least a little way to curb the storm of emotions and uncertainty that currently raged through me.

"Mom?" Lacey asked suddenly.

"Yeah, bub?"

"Is there someone here?"

I turned from where I was chopping vegetables for dinner. My stomach twisted and I reminded myself that I hadn't done anything wrong.

"Yeah, sweetie. Reid's younger brother is staying with our pack for a few days, and they told him he could rent a room here."

Lacey tilted her head, obviously confused. "Reid's brother? I didn't know Reid had a family."

"Yeah, Reid didn't either, apparently," came a deep voice from the hallway.

Lacey and I both twisted to see Mannix standing in the kitchen entrance, squinting so hard I could barely see his features.

I swallowed the sudden lump in my throat and put a smile on my face for my daughter's sake. "Lacey, this is Mannix. Mannix, I'm not sure if you can see her, but this is my nine year old daughter, Lacey."

I gave him her age details so he could curb his language if necessary.

He smiled and inclined his head. "Nice to meet you, Lacey. I'm sorry I look like this, but I still can't quite open my eyes."

Lacey hopped straight off her seat and went to him, reaching for his hand so quickly it made Mannix and me both jump. "It's okay. Do you need my help?" she asked.

Hot tears burned in my eyes. Lacey had never shown any affection toward a man other than her father. I couldn't believe she'd run straight up to him like that.

"I'm fine, Lacey. I just need your mom to show me where the bath-room is. Then I'll climb back into bed."

I walked over to him, anxious to separate my daughter from him. "I'll show you."

"I can show him, Mom." Lacey turned Mannix around. "What's wrong with you?"

I reached for her. "Oh, honey, that's not appropriate to ask."

"I've got a migraine, Lacey," Mannix told her gently, not moving his feet despite Lacey's insistence. "But I'd prefer if your mom took me. Is that okay?"

Her face scrunched up. "If she has to."

My heart lurched at her obvious disappointment. "How about you make Mannix a sandwich, and we'll meet you in the guest room?"

"Oh, yeah!" Lacey said, jumping up and down. "Do you like peanut butter and jelly?"

"Love it," Mannix said, with more of a grimace than a smile.

"Okay!" She raced off.

I took Mannix's hand, shivering at the instant electric attraction that pulsed through my body at the slightest touch. "Thank you for being so kind to her."

He shrugged. "Seems like a nice kid. Sorry I'm such a nuisance."

I led him down the hall. "The bathroom's here, to your left. Walk forward. And toilet's just in front of you."

For one single moment I considered asking him if he needed help with his pants, then backed up toward the door so fast I whacked my shoulder on the door frame, my face aflame. "I'll wait for you outside. Then help you back to bed, okay?"

He nodded, fumbling with his jeans. "Thanks so much, Amelie."

I turned away and wrapped my arms around myself, a strange sort of squeal lodged in my chest.

When I was around Mannix I felt more alive than I had in more years that I could count. And although it was fucking terrifying, I had to admit it was also exciting.

CHAPTER 5

MANNIX

After forcing down the sandwich made by Lacey, I fell asleep.

When I woke up, I could tell several hours had passed. The pain had lifted but there was that horrible hung-over effect still weighing me down. I rolled out of bed, needing to piss again and stinking of sweat.

Definitely need a shower.

I stumbled to the bedroom door and opened it. The house was blessedly dark, except for a small light on down the hall. I followed the light and found the woman I assumed was Amelie, reading under a lamp, curled up on the sofa.

"Hey," I croaked out.

She jumped, her face flashing with surprise before she said, "You scared me."

I smiled. "Sorry. I was just wondering if I could take a shower, please?"

Now that the migraine was beginning to clear, I could see she was a lot prettier than I'd realized, with long dark hair, bright eyes, and a heart-shaped face. When she got to her feet smoothly, gracefully, I was hit with a deep longing I'd never felt before. I rubbed my chest where my heart ached and coughed to try and clear the strange sensation.

"I'll get you some clean towels and show you where everything is."

I nodded, unable to respond while my wolf growled, unsettled within me.

She walked me to the same bathroom I'd used before and began pointing out the soap and towels.

"Thank you, Amelie. I really can't... tell you... how much I appreciate this." I could barely talk and sounded like an idiot, but she just smiled at me.

"I'll get you some water and a proper dinner. Take your time." She left the bathroom and closed the door.

I groaned and sank onto the toilet seat, not sure what to do with all the emotions pulsing through me.

Was I that starved for female companionship that I was hitting on the woman who was being paid to look after me? Surely not.

I forced myself to my feet and turned on the shower. Time to wash away several days of stress and grief. I might smell a bit better for my host as well.

After my shower, where I spent half the time aroused surrounded by Amelie's scent, I climbed out and dried off. What was wrong with me? A migraine had never caused heart flutters and a hard-on before.

"Shit." My fresh clothes were in my car, a long way from here.

I wrapped the towel around my waist and ventured out into the quiet house. Amelie was in the kitchen, doing dishes. The smell of comfort food was in the air.

"Hi, I, uh..." I ran my hand through my wet hair and gave her a bashful smile. I had to work really hard not to let my body spring to attention the moment she laid eyes on me. "I didn't bring any clothes with me. I'm sorry. My bag's in my truck. At your Alpha's house."

Amelie stared at me like she'd never seen a man before. Her eyes were wide, and her mouth hung partly open.

"Are you okay?" I asked her.

She was a wolf shifter, just like me. We were used to seeing people naked; it was part of the culture of our people. I might have an Alpha's physique, but beyond that, I was sure there was nothing special about me to cause that expression on her face.

She nodded suddenly and began moving around the room, almost frenetic as she tidied things that didn't need tidying. "I've made a meatloaf with mashed potatoes, gravy and corn for your dinner. Come eat, and I'll run down to Allara's place for your clothes."

I took a step toward the bedroom. "I can get them."

"No!" she practically yelled at me. "Don't go out like that, I'll... I have to chat with Allara about pack business anyway. It's fine. Just get me your car keys and I'll go."

She was acting nervous and weird. I wasn't sure why, but I did what she asked. I grabbed my truck keys from my room and slid them onto the kitchen counter for her.

"Sorry I couldn't put my old clothes back on. They were past it a few days ago."

Amelie took the keys and pushed a plate with a large piece serve of meatloaf over to me. "You eat. I won't be long."

She dashed away quickly and I sat on the kitchen stool, the scent of a well-seasoned meatloaf drifting up to entice my senses. I groaned as my stomach twisted and turned. I hadn't had a home-cooked meal for a few weeks, and this smelled incredible.

I dug in, polishing off my plate before she came back. It was perfect. Creamy mashed potatoes, buttery corn. "Yum."

I carried the plate to the sink, washed the dishes, then poured myself a glass of water. The cold liquid was refreshing and perfect against my hot throat and dehydrated body.

When the front door opened again, I made sure the towel was secured properly and turned to face her.

She was holding my duffle bag, her face pink from running, I assumed.

"Thanks so much." I held my towel knot in one hand and reached for the bag with my other. "I'll go get dressed. What time is it?"

"About ten o'clock," she answered, swallowing hard. "I'll be up for a little while if you wanna talk. Otherwise, I've got some more ibuprofen if you want to go straight back to bed."

Only if you'll join me.

The errant thought came out of nowhere and I turned away, annoyed at myself once more for lusting after a woman who was obviously just trying to be a good hostess. And she was likely involved with someone already. After all, she had a child.

"Will your husband be home soon? I don't want to upset anyone with my presence."

When she didn't immediately respond, I flicked my gaze back to her face to find she'd paled.

"Um... my husband died five years ago. So, you won't upset anyone if you want to just sit and talk. I can make hot cocoa?"

I sighed, a sense of relaxation unexpectedly washing over me. It had been a while since someone had made me a hot drink and wanted to sit and chat. It was one of the things I would miss about Alfred when I got back home—our quiet camaraderie in the evenings.

"That would be great actually, thanks. I'll be right back."

I went to my room, changed into sweatpants and a t-shirt, and returned to the living room to find her placing hot drinks on the coffee table.

"Here you go." She gestured to one of the mugs, then immediately slid into the recliner chair, leaving the sofa for me.

I sat, feeling the ache of my migraine still present in my head. "Thanks for this. You have no idea how nice it is just to stop for a minute."

She tucked her legs up under her like a teenager and smiled at me. "You've had a rough couple of weeks?"

I laughed but the sound was brittle. "Ah, yeah. My parents died when I was little, and the man who raised me—Alfred—died just over a week ago." I paused to consider the date. "Actually, around two weeks ago now. I've been on the go pretty much ever since. He told me about Reid being alive the night before he passed."

I reached for the mug of cocoa and took a sip. Perfect. Not too sweet, but the milk was creamy.

"I'm so sorry," Amelie said, taking her hair out of the ponytail it was pulled up in and tucking her long, dark brown hair behind her ears.

She looked younger with her hair down, and even prettier. Damn it.

"It's okay. He was a great surrogate father. But he was old and in pain at the end. On his deathbed, when he told me he thought Reid was still alive, I was so angry at him." I shook my head. "I shouldn't have been. I know he was only trying to protect me, but it was wrong to keep that from me. I could have found my brother years earlier, if I'd had any idea."

She smiled softly. "You were lied to your whole life. That's bound to hurt. Anger is understandable in those circumstances. Must have been tough."

"It was. But I gave Alfred a respectful send-off, made sure my pack would be okay without me there for a while, and headed off to find my big brother." I grimaced. The outcome of my journey had not exactly been what I planned.

"Well, you found him," she said in a matter-of-fact tone.

I nodded. "Yep, I did."

"Then why are you so upset?"

I stared at her. Didn't she know? "Because my brother wants nothing to do with me. He thinks I'm here to fight him for Alpha or something."

I tsked, disgusted with the very idea of it.

"You're Alpha-born?" Her tone was strange. High.

"Yeah." I shrugged. "Reid's the Alpha. I was just the spare." I'd never felt like the Alpha of my pack. Did I love my people? Would I die for my pack? Absolutely. But did I feel right in my position? No.

"You don't sound like you want the job."

I stared at her. Was that a question? "I don't have a choice. It's my responsibility to look after my pack, especially now that Alfred's gone."

"It's a lot to deal with," she said. "Losing your adoptive father, then dealing with Reid's..." She trailed off as though she didn't know how to finish that sentence.

"Rejection?" I finished it for her, my tone bitter.

She shook her head. "I don't think it's a rejection. He just... doesn't know how to process it all."

I huffed out a laugh, though none of this was funny. "Yeah. Whatever."

"I didn't mean it in an offensive way." She sighed. "I was here when they found Reid. I'm a few years older than him, and I—"

"You're kidding," I interrupted, shock running through me. "You look about twenty-five!" My age.

She grinned. "Thanks, but I'm thirty-two."

I nodded slowly. The older woman, huh?

"Anyway, I was here when they found him," she said. "Half frozen, pale as death. He didn't speak for months. It was like he'd died out there, the soul of him anyway. But his body had kept walking, determined to save him." She shook her head. "It was horrible."

"It *was* horrible," I repeated. "What my father did to him was inexcusable."

"Your father?" She blinked at me like an owl, her eyes wide and shocked.

I nodded. "Yep. He left Reid in the middle of nowhere, then came home and killed my mother and himself in a fire later that same year."

We were cursed, my family. Reid had managed to rebuild his life, and I'd only survived because Alfred had saved me. And now that he was gone, I wasn't sure what I was going to do.

"But you survived," she whispered.

"I wasn't meant to," I told her. "I should have died in that fire too. Alfred pulled me out and saved me."

There was a long silence. What was she thinking? That I should never have come looking for my brother? Yeah, that was what I was thinking now, too.

When I couldn't handle the silence any longer, I got to my feet. "Thank you so much for the care you've shown me today, Amelie, but I think I'll go to bed. I've got a long drive back home tomorrow."

She hopped up too. "You're leaving that soon? I was under the impression from Reid you'd be here a couple of days. He said something about paperwork needing signatures?"

I shrugged. "No one wants me here, least of all my brother. So, I think it's best for all of us if I return to my own pack."

"Do you have a wife?" she asked suddenly. "A mate?"

I shook my head. "No. I don't." I'd never been interested in tying a woman down to my cursed family. And if I ever had a child, would the madness of my father flow on down to them through my genes?

It wasn't worth the risk.

"Good night," I said to her, my head swimming in the strange way that I'd begun to identify with being near Amelie.

"I'll come with you and change your sheets." She hurried to stand next to me. "Nothing worse than climbing into a set of dirty sheets after a clean shower."

I smiled at her kindness. "Yeah, but I was the one who made the sheets dirty." I was certain that those sheets had been clean before I ruined them.

She kept walking past me. "Just give me a minute."

She grabbed fresh linen out of a closet in the hallway and headed into my bedroom.

I pressed a hand to my head, the pain from the post-migraine stage coming back in force now that Amelie had moved away.

I couldn't figure out if she had some sort of magical healing gift, or if there was something more significant going on here. My head was too fuzzy still.

When I swayed with exhaustion, I decided it was time to follow her.

She was just fluffing up the blankets when I walked into the room, her scent filling the air and making my wolf dance inside my chest.

"Thank you. Again." I rested against the door frame. "You've been really great about this."

She gathered up all the dirty linens, holding them in her arms. "No problem. I've been happy to help."

She went to move past me and my wolf leapt within me, forcing a growl from my throat.

Amelie jumped back into my room, and I shook myself. "I'm so sorry. I don't even know what caused that."

Her mouth quivered as she forced a smile. "It's okay. You've had a difficult few days."

"Yeah, that must be it."

This time she slipped past me without incident, and I forced myself to climb between into the freshly made bed and rest. My heart pounded, and my wolf clamored to be heard. There was something special about that woman, but I had no idea what it was.

CHAPTER 6
AMELIE

I practically ran to the laundry room after almost getting trapped in Mannix's bedroom by his wolf.

The last thing I needed was for my wolf to bond with his. Then I'd be fucked, both literally and figuratively. There'd be no escaping fate then.

Instead, I ran from him as fast as I could. I washed the sheets, went to bed, and spent a fitful night trying to get some sleep.

By the time the sun rose, I was exhausted, but I could hear Lacey getting up and moving around. I didn't want her running into a half-naked Mannix, so I hauled myself out of bed to make her breakfast.

"Good morning, baby," I greeted her as I entered the kitchen. She was already dressed for school, which was great. "What would you like for breakfast? Waffles? Toast? Bacon and eggs?"

"Is Mannix coming out for breakfast?" she asked, her face alight in a way I'd never seen before.

"Why, sweetie?"

"I just wanted to see him before I went to school, that's all."

I tilted my head at her, not sure how to approach that. "Well, Mannix could sleep a lot today, honey. He was in a lot of pain yesterday. How about you come eat, and if he gets up, then great. If he doesn't, you might see him later."

Assuming he didn't just get in his truck and go, like he was saying he would when they spoke last night.

"Ohhhhkay," she said, pouting like I'd told her she had to eat broccoli for breakfast.

"How about waffles with syrup and strawberries? I have some fresh berries from Tony."

Lacey nodded, but her gaze kept flicking toward the hallway where Mannix's room was situated.

I turned away, not wanting to see the look of yearning on my daughter's face for the stranger for whom I too felt connected. *Way too connected.* As Reid's *younger* brother, then he was definitely several years younger than me, and it felt a little strange lusting after him the way I did.

But I had an excuse of sorts. I hadn't been with a man since my husband had died.

My daughter, however, was feeling connected to him on another level. More than anything, I hoped it was just a passing interest and not part of the fated mate link I felt toward the Alpha-born male. As my blood ran through Lacey's veins, she would naturally gravitate to Mannix as a father figure, and that seemed somehow disloyal to Evan's memory.

I hurried to the pantry and pulled out the flour, eggs and sugar.

Then a door opened from the hallway and Lacey shrieked, "Mannix! You're up! Mom's making breakfast."

I didn't turn around, my stomach suddenly so twisted up in knots it took me a minute to collect myself. I concentrated on getting out the wooden spoon and bowl, then slowly lifted my head to watch him approach.

I couldn't help but notice he moved like an Alpha, slowly, and with purpose. He exuded strength and reliability.

He'd be deadly in a fight.

"Would you like some waffles?" I managed while Lacey rushed over to Mannix and grabbed his hand, pulling him to one of the stools perched near my countertop.

I couldn't stop staring at how comfortable Lacey was with him. She'd never shown affection to any of the other men in town. She barely even hugged my dad, her own grandfather.

So, what was this?

Mannix slid onto the stool, pushing his thick dark hair back off his forehead. "Yeah, waffles sound amazing."

"Are you feeling any better?" I asked, pouring him a glass of water and giving it to him before I got back into the stirring and mixing of the waffle batter.

"Yeah, definitely." He narrowed his eyes at me as though he hadn't really seen me before. "I couldn't sense a whole lot yesterday. I was kind of out of my head, so I'm sorry if I said or did anything to offend you."

I smiled and pulled out the waffle iron. "You were totally fine."

I went about slicing strawberries and getting breakfast ready while Lacey chatted to Mannix. "Do you want to come to school with me?"

I almost laughed, but kept on cooking, interested in how he would handle a nine year old girl.

"School? Really? That's cool you guys get to go to a real school. We didn't have that where I grew up."

My ears pricked up, listening to him.

"You're lucky!" Lacey gushed.

"Oh, no, I wasn't," Mannix told her. "It meant I had to get out to work and help the pack. At your age, I was building houses and helping with the farming. I would have much preferred to be at school with my friends, learning reading and writing."

"How come you didn't have a school?" she asked.

A question I wanted to know the answer to as well.

"Well, my pack was in a bit of trouble after our Alpha died. People were unhappy, and the place was falling apart. So, I helped the new Alpha to get everything back on track. But it took a while. I was only five or six years old back then."

My heart ached, listening to Mannix explain something that would have been so tough, yet make it simple so Lacey could understand.

"Well, maybe you should come to school with me," she said. "My teacher can teach you how to read and write now."

Mannix chuckled and the deep, soothing sound rolled around the kitchen, making me shiver.

"I'd love to, Lacey, but I have to get going later today. Maybe if I come back and visit Reid again, I could take you up on your offer?"

"You're leaving?" Lacey cried. "No. You have to stay."

I served up the waffles covered in strawberries and syrup and turned to address my daughter. "Mannix doesn't live here, sweetheart. If he has to go home, we can't stop him from leaving."

"But he's meant to be here, Mom. Don't you feel it?" Lacey pleaded with me, her eyes filled with more emotion than I could fathom.

I pushed the plates toward them, feeling sick to my stomach. "You two eat. I have to use the bathroom. I won't be long."

And I ran.

When I reached the bathroom, my heart was pounding. Could Lacey really feel that sort of connection to Mannix? That didn't make any sense. Why would she?

I washed my face and brushed my teeth, needing breakfast but too twisted up inside to consider eating anything.

When I made it back to the kitchen, Lacey was packing her lunch and Mannix was slowly finishing the pile of waffles I'd put in front of him.

"You okay?" I asked Lacey, reaching for her.

She tugged out of my grip, grabbing some fruit off the table and the water bottle from the fridge. "You two are stupid," she said.

Then she left.

I stared after her, my mouth open. My daughter had never spoken to me like that. Ever.

I turned back to my house guest. "I'm so sorry, I don't know what's gotten into her."

Mannix's eyes were different this morning. They were clear, bright, alert. He was noticing things he hadn't yesterday, which likely wasn't good for me.

"I think she knows something we don't," he said quietly.

I shrugged and started doing the dishes. "Kids are funny. So, should I pack you a lunch to take with you, or what are your plans?"

Mannix stood up and glared at me. "Can't wait to get rid of me, huh?"

"Oh, no, it's not that," I rushed to say, though even to my ears my voice was too high.

Mannix crossed his arms over his chest, the muscles in his forearms bulging in front of my eyes. "Then what is it, Amelie?"

"Nothing." I shook my head. "You're the one who said you needed to leave. That Reid didn't want you here."

Pain flashed across his handsome face, and I felt instantly guilty. "I didn't mean to say it like that."

Mannix sighed. "I'll go. The only person who wants me around is your nine-year-old. Not exactly a ringing endorsement for staying."

He marched off to his room, I assumed to collect his things and go.

My heart cried out for him not to leave, and my wolf prowled angrily inside my chest. I wanted to listen to my own heart, but every self-preservation warning system rang bells in my head not to.

I had to stay away from Mannix. It was obvious he was dangerous to me.

When he emerged a few minutes later, he'd pulled on a hoodie and had his bag in his hand. "Thank you for yesterday," he managed, then placed some fifty-dollar bills on my counter.

"Oh, that's way too much," I said, rushing to grab the money and give it back to him.

"No. It's not." He walked toward my door. "Bye, Amelie."

Then he walked through my front door and shut it behind him. I was left, clutching two hundred dollars and experiencing an ache in my chest the size of Texas.

"Well, crap." What should I do?

Suddenly a cell phone went off, with a ringtone I'd never heard before.

I tucked the money into my jeans pockets and ran in search of the phone. The sound was coming from my guest room. When I went inside, the noise became louder, but I still couldn't see the phone.

Then it began to vibrate in a weird way, clattering on wood.

I dropped to my knees and looked under the bed and there it was, alight and dancing.

The ringing stopped before I got to it. I reached under the bed and grabbed it, holding it tightly in my hand. *Tony.* Probably one of his pack members calling him.

Shit. Now I had to take it to him, and just when I thought I'd gotten out of his presence.

I gripped the phone hard and walked steadily to the front door.

I could call Allara. Get her to come and pick it up from me.

But I wasn't calling Allara, and I wasn't slowing down. My body had taken on a mission of its own and I was carefully walking toward the Alpha's home.

Their place was a large, two-story house at the end of my street, and with each step I took, the band around my chest got tighter and tighter. Mannix's truck was still parked in the driveway.

Was it truly possible to escape a fated mate?

Would I be able to forget him once he left?

Would my daughter?

I was only a few feet from Allara's front door now. I could hear talking inside, growly, deep voices that indicated Reid was home too.

I took a deep breath, my chest shuddering with the effort.

Then the door burst open and Mannix trotted down the steps, his eyes flashing silver and yellow when he saw me, his wolf shifter clearly attuned to my presence.

"What do you want?" His tone was bordering on belligerent, and I blinked up at him.

"You, uh... left your phone at my place."

He glanced down at the device in my hands, then took it from me. "Thanks." He glanced at the screen. "It's my pack. They must need me."

I nodded, sliding my now-empty hands into my jeans pockets to hide my awkwardness. "Of course. You should go if they need you."

He nodded, marched to his truck, jumped in, started it and put it into gear.

This time, there was no goodbye, no wave. Nothing. He just reversed out of his parking spot and drove off, taking any hope of a future with him.

CHAPTER 7

MANNIX

I drove fast and hard and didn't look back. Those bastards didn't give a shit about me. Not my brother nor his wife, and especially not the woman who'd opened her home to me over the past day and a bit.

I'd thought there was something special about Amelie, but she'd acted like I was a thorn in her side. A pebble in her shoe. Just like Reid had.

He'd thrown a set of Alpha signature papers at me so fast I hadn't even been able to get a word out.

He'd produced them, not me. I had arrived here only wanting to find and reunite with my brother. I hadn't even considered the idea of him handing over the role officially to me, but he had. And he'd had the papers drawn up while I lay in bed at Amelie's house, nursing my migraine.

That was it, as far as he was concerned. Papers signed, and we were done. So much for a blood connection. He behaved as if I'd been the one to drop him in the forest all those years ago. But I'd been *five*. And the moment I found out he was alive, I'd come looking.

I drove and drove, until my eyes felt like they were hanging out of my head. But I didn't dare stop for long. I got gas and something to eat, and stayed on the road all night.

In the end, I made it home without proper rest. Almost twenty-four hours driving, straight. But I did it. And I managed to bring back the goddamn migraine with me.

When I arrived home, I staggered out of my truck, and people rushed to meet me.

"You're back," Tony said, putting an arm around me. "You okay?"

I nodded, my head throbbing. "Yeah. Just a migraine."

"I'll get you home." Tony started barking out orders. He was my main beta and was a great help when it came to running the pack.

I was half carried to my small house, the place I'd shared with Alfred for most of my life.

"Your room?" Tony asked, and I nodded. I couldn't sleep in the master bedroom. That had been Alfred's space.

We walked into my bedroom and Tony helped me to the bed where I sat, my vision gone in one eye. "Give me a sec." Tony closed the blinds so the room became dark and came back to stand in front of me.

"Did you find him?" he asked.

I nodded. "Yeah."

There was silence in the room, and I shifted so that I could lie down and rest my head.

Tony was still there, so I waited, but he didn't say anything.

"You still there?" I asked, because the throbbing inside my head was so loud it was very possible that he'd left, and I'd missed it.

"Yeah."

"Do you want something? Or...?"

"You can tell me to butt out if you want."

I sighed and raised an arm and rested it behind my head, attempting to get comfortable. "What do you wanna know?"

There was a beat of silence, then Tony asked, "What happened? When you met him?"

I took a deep breath, fighting the pain in my chest at the mention of my brother.

"Reid? Well, he was angry, to be frank. Couldn't believe I'd come looking for him after so long."

"Seriously?" Tony's surprise mirrored my own.

"Yeah. But he got his hands on some paperwork—or his mate did—and he signed the rights of pack Alpha over to me."

"Just like that?" Tony asked.

I nodded, then stopped because it hurt. "Yeah. Just like that."

"Wow."

I would have laughed if I'd had the strength. "Yeah, shocked me a bit, but hey... at least I know he's alive, and he's happy where he is. Now I can move on with my life."

"What was he like?" Tony asked. "I remember him a bit from when we were little, but not much."

I shrugged. "He's big, like Dad was. But quiet, like Mom. His mate is the Alpha of the Northwood pack, and although I didn't see her in action, I could tell she's pretty fierce. They'd be a formidable team to go up against."

Tony chuckled. "Lucky we're not in the mood to fight them then, huh?"

"Hmmm..." I agreed, but God, part of me wanted to go a few rounds with Reid. Pay him back for not coming home. To his family. To me.

"I better get some sleep, Tony. Come wake me in a few hours, yeah?"

"Sure, Mannix. See you then." Tony left and silence descended.

I was exhausted, on a bone-deep level. I'd spent my life fighting to undo the damage my father had done to our pack, and I needed rest. Some help, maybe.

But there was no rescue in sight. No help, other than my betas, of course. At the end of the day, in relation to my future, there was only loneliness.

~

AMELIE

The day after Mannix left, Lacey still wasn't talking to me. She thought I was the reason Mannix had disappeared out of our lives, and she was angry.

She still wasn't telling me why.

"Hello? Amelie? You here?" my Alpha called through the open front door.

"Come in, Allara. Just in the kitchen." I was elbow-deep in apple pies, otherwise I would have answered the door.

She walked into the kitchen, her new son strapped to her chest, looking powerful and glowing with happiness. "I wanted to check on how you're doing."

"Oh, I'm fine. Just busy," I said, gesturing to the dozen pie crusts I'd already rolled out.

"I can see that." She smiled at me.

"How are you?" I asked, gesturing with a flour-covered hand to her bump. "Is he sleeping any better?"

"No." She groaned. "But Reid's a great help. He'll walk the baby through the night for me so I can get some sleep."

The mention of Reid had the smile falling off my face. "That's good."

I glanced down at my workspace and picked up the next circle of pastry. I had to keep busy. It was the only thing keeping my mind from spiraling down into the abyss.

"Want to sit down and chat for a bit?" Allara asked.

I shook my head. "I'd prefer not to stop. These tops will dry out. But we can talk if you want. Sit and I'll bake."

I gestured to the kitchen stools in front of me and Allara moved over and hopped onto a seat. "It smells great."

"That's the cinnamon in the applesauce."

I kept moving, stirring and rolling, waiting for the Alpha to say what she'd come to say.

But she just watched me silently, and I felt even more uncomfortable. "How's..." I hesitated, not even knowing what I planned to ask, but it didn't matter anyway because she interrupted me.

"Can I jump straight to point, Amelie? I have to feed the baby soon and my boobs are killing me."

I laughed. "I remember that all too well. Shoot." *Figuratively, not literally.*

I wasn't up for dodging bullets today.

"Well, I've been talking to Reid, and I think he needs to go visit his old pack."

I stopped stirring and looked up, trying to work out what Allara was about to say. She wasn't seriously sending her husband back to the pack that tried to kill him, was she? Well, I guess technically *they* hadn't. It was only Reid and Mannix's crazy father, but still, that was a hard ask of her mate.

"I don't understand."

She sighed. "Reid is angry. Like ballistic angry. I've never seen him like this. Whatever Mannix's visit stirred up in him hasn't gone away."

I bit my lip and forced my arm to move, stirring the cooking apples and watching them so they didn't turn to puree. "Well, it must have been a shock."

She nodded. "I know."

"He's technically the Alpha of his own pack," I said, musing aloud.

"I know!" Allara shook her head. "No wonder he's my fated mate."

My hand slipped off the spoon and touched the hot metal sides of the saucepan. "Shit!"

I rushed to the sink, thrusting my arm under the cold water. "That was stupid."

"You okay?" Allara called out, standing up now and rocking back and forth, probably to keep her baby asleep a little longer.

"Yeah, fine," I grumbled, the pain reducing to a throb rather than something that required a scream.

I reached back to the stove and turned off the burner. I wasn't concentrating enough to play with fire at the moment.

Then I twisted my body so I could still keep my fingers under the running water and look at Allara as well. "You really want to send Reid off to his old pack?"

Allara nodded. "Yeah, I think I have to. He needs to clear the air with his brother, and maybe put some other demons to rest. He didn't know his parents were dead either, so maybe visiting their graves would help him too. I don't know. But I know I need to do something to help him."

If what she was saying was true, then yes, she had to do something.

"Well, if that's what you think is best, then do it, Allara. Your instincts are usually pretty spot-on."

Was that why she'd come here? To bounce the idea off someone? Because if that was all she wanted...

"Would you go with him?" she asked suddenly.

My heart leapt in my chest.

I swallowed hard. "Me?"

"Yes, you. And Lacey, if you think she'd want to go."

A laugh escaped from my throat. "Lacey would go in a heartbeat. But me? Why would you want *me* to go, Allara?"

She stared at me, her eyes swirling with the silver of her wolf. "You're seriously asking me that, Amelie?"

I wrapped my hand in a cold cloth and nodded, turning off the water. "Yeah, I am."

She sighed heavily, like I was a child needing a reprimand. "Because from what Reid told me, Mannix is your fated mate. Is he not?"

Suddenly I needed to get back to my cooking. I found my first aid kit, smothered the burn in some cream, wrapped it up, and pulled on a glove to protect the skin.

When I turned back to my pies, Allara's smile was smug. "So, Reid's correct?"

I floured my rolling pin, my hand shaking beneath the stress. "Yes. He is."

She laughed, swaying back and forth. Talk about multi-tasking. "Don't make me pull rank on you."

I dropped the rolling pin back to the counter. "You wouldn't." I'd known Allara my whole life, and even though she was several years younger than me, I'd missed her when she left.

Since she'd come back, we'd become really close. But she was still my Alpha, and I'd follow her command if I had to.

"Oh, I would!" she told me. "I know I wasn't here when Evan died, but I was at your wedding. I know how much you loved him."

Tears prickled my eyes, and I lifted my arm to press the back of my hand into my nose. "I did."

"But that doesn't mean you have to turn your back on the future, hon. You're an amazing person with a heart the size of this state. You deserve to mate again. Be happy again."

I shook my head. "No. I can't. Not without Evan."

"Of course, you can." She spoke softly. "And believe me, living with the regret of letting love go is so much worse than chasing after it."

I met her gaze, and in her eyes, I could see the pain she'd suffered all those years without us, and without Reid.

I pressed both hands onto the countertop. "I don't know if he even knows we're..." I swallowed hard, forcing the words out. "Meant to be."

She smiled. "He probably doesn't, not yet. Poor guy had the devil of a migraine, and then you and Reid forced him out of the pack so fast his head is probably still spinning. Talk about a double rejection."

A double rejection? Is that how Mannix would see it? I blinked rapidly as the tears accumulated again. "Allara... I..."

"I know you're scared," she said gently. "But no amount of hiding in this pack is going to heal that wound in your heart. Love doesn't work that way."

I nodded, blinking and allowing the tears to track down my cheeks.

"Lacey deserves a chance at another family too, Amelie. You know she does. Mannix can never replace Evan, but for two people who both lost their families, you could maybe try to build a new one. Together."

I closed my eyes, not wanting to talk about the future when Mannix hadn't even indicated he was attracted to me.

Then, when I was able to, I took a deep breath and opened my eyes. She was right. The regret I felt already at letting him go was tearing me apart. Another few months... years... I'd drown with the weight of it all. And what about Lacey? If she was feeling a fraction of this hurt... "So, what do you want me to do?"

Allara grinned like the proverbial cat who ate the cream. "Well, I have a plan."

CHAPTER 8

AMELIE

Of course, Allara had a plan. She was a pack Alpha. What I hadn't figured on was packing a week's worth of clothes for Lacey and me into several suitcases, loading up Reid's truck, and then getting in.

"So, how far is this place?" I asked the Alpha's mate. Reid was definitely trembling, and not with fear.

Allara was right. He needed to do something about this rage that seemed to have him in its grip.

"About a day," he grunted out in reply.

"A day as in eight hours?" If it was, I was surprised we hadn't heard about Reid's old pack earlier. Most of the ones in the area caught up regularly for festivals and such events.

"No." He shook his head. "Twenty-four hours."

My jaw dropped open, and I glanced at Lacey in the back, already strapped in and grinning her little head off.

"Well, are we going to stop for the night?" I asked Reid, feeling like I was handling a cactus at the moment. "Or should I grab Lacey's blankets and pillows from the back?"

Reid glanced at me and all I could see was confusion and pain.

I made an executive decision. "Give me two minutes."

I ducked out of the truck cabin, grabbed food, water bottles and Lacey's sleeping stuff.

When I got back in the truck, I gave Lacey all her things, including the digital tablet and headphones I had for emergencies, and settled into my seat.

"Let's go then. We can take turns driving and sleeping."

Reid's fingers tightened on the steering wheel, his knuckles turning white.

I twisted to look at him. "You want me to drive first?"

He shook his head.

"Okay, then. Here's your water," I babbled, filling the intense silence with some inane chatter. "And I baked apple muffins and cookies to bring with us. So, they're here."

I patted the space between us, put on my seat belt and sat quietly.

Finally, Reid turned the keys and the engine roared to life.

"Let's go!" Lacey cried, her happy little voice filling the cabin. "I can't wait to see Mannix again."

I closed my eyes. *Out of the mouth of babes.*

I risked a look at Reid, and his lips had quirked into a tiny smile as he stared at me. "You okay?" he asked.

I nodded. "Yeah, let's just go."

He put his foot to the gas, and off we went.

Reid wasn't much of a talker, so I was glad I'd brought a book with me.

After about a hundred pages, I lifted my head, my stomach rumbling. "Anyone else hungry?"

"Me!" Lacey cried.

I'd packed some sandwiches, so I handed those out, happy when Reid took one and ate it quickly.

I handed him another one without waiting for him to ask. He took it and practically inhaled it also as quickly as the first. Good. Eating was a good sign.

When he finished, he glanced at me. "We'll stop soon for gas and to stretch our legs if you want."

"Yes, please."

"I need to go to the toilet too," Lacey piped up.

I laughed. "Yeah, me too, kiddo. Not long now."

We stopped for gas, used the restrooms and grabbed some junk food, then we were off again.

By nightfall, it was my turn to drive after stopping to fuel up. Lacey had fallen asleep in the back and Reid was looking tired.

"Hey, you wanna get some sleep for a while?" I asked him.

He shook his head. "I don't think I can, but thanks for the offer." He rubbed his face with his hand, clearly exhausted.

"You okay?" I asked him, not sure if he'd bite my head off, but needing to put it out there anyway.

Reid glanced in the back seat.

"It's okay," I told him. "She fell asleep an hour ago and she'll most likely sleep till we get there now."

"A deep sleeper. I like it."

I laughed. "Don't let that fool you. She was a terrible sleeper as a baby. Didn't sleep through the night until she was three. But she's making up for it now."

Reid smiled and I knew he was thinking about his baby.

"So," Reid began. "How did Allara get you to come on this trip with me?"

"You're kidding," I said. "She's Allara. How do you think she got me to come?"

Reid huffed a little. "She either cajoled you or threatened you. May have even used her Alpha rank to get what she wanted."

I gripped the steering wheel and made sure the way was clear before I overtook a truck going too slow. "You know her too well."

He chuckled. "Yeah. She usually gets what she wants."

"So, what did she do to you, then?"

He laughed properly this time, then shushed himself, looking into the back where my sleeping daughter still slumbered.

"She... well, she pulled rank. Let's just put it that way."

I didn't really want to know what she'd done to convince Reid to do what she wanted, but I was kind of glad she had.

We settled into the silence for a while, then Reid asked me, "Do you think it's true—about you and Mannix?"

I kept my eyes on the road. "I'm not sure how to answer that question."

"Just say whatever you're thinking."

I wasn't thinking a whole lot. It was my feelings that were the problem. "Well, I never thought I'd be interested in anyone again, so I'm not really sure what to think."

"Evan was a good guy." Reid spoke in that simple way that only men could do. "I liked him. He was a great pack member."

I nodded, not wanting to say anything that would encourage the tears that were currently clogging up my throat to actually fall.

"But not your fated mate, huh?"

I inhaled sharply, pain slicing into my ribs. "I... uh, thought so."

He'd been my first and only love. The father of my child.

Reid nodded. "I knew Allara was special, but it wasn't until she was gone that I really knew what it was like to live with a hole in my heart."

He coughed then, clearing his throat and pulling out a bottle of soda. "Want one?"

I reached for it. "Yeah, thanks. I don't usually have much of this stuff, but we'll need it if we're gonna drive all night."

"I might actually close my eyes for a few hours," Reid said, settling deeper into the seat. "Wake me at midnight, and I'll drive the rest of the way. Okay?"

It was only nine pm, so I didn't think three hours were enough, but I agreed, and soon enough, Reid's soft snores filled the cabin.

I smiled to myself. Despite being forced onto this excursion, it was rather nice to leave the pack. I hadn't traveled, ever. I'd never even left the state.

And as the state line came up and we were officially the furthest from home I'd ever been, a grin stretched my lips. I was closer to Mannix than I was to my pack now. I could feel it. And it wouldn't be long before I saw him again.

But what would I do when that happened? Allara and I hadn't really discussed that. She'd just told me to go with Reid and help him mend the rift with his old pack and his brother.

She'd also hinted I should open myself up to the idea of mating again.

I hadn't let a man in my bed in over five years. Getting married again? It was just so far out of my scope she may as well have suggested I go to the moon.

But we were on a mission, so I let my thoughts wander and I drove.

Around two am, just as my eyes were beginning to blur and I was considering waking Reid, he woke on his own.

"You let me sleep way too long," he complained.

I pulled over and groaned, stretching my back. "Well, you're awake now. So, swap?"

Reid raced around to the driver's side, and I crept over to fall sleep in the passenger seat.

The next time I opened my eyes, the truck slowed to a stop and the engine was then turned off.

"Are we stopping for a break?" I asked, stretching my neck from side to side, trying to work the kinks out of the tired muscles.

"We're here."

My eyes popped open properly and I blinked rapidly. The sun had risen, pink and orange shadows casting along the skyline.

"Where's the pack?" I asked, looking around.

We were parked next to a gate and all I could see was a long, winding driveway.

"Up there," Reid said, nodding his head at the gravel road. "They're pretty secretive, if I remember correctly."

"How much *do* you remember about your childhood?" I asked, undoing my seat belt and shifting so that blood flowed into all the areas of my body.

"I basically blocked everything out, but since I saw Mannix, lots of memories have been flooding back."

I didn't ask what sort of memories, but it was obvious from the twist of his lips, they weren't good ones.

"Are we here, Mom?" The sleepy question came from the back seat.

I turned to see Lacey's little head popping out above the blankets. "Yeah, we are, baby. We just have to work out how to get through these gates."

She squealed and jumped out of the truck, running over to the fence.

I went after her, panic gripping my throat.

"Mannix!" Lacey called out excitedly.

I laughed at her. "I don't think he can hear you from here."

A man came jogging down the path. "You guys lost?"

He was older, about forty, with a large scar bisecting one of his cheeks.

I pulled Lacey into me. "No. We're here to visit Mannix."

The man's eyebrows lowered. "He's not accepting any visitors."

Lacey put her hands on her hips. "He'll see me. Just tell him Lacey's here."

The man eyed my daughter like he wasn't sure if she was serious or not.

I smiled at him. "Would you mind just letting him know we're here?"

He crossed his arms over his chest, looking every bit like the beta enforcer he probably was. "Who's *we*?"

The truck's driver door opened, and Reid got out.

The enforcer's eyes widened, and his arms dropped to his sides as he took in the long-lost Alpha I'd brought with me. I guessed he was noting the family resemblance to Mannix. "Are you..." There was shock in his tone.

"This is Reid." I nodded at the hulking huge man behind me. I considered all the different ways to introduce him, since Reid had gone mute, and went with, "Mannix's older brother."

The beta raced for the gates, unlocking them with a key he pulled out of his pocket and pushing them wide. "You can drive up to the main house if you want."

I grinned at him, almost feeling sorry for him now. "Thanks..."

"Steve."

"Thanks, Steve. I'm Amelie and this is Lacey."

His lips quirked up into a half smile and we climbed back into the truck.

"You okay?" I asked Reid, who'd gone a strange red color in the face.

He nodded. "Let's get this over and done with."

CHAPTER 9
MANNIX

I was working on a new house foundation when Tony came running up to me. "Uh... Alpha... Mannix."

I wiped the sweat off my brow and stared at him. "Did you just call me Alpha? What the hell's wrong with you?"

"Uh... you have guests."

I laughed. "Guests? Why do you sound all pompous and... Oh, shit. They're here, aren't they?" *Amelie and Lacey.* I could *feel* their presence. Reid too, for some reason. I just *knew.*

I'd felt like crap up until this morning. Like, the worst hangover of my life. But I'd woken up feeling better.

Initially, I'd hoped it was just me feeling better about being home, recovering from everything I'd gone through these past two weeks. But now that I knew they were here, I wondered if they were the reason.

"Where are they?"

"Your place."

I groaned and put down my shovel. "Okay."

I jumped out of the ditch and started walking toward Alfred's house. When I realized I was alone, I turned around to gesture to Tony. "Come on. I know you want to meet him."

Tony ran after me and too soon, I was opening my front door and walking inside, muddy boots and all.

Inside, Tony pointed down the hallway. "They're in the living room."

I nodded, inhaling sharply past the sudden tightening in my chest. "Thanks."

I took one more step and Lacey came hurtling around the corner. "Mannix!"

She threw herself into my arms and I couldn't do anything but hug the kid back. "Hi, Lacey. How are you doing?"

"I missed you." She squeezed tighter.

Amelie stepped into the hallway and her gaze met mine with a clash that was heard through my entire body.

"Baby, you're gonna crush Mannix. Let him come through and talk to us, okay?"

Lacey disengaged her arms but grabbed my hand so we could walk together.

I didn't look at Tony because I could only imagine what his face would be saying.

The kids in the pack didn't really like me, and I'd never had a problem with that.

Lacey, however, didn't have that issue. And not only that, she ran through all the walls I'd erected around my heart and obliterated them like they were made of air.

I liked her. She felt... right.

"Come on," Lacey said, tugging me faster. "Reid came to see you, too."

When I stepped into the living room, Reid's presence became overly apparent. He filled the space like a bear.

"Hey," I said, lifting my chin at him.

He nodded back, not speaking at all.

I looked at Amelie, then back at Reid. "Can I help you?"

Reid made a strange, garbled groan noise and Amelie rushed

forward as though to protect him. "We were kind of hoping we could stay here for a couple of days."

"Stay?" I repeated. "Here?" Since when did they want anything to do with me or my pack?

"Yeah." Amelie swallowed in a way that made her throat work. "We didn't really get to talk to you much the other day, and Allara thought—well, we thought..."

She trailed off awkwardly, and I couldn't help the wry laugh that burst out of me. "That would be right. Allara thought. Yeah, well, she would."

I stormed over to the coffee table and picked up the contract Reid had signed and waved it in his face. "You signed away your rights to this pack, so just go back to your mate and your baby, and leave me the hell alone."

My heart was pounding too hard, and my teeth were beginning to shift, the sharpness of my canines biting into my lip.

Reid stalked up to me, his eyes flashing yellow. "Outside. Now."

Oh, yeah. It was on.

I turned and strode out of my house, tugging at my shirt as I went. My brother wanted to fight me, and I couldn't wait to beat his arrogant ass.

When I hit the grass, I heard his growl.

I whipped my head around to see Reid transform into a huge, black wolf.

My own shifter leapt forward, bursting through my humanity as I transformed into my grey wolf.

I dug my paws into the ground, staring at my big brother as he bared his teeth at me.

I didn't wait, launching at him.

He mirrored my move, twisting away at the last minute so my teeth found nothing but air. I snapped my jaws at him again in warning, then flew at him.

We danced and parried. His teeth tore into my shoulder. My jaws latched onto his back.

I put all my anger and frustration into the fight, but in the end, it was Reid's strength that won out.

He pinned me flat on my back, his teeth wrapped around my neck.

I didn't whine or submit, but when I relaxed my muscles enough so that it was obvious I was no longer fighting, Reid retreated.

He shifted back to human within a few steps, then stood up, naked, blood dripping down his side and over his hip.

I got to my own feet and shifted back too, panting, pain stinging my flesh where his teeth had sunk deep.

Amelie came running out, shaking her head. "You two are idiots. Come back inside and I'll check your wounds."

Logic and reason came rushing back. "Where's Lacey?"

"She's off with Tony. He took her for a tour of your pack so she couldn't see you fighting."

I was grateful for the fact she hadn't seen me fight Reid and lose. I didn't want her thinking less of me. What did Amelie think, though?

"Come on," Amelie called, cool as a cucumber.

Reid followed her inside and I walked after him. She didn't seem ruffled, but that didn't mean anything. I'd already discovered that Amelie was a master of hiding her feelings.

She'd made herself at home, pulling out a first aid kit I'd never seen before.

"Turn around. Let me see your back." She spoke first to Reid, then grimaced when she saw the damage. "Might need a few sutures but it'll heal."

She wiped at the area and pulled out some butterfly bandages, then once she was done, walked around Reid and came toward me.

I forced myself to stand still and let her inspect me, not an easy task when my wolf liked her so much and wanted to surge forward to greet her.

When she touched me, her skin was electric against mine. "Let me just wash this. Your wolf genes will sort you out."

She touched and prodded and cleansed my burning wounds, but I barely felt any pain. Her touch made pleasure push away any other feelings.

Finally, she was done, and she stepped away. "How about you both have showers, get dressed, and I'll make us an early lunch."

I nodded, not wanting to fight with her.

I pointed toward my bathroom. "You use that one," I told Reid.

Then I walked into Alfred's room for the first time since he'd passed away. There was no way I was letting Reid use Alfred's bathroom.

The sink still had his toothbrush and as I stepped into the shower, the strange, woodsy scent that I associated with Alfred rose up around me.

Grief filled me. I stepped beneath the water and let the tears run. The pain, the despair, it all swirled around me, leaving me raw and empty. And strangely hungry.

When I emerged from the bathroom, I snuck back into my bedroom and grabbed a fresh pair of jeans and a sweatshirt.

I pulled the clothes on and headed back into the living room, finding Amelie had found what she needed from my kitchen cupboards and was cooking up bacon, eggs, and toast with butter.

"Smells incredible in here," I admitted, sitting down at the dining table. I hadn't eaten in that spot since Alfred passed away.

"Well, you had lots of food to cook up, which was good." She set a plate down in front of me and served up scrambled eggs from a saucepan. "I'll get you the toast and bacon."

She served everything right to me, just like Alfred used to, and it was like I was part of a family all over again. But this one had a woman in it.

Reid arrived then, dressed in a towel.

"Your bag is over there." Amelie pointed to the hallway, and Reid disappeared again.

I grabbed a fork and began shoveling the food into my mouth.

"You okay?" Amelie whispered as she placed some orange juice down in front of my plate.

I glanced up at her, but she wasn't looking directly at me.

"Yeah. I'm okay," I said, and she nodded before disappearing into the kitchen to get more food and plates.

Then Reid appeared and sat at the table.

Amelie set food down for him, and sat down with her own plate, buttered toast in the middle of the table.

We all ate, the fight forgotten, the air clear.

I munched on my toast and listened to the sounds of people once again filling up my childhood home.

By the time we were finished eating, Lacey had returned with Tony, and Amelie set her up with breakfast too. The woman could cook well, that was for sure.

I sat back and watched them all interacting, my heart aching in the strangest way.

I'd sworn never to have my own kids, but was I missing out on something incredible?

"Reid, uh…" Tony cleared his throat. "Can I show you the town? A lot's changed since you left."

Reid got to his feet and took his plate to the sink. "I don't remember much, to be honest." He took a deep breath, as if fortifying himself. But then he nodded. "I'd appreciate that."

He held out his hand to Lacey. "Hey, kid. How about you come with me and show me what you found on your tour."

Lacey ran for Reid. "You have to see the school! It's awesome."

Reid and Lacey followed Tony out and, soon enough, Amelie and I were alone. She leaned against the kitchen counter, looking far too beautiful.

"Thanks for lunch," I managed, dragging myself to my feet and feeling the tug of pain in my back. "And for patching me up."

"I'm just glad you didn't really hurt yourself." She bit her lip.

"Why?" I asked. When she frowned, I added, "Why would you care?"

She didn't say anything, but her eyes seemed to hold the answer.

I moved closer, standing in front of her and inhaling the sweet scent that was uniquely her. "Why do I feel like I know you? Why do I feel like..." *I want to kiss you.*

I didn't finish, but she whimpered anyway, a strange, pained sound.

I took a risk, setting the plate down on the counter behind her, then moving a little closer. I splayed my hands over her hips and stepped up.

She didn't move, and once again wasn't quite looking at me.

I reached for her chin, lifting her face gently so she couldn't help but meet my gaze.

When she finally did, there was so much uncertainty and worry in her eyes, it made me pause. "Are you okay?"

She nodded. "Kiss me, please. Before I change my mind."

I pulled back. "Why would you change your mind?" Was this about her past or mine?

She came forward, gripped my shirt and tugged me toward her, pressing her lips against mine in a desperate kiss that made every part of my body light up like the Fourth of July.

Despite the way she'd pounced, I couldn't pull away. Her taste, her heat, everything about her felt totally right.

I gathered her into my arms and moaned at the pleasure rippling over every inch of my body. My heart, my soul, my wolf... every part of me was happy.

And that's when it hit me.

Shit.

She's my fated mate.

CHAPTER 10

AMELIE

Why I'd kissed Mannix like that, only the universe really knew. But there was one thing I did know. I wanted to touch him, to *feel* the connection. I had to know if it was real, or just another trick sent to test my loyalty to Evan's memory.

I could have done the seduction part of it better, of course, but even with my awkward moves and out-of-practice kissing technique, the answer came through loud and clear. And not just for me it seemed, because after a heartbeat of blinding passion where time and space stopped and we melded together like two pieces of a lost puzzle that had finally found one another, he pulled away.

No, it was more exaggerated than that. He staggered back as though he could barely walk and yet needed to put as much distance between us as possible.

He left me standing alone, grasping at the cold air between us, while he fell backward over his couch and tumbled his way onto the floor.

Ouch... could you be any less subtle, Mannix? Was my kiss really that bad?

"Holy shit." I heard his mutter before he finally got to his feet, looking more like a drunkard walking out of a bar than a guy who'd just eaten an early lunch without any alcohol whatsoever.

"Are you okay?" I called out to him, because it seemed like the right thing to ask.

Every part of me was buzzing. My lips, my skin. Every part of me that he had touched wanted more, and every part he hadn't ached for the moment it would be their turn. I was a pile of shivering, wanting flesh. Not something I'd ever felt before and a part of me was afraid of the intensity of the reaction. Was this really how it was meant to feel?

"Uh... I... Are you..." Mannix stumbled over his words, then finally asked, "How is this possible?"

He looked as dumbfounded and as shocked as I must have that first night, I realized.

"I don't know how," I managed. "But, yes, I think you're my fated mate." The pain my heart went through saying the words was worse than I could easily describe.

Evan. I loved you. I did.

"That doesn't mean we need to act on it," I added. "But if that's what you were asking, then yes... I agree with you. It feels impossible."

Mannix stalked back over to me, his dark eyes swirling with silver, his jaw tight. "You knew about this?"

Oh, fuck.

"I didn't know... exactly. I thought it might be possible though, yes." I wrapped my arms around my body and bit my lip, not liking the angry tightness I could see in Mannix's shoulder and face.

"Then why didn't you say something?" he ground out. "Why did you let me leave?"

"Let you?" I scoffed at him. "You're not a child. You told me that you wanted to go. That you couldn't stay there with Reid, and you left."

He narrowed his dark gaze at me. "If you'd told me we were mates, I would have stayed."

I growled a little, getting annoyed now. "I didn't want us to be mates, okay? I already had a husband I loved. And a child. I didn't expect to find out that I had a fucking *mate* after everything I went through!"

Mannix's gaze roamed over my face, his hands planted firmly on his hips.

He was angry and frustrated? Well, so was I.

I wanted to run, to hide. To take my daughter far, far away, so I didn't have to deal with all the feelings coursing through me. But my wolf had other ideas. When Mannix took a step forward, my wolf rose up and took over.

She wanted her mate, and he was right in front of her. So, when Mannix tilted his head for a kiss and then froze as if fighting his own wolf, I surged up to meet him. I wrapped my arms around his neck and pulled him in tight against my body.

His lips crashed down on mine and a groan sounded loudly in the room. His or mine, I didn't know, and I didn't care. I just needed to get closer, to feel loved, to feel alive again.

Mannix grabbed my ass and hauled me against him, but it just wasn't close enough. I wanted the heat of his skin against mine.

I tore at his shirt, and he pulled up my t-shirt equally roughly.

When he stumbled back, he grabbed my hand and pulled me with him. I didn't ask where we were going, I just let him lead me to his bedroom, where we undressed each other between frantic kisses. I got down to my underwear and Mannix was fully naked before I even knew what was happening. My wolf knew, though. She was humming with excitement and a sense of rightness.

I couldn't help but stop and stare, just for a moment. He was so beautiful. Muscled and smooth, with just the smallest sprinkling of hair across his pecs.

He reached around me for my bra fastening and I stopped him, uncertainty filling me for the first time. I was seven years older than him, and I'd had a baby a long time ago. My body didn't look like the girls I was sure he was used to bedding.

"Um…"

"What's wrong?" He pressed a kiss to my neck, a low growl reverberating against my skin.

"It's just… you know. I've had Lacey, and my body's not twenty-one anymore."

He lifted his head and stared at me. "Amelie, all I can see is you. And you are beautiful. You're my *mate*."

Hot tears sprang to my eyes because that was exactly how I felt about him.

I reached behind me and unclipped my bra, letting it slither to the floor.

Mannix's grin lit up his whole face as he slid his fingers into my panties and dragged them down my legs to the floor, kneeling before me as I stepped out of the circle of fabric.

But Mannix didn't get back up. He simply grabbed my ass with his hands and pulled me in closer.

"Oh... ah..." I wasn't sure about him doing that. Not yet.

But he didn't listen to my fears. Instead, he kissed me. On my belly, on my hips, then moved to lick between my thighs.

I gasped at the pleasure and heat that shot through me as his tongue found its mark.

He pulled back and grinned up at me. "Lie on the bed for me, Amelie."

I turned and rushed over to the bed, lying down on the mattress before I could let my fears run away with me.

He crawled over, prowling up between my legs and pushing open my thighs. He didn't even hesitate. He set his mouth directly onto my clit, making me buck and squeal, straight into his waiting tongue.

I gasped out as he held me steady, working his lips and tongue and teeth over my flesh. The sensations were so intense and incredible. It was like being whipped around in a storm of pleasure. I had no control, simply holding on for the ride.

He kissed me and worked my flesh until my stomach tightened and I was crying out to him to stop. To keep going. To do... something. I couldn't even think straight anymore.

Then he moved upward, leaving me aching and wanting.

He kissed my belly and then my breasts, stopping to suckle on each of my nipples. I threaded my fingers through his hair, holding him to me. I wanted to love on him as he was doing for me, but I had the feeling he wasn't going to let me. Not this time, anyway.

He lifted his head and slid his body up along mine. I moaned at the feeling and opened my legs further as he settled between my thighs. His cock was hard and thick against my belly and my core ached to be filled by his beautiful flesh.

I tugged him down to kiss him, meeting his flaming lips with my own. He kissed me deep and hard, his tongue mingling with mine and letting me taste him in the most fundamental way—with his mouth coated with my own essence as well as his own unique flavor.

Unable to think, I could only feel as he moved against me. I clung to his shoulders, digging my nails into his muscled flesh. The urge for him to be inside me was overwhelming, so I lifted my legs, wrapping them around his hips and moving my pelvis until his cock nudged my entrance.

That's when he lifted his head and stared down at me, his eyes almost pure silver now. His wolf was close to the surface, as was mine. "You sure?" His voice was hoarse with the effort of holding back.

I didn't want him curbing his desire anymore. "God, yes." I found myself wanting to beg. "Please."

He shifted slightly, nudging me softly. But I groaned and pushed against him, needing so much more.

He moaned, then thrust hard.

I cried out as his cock forged a path inside of me. Opening me up and setting me alight. Claiming a part of me I'd long forgotten existed.

He froze, allowing me time to adjust, then as I sank my teeth into his shoulder, he finally began to move.

Slowly at first, just rocking against me. He withdrew almost all the way, until I was digging my nails into his arms to pull him back. Then he drove into me hard, leaving me breathless.

He fucked me long and hard and deep, sending rivulets of pleasure through my body and tears to my eyes.

As he moved faster and his own gasps and groans grew more intense, my belly tightened and heat coursed down my legs.

"I'm going to..." I managed to gasp out just as Mannix roared above me. He thrust deep and came inside me.

His orgasm triggered mine and I screamed out as wave after wave of pleasure buffeted my system. My belly trembled as my pussy rippled around his cock, dragging every last ounce of sensation out of both of us.

We lay there for long moments, his weight on top of me and the sounds of our heavy breathing filling the air.

When he lifted himself up and slowly rolled off me, withdrawing from my body in a way that made me feel instantly empty, I rolled onto my side and faced him. He put his head on the pillow and stared at me.

Neither of us spoke, and I could see the worry mounting in his mind.

"It's okay." I reached out to cup his jaw.

He rolled onto his back away from me and stared up at the ceiling.

"Amelie, that was the single most amazing moment of my life, but I am *not* okay."

Despite being afraid that I was about to be rejected, I crawled across the space between us and nestled into him, putting my head on his chest and feeling the thump of his heart against my cheek.

He didn't push me away. In fact, he put his arm around me and pulled me in tighter.

"Do you want to talk about it?"

He shook his head. "Not really."

"All right." I closed my eyes and tried to ignore the gnawing pain seeping into the bliss surrounding us. I wanted to be happy, even if it was just in this one moment. Because, to me, what we'd just shared had been more perfect than I ever dreamed possible.

CHAPTER 11

MANNIX

How was I going to tell Amelie that I couldn't mate with her? That my family line was cursed and there was no way I'd risk my father's crazy genes being perpetuated in the future.

Part of me wondered as I lay there on my back with my mate wrapped in my arms, that maybe it wouldn't come to be. That just maybe, I could escape it. Reid had, after all. He'd found a mate, and an Alpha, at that. He'd had a child, and he didn't seem to be afraid that child would turn out like our dad.

But Reid wasn't the Alpha of my pack, and he looked nothing like our father. He may have had Dad's size, but in appearance he was all Mom. So maybe his bloodline wasn't tainted like mine.

Everyone said I was the spitting image of my father. And I wasn't risking my child's health or my mate's. If I was destined to go insane like Dad, my betas had orders to put me down. Fast. Before I killed anyone.

I would *not* turn out like my father.

But I had no idea how to even broach all of that with Amelie. Instead, I released a loud sigh.

"I'm going to have a quick shower," I told her, kissing the top of her head because I couldn't stop the compulsion.

"Now?" Amelie grumbled, sounding half asleep.

I rolled out of bed and tried not to notice how gorgeous she was. How soft her hair looked as it fell across her face. "Yeah. I won't be long. You just rest."

She nodded and curled back into the pillow, pulling the blanket up over her naked shoulder.

I backed away, then rushed into the bathroom and shut the door. My heart was pounding like an enemy pack was on my heels, and sweat broke out on my forehead.

What had just happened with Amelie... that wasn't meant to happen at all.

I flicked on the shower and let the water warm up. Steam filled the room. "Oh, God." What was I going to do?

A growl rolled through my chest as inside my mind, my human and shifter personalities fought against one another. My wolf wanted me to go back into my bedroom and make love to Amelie again, but I couldn't. I just couldn't. She'd never understand why I wouldn't give her children or fulfil the role she'd want me to play.

I stepped beneath the hot water, washing away the scent of fear and anger. Fucking *Fate*! How dare she tempt me like this? Put my mate right in my path when I wasn't able to marry her and make her truly happy. Not the way she should be.

Picking up the soap, I washed myself from head to toe, then dried myself off and snuck back into the room. Amelie was fast asleep, so I grabbed a t-shirt and jeans and headed out into the living room. The whole house smelled like her, and my cock responded accordingly.

I groaned. "Fuck."

The front door opened, and Lacey rushed in, laughing loudly.

Reid raced in behind her, his relief palpable when he saw that I was dressed and alone. "Sorry... she got away from me."

"All good." I nodded to Reid. "Thanks for giving me the time to...err... chat with Amelie."

"You two okay?" His gaze was curious.

I nodded. "Yeah. She said she was tired and needed a nap."

The edges of Reid's lips tilted up as though he knew exactly why she'd fallen asleep, but when he turned to Lacey he said, "Your poor mom drove half the night getting here. She was probably exhausted."

Lacey came up next to me and grabbed my hand. "Can we go get something to eat, Mannix? I saw a restaurant that had hamburgers."

I laughed and grinned down at the little minx. "They make amazing burgers. You wanna go?"

She nodded and gripped my hand tightly. "Yes, please."

Reid sat on the couch, yawning loudly. "I might catch a few zzzs, too. You okay with her?"

"Yeah, of course," I answered, before I even thought about it. Lacey was a great kid, and I had no problem spending time with her.

She tugged on my hand and pulled me outside. We chatted on the way to the café, and soon we were sitting in a booth holding identical burgers and sharing a big basket of fries.

"Mannix?" she asked.

I glanced up. I knew that tone. I was about to be asked a probing question. "Yes, Miss Lacey?"

"Why don't you have kids?"

I laughed to hide my awkwardness and put my burger down so I could take a sip of my soda. "Well, for one, I'm only twenty-five, and that's young to have kids."

Especially for an Alpha male.

She tilted her head. "Do you want them?"

"Do I want kids?" I repeated, stalling a bit as my heart began to thump a little too hard. "Well, I'm not sure."

I *was* sure. I didn't want them. Not my own, anyway.

She took a big bite of her burger, looking thoughtful, and then grinned. "You like my mom, don't you?"

I grabbed a handful of fries and squirted ketchup on them. "Why are you asking?"

She shrugged. "I don't know, it's just... I think Mom likes you and I don't want her to get hurt."

I swallowed hard, the intensity of the little girl's gaze rivaling that of an Alpha wolf. "I don't want to hurt your mom either, sweetheart." Especially after everything she'd been through already.

Between us, I'd lost my parents, my brother and my stand-in dad, and Amelie had lost her husband—who she clearly adored—the father of her child.

We were the walking wounded.

"Promise?" she asked. Lacey seemed too old for her years, but I knew from experience that losing a parent could do that to a kid.

I nodded. "I'll try my absolute best not to hurt her, I promise." I wasn't sure if that was possible but I'd try to let Amelie down as gently as I could.

"Okay." Lacey shrugged and focused wholeheartedly on her meal.

When we finished, we went for a walk and chatted like friends who'd known each other for years. I wasn't sure how Amelie had raised her to be so wise and fun, but she'd done a good job.

After an hour or so, we meandered back to the house. Amelie was sitting on the doorstep, staring at us with big, soulful eyes.

She stood up as we got closer and reached an arm out to her daughter. "Hey, Lacey."

"Mommy!" she cried and ran into her mother's arms. "We had burgers!"

"That's very nice," Amelie said, though her voice was thick, and I could tell she was struggling to speak. "Could you go inside and play on your iPad for a little while? I need to chat with Mannix."

"Really?" Lacey asked, her mouth practically dropping open. "Yes!" Then she ran into the house.

Amelie turned to me, thrusting her hands into her jeans pockets. "She doesn't get a lot of screen time."

I nodded. "You've got a great kid there."

"Yeah, I think so too." She seemed to change her mind about her posture and crossed her arms over her chest instead. "I think we need to talk."

I didn't want to because I could already feel where this was going. "Probably not a good idea."

She glared at me. "And why is that?"

I looked up at the sky and clasped my hands over the back of my neck. "Ugh..."

How could I even start to explain my situation?

"Mannix. Look at me."

I dropped my arms and did as she asked.

"What are you so afraid of?"

It was time to tell her the truth. I took a deep breath and let it rush out of me. "I can't give you what you want, Amelie."

"Really?" She lifted a mocking single eyebrow. "And what is it you think I want?"

"A mate," I said simply. "More children."

A strange sort of hurt flashed across her face.

"You do, don't you?" I asked. "Want all those things."

She didn't answer but I knew she did. From the pinch in her lips to the yearning in her eyes.

"Well, I can't give that to you," I told her. "I mean... I want to... but you have to understand. I can't."

"What do you mean, you *can't*?" Her voice was a whisper. "Are you married already?"

"Me?" I practically scoffed. "No! Of course not."

"Have you..." She swallowed hard. "Can you *not* have children?"

I glanced away so she couldn't see the regret in my eyes. So many times I'd almost gone to get a vasectomy so I wouldn't be able to have a child, but I'd never had the courage to go through with it.

I swallowed hard and managed to meet her gaze with mine. "I don't know. I've never tried."

"Then what are you talking about?" She covered her face with her hands for a moment before dropping them and sighing.

"Let me get this straight," she went on. "I finally face up to the fact that the father of my child wasn't my mate. That I had another decreed by Fate in this world and I've finally found him, and you... you... what? Just don't want me?"

"Of course, I want you!" I ground out. "But can't you see I'm bad news? You don't want to be the Alpha's mate in a pack like this. Our bloodline is cursed. *My* blood. It's cursed."

"Bullshit!" Amelie hissed. "Reid has a mate *and* a son! You're just afraid."

"Of course, I'm afraid!" I practically screamed. "My father murdered my mother and tried to murder Reid and me! Don't you understand? He *killed* her. And would have killed me if it wasn't for Alfred. And Reid, if it wasn't for Allara's pack. Don't you understand that? He was crazy. And I'm just like him."

"You're not like that!" She poked me in the chest, hard, but her eyes were full of tears. "So, what's that got to do with you and me?" Her lips were trembling. "You can't possibly think that will happen to you."

I looked away, fighting my own heartache and finding it impossible to meet her eyes. "It's not safe, Amelie," I said, more quietly now. "You should go. And take your daughter with you. Lacey shouldn't be here, either."

The front door suddenly flew open, and Lacey came running inside. "You're a liar! And a coward." The accusation in her gaze was almost my undoing.

My heart broke and I staggered a little as my knees almost went out from under me.

The pain I saw in those eyes, I knew too well. "Lacey, I—"

"No!" She thrust out her hand at me as though she could stop me from walking forward. "Don't say anything. If you don't want to be my new daddy, you don't have to be."

The tears were welling up in my eyes now. "Sweetheart, I..." I would have loved to be her stepfather. I hadn't even thought about that as a possibility.

She was right. I *was* a coward.

"Lacey, he's not..." Amelie tried to help, but her daughter made a wounded, angry noise, and ran out of the room. Out of the house and down the front steps.

I watched her flee into the town and beyond. I'd hurt her. An innocent child.

"I better go after her." Amelie walked past me with the tears in her eyes beginning to fall down her cheeks.

"I'll come with you."

"No!" she said, with the same unbending tone Lacey had used. "You've made your position clear. We'll be back soon to say goodbye."

Then she, too, walked away from me.

CHAPTER 12
AMELIE

I stomped off down the road, so angry and hurt I didn't know if I should let myself cry or fight through the impulse. My heart ached and my throat burned with the most terrible sensation. After so many years of grieving my husband's death, I would have thought I had no tears left. Or that I'd at least be used to the pain of loss. But no... this was a whole new fresh level of agony.

I swallowed hard and blinked rapidly, deciding that I wouldn't cry. Not today. Maybe tomorrow. After all, my mate—my true, fated mate— had just rejected me. I was entitled to a few tears, surely, but I'd handled worse, hadn't I? I could handle this, too.

I'd get through it. My daughter, however, might not. I'd never heard her speak to anyone like that before, nor had I ever heard her so upset.

She'd been too young to even remember her father. It was me that kept his memory alive for her by telling her how great he'd been, how much he'd loved her. But Lacey didn't actually remember having her daddy, and now the man she'd obviously secretly been hoping wanted the job had rejected her as well.

It was "broken hearts for all" day, it seemed.

My gaze scanned the village, searching for her among the houses, old and new. The roads weren't in the best shape, but the people grew small gardens around their homes, and I could smell baking and fresh bread in the air.

They were rebuilding, that was obvious.

"Oh! Lacey!" I called out to my daughter when I spotted her sitting on a big rock, her arms wrapped around her knees. "Honey!"

"No! Go away!" she yelled back at me before taking off, running between two of the houses and toward the forest.

I froze in place, tears welling in my eyes and falling onto my cheeks. "Oh, baby, I'm so sorry."

I wanted to go after her, but my legs wouldn't move, and the weight of my daughter's pain made it impossible to stop the tears now. How was I going to explain this to her when I didn't even understand it myself?

Mannix had gone through a lot, that was obvious. But he was letting fear stand in the way of his future, and a few days ago I would have been right there with him...head in the sand and feet firmly planted in denial.

By the time I realized Lacey really was heading into the forest and not stopping at the edge, she was gone. Damn. I shouldn't have let her go like that. She'd disappeared right into the trees, and I couldn't see her at all. The good news was she couldn't shift yet, so she couldn't have gone far. She'd probably just find a log to sit on, and mope for a while.

I took a deep breath and exhaled slowly. I had to get a handle on these emotions. I was a mother first and foremost, which meant my disappointment could be processed another day. Today, I'd pack up and head home with or without Reid. Lacey and I were out of here.

I turned and walked back to the house where only an hour ago I was making love to Mannix.

I shook the thought out of my head and walked straight through the open door. Reid was there, waiting patiently on the couch, and the moment he saw me, he jumped to his feet. "You okay?"

I shook my head. "No. It's time to go home."

"Now?" he asked. "We only got here this morning."

I knew what he was saying. We were both exhausted and couldn't make another drive like the one we'd just done.

"I know, but I got what I came here for. Answers. What about you?"

Reid glanced across the room, and I assume he was looking at his brother, but I couldn't do it. My heart was banging way too loudly in my chest, and all I wanted to do was get away from here. I ignored Mannix altogether.

"Uh, yeah. I suppose I did," Reid admitted. "But I don't think we should drive straight home."

I shrugged. "No problem. I'm sure there's a motel not far from here. We'll sleep there tonight and take our time driving home."

I lifted my chin even higher as I felt the heat of Mannix's gaze from across the kitchen. "Give me an hour to pack up and make sure I've got everything, Reid. Then we can leave."

Not that I'd unpacked, but between the three of us, I was sure our shit had spread from the car to the house and elsewhere.

"Where's Lacey?" Mannix called out, forcing me to turn my head to look at him. He was standing in the kitchen, leaning against the counter.

"In the forest. She ran off after you rejected us, and I decided to give her some space." Or that was my excuse anyway. Shock and heartbreak had been the real reasons I hadn't bolted after her. "As soon as I'm packed, I'll go find her."

Mannix's eyes narrowed at my words, but he didn't speak.

Reid coughed awkwardly, clearing his throat. "I have a few things I still need to talk to Mannix about."

"You do that." I walked over to the couch and picked up Lacey's iPad. "I'll get the truck ready."

I bent my head so I didn't need to look at either of them anymore, and set about collecting the things we'd already scattered. Sweaters, toys, water bottles.

The men wandered off and I heard them speaking in hushed tones out front. I tuned them out and focused on getting ready. Within fifteen minutes, I was pretty much done.

I walked outside with the final bits and pieces I'd gathered in my arms and looked at Mannix, trying to keep my expression blank. "Thank you for having us." I dragged my gaze away from the pain I saw in his eyes and met Reid's gaze instead. "You ready to get home to your wife and baby?"

I couldn't seem to resist the final dig at Mannix.

His main argument seemed to be that because their father was an asshole, he was destined to be one too. Ergo, no wife or baby, or even a mate.

Well, Reid had done it all and I couldn't see Allara rolling over if Reid suddenly became an asshole. Quite the opposite.

Mannix shuffled his feet. "Amelie, we have to talk."

"No," I snapped. "Unless, of course, you have something new and more positive to say?" I looked at him then and raised my eyebrows since my arms were full.

"Uh…" He stopped, then shrugged.

"Didn't think so. Okay, then. I'm gonna drop this stuff off, then go find my daughter." I twirled on the balls of my feet and headed toward the car. He didn't *want* to change his mind, that was obvious. If I was ten years younger or Lacey wasn't in the mix, maybe I'd stick around just to see if I *could* change his mind.

But I wasn't young and dumb anymore, and I had a daughter to protect and care for. I'd already endured the death of my husband and was raising Lacey by myself. If Mannix wasn't man enough—hell, if he wasn't *Alpha* enough to stand up and want me on my own merit—then he could go get fucked.

I repacked the truck with the few things in my arms, then marched back to where Reid and Mannix were still talking.

I looked at Reid, ignoring Mannix. "I'll go fetch Lacey and meet you at the truck."

Reid nodded and I turned to go, but that was when a couple of Mannix's betas ran up to us, looking worried. "Mannix! Bear shifters. In the woods."

I staggered sideways, the weight of those words hitting me hard. Not bears, damnit. No. Not when Lacey was out there alone.

My husband had been killed in a battle with bears. They were huge and vicious, and took no prisoners.

"Seriously?" Mannix was already ripping off his shirt. "But we haven't seen them for months."

"I know. But they're back and they're obviously looking for trouble."

Mannix growled. "Fuck. Okay, round up the troops, and head to the forest line. Now!"

He went to race off, and I had to stop him. I launched forward and grabbed his arm. "Who are these bear shifters?"

"Enemies." His eyes had already shifted, and his teeth began to change right before my eyes. "I need to go, Amelie. Defend my pack."

I would have rolled my eyes if things weren't so deadly serious. He was being all Alpha and perfect now, was he?

We had to get out of here. *Now.* I wasn't losing another member of my family to some bears. Oh, holy hell. Lacey!

"Okay. But which direction are they coming from? Which area of the forest?" I could barely breathe, the reality smacking me in the face. "Not the little section to the west, is it? Like, behind those houses over there?"

He nodded. "Yeah. Why?"

No! Not my baby. No. Please.

I threw the truck keys through the front door, toward the couch, not caring where they landed.

I began to strip off my own clothes. I had to get to my daughter, and I was faster in shifter form. "That's where Lacey ran off to."

A growl erupted from Mannix, and his human morphed instantly into his wolf.

"Oh, shit." Reid said, before a feral growl ripped through him as well. His shift was only slightly slower than Mannix's.

I let my own wolf take over, my maternal panic making my human self useless.

Mannix was already gone. His black wolf disappeared like lightning down the street, on his way to save his pack. And hopefully, to help protect my daughter.

CHAPTER 13
MANNIX

I raced through town, the sounds of growls in the distance making me push myself harder. We'd fought these bastards a few times over the years. They were a natural enemy, and the bears had always wanted our land.

We beat them back every time, though we lost men whenever we faced them. I didn't want to lose anyone else, but that wasn't the fact that had my heart pounding in my chest today. It was Lacey. She was out there by herself, and I couldn't endure the thought of something happening to her.

She was Amelie's daughter. And that made her special.

Please, Lacey. Walk back out of the forest. Now. Please.

I hit the boundary of our town where some of my betas were yelling and already corralling women and children into their homes.

We'd practiced this a hundred times. They knew what to do.

I threw back my head and howled, calling any remaining pack members to the fight.

Reid was suddenly beside me. My brother. At my shoulder, ready to support me. I would deal with that thought later but for now, we ran together into the dense treeline. My wolves were everywhere, and I yipped at Reid. He seemed to know what I meant, and moved to the left, running along the boundary, looking for Lacey.

I could hear the cries and growls of the bears, which were quickly approaching.

I darted through several trees and into a nearby clearing, looking around for the little girl who'd been so disappointed that I didn't want to be her daddy.

God. What had I done?

I'm coming, sweetheart.

I ran along the tree line, bolting in and out, looking for a little girl with dark hair. I wanted to shift back to human, just so I could yell out her name, let her hear me call. But I didn't dare turn back. Not with bears on the loose.

When I got to the top of a small rise, I looked down the other side, and that's when I heard her cry.

"Help me! Please! Helllppppp!"

I squinted into the distance and caught sight of two huge Kodiak bears loping through the trees. Just ahead of them was Lacey, running for her life. Those bears were toying with her. Having some fun before they stepped it up and took her.

I didn't hesitate. I raced down the hill toward her, howling and growling as I went.

As I got closer, I could see the terror in the little girl's eyes. I pushed harder when she tripped, falling down into the mud and scrabbling along beneath the trees on her hands and knees. Like her mother, Lacey was clearly a fighter. She would not give up.

When I reached her, I leapt, sailing over the top of her head and landing on the other side of her body.

I planted my feet firmly and growled as loudly and viciously as I could.

I didn't look behind me, but I heard Lacey panting, scratching at the earth with her fingers.

Run, Lacey. Run!

I lowered my head and growled as the brown bears came loping along on all fours. They stopped the moment they saw me and stood up on their hind legs.

I glared up at their forms. They were now close to eight feet tall.

Unable to hear Lacey anymore, I hoped to God she was gone, running back toward the village and safety. Relief sailed through me even as the bears dropped down onto their front paws once more and readied to attack.

If this was my time, then it was my time. But I'd go out of this world knowing my girls were safe. Amelie and Lacey. My girls. My family. And I'd managed to get to know my brother once more, even if it was only for a few days. That was something.

~

Amelie

My wolf caught wind of Lacey's scent and I raced through the forest, searching for my baby.

I reached the top of a small cliff. Now Mannix's scent also wafted on the breeze.

And suddenly, there she was, running through the forest toward me, her dark hair blowing behind her like a flag. Lacey!

I ran for her, down the hill and beyond. When I was within ten feet of her, I shifted back, collecting my daughter into my arms and holding her tightly against me.

"Thank God, you're all right." I cupped her face and pulled up her chin so I could look at her properly. "I was so worried about you, baby."

"Mannix saved me," she sobbed, tears tracking down her cheeks. "Two bears were chasing me, but he covered me so I could get away."

Two bears? A howl and a lot of growling sounded in the distance, and I pulled my daughter in to me. "We need to get out of here. Quickly."

We turned just as Reid's wolf ran up, shifting as he went. "You found her. She's okay?"

I nodded, pulling Lacey into my side. "She is. But she said two bears were chasing her and Mannix is now fighting them off." I bit my lip to stop the sob that rose. To lose two mates to bear shifter attacks... I wasn't sure I'd survive a second time. "You need to help him, Reid. Please. He..." I trailed off, unable to finish, and Reid nodded.

He pointed through the trees. "That way?"

Lacey sobbed. "Yes. Please go help him."

Reid leapt through the air, shifting on the fly.

Lacey surged in the same direction, obviously wanting to go after him, and I understood her compulsion. I wanted to go after Reid too and help battle the bears. For Mannix, and to assuage my own demons. For Evan.

But I had to get my daughter to safety, and if two Alpha wolves couldn't take these assholes down, then my assistance would be moot. If Mannix and Reid lost, then we were doomed

MANNIX

Blood dripped into my eyes from a gash on my head, but I ducked a massive paw swing and managed to get away once more.

I could have taken down one bear myself, but with both working in tandem, it was getting harder by the minute to stay alive.

I ducked again, ran around the larger one, and snapped at his heels. His claws came swinging around and I darted back.

Shit! How the hell was I ever going to take these guys down? I couldn't run because I couldn't risk endangering anyone else in town. But I needed help.

The answer came in the form of a huge black wolf, sailing over a log and running at full tilt toward me. It was Reid.

My brother has my back.

Warmth filled me even as Reid flew at the other Kodiak, tearing into its neck and chest.

The bear bellowed and the one I'd been fighting turned to help its comrade. I took a chance and launched my own renewed attack, tearing at the bear's hind legs and tasting blood running between my teeth.

Reid and I pounded into the bears, over and over, tearing at them, biting them, and taking over the fight. With two of us, there was hope in my chest instead of despair. We could do this. Together.

The beast fighting Reid suddenly turned tail and fled, running back into the forest in classic retreat style. The Kodiak I was fighting glanced after its friend and when I released my jaw's hold on his right back leg, took off as well.

I limped over to Reid and stood side by side with my brother, watching the bears run away. He didn't look too injured. He had some blood on his fur and a chunk of ear missing, but overall, he was the poster boy for surviving a battle.

I, however, was a different story. I was beginning to see spots.

Turning, I began to limp back toward town. I couldn't hear any snarling, vicious bears any longer. No howls of pain or anger. There was only silence in the forest.

Did that mean all the bears were gone? I had to find out. I needed to check on my pack and find out if Lacey had gotten back to Amelie okay.

I trudged forward, ignoring the pain in my head and legs. It wasn't far to the top of the hill. I could make it. Surely, I could.

Halfway up, I knew I couldn't. My wolf wouldn't continue any longer. I had to shift back and get some help for these injuries. I let go of my wolf and groaned as the levels of pain ratcheted up twenty-fold in my human form. "Oh, fucking hell."

Reid was beside me, instantly shifting back to human also. "Come on, brother." He spoke as calmly as one would on any given day. "Let's get you home."

He put his arm around my waist, and I managed to throw my arm over his shoulder. Together, somehow, we made it back to town.

"Thanks for the help there," I finally told him. He was taking a lot of my weight, but still allowing me the respect of being able to walk on my own two feet. "I'm not sure I would have made it without the support."

Reid, the big lug, shrugged. "Happy to help."

I wasn't sure what else to say, so I just nodded and kept going. I had to find out if Lacey got back to her mom safely. "Do you think she's okay?"

Reid glanced at me. "Lacey?"

"Yeah."

"Yep. She's fine. She was the one who told me to come find you."

Relief sailed through me, and a piece of the puzzle fell into place. That's how Reid had found me. Made sense. "Oh. Good."

"You shouldn't have gone after the bears alone." His voice was a little darker and crankier now.

I laughed; I couldn't help it. He sounded like me when I was annoyed. "Yeah, well... I can see the insanity in it now. But when I saw those bears chasing that kid..." A growl rolled through me. "I wanted to kill them on sight."

"Yeah, I must admit," Reid said, "I know that feeling. My son isn't even walking yet, and I'm terrified something might happen to him."

We'd reached the edge of the trees. My pack and town lay only a few yards away, and yet my legs were screaming at me not to continue. Black swirled at the edges of my vision.

"I think I have to sit down."

"No, you don't." Reid grabbed a tighter hold and forced me to continue walking down the street and into town. "Your people need to see you're alive and well."

I nodded and clenched my jaw tightly, hearing my teeth click together. He was right. I knew it.

"Just push through," he said. "We're not far away now."

Somehow, we made it. Reid managed to get me home, and my betas all came rushing to see me.

"Mannix! Fuck, man. You okay?"

I nodded as Reid got me to the front door of my house. "I'm fine. How's the pack? Did we lose anyone?"

One of my betas, Tommy, shook his head. "Nah. We did good. A few injuries but overall fine."

"Great," I told him, beginning to sink lower and heavier against Reid. "I'm gonna get patched up, and I'll see you guys later. Come get me if anything else happens. Okay?"

The ran off cheering, elated with the win.

I was happy for them, but I'd be even happier when I could finally sit down. Or better still, lie down.

"Oh my God. Are you okay?" Amelie came running to the open front door and threw one of her arms around me, stabilizing me on the other side of Reid.

"Yeah. I'm fine." I really couldn't see that well now. "Just need a few stitches, I think."

My legs were wet with blood, and I wasn't sure where it was all coming from. My back hurt and I was pretty sure I'd taken a bear claw to the belly at one point, but I wasn't risking looking down. Not yet.

"Let's get him inside, Reid." Her voice was quiet. Concerned.

I mock scowled at her. "I'm still here, you know."

"Not for long," she said. "These injuries are gonna make you pass out soon. I don't know how you're still standing."

I didn't either. "I needed to find out if Lacey was okay."

Then Lacey herself bolted into the room, her eyes wide with fright. "Oh, no," she whispered.

"I'll be fine, sweetheart. Don't you worry. Your mom's gonna fix me up."

My vision had narrowed. I squinted in her direction but couldn't really see the young girl much at all.

"Lacey, go find the first aid kit in the truck, okay?" Amelie's voice was sharp. I could hear the underlying fear. *Hmm. I must be pretty bad then, I guess.*

The youngster nodded, then bolted out of the house.

The moment she was gone, the world went dark.

AMELIE

After Mannix passed out, Reid threw him over his shoulder and carried him as fast as he could into the main bedroom. The room still smelled like sex, and the sheets were rumpled but there was no time for embarrassment now.

That wound in Mannix's stomach looked pretty bad. And the one in his back wasn't much better. He'd already lost so much blood.

"Here you go, Mom." Lacey panted as she ran back into the house with my first aid kit in her hands.

"Thanks, sweetheart. Could you get me some clean water and put the kettle on?"

She nodded and raced out of the room.

Reid hovered over me. "Do you think he's going to be okay?"

"Yeah, of course," I muttered, barely able to breathe through the worry and tightness in my chest. *I hope so.* "We haven't finished our argument yet. He can't die before I have my final say."

Tears leaked out my eyes, belying my attempt at humor, and I brushed them away.

Reid put a hand on my back. "Just hold on a bit longer, Amelie, you're doing great."

I nodded because my throat had closed up and I couldn't speak now. He couldn't die on me. He wasn't allowed to. That wasn't how this was meant to work.

If he didn't want me or my daughter, then fine. But he was *not* dying. He was *not*.

I pushed all feelings aside and focused on my role, assessing his injuries and blood loss. The outlook wasn't great.

"I'm going to need to do some stitches. Do you think you could stay and help me in case he wakes up?"

Reid walked around the bed to stand by Mannix's head. "What do you want me to do if he does wake up?"

I lifted my gaze from the mess of oozing claw marks and managed to smile. "Knock him out again."

Reid didn't smile back, just nodded grimly.

When Lacey brought me back some bottles of water, I thanked her and sent her away. It was a tough couple of hours of sewing flesh together and wrapping wounds, but I did it. He'd come home to me alive. It was the least I could do for the man who was my fated mate, whether he wanted me in his future or not.

When I was done, I fetched some clean blankets and draped them over his nakedness.

"What do we do now?" Reid asked.

"We wait." I wiped my forearm over my sweaty brow.

"You want to go take a shower?" Reid suggested.

I stared down at my hands, where dried and fresh blood both gathered on my skin. "Yeah, thanks."

I was exhausted. There was no other word for it. Emotionally, mentally, physically. There was no way we were driving away from this town tonight.

Lacey was sitting on the ground by the front door and, as I walked over to her, I noticed people outside. "What's going on, sweetheart?"

"The betas are here to check on Mannix." She calmly gestured to the front door.

I walked closer and glanced outside. There were people everywhere.

The men who'd been sitting on the porch obviously chatting with Lacey on her level, jumped to their feet. "Is he okay?"

"Is Mannix alive?"

"Will he be okay?"

All the queries came at once, and I noticed, not for the first time, that not many of them referred to him as Alpha. Whether that was by choice or by Mannix's decree, I wasn't sure, but it was unusual for a pack to have so much respect for their leader but not call him by his proper rank.

"He's alive," I announced, and a general cheer went up around the group. Women in the back hugged each other and two of the men surged closer.

"Can we come in?" They put their hands to the door.

"He's sleeping," I said, raising my hands to show them the mess I was in. "He lost a lot of blood, but I've patched him up the best I can. I'm going to have a shower, then I'll check on him again."

"Please." The guy at the front said. "Just us two. We need to see him."

I glanced at the two betas and tears filled my eyes once more. I knew that feeling. That deep-seated gut ache that made you desperate to set eyes on the person you loved, just to reassure yourself that he or she was still alive.

To watch them breathe. To see their chest rise and fall.

I'd never gotten that with my husband. He'd been dead by the time they brought him back to me. So, to have this moment where Mannix was alive, and I'd helped to heal him... it put parts of me back together that I'd never thought was possible.

He really was my second chance. At everything.

I'd almost lost him and my daughter in the same day.

"He saved my life," Lacey announced to the two men as they opened the door, then shut it after them. "The bears would have eaten me for sure."

I backed away from them, struggling to breathe again. "Sweetheart, you walk them through what happened, okay? I need to grab some clean clothes, then wash."

I pushed past the group and ran for the truck where I grabbed out my suitcase once more. Then, feeling the burning gazes of the pack on me, I ran for the safety of the shower.

There, within the tiled walls, I bawled my eyes out. For everything we'd all lost. For the pain we'd been through. For the fear that still crippled every choice we made.

Mannix. Me and Lacey. Even Reid, who'd been left to fend for himself so young. All of us had suffered in the past.

The hot water washed away all the blood on my skin, and I scrubbed my nails until they were red from the vigorous cleansing. I could still feel it on me, everywhere. So, I stayed under the water, washing every part of me until the water ran cold.

Finally, it was time to get out and face them.

I snuck out, changed into clean clothes, then found the house to be quiet. The pack had gone. There wasn't anyone waiting on the doorstep any longer.

I went looking for Lacey and Reid, only to find them both sitting by Mannix's bedside. "Has he woken up at all?" I whispered into the quiet room.

Lacey jumped up and ran over to me, straight into my open arms.

"It's okay, baby," I whispered, holding her close. "It's okay."

"He's going to wake up, right?" she asked as she pulled away.

I nodded, though my certainty at that point was wavering. "Of course, he will. He has Alpha blood. They heal the best, you know. Isn't that right, Reid?"

I turned toward the Alpha in the room, who nodded silently.

"Is it okay if I go play outside?" Lacey asked.

"You can," I said, "but stay close to the house, okay?"

She nodded. 'Oh, don't worry. I'm never going into those woods ever again."

I smiled at her as she left, then collapsed into the chair by Mannix's nightstand that she'd vacated. "Any news?"

Reid ran a hand through his rumpled hair. "Just got the report from Mannix's betas. The bears all retreated, and quickly. It sounds like Mannix has trained his pack well. They fight together, as a team. They do drills every week to keep them all fit and strong."

I tilted my head and stared at my Alpha's mate. "You sound proud of him." Reid had been fighting the connection to his brother since the day Mannix had turned up on our pack's doorstep.

Surely, he could see that it wasn't Mannix's fault Reid had been abandoned as a child?

"I am," Reid said, though the words were stilted. "I just—"

"What?" I prompted. "Can't get past the fact that he didn't come for you earlier?"

Reid glanced away and I knew that had something to do with it.

I sighed. "Well, that would have been a bit difficult, given he thought you were dead. I think you're blaming the wrong person, Reid."

"Yeah. I am," he said finally. "I should blame myself."

I groaned with frustration. "What are you talking about? You two were kids. *Kids*! Your father is the only guilty party in this, Reid. Not you. Not Mannix. You managed to survive and went on to be our Alpha's mate. Mannix survived and looks like he's doing a pretty good job of getting this pack back on its feet."

Reid nodded and I could see the shimmer of unshed tears in his eyes.

"Why should you blame yourself, Reid? You're not making any sense."

"I should have tried to find Mannix," he admitted. "He was just a little kid. It wasn't his fault our father was a fucking psychopath."

I rolled my eyes. "Try telling him that! He thinks he'll turn out just like him."

"What?" Reid asked, turning toward me. "What do you mean?"

I lifted my legs up onto the edge of the seat and wrapped my arms around my knees. "Mannix told me he's cursed. That he can't take a mate or have kids in case he wakes up one day and tries to kill us all."

It sounded crazy to me, but Reid nodded like he understood.

"Oh, not you too?"

Reid grinned at me. "We're all afraid of having a mate and children. Especially when you're an Alpha."

My jaw dropped. "Seriously? I would have thought it would be the opposite. That you guys would be driven to procreate. To continue the line."

He chuckled. "Yeah. You'd think so, huh? But instead, you worry about adding to your responsibilities. Mannix already feels responsible for his pack. Every man, woman and child. He worries about disappointing them. About failing them when they need him most. Adding a mate and children to that... well, not every man is built for it."

I lay my chin on my knees. "So, I should give up then?"

Reid laughed louder this time. "Hell, no, you don't give up. You two are fated mates. You'll never be happy without one another. Trust me, I know."

I smiled at that one and closed my eyes, leaning back in the chair and willing sleep to descend on me also. Reid had been separated from Allara for six years after her father had deliberately broken them up. Neither of them had done very well alone.

"Thanks, Reid."

I stayed in that chair, drifting in and out of sleep for the rest of the day and all night. I didn't leave Mannix's side because something told me that if I left, he wouldn't be there when I came back.

MANNIX

When I woke up, early morning rays of light were filling my bedroom. I hurt, everywhere, but I was alive. And that was a start.

I blinked rapidly, my eyes adjusting to the half-light.

And there she was, sitting in a chair, curled up and asleep. My mate.

I struggled to sit up and pain sliced through my belly, making me hiss. Fuck, that hurt.

Amelie sat bolt upright, blinking her big eyes like an owl. "You're awake!"

I groaned. "Barely."

She jumped to her feet, dashing over to the nightstand. "Have some water. Do you want something to eat?"

I managed to drag myself up to a seated position and rested against the backboard. "I'm fine, but how's everyone else? Where's Lacey? Is she okay?"

Amelie handed me a glass of water, smiling tentatively. "Everyone else is great. Lacey's fine, thanks to you." She slumped into the chair before me. "Thank you for saving her life. I would never have gotten there in time."

I took a sip of water. "Yeah, well, I didn't have a choice there. My wolf just took over."

She nodded slowly. "The Alpha in you, I suppose. Needing to protect a child."

It had been so much more than that. As I'd taken on those bears, all I could think of was that Lacey had to get to safety. She was too important to lose, and she was well worth losing my life over.

"Ah... yeah," I managed.

I didn't know when we'd get the time we needed to sort everything out, but I didn't want Amelie leaving. "Will you stay for a while longer? I know you were determined to go home—"

"I'll stay," she jumped in to say. "At least until you're back on your feet." She glanced toward the door. "Lacey likes it here. She's made friends with some of the other kids, and Reid is finally letting himself talk to some of your pack members."

"What do you mean, he's letting himself?" That was a strange way to phrase it.

"Well, I think he was partly afraid to get to know any of your pack. You know—in case they blamed him for leaving or staying away, or something."

I nodded slowly. "Yeah, I hadn't really thought about how he'd feel with all this."

This was meant to be his pack. His people. Instead, he'd ended up making another pack his home.

"He's getting better," Amelie noted. "I'm sure Allara is absolutely busting to get up here, so she'll come visit too. I'm positive of that."

I smiled. "Fine by me."

I moved each part of my body slowly, checking for injuries. My feet, my legs, my arms, then my torso. There were a lot of aches and deep wounds, but my head was clear. I was healing well.

"Did you patch me up?" I asked. We didn't really have doctors in town anymore. Some of the women could manage basic first aid, but that was it.

She nodded. "Yes. You needed some stitches, so I hope that was okay?"

I chuckled and sighed. "Yeah, it's amazing. Thank you. You always seem to end up taking care of me, don't you? First the migraine, now this."

She reached out and ran her fingers through my hair. "Yeah, well... you need someone to take care of you. You can't look after everyone else all the time and not receive any nurturing in return."

I turned my head, leaning into her caress. It felt so damn good. "Mmm..."

I hadn't had anyone look after me like this for as long as I could remember. While Albert had been a great mentor and surrogate father, his response to any type of injury or migraine scenario was more of a "suck it up" type of mentality.

"I'll go make some breakfast." She stood and began backing toward the door.

"Could you send Lacey in?" I called out. "When she's awake. I need to apologize to her."

Amelie stared at me, her look unreadable. "Ah... sure. Okay."

Then she disappeared.

I lay there in bed, regretting everything I'd said to Amelie yesterday after we'd made love. Here was a woman who'd already gone through so much, and I practically tossed her out of my bed and told her I could never mate with her.

Who wouldn't want to marry a woman as beautiful and selfless as she was?

I was an idiot. A fool.

And I was going to make it up to her.

I tested each of my joints, moving my arms and legs to get the blood pumping again. Amelie had done a good job of sewing me up, because I could feel myself healing with each minute that passed.

There was a soft knock on the open door and then Lacey walked in, hesitating just inside the doorway.

"Come on in, sweetheart. Have a seat."

She slid onto the chair, her big eyes focused on me. "Are you okay?"

"Yeah, of course I am."

"You saved me," she whispered. "Thank you."

I reached out and grabbed her hand, then tugged her over so she'd sit on the bed next to me. "It was my fault you ran off. I upset your mom and I upset you. And I am so, so sorry about that."

She nodded her head and began to cry. I pulled her into my arms and hugged her, letting her cry out whatever tension she'd accumulated over the past few days.

"I'm so sorry, Lacey." I hugged her tightly. "I'm so sorry that I ever made you feel like I didn't want to be your stepfather. That was never my intention."

She pulled back and stared up at me. "Does that mean you want to be my daddy?"

I took her hand in mine and squeezed her fingers. "I'm not sure," I said, and her smile fell.

I grabbed her hand again when she tried to pull away. "I don't mean it like that. I mean..." I sighed. How to communicate this with a nine-year-old? "My father wasn't very nice. And I'm worried that I won't be a good one to you."

She tilted her head and stared up at me. "But you're nice. You're nice to me, to your pack. Was your dad like that? Did kids like him? Did his pack like him the way your betas like you?"

The question was so simple but turned my world on its head. "Well..."

Everyone hated my dad. Everyone was afraid of him.

"Do you know that when Mom was stitching you up, your whole pack was waiting to hear the news? Your betas sat on the porch and talked to me, and there were women and children everywhere."

"Uh..."

"Doesn't that mean they like you? Respect you? Like our pack with Reid and Allara. Everyone respects them."

My throat tightened. "Well, to answer your question, no, I don't think the pack liked my dad very much at all."

I was too little when he died to remember exactly how everyone reacted to him, but I did remember the fear. And the ripple effect of what he'd done to his people still went on to this day.

"Then you're not like him." She jumped off the bed to stand next to me. "So, you can be my daddy, and Mom and I can stay here."

Then she pointed her little finger at me and squinted her eyes to make it look like she was glaring. "But you need to say sorry to Mom. You were mean to her. And she doesn't like it when people lie."

"Lie?" I repeated. "I didn't lie."

That was one of the things I stood for. Complete and utter transparency. It was the only thing I had some days.

She walked to the door, then turned back to face me, a happy little smile on her face. "You promised me you wouldn't hurt Mom and you did. And second, you said you can't protect me and you did."

Then she skipped out the door, taking my heart with her.

I sat there for too long, mulling over everything she'd said, the expression *out of the mouths of babes* swirling around in my mind.

When the door opened again, it was Amelie, with a plate of bacon and toast. "Are you hungry?"

I nodded. "Yeah, thanks."

I needed to eat and gather my thoughts, and then it would be time to jump with two feet into the life I was meant to lead.

AMELIE

I couldn't eat. My stomach was in knots. But I drank my coffee and watched Mannix eat his breakfast.

"I'll go clean up," I said, standing and walking toward the door.

"I'll take a quick shower, then meet you out there," he said, swinging his body around and planting his feet on the floor. He winced as though the movement had hurt him, which it probably had.

"You should rest," I told him.

Mannix stood up and smiled at me like it was any other day. "I'm healing quickly but feel dirty. A shower will do me good. I promise I'll make it a short one."

I nodded, not sure he was right to jump straight into showering, but it was his call. His body. "Okay."

"Then, can we talk?" He stared at me with a hope, an innocence, that I'd never seen in his eyes before. My heart leapt. What did that mean?

I couldn't say anything except, "Yeah, sure." But my pulse was racing like a runaway train all of a sudden.

Then I opened the door and slipped out, a squeal of nervous excitement building in my chest. What did he want to talk about? Obviously, it would be about what had happened between us, but what did he want to say now?

Had he changed his mind? And how did I feel about that?

I knew I couldn't leave him, not now, maybe not ever. Being away from Mannix would almost kill me. The connection I could feel building between us was growing by the day. Every minute I was with him, the pull toward him got bigger and stronger.

There was no going back to how we were before, but could we move forward in a way that would make us both happy?

Could he love Lacey and me? Could we build a life together amidst the ashes of our pasts?

I didn't have to wait long to find out. By the time I'd cleaned up the kitchen, checked on Lacey and texted Allara to give her a quick update on what was going on, Mannix was out of the shower and standing before me, his hair still wet.

He looked pale but better than earlier. "Do you want to sit down?" I gestured to the furniture.

He nodded, looking far too gorgeous for a man who was on death's door only yesterday. "Sure."

I hurried over to the couches and sat on one while he sat on the other.

"Where's Lacey?" he asked suddenly, glancing toward one of the windows at the front of the house. "Is she still playing outside?"

I nodded, a little surprised by the question. It had been a long time since someone other than I cared where Lacey was or what she was doing. "Yeah, she really likes it here."

"I'm glad."

The silence stretched between us until I finally asked, "What did you want to talk about, Mannix?"

"About us." His words were simple, but his tone held loads of meaning.

"Us?" I repeated, sitting straighter and taller in my chair. "Yesterday you were pretty certain there was never going to be an us."

"Yesterday I was an idiot."

I laughed out loud at that one, especially as he delivered the statement with such a deadpan expression. "Ah, you were a bit," I said. "But you also saved Lacey, and that wasn't an idiot move. Not at all."

It was a hero move, no question.

He nodded slowly. "That's what's got my mind all twisted up."

"Which part?"

He ran his hands up and down his thighs, groaning softly. "I convinced myself that I was never going to have a mate or children because the risk wasn't worth taking. The risk of..." He swallowed hard, then continued, "Turning out like my father. But then you two showed up and you both want me in your life."

I shrugged, trying for nonchalance. But inside, my heart began to race. "Yeah." *And we still do.*

"I'd never thought about the fact that I could be a stepdad or an adoptive dad, or something like that."

My heart squeezed tight, but I pushed through the feeling. "You can. Lacey wants you to be whatever you want to be to her. It doesn't mean you have to marry me or anything." Now it was my turn to swallow against the lump closing up my throat. "We can work out some sort of compromise, I'm sure."

Mannix pinned me with the intensity of his stare, then slowly shook his head. "I don't want to compromise."

My hopes fell. "You don't?" Maybe I was wrong. Maybe he didn't want us. Maybe... "Oh, what are you doing?"

He stood up suddenly and walked over to me. "I want everything," he said, and then went down onto one knee, kneeling before me.

I grabbed for his hands to pull him up. "You'll hurt yourself. Your wounds. Your stitches."

He squeezed my fingers and smiled, resolutely remaining in that position. "Amelie, will you stay here with me? Live with me? Marry me? Accept me with all my faults and failings, and... everything?"

My jaw dropped and I stared at him. "But you said..."

"I know what I said." He sighed and shook his head. "I was afraid. I'm *still* afraid."

"Then what changed your mind?" I had to know.

"Lacey," he said simply. "When I found out the bears had come to attack again yesterday, I instantly got ready to fight for my pack. Die for my pack, if necessary. Something my father would never have done. So, there's that. We're at least different on that level."

I nodded, not speaking, not wanting to interrupt him when it seemed he was on the path to enlightenment.

"But when I learned Lacey was missing and in the path of danger, I turned my back on my pack and ran for her. In that moment, she was more important than me or the pack I thought were my family. She was everything. And I know that's because she's your daughter. She's a piece of you, my mate. And if you'll have me, I want her to be *my* daughter too. Not to take her own father's place, of course, but..."

He shrugged and for a second his eyes glistened, as if he was trying to hold back unshed tears. "I want us to be a family, Amelie."

I fell to my knees in front of him, humbled by his words and by his obvious emotion. "You don't have to do this, Mannix."

He cupped my face and held me still. "I don't know if I will ever be able to have kids of my own, sweetheart. That is still my biggest fear. Would you still accept me if Lacey is the only child you ever have?"

Tears gathered and slipped down my cheeks. I hadn't thought anything he could say would have topped his first declaration, but he just beat it.

"Of course, I will." I wiped at the tears. "I'd love to have your baby, but if Lacey is enough for you..."

"She is," he said. "She really is."

"Then let's do it." I smiled despite the tears still coursing down my face. "Lacey and I will move here, and if you're still sure, we'll get married."

Mannix slowly got to his feet, tugging me up with him. "My town is still rebuilding," he said, as though warning me of something terrible. "It's been my life's work to repair the damage my father caused."

"I want to help you," I said, feeling inspired in a way I'd never felt before. "With schooling and anything else you need."

Mannix's lips tilted up. "Being an Alpha's mate in this pack won't be easy."

I laughed, happiness filling me. "I've never chosen the easy way, Mannix. I want you. I want this town. I want my fated mate."

He whooped and picked me up into his arms, squeezing me as tightly as he could, given his injuries. When he pulled back to stare into my eyes, he smiled and then he kissed me, hard.

I wrapped my arms around his neck and kissed him back, relief flooding me, enhancing the happiness in my heart. He wanted me! He wanted Lacey! We could work everything else out, I was sure.

He walked us into his bedroom, then sat down on the bed.

I pulled back and stared at him. "Are you sure you're well enough for this?"

He began tugging at my clothes, so I undressed as quickly as I could then helped him remove his clothing too. "I'm definitely well enough for this," he said. His enormous erection showed me exactly how well and how ready he was.

As I climbed up onto the mattress beside him, he chuckled. "Though, you might need to be on top for this one, sweetheart."

I speared him with a look that hopefully conveyed to him exactly how much he meant to me. "With pleasure, my mate. But first..."

I wrapped my hand around his shaft, enjoying the hiss of his breath as he exhaled sharply. "Lie back and let me pleasure you," I whispered, my eyes feasting on his beautiful body.

His eyes darkened, and he complied, lying back on the mattress and watching me avidly as I began to pump his flesh. I fisted his shaft, up and down, fast and then slow, still learning what he liked. And then I couldn't resist, bending my head to take the tip of his cock into my mouth.

His taste exploded over my tongue, and I swiped at him greedily, wanting everything he could give me, and then some. I went deeper, taking all of him into my mouth and throat, loving the sound of his groans above me. Those sounds of pleasure incited my own arousal, and my pussy dampened as if in readiness for the coupling to come.

When his groans became more feral, less controlled, and his hips began to move and buck beneath me, I pulled back. "Amelie," he huffed, his voice raspy with need. "I have to be inside you, my beautiful mate."

Every cell in my body was screaming out for more. I lifted my head and met his heated gaze. "Exactly what I was thinking, my love."

I sat up and threw a leg over his hips, positioning my pussy channel entrance just above the head of his cock. "I'll try and be gentle," I promised, and he chuckled, albeit a touch hoarsely.

"Not too gentle, please," he said. "I'm a shifter, don't forget. We heal fast." And then his words turned to another groan as I slowly lowered myself onto his hot, hard cock.

The sensation of him inside me, filling me up, was so intense I let out a tiny cry. His hands tightened around my hips, fingers clenching as he steadied me. Then I began to move, riding my mate, slowly at first and then faster, as our moans mingled together, and the delicious scent of sex rose around us.

"Jesus, Amelie, this is... God, this is *perfect*," he managed, and I gasped as the pleasure began to rise higher and higher.

"It is," I cried out. "It's like my soul is becoming whole again. Oh, Mannix, I..." I couldn't finish the sentence, could only ride the orgasmic wave as it crested and crashed over me. As I shuddered violently, my inner muscles clenching around him, Mannix released a muffled yell and came inside me in a rush of heat. And then I was off again, shuddering in yet another climax right on the tail end of the last. The intensity of it all, rushing on and on through my body, shook me to my very core.

I collapsed against his chest, forgetting about his stitches for a moment, but it didn't matter. His arms came around me and held tightly, not letting me move until our heaving breaths began to slow. He shifted his head then, smiling at me before he took my mouth in the most beautiful and intimate kiss I'd ever experienced.

When he released my mouth, tears gathered and fell. I couldn't help it. There was so much emotion racing through me that there was no other way to express it.

He reached out with his tongue and gathered up my tears, one by one. "I hope they're happy tears, beautiful," he whispered, and I smiled tremulously.

"They are. I am very happy, and I can't wait to start our new life here with you, and make a future for us, and for Lacey. It will be beautiful, I know. Because we *are* mates, and this is meant to be."

Mannix's eyes shone as he held me, and I knew that everything would be all right now that we were both on the path that Fate had decreed for us.

The path to love and happiness.

EPILOGUE

AMELIE

Five years later

It was Mannix's thirtieth birthday, and I'd raced around all day making preparations. Our new town hall was built, and I'd filled the place with balloons and streamers. The walls were lined with tables and chairs, and the pack had been cooking for two days.

After years of hard work, rebuilding and care, the pack village was looking amazing.

Allara and Reid and about twenty others from my old pack were coming for the party, and they'd be here soon.

"Hey, Mom. I finished the cake. Where do you want it?"

I turned around and grinned at my fourteen-year-old daughter. She wanted to be a pastry chef and was ridiculously skilled at making desserts. She'd created a three-tiered chocolate explosion of a cake for her stepfather.

"Wow, sweetheart, it looks amazing. Can you put it on the big table up the front near the stage?"

My strong daughter, who had recently begun shifting, carried the cake up to the front of the room. I stared after her, not for the first time feeling overwhelmed by the pure weight of how much I loved her.

Mannix and Lacey were closer than ever, and these days she called him Daddy. She had done it from the moment we told her we were going to get married.

"Hey, beautiful, how are you feeling?" Mannix asked, walking up behind me. "You didn't seem too well this morning."

I twisted around and grinned up at him. "There's a reason for that."

He frowned. "You mean exhaustion? I know you've been killing yourself to get this party done. And the school. And everything else you do."

I laughed and threw my arms around his neck. "I love our pack and everything we've achieved."

And we had achieved a lot. I'd talked to other packs in the area and managed to get help, and we had developed relationships with allies who had helped us rebuild. Our pack had grown with marriages and babies—except in our family of three.

Mannix had been quite happy not to have a child of our own for the first few years, but about two years ago, I'd gotten pregnant accidentally and then miscarried. The disappointment we'd both felt had made us both realize that perhaps our family wasn't quite complete yet.

Two years on, and I'd never been pregnant again. Until now.

"Then what's the matter, beautiful?" he asked.

I glanced over to where Lacey was still fussing with the cake. "I was thinking I'd tell you tonight, at the party, but maybe now is better."

He frowned and I knew he was beginning to worry. "What is it?"

I pressed my lips together, holding my breath. I'd been waiting over a month to tell him, but after the last miscarriage, I wanted to be sure.

"I'm pregnant."

His eyes went super-wide, then his mouth dropped open. "But..."

"But what?" I said, going up on my toes to kiss his lips. "It's not like we've been preventing it."

Mannix still made love to me each night. We couldn't get enough of one another, and I thanked the universe every day for bringing my fated mate to me.

"But... I thought..."

"Yeah, I thought so too." At thirty-seven, I'd assumed that my biological clock had ticked its last tock. "But we were wrong. I'm definitely pregnant."

"How far along?"

I tried not to smirk when I answered. "Almost ten weeks."

"What? You waited all this time to tell me?"

I shrugged. "I wanted to tell you on your birthday." And I was afraid to go through another loss with him. The last one had devastated my big, strong Alpha.

"Uh... oh..." He seemed to be totally out of words.

"Are you happy?" I asked.

He nodded and swallowed hard, his throat working with emotion.

"Happy birthday," I managed before he tugged me in for the sweetest kiss ever.

"Ew... gross. You two need to get a room."

I pulled back and laughed, tugging Lacey into our group hug and told her the good news.

"Really?" she exclaimed, her eyes going big and wide. "Oh, Mom, that's so awesome!"

Mannix pulled her into his side. "You know nothing will change with us. We still love you more than anything, and you are still my heir. The next Alpha for our pack."

Pride swelled in my heart. The day Mannix had taken Lacey as his official heir had made me fall in love with him, all over again.

She rolled her eyes, but I could see the relieved smile on her lips. "I'm happy to share the role, Dad."

We pulled her into our group hug once more, then Lacey left to go meet up with some friends.

"I can't believe we're going to have a baby," Mannix said, pressing a flat palm to my belly.

Happiness burst out of me as I cuddled into my mate. "Do you want to tell the pack tonight or do you think we should wait?"

"Oh, I'm definitely announcing it tonight." He beamed from ear to ear. "And speaking of which, I better go check on the alcohol delivery. It's due any minute."

He stopped to kiss me once more, then walked off. There was an added little spring in his step, and I was so happy I'd been the one to provide that for him with my news.

I watched him go and couldn't stop myself from cupping my own belly with my hands. It had been worth hiding my morning sickness and waiting for the right moment to tell him. The perfect birthday present for Mannix.

Now I just had to wait thirty more weeks, and our baby would be here. Fate willing.

THE END

www.ingramcontent.com/pod-product-compliance
Lightning Source LLC
Chambersburg PA
CBHW070332170726
48291CB00001B/22